COAST-TO-COAST RAVES FOR
THE 13TH VALLEY

"A remarkable portrayal of the "boonierat" and his war—the infantryman's moment-to-moment experience of jungle warfare. . . . Accurately researched and written in a simple muscular style, the book contains the raw power of combat and introduces a talented writer who was faithful to his impulse to let people know what the Vietnam War was really like."

—*The Atlanta Journal-Constitution*

"Gripping. . . . The gritty, straightforward realism in which Del Vecchio portrays men at war creates enormous drama."

—Dan Cryer,
Newsday

"The first great popular page-turner to emerge from that unfortunate conflict. . . . Describes actual combat with an authority only seldom encountered."

—*Toronto Globe and Mail*

"Because we may never know what Vietnam meant in the perspective of American history, we may have to content ourselves with simply learning how it felt to be there, and this is where *The 13th Valley* is at its best."

—Anatole Broyard,
The New York Times

"Very, very few war novels have the tensions and strength evident in *The 13th Valley*. . . . A valuable addition to the understanding of the Vietnam experience."

—*Associated Press*

COAST-TO-COAST RAVES FOR
THE 13TH VALLEY

"*The 13th Valley* . . . grabs the reader. It is the best fiction yet from the Vietnam War."
—*St. Louis Post-Dispatch*

"Tough and insightful. . . . His battle scenes are as immediate and terrifying as any in modern fiction; they practically explode off the page. And the tragic conclusion is a shocker of the first order."
—*The Denver Post*

"The total effect is tremendous. . . . Portrays the American presence in Vietnam so intensely, so graphically, so brilliantly that his explosive novel must be read by anyone who wishes to understand that watershed event. . . . The best fiction yet to emerge from the tragedy of Vietnam."
—*The Dallas Morning News*

"Few novels so completely capture the ambiance and language of warfare. . . . Rough, cynical, beyond bawdy and sometimes ugly, this book is a major step forward in the literature of a war no one wanted to know much about. . . . Del Vecchio is a talented, strong-tongued and perspicacious writer who keeps the reader in the foxhole until the book is done. This book is a 'don't miss it.' "
—*The San Diego Union*

"An impressive achievement. . . . Whoever that soldier was who exhorted Del Vecchio to write 'what it was really like' should be pleased to know that is what he has done."
—*The Miami Herald*

Bantam Books by John M. Del Vecchio
Please ask your bookseller for the books you have missed

THE
13TH
VALLEY

A NOVEL BY
JOHN M. DEL VECCHIO

BANTAM BOOKS
NEW YORK · TORONTO · LONDON · SYDNEY · AUCKLAND

THE 13TH VALLEY

Bantam Hardcover edition / August 1982

6 printings through September 1983

A Selection of the Literary Guild

Bantam rack-size edition / October 1983

12 printings through March 1990

Library of Congress Cataloging-in-Publication Data

Del Vecchio, John M., 1947–
The 13th Valley, a novel.

/51. Vietnamese Conflict, 1961–1975—Fiction.
I. Title. II. Title: Thirteenth valley.
PS3554.E4463A613   813'.54   81-70920
ISBN 0-553-23560-5   AACR2

Published simultaneously in the United States and Canada

PRINTED IN THE UNITED STATES OF AMERICA

OPM   20 19 18 17 16 15 14 13 12

ACKNOWLEDGMENTS

Grateful acknowledgment is made to: A soldier on Firebase Rendezvous at the edge of the A Shau Valley during Lam Son 719, Spring 1971.

He said to me, "You can do it, Man. You write about this place. You been here a long time. People gotta know what it was really like." And thus this book began.

To Dr. John Henry Hatcher, Archivist, The Center For Military History, to First Lieutenant Kevin R. Hart, Division Historian, 101st Airborne Division (Airmobile), and to Miss Gilbert, Librarian, The Army Library, for documents, assistance and information; To Dr. Byron J. Good and Dr. Mary Jo Good, University of California, Davis, for help with the theoretical constructs of war causation; To Lee Bartels, a soldier with the 101st Airborne at Khe Ta Laou, for assistance with the story; To Jane Vandenburgh, Susan Harper, F.X. Flinn, Alan Rinzler and Kathleen Moloney, for editorial assistance; To my parents, relatives and friends for moral support; And to the Ratcliffes, without them I would have quit after Chapter 23.

A U T H O R ' S N O T E

The operation at Khe Ta Laou, which began 13 August 1970, was part of an overall campaign code-named Texas Star. The first troops of the 101st Airborne Division (Airmobile) were inserted into the mountain jungles surrounding Firebase Barnett at 0840 hours on the 13th. The combat assault by Company A to the peak of Hill 848 occurred as described, as did many of the events included, although the story here told is a composite of events from several operations. NVA unit designations, numbers and movements are, as nearly as my research can establish, accurate. The 7th NVA Front headquarters was located in the valley. Thirteen NVA battalions did use the Khe Ta Laou as a supply depot and rest sanctuary.

The approximate results of the Khe Ta Laou operations, which ended 30 August 1970, along with the co-ordinated 1st Division (ARVN) operation in the Firebase O'Reilly/Jerome area directly south of Khe Ta Laou, were: 5 U.S. KIA, 60 U.S. WIA, 2 KCS WIA, 32 ARVN KIA, 108 ARVN WIA, 737 NVA KIA and 3 NVA POWs.

During the summer of 1970 the 101st Airborne had in its command ten infantry battalions. The 7th Battalion 402d Infantry (Airmobile) is an entirely fictitious unit. This is a novel.

The characters and their backgrounds are imaginary. In no way are they meant to depict, nor are they based upon, any soldiers, past or present, of the 101st.

The words to the Boonierat Song in Chapter 7 were allegedly written by an M-60 machine gunner of the 101st under the double-canopy of the Ruong-Ruong Valley in the spring of 1970. He added the music when his unit moved into the Elephant Valley. In late October of that year I received the words from Private First Class Charles E. 'Doc' Bell of Wichita, Kansas, who was 'keeper' of the company song. The composer was allegedly killed in action.

Note on the 12th printing, 18 January 1990

When the manuscript for *The 13th Valley* was completed in 1979, I attempted to contact 'Doc' Bell to reconfirm the information regarding the Boonierat Song. Again in 1982, when *13th* was first published, I attempted to find the original composer. Over the last eight years, numerous veteran musicians and musical groups have put their own music—from acid rock to western twang—to the lyrics. Then in mid-1989, Ray 'Blackie' Blackman of the Ripcord Association found an article in the February 2, 1970 issue of *The Screaming Eagle,* the 101st Airborne Division in-country newspaper, titled "Machine Gunner Writes Song in Spare Time." According to that article, the original lyrics were written by Randall W. Jordan of Portland, Maine, with help from ". . . the men in my company." Jordan was a gunner with the 1st Batallion (Airmobile) 327th Infantry. As of this writing, he lives with his two daughters in South Portland, Maine.

THE 13TH VALLEY

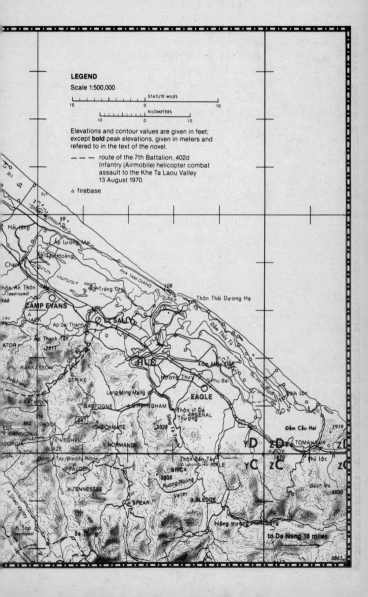

LEGEND

Scale 1:500,000

STATUTE MILES

KILOMETERS

Elevations and contour values are given in feet; except **bold** peak elevations, given in meters and refered to in the text of the novel.

— — — route of the 7th Battalion, 402d Infantry (Airmobile) helicopter combat assault to the Khe Ta Laou Valley 13 August 1970.

△ firebase

PROLOGUE

Long before the soldiers arrived the life forms of the valley had established a stable symbiotic balance.

At the most central point of the valley, in a dark and dank cavern created by the gnarled roots of an immense teak tree, a spider reconstructs its damaged labyrinth of silken corridors and chambers. Upon the outermost threads, dew glistens from a single ray of sunlight seeping through the valley mist, creeping through the shadowing jungle.

The spider—its body blood-red translucent large—stills, then jerks. The web twitches violently. The creature seems to leap forward on an arc of jointed webbed legs. A pointed claw grabs a mosquito caught in the web. Around the spider, vestiges of tunnels and prey traps encapsulate dried crusted exoskeletons. The spider perceives its home through simple clear red eyes and through a sensory bristle of exceedingly fine red hairs. At one time the home was good, food was plentiful. The spider had never needed to extend its world beyond the limits of the cavern.

The teak tree shades the spider and all the life below. From the hillock upon which it is perched, the tree reaches up for over two hundred feet, straight, massive and durable. The teak is wide at its base and gradually becomes slender as its huge branchless torso protrudes skyward, finally bursting in an imposing umbrella of boughs and leaves. For countless monsoon seasons, when the sky has broken angrily and lashed the earth, the tree has shielded plants and animals, and, for a time, the spider from the beating rain. The teak's root system has preserved the knoll into which it sinks, of which it has become a part, from the ravenous river crashing endlessly against the knoll's east side.

The tree is the oldest life in the valley—older, even, than the flood-plain valley floor which has washed down the river from the mountains and which is alive with mosquitos and leeches.

The knoll, tenacious, solid, reinforced with the unseen strength of the teak, forces the river to swirl and bend back upon itself. It is long and high, with steep embankments circling the crown, and it is strong: strong enough to hold the tree and the spider aloof from the affairs of the valley floor, strong enough to alter the course of the mountain river.

The river carries soil and rock from upland watersheds to the base of the knoll. Where the knoll forces the waters to bow, the river has deposited much of its cargo to form a beach. Sticks, branches, bamboo, whole trees have been brought down the waterway, and, catching, have formed a massive snag at the beach's north end. Riverwaters roil in the snag, back up then boil over, rushing first then sliding into the deep channel around the knoll, then lazily flowing into the broad plain beyond. Each monsoon season the river has overflowed and flooded the plain; each dry season the waters have dropped below the mud bluffs of the deepest channel.

From the muck plain of the valley floor and from the rolling hummocks of mountain erosion, elephant grass grows to twelve feet and dense bamboo thickets choke the earth to the river's edge.

The headwaters of the river are in the very rugged terrain to the east where the valley is narrow. There the mountains rise to summits of nine hundred, one thousand, and eleven hundred meters. As the river flows west down the mountains, the valley widens. Four kilometers from its origin is the knoll which causes the river to bend. At that point the valley floor is almost six hundred meters wide. The north ridge is steep, dropping quickly to the valley floor. The south ridge is lower and gentler of slope. From the numerous peaks along the ridges, small ribs extend toward the valley center and form canyons which guide sporadic rivulets to the river.

The Khe Ta Laou river valley is difficult to enter, hard to traverse. For a very long time it had remained isolated. Life in the valley is highly organized and each plant and animal form aids and is dependent upon the entire system. The equilibrium is sharply structured—a state, perhaps, which invited disruption.

CHAPTER

1

CHELINI

From that day on they called him Cherry and from the night of that day and on he thought of himself as Cherry. It confused him yet it felt right. He was in a new world, a strange world. Cherry, he thought. It fits. It made little difference to him that they called every new man Cherry and that with the continual rotation of personnel there would soon be a soldier newer than he and he would call the new man Cherry. Cherry. He would repeat it to himself a hundred times before the day ended.

For James Vincent Chelini the transition began early on the morning of 12 August 1970. He was at the 101st Airborne Replacement Station at Phu Bai for the second time; there now to receive his final unit assignment for his year in Vietnam. The air in the building was already stifling. Chelini sweated as he waited anxiously for the clerk to dig through a stack of personnel files.

"No way, Man," Chelini shook his head as he read the order.

"I don't cut em, Breeze," the clerk said. "I just pass em out."

"Listen, Man," Chelini protested. "I'm not an infantry type. I'm a wireman. That's my MOS.* Somebody screwed up."

"Breeze," the clerk shrugged, "when you get this far up-country aint nobody here ee-ven kin figure what them num-

*A glossary of military acronyms and terms appears on page 648.

bers mean. We's all Eleven Bravos. You know, you get that from Basic.''

Chelini cringed. It was one more snafu in a series of snafus that were propelling him faster and deeper into the war than he had ever anticipated. "Man," he said, restrained, "I can't be sent to an infantry company."

"Next," the clerk said lethargically.

"Hey. Dude." A harsh voice erupted behind Chelini. "Just say fuck it, Dude. Don't mean nothin." A red-haired man in civilian clothes had entered the office without being noticed. He addressed the clerk. "Hey REMF," he said in a voice of complete authority, "you seen Murphy?"

"Murphy's gettin ice cream," the clerk answered.

"You REMF fuckin candyasses sure got it dicked," the red-haired man laughed harshly. The man gestured at Chelini, who flinched, then ordered the clerk, "Square that cherry away, Man. Ya don't gotta fuck with everybody all the fuckin time." The man glided out the door and was gone.

"Who's that?" Chelini asked the clerk.

"Him? He's a crazy fuckin grunt from the Oh-deuce. Fuckin asshole. He en Murphy use ta be in the same company till Murphy extended ta get out a the field en they put him here."

"Oh-deuce?"

"Yeah, Man. Oh-deuce. Four-oh-deuce. That's where you goin, cherry. That's where you goin."

Chelini had allowed himself to be drafted and he had allowed himself to be sent to Vietnam. He had had the means to resist but not the conviction or the will. Indeed, inside, he heard opposing voices. His father was a veteran of World War II. All the Chelini men—and the Chelinis were a large Italian-American family—had served in the armed forces. James observed that having served somehow set them apart from those who had not gone. On the other side were the people of his own generation, the protestors and students, who included his older brother Victor.

In 1968, in order to avoid the draft, Victor had skipped to Canada via the New Haven underground. James told himself that that had sealed his destiny. Victor was a disgrace to the family. Outwardly, Mr. Chelini defended his older son's right to make his own decision, but inwardly, James felt sure, it tore at his father's heart. James saw his draft order as an opportunity to reestablish the family's honor.

Before basic training began Chelini signed up for a third year and a guarantee of communications school, in order, he justified it later, to avoid combat. In Basic Chelini was an enthusiastic trainee and he tried hard to learn good soldiering. In advanced training he became a telephone systems installer. This, he was certain, would guarantee his safety. No matter where he was stationed, he thought, he would work at a rear-base. He would support the war effort if needed, yet he would not really be a part. After AIT, when Chelini's orders came through for Vietnam, he told himself he would experience the war zone, exactly as he had always planned, without exposing himself to combat. He told himself that he was totally naive, that he had everything to experience and to learn.

Chelini arrived at the giant army replacement station at Cam Ranh Bay near midnight 31 July. It was dark and raining as the plane descended steeply toward the airstrip. GIs on board were fidgeting. They had been en route from McCord Air Force Base via Anchorage and Yokota, Japan, for seventeen hours. Because of the jet-lag, the confusion of crossing the international dateline, his excitement and exhaustion, Chelini didn't know if it was the thirtieth or thirty-first of July or the first of August. He had been up for twenty-five hours.

An MP welcomed the planeload of arrivals to the Republic, then said, "Go directly to the buses. In case of rocket attack on the base or ambush during convoy, remain in the buses and get on the floor." Chelini could not tell if the MP was serious. Here? he thought. He tried to look at the MP's face but was propelled with the mob toward the waiting vehicle.

What he thought was the third and last leg of his journey turned out to be a middle step. "Move your body, Troop," he was ordered, prodded, pushed. They boarded the buses by rank and service, army lower enlisted last.

"Okay, everybody," the shout of a cadre cracked as they disembarked. "Form up on the hardstand." Chelini trudged on with the others. He did not remember the bus ride. Strange, he thought. Strange to fall asleep after spending all that time getting here. Chelini stared at the installation about him, but nothing stood out. It appeared to be just another base.

Crackling static from an olive-drab loudspeaker stationed at the peak of a white clapboard building interrupted his thoughts.

"ATTENTION! Attention in the company area. Those manifest for An Khe report to the orderly building. You are shipping."

Cadre continued shouting. "Okay. Listen up. We've had a sapper attack an we didn't get em all. We don't know where they are. Sooo, stay away from the perimeter. Got that? I know you've heard Cam Ranh Bay is secure. In the past two months we've had more activity than in the past two years. Two nights ago we had a rocket attack."

Chelini was too tired to talk. He looked at his feet. "Sand," he mumbled to himself. "That's what this place is." The sand lifted with the slightest kick. It was so fine that little clouds formed around feet and rose to his ankles and then to his knees. It stuck to the sweat on his arms and face and neck. Soon itching tormented his entire body.

Processing began immediately. Chelini filled in form after form without paying attention to what they were. His money was changed for Military Payment Certificates (MPC), and he was assigned a bunk in the transient barracks. By 0300 Chelini, without having slept, was back on the hardstand with his duffel bag and a manila envelope of his records. Wearily he, and about five hundred others, waited for orders.

Helicopters had been in the air all night. Now they opened fire with mini-guns, showering the bay in a red waterfall of tracers. The firing seemed to be concentrated about six hundred meters from the processing center. Some cadre spoke of AK-47 fire, but Chelini couldn't distinguish the sounds. Most of the cadre paid no attention to the helicopters. Somehow it seemed far off. Chelini watched the firing and listened to the buzz of the mini-guns but he was very fatigued and apathetic. "They didn't even have coffee for us," he griped to a man near him. "Fuck the army, Man," the soldier grumbled back.

0400. 0500. 0600. Finally, ". . . Ivor Carton to Bien Hoa. Timmy S. Cervantes to Quang Tri. James V. Chelini to Phu Bai . . ." Chelini smiled as the sound of his name came over the address system.

0615—the first light of his Vietnam tour. The area surrounding the post was exquisite, a bay of deep blue-green waters surrounded by mountains. The temperature was already rising and it was muggy. Chelini did not notice the beauty. He looked about him and was aware of only one thing—sand. It got into Chelini's mouth and ground between his teeth.

New people continued to arrive. Some looked concerned

about the sapper attack and the helicopters firing. Chelini assured them it was nothing.

Phu Bai, Chelini thought. He looked up the location on a large, crude map drawn on the side of a processing building. He traced the route with his finger. That's about three hundred and fifty miles north of Saigon. Near Hue. The XXIV Corps is the division in that area. That's good, he told himself. It's just what I want. It's farthest north, so it's got to be cooler than here.

He was shuffled about like baggage. Line-ups, formations, order checks. The temperature kept climbing. He yawned. There was so much activity and noise, and he was so tired.

Chelini was the last passenger to board the C-130 transport going to Phu Bai via Da Nang. The noise of the uninsulated aircraft made it impossible to talk or to sleep. He felt like a zombie. The ride was rough, and he was becoming nauseous. The men sat on four rows of webbed benches that were suspended from the plane's raw metal skeleton. "If Ah was a side of hangin beef," someone shouted into his ear, "they'd a treat me bettah." Chelini did not respond.

The C-130 approached Da Nang from the sea, descended and landed. Twenty soldiers deplaned. Though he was not scheduled to disembark, Chelini, who was at the very back of the ship, got off and pulled his gear down to the pavement to make it easier for the others to exit from the narrow bowels of the plane. The rear door closed with Chelini watching from outside. The plane taxied to the runway, paused, sped forth, lifted off and flew toward the sea.

Chelini was paralyzed with exhaustion. He shuffled off with the others who had left the aircraft and then found himself left behind by the side of a taxi way. He sat on his duffel bag. The envelope with his orders and records remained on the webbed seat in the plane. He sat by the runway for a long time. The Da Nang airfield was flat and clean and everywhere white concrete glistened in the noon sun. "Snafued," he mumbled to himself.

Chelini had felt that something was not right the moment he left the aircraft, yet he was too self-conscious to yell, to make himself seen. He simply sat and thought of ways to justify what had happened. He was sure someone would take care of him.

After a while someone did come up to him. "Where you going, Soldier?" the man asked. Chelini told him Phu Bai. The man directed him to a helicopter pad that had stacks of bundles of "Stars and Stripes" newspapers at one side. A large helicop-

ter landed. Chelini helped someone load the papers, then climbed
aboard and sat amidst the bundles. His body seemed to be on
auto-pilot.

The thought of having to explain where he had been without
having a good explanation made Chelini tremble. Oh, God, I'm
AWOL. They'll court-martial me. What if something happens to
me? Nobody'll know. His body twitched. His eyes opened wide.
He kicked some of the bundles as the helicopter banked to one
side. He fixed his eyes on a man standing, peering out the left
rear porthole. The man wore a dark olive-drab flight suit and an
olive-drab fiberglass helmet with wires and a mouthpiece. The
upper front of his helmet was covered with a dark, opaque sun
visor and the sun glinted off the shield as the man looked out the
porthole. In front of him was a machine gun.

Chelini did not know where the helicopter was going. He
climbed out from the bundles and stood up. His thighs twitched
as he attempted to stand in the moving aircraft. I'll go ask the
captain, he resolved. I'll say it was a mistake. Anxiously he
began the walk up the corridor of the ship's belly. The helmeted
man stopped him. Chelini screamed a question at the crew chief.
The man pulled the side of his helmet away from his ear, but he
couldn't understand the words amidst the noise.

"Phu Bai," Chelini yelled. He cupped his hands about his
mouth. "Phu Bai."

The crew chief nodded. He motioned for Chelini to sit
down and look out the back of the Chinook.

Chelini had been in-country for fifteen hours. He had traveled over half the land, and yet he had seen nothing except
distant mountains, sand and U.S. military installations. Below
him was the city of Da Nang.

The Chinook stopped at various landing pads on the city's
outskirts. Newspapers were dropped at each location. Soldiers
boarded and disembarked.

Chelini saw large portions of Da Nang from an altitude of
three hundred to four hundred feet and a ground speed of thirty
to forty knots. He saw the large parabolic bay sided by mountainous ridges and he saw the wide river which ran inland between the
ridgelines. Straddling the river, the city seemed to be thriving.

At the edge of the bay, and running as far as Chelini could
see way from Da Nang's congestion, glistening white sand beaches
were partitioned by concertina wire. From the air he could see a

riverfront street and a market packed with food and wares and men and women bustling about. Rising above the market were three and four storey French colonial buildings, which looked like Jackson Park in New Orleans. Small second-storey wrought iron balconies extended over peasants carrying provisions—dried fish, live chickens, bread, cans of oil—in baskets suspended from the ends of bamboo sticks which they balanced across one shoulder. Chelini laughed, enthralled by the sight.

The aircraft banked back over the east side of the river, above a sampan village, then landed near a shipyard. Several wooden trawlers were in various stages of assemblage. To the north of the shipyard Chelini saw shanties built almost on top of each other from scavenged ammo-box wood and government-issued tin roofing.

The CH-47 flew away from the coast, to the sea and north. To Chelini, in his mixed state of fatigue and excitement, the trip became a fantasy, an exotic travelogue.

The helicopter banked left over the beaches and sand dunes. The dunes swelled and withered and were separated by waterways. Nestled here and there, small hamlets seemed isolated and random in a sea of sand, as if someone had thrown seeds from an earlier helicopter traveling over this area long ago and the seeds had fluttered down in a gentle breeze, scattering, some germinating and growing into hamlets, some germinating and withering in the sandy soil, some never germinating at all. As the land leveled, clumps of green and brown brush overwhelmed the mounds. Hundreds of tiny temples and tombs and small pagodas cluttered the piedmont. Between the monuments and sometimes coinciding with them, bomb and artillery craters pockmarked the land. Water filled the craters and they appeared blue or mudbrown. Chelini saw it all but he did not understand. He did not associate the sights with war.

At Phu Bai the crew chief directed Chelini to the 101st Airborne Replacement Station. Engulfed by the activity of the receiving area he walked hesitantly as men hustled briskly or jogged toward destinations. Everyone wore a division patch on his left shoulder, a black shield with the white head of an eagle with gold beak and red tongue. Over the shield in a black arch were the gold letters AIRBORNE.

*   *   *

On the morning of 2 August Chelini was transported in the back of an open topped trailer truck from Phu Bai 50 kilometers north on Highway One to Camp Evans for proficiency or P-Training at SERTS. He had slept yet a tiredness lingered in his muscles and mind. The highway passed through the suburbs south of Hue. The truck rolled north through Hong Thauy, Phu Long and Phu Loc. It crossed a temporary wood-beamed bridge spanning the Song Loi Nong. Downriver a new bridge of steel I-beams and reinforced concrete was under construction. Upstream a steel-truss bridge lay bent, twisted, ripped from its concrete footings. Chelini shuddered in awe. It thrilled him to see this: it was the first evidence of war he understood.

The trailer truck jolted at the end of the bridge and descended into a major marketplace. In the market Chelini could see hundreds of small women squatting beside piles of raw fish or rolls of bread. His eyes were shining with excitement. The world was new and fascinating. The truck rolled on skirting the scarred and shattered walls of the Citadel of the old Imperial City at Hue. There really was a war here, he said to himself. Inside the Citadel's gates he could see ancient cannons.

North of the city the truck passed fields with peasant farmers working knee deep in water or plowing behind water buffalo. They passed villages with thousands of children and hundreds of peasant hootches—some colorful, some dingy—and peasant shops which were busy selling everything from soda and soup to motorscooters.

In one village the elders came to the roadside and smiled and waved and Chelini waved back. He imagined himself as a part of the liberating armies coming into France or Belgium in an old World War II movie. At the next village the truck paused. Beside the road was a mud brick shack. To one side was a hedge, to the other, a barbed wire fence. The front of the shack was a tattered piece of canvas which opened as an awning to expose the interior. Inside, several middle-aged women stood chattering while they washed old brown bottles. Four children—a girl about six holding an infant, and two smaller boys—came shyly from behind the fence and approached the truck. The littlest boy removed a frayed baseball cap and held it out toward the truck. The boy was gazing directly at Chelini and smiling. His older brother waved and held up his right hand in a peace sign. Chelini smiled back and returned the hand gesture. The little girl with the infant approached the truck. She lifted the infant's arm and waved his hand to the soldiers. Chelini stared at her. He did not know if other GIs on the truck were watching him and the children. He imagined the children calling him "Papa" because he had brought them peace, prosperity and the knowledge of ways to ease their existence. A soldier threw two cigarettes toward the children. The boys dove for them. The soldiers on the truck laughed and began throwing gum and more cigarettes. Chelini had a sudden urge to cry.

Camp Evans was named for a Marine killed in an ambush along the Street Without Joy in 1966. At that time the base was a sparse crude outpost of tents and foxholes. In 1969 the Marines withdrew and turned the base over to the 3d Brigade of the 101st, who since their arrival had not ceased building.

SERTS training at Camp Evans intensified Chelini's fantasies of war though it was still only an exercise to him.

Chelini was assigned to a hootch and bunk and was issued an M-16. The bunk next to him had been issued to a rotund in-country transferee named Will Ralston who would become Chelini's closest friend for the next seven days. Ralston had been stationed just outside Saigon with a supply unit. "Dude, I had one gettin-over job," Ralston said by way of introduction. "We were attached to this other unit that controlled this small complex, see? But they didn't have direct authority over us, so we didn't pull guard or have any details. Then they decided to close the place up cause of the withdrawals and they sent us up here to this godforsaken hole. Fuck withdrawals, Man."

Will Ralston had arrived at Evans the day before Chelini was trucked in. He had spent the night on guard duty along the camp's east perimeter. "Dude, you aint gonna believe this place," Ralston cracked. "Down around Saigon they'd give us a 16 and three rounds just before guard. This place looks like they expectin to fight a war. You aint gonna believe the shit they got on the berm. They must be expectin deep shit, Man."

"You know how to operate that thang?" asked the Black Hat, a staff sergeant member of SERTS' cadre.

Chelini grabbed the M-60 pulled the bolt to the rear lifted the cover and put the belt into the feed tray. "Yeah," he said. "One of the sergeants came over and showed me."

"All right," the man said. "You know the rules of engagement?"

"Yeah," Ralston said.

"I think so," Chelini agreed.

"You put out your claymores?"

"Seven of em."

"Okay. You ought to have fifteen frags, twenty-one magazines each for your 16's. You got 1500 rounds for the 60 and 50 rounds for the 79. If you have to use that 60 one of you feed while the other fires. Only if yer name's Wayne or Murphy can you fire it by yourself. Do you have any questions?"

"Can we get some bug repellent?" Ralston asked.

"There'll be a truck around pretty soon with repellent and coffee," the Black Hat said. He walked off heading to the next foxhole. Every forty meters around the perimeter at Camp Evans there was a guard-duty station, a foxhole. The foxholes were designated into sectors of the perimeter and each sector had a tower for the captain of the guard and every foxhole was connected with its command tower by ground-line communication. Guards were instructed to use the phone system only in emergency or in response to the guard captain calling for a situation report. Of the next ten nights Chelini and Ralston pulled guard on six.

"Oh, Man," Ralston said, "look at this dump." It was Chelini's first night on guard and the foxhole had six inches of muddy red water in the bottom and one end was caving in. Ralston was jumpy. He attached the firing devices to the claymore mine wires and arranged them in order across the front of the hole and grumbled, "If I see anything out there—if any crazy gook thinks he's goina sneak up close—I'm goina blow his shit away."

"Calm down, Man. There aint going to be anybody out there," Chelini said. "What time do you got?"

"It's about ten after nine."

"You want to sleep first or stand watch?"

"You sleep. I'll stay up." Ralston laid a bandoleer of magazines for his M-16 in front of his position just behind the clacker firing devices for the claymore mines. He picked up his weapon, put a magazine in the well, pulled the bolt back and chambered a round. "Goddamn rain. Goddamn sand. This whole country aint nothin but Goddamn sand."

"Hey," Chelini said. "You wake me if you think you see something." Chelini lay down on his poncho on the sand behind the foxhole. "And if you get sleepy," he added, "get me up early."

"Yeah. Yeah. Don't worry about it. I'm not goina sleep with Charlie out there."

Chelini lay back using his helmet as a pillow. The sky was black with gray patches where the clouds reflected a dim half moon. It was raining lightly. A warm breeze came up from the moist fields below, outside the base. It smelled of dung. Chelini closed his eyes. He felt silly lying on the hard ground with his head in his helmet, his chest crossed by bandoleers, his thighs crossed by his rifle. He smiled. A single warm drop of water rolled off his lip and into his mouth. It tasted salty. He sat up. This must look really stupid, he thought. Like playing soldier. It was getting darker and he could feel the mist condensing on his face. The breeze was just beginning to turn cool. I'd like to have a picture of me, he thought. A picture of me like this.

The quiet rolling sound of a small truck broke in upon his thoughts. He opened his eyes. Approaching through the darkness from a fighting position farther up the perimeter was a three-quarter-ton truck. The truck's silhouette was barely visible against the night sky. The only light from the vehicle was a tiny subdued red glow at one fender. The truck stopped. "You guys want some coffee?" the driver asked quietly.

"Na," Ralston said. "You got any bug repellent?"

The driver threw them an olive drab aerosol can.

"These damn mosquitoes," Ralston whispered as he sprayed his ears. "They like to get right inside yer fuckin head and drive you fuckin nuts."

"Pass it this way, Man," Chelini said. "Hey, where you from?"

"You mean in the World? Here," he threw Chelini the can. "California, what about yerself?"

"Connecticut," Chelini said. He sprayed the back of his shirt then down the front. "What time's it getting to be?"

"Nine-thirty. You better pick up some Zs. You got it eleven to one."

"Um," Chelini groaned. He lay back down and shut his eyes.

"Hey, Man. Get up. It's ten-past." Chelini woke to Ralston shaking his boot. "Come on, Man. It's yer turn."

"Okay. Okay." He shook the sleep from his face and sat up. "Everything quiet?"

"Shit. It's so dark out there Mister Charlie could come slip right up here, tap you on the shoulder, give you an engraved invitation to your own funeral and you still wouldn't ee-ven know where he was."

Chelini slid to the foxhole and checked the box of fragmentation grenades, the M-60 machine gun, the claymore wires and the firing clackers. He checked it all by feel. He put his face very close to the 60, trying to make sure the belt was in right, but he could see nothing. "Okay, Man," he said. "Go to sleep."

It was very dark now. There was no way to distinguish the ground from the sky. In the field before him several spots seemed darker than the surrounding blackness. Chelini picked up his M-16 and aimed it on one of the spots. It did not move. Will Ralston had lain down and was already snoring lightly when Chelini turned around and looked at him. He was a spot only a little darker than the ground. Chelini turned and looked back at the dark spot which now seemed to be in the perimeter concertina wire. The spot changed shape. Very slowly Chelini moved forward. Noiselessly he picked up his rifle and clicked the safety lever from safe to semi-automatic to automatic. He shouldered the weapon again, sighted in on one dense spot and froze on it for what seemed like an hour. Then he switched his aim to another spot. The darkness crept slowly in an amoebic flow. There was no way to distinguish a target. Chelini could feel his pulse beating heavily in his neck and wrists. What the hell am I supposed to do? he asked, frustrated, frightened, furious that the army had not lighted the perimeter. Somebody could come up here and drop a frag right here in this stinkin hole with me and I'd never know it. Maybe I ought to check with the tower. Goddamn. I hope there's nobody out there. Blow a claymore first. No. Throw a frag first or pump out a round from the M-79. No, throw a frag. That won't give away my position. He stood waist-deep in the hole, the protective earth surrounding him. His hands searched the ground before him for a fragmentation grenade. He found one and lifted it, hefted it to get the feel of its weight. He fondled it to find the pin. Then he just held it and stared into the darkness slowly sweeping his gaze back and forth in a 180° arc like he'd been taught in basic training, sweeping from right to left and then farther out from left to right and still farther out and back again. Then he started the sweep again, not aiming his weapon but his eyes and ears and always fondling the grenade and feeling the butt of the M-60 against his shirt front though he did not touch it with his hands and feeling the butt of his M-16 against his side as it lay pointing forward and ready.

A few minutes past one he woke Ralston for the one-to-three shift. He climbed out of the hole and sat on the poncho behind it and then lay back with his M-16 across his legs. He thought it would be impossible to sleep. His body was taut with tension and his mind was very alert and awake and his eyes were open, staring up now into the misty blackness seeing no more than if they were shut.

The night passed without incident.

On 5 August a marathon of classes began with emphasis on airmobile tactics, basic weaponry, the official view of the war effort, the tactical situation and Vietnamese culture. Despite grunts and groans and whispered ''bullshits'' by many students Chelini would come away convinced of the sincerity and competency of the instructors.

The first training period was the round robin. Chelini had never fired any of the round-robin weapons and the power of each enthralled him, changed him, made him desire to fire them again. He volunteered for every demonstration; he constantly asked questions. First he fired an M-67 ninety-millimeter recoilless rifle. He lay beside the weapon and sighted in on a fifty-five gallon drum across a ravine in the firing range. His assistant gunner loaded an HE, high-explosive, rocket into the tube. ''Gen-tle-men,'' the instructor said in metered syllables. ''This pro-jec-tile is ca-pa-ble of pier-cing seven-teen inches of the tough-est steel known to man-kind or three feet of re-in-forced con-crete or six thick-ness-es of sand-bags. Gen-tle-men, you do not want to be on the ra-ceiv-ing end of this in-stru-ment.'' Chelini wriggled in closer to the weapons. He laid his head on the sighting pad and re-aimed. He squeezed the trigger device. The rocket exploded. Flames shot back ten feet. The noise stung his ears. He clamped his eyes shut. The projectile sailed wide of target and blew a crater into the soft dirt of the opposing hill. Chelini's heart pounded.

The second round-robin weapon was a LAW, a light anti-tank weapon. Somehow, Chelini thought, the army managed to issue every one of its instructors the same voice. ''Gen-tle-men,'' they all start out, "da-dot da-dot da-dot da-da." They all keep cadence with their speech. Chelini volunteered again.

"This wea-pon, Gen-tle-men," the second instructor was saying, "is ca-pa-ble of pier-cing e-lev-en inches of the tough-est steel known to man. Gen-tle-men, you do not . . ." The M-79 grenade launcher or thumper was next. It looked like a sawed-off shotgun with an inch-and-a-half bore. It fired forty-millimeter shells either directly at a target or lobbed in an arc like an artillery piece. Chelini stepped forward. "What's your MOS?" the instructor asked.

"I'm a wireman," Chelini answered.

"Let some of the infantry guys fire this," the instructor said and motioned him back. "You can fire the next one."

The last round-robin weapon was the M-60 machine gun. "Gen-tle-men . . . this fires seven-point-six-two mil-li-me-ter bul-lets at a rate of five-five-oh . . ." Chelini slid to the front of the line at the last moment and behind one of the practice weapons. To him this was the most ferocious weapon of all. He came away beaming, imagining himself holding a hill alone, a hero.

Next, Chelini's group was marched to a rifle range for M-16 battle-site zeroing, then to the Cobra show.

The Cobra is a narrow assault helicopter which carries its pilot and gunner in tandem. The class began with the instructor radioing-in a fictitious request for close-in tactical support.

"Holy Christ," Chelini screeched when the helicopter dove from above the group and unleashed rockets, grenades and mini-gunfire against simulated targets. "Holy Christ," he repeated. The class exploded in applause as the helicopter raked the target range.

"Gen-tle-men," the instructor shouted. "Gen-tle-men." He yelled again as the bird pulled from its dive and circled above them. "In the 101st, Cobras come in two basic configurations: ARA and Gunship. The Aerial Rocket Artillery Cobra carries seventy-six 2.75-inch rockets . . ." The instructor catalogued the aircrafts weaponry, each syllable of his speech in cadence. "Gen-tle-men, you use ARA against bunkers. You use gunships against enemy soldiers and mixed targets. This bird," the instruc-tor pointed up without taking his eyes from the class, "is a gunship. You treat it with respect. You activate it as follows." The instructor brought a radio handset up before his face. He depressed the transmit bar. "Tomahawk Six Six, this is Trainer Five, fire mission. Over."

An artillery act followed the air show. The students watched the receiving end of a barrage against the same scarred hillside. They called-in adjustments to the fire direction control center (FDC), raising and lowering the impactions, moving them left and right simply by speaking into a radio handset.

Still more weaponry classes followed. M-16 practice on a quick-fire reaction course was followed by a class on the M-33 fragmentation grenade and finally a class on claymore mines. At night they had a night-fire exercise under the illumination of artillery flares. Exhausted, Chelini and Ralston and the others marched back to their hootches. Temperatures during the day reached 109 degrees and the humidity hovered at 85 percent. On the morning march to the first range Chelini's hands swelled, his arms turned white and his joints became stiff. He had been sure the heat would make him collapse. "We got a saying up here, Duke," one cadre sneered when he protested moving. "Take two salt tablets and drive on."

The second and third days classes dealt with the history and culture of Vietnam. The culture lecture was given by a chicano sergeant. "Gen'le-men. The priorities of Mister Nguyen are: one, family and food—that mama-san an tacos; two, village an hamlet—*es su casa*; tree, district an province. Country don count. Gen'le-men, Nguyen don care too much for 'is country. Papa-san, he like tree things; 'is Buddha, 'is rice and 'is water buff'lo. He give you mama-san and he give you baby-san daughter, but don you go fuck 'is water buff'lo and stay off 'is fuckin dikes. You gotta walk in the paddies then walk in the paddies. You gonna do that for two reason, Gen'le-men. One, you walk on the dikes an you break the dikes and papa-san get screaming pissed if you break 'is dikes; and two, if somebody gonna put a booby trap in your AO it gonna be on papa-san's fuckin dikes cause everybody know that GI don like ta get 'is feet wet and he gonna walk on the dikes no matter what."

Ralston elbowed Chelini and mumbled, "You oughta write home about this. The Americanization of Gookland."

"Gentlemen," another instructor informed them later that day, "due to the push into Cambodia and the strict controls inside the Republic, the NVA soldier is hurting for food. The rice-denial program has received wide support from all the villages in our AO, and the troops from the North have very little

rice. The unofficial word is to expect a massive NVA drive into
the coastal areas for food. Also, Gentlemen, the South Vietnamese
are having a national election at the end of this month. We can
expect the NVA to attempt to disrupt the peace of the populated
areas.''

"This aint the army," Ralston cracked to Chelini. "This is
all yer dream and I wish to hell you'd wake up and let me out."

"Sssh, Man," Chelini hissed. "This is important."

"Oh, Man, don't give me that shit," Ralston said. "Don't
let em get hold of your mind."

On the fourth day of SERTS there was a class on rappelling.
It was during this class that Chelini's feelings about himself as a
soldier in Vietnam finally solidified. The school had an erected
fifty-foot tower with a simulated cliff face on one side and a
helicopter skid hanging over the air at the top of the other.
"Rappelling in the field, Gentlemen," the instructor for this
block of classes said, "is accomplished from helicopters and is
used to insert troops where the jungle is too dense for a landing.
This tactic has been borrowed from mountaineers and by the end
of this class, Gentlemen, you will be qualified to jump out of a
helicopter with nothing between you and the ground but the tail
end of the rope you will be sliding down. . . ."

First you believe it, Chelini thought, then you don't. Then
you do again. First you think we should be here and then you
think this is crazy and we're ruining the country and then you
think about the kids you've seen and how we keep the NVA out
of the lowlands. He shook his head, cleared his mind, approached the tower and climbed the ladder to the small platform
at the top. Ralston snapped more cynical comments but Chelini
did not respond. As he stood on the helicopter skid fifty feet
above the sandpit his heart pounded. The rappelling rope went
through a D-ring at his waist, around his side and over his
shoulder. For one long second Chelini paused. Then slowly he
leaned backward, feeling the rope take more and more of his
weight, trying not to think of the long drop. As his body reached
a 45° angle he closed his eyes and leaped backward, releasing
twenty feet of line. He snapped the rope taut about him; the jute
burned his gloved hands. His weight stretched the line but the
system worked. He stopped ten feet off the ground, allowed
more slack and descended.

"You snap the line on a bird like that, Troop," the instructor cautioned him, "and you'll flip the bird on top of you. You gotta be gentle." His voice was tempered with approval.

"Wow, Dude," Ralston quipped. "You gettin ta be a real gung-ho airborne-all-the-way-Sir soldier." Chelini said nothing but smiled and turned from Ralston to take a second turn on the tower. "Dude," Ralston called. "They gonna make a screaming bird out a you yet—a screaming yellow buzzard."

Classes on the last day were concerned with NVA tactics and the Chieu Hoi or open arms program. For Chelini the very last class of SERTS was scary and sobering.

"The Hoi Chanhs, Gen-tle-men," a senior instructor said, "are trained as scouts and interpreters. They work with platoons operating in areas from which they defected. In these areas they know the trails and cache sites. They know the booby-trap markers. They know the ambush sites. Gen-tle-men, a platoon with a Hoi Chanh or Kit Carson Scout is less vulnerable than it would be if it were out there on its own.

"We have with us today," the instructor raised his voice and announced, "the Senior Kit Carson Scout of the 101st Airborne Division, Colonel Phan Trinh. Gen-tle-men, for twelve years prior to becoming a Hoi Chanh, Colonel Phan commanded a successful NVA sapper company."

"Jesus!" Ralston snapped. "Look at that. A defective dink."

Chelini listened intently as the instructor told Colonel Phan's story. Phan Trinh's father, who lived in a small village near Hanoi, was actively opposed to the war in the South. Allegedly he was incarcerated and then shot. The colonel's sister and a brother were also killed, for according to tradition they came from corrupted blood and thus were or would be infected with the same thoughts as their father. Phan Trinh was warned by a close friend in a staff position that he was to be recalled to North Vietnam to be interrogated—to see if his blood contained the obsessions of his father. Instead of facing charges of being the son of a radical, Colonel Phan, with a heavy heart, knowing he would never again see his homeland, defected to the south by simply slipping through the wires at Camp Eagle at night and walking up to the Division Tactical Operations Center. There he waited for daylight then defected to the Assistant Division Commander.

For this class the students were instructed in the stringing of barbed wire and the installation of claymore mines, trip flares and rattles. The class was asked to construct a simulated perimeter defense. Chelini was one of six men chosen to build the position and he took extra care to make the wires taut and to keep the strands close to each other. In the wires they implanted trip flares and stone-can rattles. Behind the first set of tanglefoot and under a coil of concertina Chelini hid a claymore in a clump of grass. ''That'll get em,'' he chuckled to the other volunteers.

After the perimeter was completed Chelini and the class watched quietly. Phan approached the exterior of the newly laid position. He was clothed only in a loincloth. With him he carried a small pair of wire cutters, a dozen sachel charges, a blade of grass in his mouth and on a string around his neck a small flat piece of wood. He lay very still in the grass before the wire. Slowly he moved his left arm forward then his right leg, his right arm, then left leg. As he inched forward like a lizard Chelini watched in awe. If Ralston was talking Chelini did not hear. They could come in like that anytime, he thought.

Phan reached the first wire which was about two inches off the ground; he removed the blade of grass from his lips. Slowly, cautiously he stroked the area before the wire, then above the wire and finally as far past the wire as he could reach. He was satisfied there were no trip wires for flares. Again, very slowly he slithered over the wire, one arm, one leg at a time. He slithered into the heart of the entanglement. Phan went over the lowest wires and under the rest, never seeming to touch any, always keeping his body suspended only minutely off the earth by his fingers and toes. He was incredibly agile—almost liquid. As he flowed through the defensive concertina strands his sinuous muscles rippled. Between each movement he placed the flat piece of wood on the earth, placed an ear to it and listened for the movement of the defenders. When he found a trip wire with the blade of grass he moved his cutters—first checking the wire for tension to insure that some alert GI had not spring-loaded the trigger mechanism—and snipped the wire in two.

He proceeded through the emplacement until he came face-to-face with Chelini's claymore mine. The sapper removed the electrical blasting cap from the mine, turned the mine around and aimed it at the audience. Once inside the perimeter he crawled to the instructor and placed his sachel charges carefully about and between the instructor's feet. Finally like a serpent Phan slid back through the wire, re-arming the claymore on his way out. Once out of range he threw several stones into the perimeter.

"GENTLEMEN!" The instructor screamed. Chelini jumped. "MOVEMENT IN THE WIRE! BLOW YOUR CLAYMORES! . . . You will eliminate your own life-support systems by aerating your lungs and heart group with six hundred tiny holes. Gentlemen, a hand for the master." There was a long round of applause.

Most men received their unit orders the last day of the SERTS training course and reported directly to their units of assignment. Will Ralston was sent to division headquarters as a supply clerk. On 12 August Chelini was returned to Phu Bai to obtain his unit assignment which had been intercepted and audited because of the earlier loss and delay of his records. The new mimeographed orders—DEPARTMENT OF THE ARMY, Headquarters 101st Airborne Division (Airmobile), APO San Francisco 96383—assigned James Vincent Chelini to Company A, 7th Battalion, 402d Infantry.

CHAPTER

█████████████████████████████████████

2

█████████████████████████████████████

EGAN

For a long time, long enough for the other passengers to move from sight, Daniel Egan stood by the landing strip. The warm air against his skin felt thick. The pervasive pollution of burning fuel oil and feces that came from bubbling waste cauldrons tended by motionless papa-sans clung to the sweat on his neck. I'm back, he said to himself. Unintelligible screeches from unseen children split in his ears. Back, he nodded. Back in Nam. There was a feeling of disgust in the pit of his stomach. It was not the air; it was something else. He grabbed his suitcase, swung it off the ground, up, over him then allowed the bag to crash down atop his head. He balanced the suitcase and began slowly ascending the slight incline toward the cluster of buildings. He heard a clashing of gears, mental gears grinding. "Fuckin place hasn't changed," he said softly. "Fuckin place never changes."

He paced up the path slowly, the suitcase shading his head. Without altering his metered pace he produced a package of Ruby Queen Vietnamese cigarettes. The package was pale turquoise. On one side was a drawing of a family—the father wearing a helmet, the mother in a conical straw hat and the child bareheaded. On the other side there was a charging infantryman in silhouette. He removed a short fat cigarette with his lips and returned the pack to his pocket. The smell of the tobacco was harsh. With his right hand he took a book of OD moisture-resistant matches from another pocket, bent the cover back, rolled a match so the tip was on the striking surface and snapped his fingers to strike. He lit the cigarette and blew the match out. "Fuck it," he whispered. "Don't mean nothin."

He continued his perfectly metered pace all the while scanning the installation before him, the path he walked on, the sides of the trail. Don't nothin move, he snarled. Don't nothin fuckin move. The thought felt good.

Egan had spent the preceding six days on R&R in Sydney, Australia. From King's Cross he had returned to Phu Bai via Tan Son Nhut and Da Nang. In his new civilian clothes he felt clean and the Nam atmosphere disgusted him. Yet it was not the air. Nor was it the war. He shook his head almost imperceptibly. "Drive on, Mick," he whispered.

Daniel Egan was a thin man, five-ten but only 150 pounds. He had played football in college at 185 but he'd lost much of the bulk of a linebacker after he'd quit playing in his junior year. He'd lost twenty more pounds on the booonierat diet. What remained was bone and tight muscle, a shock of red hair on a head where freckles had sunburnt to large brown blotches and light blue eyes that seemed to say, "Don't ask."

In Sydney, with a bitchy little Sydneysider, he had discovered moments when the Nam was forgotten. There was nothing in Sydney to evoke thoughts of Nam. His thoughts there had been of other things and the only reminder of Vietnam had been himself.

He searched the trail automatically now, unconscious of the scrutinizing jerkiness of his eyes. At Sammy Lee's Cheetah Room on Pitt Street he had found a lady. The moment had been awkward but then he had always had awkward moments with ladies. He smiled inwardly. How quickly he had adjusted to the civilized world. It had startled him each time he remembered the appropriate thing to say or to do. It was there, he thought, with her, that I got this feeling. But it wasn't her. He started. Suddenly he realized he was searching the trail, searching for booby traps. The gears of his mind chattered, resisting for another moment, then meshing, changing. Healthy animal paranoia returned; he felt comfortable.

When Daniel Egan originally arrived in-country he did not understand what he was seeing. The contrast between Nam and the World did not seem immense. Now the contrast was numbing. He stared at the Nam around him. Much of it was beautiful. It had been a long time since he had seen the beauty. In February of '69 as a new Shake'n'Bake sergeant, Egan had walked up this same path for his initial in-processing to the 101st. He had been apprehensive but he was determined to make a good showing of himself. At that time terrorist/sapper probes of the perimeter at Phu Bai and in the surrounding villages were not uncommon. Enemy rocket and mortar explosions bi-weekly disturbed Phu Bai life. By August 1970, with the ever-increasing effectiveness of the 101st and its Vietnamese counterpart, the 1st ARVN Infantry Division, Phu Bai was nearly totally secure. The last 122mm rocket had landed within its perimeter on 11 November 1969. Except for the grunts in from the line units, who were seldom without their M-16s, no one carried weapons. Phu Bai had become a casual post, a place where permanent personnel wore starched jungle fatigues and spit-shined jungle boots and worked an eight-to-five day.

As Egan approached the buildings of the personnel center he became aware of the ever-present thumping of unseen helicopters and then of the strange feeling in his gut.

He had first gone into the jungle in March of '69 with Company C, 1st Battalion, 502d Infantry. It was the beginning of Operation Kentucky Jumper, an assault on NVA base camps and supply areas in the A Shau Valley. The first day with his unit his company was mortared and seven men were killed. The next day they were mortared again and he swore he'd never stay in the field. For thirty-three days his unit made regular contact, culminating with the Battle of Dong A Tay, Bloody Ridge, 26 April '69, where ninety NVA soldiers were killed. US casualties had been reported only as "heavy" but Egan found 50 percent of his platoon no longer existed.

After Dong A Tay the battalion was extracted and moved to the rear for a brief stand-down and in typical guerilla style the NVA retaliated as hard and as fast as they could. In the middle of the first afternoon of relaxation Egan's company area was hit by fifteen 122mm rockets and he came closer to getting blown away than when he was in the boonies. The rockets were indiscriminate, impersonal and impossible to stop once they were in-coming. Egan and his friends low-crawled, scrambled, dove into the trenches. A man named Simpson, lying next to Egan in the trench, was hit by a stone ricocheting from the blast of a 122 exploding only feet away. The stone shattered Simpson's left knee and the joint lubricating fluid reacted within his veins, clotting the blood. Within minutes Simpson was dead.

Egan freaked. He cussed out his company commander. He

screamed at the battalion commander and he told the first sergeant he was going to scatter his shit to the wind.

Two days later he found himself back in the boonies, humping a ruck with Company B, 1st Battalion, 506th Infantry, and within ten days he was a squad leader on the Laotian side of the A Shau. Operation Apache Snow commenced. It took Egan up Hill 937, Dong Ap Bai, Hamburger Hill. That battle pitted one ARVN and three US battalions against the reinforced 29th NVA Regiment. The 29th was dug into the mountain's crest. Enemy resistance was softened by a thousand tons of bombs and sixteen thousand rounds of artillery but the NVA tunnel and bunker complex was deeply buried and the final infantry sweep required bloody, close-in fighting.

With his platoon pinned down by intense automatic weapons fire Egan maneuvered his squad close to the enemy bunkers. Then under the suppressive fire of his fire teams he insanely charged the bunkers with fragmentation grenades. He destroyed two emplacements and killed four NVA soldiers. His thoughts began to slide backwards, to become primitive. His behavior became guided by a more fundamental code. Months later he was awarded a Bronze Star medal with V-device "for heroism in ground combat against a hostile force." He spat at it.

Egan's eyes darted back and forth across the Phu Bai base. Keep yer ass covered, Mick, he told himself. Keep yer eyes en ears open, yer mouth shut. Just cause yer paranoid don't mean they aint out to get ya.

After Hamburger Egan began to feel that he had become a machine. He had seen new friends die: six men from his company, two from his platoon, one from his squad. And the wounded. That was worse. But he did not freak—not immediately. He became the machine, hard and invulnerable. "Don't mean nothin," he had learned to say. "Just say, 'Fuck it,' and drive on."

On the third night of the stand-down after Dong Ap Bai Egan got very drunk and very stoned and his old indignation revived and he stood in front of the brigade officer's club screaming. "FUCKERS. MOTHER FUCKERS. COCKSUCKIN MOTHER FUCKIN REMFS. I'M HOLDIN YOU PERSONALLY RESPONSIBLE FOR GREER EN MILLS. EN FOR KANSAS CITY. I'M HOLDIN COURT. ME EN GOD. RIGHT FUCKIN HERE, FUCKERS. RIGHT FUCKIN NOW. YOU FUCKIN PIGS. YER GUILTY. YER GUILTY OF SENDIN KANSAS CITY EN MILLS EN ME UP THEM FUCKIN HILLS.

YER GUILTY OF SENDIN MILLS EN GREER UP INTO THEM FIFTY ONE CALS. I'M SENTENCING YOU ALL TO DEATH BY M-A. FUCKIN LIFER PIG REMFS . . ."

Someone had hit Egan from behind and had carried him off to a bunk. The next morning he had found himself an E-2 Private with a choice of standing court-martial for attempted murder or of transferring to the 7th of the 402d. He chose the transfer. Over the next few months he became more paranoid, more defensive, more closed. He became sly. They called him The Boonierat. When men got together during stand-down they would swap stories of the things they had seen him do. "You wanta see something beautiful, Man?" an infantryman would say to another when they were drinking. "Then you oughta see Egan in contact. Him and maybe Pop. Nothin can touch em. Man, Egan is so fast, so powerful . . . Man, it's like . . . it's like beauty. It's just beautiful." And the second soldier would say, "I know. I seen him once. That 16's like his hand, like he was born with it. I seen him kill four dinks with four rounds. And they was firin at him. I shit you not."

And Egan became cunning.

Somebody's always fucking with somebody in the rear, he thought as he approached the Record Center Building. Fuck the Army. Fuck the green machine. Salute this pig. Salute that pig. Egan paused as thoughts ran in his head. If a pig wants ta get rid of a dude he had him assault 937 or Bloody Ridge and he says it's for the Glory of the Infantry. Demented Fuckers. Half the time the dude don't get wasted. Somebody else gets it. Dude aint supposed ta get blown away. He's just fuckin there. And dudes plantin frags. Demented Fuckers on both sides can't shoot straight as I can piss. Some innocent dudes always get fucked up and blown away.

In August of '69, when the 7th of the 402d was sent to secure Bach Ma—the 1500-meter high peak that rises from the sea and overshadows the lowlands of Phu Loc—Egan knew he had been sent, once more, to the boonies to be killed. He hadn't fragged an officer, he wasn't under suspicion. But he'd opened his mouth too wide and the irritation his arrogance caused was reason enough. Sly babe, sly, he'd repeat to himself. Keep it cool, Mick. The terrain at Bach Ma was steep and treacherous and the winds at the top gusted to one hundred miles per hour. The NVA had the good sense to leave the Americans with nothing to fight but the mountain and the jungle, and the terrain took its toll in wounded.

Egan stood thirty meters from the door of the in-processing station. He stood stock-still for minutes. Newly arriving personnel sauntered in and out of the building in their new boots and new jungle fatigues. It's cause a me you fuckers can tricky-trot around here without worryin about Charlie doin a damn-damn on yer heads, Egan thought. You must be gettin soft, Mick. That's what R&R does to ya. Maybe that's it. Twenty-six en a wake-up. Don't fuckin mean nothin.

As if he had never stopped Egan resumed his metered pace. He walked, almost glided, into the in-processing station.

"I tell ya, Man," a young soldier was whining to the personnel clerk, "I'm a wire man. I can't be assigned to an infantry unit."

Chicken shit, Egan thought. The young soldier and the clerk disgusted him. He inquired harshly about his old friend Murphy then he snarled something at the clerk and at the new soldier and then left.

In late January 1970 Egan came to the rear for a few days to sign papers extending his tour. By lengthening his time in-country he received a drop of one hundred and fifty days from his enlistment. This meant that when he returned to the United States, instead of having five months remaining in the army, he would be immediately discharged. The first night in the rear Egan settled into a hootch with friends to have a party. A new supply sergeant, a young man with plans of making the military his career, had been assigned to the same hootch the day before. For the young lifer the hootch assignment was temporary, for, as a career man, he would soon be assigned to a more comfortable billet occupied only by other career NCOs. Egan and his friends broke out a little dope and the new young lifer threatened to report them all for being heads.

"Look, REMF," Egan snarled aiming a bony hand at the man's eyes. "I happen to be the best mother-fuckin sergeant in this AO. I been humpin ruck in those mountains while you been suckin down whiskey at the NCO club. I know my shit, Man, and I do my job better'n any mother-fuckin REMF. You ever even been under a ruck? You couldn't even pick my ruck up. You aint ee-ven worth havin a dog walk yer slack. I'm goina explain somethin to you, mothafucker, and then I'm goina decide if it sunk in and then I'm goina decide if a sapper's goina cut yer balls off in yer sleep. Now you listen. I'm on stand-down, my own personal vacation from two months in the bush. That's two months, twenty-fuckin-four hours a day with no fuckin slack. We don't booze it out there. We don't blow no weed. What fuckin right you got to resent my relaxin?''

"Wow, Man," one of Egan's friends said, "this dude's a real bummer. Let's go up to brigade and party. I know some cool dudes up there."

For the next two days no one spoke to the new supply sergeant. Word passed through the entire battalion and brigade area that the new E-5 lifer in Oh-deuce supply was a bummer.

On the third evening after the encounter Egan found the man alone in his hootch. He was sitting in silent dull light on his cot, his head in his hands, his elbows jabbing his knees. "Hey," Egan called. "It's cool, Man, ya know. It's okay." Egan sat down next to the supply sergeant. The sergeant apologized and they laughed. Egan removed a pack of joints from his fatigues, lit one and continued rapping. He got the lifer to take a puff too, and then they smoked another joint and another and another and they laughed and joked. Five of Egan's friends came in and joined them. They brought in candles and a radio. They let the sergeant laugh and talk and smoke the dope. None of them smoked. They all laughed because they knew they had the young lifer. On Egan's cue someone turned the radio off and everyone became silent, everyone except the lifer who was still laughing. The silent men with the candles walked out leaving the sergeants on the cot. "Hey," Egan chuckled. "It's cool, Man, ya know. That's the Nam." Then he too left and the young lifer was again alone and he knew he was caught and he became depressed and withdrawn. The next day Egan returned to the field via the supply pad. Egan punched the new supply sergeant on the shoulder, winked at him and said, "That's the Nam."

It's all the Nam, Egan said to himself as he walked beyond the Personnel Center toward the cantina. It don't fit onto the mind of the World so yer head shifts. It all makes sense.

"Fuckin REMF suckin down ice cream," Egan screamed when he found Murphy. Daniel Egan and the Murf had been boonierat brothers in Company A, 7/402, from June to December '69. The Murf hated the bush and Egan hated the rear. In December Murphy agreed to extend his tour by six months in exchange for a job at Phu Bai. He became a personnel clerk.

When he left the 7th of the 402d Egan was irate. The Murf had abandoned him. For five months they did not see each other although when Egan extended his tour in January for the one-fifty drop the Murf hand-carried Egan's paperwork to insure nothing was fouled up.

Both men with nearly a year and a half in-country were tied by old times and impatient disrespect for the newfers and for the army in general. Whenever Egan was in from the boonies he looked up the Murf for a set.

Murphy was sitting behind the main personnel building at a round, unfinished wood table. Green-brown camouflage parachutes hung over the entire area and the shade felt good. Murphy was sitting alone, reading Anthony Burgess' *A Clockwork Orange*. "Bog, Bratty. Dig this shit. Good ta see ya," Murphy laughed. "Egads, Egan, let's steal a jeep and score. You gotta be stoned to the max to read this book. Have some ice cream. Hey, how was them little Aussie ladies?"

"Oooo, Murf. We licked and fucked and sucked all night long."

"Shee-it. I thought you said yer heart belonged to a lady back in the World."

"It do, Murf, it do. But I wasn't talkin bout my heart."

Murphy chuckled then asked, "You got time for a set? I'm clean out a dew but I can get headquarters' three-quarter if you got the time."

"I don't know," Egan said looking at his watch. "I'm gettin kinda SHORT for this shit."

"Oooo! I know, Man, I know. Twenty-eight and a wake-up."

"Murf, you'se a cherry. Twenty-six and a wake-up. Let's do it to it. They don't grow good shit in the World."

"Did ya stay at the Illowra Lodge like I told ya?" Murf asked.

"Yeah, oooo-oo! Let me tell ya . . ."

"Dynamite lady at the switchboard, huh?"

"Yeah, yeah. Let me tell ya . . ."

"Told ya I'd take care of ya didn't I? Does ol' Murf take care of his buddies? Huh? Aint nothin ee-ven too good for my boonierat brothers."

"Let me tell ya . . ."

"Shit, Man. Did you score on that honey at the Illowra? You son of a bitch. Did ya score on the Murf's old lady? I was goina go back there . . ."

                    *   *   *

They drove north on Highway One past Eagle and through
Hue. They continued up the road ten kilometers to a low-lying
area just before the steel truss bridge that crossed the Sông Bo,
then they turned to the left and followed a rutted dirt road to the
hamlet of Ap Lai Thanh. Egan and the Murf rode in the back of
the three-quarter-ton truck, sitting on the sandbag-lined floor—in
case the truck hit a mine the sandbags were supposed to stop the
shrapnel. Two other men from the base at Phu Bai were in the
cab. While the truck rumbled down the dirt road dust swirled in
over the open back. Egan's civilian clothes were filthy. Murf's
fatigues hardly showed the dirt. Two kilometers down the road
the truck slowed and struggled through muck where irrigation
water from broken dikes flowed toward the river. Up the other
side of the mire the truck halted and Egan and the Murf jumped
from the rear. The truck drove off. Instantly fifteen tiny children
surrounded them and ushered them off the road. Murphy knew
the mama-san and the children. The kids asked for candy and
cigarettes. One lad reached up to admire Daniel's watch. The
little ones were respectful, the older ones mostly shy.

"Egan, I'll be with you in zero five," Murphy said, disappearing into the house while Egan played "Who You" with the
children, gently poking one then another in the ribs. "Me Daniel.
Who you?" The children laughed and hung at his legs. In a short
time the flow of little bodies carried Egan into the house. As he
entered the oldest daughter exited.

Murphy was standing behind Mama-san. Egan bowed slightly
and said, "*Chao ba,*" which was one quarter of his Vietnamese
vocabulary. Murphy jerked his arm and whispered harshly, "Don't
stand with your back to the shrine."

The two Americans and all the children and two dogs and a
mourning dove and the old women relaxed and the adults sat
down. Murphy said something in Vietnamese to the old women.
A young daughter came in with two glasses of citrus and water
with ice. "You pretty baby-san, thank you," Murphy said. The
children increased in number to about thirty.

Egan looked at the pretty girl with the citrus drink. She was
eleven, maybe twelve years old. He thought she was beautiful.
Her skin was a perfectly clear copper color. Her large brown
eyes flashed over him, looking at his civilian clothing. Straight
jet-black hair fell across her shoulders to the middle of her back.
She was petite, delicate, fragile. Like Stephanie, he thought. As

he accepted the cool glass from her he noticed how fine her hands and fingers were. Then she was gone.

The house was made of boards from discarded mortar munition boxes. The floor was packed dirt. The building had no heating system, no plumbing and no electricity. For fire safety the kitchen was in a separate shed behind the house. The house smelled of fish and mildew. "Nice place you've got here, Mama-san," Egan said slowly in a respectful voice.

"Not too shabby, huh?" Murphy said quickly. He winked and added, "Mama-san makes beaucoup dinero off my orders, eh, Mama-san?"

Egan looked closer. There was a small altar on one wall of the main room. On it there was a crucifix, several candles and a lacquered bowl with rice and small wooden fish soaked in nuoc man. Above the altar in a scant white plastic frame there was a photograph of Pope Paul VI.

Murphy was now speaking in Vietnamese to the small old woman, who seemed very happy to see him. She was a weathered old woman. For many years she had worked in the rice paddies under the scorching sun and her skin was wrinkled and grayish brown.

Mama-san had lived all her life in this area which had become known as the Street Without Joy. She had been here in July 1953 when the French attacked Regiment 95 of the Viet Minh. The French first encountered little resistance on that operation. At the village of Dong-Que, where this woman had been born and raised, a fire fight had erupted. The French field commander had called in artillery and soon shells from the 69th African Artillery Regiment of the Foreign Legion pulverized the tiny bamboo and rice thatched huts. The village burned but the people remained hidden. An artillery shell dropped through the roof of the Viet Minh's main building and the round continued into a concealed ammunition bunker below the floor. There had been a tremendous secondary explosion which shook the entire village. French tanks and infantry closed in. The Viet Minh, following their standard defense pattern, a pattern the Viet Cong would use for the next twenty years, forced the civilians out of their safety dugouts. The villagers flooded the hamlet square and the paths and the road. Under this cover the Viet Minh cadre and troops began their withdrawal.

French forces had totally surrounded Dong-Que. The Viet Minh unit, the 3rd Company, Battalion 310, 95th Regiment,

Viet-Nam People's Army, along with many civilians had been destroyed. Mama-san's father and two brothers, all fishermen, were killed.

Mama-san and the remainder of her family moved south to another village where her father's brother became the assistant government administrator. He was killed in the spring of 1954 when the Viet Minh again infiltrated the Street Without Joy.

In July of '54, after the Geneva cease-fire, the Viet Minh's 95th regiment evacuated the area. The new government relocated Mama-san's village to Ap Lai Thanh. In 1962 Mama-san's only living brother was killed in an ambush when new enemy troops again infiltrated the area. The new force was called Viet Cong yet it again was the 95th Regiment.

US Marines stormed the Street Without Joy in 1964 and 1965. Again Mama-san was uprooted. Her village was cordoned off. All civilians were directed to gather their effects and relocate to the refugee camp three kilometers northwest of the Citadel at Hue. The village was razed, the ground plowed under. The area became a free-fire zone.

On 31 January 1968 the North Vietnamese 800th, 802d, and 804th battalions along with Viet Cong elements of the Hue City Committee of the Communist Party assaulted and captured the Citadel and the city and many of the surrounding villages. Sometime between the onset of the TET Offensive of '68 and February 25, when the last NVA soldiers were driven from the area, Mama-san's husband and eldest son, a good-looking boy of nine, were killed. She did not know how or by whom and she did not care.

In the spring of 1970 with the help of the 326th Engineer Battalion of the 101st Mama-san and nine hundred other refugees resettled Ap Lai Thanh.

Mama-san had cried many times. She had seen many soldiers. Now she told Murphy in Vietnamese, she wished all the soldiers would go. "If they stay," she said, "it will only be more hardship. I will cheer the peace when all soldiers are dead. Today our lives blossom; today we open ourselves to the sun. Tomorrow we will have no petals for the sun to warm."

The soldiers sipped their drinks. A little boy was sitting on Egan's lap and holding the mourning dove. The bird flew from his hand to Egan's shoulder and then to the top of the boy's head. The bird perched briefly and returned to the boy's hand. All the kids laughed and Egan laughed and blushed and laughed again. Mama-san's oldest daughter returned with a package wrapped in brown paper.

Murphy did not know where Mama-san got the dew but he knew it would be good and the price was very fair. He purchased twenty decks of O-Js. The O-Js were thin, perfectly rolled marijuana cigarettes soaked in an opium solution. Fifty O-Js to a deck. Mama-san sold the twenty decks to Murphy for two hundred and fifty dollars greenback. She would then turn the American money into seven hundred dollars worth of piasters and Murphy would sell half the dope to more timid GIs for five hundred dollars MPC.

More children ran into the house. They had been waiting outside: sentries. "Your friends back," an older boy said. "Must go. Em-peees at end of road. You go now."

Egan had kept his attention on Mama-san while she and Murphy spoke and while he played with the children. The old woman now turned to him and said, "I wish you a thousand years. *Chuc ong may man.*" She turned to Murphy and in Vietnamese invited them to come back on Wednesday night to play cards.

Egan and Murphy got up and thanked Mama-san and the eldest daughter. They ran to the truck. *"Cam on ba, Mama-san,"* Murphy shouted. "Yes. Thanks again," Egan added.

The little boy with the mourning dove ran with them to the truck. As Egan climbed up the bumper and began getting into the bed the boy grabbed his leg and cried, "Merry Christmas."

They lay quietly on the sandbags on the floor of the three-quarter as the truck made its way back to the highway and past the MP patrol. Egan felt nauseous. Not nauseous but . . . It was that feeling again. Something had happened to him on R&R and he had not known it. He was getting short. His tour was almost over. He was down to twenty-six and a wake-up and he had gotten a new taste of civilized life. Maybe, he thought. Maybe it was the lady. She had reminded him of Stephanie. A chill ran through him. Not yet, Mick, he said to himself. Don't think of her yet.

"We're clear," Murf shouted, laughed, after they passed through the first village. They sat up.

"You comin up Wednesday?" Egan shouted back.

"Not anymore, Bro. I'm too SHORT. This used ta be a good place though. Mama-san's been like a mother to me. I'm

serious. I got to know her and the kids. No fuckin around.
Really nice people. Baby-san plays a mean flamenco guitar.
She's been teachin me. All the men are off fightin a fuckin war,
I think. You'd know more about that shit, though.'' He paused
to chuckle. ''Hey, can you stay for a coupla days? Aint nobody
goina miss ya. I'll send word ta yer XO that yer plane crashed en
you gotta row back from Australia. You can crash at my hootch.''

''Like to, Murf, but . . .''

''Aw, come on, Eg.''

''I'd really like to, Man, but . . .''

''But! But my fuckin ass. You still got that crazy fuckin
sense of responsibility? Yer fuckin crazy. You know that? Yer
gung-ho. What the fuck they goina do if yer a day late—send ya
ta Nam?''

''Murf. The L-T might not even ask me to go back to the
boonies. I'm pretty short and he knows I'm short. If they already
went out . . .''

''Oh-deuce goin out in the mornin. I talked to El Paso
yesterday. He said yer goin up north. They're goin after a
headquarters complex or somethin.''

''Look,'' Egan said firmly, ''if the L-T says I don't have ta
go, I'll be back for a set tonight.''

''Egan,'' Murphy shook his head in disgust, ''you're a
ridiculous person.''

At Phu Bai, when the three-quarter returned, Daniel Egan
found a jeep from his battalion waiting for him. In the back of
the jeep with duffel bag and gear was the young soldier who had
been whining to the clerk. He looked miserable.

C H A P T E R

3

L - T   B R O O K S

Under the cap the lanky black man sat motionless, sat as if his entire self were his eyes and brain and thoughts and his body did not exist. Ovals of sun seared the long tops of his thighs and across his shoulders an ellipse of sun burned. The sun struck his chin and the heat radiated to his teeth. The skin of his neck and jaw glimmered with the sweat of a man acclimated to tropical heat, a film of perspiration, not dripping beads. His mouth and nose and eyes were undistinguishable in the dark shadow cast by the oversized bill of his baseball-style cap.

Lieutenant Rufus Brooks sat on the two-foot-high wooden retaining wall which deterred monsoon rains from eroding the footings of Company A's headquarters. He had been sitting on the wall, his arms relaxed and hanging, his large hands limp on the retained earth, motionless, for nearly two hours.

Would you like a shot at an enemy headquarters? The GreenMan's question resounded in his head. Would you like . . . ? He concentrated on those words. He had been in his room at the rear of the company hootch thinking about war and about conflict, about his wife and Hawaii and about, DEROSing or extending, when the GreenMan had come to him all smiles and beaming like a salesman. "Would you like a shot at an enemy headquarters, Rufus?" the GreenMan had asked, and without a thought, like a pre-programmed automaton, he had answered enthusiastically, "Yes Sir." The GreenMan left as quickly as

33

he'd come, left the lanky black lieutenant with no details, with only his own thoughts about war.

"Minh say First Brigade, she moving," First Sergeant Laguana babbled, bursting into his room, bursting into his thoughts.

"Yup. I know," he had replied. "That rumor's been around . . ."

"Yes, Sir. *Es verdad*," the first sergeant had nodded at him. "But thees one, Sir, Minh, he get . . ."

"Yeah. Yeah." He had mimicked the first sergeant's nod. "Minh's always got a reliable source. Remember last time? He had us moving . . ."

"Ooooh, yeas, Sir. It almost come true. You know even our rumor control report it."

"Stop." He snarled at the smiling chicano. "Don't say another word about any rumors. If I hear . . ."

"Yes, Sir. That true. I don't say nothing. I tell Minh too. This time Minh, he say he hear it from Military Intelligence. He say they interrogate two NVA. He say they say First Brigade gwon to Da Nang. Hard Intelligence. *Es verdad*. We gwon be withdrawn."

"Sergeant, that rumor started when the first boonierat assaulted in this country. Now you maintain silence. Is everything and everybody ready? Did we get enough rations for all the platoons? Did Supply send over a new barrel for Whiteboy's 60? Get that done, Sergeant. I don't want my men on that CA tomorrow with only half the equipment they need." The lieutenant had jerked open the flimsy door of his tiny room, entered the orderly room, then marched out of the hootch and slammed the second door shut. He'd glanced left and right, walked to the retaining wall and sat.

There was activity everywhere in the battalion and company area. Fifty meters to his left there was a basketball game being played; slightly farther away and to his front a crowd of men sat on the shaded stage of the theater. Behind the theater one of his platoon sergeants had his entire platoon formed up for an equipment inspection. Sergeants and lieutenants, company executive officers and clerks and supply personnel distributed C-rations and ammunition and batteries. Operations officers studied maps and intelligence reports and conferred with company commanders about moves and counter-moves. Supply officers studied lists of articles and projected needs and resupply dates and thought up excuses for the unfilled requests for boots and clothes and firing pins and replacement barrels for the worn M-60s. He sat on the wall and watched the activity with disgust yet without concentrating.

"Hey, L-T. We got any more frags?" someone asked. The lieutenant canted his head toward his headquarters hootch and said nothing. The man left. "L-T, Supply won't issue me a pair of boots." He did not move. This man also departed. "L-T, my ruck's busted. Can I DX it?" The man looked at the lieutenant and waited to be acknowledged and waited and finally walked away.

"What's the matter with the L-T?" someone said from behind him. "I don't know," someone else whispered.

Word spread: leave the L-T alone.

Before him there was a newly excavated eighteen-inch-wide by forty-inch-deep trench. It had been dug mechanically by a trencher a week earlier. If the battalion received in-coming rockets during their refitting stand-down the men could wait out the barrage in the depths of the trench. The L-T's eyes fixed on the trench. They never do it right, he thought. They never go all the way. This trench is so straight . . . he saw an image . . . it should zig-zag . . . an image of a rocket exploding, erupting at one end of the trench, dominoing the soldiers within, falling in order to the other end. "No one ever thinks," he mumbled quietly. His eyes followed the trench to the end, the thought sped on seemingly unconnected to his utterance. Hawaii sped into his thoughts. He chased it away. I always look objectively at others, he thought. They come to me for advice. They always have. Why can't I get a handle on my own situation? He chased that thought away too and for a time nothing replaced it. The lieutenant sat motionless in the sun.

Brooks' army training began with ROTC elementary classes in Military Science. He spent six weeks in basic training after his sophomore year, Advance Course after his junior and upon graduation, along with a degree in English, he was commissioned a Second Lieutenant in the US Army. The next year Brooks entered a Masters program in Philosophy at the University of California at Berkeley. He did well but academia antagonized him. So many things seemed to be pulling at him. Active military duty was postponed by graduate work but the weight of it in the future, the financial strain, a new wife and the political tension on campus made him decide to leave school. In January of 1968 he took a leave of absence.

By June he had entered the army and in February of 1969 Brooks arrived in Vietnam. He was assigned to the 101st Airborne Division (Airmobile) as an aide to the Division Chief of Staff. At the time of his arrival there were no black officers on the primary staff at division headquarters. The highest ranking black man in the tight group known as the Decision-Makers was an old master sergeant whom Rufus called "Uncle Tom," and who chided Rufus back: "Uncle Tom, Sir." The senior NCOs and some of the general officers privately referred to Brooks as Tango November, their token nigger. In response to that atmosphere Rufus tended to verbalize his criticisms. He felt threatened. He believed he was more intelligent than the commanders. He was certain that he was better educated.

"Excuse me, Sir," he would say to a deputy commander, "but Sir, would you explain to me, Sir, so I may explain to the young black troops, Sir, why we use most of our blacks in line units and very few as clerks . . . Oh, I see, Sir. I see. I'll tell them that, Sir, and I'm sure they'll understand. It's just a matter that there are not enough blacks qualified to do the job of a clerk, according to Army Qualification Examinations . . . thank you, Sir . . . No, Sir . . . I assure you, I'm one fine ambassador from division headquarters to the troops, Sir."

For five months, long enough for it to be proper to transfer him and for that headquarters to receive a black major and another black lieutenant, the chief of staff withstood Brooks' insinuations and critical panache. In late July of '69 Brooks received orders for the 7th of the 402d. First he served as an undistinguished platoon leader with Bravo Company where he was under the field command of a watchful, non-delegating captain. The commander allowed no independent platoon decisions. Still, field duty and the jungle thrust Brooks into a position of constant responsibility and decision making and he made his share of mistakes. He softened and amongst the combat camaraderie and jungle existence he reverted to his previous quiet manner.

Just prior to Thanksgiving Rufus was assigned a rear job with battalion operations where the stricter military bearing was tedious and again he fell to chastising his senior associates. Within six weeks and after the death of the reconnaissance platoon leader from Echo Company, Rufus was back in the field commanding that same independent combat unit. "You gettin kinda short for that stuff, Ruf," one of the other young officers cautioned him. "You don't have to do that, you know. You spent enough time out there. Hell, you owe it to yourself to stay out of the boonies."

With Recon Brooks produced a fine combat record and gradually he went from being called L-T B to L-T Bro. Privately his men called him L-T Beautiful or Buddha. They said he had karma, they meant he was charmed. Brooks had an instructive, informative and quiet manner with his men. When time and circumstance allowed he would explain the situation to as many men as possible and he would ask and often act upon their opinions. He did his share of the shit jobs too and his men knew it. He chose the game, defined the rules and made sure every man below him understood. What they didn't know, he taught them. And he provided the spirit, the spirit to win. Brooks maneuvered his unit into and out of difficult enemy areas without sustaining casualties. His men CAed into the middle of firefight and no one was wounded. They were inserted onto hot LZ, red smoke, their birds would take fire and their LZ would be booby-trapped and they would come through unscathed. Other units would come in behind them and a sniper would blow one of them away or a pop-up mine would level a squad. He brought out the best in his men. He considered himself to be an intellectual but he made every man his equal. He believed there was no such thing as a stupid person: "Every man has the capacity for very complex thought," he would say. "Sometimes you just have to make him use it."

After four months with Recon Brooks was awarded the command of Company A. He was held in jealous esteem by other company commanders. During the spring offensive drive to the west of Hue, around Firebase Veghel, Brooks' Recon Platoon accounted for forty-four of the battalions' NVA body count of 147. During the late spring and early summer sweep-up operations along the Song Bo, from Three-Forks south to Highway 547 and west to Firebase Zon, Company A, under Brooks, accounted for twelve of the battalion's twenty-one NVA KIA. Again his unit sustained few casualties. Brooks was the only lieutenant in the battalion to command a company. Normally companies are commanded by captains and the other companies of the Oh-deuce were. The captains were superior competitive leaders. Their combat records were very important to them. Rufus

Brooks said he didn't care. His instructive nature and his quiet self-confidence led to his men's belief that he had attained enlightenment. He was long overdue for promotion but his earlier ratings for insubordination had caused postponement.

By August of '70 Brooks had become a cool calculating commander yet he did not really like the army and he certainly didn't like being in Vietnam. He longed to return to his life in San Francisco, to the quiet of school and mostly to his wife. He hoped never again to wear anything green. Yet, for a reason he kept to himself, after he had been in-country eleven months, in January '70 Brooks had extended his Vietnam tour and requested continued combat duty. His overseas tour was due to end in late August. He was now contemplating extending again. His three-year active duty obligation would keep him in the army to June '71. With the American troop withdrawals and the reduction of overall military manpower, there was the possibility that if he extended until January, he might be discharged upon returning to the States. The prospect of spending a year in the army in the States, living in one world during the day and another at night, appalled him. Could he subject his high-strung wife to the demands of an officer's wife? Could he afford an additional six months' separation? Was there really a difference?

First Lieutenant Rufus Brooks glanced at the trench before him. He turned his head toward the basketball courts and then swept his vision across the theater seats and the stage and over to a group of men packing their rucksacks and cleaning their weapons. In the office behind him the first sergeant was cackling to the clerks.

The voice irritated him. He shook his head imperceptibly. It's been a long road, he said to himself. It's been a battle all the way and still there is a conflict in every aspect of my life. Would you like a shot at an enemy headquarters? Would you like to DEROS? Would you like to keep your wife?

CHAPTER

4

The battered jeep from Alpha, 7th of the 402d, lurched over the ruts at the Phu Bai gate, jolted past the Vietnamese concession stands and the Korean souvenir shops and shuddered up the soft shoulder onto Highway One. Chelini grabbed the bottom of his seat with his right hand, hooked his feet beneath the seat before him and, with his left arm, managed to keep the baggage from careening out of the vehicle. He glared at the oblivious driver.

The driver was a blond boy, eighteen or nineteen, whose face could have been used on recruitment posters. He appeared cheerful and very absorbed in his driving. He may have been myopic. He did not speak.

In the front passenger seat was a captain who said he was from First Brigade S-5, Civil Affairs. He was returning from his third R&R, this one to Bangkok. "Hope I didn't keep you boys waiting," the captain said. "One of the clerks there said there'd be a vehicle from the four-oh-second and that you'd have room for me. I appreciate that. I don't like to wait. They're sending over a vehicle from brigade but it won't be here for another twenty minutes. Hope I didn't keep you too long."

In the rear seat beside Chelini was the man in civilian clothing who had come into the personnel office while Chelini argued with the clerk about his assignment. Below his red hair and beneath his sunburned skin the man snarled. He had not looked at Chelini when he'd thrown his suitcase on top of Chelini's duffel bag. He hadn't spoken while they waited for the

39

captain. Chelini was cramped in the small back seat with luggage piled about him. The red-haired man lay sprawled across most of the seat, his left foot out the side of the vehicle and his right reaching to the shift lever between the front seats. The sun glimmered off his scowl. His eyes appeared closed.

The vehicle's suspension clattered and the drive train whined as they drove north past the first cluster of bustling street-side shops and shanties.

The roadway was crowded with men in military uniforms or western dress or loose black trousers with loose fitting long shirts and with women in the traditional sheath dresses and silk trousers, all riding on Hondas or Vespas or Lambrettas. Old black Citroen sedans, long, low-slung, with high fenders and wide running boards, seemed filled with dozens of Vietnamese. There were colorful three-wheeled lorries and at one point a small, very ornate panel truck passed, going the opposite way. The truck was red. Its painted headlights were huge pupils in white and green eyes, the fenders yellow and black dragon legs. A dragon body rippled yellow and blue and green down the side. The roof of the truck was a pagoda roof with swirling corners and peaks surrounded by blue sky with white fluff clouds.

"Wow!" Chelini said. "You see that?"

"Hearse," the red-haired man snapped.

"Where you boys from?" the captain turned and asked.

"Connecticut, Sir," Chelini answered.

"And you?"

"Oh-deuce," came the curt reply. The captain returned forward and looked at the driver who seemed oblivious to the question and said nothing.

Amongst the civilian traffic US and ARVN military machines rumbled, carrying supplies and personnel. The trucks were heavy, squarish, made of thick steel plates. Here and there were the amphibious pod-shaped vehicles with huge black rubber balloon tires of the military police.

The driver nodded and flashed a peace sign to every American driver who passed in the opposite direction. "Right on, Bro," one yelled. "*¿Que pasa?*" shouted another. "There it is, Babe," screamed a third. The captain shuffled about in the front seat and stared at the passing villages.

"See that village, boys?" the captain said. "That was one of my first. We resettled the people there. They'd been driven out during the '68 TET Offensive. VC burned the place to the ground but I had them back in and resettled by the end of September last year. Now it's one of the boomingest places south of Hue. I got the three-two-six engineers to come in with their bulldozers and build up foundation pads for the houses and then I had them help the people put in a culvert system. You know, that village flooded sixteen of the last twenty years. Amazes me these people put up with it. You'd think they'd have figured out ways to stop the flooding a long time ago but they seem to think it's inevitable or something. Damn people won't get up to help themselves half the time.

"Anyway," the captain continued without looking to see if anyone in the jeep was listening, "I had nine thousand refugees from north of Hue in camps along this section last year. Nine thousand right in here. I can hardly remember how they all fit. There's only four hundred left. All the others have settled back to their original villages. Except the Montagnards. They're mostly still here but we've got a new village site picked out for them that their chief just okayed. Out on 546. By Lang Minh Mang. You boys know where that is?" The driver remained oblivious. The red-haired man said nothing. Chelini waited. He was about to say, "No Sir, where is it?" but without the others replying he hesitated, then decided not to reply. The captain fell silent. The driver continued to nod to the passing military vehicles.

Paralleling the roadway were two sets of rails. As the jeep approached the turnoff for Camp Eagle, a combination freight-passenger train, the daily from Quang Tri and Hue over the Hai Van Pass to Da Nang, chugged slowly south. The engine appeared to have been made around the turn of the century. Its big black cylindrical boiler lay atop a flat platform sided by large spoked wheels. A small boxy cabin was welded to the back. The engine pushed seven empty, ancient and dilapidated cars: two flatbeds, two wooden boxcars and three gondolas. Behind the engine was a caboose and following that, twenty-eight vintage wooden passenger cars and boxcars packed with people and goods. Atop each car behind the engine sat a Vietnamese soldier armed with an M-14 rifle.

"That looks kind a stupid," Chelini said.

"Better ta blow away the empties up front, Cherry," the red-haired man growled.

Chelini looked at him. His eyes were closed, his jaw slack and his mouth open. He had to be asleep. How could he know there was a train there?

The jeep entered the dirt road after the train cleared the intersection. At the corner two American MPs were playing with half a dozen children in front of a ramshackle, weather-beaten bunker. Chelini waved to the children and two waved back. He smiled. He looked at the bunker. It was high above the ground, circular, made of layers of sandbags stacked atop rusting, dirt-filled fifty-five-gallon drums. The sandbags had rotted and frayed. Dirt spilled badly from one side causing the entire tower to list. It stood alone and Chelini could not determine its original function. Behind the bunker he could see a junkyard or salvage yard for the squashed carcasses of corroding military vehicles.

Further down the road were garbage dumps. Scavenging amongst the clutter, old Vietnamese women, darker-skinned than those along the highway, Montagnards, collected bottles and cans and pieces of wood. At the finding of a belt by one digger all the ladies gathered around her and shrieked and cackled. It gave Chelini a creepy feeling yet he enjoyed watching the scavengers. Beyond the dumps the jeep passed a vacant firing range where children were searching the clay for expended cartridges.

As they traveled the road became progressively drier and they rode into thicker and thicker lingering clouds of dust from passing vehicles.

"Why do you do that?" the captain demanded of the driver.

"Do what, Sir?" the driver asked.

"Nod like that. To everybody. Do you know every one of those drivers?"

"No Sir."

"Do you think this is some country road? Are you some kind of hick or something?"

"No," the driver answered.

"Then why do you do that?" the officer demanded again.

"I'm an enlisted man, Sir," the driver said, "and so are they."

Chelini chuckled inwardly. He wanted to flash the finger at the captain's back but he didn't dare. The red-haired man opened his eyes for a second and gave the finger to the officer. Then he nodded to Chelini and closed his eyes again.

The terrain changed subtly from the greener piedmont at Phu Bai and along Highway One to the dry red-brown of the foothills. Strings of barbed wire, stretched and looped concertina and pegged tanglefoot, extended from bunkers to a tiny guard-house with a small sign announcing, "CAMP EAGLE—GIA LAI GATE." A lethargic MP glanced up from a paperback and nodded them through. With his left hand out the side of the jeep, below the captain's view, Chelini saw the driver flash an inverted peace sign.

The jeep jostled down the rutted dirt road away from the perimeter line and through an area of open nothingness. Rooster tails of dust rose from the wheels. Old Marine Corps Quonset huts appeared to the right in a shallow draw. In front of one half-cylindrical building was a red and black sign shaped like a bulldozer, "Home of the 326th Engineer Battalion (Airmobile)." A little further on to the left a line of trucks were awaiting gasoline at the 426th S & S fuel point. Beside this was headquarters for Company A, 5th Transportation Battalion (Airmobile). Chelini glanced back. Behind him dust formed an opaque wall. As each new unit appeared he squirmed in the seat and squinted through the dust searching for the headquarters that would house his assignment. Next unit down the road was the 801st Maintenance Battalion looking like a giant bunker complex. All these support units were airmobile and Chelini began to understand what the SERTS instructors had meant when they said everything in the division could be picked up by helicopter and moved.

Where the road turned from west to north there stood the hangars of Eagle Dust-Off, the division's medical evacuation helicopter unit. The hangars were open. In one Chelini could see mechanics working on the jet engine of a ship. In another six men were playing basketball.

They came to the infantry areas: 1st of the 501st, 2d of the 327th and at the westernmost point of Camp Eagle, down the hill from brigade headquarters where they delivered the captain, where the jeep slowed and crept and turned, Chelini suppressed his excitement at seeing the 7th of the 402d.

During the ride back to Phu Bai and the jeep trip through Camp Eagle an anxiety plagued Egan and would not allow his muscles to either relax or tighten. In the jeep he sprawled across much of the rear seat. He felt like a plastic garbage bag filled with oil or pudding. He kept his eyes closed against the harsh sun. The jeep jolted, his head snapped on a limp neck. Don't mean nothin, Egan moaned to himself. It don't mean a fuckin thing. Through his shut eyes he could feel something glinting

silver in the sun before him. He cracked the lids, dust and glare
stung and he closed his eyes more tightly. Something glimmered.
An amber glow through a draft at Louis' Tavern in Paddington
just south of Sydney or the instruments and light show at Whiskey-
A-Go-Go. He opened his eyes again. The cherry beside him was
awed by the antique which served as a cargo and commute train.
Egan shut his eyes and said something but he did not hear his
own voice. The jeep turned and his head flopped on his neck.
The glitter turned. It was coming through an ice cube in a cool
drink of citrus with water. The glass was moist, wet on the
outside, dripping over the small fingers holding it. Wet fingers,
fine and fragile. Over the glass oval lip, beyond the glint of the
cube, between outstretched delicate arms the face of a dark-eyed
girl glistened, looked at his face then cast down.

He opened his eyes. They were passing through the Gia Lai
Gate. Back, he thought. Mick, you're back in the motherfuckin
Nam.

The dust clogged his nostrils and he began breathing through
his mouth. The dust dried his throat. The captain was fussing.
Egan didn't want to hear it. He squeezed his eyes harder and
shut his mouth and sucked air slowly through a slit between his
chapping lips. Through his eyelids the warm sun was Mexican
fire opal refracting on a ring on her finger on a warm spring day
in a small town in western New York.

It was that light, that certain light, that glare that hit him
across squinting eyes. That glistening would trigger in his mind
the thoughts and memories and questions which would not stop.
There it was in his mind, on his mind, the affair, the beautiful
Stephanie. Their love had blossomed, withered, reblossomed,
matured and withered again, and it was still with him, on his
mind, never out of mind. A haunting relationship which periodically reran itself in his brain and tortured him. The story would
be in his mind for ten days or two weeks and it would produce in
him a sadness, a loneliness of a depth only an infantryman in a
war zone could feel so deeply, could hurt over so much and then
at times could so completely forget for weeks and weeks. Then it
would spawn again and begin its run, embellished as memories
often are until one cannot separate the real from the imagined.

The glint on Egan's eyelids triggered the memories. She
was as delicate as Mama-san's daughter. She had pale skin and
large lovely eyes that sparkled. Egan fidgeted. That was the
feeling. The jeep, with the driver and the captain from S-5 and

the cherry, rumbled down the dirt gravel road shaking the earliest moments of his relationship with Stephanie and jumbling those with more recent thoughts of Mama-san's daughter and of his R&R ladies.

The jeep whipped. Egan opened his eyes. He sat up, licked his lips. He glared at the approaching units and at the road choked by the dust of every vehicle which had passed for an hour. Egan looked at Chelini and at the back of the captain's head. He turned and spat dry mud from his mouth. Crazy cherry, he thought. At least he's got the brains to keep his mouth shut most of the time. I'll give him that.

Now Egan could not close his eyes. The driver brought the jeep up to the First Brigade Officer's quarters where the vibration of a generator could be felt beneath the rock music on the stereo set it powered. "Motherfucker," the driver said as he turned away from brigade. He had a low mild voice. "Motherfucker didn't even say thank you."

The jeep slowed and entered the battalion area. An old white soldier was chewing out a lethargic black soldier by the basketball courts. Charlie Company was in informal formation with its gear spread out. Platoon leaders and platoon sergeants and company commanders were meandering and checking and asking questions. A supply truck was unloading cases of C-rations by Recon's hootch and the clerks from S-1 were preparing the stage at the theater for a floor show. It was already difficult to remember what the World had been like. Egan could not even be sure if the eyes of the gypsy in Sydney had been blue or green or brown.

"Fuck," he growled. "Just fuck. Twenty-six en a wake-up." Oh man, he said to himself. Twenty-six en a wake-up. If we can just keep from hittin the shit. Twenty-six en that Seven-Oh-Quick Freedom Bird's goina drop me off in Stephanie's AO. Echo Tango. Sierra.

When the jeep stopped before Company A's headquarters the dust which had tailed it along the road and into the battalion area caught it, swirled and engulfed the vehicle, passengers and all those who were within a five-meter radius.

Brooks stood up coughing. First Sergeant Eduardo Laguana came out of the hootch, ineffectively swatting the dust away from his face. "Turn that thing off," Laguana shouted. "You try to drown the company commander?"

"Hey, L-T," Egan called as he hopped from the jeep. "What's happenin? ¿*Que pasa*, Top?"

"Say hey, Babe," the lieutenant greeted Egan. "You know, Danny, I knew you were coming in right now."

"Yeah, L-T. That's my aura. You tuned into it. I've got one hell of a strong aura."

"No. That wasn't it. I could hear Top up there in the office. He just got a call from brigade. Somebody complaining about my troop's military courtesy. I knew it had to be you."

"That fucker complained? Fuck im. Hey, what's happening anyway? This place looks like a giant cluster fuck."

"How was your R&R?"

"Short, L-T. Too fucking short."

"You," Brooks pointed to the back of the vehicle, "you must be Choo-lee-nee."

"Yes Sir," Chelini said and he awkwardly saluted the lieutenant from his cramped seat beneath the baggage.

"Yeah? Hum." The lieutenant sized up the neophyte with sweeping glances. "I'm Rufus Brooks. This is First Sergeant Laguana and you've already met Platoon Sergeant Egan. Top," Brooks thumbed at Laguana, "will get you squared away with a bunk for tonight and a ruck for tomorrow and all the paperwork Personnel requires. S-1 says you're a wireman."

"Yes Sir," Chelini said. "I work on telephone systems."

"Hum," Brooks stroked his chin. "A telephone man. Yeah. Good. You're going to be Daniel's RTO."

"What?" Egan said, startled. "L-T? This cherry goina be my RTO?"

"Yeah, Daniel. Tompkins extended for a clerk job with supply. Now," he added laughing, "you got zero five to get out of those civvie threads and make a strack troop of yourself. You and I are going to catch a bird to Evans. They're briefing us about tomorrow's CA. I want you to come up with me."

"You come here, Scholdier," Sgt. Laguana said to Chelini; "we get you squared way. Bring jor equipment and we lock it away."

"Pop, De Barti, Thomaston and Whiteboy are up there already," Brooks told Egan. "And Caldwell can't make it. Hey, tell me, really, how was your R&R?"

Egan looked at the lieutenant and chuckled. "God fuckin damn, L-T. Shee-it. That cherry's goina be my R-fuckin-TO! I thought they'd drop him off with the Delta Darlins. I just get back en you loadin my ass with briefins en CAs en cherries. Now you wanta hear a cock story. And, Man,'' Egan paused, ''do I got some good shit to lay on you. Let me tell you bout the tattooed lady.''

"Come on, Danny," Brooks said stepping forward and putting his arm around Egan's shoulders. "Tell me about it."

CHAPTER

5

Chelini waited outside the orderly room shack for the first sergeant to call him. He felt completely lost. This was not a training unit where everyone was new or a replacement station where everyone was transient. This was the infantry, a permanent assignment and he was an outsider. The men were busy in closed groups or loafing in closed groups.

The battalion to which Chelini had been assigned was on the last day of a five-day refitting and training stand-down. Before stand-down the men of the Oh-deuce had spent 105 days in the boonies, up the Sông Bo and Rao Trang rivers, on the hills by Firebases Veghel, Ripcord and Maureen, and in the swamps west of Quang Tri City. They were the division reaction force. It was not uncommon for them to be extracted from one jungle only to be inserted into another.

Chelini went to the screen door of the hootch and tried to see inside. He could see nothing. He turned and scrutinized the battalion area. Before him was a quadrangle surrounded on three sides by buildings. On the far side a steep hill rose to a helicopter resupply point.

At the center of the quad there was a boxing ring and a PSP basketball court. By· the court the old white soldier was still chewing out the same lethargic black boonierat. From where Chelini stood the words were unintelligible. The black soldier had very dark skin. He was shuffling his feet in the red dust, casting upward scowls from a down-hanging head, bouncing and jiving with his knuckles on his hips. The old white soldier was shorter than the black man and much heavier. His head was round and bald on top with the sparse hair at the side shaved. The skin was very red, as if blood was trying to escape.

Very near Company A's office was a narrow moldy structure with a boat on the roof. Five white enlisted men with deeply tanned arms, faces and necks and pallid torsos carried olive drab towels and shaving gear into the shower house. They joked and fooled and slapped each other with the towels and stepped gingerly over the muck patch which flowed past the four-holer EM latrine toward the drainage ditch. They did not even look in Chelini's direction.

Close to the screen door of the office where Chelini stood two men converged, stopped and commenced a strangely ritualistic clapping and shaking of hands and forearms and slapping of each other's shoulders and tapping of each other's fists. One of the men was black, dark brown, not as dark as the soldier at the quad's center; the other was light brown, the color of wheatbread. The ritualized greeting went on for what seemed a long time.

Chelini turned. A clerk opened the screen door. The first sergeant called him in by methodically curling one index finger. Chelini gulped. The first sergeant fumbled with a stack of papers and forms. His desk was clear of everything except essentials. He dusted the land-line telephone with his hand and directed the clerk to empty the trash containers. Then he handed Chelini the forms and a pencil. "Complete thees," he said and turned away. Chelini nodded. Holy Christ, he thought. I'm lost. I'm stuck. I gotta get out of this unit. Chelini glanced at the forms briefly and began filling in his name on a weapons card. He looked up, out the door. The dark black soldier from the center of the quad had joined the black soldier and brown soldier at the front of the office. The greeting rite of raps and slaps and shakes began again.

"Troop," the first sergeant said. Chelini jumped. "Can't you write any faster? You scared of that pencil?"

"No, I just . . ."

"Troop, you a college graduate, aint you?" Oh, shit, Chelini thought. Two strikes against me already. "You let pencil run you. T'row that pencil down."

"T'row it down?"

"Yeas. That what I said. T'row it down." Chelini dropped the pencil. "Chee!" the first sergeant shouted. "What it do? It don't jump up and bite you, do it? It's daid, Scholdier. Now pick it up and run it.''

Chelini began signing the forms. Oh shit, he thought. How'd I get stuck in an infantry unit? They put all the dumb kids in here. Of all the places to be assigned. I wonder what happened to Kaltern from basic. He had a good head. Or Baez from AIT or Ralston. They were some okay people and now I gotta get stuck with a bunch of high school dropouts.

"Troop," First Sergeant Laguana said, "you getting some very expensive equipment. You getting the best weapon in the world. You know that? When you get here at Eagle no magazine in weapon, hokay?" The first sergeant picked up Chelini's weapons card and brought it close to his face. "When you on berm guard you lock en load. You lock en load on helicopter for CA, hokay? On CA you keep the chafety on. If you on the first chopper you go in on automatic, hokay? I don want none my troops schot." Chelini nodded and nodded. This guy's an idiot, he told himself.

The three men who'd been in front of the office came in. The first sergeant ignored them and they ignored him. Chelini looked up. The nearest one nodded and winked. Chelini nodded back. The dark black soldier saluted Chelini with a clenched fist. Chelini startled, stared. He nodded agreement. He was frightened not to. He knew he'd been assigned to a unit of crazy racist psychopaths. The first sergeant picked up the remainder of the forms and scrutinized each. "You getting the best radio in the world," Laguana said. "You know that? You getting seven hun'red channel. You know that?"

"Hey, Babe, we got us a new RTO," the dark black man said snapping his fingers. "Oh Babe, that fucka gowin kick yo ass." He gave Chelini a second power salute. Chelini smiled dumbly and nodded and made a half-hearted attempt to emulate the gesture and the black man laughed.

"Hey, Top," the brown man laughed. To Chelini the laugh seemed bitter. Oh Man, he thought. These guys would slit your throat for a cigarette. "You got a new wristwatch." The brown man grabbed for the first sergeant's arm but the NCO pulled it back. Shit, Chelini thought. Even the first sergeant's scared of them.

"What choos want?" Laguana snapped. "Jackson. Out," he said to the dark black. "Doc. Out," he added. To the brown man he said, "El Paso. You stay."

The two black men departed after chiding and jiving the first sergeant. The light brown soldier stayed.

"Hokay, now I get a rucksack." Sergeant Laguana reached beneath his desk and with a theatrical flip of the wrist produced an aluminum frame with a nylon bag attached. "Thees," he said, "is rucksack. Thees rucksack weigh one pound. By the time I schow you, we get you a P-R-C twen'y-five, chow, ammo and canteen . . ."

"That motha's goina weigh a hundred pounds," El Paso inserted.

Chelini shifted toward the brown soldier and a bit out of the way. El Paso was older than Chelini had thought when he'd first seen him standing in front of the office.

"Troop," Laguana addressed Chelini trying to ignore El Paso again, "you gon carry everyt'ing you need right here. Here, you try it on." Chelini reluctantly reached for the rucksack.

Laguana scowled and walked into the back storeroom and returned with a PRC-25 radio. Then he left again and returned with a case of C-rations. He dropped that on the floor by the growing pack and disappeared into the back room singing to himself. El Paso fitted and secured the radio inside the ruck's main pocket. He fastened it in such a manner that it could be easily removed and carried separately.

"Hey," El Paso said. "Ask Top to give you two extra pair of bootlaces. He'll be okay to you now cause you're new. You won't be able to get them later."

"Thanks," Chelini said. He wanted to ask the brown soldier questions but he was wary.

Top returned with four one-quart canteens, an empty steel ammo can, an M-16, eighteen empty magazines and eighteen boxes of cartridges, four fragmentation grenades and two smoke grenades. He dropped the equipment on the pile and whistled his way back to the storeroom.

"Hey," El Paso yelled at him, "get him some more canteens. This aint enough."

"Thas enough," Laguana yelled back.

"Guy's a fuckin shithead," El Paso said. "I won't tell you, though. You can't tell one man about another." El Paso set to work filling the rucksack, carefully ordering items with the attention he would give to his own gear. Chelini watched him. "Shit," the brown man said. "Ham and lima beans. Taste like shit. Worst Charlie Rat there is. You oughta throw it out. Aint worth humpin. These, canned fruit and pound cake, they're worth their weight in gold.''

The first sergeant returned with four radio batteries, a machete, an entrenching tool, a claymore with wire and firing device, a poncho and poncho liner, one olive drab towel, a web belt, ammo pouches, helmet with liner and cover, a long and short antenna for the radio, and small bottles of LSA and bug repellent. El Paso continued sorting through the food asking Chelini what he liked and throwing what he himself didn't like to one side. From the heavy cardboard of the C-ration case El Paso cut a broad section and fitted it on the inner side of the ruck so it would lie between the lumpy cans and batteries inside and Chelini's back.

"Look at this shit," El Paso said. "Take the batteries but see that you get somebody else to carry one of em. Fuck the E-T and the claymore. When you hump a Prick-25 you can't carry all that shit. Machete's optional. Top'll have you humpin two hundred pounds if you let him. Make sure he gets you more canteens." El Paso tied the empty ammo can, a small steel box with a watertight seal, to the base of the ruck. "That's where you keep all your personal stuff," El Paso said. "Toothbrush, writing paper, extra socks. Everything that's you and not the army." Then he said, "Dump your duffel bag out." Chelini emptied his duffel bag onto the floor. "You can't carry any of that stuff," El Paso said. "You can maybe take a book and you gotta take your razor. Top'll lock away any personal shit you got. The uniforms go into the company clothes fund. You might want to keep out an extra T-shirt but that's all."

First Sergeant Laguana returned again and handed Chelini an extra pair of bootlaces. "Don let nobody see thees," he smiled. "They always try an take them from me. I gotta keep thees locked up."

"Top," El Paso looked up angrily. "You're an ass."

"Jus go trim that mustache," Laguana shouted.

"Don't harass me. I'll get the Human Relations Office to slap the back of your head. This place is fucked up."

Laguana bent down to check and adjust the straps on Chelini's rucksack. "He Company Senior RTO," Laguana said proudly trying to mollify the young brown soldier.

El Paso pushed Laguana away. He grabbed the ruck. "Don't fuck with my RTOs," he said. He turned to Chelini. "Try it on."

"He schow you how to put the ruck together pretty good, eh?" Laguana smiled. "Oooo, you gon cuss me. Now I got somet'ing to do. You go cut that mustache. Now get out."

"Hey, Top?"

"Out."

"If you don't listen to me I'll tell the IG."

"What you want?" The first sergeant feigned exhaustion.

"About my R&R request. I'd like to change it from Bangkok to Sydney. Like Egan's."

"Can't."

"Why?"

"Out."

"I want to talk to the L-T."

"He aint in."

"You aren't going to let me see him."

"Get out of here you chon-of-a-bitch," the first sergeant erupted, jumping out from behind the desk, his eyes bulging and his fists clenched.

El Paso ran out of the hootch. He called back through the screen, "I'm only teasing you, Top. Cut yourself some slack." He walked away mumbling, "That stupid asshole. He doesn't have any right to tell me to trim my mustache. Son-of-a-bitch. Gives us Chicanos a bad name. Can't even speak English."

Chelini staggered out of the office hunched under the weight of the ruck. He plodded down to the boonierat shacks behind the theater. The weight of the rucksack was immediately oppressive, the shoulder straps cutting. Surrounding the hootches were the shacks the boonierats occupied when in from the bush. There were only half a dozen of these and when the entire battalion was in on stand-down these shanties were supplemented with twelve-man tents. Now, the tents, with their sides rolled up, filled the gaps between the hootches behind the theater. Chelini entered the hootch the first sergeant had told him was for the second squad and command post of the first platoon.

The hootches were all the same: the architectural essence of the 101st. These modular buildings dotted all the base camps. They were elevated on cinder blocks laid on the earth. Floor joists ran from block to block and to these a flooring of 4 x 8 half-inch plywood was nailed. The standard building was sixteen feet wide and thirty-two feet long, stud-framed to a height of five and a half feet with a pitched roof rising to ten feet above the long center axis. The sides were again 4 x 8 sheets of plywood laid horizontally and tacked to the stud framing. This allowed eighteen inches of open space running down both sides for windows. Roofs were corrugated galvanized iron sheets which absorbed the dry-season heat and made the hootches ovens or resounded with and amplified the rain of the monsoons, making enough noise to drive a man crazy. There was no heating. Electrical wires ran to the buildings but were not connected to a power source. The offices and buildings for rear-echelon personnel were of similar design, though more refined.

Chelini looked down the long low narrow barracks. It was somewhat like a tunnel with windows. There were two rows of canvas cots. On some of the cots various articles of field gear lay exposed. Rucksacks were scattered against the walls. The floor was covered with dry brown dirt and the wood was splintered. In the far corner a man lay on a cot. He had on no boots or socks, no shirt. He wore a pair of OD boxer shorts and a Star of David on a black bootlace around his neck. The man was emaciated. Lying down he appeared nearly six feet tall, 140 pounds at most. His ribs rippled the chalky white skin of his chest. Across his shoulders were red-yellow acne bumps. On the man's hollow stomach was a small black cassette tape recorder.

"Say hey," the man said when he noticed Chelini staring at him. "You a cherry? Pick yourself a bed. Last chance for a good night's sleep."

"All these taken?" Chelini asked.

"That one's not." He indicated the cot across from him, which was missing a cross bar at one end where the canvas sagged. "Who you goina be with?"

"Company A."

"Damn, you are a cherry. This area is all Alpha Company. I mean which squad. This hootch is for the first platoon."

"Oh. I'm supposed to be with the command post. The first sergeant said I'm goina be Sergeant Egan's RTO."

"Ha! You Egan's cherry. He's okay but he's goina hump yer ass off. That man likes ta walk. What's yer name? I'm Leon Silvers."

"I'm James Chelini. People usually call me Jim."

Silvers sat up and put the cassette down next to him on the canvas cot. He looked shorter sitting but he looked just as thin. "I was just listening to a tape my family sent. It was my folks' anniversary last month and my father was officiating at the dinner table while everybody was talking.''

"Oh,'' Chelini said. He was at a loss for something to say. "Ah, where is everybody?''

"Around. Half the dudes are on guard.''

"Where are you from?'' Chelini asked. "I mean . . . back in the World. I'm from Connecticut.''

"Really? Where?''

"Bridgeport.''

"Ha! You shittin me? I'm from Stamford.''

"Wow! You're the first person I've met from Connecticut. Except for basic. How long have you been here?''

"Me? Seven months. But let me give you a tip. Don't go around asking everybody you meet how long they've been here. You can get only two responses to that question. Either somebody is really short and they're goina yell 'SHORT' or they're goina interpret it as though you were asking them like how they made it so long without getting their shit scattered. It's kind of a bad omen. You don't want to ask everybody right off where they're from either.''

Chelini stared at Silvers. The skinny man's eyes were very pale hazel and they bulged from their sockets as if his brain were pressuring his eyeballs and forcing them out of his head. He had prominent cheekbones and a very prominent Adam's apple. Most of his body was white but his arms below where a short sleeved shirt stopped and his neck and face were weathered red-brown. "I didn't mean to ah . . .'' Chelini shrugged then blurted out, "It's just that everybody sees I'm new and calls me a cherry and I guess without thinking I just say, 'How long have you been here?' ''

"Hey, I know,'' Silvers laughed. "It don't really mean nothin.''

"That's another thing. Everybody I've met around here says that. 'It don't mean nothin. It don't mean nothin.' Why does everybody say that?''

Silvers winked and shrugged, "I don't know. You know. It don't mean nothin.'' He laughed. "That's what happens when guys live together. Everybody says the same things.''

Silvers lay back again and Chelini arranged his gear on the cot that Silvers had indicated. Chelini rummaged through his rucksack then cleaned off the cot by slapping it and raising small dust storms. Silvers turned his tape player back on and continued listening. Then he stopped it and said to Chelini, "Hey. You want to listen to some of this? It's kinda funny. My brother's talkin about racing. He just bought a super-vee. Both my sisters and their husbands are there. The oldest one and her husband just got jobs at Yale. My other sister teaches high school and her husband's just been laid off by Sikorski. Listen to this." Silvers' large eyes watered with mirth.

"Leon, we just finished stuffing ourselves with cream puffs," one voice said.

"That's my oldest sister," Silvers injected.

The same voice continued. "I wrote to you about the farm we're going to be buying, maybe. If you think you want a writer's retreat there and join in with us, I told you, you could pick up one of the shares."

"Unless you'd rather travel to Europe with me, racing," a male voice joked.

"Unless you'd rather come to London with me," came in a second female voice.

"Unless you'd rather stay on welfare with me," quipped a voice in the background of the taped conversation. "Thirty-nine weeks you're eligible for."

Chelini stopped fiddling with his gear. He looked at Silvers and smiled. His stomach relaxed.

The tape continued. "He's going to be on welfare," giggled the first female voice. There was a short pause then Leon's sister said, "I can't really remember what I wanted to tell you. I guess there isn't really anything to tell. When you get home we'll have a good blast."

"Nobody's going on welfare around here," a strong matronly voice commanded. "Really, Leon. The way they all carry on. Everyone is doing just fine. Now don't you tell Leon your problems. I'm sure he's got enough of his own to worry about."

"Leon, dear," the second female voice came on again, "how are you?" There was much laughing in the tape. "As you know, Sheldon and I are going to London and Dublin in about a month-and-a-half even though we can't afford anything at the moment. And good things of course come in packages of three. Sheldon has been laid off; our car was stolen; and I might not have a job next year because I had another tiff with my department head but I'll write you about that. He's really being assinine and is quite a jerk. Similar to your major or colonel you wrote about having so much trouble with. The situations are parallel even though one is education and one is military. And here's mother, Leon. I wish you were here with us.''

"Mother can't say a word," said an older male voice. "Isn't that amazing? Are you at a loss for words, Mother?"

Chelini did not look at Silvers now. This was too personal. Chelini was embarrassed for the gaunt man. Silvers simply lay back and listened, shut his eyes and laughed.

The tape continued. Leon's brother said, "Leon, you look very strange. You're only about six inches long. You've got a silver head and a black thin body. What are you doing to yourself? Has the army turned you into a piece of plastic?"

"Yes, Leon," said one of the sisters. "We're all looking at the microphone pretending it's you." There was a loud "Ouch!" "Sheldon just burned himself passing me a cordial over the candles."

"Just a minute," Mr. Silvers controlled the conversation. "I'm going to tell him one of the Playboy jokes." Laughter. "Mother won't let me tell you a Playboy joke. You're not old enough."

"That's not a good image for a father," Mrs. Silvers said.

"You see," continued Leon's father, "there's this girl who goes to Harvard to take a sex education course and she refuses to take the course because the last lesson is an oral exam." There was more laughter.

The conversation went on and on. It made Chelini think of his own family. He laughed when the people on the tape laughed. He pretended he knew them. It made him feel close to Silvers. Finally Leon's older sister's husband, who hadn't yet spoken, said, "Leon, I hope you got the address of the guy who's putting together stories and poetry by Vietnam veterans. We expect to find some of your writings in that anthology. I'm sure any number of those things you've written would be appropriate."

"Leon," his father said, "you make sure you get clearance for anything you send. And let them change anything they say must be changed."

"Pa," the brother-in-law said, "don't tell him that. He can write what he likes. This isn't World War II."

"Umm. Mother wants me to stop this tape. I don't know why. We've got an hour left on it."

"Stop it until we have something to talk about."

"Let's you and I argue. There she goes, see?"

"Just like always," Leon's brother said. "A touch of home, Leon."

This was followed by the sound of people talking to each other with no one speaking directly into the microphone. There was some jumbled talk of his father selling a portion of his business then Mr. Silvers said clearly, "All things being equal, this year, after you come back, I think Mother and I will pretty definitely go to Europe for about three weeks."

"Leon," his mother said, "you can come with us. We're going to put the machine away now and later I'll finish the tape to my son. You all had your turn. I'm going to talk to him in private."

"Shit, Man," Silvers said to Chelini as he clicked off the recorder, "them folks gettin down. Hey, you been over to the Phoc Roc TOC yet? That's our little club. Let's get a beer and I'll introduce you to some of the dudes."

"Wait a minute," Chelini reared back. "Let me think. I've seen so many people already I can't keep them all straight. There was an old man, I mean old, screaming at a dude by the basketball courts. Then three guys in with the first sergeant. There was Egan and the lieutenant. Top was getting me a radio and a rucksack. He told me to get a haircut and this Puerto Rican guy to cut his mustache. Couple of brothers slappin themselves silly . . ."

"That's the dap. It's kind of a way to say hi." Silvers paused. Chelini didn't say anything. "Here, give me your right hand. I'll show you an abbreviated dap so you can greet the brothers." Chelini held out his hand. Silvers put out his fist. Chelini balled his right hand as Silvers tapped his twice against Chelini's. Then he rapped the back of his fist twice, then the top and the bottom. Silvers opened his hand, motioned for Chelini to follow, slid the palm over Chelini's upturned palm. He snapped his fingers. "You'll get it," Silvers said. "Let's see. The old dude had to be Zarnochuk. Old Zarno. He's battalion sergeant major. Chews everybody out. Hardass, Man, hardass! Who else?"

"There was that Puerto Rican . . ."

"Oh shit. El Paso. Don't ever call El Paso a P.R., Man. He's Chicano. Mexican. History major from the University of Texas. He got a year at law school finished before the draft got him."

"Jesus! Is that right? Man, he gave the first sergeant a bad time. The other two were both black, I think their names were, ah, one was Jackson and the other was Doc."

"Ah, El Paso always gives Top a hard time cause Top's such an ignorant shit. Jackson's from Mississippi. Doc. That's gotta be Doc Johnson cause he's the only black medic we got. Doc's from Harlem. He's company CP medic. El Paso's senior RTO. Jax is a rifleman in my squad—fire team leader if we had enough guys to have fire teams. All those dudes been here forever." Silvers had put on a pair of shower togs and had pulled on a pair of jungle fatigue pants while he talked. He put on a fatigue shirt and picked up his hat. "Come on. Let's get a beer. I'll show you where the barber's hootch is. You in the Oh-deuce now, Cherry. You gotta get your shit together."

C H A P T E R

6

They did not look at each other while they spoke but only squinted ahead toward the building. "Why we goin to this fuckin briefin?" Egan asked. "I mean, why this briefin? We never go to briefins."

"We never go," Brooks answered, "because we always . . . we're always in the boonies."

"L-T, you been ta briefins before. You know they aint goina say nothin."

"Come on, Danny. You really can't tell. We might get something. Besides, the colonel wanted a good showing for the Third Brigade CO."

"Shee-it. REMFs givin the briefin only do it so they can kiss the colonel's ass. And the colonel, he only goes cause he likes to have his ass kissed."

"Maybe so."

"They already worked everythin out in the TOC before. Or in the colonel's office or in the general's hootch while the old man's ballin some gook whore."

"Shhh. Looks like they're already under way."

In the 101st Airborne Division (Airmobile) it was not atypical for a battalion from one brigade to be placed under the operational control of another brigade for short duration assaults. Airmobility produced a functional efficiency in the deployment of forces which previous warfare had never matched. The helicopter made it possible for entire battalions to be under the operational control of one commander in one area one day and under the control of another commander in an area a hundred kilometers away the next day. If the men didn't have to disembark and slowly trudge by foot about the jungle mountains it would almost be possible to have only one set of boonierats. The army could have twice the commanders with their command posts and maps and charts and electronic surveillance devices and half the ground troops and simply airmobile the troops, op-con the boonierats, in a continuous hopscotching. Troops would no longer belong to a commander but to several commands and the casualties of one real unit could be spread over the various on-paper units. The quicker infantrymen could be moved, the fewer infantrymen would be needed. Theoretically there would have to be more support and transportation troops and the endless deployment, redeployment, redeployment from fight to fight might be hell on the soldiers. That was reality for the one-in-ten American soldiers in Vietnam who were the infantry. One-in-ten was the lowest ratio of line soldiers to support troops in American military history.

The 7th of the 402d was the division reaction force, the cooling unit to be extracted from its AO at any moment and inserted about a hot spot until cooled then extracted and inserted again. Brooks and Egan felt uneasy in the Third Brigade rear. They entered the briefing hall as unobtrusively as possible.

"Gen-tle-men," a young second lieutenant was saying, "the governing mission of this operation is to conduct airmobile operations in support of the Armed Forces of the Republic of Vietnam, to locate and destroy enemy units and base camps and to interdict enemy movement into the lowlands. Our operations provide the secure environment which is enabling the GVN to pursue the national objectives of political stability and socio-economic development. In support of this mission we will be operating from two headquarters; the main headquarters here at Camp Evans and an advance light TOC on Firebase Barnett. The topographic briefing will be delivered by Sergeant Marquadt. Sergeant."

Egan and Brooks mingled silently with the company grade officers and enlisted men standing behind the seven rows of seated personnel. The room was bright, lighted by three rows of fluorescent lights and the glow through the translucent shades drawn across the window openings. The room was stuffy. Sev-

eral senior NCOs sitting in the third and fourth rows were
smoking pipes. EM in the back smoked cigarettes. The air about
the lights and by the shades was tinted blue. People were shuffling in the chairs and shifting from foot to foot behind. Voices
murmured.

The Third Brigade commander—self-named Old Fox—sat
sideways in his chair in the front row. The remaining seats in
that row were vacant. The second row was occupied by the
battalion commander from the 7/402, Lieutenant Colonel Oliver
M. Henderson—The GreenMan—and by various commanders
from artillery and supply units. In the third row sat the Air Force
and Vietnamese liaison officers, intelligence and operations officers and NCOs. Behind these were more staff personnel, officers,
NCOs and clerks and in the last rows the company and battery
commanders and platoon leaders who had arrived early enough
to get a seat. Standing, leaning against the windows and the back
wall and against each other were the majority of lower ranking
enlisted personnel and late arriving junior officers. Among these
were several men from Company A including Jonnie 'Pop'
Randalph, platoon sergeant of the 2d platoon, Lieutenants Frank
De Barti and William Thomaston, platoon leaders of the 2d and
1st platoons, respectively, and Clayton 'Whiteboy' Janoff, a
squad leader from the 1st platoon who'd only come to accom-
pany Lt. Thomaston.

Egan and Brooks found an open space at the center of the
crowded rear section, stood side by side in an informal parade
rest and faced forward. "Hey," Egan nudged Brooks, "can you
believe this REMF mentality?" Brooks did not respond.

"Thank you, Sir," Sergeant Marquadt said insolently. The
sergeant approached the podium with an extended chrome swagger.
Behind the podium and indeed covering most of that wall of the
building was a topographic map of northern I Corps. The map
was fourteen feet wide, eight feet high. It was a composite of
twenty-eight smaller topographic maps, each covering a grid of
27.5 x 27.5 kilometers. At the top the DMZ was depicted by two
roughly parallel lines seven kilometers apart. The Laotian border
was marked in red to the left. Jungles were in dark green, clear
forests in light green, lowlands and swamps in white with light
blue symbols for rice or marsh grass. The entire map had a
brown under-hue from the thin topographic lines circling up to
the mountain peaks and opening down the valleys, becoming
denser as the terrain steepened. To the right was the Gulf of

Tonkin in pale blue. Various areas were dotted with red triangles indicating hilltop firebases.

The maps were of a scale of 1:50,000. Infantry units carried those sections in which they operated. Artillery units used the maps in their FDC (Fire Direction Control) to plot missions. At the base of each map, in the key printed in English and Vietnamese, were the disclaimers: DELINEATION OF INTERNAL ADMINISTRATIVE BOUNDARIES IS APPROXIMATE, and DELINEATION OF INTERNATIONAL BOUNDARIES MUST NOT BE CONSIDERED AUTHORITATIVE.

"Gentlemen," Sergeant First Class Emil Marquadt boomed, "the operational environment is a long occupied, extensively developed and heavily defended supply and logistic base, staging area and communications and transportation center. Resident forces include administrative, logistic, quartermaster and transportation units with organic security as well as some tactical units . . ." Aw, come on, Man, Egan thought, raising his eyes to the ceiling. ". . . Central to the landform of this operational area and determinant to the direction of attack is the Khe Ta Laou river valley which runs generally east-west."

Sergeant Marquadt swung his chrome swagger and slapped the map. He was a large heavyset man with a ruddy, slightly disfigured face.

"Gentlemen, this valley is twelve air kilometers long. With the exception of this one major bow the river runs straight through the valley." Marquadt traced his statement on the map with the tip of the swagger. "The headwaters of the river and the origin of the valley are in the rugged terrain here, to the east." His voice rose and fell as he traced up and down the terrain. "The floor of the valley varies in width from 200 meters at its narrowest point to about two kilometers where it enters the Da Krong plain," he boomed. "The Khe Ta Laou will be the single most useful navigational aid for aircraft flying under conditions of restricted visibility."

Marquadt belched into his closed left fist and glanced at the brigade commander sitting isolated in the first row. The commander gave no indication of recognizing Marquadt's presence at all. The sergeant quickly continued. "There is a distinctive feature, a single, very high tree on a knoll where the river bows, which can be located visually from anywhere in or above the valley. It will serve as good navigational reference. You might want to note it on your maps at YD 148321.

"The valley floor is a brushwood area consisting of grass, bushes, secondary scrubs and elephant grass. The brushwood is discontinuous and varies in density from extremely heavy to moderate. In areas, particularly in the eastern end of the valley, this vegetation forms a canopy covering the river.

"The landform of the ground north of the Khe Ta Laou . . ."

Egan yawned loudly. He stretched his arms, rolled his shoulders. He looked around. Mick, he said to himself, these are the assholes who control your life. Fuck em. Twenty-six en a wake-up.

"Gentlemen," Sergeant Marquadt bellowed, catching Egan's attention again. He was looking toward the back of the briefing hall where the infantrymen were easily distinguishable from the staff and rear personnel by their worn rumpled uniforms. "I spoke personally with several LRRPs (he pronounced it "lurps") and they asked that I convey to you . . ."

"Sergeant," the brigade commander interrupted gently without turning, "may we stick to the topography of the valley?"

"Yes Sir. Excuse me, Sir." Marquadt regained his composure and continued with his prepared remarks. "The north wall is covered with single- and double-canopy jungle. The single-canopy forest averages twenty meters in height with scattered . . ."

I wonder what he was going to say, Egan thought. Egan looked at Brooks and he could see the L-T was also distracted.

". . . at the western end of the valley, here, there is a thumb of Laotian territory protruding into the Republic of Vietnam. Highway 616, a major artery of the Ho Chi Minh Trail, runs up this peninsula and connects with supply routes in the hills near Lang Kerie, here, at YD 020295. From this junction . . ."

Why'd the Old Fox cut the dude off, Egan asked himself. Fucken typical.

". . . Gentlemen, these are the highest mountains in I Corps. It will be rough out there . . ."

That's what he wanted to say, Egan said to himself.

". . . Or you can look east down the Rach My Chanh across to the Sông Ô Lau. Looking east you will be able to count eleven ridges, each lower than the one closer to you. Eleven ridges with the shadows of twelve valleys reaching east to Hue. Gentlemen," the voice boomed to the back of the room again, "from this perspective, you are standing on the 12th and highest ridge, with your back to the 13th valley."

"What the fuck's this guy saying?" Egan's whisper exploded.

Brooks attempted to quiet him with a stern disapproving glance. "L-T, what the fuck did you bring me here for?" Egan snarled through clenched teeth. "I ken read a fuckin map. I don't need this fucker tellin me the fuckin valley runs east ta west."

"Hush up, Danny."

"Jesus H. Christ."

"Sshhh."

". . . There is a paucity of natural helicopter landing zones in the operational area," Marquadt continued.

"What's that mean, L-T?"

"Scarcity. Means we're going to have to cut them."

". . . the few which do exist," Marquadt said, "are usually one-or-two ship landing zones requiring hovering approaches and departures and are so obvious they will probably be defended or booby-trapped. It will be desirable and necessary to construct new landing zones. Insertion LZs for the airmobile combat assault will be constructed with USAF-delivered weapons at locations jointly selected by ground force and air mission commanders.

"Gentlemen." Marquadt closed his chrome swagger. "Thank you."

People shifted. A mumble rose in the hall. Brooks and Egan straightened, stretched their backs. Egan was pissed. Marquadt sat down. The young lieutenant introduced a nervous buck sergeant in heavily starched fatigues. The buck sergeant was from the weather service.

"Sir," he nodded to the brigade commander, "today's forecast for the coastal staging area and headquarters area is continued hot, humid and partially cloudy. Humidity: 60 to 90 percent. High Tuesday was 97 degrees; low 81 degrees. Today's high was 99 degrees; low 80 degrees. Sunrise tomorrow is 0635 hours; sunset 1924 hours. Rainfall to 1500 hours today has been zero; for the month 1.42 inches. Valid period of this report is 1500 hours 11 August to 1500 hours 12 August. Screaming Eagles have been in Vietnam 1850 days.

"The operational area is affected by winds, clouds, precipitation and ceilings of both the northeast and southwest monsoons during seasonal transition. Weather over the operational area: Cloudiness will occur over the Annamite Mountain Range. Ceilings will average 2500 to 4000 feet. The border areas will experience mostly scattered clouds . . ."

Egan was going nuts. He felt trapped.

". . . if the primary winds come from the southeast scattered thunderstorms and showers with bases of 3000 to 4000 feet will develop over the operational area by mid-afternoon . . ."

Egan looked at Brooks. Brooks seemed to be listening intently. Egan squeezed his hands into fists.

". . . fog, rain and clouds will characterize the early morning weather and may preclude employment of close tactical air support. Visibility in the afternoon will be sharply reduced by a combination of natural haze and flying into the sun."

Rufus Brooks heard only portions of the weather briefing although he made a conscious effort to pay attention. His thoughts distracted him. The buck sergeant sat down and the second lieutenant introduced Major Homer J. Walker, Third Brigade Intelligence Officer, to recount recent activity and to establish an intelligence basis for the operation.

Major Walker seemed the absent-minded scientist who finds briefing his colleagues on his work a distraction from the work itself. He spoke laconically into the papers he held on the podium. "Ah . . . in the past several months . . . as I'm sure you're all aware . . . enemy activity in our western AO has increased significantly. Let me, ah, recount, ah," the major shuffled pages of notes, "ah, some of the activity. The NVA apparently is trying to muster an offensive up here in response to the recent Cambodian thrust. As you know that operation, for the American units involved, ah, ended 30 June. Screaming Eagles of the 3d of the 506th op-conned to the 4th Infantry Division participated in the areas around Prek Drang. Very successfully. Since then we have uncovered apparent build-ups both directly below the Demilitarized Zone and along the Laotian border. During the second and third weeks of July aircraft of the 2d of the 17th engaged an estimated 400 new enemy soldiers around Khe Sanh killing, ah," the major fumbled in the pages again, "209 of them. Elements of the 3d of the 187th discovered a mass grave on 25 July by Ba Da at YD 295315. They observed numerous bodies but stopped the search and did not obtain a definitive body count because of the smell.

"Activity during the first eleven days of August has increased significantly along a frontal corridor from Firebases Airborne and Goodman in the south up through Maureen, Ripcord, O'Reilly, Jerome and Barnett. On 1 August, the 2d of the 17th killed ten enemy south of Firebase Jerome. Three kilometers

north of Goodman the 3rd ARVN Regiment engaged an estimated . . .''

Neither Egan nor Brooks could sustain interest in the report.

''. . . killed and five 12.7mm machine guns captured . . .
On 6 August D Troop 2nd . . . the ARVN Hac Bao . . .
Thirty-six cases AK-47 ammunition, one hundred 82mm mortar
rounds and 15 rucksacks. The equipment was evacuated . . .
Four 122mm rockets impacted in Hue City at an ARVN deten-
tion center killing 14 detainees and wounding 89 . . . On 9
August Firebase O'Reilly . . . ARVN Regiment engaged and
killed 11 NVA . . . vicinity of Firebase O'Reilly reported sighting 800 NVA on a ridgeline. In response to this sighting 26
tactical air strikes and 36 aerial rocket artillery sorties were
expended in the target area . . .''

There was something significant, Brooks thought.

''. . . Three nights ago, Ranger Reconnaissance Team Quebec 16 reported spotting four 5-ton and five 2½-ton trucks filled
with troops coming up the road to Ta Laou at YD 091329. That
road is indicated on your maps as a footpath. The reconnaissance
team did not engage the enemy . . .''

Trucks to Ta Laou? Brooks asked. That's only ten klicks
from where we're going.

''. . . Evans, 122mm rockets impacted in three locations
about the base during the past week resulting in the destruction
of one UH-1D helicopter . . . Remote area monitors have shown
heavy activity in the area of your objectives. Magnetic and
acoustic detectors indicate some movement of heavy equipment
in the Khe Ta Laou valley. Our newest gadget, ah, the XM-3
Airborne Personnel Detector Device or People Sniffer, indicates
a massing of human beings in the Khe Ta Laou valley.

''Captured documents and PW interrogations indicate the
following units and strengths within the operational area: 7th
NVA Front Headquarters, estimated strength 200; 812th NVA
Regimental Headquarters, estimated strength unknown; 5th Infan-
try Battalion, 812th, estimated strength 600; and the NVA K-12
Transportation Battalion, estimated strength 200 . . .''

Would you like a shot at an enemy headquarters? Brooks
thought of the GreenMan's question. He wouldn't. Not a Front-
size headquarters?

''. . . Lastly, the Government of Vietnam National Elections are scheduled to be held 30 August. The number of VC/VCI
related incidents against the local populace of Thua Thien Prov-

ince has increased significantly from 38 in July to 23 in the first ten days of this month. There has been a slight increase in sabotage and assassination incidents and a significant increase reported for propaganda with indications the NVA may try to disrupt the elections.'' The major looked up from the podium, glanced then nodded toward the Old Fox and returned to his seat.

Daniel Egan had nothing but contempt for the briefing officers. Shee-it. I've heard all this crap before. These guys with their little black boxes. One dink sits by a box with his cooking pots and walks back and forth and they got a whole regiment moving into a valley. Egan shifted his weight and with the movement his thoughts shifted, fell to his feet. Egan's feet were already sore from standing. If there is one thing of importance to an infantryman it is his feet. Egan caught himself listening to various portions of the briefing and criticizing everything he heard. His feet irritated him and the briefing made his feet hurt worse. During the meteorological section he cursed the irrelevance of the forecast. He had spent enough time in the mountains of northern I Corps to know that neither mountains nor weather nor commanders cared about or respected his feet. Fuckin rains in the mountains all the fuckin time. When it aint rainin it's so fuckin socked in ya can't get a bird in fer resupply half the time. Early morning showers! That man's got his head way up his ass. How come ever time we go out it's raining on our heads and soakin our feet? These poor feet. Took me all my R&R to get em clean and then they weren't really clean an that fucker's got the brass balls to say early morning fog and showers.

Once Egan's thoughts broke from the briefing, he relaxed. He allowed his thoughts to play in his mind. His eyes closed, then opened then closed almost all the way, open just far enough to allow a sliver of light to enter. A drop of saline solution filled the slit and the light passing through it was refracted into a blur rainbow. It pleased him. If he could only keep his eyelids perfectly still. Images formed in the wash of color. His eyes flinched. The minute images were lost, new ones formed. He forced the image into the shape of a girl, a young woman. The image was not clear. The harder he tried to focus the more his eyelids jumped. He lost the image. He took a deep breath, exhaled very slowly and thought of his girl back in the World.

He could not conjure up a picture of her but he could think the image in words and describe the way it should be or at least the way he thought it had been. There had been times when he could not think of anything or anyone else and yet there were times, months at a time, when he did not think of her at all. He had not seen her for almost two years. They wrote each other sporadically. He kept her letters in the ammo can at the base of his rucksack. Whenever he wrote it seemed a letter from her crossed his in the mail. They were very similar, yet they never seemed to be able to occupy the same space at the same time. Of all the people he had ever known it was for Stephanie he harbored the warmest feeling. Thoughts of her warmed his insides. She and only she had ever brought a warmth to his soul. Before her he'd felt an adolescent, a person only half-developed. With her he had been a man fulfilled. After her, without her now, there was a hunger, a craving for something else to bring out the fervor.

I love you, he whispered to her image. He heard himself say it in his mind. But it was just words now and there was no feeling attached to them. The warmth was not there. Perhaps it had been too long. Fuckin lady. Always on my mind. She comes up and I can't tune her out. Stephanie. Goddamn you, Stephanie. It aint fair. I gotta think of you all the fuckin time and I don't even know if you ever think of me. Women! They aint nothin but unhappiness.

The second lieutenant introduced Major John Serpico, Third Brigade Operations Officer. "Thanks, Billy," the major said to the young lieutenant. "Gentlemen," he hissed. He had the voice of a large snake. "Gentlemen," the major hissed again to settle the rumble of voices that had arisen. "You are all familiar with the Khe Ta Laou Valley as so ably described by Sergeant Marquadt." He spit the word "ably" with contempt. "Gentlemen, I would like to tell you what we are going to do to that valley. First, though, allow me to explain to you where you will all be.

"Barnett will be occupied for the duration of this operation by Battery A, 2d of the 319th Artillery, one-oh-five millimeter howitzers and by Battery C, 2d of the 11th, one-five-five millimeter howitzers. Barnett will be secured by Company C, 7th Battalion, 402d Infantry. The Recon platoon of Company E, 7th of the 402d will be on-site reinforcement for the infantry units that will be in the valley. The above artillery units will stage from here at Evans. Company D, 14th ARVN Artillery, one-oh-fives, will remain on Barnett. Working north of the hill and the

ridge will be the 2d Battalion, 3d ARVN Regiment of the 1st
Infantry Division, ARVN. The 2d Battalion of the 1st ARVN
Regiment will redeploy to areas surrounding Firebases O'Reilly
and Ripcord.

"Now, Gentlemen, very quickly we come to the essence of
the assault on the Khe Ta Laou. Intelligence suspects there is a
regimental or larger size NVA headquarters someplace in the
valley and that someplace is suspected to be in or around the
center of the valley or on the cliffs. It will be the mission of the
7th of the 402d to assault various locations within the Khe Ta
Laou and to break up the little tea party the NVA is having there.
The 7th of the 402d will stage at LZ Sally tomorrow morning. If
the weather in the valley is clear Company A will CA to Hill 848
at YD 198304. Company B will be inserted on a mesa LZ just
west of Firebase Barnett at YD 174329. Company C will be
airlifted to Barnett. Company D will CA to Hill 618 at YD
145335. The Recon and mortar elements of Company E will be
airlifted to Barnett where the reconnaissance platoon will become
the first reinforcement element if any of her sister units need a
hand.

"Gentlemen, each unit commander will receive a more
detailed plan as to the exact pick-up times and his individual
objectives. I would like to say at this time the following: this
operation has become necessary, in part, due to the recent siege
of Fire Support/Operations Base O'Reilly. It appears that the
logistical and command support for the NVA operation against
O'Reilly comes directly out of the Khe Ta Laou. During this
time of troop withdrawals, Gentlemen, we must insure the safety
of our units, our rear areas and the coastal lowlands. Thank
you."

The briefing continued through its various stages with Signal and each of the supply and aviation units going into details of
their preparation and available faculties. Each artillery unit reported on the number of rounds it had on hand. Tracker and
Scout Dog unit leaders reported on the health and strength of
their units. The Air Force liaison officer made a brief statement.
The longer the briefing lasted, the more the listeners shuffled and
fidgeted. Virtually every speaker addressed the brigade commander only and with information certainly cleared by him in
previous private sessions.

Lieutenant Brooks looked at Daniel Egan and he could see
that Egan's mind was someplace else. Brooks glanced at Pop

Randalph who was leaning against the wall staring at the drawn shade. Whiteboy seemed to be sleeping. The lieutenant sighed. In the seats before him were the backs of men's heads. Ordinary heads. There was nothing special about the back of a man's head, nothing to differentiate it from the back of the man's head to his left or right or to his front. Some of the heads were larger than others, some had more hair, one or two looked a bit square or triangular or cone-shaped. A few had dark black or brown plastic ear pieces from glasses aiming behind them. The Third Brigade commander had dark hair cut so short it looked like a five o'clock shadow. Colonel Henderson's blond hair was slightly longer than the Old Fox's stubble. The tips of his ears shone pink against his golden fuzz. There was one thing Brooks noticed about all the seated men which did stand out from the backs of their collective heads—all the seated men had white skin. For a time he thought about that but it did not really interest him anymore and soon he found himself simply staring at this ear or that bald spot and wondering what it was like to hear through that ear or what was going on under that bald spot.

The more Brooks stared at the backs of the heads the less he saw and the more his thoughts drifted. When a man spends long periods of time alone, and for all the camaraderie of the infantry, infantrymen while in the jungle spend most of their time alone, a man conditions his mind to be the place where most of his time is spent. Themes develop. An infantryman easily falls to thinking about his themes. Sometimes they are dreams, sometimes desires, sometimes compulsions, sometimes obsessions.

I met her in an unusual way, Brooks said to himself as if he were telling the story to a stranger. I had this friend, Tony, from playing basketball. We were close and I got to know him and his family very well. Tony came from one of the old Italian families that lived off Columbus Avenue in North Beach. We used to go to his house on weekends. Brooks paused. Maybe he'd tell the story to Egan. Tony came to my folks' flat in Oakland once but I think he felt uncomfortable and we never went back there. I think whites are usually more uncomfortable in black neighborhoods than blacks are in white neighborhoods. I'd been to Tony's house so many times I wasn't uncomfortable at all. This time we'd gone up to his house for the weekend and his mother made us go to church with her. She took us to Peter and Paul's, an old

Italian cathedral with candles in little red glass cups and statues all over.

Anyway, I met her indirectly through Tony, at a mass in the cathedral. There were all these little old Italian ladies in black in the first few rows on one side. On the other side are a dozen little old Chinese ladies. Behind the old ladies the church was full of lots of families but Tony's mother decides we're going to sit right up front. I think she might have wanted to let some of those devout old dagos know she was saving this heathen's soul. I'm not feeling bitter, hey, she was Tony's mom and she was always nice to me. Up we go to the front. I'm the only person in the church who's wearing white or has black skin. I was very self-conscious. I think even Tony was too. Not about me. Just about being in front of all those people and having them staring at the back of our heads. I glanced around some, standing, kneeling, sitting, trying to see if there were any other brothers in the church or if there was anybody who was taller than these little ladies who were all about five feet tall. Over among the Chinese ladies there is a Chinese family all sitting around one little lady and they have a sister with them—not a nun—a really beautiful black lady, and she is looking at me. Right in the middle of a Dominus Nabisco, those are the people who make the wafers, I begin to giggle and so does this sister so when all these people get up to go to the altar we both get up. I thought Tony would fall off the pew, so I said to him I'd be at the back of the church or I'd meet him outside, and this lovely lady and I head to the back of the cathedral. I swear to God, that's how we met. Two blacks in a dago church in the middle of Chinatown.

Brooks chuckled to himself. A slight smile crossed his lips. He glanced at Egan and continued telling the story. We slipped out of the church, giggling through the vestibule and down the steps. The sun was warm and it took the chill out of the rawness of the San Francisco morning. Across the street was a park. It was filled with people worshipping the sun or throwing Frisbees or jogging. We sat on the grass facing the cathedral and talked and watched for the people to begin coming out.

Brooks paused again. He stopped the narrative and tried to recall exactly what he and Lila had said that first morning five years ago. He could not remember. He tried to reconstruct a feasible facsimile of the conversation but it did not sound right. He could not remember. Why is it, he thought, you can remember the words of an argument word for word but you can't recall what was said when the times were good?

Several nights before his wedding, he recalled, he told his father the same story about meeting Lila. He was sure he had remembered then what he and Lila had said. He and his father and his mother's brother had been sitting in the kitchen of the Oakland flat. It had been a hot muggy night in September of 1967. They had been toasting him and teasing him and drinking more and more until all three were very drunk. Brooks paused and tried to recall the teasing and joking. Nothing. He remembered his father becoming bitter. "How you going to sup-sup-port that wench?" he slurred. "They aren't going to pay you to play bask-basket-ball no mo." The old man began to beat his fist on the table. "Know what you gotta expect? From life? A kick-in-the-ass. That ishn't the half of it. They'll turn you around en kick you in the balls and when you fall they're going to kick you in the head. If you don't hit em furst." Then old George Brooks said something about technology making men obsolete and interchangeable and interchangeable meant dispensible and dispensible meant cheap and a black man was the cheapest throwaway that industry had. Brooks thought about that for several moments. He thought about remembering the bad parts of good times and it saddened him. Then he said to his father, "We're even cheaper in the infantry, Pop."

A rumble of voices rose in the briefing hall and everyone shifted and stretched and the seated men rolled their heads. The Old Fox had stopped a baby-faced second lieutenant in the middle of a sentence. "That's enough, Lieutenant." The young officer looked shocked and shattered and he was not sure if he should remain at the podium or if he should be seated. The Old Fox remained seated and facing the map with his back to the group. "Gentlemen," he said in a low voice. "Thank you all for coming this afternoon. I have a few comments to make." An absolute hush fell. Men let their cigarettes die. The roar of helicopters in the distance became the only perceptible sound.

"Gentlemen, I would like to stress the strategic importance of this mission." The commander's diction was perfectly measured. "Two months ago, one of my bases, Firebase Ripcord, came under siege by the enemy. For nearly twenty-five days you men heroically defended that hilltop while inflicting heavy casualties upon the North Vietnamese and while intradicting their movement and supply lines to the lowlands. During this time the news media continually reported our light casualties as significant and editorialized the reports—asking why we were defending a mountaintop in the jungle during this advanced state of Vietnamization.

"Gentlemen, we closed Ripcord not due to enemy pressure which was very heavy, but due to American media pressure which was stronger and against which we had no adequate defense. When we closed Ripcord we moved the men and the guns to Firebase O'Reilly. It took us less than ten hours to evacuate Ripcord and have O'Reilly fully operational. It took the enemy over three weeks to react and adjust to a point where the pressure on O'Reilly has drawn the attention of our friends in the press. O'Reilly, however, was turned over to the ARVN and our press friends could not care less about their success or failure. That is not the story they are looking for.

"Now, Gentlemen, we are moving back into the area to assist the ARVN. Gentlemen, this time, I am not going to stop. With the Ripcord and O'Reilly operations we sought only to neutralize the enemy, to disrupt him and to keep him in the mountains. With Barnett, Gentlemen, we are going to deliver a decisive blow.

"For years the Khe Ta Laou Valley has been overlooked by allied commanders. I do not know why. Sergeant Marquadt did an excellent job placing this valley for us. This is a communications headquarters and a major supply distribution point. I believe, Men, that not only has the North engineered its operations against Ripcord and O'Reilly from this narrow gutter in the hills, but I am positive, and we have the intelligence material to back it up, I am positive, Gentlemen, that all major operations as far back as TET of '68, and possibly earlier, have been directed from this untouched valley.

"We have intercepted some very revealing documents placing the headquarters for the 7th NVA Front within the Khe Ta Laou. The headquarters of the 812th Regiment is in the same complex. That's affirmative. Many other NVA units have used this valley as a base area, a sanctuary. They return to Khe Ta Laou to rest and regroup and we overlook them. A major command and communications center and an R&R retreat and we overlook it. Have overlooked it. This valley is a tiny COSVN in the north and, Gentlemen, I want to destroy it.

"We have pursued this for three years and have never been able to find it. Think why, Gentlemen. This tiny valley, this narrow insignificant gutter, is surrounded by some of the highest mountains in all of Vietnam. This valley will be difficult to enter, hard to traverse. That is why it has remained isolated and untouched. We have been lazy.'' The voice of the Old Fox echoing off the front wall of the briefing hall rose and fell. At one moment it seemed very excited, the next very flat. Always the words came perfectly measured.

"To the west the Khe Ta Laou virtually opens into Laos. To the north the plains are patrolled by a mechanized brigade with no ability to penetrate the ridges surrounding our objective. To the south we have the giant A Shau, a valley we have fought in every year since we—since Screaming Eagles arrived in Vietnam—a valley good for a battle but poor for headquarters. And between, Gentlemen, between.'' The colonel clapped his hands together. He gripped each hand with the other and kneaded them together. "Between, the enemy has sat calmly for years, retreated for years to this narrow sanctuary too insignificant for allied forces to be concerned with.

"Gentlemen, I'm concerned. This will be one of my last operations before I rotate to a duty desk in Washington. I want to leave this country safe. I want to leave our area clean so when the ARVN assumes total responsibility for its own land, we will have left them with a chance for success and not with the seeds of failure.

"This is the last NVA stronghold in I Corps. We can kick the enemy out of our AO, out of this valley, out of I Corps and out of this country. Gentlemen, it is up to us. We are about to embark upon a historic mission. We must take the world, Gentlemen, as we find it and make it like we want it. We have the equipment, the mobility, the tactics. Air mobility has come of age. We have the planners, the commanders and the men who know how best to exploit this new ability to strike fast and strike hard.

"Gentlemen, the NVA does not want to make contact with troops of the Third Brigade. They do not want to make contact with the 7th of the 402d SKYHAWKS nor with any battalion of Screaming Eagles. A guerilla force must make contact on its own terms and the 101st no longer allows the North Vietnamese to specify the terms. Since the 1968 Tet Counter-offensive the NVA has lost too many men and too much equipment to Screaming Eagles for too little return, for no solid return. Word has come down from opposition commanders, 'leave the 101st alone.

Pick on easier targets.' This has created problems for their field commanders. They can pick on the 1st ARVN Division but Screaming Eagles stand in close support of the 1st ARVN. NVA commanders in the field have decided to pull back, pick a few lax targets, a few targets to keep the media pressure on our backs, and to build their strength until we are too weak from withdrawals to respond.

"This is going to be a massive operation in terms of tactical impact, if limited in scope, manpower and equipment. For security, as always, no one has been told of these plans until this briefing. I am going to ask you not to tell even your men of the location of this operation or of the overall objective. We are on to something very significant. We do not want to make an announcement. If all we come up with is a few tons of rice, there is no point in having the press make us out to be fools. In hindsight, Cambodia was a very great victory, but if you've read your papers, the press has crucified us for not having reached our announced objective. If it had never been announced we were looking for a COSVN the incursion could never have been labeled as a failure. They were wrong but let us not fall into their trap. Let's do it first and release the results later. Action, Gentlemen, speaks louder than words.

"Now is the time. Let us embark upon our rendezvous with destiny. Thank you."

CHAPTER

7

THE PHOC ROC TOC

The big soldier sat alone at the bar brooding. Except for Molino and himself the Phoc Roc TOC was empty. The Phoc Roc TOC was not the official name for the enlisted men's club of the 7th of the 402d however the phonetics expressed an essential emotion all infantrymen bore about those 90 to 100 pound rucksacks carried on their shoulders and backs. Normally the last portion of the name, TOC, an acronym for Tactical Operation Center, was eliminated and a soldier would say to his buddy, "Let's go get a beer at the Phoc Roc." After a time the name lost its meaning. No one remembered its origin or thought about its phonetics. Even the battalion commander referred to the EM Club as the Phoc Roc.

The Phoc Roc was typical temporary hootch construction, wider, a single room 24 x 32, with a galvanized iron roof. Inside, along the back wall was a bar of singed and sanded plywood iced with high gloss polyurethane. Red vinyl had been carefully tacked to the bar's front and padded gray vinyl covered the edge between top and front. Before the bar twelve small round red and gray Formica tables were randomly scattered, some without chairs, some with four or five.

During the rear-area workday the club was off-limits although on hot dry season days men would enter, buy a beer from Spec Four Molino, chug it on the spot or conceal it in a large fatigue pocket and return to work. As the sun descended and the Phoc Roc cooled and the workday came to an end, men would come in, buy beer and stay.

"What'll it be tonight, Joe?" Molino'd sing out as if he were on stage as the first REMF arrived after mess hall dinner.

"Got anything different?" the REMF would say.

"Got Fresca. Got Bud. Got Millers and Schlitz. Even got a special on Fresca. Two cans for the price of none. Drink one, get one free. Drink two and you get a six-pack. Drink three and I'll call for the Doc. What'll ya have?"

"Gimme a beer. How come you got so much Fresca? Why didn't you buy Coke or somethin?"

"They only got Fresca at the PX. Dudes down south swipe all the Coke and good shit. Zarno said he'd see bout gettin some Coke from the gooks cause Lyn told him they got beaucoup cases of it in her ville. She says the cowboys trade medical supplies for it. They take the medicine from the villagers after Doc's MEDCAPs and get the Coke blackmarket cause they know we can't get it up here and they know they can sell us that shit cause everybody hates Fresca."

"Fuck it. I'll drink beer. Got anything hard? . . . Not that, asshole. I mean booze."

"Suit yerself," Molino'd say, "I got some special reserve but Zarno don't let me sell it in here. They got plenty at the PX. You oughta go up and buy some. Hell, it's cheap as Fresca. Special on vodka this week—seventy cents a quart."

Stacked behind the bar forming a solid barrier of cans were cases of Fresca, Budweiser, Miller and the various other beers. Amongst the stacks, a foot off the floor, was Molino's bed, twenty cases of Fresca covered with a filthy cotton mattress. Above his bed, supported at each end by columns of Fresca cases, were four orderly shelves packed with books and record albums. Shelf one contained classic works and LP records, shelf two military manuals for promotion board study, shelf three paperback and cockbooks and shelf four histories and cultural, political and economic studies on Vietnam. Molino, along with his duties as club manager, was battalion librarian. He checked the books in and out and levied overdue fines at one cent per page per day on the manuals and fifty cents per day on the books. He did not worry about losing the shelf supports.

The big soldier sitting at the bar late in the afternoon of 12 August was called Whiteboy. He was a very big, very pale soldier with thick lips and a pug nose. He couldn't have cared less about the Fresca or about Molino's books or about returning to the detail to which the first sergeant had assigned him. He was seated on the only stool in front of the bar. Since he'd returned from the briefing he'd been sitting on the stool, chatting infrequently with Molino, listening more than speaking, drinking Budweiser, playing solitaire and glancing about with disgust.

"Lahff's lahk cards," Whiteboy drawled slowly. "Lahk Ah've been wonderin. If Ah played these cards afta shufflin um four time stead a fahve, would Ah have won? Ah don't reckon Ah know why Ah had ta shuffle um one mo time. Ah only got four cards up there. Lahff's lahk that."

"Come on, Man," Molino shot back in quick short words. "What the fuck's eatin you?" Molino changed the record. Very carefully he wiped the dust from the Isaac Hayes disc before putting it in the cover and returning it to the first shelf.

"They stickin it to us ah-gain," Whiteboy said. "They found um a whole pile a dinks and they stickin us ah-gain. Ah sho do wish Ah could stay back heah this one time."

"Hey look," Molino said. "I'll tellya somethin. I been here and I been there in the bush."

"Ah know that," Whiteboy said slowly.

"I was in the bush most of '69 and most of this year. I was up on 714 and 882 with Bravo."

"Ah know that too," Whiteboy said placing the cards on the bar for another solitaire game. Molino always reminded the boonierats that he had been one of them. He was a REMF now and the reminder grated on Whiteboy as he added a second layer of cards then a third. Whiteboy's hands moved skillfully, as quick as his speech was slow.

"They blew away a lot of our people," Molino said slower, morose, reflecting with calculation. He added with half a smile and a twinkle in his eye, "Then I got this job as club manager. The old man wanted me back in the bush. I said, 'I can't go back.' He says, 'Why?' I say, 'I've got this heart murmur.' He says, 'What?' And I say, 'Yeah. I got this heart murmur.'" Molino bent forward, cupped his left hand to the left of his mouth and stage-whispered, "It keeps murmuring, 'Don't Go. Don't Go.'"

Whiteboy guffawed unwillingly. He did not speak. Molino began again, "I'll tellya somethin, Whiteboy. The rear aint what it's cracked up ta be. It's a real horror show. That aint no shit. I mean it. I'm more scared back here than I was out there. Ya know, I built me a bunker behind this place so it aint too far in case of incoming. Shee-it. Eagle got mortared five times last month. Okay. Nothin landed down here but one blew a dude away up at division. Why you think I keep the music so low? It's so I can hear the rockets before they get here.''

"Shee-it," Whiteboy said. "That doan do no good. If it's goan land on you, you aint goan heah it. You only heah um if they passin on ovah."

"I don't care, Man. I'll tellya, ya do unnatural things back here. Don't never take a shit after dark. If ya gotta piss at night ya go to the door. Aint no way ya ee-ven walkin down ta the piss tube. Watch these REMFs, Man. They always keepin one ear on the rap and one listenin for rockets. They got me paranoid. They worse than the field. Every time somebody drops somethin they pausin ta check it out. Shee-it. I don't even tuck in the mosquito net. It might take half a second longer ta get outa bed. I'll tellya, Man, I feel more like a savage back here than I did in the bush. These dudes back here, they all lookin out for number fuckin one. Last time the rockets hit, Man, all these dudes jumped into my bunker. I couldn't even get my fuckin ass in. Shee-it. Echo's pumpin out mortars, rockets are comin in one every half minute. Reaction team's runnin round lookin for the cannisters, Cobra's come up and begin nailin down the perimeter. I figure we got us a ground attack."

"Whut happened?"

"Shee-it. All these REMFs sittin in my bunker, bare ass half of em, their dongs hangin out, all jabberin away about what they was doin when the first rocket landed. What action *they* took to get ta *my* bunker."

"Whut you do?"

"Shee-it. I'll tellya. It's a rotten helpless feelin. You race to the bunker. You just lay there, Man. Listenin. Listenin to those goddamn fuckers schuss over yer head and explode right behind you. Can't stop em. Can't shoot em."

"Dammit Milleenee, whut you do?"

"Mo-lee-noh. You mean to the REMFs in my bunker?"

"Yeah."

"Oh. I took two cans of Fresca. Shook em up, pulled the tops and threw em in. Then I got my 16 and joined the dudes on the reaction team."

Whiteboy guffawed again.

"Hey look, Man," Molino said softly, changing his tempo again, "it aint goina be bad. You know the way them briefings are. You aint ee-ven goina have another 714. Man, the dinks have dee-deed. They've split, Man. You aint got nothin to worry about.'' Molino hit Whiteboy with a light jab on the shoulder. Beneath the loose skin Whiteboy's muscles were rock hard. "Snap out a it, Man.''

Whiteboy picked up the cards again and shuffled. He had the strong hands of a mechanic. His fatigue shirt was stretched tight across his wide back. The shirt sleeves were rolled back two turns and the cuffs fit tightly about his heavy muscled forearms. Whiteboy usually moved slowly yet immediately upon seeing him other soldiers knew he could move quickly and with great force if he wanted to.

"Ya know," Molino said, still trying to change Whiteboy's mood, "I put in for Nam. Boy was I dumb. My brother was killed here in '66. I'll tellya somethin. Anybody who signs up for Nam is an asshole. What good does it do? It don't bring nobody back. My mother got ten grand for my brother. Ten thousand big ones. I'll tellya somethin. She aint gonna get my money. Aint nobody spending my ten grand.''

"Ah don't got that long ta go," Whiteboy said. "Ah'm goan ETS out a heah in two mo months. Ah don't know whut Ah'm goan do. All Ah know is mah sixty an these cards. An mah sixty don't lie an neither do these cards. Ah got ten up theah this time. Guess Ah'll be goan out with all them othah dudes. But Ah'll tell you, Milleenee—they's stickin us ah-gain.''

Whiteboy, Sergeant Clayton Janoff, the biggest man in the Oh-deuce, was machine gunner and squad leader of the 3d Squad, 1st Platoon, Company A.

As dusk settled men entered the club. Music and whistles and catcalls, floor show language, shrieked in from the theater. Men came in dressed for guard duty then left and others replaced them. No one sat at the bar. When all the chairs became full men stood in clusters but no one stood at Whiteboy's bar. Whiteboy did not acknowledge the presence of the other men. He did not even turn around. He spoke laconically with Molino and continued laying cards down, playing out the solitaire hands, picking them up and shuffling. He hummed and whistled to himself as he watched the cards, occasionally singing, then returning to his thicklipped whistle.

"What's that . . .'' Molino started, was interrupted with the selling of beers, "what you whistlin?'' Whiteboy did not answer. He did not look up from the cards. "You whistlin

'Boonie Rats'?'' Molino asked. Whiteboy looked up from the
cards on the bar. There were only three scoring above the game.
His large hands encompassed the game and shoved the cards into
a pile. He said nothing. "That's what I thought," Molino said
sighing, looking far off into the small club. "That aint the way it
goes. It goes like this." He whistled the tune, quiet, melodic.
Then he sang the first verse of the first stanza. *"I landed in this
country,/ One year of life to give,/ My only friend a weapon,/ My
only prayer, to live."*

"Ah figger Ah do it good as the nex fella," Whiteboy said
slowly.

Whiteboy whistled the tune in near monotone. Molino spoke
the words to the remainder of the first stanza to Whiteboy's flat
whistling, trying to elongate the big soldier's beat on long notes
by stretching the vowels of his speech. *"I walked away from
freedom/ And the life that I had known,/ I passed the weary
faces/ of the others going home./ Boonie Rats, Boonie Rats,/
Scared but not alone,/ Three hundred days more or less,/ Then
I'm going home."*

"What the fuck!" A seated soldier said loudly to the men
he was seated with. He rose and strutted to the far end of the bar.
The Phoc Roc's music system had an amplifier powerful enough
to blow out the building's flimsy walls. The soldier turned the
volume up drowning Whiteboy's and Molino's duet and the
shrieks and hoots from the theater.

"Keep yer mitts off the dials," Molino commanded loudly.
He threw his fists into the air feeling Whiteboy behind him.
"Watch yerself, Cool." Molino turned the stereo volume down,
snarled at the soldier, replaced the record that had been playing
with a Cat Stevens album and played "Moonshadow."

> *If I ever lose my mouth,*
> *Or my teeth, north and south,*
> *Yes if I ever lose my mouth,*
> *I won't have to talk.*

"Here come Doc Johnson and the dudes," Molino announced to Whiteboy. "Floor show must be bad."

"Ef I ever lose my feet," Jackson sang to Doc and El Paso
as they bopped to the bar, Jax' head down, eyes closed, hunched
forward, jiving, snapping his fingers, *"All my toes hunt gook
meat/ Ef I ever lose my feet,/ I won't have ta hump."*

Jax looked up, hand out, Molino filled it with a beer. "Hey Dago, *¿que paso?*"

"What's happenin's happenin." Molino exchanged a short dap with the soul brother.

"I din't know, my friend Dago, gave beer en toys, to Whiteboys."

Whiteboy shrugged. El Paso and the big soldier exchanged an extended handshake though not quite a dap.

The club filled as more soldiers came from the show in the theater. Outside it became darker and cooler. Inside the men formed into groups around the tables. Most of the soul brothers stayed to one side. The whites formed two groups, one by the bar and one by the door. The chicanos gathered in the middle and mixed with the fringe groups. There were several blacks in the predominantly white group by the bar and several whites in the black group at the side. Whiteboy, Doc, Jax and El Paso picked the last empty table which was in the center of the room, confiscated eight chairs, sat and drank.

EM clubs generally were restricted to enlisted men, privates to corporals and specialist fours. Some clubs allowed spec fives and E-5 sergeants. The Phoc Roc attracted all the younger men of the 7th of the 402d. No one was surprised to see a young officer or a young anti-army NCO. Lifers stayed away.

When the floor show ended the club was deluged and a hundred now packed the single room. Molino turned the music up but voices and laughter drowned most of it. The entire club seemed to be in an early, happy, joking stage of intoxication.

Chelini and Leon Silvers followed six blacks into the club. To the left the blacks meshed with the group of soul brothers and daps were exchanged all around.

"Good evening, ladies and gentlemen," a tall white soldier announced into a beer can as Chelini and Silvers moved to the bar, "and welcome to ABC's Wide World of War. Tonight we take you to the jungles of the Republic of Vietnam for the finals of the ancient sport of hand-to-hand combat."

The men standing around the tall soldier laughed and urged him on. Someone shouted, "Go to it, Rafe."

"In the finals tonight, which, by the way, are taking place in this spacious Thua Thien arena outside the Citadel, we will see bold, courageous and humble Joseph Gee Eye pitted against the Little Giant, snarling screaming Charles V. C. Cong."

"Yea, Charlie!" someone yelled. Silvers bought a beer for Chelini and himself. They stood to one side and watched.

"Joe, from Sometown, Anystate, weighed in prior to tonight's engagement at 187 pounds. He has a 41-inch reach and stands six-foot-one.

"Charlie, from Sauhnmhamlet, Upnorth Province, weighed in at 58 kilos, ahhh, that is 127 pounds. He stands five-foot-five and has a 34-inch reach.

"I think I just heard the sound of barbed wire being snipped— 'The National Anthem.' We are about ready for the start of tonight's fight."

Chelini felt slightly self-conscious. His new haircut was lifer-short and his fatigues newfer-new. He stayed close to Silvers and tried to look inconspicuous.

"I noticed at the beginning of this broadcast that Joe had been in his bunker working up a high on Laotian Red. You should note that Joe has several M-67 frags hanging from his belt, a bandoleer of 5.56 M-16 magazines and a black plastic weapon made by Mattel. Bayonet is affixed."

"Sock it to em, Joe." The club was becoming rowdy.

"Could we please have a little quiet here at the broadcast booth? Here at my right I have the pleasure of having Willie Moreland, who, as you know, is an internationally recognized expert at this sport. Last year, before he retired, Willie was captain of the southern All-Star Team which played the north to a 40,000 to 200,000 deadlock. Willie, the fans and I would like to know how you think Joe will open up tonight if he wins the toss of the coin. Would you comment?"

The soldier turned to the bar then turned back with his shoulders hunched and his head cocked back. "Hey, this guy's really good," Chelini whispered to Silvers.

"Yeah," Silvers said louder. "That's Ridgefield. He's from Alpha too. Like us."

"Well, Jim," the soldier continued in a high voice, "as you know we like to encourage the boys to open with a bang. Sometimes a short burst will be effective."

The tall soldier turned again to the bar and returned as the announcer. "And what if Charlie wins the toss? Do you think Joe will be able to open with the same move?

"No, definitely not, Jim. He will probably open with a vertical butt stroke series or maybe a long thrust and hold. It really depends then on what VC, ah, Jim, you don't mind if I refer to the boy from the north as VC do you?

"No, not at all.

"Well, Jim. If VC pulls something unusual, Gee Eye may have to counter with something unusual.

"I hate to interrupt you, Willie, but I just noticed that Chuck has a Samurai sword and two bags of plastic explosive. That is kind of unusual, isn't it?

"Yes, Jim, it is. VC usually moves with a minimum of weight and that's a mighty large sword. He usually depends on speed, you know.

"From my seat high above Firebase Kathryn I can see that Charlie has won the toss of the coin. He's opening with a diversionary tactic. I see some blue-white flame off to the left.

"Jim, I think Gee Eye is groovin on the flames . . ."

"Come on," Silvers nudged Chelini, "Let's go over there where Doc and Jax are." They worked their way through the crowd, bodies parted before them and closed behind. At the table in the middle Jackson jumped from his seat.

"See that," Jax shouted holding up his fists. "Fast as rockets." He jumped into the air and spun fully around firing both hands at imaginary targets. "Mean, babe, mean. That's ARA—aimed right atchya. Don't mess with this dude. Floats like a butterfly, stings like a B-52."

Five other soldiers were now sitting with Jax, Doc, Whiteboy and El Paso. Others stood by the group listening or watching. The center group seemed to control the club's mood.

"Hey," El Paso shouted, "the Jew's comin ta join us. Watch yer MPC, babes; he looks like he's got some dirty pictures to sell."

"Hey, Molino," one of the soldiers surrounding the seated group at the table called, "give the Jew a Fresca, on me."

"Hey," Silvers addressed Chelini. "This is El Paso and Garbageman. That's Doc and Jax. Whiteboy, Numbnuts, Boom-Boom, Monk and Brunak. Got that? This is Cherry."

"Yous just come in from the show?" A seated soldier asked, then added, "That was a real downer."

"Those Filipino strippers were the worst I ever seen."

"I liked the one with the big jugs."

"That's plastic, Man. Gooks got little tits."

"Oooooh, Man. Forget them," El Paso said. He nodded

toward Doc Johnson. "Doc and Top went to the *ville* and brought some ladies back."

"OOOoo-OOOo," a soldier whistled. "We are gonna have fun tonight."

"Doc. You made sure them ladies is clean, didn't ya?"

"Who you think you playin with, Mista?"

"How much?" Silvers asked.

"For you, Jew? One shot? Back a the line? Pound a flesh and 100 piasters."

"He aint gonna have ta pound his flesh tonight," Boom-Boom laughed.

"L-T's pickin up the tab," Doc said, "with his own bread."

"Man," Jackson spoke up. "They's ugly. Ugglee, I mean. One so ugly she gotta sneak up on her meals ta get somethin ta eat."

"Yeah, but it's big," Numbnuts said.

Someone stuck his hand over the table and formed a circle with his thumb and forefinger and laughed, "This big?"

A soldier who'd been there formed his arms into a circle over his head. "No, Man. This big. It's so big you kin stand back a hundred yards and throw grenades inta it." Everyone laughed.

Chelini felt even more self-conscious being near the center group. No one addressed him. Men at the fringe of the seated group stuck their ears in for a bit then went back to drinking beer from cans or looking about or talking more softly to others standing at the fringe. Chelini looked at the bar. The man who had announced the hand-to-hand sporting event was now sitting on the bar simulating the sound of an early radio broadcast. "Aaaahh, this is rumor control reporting directly to you out there in radio land from the Phuc Ruc TOC," the voice whined. "Rumor here has it," the voice went on with crackles, "that the Big Screaming Yellow Chicken himself, CO of the flock, has personally requested to put your sweet asses under the operational control of the Third Brigade for a brief trip to the DMZ. Rumor has it that the Screaming Bird was so impressed at how good you is, he thought kindly enough to arrange a direct scrimmage for you with Uncle's little men. Big Bird offers his condolences for not being able to participate hisself . . . ."

Soldiers near the announcer cracked with laughter and stoned giggling. The man continued. "At early dawn, on good sources, rumor has it here at control HQ, that is right, right here at Hotel Quicksilver, that the men from Uncle have called for . . .''

Chelini turned halfway back to the table. A man beside him was saying, ''. . . R&R. I said to her, 'The way I'd really like to try it next is in a bathtub full of peanut butter.' And she coos, 'Oh, Bill. You're so sensual.' So . . .''

Another conversation spilled into Chelini's ears. ''. . . if Yastrzemski can't get Boston inta the Series . . .'' ''Yer fuckin nuts, Duke. Boston's in the cellar. They . . .''

Chelini turned back to the table. Jackson was looking at him. He nodded to Jackson and grinned an indecisive grin. ''Don't they teach you nothin, Man?'' Jackson accused him.

''What? I mean, excuse me?'' He had not expected anyone to address him.

''Don't they teach you cherries nothin?'' Jackson said standing up. He pulled Chelini toward him, into the focal point of the group's attention. ''Prepare yo mind, body and soul, for the number one GI Joe of Attack Company Seven of the Four-Oh-Two. Jax' here to square away you.''

''What?'' Chelini asked sheepishly.

''Yo dog tags, Man.''

Silvers looked at Chelini and shook his head.

''Take em off,'' Jax ordered.

Chelini removed a chain from around his neck on which the two identification tags hung.

''Boy. Now yo gowin take off yo boots,'' Jax said.

Chelini looked past Jackson to Silvers. Silvers shook his head in confirmation and pointed a finger in mock disgust. Chelini bent over and began untying his bootlaces.

''Sit in my chair, Boy,'' Jax ordered.

Chelini sat down and removed his boots. Everyone in the group had become serious. Jackson took one boot and handed it to Doc. He took the other boot and handed it to El Paso. Chelini looked at his boots and blushed slightly. The boots still looked brand-new. Doc and El Paso unlaced the boots down to the first eyelets. Silvers grabbed Chelini's chain and removed the dog tags and handed one to Doc and one to El Paso. The two men with the boots took the tags and slid them onto the laces and began relacing.

''You cherries,'' Jackson said. ''What Doc gowin do when yo loose yo head, when yo dead. Yo got only one head, yo know. So. Yo got two feet, neat. Chances yo loosin two feet is lots worse than chances yo loosin one head.''

Doc handed the boot to Whiteboy for his approval and El Paso passed the other to Garbageman who passed it to Happy who passed it to Silvers. They all approved. Whiteboy and Silvers tossed the boots at Chelini. Chelini covered up and let the boots hit him. Jackson began to laugh and everyone laughed. Chelini laughed so hard he couldn't get his right boot on.

Jax nudged Chelini out of the seat and sat down smiling. He pulled a black and chrome hair pick from a fatigue pocket and stuck it into his short Afro hairdo. He fluffed the black frizz and then scratched his scalp slowly with the long chrome teeth. He eyed Chelini.

"Whatchu think of this cherry, Jax?" Silvers asked.

Jax smiled but he did not answer. He had not yet judged Chelini. About him the laughter continued and the conversation flowed back to the floor-show strippers. Ridgefield had a new mock radio program going by the bar. At several of the tables soldiers were breaking out bottles of hard liquor they had brought into the Phoc Roc. As the whiskey and bourbon were passed, swigged, chased with beer, the noise level rose. Jackson continued eyeing Chelini.

Although he hid it well William Andrew Jackson was very defensive about his dark black skin and his broad flat nose and his full lips. He was defensive about his background.

As Jackson sat watching Chelini, smiling, smelling the stale beer smell of the Phoc Roc, not hearing the ruckus, his mind played games with images and odors from home. Jackson had been born and raised in a depressed area of rural Mississippi, an area known as Nigger Hollow. For some perverse reason the Hollow attracted odors. If an animal thereabouts was dying it came to the Hollow to lay its broken body down and during the day the whole area smelled of carrion. At night there was always the smell of skunks. When a person from the Hollow made a trip to town the smell preceded him and remained there long after he left. That embarrassed Jackson when he was young. The thought embarrassed him now.

Jackson shifted in his seat and chuckled at something everyone else was chuckling at. He still was not sure where to place Chelini. Chelini seemed sharp, smart, a sleeper.

At seventeen Jax fled from his past, fled into the army. The army gave him a better life and it gave him pride. He earned a high school equivalency diploma, advancement to Private First Class and he learned the skills with which to kill. After AIT Jackson, proud, spit-shined and shaved-head, returned to the Hollow. A brief wild fling with the eldest Wilitts girl ensued and before his leave was over, he married her. Two weeks later he was in Vietnam. Two months later, after he had already been awarded his first Silver Star, the letters began and at first they embarrassed him. Not his wife but his new brother-in-law wrote to remind Jax of the suffering black people had endured because of white men. His brother-in-law, Mathew Wilitts, renamed himself Marcus X. The letters were full of Black Power and revolution. The initial embarrassment became agitation in Jax. He exploded, allegedly attempted to frag an officer, was court-martialed and was sent to L.B.J., Long Binh Jail, for a three-month cool down. After a time the letters no longer agitated Jackson though they still hurt him. Jax wanted to be racially militant but he did not have the true militant's fervor. He had no hate. He had resignation. Maybe he would hate this cherry. Jax would not make up his mind about Chelini for two days and then he would change his mind almost daily thereafter.

When the laughter settled down again and he could keep himself from choking on the laughs Chelini stared at Jackson, then Whiteboy then around the table. These people are really okay, he thought. If they're willing to laugh at me and let me laugh with them then it must mean something good. He detected no resentment.

Part of the crowd from the surge into the club had left and the Phoc Roc was less crowded but still noisy. Some had left to form private parties, to get stoned or to get drunk or just to get a longer night's sleep. There was more room to move about and the group at the table in the middle acquired several more chairs. Chelini and Silvers pulled up chairs at the side.

"Can I ask you guys some questions?" Chelini asked the soldier next to him.

"Whatcha think you just did?" a soldier from the far side of the table laughed and they all chuckled again and drank more beer.

"No, I mean, like can I ask a serious question about tomorrow? I feel a little funny. I don't know what I'm supposed to do."

"Just do what we do," El Paso said.

"I'm not an eleven-bravo," Chelini explained. "I'm supposed to be a wireman."

"I'm supposed to be a cook," Happy said.

"Ah'm supposed ta be home and out a heah," Whiteboy said.

"I won't never supposed to come," said Brunak. "As a matter of fact, I think I'm goina sky. Doc, what's that bitch look like you brought back?"

"She's number fuckin one."

"She's ugly, Man."

"I'm comin too," Numbnuts said.

"Shee-it," Boom-Boom said. "If you ever saw a pussy you'd throw rocks at it."

"Count me in," Garbageman said. "I've gone too long to care what it looks like. I aint goina eat it."

Boom-Boom rolled back in his chair. "Don't give Numbnuts no ideas."

Brunak, Garbageman and Numbnuts rose and Boom-Boom rose too and they all left, leaving seven soldiers at the table.

"What are you worried about?" El Paso said to Cherry.

Chelini felt conspicuous again but he forced himself to speak. "I don't know what I'm supposed to do," he shrugged. "I don't know a thing about the field."

"It's like this," El Paso said. "You just do everything everybody else does. And you do it quiet. We don't make any noise."

"After the CA . . ." Jax said, "CAs is excitin, Man . . . but after the CA maybe two days it all jest humpin yo ruck up every mountain like a bear. Yo goes over the mountain ta see what yo ken see and what yo see . . ."

" . . . is another mountain."

"Yo got it, Cherry. Check it out. One after nother like the fuckin bear."

"Thaht ruck goan kick your ass," Whiteboy drawled. "And thaht weapon goan get so heavy you're goan cuss it like tits on a bull, til when you need it then you goan wonder how it done got so light."

"We had one dude," Jackson said, "up at Bach Ma. We called him the Shepherd cause he wouldn't carry a weapon. Yo dudes remember the Shepherd? Carried a long stick instead. Called it his staff."

"That asshole."

"What happened to him?" Cherry asked, disbelieving.

"I think somebody shot him for sleepin on guard," El Paso said.

Chelini chuckled briefly. The others remained silent as the point struck very fast and Chelini stopped chuckling.

"Look," Doc said. "You do what you gotta do. First bird in is bad. B-A-D—if the dinks don't want ya on the ground. Usually it the second bird theys after. If they can blow that one away they can waste the dudes that come in on the first bird and the other birds can't land cause the second bird messin up the LZ. If we get three birds in theys gonna dee-dee."

"If the dinks are out there, we'll do em a J-O-B," Happy said from behind Jackson.

"Kick ass—take no names," Jax said.

"Scatter their shit to the wind," Happy added.

"Nobody gets blown away unless we make a mistake," Silvers smiled. They all began smiling now and Cherry couldn't tell if they'd been serious or if they'd been teasing him the entire time. "Course," Silvers said, "it may be a mistake to be here in the first place."

"Hey Monk," El Paso said. "Tell him the story about the dude with the bagpipes. I like the way you tell that one."

"Christ," Silvers chuckled. "The war story of all war stories."

"This aint no shit," Moneski said. Moneski was a small, squarish-looking soldier who'd said very little but who had drunk a lot of beer and smoked a lot of cigarettes while the others were BSing. He drew his head back, belched as loudly as possible and said, "Well, t'was a feller we had here one time that use ta tell a story about a unit he was in down south on an earlier tour. I forgit his name. I think it was McDonald. Yep. Some dude in his old unit come cross this idear on how to keep everybody from gettin killed. Units down south, Man, they're fucked up. This dude figgers the NVA and the VC aint never but never heard no bagpipes. He figgers he can create enough noise so next time they get sprung in an ambush he goina be able to scare everybody away. He says they gets into a firefight, ah, that is McDonald says they hit the shit bout two weeks after this dude comes up with his bagpipes. All of a sudden, from someplace in the middle of nowhere comes this horrible screechin sound. It sounds so bad, McDonald says, that everybody stops firin. Even the NVA stop firin. Then McDonald says that crazy motherfucker stands up and starts marchin forward screechin and screamin on his instrument. Then everybody starts rushin around, pullin out frags, attachin more belts to the 60s, gettin set to charge up behind this dude when, WHAM. That crazy motherfucker standin up with his bagpipe gets it right square in the head, right between the eyes. Boom. Naaughk. Ginggg.''

"Mothafucka gave away his position," El Paso smiled.

"Well," Monk continued, "that aint the half of it. McDonald says they go out and rout the NVA anyway. Then it turns out that sometime later they in the same area and they catch this NVA feller. And MI's talkin to him and gettin a little information, cache here, booby trap there, you know. MI, they begin gettin this dude's history in combat and this little dude begins talkin about that crazy time when they ambushed a bunch of USAs right in that same AO and there was a crazy dude with some bagpipes. That dink look up at the dudes from MI and says, 'This crazy Americano start playin him bagpipe right in the middle of the firefight and everybody stop shooting. I never hear bagpipe play so bad before,' the gook says. 'That man not fit to call water buffalo with bagpipe. My squad, we all look at each other and laugh. Then we draw straws to see who gets honor of returning honorable peace to our ears and Tho, my friend, he wins and he places bullet in middle of bagpipe man's head and for a little while everything is quiet again and only the sound of rifles can be heard.' ''

"Shee-it," Cherry said. He was now a little drunk himself. "You guys have been just playin with me."

Whiteboy guffawed and everybody laughed and Whiteboy said, "Cherry, you doan gotta worry bout nothin. Doan gotta worry bout the bullet with your name on it. It aint been made yet. The one you gotta watch for is one thaht sez 'To Whom It May Concern.' '' Whiteboy guffawed even louder and most of the soldiers laughed at his laugh.

More soldiers departed the club and the noise level fell to where the music could be heard again. The Monk left and Whiteboy became so drunk he laid his head on the table for a rest and passed out.

"Hey," El Paso announced, "we've got some latecomers. Hey, L-T, Egan, over here. Hey L-T, guess what? We got us a psychologist. Now we got us just about everything."

"Yous guys still drinking?" the lieutenant asked. Jax handed the lieutenant a beer. "Say hey, Little Bro," Brooks grasped

Jax' hand in a soul handclasp. "We're movin out at oh-four hundred."

"That aint nothin, L-T," Whiteboy said raising his head about three inches off the table. "We sh'till got fo hours ta party."

Egan did not sit immediately at the center table. He went to the bar and bought a case of beer. Ridgefield was there joking quietly now with his closest friends, Snell, Nahele and McQueen. Egan nodded to them. Ridgefield nodded back with detached respect. They were the informal leaders of their respective platoons and the competition between them, although concealed, was ardent. Their styles were very different. Ridgefield was Rafe the Rapper, always joking and entertaining. He was a very good soldier. Egan was quiet, disciplined, the man who would take any risk to protect his men, a soldier's soldier, The Boonierat. Egan left Rafe a six-pack, grabbed a seat and pulled up at the center table.

Alpha Company, 7th of the 402d, like all infantry units in the 101st in which officers were rotated more quickly than enlisted men, had developed a substructure of leadership. In the year preceding the assault on the Khe Ta Laou Company A had had four commanders. There had developed a structured bureaucracy within Alpha in which was placed a significant degree of decision making. The bureaucracy was mostly comprised of old-timers: platoon sergeants, the senior RTO and medic and several riflemen. Jackson, Doc Johnson, El Paso, Whiteboy, they were the core, the nucleus, the very heart of the company. They had been through it all together, for ten, fourteen, sixteen months. Each had had his reason to extend his tour in Vietnam although the only reason anyone ever admitted was that his hate for the army had driven him to extend his tour until he would have less than one hundred and fifty days remaining in his enlistment when he DEROSd. With less than one hundred and fifty he would be automatically discharged. Ridgefield and his friends were the bureaucracy at platoon level in 3d Plt. Egan was it in 1st. As platoon sergeant Egan ran 1st Plt. The platoon leader, Lieutenant Thomaston, deferred all the tactical as well as the daily decisions to Egan. Thomaston put his authority behind Egan and followed. At company level the bureaucracy was a mix of CP old-timers and the platoon bureaucrats.

Brooks had been in-country for seventeen months. He'd been with the 7th of the 402d for thirteen of those months and

with Company A for three. They accepted him though he was
not one of them. He was the commander, the computer center,
the brain of the unit and these men were now *his* heart, ears and
eyes. They were like one body. Men like Silvers and Moneski,
Lairds and Brunak were the skin. They were essential to have
but somehow not an inside part. Chelini was a new cell and
neither he nor the others knew how he would grow.

"If it aint Bro Boon," Egan laughed at Jackson as he pulled
up his chair.

"Is that Bro Boon like in Bro Coon," Jax intonated with
mock arrogant disgust, "or is that Bro Boon like in Bro
Boonierat?"

Egan reached over and exchanged a dap with Jax and said,
"Bro Boonierat." Then he looked around the table and greeted
each soldier with a nod. To Egan's right was El Paso, then
Whiteboy with his head back on the table, then Doc, Jax,
Silvers, Cherry and L-T B. They spoke quickly, easily, except
for Cherry, without restraint.

"Who's a psychologist?" Brooks asked.

"Cherry here," Silvers answered.

"Great."

"Ah, I'm not really a psychologist. I've got a degree in
psych. It's just a B.A."

"Egan's an engineer," Brooks gestured toward Egan, "and
El Paso's in history and law."

"L-T is a Philosopher," Jax said proudly.

"It's good to have someone with a new perspective,"
Brooks said. His speech was confident, the voice of a teacher
well versed in his subject and in control of his pupils. "We can
use all the help we can get," Brooks said. "What we try to do is
bring everything we have to everything we do in every situation,
then we choose the best way to go. I'll be looking to you for
contributions."

Chelini shrugged his shoulders. He wasn't sure if he should
speak. "I don't know anything about this," he said.

"You will," El Paso laughed. "You will soon enough."

"We all have different methods of ordering the world around
us," Brooks said. There was no note of condescension in his
voice. "The method of historical extrapolation, the engineering
method of generating alternatives, scientific analysis and common sense are all valid manners of seeking truths or forecasting

probable results of alternative courses of action. Do you understand?"

"Yeah," Cherry said seriously. He was not certain he understood but everyone else seemed to understand. He wasn't about to say no.

"We're happy to have you with us," Brooks said. "With Jax for an inductive leap and Minh for an Eastern mind . . . where's Minh anyway? . . . and Whiteboy putting it together with his diagrams on the ground, with everyone pulling together, contributing, this unit runs safe and smooth."

"Yo a boonierat now," Jax said with pride. He was always proud when the L-T spoke. "Doan ever forget it."

"Ya know," Egan said, "early in the war, guys used to be sent here and right off they had them setting up bases and perimeters that had to be defended the night they arrived. I remember, just after I got here, talkin to guys who'd come in around Da Nang. They arrived, some of em, in '67. They'd say that they'd come from the World as a cherry unit and the entire unit would be moved to a ville or someplace to defend and they'd be there the day they arrived. No SERTS, no in-country processing stations, no battalion P-training. Just right to the boonies. They didn't even have time to get acclimated. That's why so many of em had their shit scattered. They weren't comin in as one cherry among one hundred dudes with time in-country. They were virgin units who'd never been shot at. Didn't take long before they knew the score but by then only half of em were still around."

"Cherry," Doc said, "we gonna take care of you."

"There's a lot of crazy fuckin dudes in this battalion," Silvers said. "They think they're gettin over on the green machine. They say, 'gotta get over on them cause they gettin over on us.' That don't ee-ven cut it."

"Only dude yo gettin over on in the boonies ef yo ghostin is yoself," Jax added.

"Some people back here are on fire," Brooks warned. "Anti-war, anti-government, anti-white, anti-black. Leave that stuff back there. I want you to be anti just one thing—and that's anti-getting killed."

"That, I can be," Cherry tried to joke. The others did not laugh.

"Politics don't have no place out here," El Paso said.

"Shee-it," Doc nudged Jax, "Jax plannin a revolution back in the fucken World. By his fucken self. But it aint fo the bush. Neva hear the man talk bout it. Neva." Now Doc could not hold it and he laughed loudly and slapped the tabletop. "Neva."

"I got some dudes need dealin on," Jax scowled.

"We all got dealin ta do," Egan said, "but not out there. This is our company and we don't let no one fuck it up." Egan's voice was harsh, unmistakably serious. "All the papers from the World, they all the time tellin how this place is fucked up," he said. "Everybody gets letters askin why we so fucked up. Mothers cryin, askin if their little Joey-boy is smokin dope or rottin with the sif. Tellin em ta cover his ass, take care and come home in one piece cause nobody there wants ta take care of a two-piece man. Man, they just don't know. This here's a good unit. We're winnin this fuckin war." Egan shouted at the table. "Winnin it by our-A-number-fuckin-one-selves. You should a seen this place two years ago." He directed his voice not to Chelini but to every troop newer than he. "Two years ago the NVA had I Corps by the balls. Last year you couldn't ee-ven go out to Birmingham without a convoy. Now you can walk down 547 all the way to Veghel without a weapon and you'll be safer than drivin down Route 22 from Allentown to Harrisburg. Shee-it. We are A-okay. We don't want no fuckups in Alpha."

"When yer kids ask ya," Doc got carried away in Egan's speech, " 'Who the night belong to over there?' tell em, 'The night belong to the Oh-deuce.' "

"Right on!" Jax shouted.

"Hey, why you comin down so hard on the cherry?" Silvers asked, calming them. "He hasn't done nothin."

"It is my job to see we all work together," Brooks took over again. "And we all get out of here in one piece. I don't care about your politics, just your sorry cherry ass. Don't let any dudes fuck with your mind."

"We talk about the revolution comin," El Paso said, "and about the trainin we're gettin, but that's not for here."

"And bout wastin Jody's mothafuckin ass for messin with our ladies," Egan added. "But that's when we get back."

"We soldiers," Doc said. "Boonierats. Brothers. Here we are one."

"There it is," Jax said. "Unanimous. We are the one gonna take charge. A new World order wid all power to the people. Blow em all away. I aint gowin back out. I jus decide. It's time fo peace. I declarin peace here en now so I doan have ta fight on two fronts.''

"That's cool," Doc said. "Let's declare it over and have peace.''

"What's so God-fuckin-whore-good about peace?'' Egan scoffed. "Jesus! Peace is a fuckin bore.''

"Egan, yer crazy," Silvers said.

"Shit. Maybe we oughta eliminate all the ways to die," Egan snarled. "No more war. No more cars. No more fires or heart attacks. We'll outlaw all that. Pass a law. Nobody can die on Sundays. Then everybody can get cancer and sit around and watch their bodies rot. War aint so bad. It's natural, a natural state. Why is everybody fuckin with nature?''

"There's one thing for sure," El Paso said. "There's one thing totally indisputable throughout history. Everyone, no matter how good or important or bad, everyone, in the end, dies. Death aint no sin.''

"Yeah," Egan said, "and I don't know if killin is either.''

"Aren't you guys carrying that a bit too far?'' Cherry asked.

"No," El Paso said quickly. "I don't believe death is important. What is important is how you live. While you're here, how do you justify your existence. When it's all over it won't be enough to say, 'I never killed a man.' ''

"However," Brooks said slowly, always in control, "it might be enough to say, 'I saved a man's life.' ''

The conversation continued, the soldiers kept drinking. At times they spoke passionately, at times they laughed undefensively. To Cherry it seemed everything they did, everything they said, was done purely to educate and to socialize him into the new culture. For his part he listened intently and tried to repay his perceived debt by buying beer. Several times he went to the bar and purchased a round from Molino. On his return to the table he served the beers as if he were a waiter.

At nearly one in the morning Cherry rose and went out to the EM four-holer and defecated for the first time in two days. Phhoo! he thought. Must be nervous. Me in the infantry. I can't believe it.

Yet he fully believed it. His head buzzed. He was beer-warmed. Somehow too he felt warmed by being in the infantry. Here, in the 7th Battalion, 402d Infantry, he would learn war in a way he would never learn war in a signal battalion repairing wires or setting up telephone systems. A wireman or an infantryman. There was no comparison. One was the real thing, one was make-believe soldiering.

Soon, he thought, I will know war. I will learn from these crazy men. Death is not a sin and neither is killing. Crazy. How can anyone say that? How can one of them say that and nobody even flinch?

When Chelini re-entered the Phoc Roc TOC he tried to see them from a different perspective, as if he were one of them. They're really tight, he thought standing inside the door watching the center table through moving bodies and smoke. They're like brothers. He worked his way through a group of soldiers dancing. At the table Chelini sat down in his same seat. They had reserved it for him.

More men left the club and the various groups thinned until there were only a half-dozen seated blacks to one side, a dozen or so whites standing at the bar and the group of men seated at the table in the center.

Jax was again talking about settling a score. "I gowin blow that mothafucka off the face of the fucken World, that white fucken honky. It time the white man in this country learn that the black man is a man. Those that doan learn, burn. Simple as that."

"Amen," Doc said.

"Hey," Egan said, "I know some pretty cool white dudes."

"Honkys," Jax spat.

"That's yer problem, Jax," Egan snapped. "I can accept the black race as equal to the white race—every fuckin bit equal. It's you that can't accept it. You keep yerself down."

"Doan give him lip, Man," Doc said. "He's drunk."

"I aint fucken drunk, Nigger," Jax leered at Doc.

"Hey," Brooks stopped them. "Keep that shit out of this company. Why do you guys always have to bicker? Why the conflict? I've been thinking a lot about this," Brooks said. "You know, the way we see something determines how we react to it and the way we're taught about it determines to a great extent how we see it. All whites are not honkys. All blacks are not niggers. The culture . . ."

"Honkys," Jax yelled. "Oreos en honkys."

That quieted them. They sat angry, not looking at one another. Doc took out a pack of cigarettes, took one, lit it and threw the pack on the table. Silvers, Egan and the L-T helped themselves. Conversation at the fringe of the group had stopped as they had become louder. Now murmuring picked up about the group. Chelini did not know what to make of the talk. Jax was in a huff of anger and beer. Someone farted. The odor was disgusting.

"Who done that?" Doc said.

"Done what?" Whiteboy asked raising his head.

"Done stinked up the fucken table."

"Won't me," Whiteboy said.

"Hey, Eg," El Paso said to change the subject. "Rumor has it you was shakin with a tattooed lady in Sydney."

"Man," Egan smiled, laughed. "The tattooed one was a dog but let me tell you bout Michele. Sweet sixteen, round-eyed Michele . . ."

"Fuck you with that roun-eyed shit," Jax' teeth flashed with hate. "Mothafucka, what you mean is white."

"Fuck that shit," Silvers said disgustedly. "I'm goin. Look dudes, it is like gettin really late, like inta the tee-tee hours of the mornin. I'm goina crash. Catchya at first light."

"Hey," Brooks said. "I'm going too. We've got to be ready to move in three hours. All of yous should get some sleep."

"Whiteboy. Hey. Come on." Silvers grabbed the big soldier and shook him. "I'll lead ya to the hootch. You comin, Cherry?"

As the L-T, Whiteboy and Silvers left, the awakened Whiteboy bellowed out in coarse drunken monotone a verse from "Boonie Rats."

> *The first few days were hectic*
> *As they psyched my mind for war,*
> *I often got the feeling*
> *They're trying to tie the score.*

The mood of the soldiers remaining in the Phoc Roc instantly mellowed. At one time there had been a light black or dark white soldier, no one knew which, who would come to the

Phoc Roc and sit in the corner by the stereo. From a small leather case the man would produce and assemble a clarinet. The stereo would be turned off, the lights lowered. Musical notes connected by a blue ribbon of jazz would wind out, spiral up fluttering into the darkness.

Jax and Doc leaned back, the music was in them. Egan said the words in his mind. Between the stanzas where the clarinet player would trip up and down the scale in the way good jazz musicians do, Egan saw, not heard but saw images in his mind of lines and patterns, a graphic presentation in his head of static then kinetic forces, then flashing shapes, then flowing visual patterns, then the motions of Stephanie. Egan forced the image away and looked about.

The entire club was silent. Then from behind the bar, very softly at first, Molino's voice could be heard. As he sang some of the soldiers sang with him or just hummed beneath the words.

> *I landed in this country,*
> *One year of life to give,*
> *My only friend a weapon,*
> *My only prayer, to live.*

> *I walked away from freedom*
> *And the life that I had known,*
> *I passed the weary faces*
> *Of the others going home.*

> *Boonie Rats, Boonie Rats,*
> *Scared but not alone,*
> *300 days more or less*
> *Then I'm going home.*

> *The first few days were hectic*
> *As they psyched my mind for war,*
> *I often got the feeling*
> *They're trying to tie the score.*

> *The first day with my unit*
> *We climbed a two klick hill,*
> *To find an enemy soldier,*
> *To capture, wound or kill.*

Boonie Rats, Boonie Rats,
Scared but not alone,
200 days more or less
Then I'm going home.

The air was hot and humid,
The ground was hard and dry.
Ten times I cursed my rucksack
And wished that I could die.

I learned to look for danger
In the trees and on the ground,
I learned to shake with terror
When I hear an A-K round.

Boonie Rats, Boonie Rats,
Scared but not alone,
100 days more or less
Then I'm going home.

'SKYHAWKS' is our motto,
'AIRBORNE' is our cry,
Freedom is our mission,
For this we do or die.

Boonie Rats a legend
For now and times to come,
Wherever there are soldiers
They'll talk of what we've done.

Boonie Rats, Boonie Rats,
Scared but not alone,
50 days more or less
Then I'm going home.

They say there'll always be a war,
I hope they're very wrong,
To the Boonie Rats of Vietnam
I dedicate this song.

Boonie Rats, Boonie Rats,
Scared but not alone,
Today I see my Freedom Bird,
Today, I'm going home.

Within seconds the soldiers returned to the beer stench reality of the Phoc Roc. Doc offered to buy a last round. It was 0120 hours.

"You know," El Paso began slowly, setting the pace for the succeeding talk, "ten centuries from now history here and in other solar systems may view our involvement in Southeast Asia along with colonialism and neo-colonialism as nothing more than a rapid manner of destroying traditional cultures and supplanting them with an ethos susceptible to the spread of technology—a planet of earthlings with a common energy advantageous to the exploration of the universe."

"We aint gowin be roun ta see," Jax said. "I'm concerned bout me en my kid. I'll let my kid be concerned bout further inta the future. My chil's gowin grow up in a new world with a papa it ken be proud a."

"That's right, huh?" Egan said reaching over and rubbing Jackson's tight curled 'fro. "I'm sorry, Jax. I forgot to congratulate you. Ol' Jax goina have a kid."

"Yep. I'm gowin have me a beautiful little black princess an I aint ee-ven gowin let a white man look at her. Then later on, I's gowin grow half-a-dozen of the baddest, meanest ball playin badasses anybody ever seen an anybody come near their sister gowin get banged up side da head, til they dead." Jackson paused for breath, then said, "You know, Eg, that lady you always talkin bout in yer sleep. You ought go back an tie that lady down. Time's a runnin, Bro."

"That was a real bummer," El Paso pursed his lips. "What the L-T's old lady did."

"What'd she do?" Egan asked.

"You mean, Man, he didn't tell ya?" Doc was shocked.

"No. What happened?"

"I thought you two was tight, like this," Doc held up his hand and crossed two fingers.

"When we got in for stand-down," El Paso said, "he got a set of papers from her lawyer."

"Say again."

"Yeah," Jax said. "She suin his ass fo a dee-vorce."

"Shee-it. Fuckin ladies. L-T said somethin bout them havin problems but he didn't tell me that."

"Man," El Paso said, "you gotta know two things about ladies. One, you can't pay attention to them and expect them to

pay attention to you and, two, every lady wants every dude to
desire her ass. They all want to trap you then leave your sorry
ass in the lurch. That's what happened to the L-T. He got
trapped.''

"Women," Doc said. "Women. They all the time doin
somethin jus so you can't expect why. They's like the dinks. If
you expects them in the valleys they's gonna be on the hills and
if you expects them on the hill they's gonna be in the valley.
Women like that. They figure out what you expects then they do
jus the opposite. They know they gotta keep a dude jumpin. A
dude's like a dog with a cat. Ever watch a dog with a cat? Ol'
dog trippin down the block sees ol' cat layin on the stoop. Ol'
dog doan give a rat's ass. Cat says, 'Well fuck all. That man
'pose ta want my ass.' An ol' cat leaps off in front of ol' dog and
burns down the block. Dog says to hisself, 'Shee-it, Man. Dare
she go. She must be a real somethin an all the time I thinks she's
over the hill.' See, ol' dog now thinkin he missed somethin
special and he cranks up his four-on-da-floor, chirps his rears an
burns after her. The thing ta ol' cat da chase. Always gotta have
a dude chasin em. Ol' cat goes inta da ally, up da garbage cans
an up top da fence. Dog growlin and snappin and cussin up a
ruckus an dat cat, she up dere stretchin out her rear legs, you
know, spreadin em, spreadin them toes and lickin herself like the
dog aint ee-ven dere. Man, you wanta be ol' dog. That aint even
cool. Sometime a dude got plenty of brains for dealin on dinks
but he loses his powers when applyin it to pussy.''

"How is the lieutenant taking it?" Cherry asked.

"Weren't you listenin?" Doc said. "I jus told you."

"Bro," El Paso turned to Egan, "I wanted to talk to you
about it. L-T's takin a heavy. Given him a bad time like your
lady did you.''

Egan shrugged slightly. "Yeah. I thought they were okay,
ya know. Life's hard, Man. See Jax, that's why I aint tied down
to that lady. It's simple as that. Life just aint easy. You gotta
struggle till you die and all you can do is make the best of it and
sometimes that aint much.''

"Egan," Jax shook his head annoyed, "yo a middle-class
white dude, how yo ee-ven spout that shee-it?''

"Don't change nothin, Man. You can have dough out the
yang, yer lady splits and yer fucked. No fat whore goina change
that.''

"Fat whore? Yo crazy, Man. Yo crazy. Yo want some skinny womanwench. Yo always talkin bout that 'lithe lean roun eye.' Maybe yo like some a these dinks. They got no tits. They got no ass. That what yo want, Man. Yo nuts. My ol' lady's fat and yo always dischargin that shit bout skinny tight cunt like my ol' lady a nigger bitch in honkeyville. Give me a woman who's got nice . . . nice . . . nice junk I can hold."

"Give me a woman," Egan said unscathed by Jax' allegations, "to whom I can dedicate myself. I need a woman who will dedicate herself to me one hundred percent."

"Man, you like the ol' dog," Doc said sadly. "Maybe you's sufferin from *optical rectalitis*."

"What's that?" Cherry asked.

"That," Doc winked, "is when the nerve from the eyes cross the nerve from the rectum and short circuit. Give a man a shitty outlook on life."

"That's a white man's disease," Jax said. "Yo dudes got a strange way a lookin at things."

"Man, do you realize," Doc said, "that while you worryin bout yer skinny cunt there are people back in the World, I mean, Man, in the World, right in the US of A World, who have to steal to eat. You white mothafuckas doan know that."

"I know that," Cherry said, "and I think you're right. But I think it's only a portion of the overall picture . . ."

"Doan try to whip no L-T philosophy shit on me." Jax spit.

"Jesus H. Fucken Christ," Egan shot back. "What the fuck's with you. You been ridin my ass since I came in. I'll give you somethin ta ride . . ."

"Wait a minute," El Paso shouted. "Cool it."

Doc had a sudden surge of hate for Cherry and Cherry's condescending tone. "What makes you think you know so much?" Doc yelled. "Just cause a man's black, mothafucka, and jus cause he's not as educated as you, mothafucka, doan mean he aint smart as you." Doc's shouting rattled the walls of the Phoc Roc and men in both the black group sitting at the side and the white group at the bar stopped their conversations to listen, to get ready. There was more in Doc's voice than anger.

"Look," Egan shouted back, "that fuckin cherry's bout right. No nigger in the world can claim they don't have one fuck of a better life now than they had twenty years ago or ten years

ago or even five years ago. Look at all the legislation that's
come down in the past ten years givin every nigger a fair deal."

"Blacks," Doc yelled at Egan, "is fuckin tired of a fucken
Congress that say we gonna pass a law that make everythin right.
Fact is, it don't."

"Who you callin a nigger, honky?" one of the black soldiers from the group by the side jumped up.

"Who you callin a honky, nigger?" a white soldier from
the bar stormed up to the black soldier.

"Cool it," El Paso yelled.

"I'm goina bust dat mofugga in da head," the black soldier
snarled toward Egan and all the other blacks fell in rank behind
him. The whites by the bar grabbed up their beers and circled the
other side of the table in the center.

"Cool it," El Paso yelled again.

"That fuckin nigger's always spoutin that shit," another
white soldier rasped.

"Dats fuckin honky jive," the black soldier who'd first
jumped up said.

"Who you callin a honky, Nigger?" Jax stood defending
Egan with a smile.

"Yeah," Egan stood, laughed at the white soldier, "and
don't you go callin my Bro a nigger, Honky."

Jax and Egan sat down and El Paso waved the blacks back
toward their table. He turned to point the whites back to the bar.

"Watch it, mothafucka," Doc laughed at the white soldier
who'd first come over and who stood nearest. "I'm ETS in thirty
an if you aint careful I'm gonna look up your sister and give her
a thrill." Doc turned and winked at Egan who began to laugh.
Then the white soldier swung from the hip and hit Doc in the
back of the head.

For one second, as Doc's whole upper torso shot forward
and his head, slamming against the table, his forehead catching
the edge of a beer can, spit blood, the entire room suspended
motion. Doc's head and body were the only moving parts in the
three-D still life. A latent pulse throbbed, rebounded, then bodies converged about the table in the center.

The outside imploded upon the concentrated nucleus, the
center growing denser with bodies, the bodies flaying quicker to
keep from being crushed.

Molino turned the lights off then on and off. "Hey! Stop

that! Hey! Okay! That's enough! Closing time! Everybody out. Watch my motherfuckin stereo. Get the fuck out a here. Everybody out. Fuck off! Stop that! Get the fuck out.''

"Grab the Doc's other arm,'' Jax shouted at Cherry. "Let's get out a here.''

Egan and El Paso covered the retreat with a few well aimed punches and the five from the center split to the door while the two groups, black and white, thrashed savagely at each other in the dark.

CHAPTER

8

The moon had begun its ascent through the high mist. It climbed slowly, quietly, smoothly, seeming to diminish in size as it rose, seemed to contract and intensify. The night had become cool-humid tropical. Through the night the moon cut strong yet cast indistinct dark nebulous shadows, images of window frames against chairs and images of chairs and desks against a man and images of the man cast with all other images in a continuous conglomerate darkness onto the floor of Alpha Company's headquarter hootch.

The back room of the hootch was windowless and dark. He did not sit there. It was hardly a room, his room area, sectioned off by locked personal equipment cages and company equipment stores and sided by empty rifle racks. Lieutenant Brooks' bunk sagged beneath his cleaned equipment. His rucksack was packed, canteens full, sitting in the center of his cot. His helmet and weapon lay against his ruck. A web belt with canteen, four ammo pouches and four fragmentation grenades rested across the foot of the cot. He had checked and rechecked the equipment in the dark, had assured himself of its readiness then had gone to the front of the hootch and sat at the company clerk's desk.

His mind was running, reflecting on theories of international conflict, deliberating problems of his own personal life. He stared at the desk, the floor, the shadows. It seemed so clear yet he could not find the words for it. An explanation of the cause of war was here, right here, coming together. And with it, with these revelations, were the nagging last letter from his wife and the forms he had just received from her attorney.

For a long time he sat at the company clerk's desk staring into the eerie light filtering through the screened windows to his side. He did not turn on the electric light nor did he light a candle. He sat in the chair behind the desk and held the letter and the newly arrived forms at arm's length.

Rufus and Lila, he thought. We were something special. How did this happen? Where did it start? It had been a fairy tale. From the moment of eye contact in the cathedral he had never doubted the specialness of their relationship. He thought of specific times, of their first walk, a stroll in Golden Gate Park through the flower show. He thought of early walks through the financial district where they window-shopped, when they discovered once again their perfect match. How could this have happened? Am I ignoring our early fight, our few bad times?

Very early, perhaps their first day together, she had told him her recent experiences with love. She had lived with a man for two and a half years, she had said. One day the man came home and said he had fallen in love with a secretary in his office. In two weeks, Lila told Rufus, the man had moved out. He hadn't let it die there. He told her that he had never really loved her though he did not know it until he felt real love. Lila said that six months after he left, her ex-man married the secretary and even sent her an invitation to the wedding. "I was really hurt when he left," she had told Rufus, "especially with that 'I never really loved you' stuff."

Rufus had told Lila that he understood where the man was coming from. He had said, "I've been there. I might be there now if I were living with some lady." She had smiled when he said that. To him, her face seemed to glow. Rufus had said, "A man needs lovin whether he's in love or not. That man probably really liked you very much but, well, that's the way it goes sometimes." "Humph!" She had reacted yet her eyes still shone and Rufus knew he was in love. When had that been? She had been bitter about the man and that had made her all the more beautiful.

He pictured another time. A night in the park when she had sung soft blues songs and they'd kissed and he'd put his head in her lap as she sang. He could see them there now as if he were a third person watching young lovers from across the path in the park. He longed to be the man with Lila in the image in his head.

In the strange darkness Rufus thought of the days and nights in the park, at parties, after basketball games, on study breaks. He thought of the plans and the planning that surrounded their marriage and of the graduate school nights when he sequestered himself and his books in the tiny den and she'd paint or other nights when she'd have a gig and be singing at a club and he'd not be able to go because of the studies, the papers, the deadlines. He'd be furious, raging within, raging without while she was gone, jealous and fearful. Yet he'd say, "I understand. I can't hold her too tight."

Lila was a striking woman with a beautiful face and taut body. Her dark skin had an undertone of red which she accented on her rounded cheekbones with a touch of rouge. She'd wear her hair parted in the center, pulled tight about the crown of her head by a colorful band and then frizzling out and down to her shoulders. He could not help but love her. She was poised and intelligent, active and lovely. She painted and sang and modeled for local boutiques. Rufus loved Lila first for her beauty and then for everything else about her.

Now here in a busted shanty infantry company headquarters, Rufus asked why. As he thought his stomach churned. Would these letters and forms affect his ability to command? And, he thought, Lila, how can I overcome Hawaii without you?

For many soldiers Vietnam was depression, despair, a valley of terror. Much of the anxiety came not from the NVA nor from the jungle. For many soldiers there was no war, they never saw any of it in the giant rear base camps and beaches. But anxiety came from being away from wives and friends and family and being totally out of control in a life where control seemed the utmost criteria for survival. It was an old story and Rufus Brooks knew it.

The story was as old as mankind, as old as war: the Dear John story. For American soldiers in Vietnam the story was probably more common than for GIs in earlier wars. The war was unpopular. Could any soldier really expect something more from his woman? The war was immoral, wasn't it?, with all the indiscriminate killing, the bombings, the napalm, the defoliants. By extension then, were not the soldiers immoral too? Could anyone expect any righteous woman to stand by a barbaric man? By 1970 it had almost become the patriotic duty of a wife or girl friend to leave her man if he went to Vietnam. Why should Lila be different? Why should she be true to a boonierat, a commander of boonierats, the operator of a death machine?

Rufus looked at the letter.

Wednesday
July 15, 1970

Rufus—

How is the soldier? I spent yesterday with my mother and sister. We went back by the old flat and around. Then my sister and I went up to the Marina to watch the sailboats and then over to GG Park for the flowers. It brought back a lot of memories of the walks you and I used to take.

Did I tell you I got a new job? It's with a small art gallery that just opened up on Union Street. The job is giving me an opportunity to really learn that end of San Francisco and also it is giving me an opportunity to see some good works and a lot of junk. I know I can do better than most of it if I just could get myself together to do it. I think I'm losing my ability to paint or to sing. Goddamn! I'm just going to let it all out. It's killing me, this, this being trapped in a marriage in which one must deny oneself in order to let it be. I have sacrificed my painting to establish a home, to establish your home and to be responsible to you and to not feel like a moocher. At times I hate myself for being what I've been in our relationship. It has not been easy for me these past months. God! I haven't seen you since Christmas—I don't know why I have a home for *us* at all. But I can imagine it was hard for you to return to army life too. Or was it? You can rest back on your orders. I must have misunderstood what you said in Hawaii last Christmas. You gave me the idea that you respected my feelings. You're not supposed to mess up people who care about you. If you can't care at least a little, you should just leave them alone.

Don't think I'm getting a kick out of writing this, because I'm not. I would have preferred to talk to you, but that obviously can't happen. I would rather have a reaction to what I've been saying, but with you I'm used to doing without. I always wanted to bring you into my land of fantasy and then together we could make it all real but you've denied the fantasies and have made them impossible.

Rufus, I do not want to be mean. I don't want to be bad to you, but everyday this eats at my heart. I think we must separate and go our own ways. Sometimes I lie in bed and think how nice it would be to be touched by you and I think of our early years. Then I think of that *Goddamned Army* which you joined and how it's become you and squeezed out the man I knew. I think about Hawaii and I don't want any part of it. I hated you, what you turned into, what you were in Hawaii. You and your Goddamn men. I don't know you anymore. I can't love a man I don't know.

Rufus, you're an SOB. How any man can think he's so right and be so wrong is beyond me. At one time I would have called you a real prick, but since Hawaii that doesn't seem to fit too well anymore either. You had me convinced I was completely inadequate. I'm really sick of this.

Lila

Rufus Brooks laid the letter down on the desk top, leaned forward and with his elbows on the desk and his hands in his hair, he closed his eyes. He sat there and let his mind flow sadly, not actively directing his consciousness, not inhibiting the fusillade of images and half-developed thoughts, letting his thoughts run from him and Lila. Behind the flow there was a near static image, an image of himself standing on a darkened basketball court in a very large empty gymnasium. He stood with the ball, swinging it in slow motion high over his head, high, keeping it out of the reach of a transparent defender, over his head, well behind his head with both hands, he looking for someone to pass it to, ready to snap the ball with his strong wrists, ready, except, he had no teammates.

He shifted his head to one hand. His brow was wet in the coolness of the tropical night. The vision changed. He had just returned from the Nam and she, his wife damn-it, and he were in a swank club and a group of white men began harassing them and patting Lila on the ass and rubbing her thigh. Rufus remained calm and delivered a soft warning. The white men had been drinking and words were of little use. White men never listened to black men anyway. Very calmly he rose against the boisterous group, no, groups, of whites. Three large fair-skins encircled him laughing and taunting him and a fourth sat next to Lila, next to his wife, and he put his hand on her thigh, high on her thigh. One of the whites swung a heavy fist and cursed, "Fuck off, Nigger." Rufus ducked the swing and jabbed the biggest man in the middle of his face, in his eyes, Rufus with his large strong hands, fingers out, going into the big man's eyes, digging, hooking down and pulling out, using the momentum of the pull to propel his own body forward, kicking sideways with his right foot into the third white man's balls. Then standing still and tall as they scattered, apologizing, 'Excuse us, Sir,' 'Pardon me, Mr. Brooks,' and the two on the floor crying, all knowing not to mess with The Ruf and His Lady.

Brooks sat back, opened his eyes and took a deep breath. He craned his neck back and then looked back at the desk, at the letter and at the forms. He had received the letter on 3 August and had read it only once in the field. The forms arrived yesterday.

FILED July 17, 1970
SUPERIOR COURT OF CALIFORNIA, COUNTY OF SAN FRANCISCO

IN RE THE MARRIAGE OF
PETITIONER: Lila I. Brooks
   and
RESPONDENT: Rufus William Brooks
PETITION (MARRIAGE)
1. This petition is for:

      ☒ Dissolution of marriage pursuant to

      ☒ Civil Code Section 4506 (i)

Petitioner has been a resident of this state for at least six months and of this county for at least three months immediately preceding the filing of this petition.

2. Statistical Information:

.

.

.

    d. There are *none* children of this marriage including the following minor children:

  SUPERIOR COURT OF CALIFORNIA, COUNTY OF SAN FRANCISCO

PLAINTIFF: Lila I. Brooks

DEFENDANT: Rufus William Brooks

NOTICE AND ACKNOWLEDGMENT OF RECEIPT

TO: Rufus William Brooks . . .

"Fuck it," Rufus mumbled without listening to himself. "Don't mean nothin.'" He did not believe his words.

    In the room lighted only by the rising moon he uncovered the clerk's typewriter and inserted a sheet of paper.

Early morning,
13 August 70

Dear Lila,

    We all make those little mistakes once in awhile which have far reaching repercussions, lasting sometimes, through a perverse geometric progression of events, for all our lives. Little things like signing up for ROTC way back in 1964 in order to have money for school. Little things which control one's existence far into the unseen and unknowable future. Hawaii and its repercussions have been very heavy with me since that brief interlude and I know it will affect me, both of us, all our lives. However, it need not be paramount to our every decision, it is something I believe we can cope with, can live beyond and can reduce in the future to relative insignificance. That reduction will require our mutual effort, an effort that I can not begin until I am again back home with you. There are numerous problems that demand my immediate concern, complex problems I am obligated to address while I am here. I can do little to alleviate your distress except to say I will return soon and I love you and want you and want to make your fantasies real.

Earlier this week I spent two days writing to the parents of several of my own men who had been wounded. I also helped the company compose a joint letter which we mimeographed for all our families. In the past several months many of my men's families have received malicious hoax calls. The calls are primarily related to false reports of death, missing in action and desertion. They cause an adverse and traumatic impact upon the unwary and the repercussions upon the man in the field finding his family thinks he's been killed and are making plans for his funeral are disastrous. My utmost immediate concern is for the welfare of these men. When I leave here I will leave that concern behind.

In your last letter you mentioned your desire for a separation. How much more separated can we be? My options are clear to me. I have 10½ months of military obligation remaining. I can extend here for 5 months and arrive there a free man or I can be home in 20 days and then I must serve the 10 months on active duty in the States. I can request duty at the Presidio but the probability is low that I will be granted it. I have already set the papers in motion to return, though I have also submitted my extension request. The final decision must be made by 21 August. On this I hope to hear from you prior to that time.

Brooks paused from typing the letter. He leaned back in the chair with thoughts of a time in their marriage before the army. He had been a graduate student and the pressures on him seemed to be increasing from all sides yet he was coping, he thought, very well. It had been Lila who had . . . had what? He could see himself in the small kitchen of their walk-up. The sun was just rising. Rufus was reading over class notes and Lila grudgingly preparing breakfast. There was no specialness in the room.

Look, my love, Rufus had said to himself preparing it to say to Lila. Look, my love, something is going wrong between us, has gone wrong between us and I want to set it straight. That's all I would have to say, he had thought and we could return to delightful times. If only I could figure just what the problem was. No not I. We. We must do this together, he had told himself, for if I were to set upon it alone she would resent it. Resent. That's part of it. I resent her . . . her . . . her what? We aren't making love with anywhere near the frequency we did at one time. No, that's not it. I resent that but that's a symptom not a cause. She had seemed depressed at that time also. And her depression had fed his resentment. Why can't she just accept things as they are, work for them to be better but accept those things that are as neither bad nor good? He had risen and seen the sun and thought, ah, today, another day in my life and the sun is out. Then he had woken her and she'd seen the sun and acted as if she'd been betrayed. How dare you rise, her gestures seemed to say. How dare you rise before I'm ready. And she resented the sun. Or she resented the clouds. Or the getting dirty of things. Nothing is constant, he had prepared to say. Everything is flowing. Clean dishes or rooms getting dirty is part of it. He had resented what he thought was her attitude. He had resented the feeling that once done things should stay done. The more he had thought about it the more he found he resented even thinking he had to tell her these things, tell her life is flowing and not static and that the reason she was depressed and found trouble coping, wanted to hide in bed in the morning, was that she was trying to stop life. "It doesn't work that way," he had whispered to himself. You have to ride life like a wild horse or like the wind, he prepared the statement. Enjoy life while you're in the saddle. Direct what you can. But don't try to cope with it by attempting to tame it. You can't. It will flow with you or without you and your efforts to stop the flow will only produce depression.

"If you're going to start preaching to me again," Lila had said, "don't. I don't want to hear it."

"I wasn't going to say anything," Rufus had said.

Brooks leaned forward, scratched his chin and returned to the typewriter.

Lila, I want to tell you something I found tonight. In a discussion with several of my men, I should call them my friends, I could feel the old Rufus return. We were discussing the war and racial conflict—they bicker as if they are trying to place blame on someone other than themselves or their particular ancestors—when it came to me . . . a semantic determinant theory of war. I can feel it, see it, hear it. It may be the most significant lesson that I or anyone may learn from Vietnam.

I must analyze this, concentrate upon this, answer this. What causes war? The situation here is perfect for study. I've brought with me all my knowledge of philosophy. It is dusty and tarnished but it is here, in me. And here are all the elements of war about me. Here are all the major races of mankind, representatives from every socio-economic group, from every government-politico force, all clashing. And the language groups: English, French, Vietnamese, Chinese, American technologese, Spanish. Here a democracy upholds a dictatorship in the name of freedom while a dictatorial governing group infiltrates five percent of its nation's population to a different country in the name of nationalism. The answer to the question must be here, waiting to be discovered.

Brooks paused again. In his mind he formally composed his thoughts. Hawaii and pre-army times kept springing into his thoughts. It took a strong effort to repulse them.

Differences! Inter-people differences and people's reactions, people's paranoia. Do we frighten people with our differences? Do others who are different frighten us? The more insecure we are the more defensive we become. If our personal insecurity is built into our national or racial character, passed down from generation to generation, then in order to alter our defensiveness, we have got to change our basic character. And what forms that character? What passes it down?

LANGUAGE. Thought structured by language. And WHOSE language? English. The white man's language.

The causes of war run very deep in white American culture and to this culture black America is being assimilated or perhaps it would be more accurate to say, digested. Our world is coming apart and it is imperative that we analyze the causes and help our world develop a different perspective about conflict.

Oh Lila, I hope I am not begging the issue between us by digressing. I know that I have failed you, for 18 months have not been a husband at all. Not even a man to you. What? I do not know. An idea, a past tense image that has lost reality? You existed in my soul long before you came into my life. Now you are withdrawing, and in so doing have perhaps withdrawn the essence of my being. From so great a distance, just when one withdraws the other can not know. Now, with these papers before me, papers printed weeks ago, the loss comes to me in past tense, comes to me at a time when perhaps your own feelings have changed and the emptiness I feel is, in reality, refilled. I have attempted to reconstruct what you must have gone through, what you must have been going through, the thoughts, the anxieties, at the time and just prior to the time you allowed these papers to be sent. I'm sure you suffered silently with the decision for many nights until finally, with nothing to counter the flow of your thoughts, you knew there was no other way.

Lila, I must decide by the 21st of this month to either extend to January and obtain the 150-day active service reduction or to DEROS from here in 25 days and have ten months remaining to serve. I will wait to decide until the 21st in hopes of hearing from you before then. May I say again, you mean more to me than anything I have ever known. I know I can return, revert to the man you married, grow quickly in the direction in which you've evolved, become a unity of spirit with you. You have always been my soul and I believe I have been yours. Before separating our spirits, and this I plead, allow us a chance to reunify. There is in me still the same man you married. He may be blunted by the experience of war, by the army more than the war, but he is not dead.

Lila, I love you.

Rufus

CHAPTER

9

P I O

The moon was higher now. It was blunt not crisp, an immense lopsided ovoid emitting soft light into a hazy sky where stars are dim and do not twinkle. Cherry followed Doc and Egan over the drainage ditch by the EM four-holer and up the graveled dusty road toward brigade headquarters. El Paso and Jax had decided to return to their sleeping area but Egan had said to Doc, "Let's go up to brigade and do our heads a favor," and Cherry had been pulled along in the excitement which followed the brawl at the Phoc Roc.

"How's your head?" Egan asked Doc. He stopped the black man in the middle of the deserted road to inspect the cut on his forehead and feel the lump coming up on the back of his head. "You're okay," he said. "Let's see if Lamonte and the dudes are partyin."

"Them white folk," Doc said. "Them are some crazy mothafuckas. Sucka'd me right up the backside a my head. Mothafucka. Hey, Man," Doc said to Cherry and Egan as they resumed walking, "I wanta jus say thank you fo helpin me out a there. That mothafucka nailed the backside a my head but good."

A few steps farther Doc turned to Cherry. "You handle yourself pretty well. I see you dealin on that one dude and I says, 'Cherry's gonna be al-fuckin-right.' "

"Them Delta Company mothafuckers," Egan said looking straight ahead as they walked, "losing their fuckin cool. God fuck. Suckered you but good. Wish I'd gotten a better shot at the mothafucker."

118

"Cherry nailed the fucka," Doc said.

"I'm not sure," Cherry said glancing first at Egan then at Doc and then back at Egan. "I'm not sure I got it all straight what happened."

They spoke quickly and quietly as they walked, their words running into each other as the words of men will do when adrenaline is still flowing though the fight is over. "We was jus teasin each otha," Doc said. "Except fo Jax, Egan here my Main Man. Like best friend."

"You coulda fooled me in there," Cherry said.

"We were just discussin," Egan said. He was embarrassed by the warmth of Doc's statement.

"You was really dealin on that one fucka," Doc said. "Eg, your Cherry gonna be al-fuckin-right-on."

"Hope I didn't hurt him," Cherry said. "I've never hit anybody like that before. Not that hard."

"He had it comin," Egan said.

"I think I might of broken his nose. I felt it crunch. I'm really sorry."

"Sorry! Sorry, Mista?! You broke that dude's nose, he gonna be the happiest luckiest mothafucka round. You maybe saved that man's life, Mista, if you broke his fuckin nose. You know that?"

"Hey," Egan said wanting to change the subject, "these dudes up here are really into their dope. Don't be a bummer. Okay?"

"We oughta invite Lamonte out with us," Doc said. "He'll wanta go."

"Yeah," Egan answered. "Cherry, you know anything bout pot protocol?"

"About what?"

"These dudes really got a rigid way of doin their dew."

"Ah, you're losin me. Their what?"

"God fuckin damn. How'd you get to be such a fuckin cherry?"

"Their dew, Man," Doc said. "You know, like in the morning the dew is on the grass. Dig?"

"Look," Egan stopped in the road again. He turned to Cherry and stopped him. "There are about ten dos and ten don'ts at a set. Those dudes find it necessary cause a downer'll wreck a high and that's UN-For-givable."

"I'll watch it," Cherry said.

"No. Just let me tell ya. After they torch up a bowl be powerful mellow. Like never pass an unlit bowl; never reach for a bowl til it's passed; never let your rap put the bowl out."

"Yeah, dig?" Doc added. "Never rap anyone inta a bummer and never keep a dude's lighter after lightin a bowl.

"Bowls pass to the right up at brigade. Take a toke and pass the bowl. Dig?"

"Hey. Okay," Cherry said. "If you see me doin somethin wrong, tell me. Okay?"

They continued up the road a quarter of a mile and turned at the break in the low sandbagged wall that preceded the trenches for brigade rocket security. No one was about. It was 0145 hours. Behind them, beyond the Oh-deuce, beyond the perimeter, illumination flares popped and slowly sank against the black wall of the mountains. Up the hill before them were half-a-dozen hootches. At the right end of the line were the quarters for the Vietnamese interpreters then the hootch of the attached personnel then, the APO, the Military Intelligence Office, the PIO and Civil Affairs office and finally the MARS station. All the offices were vacant, the interpreters' hootch was dark and silent. From the quarters for the attached personnel music drifted, oozed from the glow at the edge of the windows. The music seemed to have a difficult time squeezing through and expanding in the thick air. At irregular intervals the blast of artillery from the batteries deeper into Camp Eagle interrupted the music and the woosh of the mortar flares streaking skyward then popping, igniting and gently whizzing to earth added an eerie harmony to the sounds.

Egan, Doc and Cherry entered the hootch from which the music seeped. The interior had been sectioned off with plywood sheets forming six rooms with a narrow hallway down the center. A single incandescent bulb lighted the hall. A mural had been crudely painted on the wall of the first room to the left. The scene was a country road running back into green grassy hills with clusters of rounded trees here and there and fences paralleling the road over the hills, in and out of sight, finally disappearing at a vanishing point. A sign in the foreground had arrows pointing in five different directions: Quang Tri–78 km; Saigon–514 km; Big Moose, Montana–19,757 km; N.Y.C.–24,460 km; and one arrow pointing straight up, Moon–386,800 km ± .

Wooden ammo crate tops served as cafe doors for the room.

Egan, followed by Doc and Cherry, pushed the doors aside and entered. Inside the room there were three men. They had been talking sporadically. Two of them sat behind a bar on high stools and the third sat on a footlocker turned on end. The bar had been the old bar from the Phoc Roc which the men had scavenged.

The room was dingy. At each end a cot was covered by sloppily hung mosquito netting. Above the cot to the left was a stereo receiver/amplifier and 8-track tapedeck. Above the bunk to the right was a bookshelf full of volumes varying from *The Working Press* by Ruth Adler and *The Information War* by Dale Minor to a volume of Shakespeare and Joseph Heller's *Catch-22*. Hung below each shelf was an M-16 rifle and a bayonet. Below the rifle to the right there hung a crude sign:

IN MANY COUNTRIES POLITICIANS HAVE SEIZED ABSOLUTE
POWER AND MUZZLED THE PRESS;
IN NO COUNTRY HAS THE PRESS SEIZED ABSOLUTE POWER
AND MUZZLED THE POLITICIANS.

The man to the right behind the bar was thin and slight. He had long straight brown hair, longer than regulation. He wore civilian clothes, a western shirt with embroidered shoulders and blue jeans. He was known variously as Lamonte, PIO or Photog. Lamonte was an Army Information Specialist—Journalist, Spec. 4, assigned to the 1st Brigade Public Information Detachment. He was an infantry correspondent and he took himself and his job seriously. He traveled repeatedly with the same twelve infantry companies and he became close friends with many boonierats. Amongst them he was known as the Boonie Rat Correspondent.

Everyone has always portrayed infantryman, boonierat, as dumb. Everyone, except anyone who has ever been a boonierat. Boonierats were not dumb. Lamonte often emphasized this fact in his stories. He liked to tell people, especially soldiers, that the average soldier drafted into the army in 1969 had 14.4 years of schooling. "A junior in college," he would say. "This army is probably the most highly educated army ever, anywhere."

Beside Lamonte stood a heavy soldier in jungle fatigues. He was Lamonte's replacement. He'd been in-country two months though he had only limited field experience. His name was George.

On the turned up footlocker was Le Huu Minh, the Vietnamese scout and interpreter of Company A. Like most Vietnamese he was small by American standards, just over five feet. GIs called him Minh or Little Minh in deference to the South Vietnamese general and political figure known as Big Minh.

Whenever Lamonte and Minh were in the rear together they discussed politics and current events.

"I heard on your radio today," Minh had been saying in his soft precise English, "your federal tribunal reaffirm your chain-of-command courts."

"Oh, on My Lai," Lamonte said. "Yep. The courts ruled . . . Egan!" Lamonte shouted as the three entered. "You ol' rattlesnake, good to see ya. Doc! Jesus H., what happened to you."

"Ah, nothin, Man. Dig? Doan mean nothin."

"Yer the first ones to the party," Lamonte said. "How bout a Coke? You know, if you don't want to drink anything alcoholic."

"No thanks," Egan said shyly.

"We're goina be up for quite a while tonight," the correspondent said.

"We come over to ask you out with us in the mornin," Doc said. "What are you doin?"

"That fuckin major. He and that fuckin asshole butterbar lieutenant we got. They keep killin my stories. I'm workin on an article about censorship. But I'm through for the night." Lamonte stacked the scattered pages, bent down behind the bar and came up with two cans of Coke. "Here. Hey, this is my new cherry, George. This is Egan and that's Doc and . . ."

"This is Cherry," Egan said. "Lamonte," Egan pointed, "George and Minh. Minh's from Phu Luong," Egan addressed Cherry. "You know where that is."

"I do?" Cherry said.

"Yeah," Egan said. "Remember when we came in today, with that asshole captain from brigade? Remember?"

"Yeah," Cherry said. Doc had given Minh a power salute. The two now were power handshaking.

"Remember that village he was rattling on about?" Egan asked.

"I thought you were asleep."

"I haven't slept in 17 months," Egan said. "That village is part of Phu Luong. Minh lives down on one of the criks behind the village center." Egan turned back to Minh. "You gettin round," he said.

Minh smiled a shy respectful smile. Lamonte opened the sodas and handed them across the bar for the men to share.

"No," Egan said, "I think I'm imposin on you guys. We just come over to tell you we're ruckin up at oh-four hundred. We don't want to impose on you."

"You just think you're imposin because you don't understand, Man," Lamonte said.

"You know what it is?" George chuckled.

"He's in bad shape," Lamonte nodded toward George.

"Yer standin on that side of the bar," George chuckled again. "By yerselves."

"That's what it is," Lamonte agreed. "Why don't you shut the doors. If that hall light wasn't on out there this place would look real cool." Lamonte took a tensor-lite from the bar and placed it on the stereo shelf with the beam aiming at the ceiling. "Why don't you go out and shut off the light, George?"

With the hall light off and the tensor beam against the ceiling the room lost its dinginess and became almost cozy. "Where you all from?" George asked.

"Oh-deuce," Cherry said with private pride.

"How long you all been in-country?" George asked.

"Shit, Dude," Lamonte interrupted. He pointed at Egan, "That man's been here since before I was. Man, Egan was a cherry way back when Christ was a corporal. And Doc! God! Doc came here right after Genesis. Doc, you don't look too good. How you feel?"

"Man," Doc expelled the word from his throat after taking a swallow of Coke, "my head burn and I feel all this pressure on it. But Man, my body is cold, dig? And I got a mean case a the chills and my feet is freezin. I'm five thousand years old, Man, an I feels like a five-thousand-year-old piece a shit." Everybody laughed and Doc laughed the hardest.

"I got somethin to fix you right up," Lamonte said, smiled and the others laughed again. "We got a new, super-mellow one-hit bowl and some stash that'll warm ya up and ease the pain."

George reached up behind the books in the shelf and produced an eighteen-inch-long bamboo tube. The tube was almost two inches in diameter. The bottom was sealed by a natural sectioning of the bamboo. The top sectioning had a small hole drilled in it. About midway up the side of the tube a tiny carved bowl on a long stem had been inserted at an angle into the only other orifice in the tube. George handed Lamonte the pipe and Lamonte carefully, methodically, removed the bowl and stem from the tube and laid the tube on the bar. From under the bar he produced a bottle of white wine. He very slowly poured the wine into the orifice in the tube gradually raising the top so the wine did not spill out from the mouthpiece.

"Where you going out to tomorrow?" George asked Egan.

Lamonte gazed up at George in amazement at the inappropriateness of the question. Stoned George was oblivious.

"Just into the boonies," Egan said. He looked distrustfully at Minh from the corner of his eye. Then he turned to Minh, "You comin out?"

"Yes," Minh said. "I am ready. I will be on the pad when the helicopters arrive." Minh's voice was an octave higher than Egan's. He spoke English more precisely than most American soldiers though he added an intonation to the words which made his speech oddly like singing. He was proud of his diction and extensive vocabulary.

Lamonte gently placed the bowl stem into the tube and then filled the tiny bowl with finely ground marijuana leaves. He handed the pipe to Doc. "Let's get your head squared away," he said. Doc took the tube and holding it at an angle so the bowl stem was in the wine but the wine was not high enough to flow up the stem into the bowl, he placed his mouth over the upper end of the tube. Lamonte clicked his lighter and held the flame over the bowl as Doc sucked. The dried leaves glowed to amber red coals. The smoke bubbled through the wine then cooled in the air chamber below the mouthpiece finally passing through and into Doc's expanding lungs. The coals died. Doc shut his eyes, held the gases in and handed the tube back over the bar to Lamonte who reloaded the bowl.

"Damn," Doc opened his eyes wide, exhaled and bellowed, "that's one mean mellow bowl."

Lamonte handed the one-hit bowl to Egan and fired it as Egan sucked then reloaded it for Cherry, George and finally himself. Little Minh declined to smoke which was typical of all the 1st Brigade Vietnamese interpreters and scouts. Smoking, like drinking alcoholic beverages, was a very social way of relaxing in the rear-areas. The men who smoked usually maintained a lower profile than the men who drank. There were men who only drank and others who only smoked, the juicers and the heads, but most men did both and some men did neither.

Lamonte and the crew laughed and joked and passed the bowl several more times. Then Egan took some OJs from his pocket and they passed the opium joints around until everyone was feeling very relaxed and introspective.

Cherry picked up some papers Lamonte had written and read them slowly, concentrating on the images of each word, each letter of each word. The dope gave him a pleasant tight sensation at the temples and across the top of his head. Slowly he pieced it all together.

'Hello Kiddo.' That's a line from a movie I saw about four years ago. 'Hello Kiddo, Kiddo hello.' I think it was *David and Lisa*.

Lots of things have been happening around here. So many things that I'm dying of boredom. Brian Thompson got killed yesterday. Bill Martin caught a piece of shrapnel just below the navel but it wasn't too bad and he didn't even have to be medevacked. They're allowing him to stay in the field with all his buddies who all want to look for the NVA who killed Brian Thompson. As a matter of fact they are going to look for any NVA and try to shoot and kill them. Brian Thompson or no Brian Thompson, they'd probably do it anyway. They killed three soldiers, NVA type, today. They probably were not the ones who got Brian but if they could have gotten Brian or Bill they probably would have. Not any more, though.

Lots of people have been killed in the last few days. Probably some of them were from Colorado. Probably some of them were killed in Colorado or Kentucky or even California. Some of them weren't even in the Army. Some of them were probably too young or too old to be in the Army or the Navy or even in the Air Force for that matter.

Isn't it wonderful the ways, all the ways, that people die? And just think of all the stuff people will do for you after you die. Why, as I understand it, somebody will replace all your bodily fluids with formaldehyde and other good tasting chemicals. Then someone will put you in a plastic bag. That isn't really for you. That's for other people. They don't want to smell your BO.

Arnie Thompson, he's not related to Brian . . . Brian is a black man or was a black man . . . Arnie is a white man and still is, all of Arnie except his liver which he has succeeded in turning black with some stuff you can buy over here in a bottle . . . you can buy it back there too . . . Arnie was telling me last night about Lieutenant Anderson. Lt. Anderson was a devout Mormon, Arnie said. I didn't know the lieutenant. The day before the assault on Ripcord, Arnie told the L-T that he'd kill him if he ever left the body of an American up on a hill. Evidently the L-T had done that on an earlier assault attempt.

So the next day the lieutenant is a changed man. And he's got the courage to charge up the side of Ripcord . . . For the Glory of the Infantry. Someone had earlier suggested to the generals that they withdraw all allied troops and send in air strikes and B-52s and stuff like that but the generals wanted the victory of Ripcord for the Glory of the Infantry, too.

So, L-T Anderson from someplace in Indiana and his men go up the side of Ripcord to reinforce the sieged troops at the top, up ol' Ripcord with the pride of the Queen of Battle. Arnie never said why the generals wanted them to assault up the side of Ripcord. He never told me why they didn't just pick up his company and fly them up there and let them assault down if they really had to assault. Anyway, Joey, L-T Anderson's RTO, gets lost or something. Actually he had his head splintered. Not bad enough to kill him. Arnie found him at the bottom of the hill later. Good Mormon Anderson is up on the hill looking around for Joey when he gets his right arm and left hand and both legs blown off. "My arm, it isn't there," he says to Arnie. "No Sir. Your arm isn't there." "And my hand is gone too," Anderson says. "Yes Sir. Your hand is gone too," Arnie tells him. Arnie had tears in his eyes as he told me this. I'd been feeding him wine and scotch and listening. I wasn't drinking myself because I had a bad case of the shits.

"Well," Arnie says, "I wrapped up his arm and his legs and called for a medevac but they were all busy and it was going to take some time." Arnie's been around for some time. He's old. Maybe forty. His face is pockmarked.

"It were two hours later that man died," Arnie whispered with tears rolling down his cheeks. There were not a lot of tears. Just one on each side. Arnie isn't the kind of man to bawl. "That man died right here," Arnie said holding out his arms. "Right here, of a sucking chest wound that he didn't tell me about," Arnie said.

And it was all so they could go up the hill and kill some North Vietnamese who were there only to kill some Americans or some ARVNs or maybe a ROK or two. Lt. Anderson never did find Joey. Joey is back in the World now. Arnie was saying he'd kill a man if he ever left another man behind on the battlefield. Isn't it wonderful what people will do for you after you are totally unable to do anything for yourself?

They'll do even more for you than that. They'll get your insurance money and spend it on a lot of flowers and on a great hulk of marble or granite and on a hole in the ground. Maybe there will be a little left over for gas money so they can go to the movies and forget why you died.

Come to think of it, it was David who said to Lisa, 'Hello, Kiddo, Kiddo hello.' Yes David who wouldn't let anyone touch him and Lisa who was so into poetry she would speak only in rhyme and everyone thought they were crazies.

The real crazy was Brian Thompson. I was talking to him the night Delta Company had a ground attack on their position. That was two weeks ago. Delta was on the hill across from us. We felt sorry for them and very helpless because we couldn't help but could just listen to the firefight all night long. That night Brian told me he wanted to get the Medal of Honor. 'They's gointa put me in for it cause a the way I react in the field,' he said. Later I asked the captain if any of his people were up for medals and he said no. "Lots of the people in the company now are cherries," the captain said, "and we haven't been making a lot of contact. I had one man who DEROSd who is in for a Silver Star but none of the men we have now."

Cherry looked up from the pages. He looked at Lamonte and at Egan and Doc and George, all who were laughing at something George was doing. Minh was laughing too but his laughter was more subdued because he was not stoned. Doc passed Cherry his OJ and George passed Cherry half an oatmeal cookie.

"You really got a rap, Man," Lamonte said to George.

"No foolin, Man. But it sure took you a long time to say that." The opium and marijuana slowed all their speech considerably and it shortened their attention span.

"Oh," George groaned to the general laughter. "Open up a can of tamales, Man. We got a can of tamales."

There was more laughter and Cherry laughed too although he was feeling strange from what he had read and from the dope. He did not feel a part of the group any more. Lamonte opened the can and dumped the contents onto an old, broken china plate on the bar. "Wow! We're goina have ta cut these into threes," he said.

"I do not like tamales," Minh said.

"Good," George said. "Then we can cut em up into two-an-a-halves." They chuckled again. "I told you that thing about 'you cut—I pick,' didn't I, Lamonte?"

"I don't know but I was just cuttin on this thing for about five minutes with the back side of the knife."

"You still are," Egan laughed.

"There is a collusion set up against you, Lamonte," Minh said.

"Is that your word for today?" George asked.

"No. That one I learned yesterday."

"Doc. Here," Lamonte said passing him a tamale slice. "No. Doc," he said when George reached for it.

"I'll pass em around," George said.

"There you go," Lamonte said as he passed out the remaining slices. "Augh . . . that's no fair. I got a nub on mine." Then he added in falsetto, "Devil made me do dat."

"Hey," Doc said seriously, stoned serious. "You all pretty educated. Maybe you can tell me. I've asked sergeant majors, majors, captains, lieutenants, EMs, buck sergeants, master sergeants. Why do the army do this shit? Huh? Huh?"

"What shit?" Cherry asked.

"It's bad enough we gotta come in the army and then leave the army and depart our friends. But the war . . . Why? Give me one good logical goddamned reason, Mista. One."

"The war come, ah, the war comes before the army, ya

know?" George said. Lamonte glared at him and shook his head
and George added, "Well, maybe not."

"I mean, like all the people you know in the World," Doc
said simply going on, oblivious to George, "Blond who used ta
be up there. Way down there. Great guy, blond hair. Use ta
always be drunk all the time . . ."

"Yeah."

"Do you know me en him been here since '68 tagether. I
was in the Cav, Airborne Infantry. In the Elephant Valley up
north."

"North of the A Shau?"

"Walkin," Doc said. "Walkin. Walkin toward the A Shau
Valley. And after we left the A Shau we were supposed ta go ta
the Ruong-Ruong. Which we did. They all three is right there,
right?"

"Yeah. North, middle and south," Lamonte agreed.

"Do you know when Blond said good-bye ta me tanight, no
Man, two nights ago, both of us cried, Mista. I'm not bullshittin.
He was on the mothafucken LZ when I got those two SKS
rounds in my legs. I was there on the chopper pad. I saw him. I
met Blond before, on Firebase Geronimo when he was with
Seventh a the Four-Oh-Deuce. Recon. Both a us cherry in-
country: 1968. But he was here before me an . . . well, he was
here bout three month before me. He got here round August a
'67. I got here November 17th, 1967. I left March . . . March
22d, 1968. I got wounded January, ah, January . . . ah . . . I
fergot the date. I try ta keep it far from my mothafuckin mind.
Like you nevah hear me talk bout it, right?"

"Right."

"I see Blond on Geronimo the day I got wounded. When I
was goan out in the chopper, one Power Sign, one Peace Sign."
Doc held up one clenched fist and one V-fingered hand. "I'll see
our brothers later. Right? I didn't go ta Japan. I didn't go ta the
Philippines. I didn't go ta Korea. Ya know, those big hospitals. I
went to Cam Ranh Bay en came right back. Right back. Dig it?"

"Yeah."

"I was Medic. I was medic humpin. Ya know what I mean?
I was medic with the 1st Cav. Combined operation. Recon jus
walk off Leech Island. Went ta Curahee. Dig?"

"Yeah."

"They was comin off Curahee goan toward Berchesgadten.

And they radio inta Berchesgadten an say they was comin in.
Berchesgadten say, 'Don't even come here. We gettin hit.' They
had ta turn around and come back. They radios in and says they
comin back. They say, 'Don't come back here, we's gettin hit.'
I'm hearin all this conversation. Dig it? Blond was walkin slack.
That time he was walkin slack. They had a brother . . . black
guy like me . . . Black Brother, ya know what I mean? Man,
listen. Him en Blond, he was walkin behind Blond an a RTO
was walkin right behind him. I'm not bullshittin ya. We was
walkin down the Hoi Sanh Trail. Okay. Blond, they was comin
up the Hoi Sanh Trail. We was comin down the Hoi Sanh Trail.
We dug a trail watcher. So instead of sayin the trail watcher saw
us . . . most likely he know we saw him, that's why he dee-
deed, we didn't go chasin him cause it was comin on night, the
L-T says, 'Let's move up above bout maybe 250 meters.' Good
thing we did. Cause that night, that night, Mista, that night, that
spot where we seen that mothafuckin trail watcher at, got fucked
up.''

"Mortars?"

"Mortars, RPGs, frags, everythin. B-40s was comin in on
that mothafuckin spot where we started ta stay. It's a good thing
that the L-T had sense. Dig it?"

"Right."

"En the dude says, 'Blond, Look Out! RPG!' He hit Blond
in the back a the head with his M-16. Blond fell ta the ground.''

"Blond, that guy in radar?" Lamonte asked.

"Yeah. Me en Blond was humpin tagether from '68. Blond
en me, we hugged each other, kissed each other. Ya know Man,
like this, side-ta-side. We shook each other's hand, Man. Man,
shake my hand. Ya know? Shake my hand. Ya know, we shook
each other's hand. Ya know what I mean. I put his hand ta my
heart, Mista PIO, like I got your hand ta my heart and I says,
'Blond, do ya feel it.' He say, 'Brother Doc, I feel it.' I says,
'Guess what Blond?' I says, 'You got soul.' He say, 'Brother
Doc, you been wantin ta tell me that fo a long time.' I says,
'Yeah Blond, I know it.' En he say, 'En I'm goan home now en
I know you really mean it. If you had told me any other time
before this, when even we was humpin back in '68, fightin, ya
know,' he says, 'I would a had some kind a doubt, some kind a
thought. But I'm goan home now and I know that you really
mean it.' I put my hand to his heart. This way. En I say, 'Blond,

I really feel it.' En Man, we cried. Right there in his mothafuckin hootch, jus a while ago, Man. We cried. We actually cried, Mista. I'm not bullshittin ya.

"Why do the army do that, Mista? Why? You all pretty educated. You tell me."

"No, Man," Egan said. "Doc, nobody can tell you why. It's just like that."

"Hey, Mista PIO, you tell me."

"No, Doc," Lamonte said. "I can't tell you neither."

"You know, Man," Doc said. "We got us a new cherry here, a new white cherry who gonna be oh-fuckin-kay. Lots a white dudes okay. Dig? Lots a Brothers okay too, Man. Dig?"

"Yeah."

"Yeah."

"See, but when they get back ta the World we all turn inta mothafuckas. You know what I'm sayin? Man, you know what I'm sayin? Why? Tell me why, Mista?"

"Don't mean nothin," Egan said. He removed two OJs from his shirt and handed one to Doc and one to Lamonte and lit them both.

"I think it is time you all go," Minh said from the far end of the bar.

"Yeah, I think so too," George said. "It's three-twenty. What the fuck you guys doin in my AO at three-twenty?"

"No," Minh said. "I mean it is time you all leave my country and let us work out our separate peace."

"Minh," Egan said, "you know, if we were all to leave, even if we negotiate a separate peace, that won't mean peace for your country."

George mumbled, "That's like oh three-hundred and twenty."

"This is true," Minh said. "But, my friend Egan, then the war will be a Vietnamese war and not an American war. Your money is too much and now I do not recognize my own home. Your president must have you leave."

"Oh-three-two-zero," George muttered. "Up at oh-four-three-zero."

"Man, you really out of it," Lamonte said to George. "You are really wasted."

"Time to sky up," Egan said lifting his body as though he were lifting a great bulk weight.

"One more hit," Lamonte said. His eyes gleamed. "Get the shotgun."

"Oh shee-it," Doc laughed. "You gonna blow his mind away."

The shotgun was a tube of seven Coca-Cola cans taped together end-to-end. Grass, bulk marijuana which could be purchased by the sandbag for ten dollars MPC, was burned in the second can. The shotgunner blew into a large opening in the first can and the smoke flowed and swirled up and down and cooled in the five following tins until it peed out a tiny puncture at the end of the tube, until it sniped out in a thin straight line where the shotgunnee could stand back eight or ten inches, mouth gaping, and swallow the smoke stream.

Lamonte loaded, lit and fired. The shotgun worked its way about the room, Lamonte shotgunning his honored guest, Doc. The Doc gunning Egan and Egan George and finally George gunning Cherry. Cherry couldn't stand after the hit and Egan gunned Lamonte and Lamonte reloaded the tube for a second round.

Cherry sat on Lamonte's cot and stared into the room and beyond. What am I doing here, he thought. I'm just a kid, just a dumb kid. These are just kids, he said the words inside. The thought was a jumble of words and phrases, of pictures whirling and of names as ideograms. Kids from the suburbs, he thought. Rich kids. We're kids who've dreamed of far lands and exotic places, of the lands and wars of Hemingway and Mailer. Kids dreaming of seeing hobo jungles and shanties and of jumping a Steinbeck freight and of seeing America and the world. I've seen Daytona and Ft. Lauderdale at Easter and Cheyenne during the Round-Up but I never saw a dust bowl or mass poverty like the descriptions of the Depression by my folks or by the television. How the hell does an American middle-class white kid see what life is like if they get rid of all the rough edges? Shit. The L-T is as middle class as I am. And Doc. That's not poverty he comes from. Or El Paso, a low class peasant? With a college degree? A year of law school? That's not poverty. Jackson? Maybe. But he's makin the almighty greenback right now more en me. Spec 4. That's about four-hundred a month with combat and overseas pay and he's gotta be gettin an allotment for his wife and he'll get another hundred for his kid. Maybe six bills a month. Then poverty's gone. So come to Asia and see the poverty. See the poor fuckin gooks with their Hondas.

The music in the hootch was turned up. It blared in through his ears. Now he could not feel his body. Everybody was laughing at him. Everything was sprinting in his head. Everything was clear, so clear. He squinted and the candle flames starred and shot rays in every direction. A flat star first, lines, a halo, glowing growing into a sphere halo and the lines glowing exploding fuzzy clear beams shooting speeding toward him, fire reaching penetrating his eyes. Cherry closed his eyes. He could see the future. The light revolved, rotated, the light stood still and he revolved and rotated. He tried to duck the light then the colors. All colors. They were all giggling at him now.

"Oh, the colors," he moaned.

They all laughed harder.

"Oh, the colors," he bellowed. "The colors. They're . . . they're speeding right through me. The fire is speeding through you."

"Jesus, Egan," Lamonte chuckled, "you got a super cherry. He's really funny."

"Come on, Cherry," Doc picked him up. "You gettin silly."

Cherry put his arm around Doc's shoulder. "Colors, wonderful colors. Colors with jelly. Covered with jelly." He began chuckling then laughing hysterically.

"He's cool," Lamonte laughed. "He's really all right."

In five hours they would be high again, this time in the air, CAing to the Khe Ta Laou River valley.

AUGUST 1970

SIGNIFICANT ACTIVITIES TO DATE

THE FOLLOWING CUMULATIVE RESULTS FOR OPERATIONS IN THE O'REILLY/BARNETT/JEROME AREA WERE REPORTED FOR THE TEN-DAY PERIOD ENDING 2359 10 AUGUST 70:

97 ENEMY KILLED, 15 BY US—82 BY ARVN; 18 INDIVIDUAL WEAPONS CAPTURED BY ARVN; 14 CREW SERVED WEAPONS CAPTURED, EIGHT BY US—SIX BY ARVN. FIVE ARVN SOLDIERS WERE KILLED IN ACTION AND 33 WERE WOUNDED IN ACTION. US CASUALTIES WERE TWO SOLDIERS WITH MINOR WOUNDS.

ON 11 AND 12 AUGUST A TOTAL OF 112 ENEMY WERE KILLED AND 17 CAPTURED IN THE VICINITY OF FS/OB O'REILLY. SMALL ARMS CONTACT BY ELEMENTS OF THE 1ST AND 4TH

BATTALIONS, 1ST REGIMENT (ARVN) ACCOUNTED FOR 19 ENEMY KILLED. THE 2D SQUADRON (AMBL), 17TH CAVALRY (101ST) KILLED 23 AND TACTICAL AIR STRIKES (USAF) AND AERIAL ROCKET ARTILLERY (101ST) KILLED 70. ONE ARVN SOLDIER WAS KILLED AND 11 WOUNDED DURING THE TWO DAYS OF CONTACT.

Throughout the book, "Significant Activities . . ." have been adapted from Defense Documentation Center document AD 515195: *101st Airborne Division, Operations Report—Lessons Learned for the period ending 31 October 1970;* declassified 11 November 1977.

CHAPTER

10

13 AUGUST 1970
STAGING

The moon was yellow, low on the horizon, just above the blackness of the mountains. Straight up was blue-black. Eighty-four men sat, leaned against their rucksacks, lay on the ground with the chill of the earth passing into their muscles and bones, eighty-four men trying to catch a few moments sleep, trying to have time pass without tiring them more than they were already tired. They lay quietly in the deep monsoon-carved gullies surrounding the landing strip, trying not to think, trying to sleep on the gravel and stone and hard clay of the ravines of the staging area. Twenty soldiers in this ravine; thirty in the next; twenty-four in the one across the landing strip. A few sat back-against-back on the tiny hard ridge dividing the ravines, sat smoking, the faint glow of cigarettes swinging in the darkness.

To Chelini the strip looked like an eighth-mile mini-dragway; to Jackson like an oasis above the ground mist cloaking the surrounding rice swamps; to Minh like an immense multi-legged dragon with eighty-four sucklings squeezing and squirming in the gullies of its legs. The monsoons of last winter had eroded the sides of the strip and gullies had cut deep into it and had grown to sharp V-shaped ravines. The dry season sun had baked the ocher clay and red stone gravel into one solid narrow mesa. The strip had been grated and rolled flat but the lesions had been allowed to remain for they served as trenches.

In the darkness of the pre-dawn a second wave of CH-47 Chinook helicopters approached the staging area. Nothing at first, only a feeling of their nearness. Then powerful headlight beams visible high over the South China Sea, then a slight vibration in the air, then the harsh slapping of rotor blades spanking the sky. Men unable to shut their eyes, to keep them shut, to keep from watching the approaching helicopters, to keep from feeling time's slow forward pacing.

On the strip a strobe light flashed, an RTO spoke directions into the handset of his radio, moving in the flashes like a character in an ancient film flickering. The dark silhouettes of the birds grew in the sky, the noise became larger enveloping the strip in quick pulsations, shattering the air. Chelini watched fascinated, as pathfinders guided the birds in with long red-tipped flashlights. The strobe went out, the helicopters descended, hovered, descended. In the blackness of the trenches men hid behind their rucksacks and pulled their shirts up tight around their necks. Some men covered their heads with olive drab towels. Cherry watched naively. The rotor wash from the big birds sent dust then sand and stones hurling from the landing strip into the trenches. The birds set down, tails opened releasing more infantry troops, more boonierats scurried to the protection of the trenches. The helicopters lifted and blasting sand lashed the ravines again.

"Okay, People," someone yelled. "Down here. Charlie Company down here. Don't go mixin up with Alpha."

Again it was quiet. The men in the first ravine rolled back, shook the sand from their hair, dug the sand from their scalps and from under their shirts, rolled back onto the hard gravel, exhaled the smell of jet exhaust, lay and attempted to rest. Cherry spat dirt from his mouth and tried to clear his eyes and ears of the sand. Now one hundred fifty-two infantrymen waited, rested, waited restless.

The sky grayed. At the helicopter pad on the ridge above the battalion base at Camp Eagle a Huey helicopter arrived and touched down. Supply personnel, hunching beneath the rotors, carried armloads of OD green equipment to the bird and stacked it on the steel floor. An operations officer and a supply NCO boarded and the Huey lifted. Two companies of the 7th Battalion, 402d Infantry had already rucked up, boarded the large CH-47s and had flown to LZ Sally. At 0605 hours, first light, the third wave of Chinooks departed Camp Eagle for the twenty-eight kilometer flight to the combat assault staging area.

The staging area for the combat assault was on the western

edge of LZ Sally, a tiny outpost situated between the sprawling headquarters and base camp of the 101st at Eagle and the division's 3d Brigade base at Camp Evans. From the staging area the third flight of CH-47s looked like a line of awkward sea gulls. They approached from a point over the Tonkin Gulf where land, water and sky merged to a long thin green-blue-gray line. Again the Chinooks became larger, distinct in the graying sky. Again the air broke with the deep slapping noise from the blades.

"Oh God," Cherry muttered to himself. "Here they come again." He rolled on his side, his rucksack between him and the landing helicopters and he watched the monstrous OD bellies drop slowly, watched the sixty foot rotors blur until the wind and dust became so violent he had to close his eyes tight and wrap his arms about his head and bring his knees to his chest to keep the wind from penetrating.

Three companies ordered themselves in the ravines. Two more companies, three scout dog teams and three sniper teams were scheduled to arrive by 0800. At 0817 the combat assault to the Khe Ta Laou River valley would begin.

On 15 May 1970 the 7th Battalion, 402d Infantry was reorganized under Department of the Army TO&E 7-35F. Headquarters and Headquarters Company was organized under TO&E 7-36F and the rifle companies under TO&E 7-37F. A few months later Companies D and E were added. Company E was a weapons support element with 81mm mortars and 90mm recoilless rifles. A reconnaissance platoon that was designed to work as a highly mobile rifle platoon or in six-man recon teams under direct control of the battalion commander was attached to Company E.

Officially an airmobile infantry battalion organized under these TO&Es at full strength had the capability to: close with the enemy by means of fire and maneuver in order to destroy or capture him; repel enemy assaults by fire, close combat and counterattack; seize and hold terrain; conduct independent operations on a limited scale; maneuver in all types of terrain and climatic conditions; and to make frequent airborne assaults.

At full strength the rifle companies fielded 121 men plus six attached personnel. A company consisted of three platoons and a command post. Each platoon had three 12-man squads and a platoon CP. A squad consisted of seven riflemen, a thumper man (M-79 grenade launcher), an M-60 machine gunner and an assistant gunner (the AG carried an M-16), an RTO (carried an M-16) and the squad leader.

Platoon CPs consisted of the platoon leader (usually a 1st lieutenant), a platoon sergeant, a medic (attached) and an RTO. The company CP was headed by the company commander and had three RTOs. Attached to the main CP were the company medic, an artillery forward observer (usually a lieutenant) and a Kit Carson Scout, a Vietnamese interpreter-scout-liaison.

On 13 August Company A was at 68% strength. This was typical of the entire battalion. Bravo Company was at 70% strength, Charlie at 59%, Delta 66%, and the Recon Platoon of Echo at 74%. HHC stationed at Eagle was at 81% strength.

A military unit tends to have a character of its own, an identity comprised of its history and traditions and of the personality of its commander. A squad becomes an extension of the squad leader, a platoon a compromise of the platoon leader and platoon sergeant; and the company, the body of the captain or lieutenant who leads it. Battalion tends to be the last level where the brunt of a commander's whims, likes and dislikes are felt by the individual soldier; yet even at brigade level the colonel marks the collective personality of the units below and again at division and corps and army. At the beginning of August 1970 there were 403,900 US military personnel in Vietnam: 293,600 Army, 22,600 Navy, 48,200 Air Force, 39,300 Marines and 200 Coast Guard; all deriving a multifaceted American personality from the leadership of MACV in Saigon and from the Pentagon and Joint Chiefs and on up to the President, Commander in Chief of all US military forces.

The division personality of the 101st was hard-ass spartan, perhaps the most spartan of all army units in Vietnam. The division ethos was purposefully directed and developed from the style, zeal and *esprit de corps* of the airborne of World War II. Tradition, heritage, rugged, tough and *Airborne All The Way;* that was the 101st Airborne. The 101st had stormed through Europe at Eagle's Nest and Berchesgadten and Zon, had endured the Battle of the Bulge at Bastogne with General Anthony C. McAuliffe's famous 'Nuts' reply to German demands for surrender, had jumped into Normandy on D-Day. In Vietnam the firebases were named after World War II locales and slogans: Veghel, Bastogne, Eagle's Nest, Ripcord, Airborne, Checkmate, Rendezvous and Destiny.

In 1969 the division became Airmobile and by 1970 most of

the troops no longer were hardcore jump-qualified paratroopers. However, most of the senior officers, the leaders, were.

Lieutenant Colonel Oliver Henderson, the GreenMan, ran the 7th of the 402d. He was a strong commander. The stronger a commander the more he affects the men he commands. Henderson ran the 7/402 with stern exacting leadership. He allowed himself few luxuries and he allowed his troops none. Henderson seemed to be unaware of American troop withdrawals and the winding down of the war. He was busy fighting. His 'SKY-HAWKS' battalion was a proud fighting unit.

Each infantry unit had a particular spirit of independence. This too was planned. Each company, each platoon, each squad and each man was independent and responsible for himself or itself, first and then responsible up the chain of command, link by link. The infantryman, infantry unit, ultimately, like no other military entity, operates alone. Some commanders expected their soldiers to execute orders like automatons but this, especially after the exposé of My Lai, was neither the official nor the most prevalent style and it was not the GreenMan's style. Soldiers were expected to follow orders but they were also expected to know the rules of the host country and of international warfare. If a superior did not follow the rules a soldier was expected to protest. More often soldiers were expected to interpret their own situation to determine the optimum course to accomplish the military objective. As an outgrowth of My Lai, no longer was an American soldier able to excuse barbaric actions by saying, "Sir, I was only following orders." The GreenMan strongly emphasized that each individual was part of his own leadership and he was responsible for his actions.

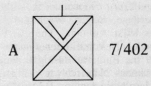

The following chart outlines the organization and personnel of Alpha Company, 7th Battalion of the 402d Infantry (Airmobile) on the morning of 13 August 1970. Symbols:

AG—assistant gunner   M60—machine gunner
FO—forward observer   M79—thumper man
KCS—Kit Carson Scout   RTO—radioman
M—medic   SL—squad leader

COMMAND

1st Lt. Rufus Brooks—Commanding Officer
1st Lt. Emory Wurzback—Executive Officer
1st Sgt. Eduardo Laguana—Top Sergeant

FIELD COMMAND POST	REAR STAFF
1st Lt. Rufus *L-T* Brooks	1st Lt. Emory Wurzback
Sgt. Alexander *Doc* Johnson—M	1st Sgt. Eduardo *Top* Laguana
Sgt. Rafael *El Paso* Pavura—RTO	Sgt. Mitchel King—Company Clerk
Sp4 Bill Brown—RTO	PFC John Swenson—Supply Clerk
Sp4 Tim Cahalan—RTO	
1st Lt William *FO* Hoyden—FO	PFC Mike Sheehan—Armorer
Sgt Le Huu Minh—KCS	

1st PLATOON
COMMAND POST

1st Lt. William Thomaston—Plt Ldr
Sgt. Daniel Egan—Plt Sgt
Sp4 James *Cherry* Chelini—RTO
Sp4 David McCarthy—M

1st SQUAD	2d SQUAD	3d SQUAD
Leon Silvers—SL	Joseph *Monk* Moneski—SL	Clayton *Whiteboy* Janoff—SL & M60
Steven Hoover—RTO	Robert Growitz —RTO	Daniel Andrews—RTO
Lee Marko—M60	Vondel *Boom-Boom* Beaford—M60	Justin Hill—AG
Bryan Brunak—AG	Albert *Smitty* Smith—AG	Melvin Harley—M79
Marty *Numbnuts* Willis—M79	James Polanski—M79	William *Cookie* Frye
William *Jax* Jackson	Robert Murphy	Greg Kirtley
Thomas *Happy* Lairds	John Hall	Joseph Mullen
Bo Denhardt	Ellis Michaels	

2d PLATOON
COMMAND POST
1st Lt. Frank De Barti—Plt Ldr
SFC Jonnie *Pop* Randalph—Plt Sgt
Sgt. Paul Calhoun—RTO
Sgt. Woodrow Hayes—M

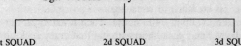

1st SQUAD	2d SQUAD	3d SQUAD
Camillo Baiez—SL	Alex Mohnsen—SL	Larsen *Catman*
Richard Shaw—RTO	Ezra Jones—RTO	Catt—SL
Ronald Pettington —AG	Mike Smith—M60	Carlos Fernandez —*RTO*
Michael DeSouza —M60	Jerome *Garbageman* Clement—AG	Homer Broadhead —M60
James Woods	Dewey Greer—M79	David Easton—AG
Sylvester Price	Bob Roberts	Raymond
William Riviera	Ralph Sklar	Humpphries
		Theodore Hackworth
		George Ibock

3d PLATOON
COMMAND POST
1st Lt. Larry *Boy Asshole* Caldwell—Plt Ldr
SSgt. Donald White—Plt Sgt
Sgt. Stan Kinderly—RTO
PFC Darryl Korman—M

1st SQUAD	2d SQUAD	3d SQUAD
Rafe *The Rapper* Ridgefield—SL	Andrew Spangler—SL	Bobbie Hampton—SL
Terry *The Reverend* Snell—RTO	Johnny Jenkins —RTO	Charles Smith—RTO
Don Nahele—M60	Kurt Bowerman —M60	James Cooley—M60
John *Queenie* McQueen—AG	David Tischman—AG	Juan Rodriguez—AG
Phillip Leahman —M79	James Arasim	Robert Craig—M79
Carl Adams	Harry Brown	James Roseville
Michael Bozarth	Louis Phillips	Eddie Hudson

During the pre-dawn Cherry had lain bewildered and silent in the trench at LZ Sally. He had been silent yet he had wanted to talk. He had contemplated asking Jackson something but he could not think of anything to ask. He could not rest. The anxiety about the coming combat assault had caused his muscles to tighten, his stomach to squeeze.

He had been up at 0400 hours. Then it had been hurry up to chow, hurry up and pack, hurry up lug that crazy ruck up the hill from the battalion area to the Oh-deuce pad then wait. At 0440 he had hurry-upped into the Chinook and at 0503 he had hurry-upped out of the bird and into the trench. Then he had waited. "Hurry up and wait," he had muttered. "SOP. Standard Operating Procedure."

Throughout it all no one had spoken to him. It was as if he had never met them. It was as if he had not spent the entire night drinking and smoking and talking to them. Again he was an outsider.

It was still cold in the trenches and it was uncomfortable. Restlessly he fiddled with his helmet, his weapon, the radio in his ruck. He fiddled self-consciously, quietly, trying not to disturb anyone, hoping someone else nearby would be fiddling with his equipment also so he could speak. Cherry lay back and closed his eyes. He tried not to force them to stay shut but tried to allow them to remain closed of their own relaxed accord. His eyes would not cooperate.

The sky grayed. The silhouette of mountains to the west turned green-black where the lifting darkness accentuated ridges yet remained jet-black in the canyons. Within the ravines darkness still hung. Laconic chats and extended grumbles disrupted the close silence, the tiring rest.

Doc was suffering hangover pains and pains from the lump on the back of his head and the laceration on his forehead. The thought of the open wound irritated him. "What a sucka. Man, a cut's a real sucka. Fuckin helmet rub it and keep it open for all them bacteria. Mothafucka gonna get infected. Can't wear no fuckin helmet." Doc tied his helmet to the top of his rucksack, shook the pack to be sure the helmet was secure and that it would not rattle when he walked.

"That a good cut, Doc," Jax said. "Wish I had a cut like that. I think I's catchin cold. That good too."

"You need somethin fo it?"

"No way. Not yet. I got this cold now an I's gowin keep it."

"You need somethin."

"I needs this cold, Man. Sound pretty bad, huh?"

"Sounds bad."

"Like bronchitis?"

"Gettin there."

"Yeah. Good. In three or fo days I get pneumonia. Gotta keep smokin."

"There's mo cig'rettes up in the sundry pak."

"Yeah. I's got get me sah mo. Yo need any?"

"I got em."

"Ef I's get pneumonia in a few days you gowin send me in on resupply fo a week a bed rest."

"If you gets pneumonia."

"I's bet I can pull that out ta a month profile," Jax said. He pulled out his hair pick and fluffed up his 'fro. He said, "Then with the rains startin they aint ee-ven gowin send ol Jax back out. I's gowin sit in that hootch all day with my water bowl an get fahhcked up. Let everythin pass til—WHAM! E-T-S."

Morn's early pallor penetrated the last light of the moon, permeated it, diluted it and finally diffused it until the moon disappeared. The fourth wave of Chinooks deposited Delta Company at LZ Sally. Warm sun assailed the ocher clay. The ground became warm then hot; the air lost its morning heaviness, the paddies their mist. The sun became blinding. In the ravines 246 boonierats huddled, covered their heads and eyes with towels or buried their faces beneath olive drab helmets still hoping time would pass without their having to endure its long uncomfortable minutes, its lagging dragging slow minutes, still waiting for the assault to begin. Slow minutes only a soldier knows. No, they are not like the minutes in a locker room before the big game nor like those backstage minutes before the opening night curtain rises. They are unique minutes. Soldier's minutes. Boonierat minutes, undistinguishable minutes, undistinguishable millennia, unsavored, endured lonely minutes 13,000 miles from home. Once the assault begins the minutes will be different. They will be filled minutes. But these. These minutes. These. Perhaps the last minutes.

Above the first set of ravines the platoon sergeants of Alpha surveyed their men; Egan from the first; Pop Randalph from the second; Don White from the third. They spoke slowly and easily, the mark of old-timers. They laughed at each other's quips and gestured toward the fuck-ups and laughed and cursed. The light skin of Egan's face was already beginning to re-blister from the sun. Pop's face, tanned deep red-brown with concentric creases surrounding watery red eyes, was dirt splotched where helicopter dust stuck to sweat. Don White, tall, wiry, coffee black, shrugged an unconcerned shoulder to the sun and lightly mocked Egan as Egan wiped salve on his lips.

"Mothafuckin cunt whore son of a bitch," Egan mumbled scraping sand bits from sun blisters on his face and arms. "I hate these mothafuckin Shithooks and this fuckin REMF sun."

Egan bent down and rifled through a sundry pak at his feet. The box contained candy and cigarettes, razor blades and shaving cream, toothpaste and brushes, writing paper, pencils and various odds and ends. The other sergeants picked through the box too. They left the box open for anyone who wanted to come up. Sporadically troops approached, took the candy and the cigarettes and returned to the ravines. Egan bent down and picked up a package of light blue stationery, then he rose, spat toward the trench and sauntered away. Fuck it, Mick, he said to himself. Drive on. His platoon was in order, had been in order for two hours. Echo Company still had not arrived.

Company commanders and operations officers and NCOs from Intelligence formed small groups on the landing strip. They had long since hashed and rehashed the operation schedules and objectives and now stood mostly silent, waiting to be under way. The sniper teams came in by Huey and reported to their assigned companies, dropped their rucks and regrouped on a small sharp ridge between the ravines of Alpha and Charlie companies. They too were mostly silent, smoking, checking their rifles and scopes.

The platoon leaders of Alpha joined Pop and Don White by the sundry box. All three were first lieutenants, young, in their early twenties, white, all-American ROTC officers. Two carried M-16s. Lt. Larry Caldwell carried a CAR-15. Pop sneered at him and the carbine and thought, that piece a shit. That weapon couldn't hit a water-bo at two paces. Goddamn barrel's too short, the buffer don't sweep right and the damn thing jams evera other round. Wonder why Brooks lets Boy Asshole carry it.

In the trench below them one man finished reading a Fantastic Four comic book. He passed it to the man next to him who

had been studying a worn skin magazine. That man passed his
material to a man sitting up the ravine wall who had been
reading a book on the religions of the people of Vietnam. The
man on the ravine wall put the book down, glanced at the
magazine, passed it on and returned to his book. The sitting and
waiting became unbearable so men stood and waited. There was
nothing else to do. It was impossible to rest anymore. Some men
hunched over their rucksacks and adjusted the straps and ties and
checked the pins on the grenades tied to the sides of the pack,
tightening anything loose, checking the extra ammo to insure its
easy accessibility. Other men cleaned their rifles, cleaned, polished, applied a light coat of LSA oil. It was the most repetitive
action of the infantry, cleaning weapons. Soldiers disassembled
their rifles, cleaned them, assembled them, checked them and
then began again. Time passed.

Bellowing laughter exploded in a gully halfway down the
landing strip, one very loud guffaw followed by secondary eruptions of giggles and chuckles. Men in other ravines stood and
looked, strained their necks to see. Cherry climbed a step up the
ravine wall to witness the joke. A smile came to his face. Yet the
looking seemed to extinguish the joke and the gully quieted and
the soldiers returned to their immediate worlds.

The restless infantrymen in the trenches and their clustered
sergeants and lieutenants and captains on the landing strip represented a collective consciousness of America. These men, Chelini, Egan, Doc, Silvers, Brooks, all of them, were products of
the Great American Experiment, black brown yellow white and
red, children of the Melting Pot. Their actions were the blossom-
ing of the past, blooming continuously from the humus of decayed antiquity, flowering from the stems of living yesterdays.
What they had in common was the denominator of American
society in the '50s and '60s, a television culture, the army
experience—basic, AIT, RVN training, SERTS, the Oh-deuce
and now the sitting, waiting in the trench at LZ Sally, I Corps, in
the Republic of Vietnam.

A feeling of urgency, a contagious expectation swept over
the men. The terrible enduring of minutes gave way to impetu-
ous movement and thought, accelerating gradually, continuously,
as lift-off time approached.

At the north end of the landing strip Egan sat alone his legs
dangling into a ravine. He was thinking of the World again, his

non-Nam, pre-Nam World. I never did send her those sketches, he thought. He pictured the drawings of two homes that he had designed for a pre-architecture course. In their student days, his and Stephanie's, he had sketched homes for her and she had designed interiors for him. In their heads they worked for each other yet they seldom actually sent the works to each other. Fuck it, Mick, Egan said to himself, I'll bring them to her when I get back. He stared for a moment into the paddies before him then at the writing paper on his lap. He began a letter to Stephanie. He did not include date, time or salutation.

> You are on my mind again. It is three years, maybe four now, since we lay on the freshly mowed lawn in the sun of mid-spring's warmth. Maybe it is longer. Perhaps it is five years since we walked down darkened city streets in the quiet of pre-dawn or since we first sat on the floor in your room and listened to Sandy Bull's *Fantasia*. I remember every moment, every word we said, everything we did. I do not know why my time here has not blunted my memory of you. Days with you stand out as if they were happening today, even with all that has happened between. I think I laughed a lot. You'd have to tell me for I don't laugh like that anymore and it is possible I did not laugh then either but simply think I did when I think about you and me. I need to know if we ever really had what I sense we had or if it is just something in my mind now and it never was a reality.
>
> When I was drafted—I wasn't drafted. I enlisted. Did you know that? Was I that honest with you? I think you knew that whether I was honest or not. I have experienced it now, all and more than I wanted and I think now I could have stayed there with you and you would have been all the experience I'd ever have needed. But if I'd not gone I would have never known. Stephanie, we are starting a new operation this morning and I must get busy. I'll continue this later.

Leon Silvers sat in a trench with Minh, Whiteboy and Doc. He also was restless. The others were fidgeting but not talking. Silvers opened his journal to make the day's first entry.

> Day 223—I look around me at my boonierat brothers and their sincerity amazes me. My own sincerity amazes

me. I do not know if I am or am not my brother's keeper or if I should be. I do not know if it is morally proper for my country to attempt to assist another to stop the infiltration from a third. I do not know if we should fight and spill our blood and have those we try to rescue spill theirs and again spill much of our enemy's. Perhaps we should not. Perhaps we should not have gone to Korea either. Or to Europe for the First and Second World Wars. I don't know if morality has anything to do with it, yet I look around and see these young men here about me. How can we feel this responsibility? Is that not morality?

> All mankind is my brother.
> Am I not my brother's keeper?
> If then, one of my brothers
> Turns against another,
> Am I not responsible to maintain
> The latter's keep?
> All mankind is my brother.
> I do not wish to side with one
> Brother against another.
> I do not wish to have a brother
> Against me.
> But if all mankind is my brother
> Mustn't I be the keeper
> Of my brother in need?

Why do some of my boonierat brothers think we should withdraw completely? Would we then not be like so many Jews in the 1930s allowing the world to push them around? I look about me and I know these men believe as I do, most of them at least, we must be here. If we were to leave, it would be immoral. Once we behave in an immoral way, we will lose our spirit and wander in the wilderness.

Silvers stopped writing. He looked around. It was very warm. There still was nothing to do. He removed a sheet of paper from the back of his journal and began a letter to his brother.

Friday, 13 August 70

Ab,
        So your old lady wants you to marry her. No sweat, GI.
Want me to discourage it? Can do. Can do it in a very tactful
way. Tell her first you can't wed til I get back, which really
you can't. I gotta be there. That's about five months off and
nobody gets married in January so you got it made at least
til spring. I've got a year after I leave here and no telling
where they'll send me that I won't be able to get back from
so that puts it in winter again. Maybe what you should tell
her is like this—tell her you want to get married in Europe
while you're racing formula 3 or 2 (if you can rob a bank).
What could possibly sound more romantic than getting
married in the pits at Monte Carlo just after your oil cooler's
sprung a leak and put you out of the race? The cars are
still zinging by. You are covered with oil and depressed.
Your bride is in a white leather suit of hot pants and vest
(no bra) and boots. Just the sound of the whole thing will
make your lady want to put the ceremony off til then. And
that is, at least, a stay sent from the governor himself.
        Now then, to the business at hand. What are the specs
on the Hawke Super Vee? Is it a good car? Have you seen
the new Lola and all the others? I find myself rather
anxious over this buy. You salesmen can be sold anything.
Are you going to drop down to 145 pounds? I've a feeling
this could be a big year. I don't mean big money-wise, but
big for the breaks for the rest of your career.
        I'm seriously thinking about joining Uncle Jake in
business. He wrote to me with a real nice proposal saying he
wants me to get my travel business license and open up an
agency for him and me. I could really get into that, I think.
I have got to have my own place or a place that is like
half mine but where the other half doesn't come around.
        I'm going to enclose some notes on the Southeast
Asia situation as I see it. Maybe you'd like to read them to
some young ladies and then have them meet me at the
airport with their panties at their knees. Two months to
R&R. I'm going to fuck myself to death in Bangkok.

                                        More later,
                                        Leon

*   *   *

First Lieutenant Rufus Brooks sat alone on the edge of the landing strip, staring west. The heat of the sun was on his back and on the light black skin of his neck. He stared beyond his men's restless shifting in the trenches, beyond the rice farms where peasants had appeared seemingly from nowhere, beyond the foothills with their clump greenbrown brush, staring at the mountains. Had there been a thousand more troops surrounding him or none at all, it is inconceivable he would have noticed. I had her convinced that *she* was inadequate?! he thought. He sat still but in his mind his head shook woefully back and forth.

"Hey, L-T," Egan said softly. He had come from the end of the strip where he'd been sitting, writing. Egan sat down beside Brooks. He looked toward the object of the L-T's gaze. "What's happenin?"

Rufus Brooks did not look at Egan. After a short silence he said, "I was just thinking about last night." He did not want to mention his wife.

"Yeah," Egan said. "That got to be a pretty heavy rap."

"Yeah," the lieutenant agreed. They were both silent for a moment. Brooks knew Egan had come to console him but he was not yet ready to talk about it with anyone. Brooks said, "Do you know what causes war?"

"Yeah," Egan said relieved. He also was not yet ready to talk though he felt a duty to their friendship. "It's when people shoot at each other over land. If they just do it, it's a feud but if they got some crazy mothafucker leadin them, then it's a war."

"No," the lieutenant said. "It's how we think. People think themselves into wars." He was happy to talk about war causation.

"I didn't think me into this one," Egan said.

"That's not what I mean," the lieutenant smiled though he was still looking at the mountains. "I was thinking mostly about cultural differences and how they affect our thought patterns and perceptions and actions."

"Yeah," Egan answered. "You can see it. I don't know if I ever really thought a lot about it before."

"You know, the causes of war are very deeply seated in white American culture and black America is being assimilated by that culture. This is an impossible war for black Americans to understand."

"It aint too easy for whites either," Egan said instinctively defending his race. They were silent again.

"What I mean," Brooks said mildly, "is that the roots of war are in mankind, in each individual and the individual is manufactured by the traditions of his culture. A man is like a rough casting entering a machine shop. He's already made but the culture he's brought up in is going to sharpen his edges. That culture is going to re-form him, cut away at his humanity, mill him down to size and get rid of what the culture doesn't think is necessary or efficient or beneficial." Brooks was sounding like a professor again. "Traditional black culture," he said, "cuts out the war-causing metal; traditional white culture accentuates it and sharpens it."

"Hey," Egan countered defensively, "you're the L-T. You're the boss man. You tell me."

"Oh Danny, I don't mean you and me specifically. I'm just talking. I want to think this out. If I go back to school, maybe I'll write it all down. I kind of started on it last night. It doesn't mean anything."

"Fuck it, L-T. Don't mean a fuckin thing. Now, what's happenin? We goina get this clusterfuck in the air?"

"Yeah, soon. How's your cherry doing?"

"I don't know. He's goina be okay. I'll go talk to him. Get him psyched up."

As Egan rose Sergeant First Class Jonnie Randalph came toward him and the lieutenant. Brooks continued sitting, staring to the west. Behind him Egan gestured to Randalph. Egan's hand was at his own temple and his head was cocked toward Brooks, his hand twisted back and forth indicating that the L-T might have a screw loose.

"Mornin, Sir," Randalph said as he sat next to the lieutenant. "Somebody said yer ol gal sent ya a Dear John. Thought I'd come by an cheer ya up some."

Jonnie Randalph, platoon sergeant of the 2d Platoon, was at the mid-point of his third tour in Vietnam. He was thirty-six years old but looked sixty. He had been with the 7/402 on and off for fifteen years and had spent all his Vietnam time with the 'SKYHAWKS' battalion. In a society where the youngest man is eighteen and the mean age is twenty-one, a man of twenty-five seems old and a man over thirty is ancient. It was uncommon to find a man as old as Randalph humping a rucksack. The boonie-rats called him 'Pop.'

"Pop, you old drunk," the lieutenant smiled, "have you got your platoon all squared away?"

"Yea Sir. They been fine for a long time now so I thought I'd just come over heah and git ya fine too."

"Thanks," Brooks said laughing.

"Yea Sir. Happens to bout everabody. Happened ta me bout six weeks inta my first tour. Just bout the best thing evera did happen ta me."

Brooks could not keep from chuckling as the small leathery old soldier slapped his knee, rolled his head around and chattered softly. "That gal a mine, why when I got back I looked at her and you know she's got her legs crossed like this"— Pop flopped his right leg over his left—"like her cunt's made a gold an I'm bout ta steal it. Well, Sir, we done it up right. There's just one way ta do it, Sir. When you get back you an ye ol gal jump on one a them dee-vorce charters ta Alabam. Ya just go there with everabody else one weekend an they pro-nounce ya all dee-vorced. That's what we done. Lordie! Then ya all come back on the same flight an ya all are a'ready dee-vorced so ya can party. Dang best ol party me an my ex eva went ta. Regular downhome orgy."

The sun seared the staging area. Soldiers clustered. Leon Silvers, Doc, Minh and Whiteboy formed a closed foursome.

"Whut do you find ta write about au the time?" Whiteboy asked Silvers.

"Everything," Leon said.

"Naw, Ah mean lahk whut?"

"Everything, Man. If you just let your mind use itself, you'd have hundreds of things to write about. I just write about what I is and what I think."

"You mean like you write bout this place all the time?" Doc asked.

"Shee-it," Whiteboy laughed. "We aint done nothin in Ah doan know how long cept hump them fuckin trails up en back. Up en down them fucken mountains. Humpin til one hill doan look no different from no othah hill en one NDP doan look no different from the las."

"Whiteboy," Silvers said, "just because there isn't somebody there every minute to tell you how to think or what you're seein doesn't mean yer mind is supposed to stop. Look at this strip. We've never left on a operation like this one."

"Yeah? Whut about Ripcord when we was gonna go in there en bail em out?"

"Damn," Silvers said. "You remember that mothafucker?"

"Yeah," Doc said. "We was gettin the word second-hand all the time. Man, dint nobody know what the fuck was happenin."

"Yeah," Whiteboy said. "Ah remember they sayin theah was fifteen dink reg'ments out theah. They was s'pose to be like ants movin up the side a the hill. They was losin whole comp'nies."

"That is the way it was," Minh entered the conversation. "I talked with a scout who was there. They had human wave attacks."

"Yeah," Doc concurred. "They say when the last bird was leavin that sucka the dinks was on top throwin smoke grenades tryin ta get the birds back in. That sucka was completely overrun, Mista. OVERRUN."

"They lost some artillery tubes up theah and Ah heard the gooks got em."

They were speaking to pass the time, entertaining each other with old tales. Chelini could hear the discussion. He wanted to be part of it but he did not know how to get their attention. He listened for an opening.

"They spiked them tubes with thermite grenades," Silvers said authoritatively.

"Yeah," Whiteboy agreed. "But they dint destroy em all. Ah heard the gooks got some of em off the top."

"No," Silvers insisted. "They brought in the fast movers and bombed the entire hill and destroyed everything. Shee-it. Remember those days when it was bein overrun. It was supposed to be any minute and we were goin out."

Doc said emphatically, "We sat there fo three days. Three days, Mista."

"Yeah. Shee-it."

"When they give each a us a plastic bag a plasma Ah near shit mah pants. Ah was so scared sittin theah Ah was shakin lahk a leaf in a twister."

"Man, when they finally told us Ripcord'd been overrun I was one fully relieved mother. I think I wrote a dozen letters in those three days."

"Ah'll tell you, that was the only time Ah ever heard a the 101st losin men. But Ah wasn't gonna write home about it. The way Ah heard it, theah was wounded left behind."

"Yeah," Silvers said. "That's somethin that should be written about. Man, I just write notes to myself so I'll remember

what this place was really like. I don't want to be spreadin any
bullshit when I return. That's the whole trouble with this war.
Everybody's tellin war stories and nobody's tellin it the way it
is.'' Silvers paused. He turned to Minh. ''Hey, Minh, what's the
word you got about where we're goin?''

''I think I only know what you already know,'' Minh said.

''Come on, Fucka,'' said Whiteboy. ''What do the othah
scouts say about wheah we goan?''

''They say it is a bad AO. But you have already heard that.''

Until 1968 Le Huu Minh had never supported any of the
numerous governments of South Vietnam. He had not supported
the communist National Liberation Front or the North Vietnamese
infiltrators or the American presence in his country. Until 1968
he had been an anarchist. Like many of the young men from the
city of Hue and the surrounding province of Thua Thien, Minh
was highly educated and believed strongly in the autonomy of
his region. As a student he was fond of quoting the ancient
Vietnamese saying, ''The authority of the government stops at
the hamlet gate.'' To Minh that saying had many facets. A
national government had authority only down to the province, a
province government only to district, district only to hamlet and
hamlet only to the doors of a man's home. No one had the right
to intrude upon a family and no member of a family had the right
to intrude into the thoughts of an individual. That was the natural
course of the universe.

Minh had been born in the village of Phu Thu, twelve
kilometers south of Hue. Like most peasant boys he worked in
the rice paddies from the age of four and by six he was responsible for his family's two water buffalo.

In 1958 most schools in South Vietnam were still segre-
gated between Europeans and Asians, a vestige of colonial days.
For Europeans education was universal, for Vietnamese it was
nearly universally prohibited. Unlike most of the boys of his
village who never received any formal schooling until conscrip-
tion forced them into military training, Minh, at ten, was enrolled into the French-built Catholic school in Phu Luong. At
fourteen Minh left his family and entered Quoc Hoc High School
in Hue, the same school that had been attended by Ngo Dinh
Diem, Ho Chi Minh, Pham Van Dong and Vo Nguyen Giap. In
1966 Minh became a student at the University of Hue, one of
three universities in South Vietnam. The school had five colleges—

Law, Medicine, Letters, Science and Pedagogy—scattered throughout the city, and it served some 3000 students. Minh was enrolled in the School of Letters, a very big step for a peasant boy.

Hue University was the Berkeley of Vietnam, a center of political activism and controversy, a haven for Vietnamese draft dodgers and a source of falsified identifications. As long as a male had identification proving he had not yet reached his eighteenth birthday, the military would not, could not draft him. At the university there were men who had been seventeen years old for years.

Hue itself was a beautiful city and the most independent city in all of Vietnam, North or South. The old Imperial City with its Palace of Perfect Peace, its villas and gardens, temples and ancient palaces, embodied the glory and traditions of the past. Wide boulevards paralleled the beautiful parks along the River of Perfumes, an ancient name derived from the choking lotus that thrived in the deep meandering waters. Old French Citroëns rolled past tile roofed houses inside and about the Citadel and past the long villages of sampans floating in the sweet smell of the river.

Hue was established in 1687 by Nguyen dynasty warlords, who built two great walls stretching from the sea to the mountains designed to help them defend the South from the Trinh warlords of the North. The walls were built just north of the present DMZ, a line that had traditionally divided the countries. In the late 1700s Quang Trung, who united all of Vietnam and drove the Chinese out of Hanoi and the North, proclaimed himself emperor and ruled from Hue. The city became the national capital. In 1802 Gia Long captured Hue with French assistance and he re-established the Nguyen dynasty which lasted for 81 years. Under Gia Long the impressive, nearly impregnable Imperial City, the multi-walled Citadel, was constructed. In 1883 the French bombarded the Citadel and captured the royal court. From then until 1939 Vietnam was ostensibly ruled from Hue by emperors condoned by the French colonialists and then until 1945 by emperors condoned by the French, who were in turn controlled by the Japanese. In August 1945 the last Vietnamese emperor, Bao Dai, renounced his throne to the Viet Minh revolutionaries. The French returned only to be ejected in 1954. Over the next six years lines were re-drawn for the North-South conflict.

No longer a national capital, Hue became the scene and

center of dissent, the heart of the 1963 Buddhist uprising against the Catholic regime in Saigon and the center of the Vietnamese intelligentsia. The spirit of *Giai Phong*, liberation and independence, increased and fostered numerous political factions. It was to one of these factions Le Huu Minh attached himself and developed his own strong political beliefs and it was with this splinter group that in the fall of 1967 Minh joined the alliance of the Right Bank Resistance. As he plotted for the general offensive and uprising that would liberate Hue from the oligarchy of Americans and Catholics and the Saigon puppets, Minh never thought that a replacement machine of northerners might be both more repressive and more exploitative. It never occurred to him that the northern political machine might fully replace the current regime and exclude his faction. As a member of a splinter group Minh knew little of the plans for the offensive, but as an activist he was able to state the needs and reasonings behind it. The TET Offensive against the city of Hue, against his city, by the NVA 800th, 802d and 804th Battalions began his cruel awakening to the realities of power.

Chaos, that most wonderful word to an anarchist, became terror. The NVA and Viet Cong, in control of the Right Bank from early morning 31 January 1968, systematically hunted down and executed an unexpectedly long list of targeted people, a list that included apolitical doctors and missionaries, Buddhists, Catholics, university professors and students. By the end of the first week of the Year Of The Monkey Le Huu Minh found himself sheltering enemies of the people. The city was in shambles. Virtually every building south of the river had been smashed jagged by mortars or rockets from the opposing armies. Triangulated steel truss bridges over the River of Perfumes lay twisted as if they had been constructed of rice paper and bamboo. Behind the heavy walls of the Citadel the fighting raged. Minh was exhausted, nauseous, for weeks. The land and city he loved had been devastated.

In July of '68 Minh *hoi chanh*-ed to an American MP. He was interrogated and released. Peace had returned to the lowlands and American memories are very short. But peace was not in Minh. He convicted himself of war crimes. Again Minh gave himself to an American MP and again he was interrogated. He pleaded to become a scout and was finally accepted into the Loc Luong 66 program, a program for ex-VC and ex-NVA who had 'rallied' to the GVN.

Minh was shipped to Saigon for indoctrination and then to Tam Ky for training. From Tam Ky Minh was assigned to the 101st where he underwent additional indoctrination at Camp Eagle. Minh was shipped to Camp Evans, buddied-up with an American line unit soldier and "oriented" for eight more days. Finally Minh and his buddy went through the standard SERTS training. Upon completion of the program Minh was assigned to the unit of his buddy, to the Reconnaissance Platoon of Company E, 7/402, as a Kit Carson Scout. As his ability to speak English improved he moved up to better jobs, first to S-5, Civil Affairs, where he worked as interpreter for MEDCAPs and then to Senior Scout for Headquarters Company. With the arrival of higher ranking Vietnamese soldiers Minh was demoted and became the scout for Company A.

The perpetual smile on Minh's face angered Whiteboy. "Damn gook a'ways laughing at us," he would say when Minh was not around. Minh was a foreigner; he could never be part of Whiteboy's Alpha Company. "Minh, you lit'le fucka," Whiteboy said, "the Jew asked you a civil question. Why doan you give him a straight answer?"

"Whatcha gettin on his case fo?" Doc said. "He tellin ya it's goan be a bad mothafucka. Goan be another 714. Huh, Minh?"

"I do not know," Minh said still smiling. "I hope it will not be so."

"Fuckin ay, dammit, best not be," Whiteboy snapped. "Ah've ordered me a Super Sport ta hop up when Ah get back home an Ah sures hell expect ta be theah when it arrives."

Minh continued to smile. The muscles of his face ached from smiling but it was his only response to the Americanisms which he did not understand. Later, if he was alone with Doc or possibly El Paso, or if he were in the rear with Lamonte, he would ask questions and he was often surprised to find that many of the American soldiers had as little understanding as he of 427s or 352s or Holly four-barrels which were not weapons. Minh had often been surprised and pleased to find that Americans smiled outsider smiles just as he.

But with Minh it was that way more often than not. The creases from the constant smile on his face became deep and permanent. The Americans looked at the dumb smile and they saw the misunderstanding in him and they saw their own lack of knowledge of Americana and they hated him because of it. Minh knew he was an outsider and this scared him when he was in the boonies. He feared that if Alpha got in trouble, became pinned down in contact, the Americans would not jeopardize their lives to save his. Minh was thus overly cautious and the American soldiers thought him a coward. In turn Minh hated most of the Americans he served. There were individuals, El Paso and the L-T and Doc, whom he developed genuine friendships with, symbiotic intellectual relationships, exchanging and defining against each other their cultural heritage and in that, themselves.

In his village and among his city friends Minh was also an outcast. To them he had become Americanized. The riches of the wealthiest land on earth were at his disposal. He was a farmer milking the great cow, prostituting himself and his country for material benefits. Minh was a man alone with broken ties to his culture and with shallow ties to the American military presence.

"Hey," Silvers said, "you know what I was just remembering?"

"Yeah," Doc laughed. "I'm inside your head."

"I was remembering when I first came in-country," Silvers said laughing along with Doc. "I remember we had just gone through in-country training and, ah, everybody was still scared. There was so much that was unknown."

"Damn"—Whiteboy drew the word out for extended emphasis—"that so far back, Ah can't recollect none a it."

"I remember it very clearly." Silvers gazed into the ground then looked up. "Or at least this part. I remember we didn't know where we were going or what it was goina be like. During training we kept hearing about this one battalion that had been mauled really badly and we still hadn't gotten our assignments as to where we were goin. I remember goin into the EM club there and getting a beer. I had just gotten assigned to Alpha Company, 7th of the Four-oh-deuce. And the guy says to me, 'Where you going?' I said, 'Alpha Company, 7th a the Four-oh-deuce.' And he says, 'Here.' He says, 'Here. The beer's on the house.' This cold chill ran up and down my spine. I thought, 'Oh God, it's all over. The minute this guy hears where I'm goin he gives me a free beer.' "

Doc and Minh laughed and Whiteboy said, "You really remember au a that? Ah doan know. Ah got two mo months then Ah'm gettin out."

"What you goan do?" Doc fed Whiteboy the question.

"Ah'm gonna do, Ah guess, just lahk ma daddy did. Think Ah'll get on with the railroad. Ah'm sure my daddy can get me on as a brakeman or sompthin. Ah got a letter from a friend the othah day and he says mah ol sweetheart's had a kid an looks lahk a Sherman tank. Ah guess Ah'll just drift a bit then get on with the railroad but Ah doan really know."

"What about you, Doc?" Silvers asked. "What are you goina do?"

"Too early ta say yet," Doc dodged the question. He would like to have said he was going to continue his education in medicine, become a nurse or a technician or even a doctor, but he believed those things were beyond the hopes of a poor Harlem black. "I think I'll jus get out first," he said. "What bout you, Minh? We know the Jew goan buy a respectable whorehouse but what yo gonna do? You in fo the duration."

"To me," Minh said, "it is most important for peace to return to my country and for all of you to go home. We do not have futures as long as the war continues and as long as your army is in my country."

"God A'mighty," Whiteboy snapped. "We're heah bustin our guts out for you lit'le fuckers and au you can think of is throwin us out."

"Why you gettin on his case again?" Doc said. "If I said to you it's time yo left yo'd say 'Right On!' and thank me. Shee-it. Minh, I say thanks fo wishin me the fuck out."

"Ah, fuck this shit," Whiteboy said and strode up the ravine.

Whiteboy moved his great bulk smoothly, stepping lightly over Jackson and around other soldiers, over Cherry and up the loose gravel incline onto the landing strip. Cherry had been following their conversation on and off and as Whiteboy stepped over him he smiled trying to indicate to Whiteboy his own approval of the big soldier's position. Whiteboy did not acknowledge him and as he passed Cherry thought, that guy, he shouldn't treat Minh like that. Whiteboy proceeded past the lieutenants and the sergeants to the devastated sundry pak where he grabbed a new deck of playing cards. Whiteboy nodded to Pop who was standing with Don White guarding the remaining supplies. The big soldier flexed his muscles, squinted up and down the strip and returned to the ravine.

All the men in the ravines were sweating. The sun had turned the small canyons into ovens. The men chatted blindly.

Some men opened canned C-ration fruit. Others munched candy bars. They shared the fruit and candy, sometimes passing food between groups.

Whiteboy sat again with Silvers, Doc and Minh. He broke the seal on the deck of cards, removed the jokers and began to shuffle.

The last wave of Chinooks approached. Whiteboy held the cards tight. Troops turned their backs to the storm of the descending helicopters, a shower of loose landing strip pelted their worn fatigues even though the CH-47s set down at the far end of the strip. Echo Company and the scout dog teams disembarked. The big birds lifted, climbed, swung toward the sea and were gone.

Jax got up from near the card game, walked up the ravine to the sundry paks, removed a can of shaving cream, shook it up then artfully designed a large elliptical peace symbol on the hot hard ground. El Paso came up behind Jax, looked at the peace symbol, tapped Jax on the shoulder and said, "Never happen."

"Na, Dude," Jax responded, "doan be a fool. Yo gowin be outa here and I gowin be outa here before it happen but I bet ten ta one Cherry doan pull no full tour."

In the trench sitting back against his ruck, sitting beside Jax' ruck, Cherry scratched sand from his scalp. Dust and grit stuck to his sweating arms and neck. He was miserable. He was still alone.

The staging area was now a cluster of hundreds of individual activities. Cherry was surprised, as he looked up and down the strip, to see so many men. In a ravine behind him a platoon sergeant snapped at the troops from Charlie company. "Come on," the voice demanded. "Turn in all your pot. Let's go. Pot, pills, hash. All that shit. Come on now, I know you got that shit. I'm going to go for a walk. Go up and throw it in the sundry box. No questions asked. If you don't turn that shit in, I'm going to find it on you. If I find it in the boonies, yer goina be in a world a hurt."

"Shee-it, Egan," a voice boomed out. "I don't know how you kin smoke them gook cigarettes. They smell like they come outa the asshole of a dyin gook whore."

Egan was coming down the ravine. Cherry did not look up though he followed Egan's approach with his peripheral vision. Egan was looking directly at him. For the first time Cherry really noted Egan's physical appearance, noted the ill-fitting faded and torn fatigues draped over the wiry thin body, the dilapidated jungle boots worn bare of color, the jungle sores and sun blisters and scars on Egan's face and arms.

Egan squatted beside Cherry and in a voice coming from low in his throat he said, "Aint this a fucker?"

"This? What?"

"This," Egan said looking Cherry up and down and then straight in the eyes. "You doin okay?" he demanded.

"Yes."

"Aint this a bitch though?"

"What?"

"This havin ta go look for em," Egan said teasing Cherry with the half statement. He spoke at Cherry, aimed his voice at Cherry's face. "My bag is killin gooks," Egan said. "I really love it. Didn't I tell you that last night?"

"Ah . . . no . . ." Cherry stammered.

"I remember the good ol days," Egan said. His eyes shone. "Tet a '69. It was tremendous. We had gooks runnin around the battalion AO. Right in Eagle. Man, they'd gotten through the perimeter. This is a fucker but back then you didn't even have ta go lookin for em. Shee-it. Now you don't find enough ta fill an ant's asshole. But before—you could just walk out in back a the orderly room and shoot a few."

Cherry stared at Egan. Egan was glaring him in the face. Cherry looked away, frightened. My God, he thought, this character's sick. Cherry looked down at his knees. He still wore one of the uniforms he had been issued at Fort Lewis. It struck him how new his fatigues were. He looked up at Egan then past Egan and he realized that he, of all the men in the ravine, had on the only new uniform. His skin was the only clean skin, the only skin without sores and scabs and bandages.

Egan's voice rose in an eerie whisper. "Maybe we'll get ta shoot some gooks today—shoot em right through the fuckin head. Would ya like that? DAMN! War is good. Really good. You love it, don'tcha? Don'tcha?" Egan leaned forward pressing Cherry for affirmation.

Cherry trembled imperceptibly. "War," Egan said forming his lips into a trumpet and sensuously blowing the word at Cherry. "They send you to the far corners of the earth. You hear the blasts of artillery and bombs. You get weapons, helicopters. You can call all heaven down, all hell up, with your radio. War. It's wonderful. It don't make a gnat's ass difference who the

enemy is. Every man, once in his life, should go to WAR."
Egan harshly flicked the butt of his cigarette across the ravine
then spat into the earth between himself and Cherry.

Cherry hesitated, then muttered, "Yeah, but is it right?"

"Winning makes it right," Egan snarled. "You can count
your cherry ass on that."

"What about the corruption?" Cherry asked more aggressively.

Egan snapped harsher, "Corruption?! What corruption?
Thieu? Are you goina tell me if the gooks win, they won't be
corrupt? Do you think they'll be better? Do you think their
honchos won't rape and pillage? You can kiss my ass. You're
missin the point. Fuck the honchos. It's us or them. WAR! May
the best man win. WAR. Beautiful WAR. When yer kids ask ya,
'Daddy, who'd the night belong to? Daddy, did you kill anybody?'
tell em the night belonged to Egan—and he killed everybody."

Egan stomped away. Cherry did not look at the men about
him. He was sure everyone was staring at him. He breathed
deeply trying to gain control. Things had been coming together
slowly for him. At first everything seemed detached from every
other thing; each incident, meeting, conversation seemed to be a
separate entity. Then things began to blur; one incident became
indistinguishable from another, the starting and stopping in time
and physical arrangement became all screwed up in his mind.
Egan's tirade had suddenly caused a connection, a clear slash of
reality through the haze. It was the beginning of understanding,
the beginning of Cherry's loss of innocence. Chelini was at war.
"You are finally goina see it," he mumbled to himself. "You're
finally goina be a part of it."

Off the landing strip at the beginning of a tiny divide
between two ravines of Alpha Company troops, Lieutenant Brooks
re-briefed his platoon leaders, forward observer and two platoon
sergeants. In one hand he held a map of the operational area, in
the other his M-16 rifle. "Birds will be here in one-three," he
said. "They'll land at thirty-second intervals. We're going up in
platoon order, first, second and third. Have your men arranged
in pick-up order. Where's Egan?"

"I think he went off to write a letter to his lady," Lieutenant Thomaston said.

"Tell him to get moving. Okay, let's break it up. Have em
get em on."

Lieutenants Caldwell and De Barti walked off with their platoon sergeants. Lieutenant Thomaston strode over toward where Egan stood cussing.

Seven men approached Brooks from the center of the landing strip. They were dressed in smartly tailored, well starched fatigue uniforms. Leading the group was the 3d Brigade commander. He wore a spotless helmet with a freshly starched cloth helmet cover. On the front of the cover were embroidered gold letters spelling out OLD FOX in a horseshoe wreath. Inside the wreath was the silver eagle insignia of his rank.

By the side of the Old Fox was Lt.Col. Henderson, the GreenMan. Both men wore web gear over their fatigues and both carried .45 caliber pistols in polished leather holsters. Their boots were so shined that somehow the dust of the strip had not dulled or coated them.

Behind Henderson was his aide and behind the Old Fox was his entourage of aides and advisers. The commanders approached Brooks together while the aides hung back a respectful three or four feet.

"Good morning, Sir," Lieutenant Brooks saluted.

"Good morning, Lieutenant," the two senior officers saluted in unison.

"Lieutenant Brooks, I do not think I have had the pleasure of your acquaintance before but I've heard nothing but positive reports about you for the past week. I'd like to say it is an honor to have you in my command."

"Thank you, Sir," Brooks replied uneasily.

The Old Fox spoke perfectly, weighing each word for effect and calculating the response each received. "Brooks, I am the Colonel, The Man, The Old Man if you like. And what I say goes."

"Yes Sir."

"Lieutenant, if there is one thing life has taught me it is this: You have to pay for what you get. Don't you agree?"

"Yes Sir."

"You have to pay for liberty, for freedom, for justice."

Christ, Brooks thought. What am I in for now?

"I want to tell you something about war, about this war. I want to impart to you lessons I've learned that seem to be lost on our youth today. I'd be very pleased, Lieutenant, if you'd impart this lesson to your platoon leaders and NCOs. I'd be very pleased if my words filtered down to your brave men. How old are you, Lieutenant?''

"Twenty-four, Sir."

"Twenty-four," the Old Fox repeated quietly, shaking his head. "Lieutenant," he said louder, "this infiltration is like a cancer to this nation. It's like a tumor which we've attacked. We've halted its growth and possibly reversed its gnawing, rotting progress. When Marines first landed in I Corps back in '65 most of their contacts were made within five to eight kilometers of the cities. In '67 and '68, with the exception of the Tet Offensive and Counter-Offensive, the fighting had moved into the jungles and away from the populated lowlands. Now, Lieutenant, we are in the mountains thirty, forty, fifty kilometers from the cities we must defend. A lot of Americans have paid dearly for this protection and we have been paid back. We have checked this cancer. But until the victim is strong enough to combat this disease by himself, our aid is paramount to his survival.''

"Yes Sir."

"One of our problems is public opinion, Brooks, and you and your men are part of the public. That's why I want to address you personally. The North has never publicly admitted either to infiltrating the South or to its ultimate objective of conquering the South. That lack of a clearly stated objective has tricked many Americans into questioning whether their objectives, so fully exposed by our intelligence network, are indeed real. Many Americans simply do not believe it or choose not to believe it yet we are about to tangle with a massive element of NVA regulars—infiltrators.

"The purpose of our being here is to defend South Vietnam, not to occupy or to dominate it. We are an army opposing an army. They are an army who has come to conquer. We may well try to capture or control the same objectives but our intent is not identical. We are defenders, not aggressors. As President Johnson once said, 'Aggression unchallenged is aggression unleashed.' We are here to challenge the aggression from the North. Do you believe that, Lieutenant?''

"Yes Sir."

"Good, Lieutenant, because if you believe in what you are fighting for, if you support the cause, you are more apt to be willing to die for that cause. If you do not believe in what you are fighting for, you fight badly. If you fight badly, you are

more apt to lose and more apt to die. It is a paradox of traditional
warfare that if you believe in the cause for which you fight, you
are more apt to risk your life, more apt to win, less apt to fight
badly and less apt to die. More risk but less death. That,
Lieutenant, is why you and your men must believe in what we
are doing.

"We are the strongest, toughest, hardest fighting division in
the Army. But by the news releases that I see every day, one
would think we are a bunch of pansies. Lieutenant, I believe in
our just cause and I want you to know you are backed by our
every asset. Either we shall all pull together, fight together or we
shall die together. That's the way it is. Lastly, Lieutenant, you
would not be here, your men would not be here, if your country
did not need you. Believe me, Lieutenant, your country will
repay you many fold."

The Old Fox saluted Lieutenant Brooks, awaited a return
salute, executed an about-face and marched toward the commander of Charlie Company. Colonel Henderson waited until the
brigade commander was a dozen paces off then said smiling,
"Rufus, that man's on our side and I'm sure he likes you. You
might get a personal letter of recommendation from him for your
file. Now I've got several operational changes for you and
clarification and delineation of objectives. May I see your map?"

In the corner of his vision Brooks watched the Old Fox and
his entourage as they approached then encircled the commander
of Charlie Company. He lifted his map for the GreenMan with
detachment, momentarily concentrating on the Old Fox.

"Rufus, you'll CA to 848 as planned," the GreenMan
spoke excitedly. "You'll work west across the ridgeline and
north down this finger and then onto the valley floor here and
then work toward this knoll as best you see fit." The GreenMan
pointed to the center of the valley on the map where brown
concentric circles indicated an elevation rise. He studied the map
as if he were planning the operation for the first time, directing
attention to topographic details with his stubby clean fingers.
"This knoll is your ultimate objective. I see it taking ten to
twelve days to clear this AO.

"There's a strong enemy force in this valley. We've added
a reinforced company from 3d of the 187th to secure Firebase
Barnett and this is going to give us two additional maneuver
elements. As you know Bravo Company is going to assault here,
northwest of you. They'll set up a blocking force on the north-

eastern end of the valley. Charlie Company will not secure the
firebase. Instead they'll be inserted here to the west and secure
that flank against any additional enemy units coming up the
valley and block any units trying to escape. Delta Company will
go in here and set up a blocking force on the north escarpment
and check out the caves. Recon will be inserted directly behind
you, here. They'll follow you by a day or two until they reach
this point on the south ridge where they'll close off any NVA
travel between this valley and the O'Reilly area. Each of the
blocking forces will search their areas for bunker complexes and
enemy concentrations. But you, Rufus. You're going to be the
rover.

"I want you and your men to check out the valley floor and
to work toward this knoll. Have you got that?"

"Yes Sir."

"Rufus, I'm looking for a fight," the GreenMan said exud-
ing enthusiasm. He boasted, "We are hos-tile, a-gile, and air-mo-
bile. I don't know how much of a cancer these NVA are. I don't
pretend to know what the political picture is. But what I do
know, Rufus, is how to fight. I know how to find and defeat the
enemy and how to do it with the least casualties. I promise you
the utmost support. I know what you've accomplished in these
mountains and I know the sacrifices you and your men have
made. You are a natural born soldier, Rufus. A real jungle man.
Your sacrifice has bought time for the people of our area, from
Quang Tri to Hue and all the way south, and it has brought peace
to this population. We can't fail them now. We don't allow
failure."

Brooks kept his face down to the map while Henderson
spoke. He's like a chubby little kid, Brooks thought. Like a little
kid playing with tin soldiers on a dirt mound in his backyard in
the middle of Missouri or some place. He's having a good time
now. That's cool. It's partly because he plays so well that we're
good. Because we're good our opponents cut us some slack. It
makes it easier.

"Rufus," the GreenMan continued, "you are a thinking
human being. Your men are intelligent and experienced. I'm not
going to send in a lot of plays from the sidelines. You be your
own quarterback. And Lieutenant, we are playing for keeps. I
know you know that. This is the big game, Rufus." The GreenMan
checked his watch. "The Air Force has prepped ten landing
zones. We'll use five; five are diversionary. You've got a good

company, Rufus, a goddamned fine company. Best in the battalion, in my opinion. Maybe best in the whole goddamned division.''

"That's a real honor for a first lieutenant. If things work out well we'll see that you get that promotion to captain. Who knows, maybe we'll get you a Silver Star. That always looks good on a young officer's record.''

"We're ready, Sir," the colonel's aide interrupted. "The birds are due here in zero-three.''

"Thank you." The GreenMan paused and looked Brooks coldly in the eye. "Best get your men lined up," he said, his chin tight and hard. Then he saluted Rufus Brooks and said, "For the Glory of the Infantry, Lieutenant.''

CHAPTER

THE CA

The sound of helicopters had pulsated in Cherry's ears all morning. Now the air became saturated with the roar of jet engines and the slap-thumping of rotors. Cherry saw eighteen slicks racing toward the landing strip from the south, Huey UH-1Ds, small birds compared to the massive Chinooks, approaching low-level in a line looking like a flying race down the dragway, helicopters speeding bearing down on top of him. Behind the first heat a second squadron of eighteen birds appeared. Behind those a third. High in the air to the west, waiting to rendezvous with the troop ships, were a dozen Cobras.

". . . for the Glory of the Infantry, Lieutenant," the GreenMan saluted Brooks and walked away.

"Hey! Okay," Brooks yelled into the ravines. "Get em on. Get up here."

Egan emerged from a cloud of thick grape-juice smoke, marker grenade, billowing up in an opaque column, thick hot purple smoke that jetted from the canister, billowed up into a mini-mushroom cloud cooling on the top and sides, tumbling down the exterior of the rising column, waterfalling, slow-motion splashing onto the landing strip and cascading into the ravines. Egan raced into position as the first bird braked.

Brooks locked his gaze on the first bird. In the back of his mind unvoiced objections spawned, trickled toward the center of his brain, 'the big game—quarterback—fight or die—sidelines,' words swept in, thoughts seeped, surged to be expressed then

floundered in the war machine noise and action and washed to
tiny enclaves.

A PsyOps bird swooped down and hovered a hundred meters to the east of the staging. It had a cluster of sixteen loudspeakers mounted on its right skid. Acid rock music blared at
maximum volume and mixed with the helicopter noises.

Men in the trenches scurried. "It's light," Jackson yelled to
Cherry as he heaved his rucksack skyward, twisted beneath it
and slipped his arms through the straps. The ruck became part of
his body.

"Yeah," Cherry yelled. He laid his back against his ruck,
forced his arms through the shoulder straps, sat up, rolled to his
knees and stood. The ruck with the radio gouged his lower back
and the weight already hurt his shoulders. Again a dust storm.
Again sand in his ears and eyes and in the sweat under his shirt.
The straps from the ruck ground the sand into his skin.

The first six helicopters lit upon the landing strip diffusing,
scattering the purple smoke. Daniel Egan, Lieutenant Brooks and
Lee Marko hustled, boarded the left side of the first bird. El
Paso, Doc Johnson and Bryan Brunak clattered in from the right.
The bird was immediately airborne. Cherry ran toward the first
bird too. His eyes were seeing more quickly than his mind was
processing. The helicopters were from Company C of the 101st
Assault Helicopter Battalion, The Blackwidows. They had distinctive blue diamonds on their tail booms. Cherry read the name
Charon in the diamond and the words *To Hell and Back* written
on the small olive drab door of the pilot's compartment.

"Come on, Cherry," Jax yelled. "This one ours. Yo doan
wan a leave Eg an Doc out there alone, do ya?" Cherry raced
back toward Jackson and the second bird. This helicopter was
named *Sybil* and was inscribed, *Follow Me*. Cherry stepped onto
the skid, jumped, spun through the bird's open side and plopped
his ass and ruck down onto the metal floor. He sat next to Jax
with his legs dangling out the door of the helicopter. Lt.
Thomaston, Numbnuts, Bill Brown and Happy Lairds scrambled
in with them and the ship lifted. Its tail rose, the rotors whacked
the air, the bird dropped its nose, accelerated forward gaining
altitude. To Cherry's left a doorgunner sat behind a machine gun
mounted on a black iron swivel. The gunner wore a flight suit
and aviation helmet with the dark visor down. He looked like an
armed green astronaut.

Jackson leaned back. "He aint nevah been on a CA b'fo," Jax yelled.

"Well, check it out," Thomaston shouted back. The doorgunner said nothing. "You just follow Jax," Thomaston leaned forward and screamed to Cherry over the noise of the helicopter. "We'll be there in about twenty."

The bird banked sharply west, dipped, banked. This is like the first hill on a giant roller coaster, Cherry thought. Suddenly he could feel his ass and the back of his legs sliding on the metal floor. He was falling. The bird was getting higher. He leaned back. His legs dangled below him in the unsupporting air. The bird banked steeper and Cherry could feel the weight of his pack forcing him out and down. He grabbed the support post between him and the gunner with his left hand. With his right he squeezed his M-16. Next to him Jackson, with his rifle cradled in both arms, seemed relaxed. Next to Jax the lieutenant shifted casually to a more comfortable position. All three had their legs hanging out the helicopter's open side. As the bird continued to climb and bank the three soldiers cramped into the other side seemed higher than Cherry. Cherry's ears popped. His eyes popped. The soldiers on the other side might tumble onto him, might push him out. His left hand squeezed tighter, his arm strained. Then the helicopter leveled into position behind the lead bird and again all the soldiers were level on the metal floor. Cherry wiggled and eased his grip on the support post and breathed deeply. Four helicopters fell in line behind them, six Huey slicks carrying the command post, the first platoon and the military journalists Lamonte and George in bird three. The air in the birds was cool and clean.

Above and in front of the lead slick a Cobra gunship with its mini-guns, cannons and rocket pods hung. Twelve more slicks carrying the remainder of Alpha Company joined the convoy. Four more escort Cobras surrounded the first wing.

The convoy progressed rapidly above the coastal plain and piedmont and into the foothills and finally into the jagged mountains. The birds followed the twisting Sông Bo River southwest to the Rao Trang, then flew westward toward Coc Muen, a landmark peak at 1298 meters and north along a high ridge and into the valley of the Rach Mỹ Chành and then due west. Below, the valleys were mist-filled, the ridges sun-baked. The helicopters climbed, flew west climbing, always climbing. The air became cold.

"Where's Martini?" Cherry heard Thomaston shout. "I didn't see him. Isn't he coming out?"

"No," Jackson yelled back. "His little brother was in a car accident last week. They shipped ol Martini's ass back fo the funeral."

"Oh. That's too bad."

"Yeah. Doc says the kid was only thirteen."

As the helicopter raced up the Rach Mỹ Chánh Canyon a refrain from basic training entered Cherry's mind. During his first weeks in the army, at the beginning of each class, he and his classmates had had to chant their company slogan before the instructors would allow them to be seated. Cherry had been with Company A, 5th Battalion, 3d Basic Training Brigade. The refrain throbbed in his ears in beat to the rotor thwack.

> *Action Alpha A 5 3*
> *Best damn company in the infantry*
> *We'll meet the test*
> *We'll beat the best*
> *Goooooo, Alpha.*

Goooooo, Alpha. It became louder and quicker. Then the thought, second bird. Cherry tightened. "They try to blow up the second bird," he remembered Doc saying. Oh Christ! he thought. Then a hundred voices strong, *GOOOOOOO, ALPHA.*

The top of 848 had been pulverized. At 0735 hours Air Force fighter/bombers dove upon 848 and released six 250-pound bombs. They and other bombers passed the hill and bombed nine other landing zones and diversionary sites. At 0745 more bombers came and dropped napalm canisters on the LZs, setting the smashed brush on fire. Ten minutes later airmobile howitzers from the surrounding firebases and self-propelled eight-inch guns from Camp Evans released barrage after barrage. Fifty-six rounds of high explosive cratered 848 blowing the burning vegetation from the hilltop and smashing and tearing trees on the hillside. The troop ships lifted from LZ Sally at 0817 hours. One minute later ARA Cobras swept across Hill 848 firing flachette and HE rockets into the broken earth and the rising circumjacent jungle. The earth heaved again and again and settled back upon itself in hot drying clumps. ARA went off station and from 0831 to 0837 more artillery blasted the landing zone.

The scenario was repeated on each LZ around the valley and on high peaks that could serve as future firebases. At 0839 the lead escort Cobra had Hill 848 in sight.

Simultaneous with Company A's convoy the command and control (C & C) birds of the brigade and battalion commanders entered the valley and slicks began inserting Recon and Bravo. At Firebase Barnett the ARVN security force and a battery of 105 howitzers prepared to be extracted, exchanged for American units from the 187th Infantry and the 319th Artillery. A pathfinder team landed at Barnett to organize the air traffic and to load-unload the slung cargo from the Chinooks, the guns and ammo for the artillery, 500-gallon blivets of water and fuel oil, and steel CONEXs set up as portable TOCs and FDCs. Within twenty minutes of the first ground troop insertion the new battery was to be laid, registered and ready for a fire mission.

Cherry nervously scratched sand from the side of his head. The breeze coming into the helicopter was invigorating. His heart was thumping. From high above the jungle the deep green had looked inviting and virgin. Now the land started to rise while the helicopters maintained their altitude and suddenly they were darting single file up the canyon below the ridgelines. The jungle looked threatening. Jax shook Cherry's arm. "Lock-n-load. We're gowin in. Pilot reports Recon got a hot LZ."

Goooo, Alpha. Gooo, Alpha. Cherry's heartbeat quickened. Second bird. *Goo, Alpha.*

The line of slicks approached the LZ from below, coming up the canyon, climbing to the peak. The lead escort Cobra, now directly above the first slick, opened with a fusillade that showered the landing zone with mini-gun fire, nailed down the hilltop with flachette rockets, thousands of tiny nail-like arrows burrowing into the soil, and blasted the already shattered vegetation with 40mm grenades. The peak became a smoking volcanic eruption of bright flashes and small black mushroom clouds. The four escort Cobras shot across the summit, peeled off to the sides and savaged the surrounding jungle ridges and canyons with more rockets. The missiles consumed trees and thick vegetation in bursts of white-red fire and large gray smoke thunderheads.

Cherry's eyes darted to the doorgunner behind the machine gun. The man was intent on the jungle. Suddenly the bird was above the canyon, at the summit, in double intensity sunlight. To the west a long narrow virgin valley burst into sight. The bird crested. Cherry clicked his rifle selector from safe to automatic.

Goo Alpha. Go Alpha. Go Alpha.

The tail of the helicopter dropped as the bird skidded in the air. The doorgunner opened up with the machine gun spraying suppressive fire down the side of 848. The explosive barking was ferocious in Cherry's ears, crack jolting shivers throughout his body. Adrenaline raced. All thoughts stopped. The ground enlarged, filled his vision. The slick stopped, hovered six feet above the peak. Jackson leaped. Cherry leaped. His rucksack smashed him down into the earth, into the soft exploded peaks, soil covered with shattered debris. The tinder was smoldering from the napalm and craters pocked 848. Cherry rolled and scrambled madly from the barren hilltop toward a small bush in the encircling concealing jungle. He slid down the incline into denser foliage and searched the jungle directly before his eyes for the enemy. For all the explosive force and shrapnel it had received the jungle looked unscathed.

Slicks came into the LZ every thirty seconds. Doorgunners pelted the surrounding hills. Heavily laden boonierats jumped from the birds and scrambled off the LZ and into the jungle and disappeared. The choppers lifted tail first then rolled left accelerating down the mountainside, gunners continuing to pump rounds into the dense growth. The perimeter expanded with each arrival. The hilltop remained empty.

"Fucken jungle," Egan sang out. He was standing at the edge of the LZ just below the peak. He had shed his rucksack. He held his M-16 casually at his side. Egan sauntered around inspecting perimeter security. "Fuckin jungle can really take it."

Jackson removed his helmet, turned it open-side up and sat in it. He took a chocolate disc from his fatigues and began eating it. "Hey, Cherry," Jax called throwing him half of the candy. "Heah. Yo owe it to yoself."

"Where's my RTO?" Egan shouted.

The birds of the second wing reached the LZ. Without firing they set down, the troops disembarked and the birds left.

"Cherry!" Egan shouted. "Where is that mothafucker? Cherry. Get a commo check with El Paso. We're goina secure this side. Second platoon over there. Jax, tell Whiteboy to move his squad forward about fifteen meters and set up a point covering that trail. Watch for booby traps. L-T found signs of dinks

on the other side and there's old bunkers on top blown ta shit.''
Egan circled toward Lee Marko.

The third platoon came in and disembarked quietly, only the
slapping of the rotors on the cool mountain morning air breaking
the silence. Then all the helicopters departed and the jungle was
very quiet. It was 0851 hours. The day was clear with a slight
breeze. To Cherry the jungle was very beautiful.

CHAPTER

█ 12 █

HILL 848

Beneath the flying marvels of modern warfare a transformation subtly seeped from soldier to soldier about the hilltop. Finding the bodies hastened the change. Alpha reverted, returned to the most traditional soldier life form, the walking marching humping hunting legions, the infantry. Airmobility brought them to 848 but from there they would go on foot.

With Alpha safely atop 848 and Recon on a lower peak 900 meters due north the command decision was made to insert all other units as planned. The operation's momentum increased. Helicopters seemed to swarm everywhere at once over the Khe Ta Laou. Companies C and D began their insertions. Two kilometers north of 848 the American/ARVN unit exchange on Barnett commenced. Infantry units arrived by Huey and American security teams relieved ARVN security teams. Chinooks could be seen arriving with American airmobile 105mm howitzers slung-loaded and departing with slung-loaded older style 105s of the ARVN artillery unit. Just east of Recon's LZ Cobra gunships came on station and could be seen working over a draw. Tiny black mushroom clouds erupted in silence below the helicopters. The jungle-muffled karRump reached 848 so much later than the sight, the sound seemed incongruous.

From training and fear, Alpha troops ordered themselves into a tight defensive perimeter below the peak, concealed in the brush. This was front-line Nam. The differences between the boonies and Phu Bai were as great as the differences between

Phu Bai and the World. Few people experienced the difference,
few recognized it. Da Nang was a forward area to military
personnel and journalists who lived in Saigon. Phu Bai was
forward to Da Nang, Eagle forward to Phu Bai. Combat and
firebases such as Bastogne and Veghel and Khe Sanh were front
line compared to Eagle, but to the guys humping rucks in the
mountains, everything was rear.

Platoon sergeants immediately organized recon patrols and
before the unit had been five minutes on the ground squads were
reconnoitering south, east and north. Lieutenant Brooks, the
platoon leaders and boonierat advisers clustered at the center of
the defensive ring to discuss first impressions of the new AO, to
reaffirm the order of movement and to prepare to walk west, off
the hill toward an objective they would not reach for thirteen
days.

Below them, perhaps two kilometers west of 848 and extending perhaps fifteen kilometers to the foothills of the Laotian
border, the Khe Ta Laou Valley was flooded, completely obscured,
by a continuous white mistcloud which filled the long valley
halfway up the north escarpment and overflowed through spill-
ways between south escarpment peaks. The view of the valley
from the summit of 848 was magnificent. In the middle of the
immense fog sea, like a jade island in a whipped cream ocean,
the top of a single tree broke through the mist and rose to glisten
in the sun. Boonierats clustered to the northeast corner of the hill
to peer into the valley they had heard held an NVA headquarters.

"Sir. Sir," Pop Randolph called. "Sir, theah's a daid gook
down heah. He's all blowed up an covered with dirt. He's got
two Chi-coms an a sachel charge with'm."

"Well I'll be dipped in shit," Garbageman said.

"Go git the L-T."

"I'll git um, Pop," a third soldier volunteered. "I'll git um
but I'll be dipped in shit, too."

"We aint been heah but two minutes," Pop smiled, "an
a'ready we got us a body count."

"There aint much left a him," Garbageman laughed. They
were standing about a depression of soft earth and mulch just
below the crest of the LZ. Garbageman snickered, stepped over
the depression and climbed toward the peak to see if the L-T was
coming.

A fourth soldier from 2d Plt brought Pop an entrenching tool, a short, collapsible shovel/pick. The old platoon sergeant stepped into the depression, straddled the low spot and began to dig, gingerly picking away at the mulch. Immediately thick odor rose. "God A'mighty," he sang out cheerfully. "We got us a gook. We got us a gook. We got us a gook all blowed ta shit hell en highwater."

Other soldiers clumped about the old boonierat picking at the slime in the hole. The commotion attracted more soldiers and they crowded closer attracting more until nearly all soldiers from that sector of the LZ's perimeter surrounded Pop and the hole and the mob trapped the rising spreading disturbed stench of decaying human, trapped the odor and held it motionless. Pop stirred the muck with the tiny spade, consciously avoiding acknowledging the gathering, humming in the limelight, slime oozing about his boots. Soldiers at the edge of the mob pushed forward to get a glimpse. Those in the middle swayed in two-way traffic driven forward by curiosity and by the pressure from behind. Soldiers at the center laughed, gulped, tried to stop their lungs in mid-stench inhale, tried to escape. Someone vomited. Still the circumference about the pit tightened.

"We got us a gook. We got us a gook," the refrain passed from man to man, from inside to out.

"Don't they ever wash?" someone yelled.

"That dude aint got all day protection," called another.

"Hey! Break it up!" The voice of the company commander exploded angrily. "Break-it-the-fuck-up!" Brooks yelled in a harsh uncharacteristic voice. Spectators parted to let him and Garbageman approach the hole. "Break it up," Brooks said harshly again, aghast that his troops, including his eldest NCO, would cluster so stupidly. "Where are you supposed to be? One round would get you all. Get back to where you're supposed to be. Who's covering the perimeter?"

Brooks stood stone still, stared at his troops. Men shuffled sheepishly away, glancing furtively toward the commander, ashamed by the most elementary of reprimands yet still curious. When the cluster dispersed Brooks asked calmly, "What do you have, Pop?"

Garbageman joined Pop in the hole. El Paso and De Barti stood behind and above Brooks. All five men stared into the pitted moist earth.

"I aint sure, Sir," Pop said. He smiled at the commander.

"He aint been daid more'n a week, Sir. Looks like he was in this heah hole when a arty round decided ta share it with'm." The old boonierat backed out of the hole and handed the entrenching tool to Garbageman who immediately assumed Pop's position in the mulch and began shoveling. The sides of the foxhole had caved in and the dirt was clumped and black and loose. Hundreds of flies hovered and landed and hovered and relanded with each disturbing movement of the shovel.

"He had im a US pistol belt," Garbageman said, lifting a slashed soggy belt. "Damn. He had boocoo shit in here with'm." Garbageman dug deeper and disinterred first a twisted belt of RPD cartridges then three more satchel charges and two aerated ponchos then four more Chinese-communist grenades and assorted personal and food items. Then Garbageman lifted a large brown muck-covered chunk. He examined it closely then backed off and laughed. "His foot's blown off." He lifted the chunk on the shovel blade and displayed it.

"Bout a size nine I'd say," De Barti said and he too laughed. "Pee-uu! Dinks always smell that way?"

"This Tootsie-Roll don't taste so good," Mohnsen, the squad leader of Garbageman's squad, said as he joined them. "That sure is one helluva mess. Do ya gotta dig it up?"

"We gotta dig it out," De Barti smiled. "Intelligence. You know that. An intelligence report."

"Here's his ribs," Garbageman said producing a decayed shattered human torso. "Looks like a dog's, don't it?" The body was very decayed and small pieces came up with each shovelful.

"Well, Sir," Pop smirked, "the ribs is theah and theah's a foot. We don't got enough ta put him tagether yet. Got by artillery. I'd guess a dee-rect hit."

"Got a gook killed by small arms fire. Killed today by small arms," De Barti corrected laughing. "Blown away just now by small arms fire. That son of a bitch is blown ta shit, isn't he?"

"Killed by artillery," Lieutenant Brooks said flatly.

"Sir?" Pop Randalph questioned. He knelt down by the pit. "Sir, theah's three sandals in heah. I think theah was two of'm in the hole. Must a been a dee-rect hit."

Garbageman lifted more satchel charges and grenades and some empty C-ration cans and more pieces of human body. The area about the hole became littered with ration cans and debris. Deeper Garbageman found two Chi-com gas masks and more

RPD machine gun rounds. "Hey Pop, there's his head," Garbageman giggled.

"I wonder what that silly sonabitch was doin with it so low," Pop winked. "Reckon he was kissin his ass good-bye?"

"Think we oughta call him a Medevac?" De Barti laughed.

"Can't you find his weapon?" Brooks asked flatly.

"Maybe he was layin on it," Pop suggested.

Lieutenant Thomaston, carrying a belt of M-60 ammunition, approached the group around the hole. The cartridges in his hands were bright shiny new. "Goddamned ARVNs, L-T," he complained to Brooks. "They must have left this here. Damned ARVNs. It's like they're resupplying the dinks."

The odor from the pit nauseated Brooks and he stepped upwind to look at the ammunition. "Oh Christ," Thomaston stepped back. "What's that? What did him a J-O-B?" Thomaston scrunched up his nose and stepped further back.

"He don't smell near half as bad as the one we found on that other LZ," Pop chuckled.

"El Paso," Brooks said, "write down what we find and give the list to Cahalan to call in. We'll stay here until the patrols are back in. Pass the word to chow down. We'll move out at 1030 hours."

"Chow down," Garbageman sang from the hole. "Everybody chow down. Sounds fine ta me. I'd like mine medium rare. How bout you dudes?"

"Get to the bottom of that fuckin stink pit," El Paso snapped.

"Wanta help me stir the soup?"

"Fuck you."

The transformation from base camp soldier to boonierat continued amongst the light-hearted quipping, eating, smoking. Half the troops removed their helmets and tied them to their rucksacks. Helmets were required in the 7/402 but the wearing of them was not enforced in Alpha. Many of the boonierats felt the encumbrance of the heavy steel pot was not worth the slight probability of protection from a glancing bullet or piece of shrapnel. Against a direct hit a helmet was considered useless. Brooks replaced his with the odd-style baseball cap; Egan wore a tight-fitting broad-brimmed boonie hat that hid his red hair. Some men stripped off their shirts. Blacks, like Jackson, put only an olive drab towel over their shoulders as a cushion against the rucksack; whites, like Whiteboy, with skin that could be seen through five meters of dense jungle, covered their torsos with olive drab tee-shirts. Infantrymen in the 101st did not wear flack jackets in the boonies, the trade-off of protection for encumbrance not being worthwhile.

Daniel Egan searched the recesses of his mind. He had satisfied himself his platoon's segment of the perimeter was properly manned and defensible and that his patrols were out reconning. He sat alone in a bush and let his mind grind again, brood again, clash within itself, transforming itself, preparing for the responsibility of a platoon sergeant, for the alert paranoia the field demanded. A giant click, a massive gear grind began.

All the collective lessons of ten years of American involvement snapping into place in his head, all the collective lessons learned, forgotten, relearned by tens of men, by tens of thousands. The lessons were there in Egan's mind, there from almost eighteen months of combat duty, there from his heritage as an American, as a man, as a human being. All that need be done was to relax, allow the mind to shift, to tap the data banks of 10,000 years of human warfare perhaps 100,000 years perhaps for the entire age of man perhaps earlier. The adjustment was not easy. Egan fought it. All men fight it. Egan's mind balked. His direct experiences were close and easy to grasp, to drop him into the channel which flowed back, inhibited but deep and straight for a million years to a million years of data. And his enemy, Egan thought, conceived without words, knew, they too would bring the collective lessons of tens of millions of men from tens of thousands of years of fighting, of fighting North against South, brother against brother, the same pattern from antiquity to post-Geneva, the enemy with a mind-set developed by tens of billions of man-years of war all brought to the battle for the Khe Ta Laou. And the land, Egan thought. No experience needed. That he knew for sure, felt for sure. The land knows all, has seen all, has always known it, has always absorbed the blood and returned men to their humus components. Egan's mind shifted. He was there. He was ready. He was relaxed. He rose with his M-16 dangling lightly in the fingers of his right hand, rose and walked back to the company CP.

Cherry sat alone, in awe of where he was and how he had arrived. Up the hill behind him soldiers were laughing and cursing loudly. He sat quietly, alert, half-hidden, scared. His forearms ached. He rolled his arm over and looked. Both forearms were scraped and burned and bruised. Below his right elbow there was a two inch long incision surrounded by blood and a crusting scab. Cherry did not remember it happening. Thinking about it now he figured he had bruised himself while jumping from the helicopter. He looked down into the jungle then to his sides then to the laughing men. Since the moment after insertion when Jackson had given him the chocolate candy disc and he had checked in with El Paso, no one had spoken to him.

Just north of where Cherry sat, slightly higher up the peak, Jackson and Silvers were eating canned C-ration fruit cocktail from one can with one white plastic C-ration spoon. Jax was lying on his side trying to catch some Zs between passes of the fruit. Silvers was leaning against his rucksack, reading a July 13th copy of *Newsweek*. They had spoken little since moving into position above the rest of 1st Sqd. "Hey," Silvers poked Jax. "Listen to this."

"This," Jax yawned, "I can miss."

" 'General Creighton Abrams,' " Silvers read aloud, " 'American Commander in Vietnam, is reported increasingly concerned about President Nixon's plans to withdraw 50,000 more U.S. troops from Vietnam by October.' Think maybe I'll get a big drop?"

"Na," Jax rolled onto his stomach. "By the time yo get a drop, I'll be a pop. They aint gowin let yo out—word's out. All Jews stay. Blacks leave today."

"Hey, Jax," Silvers said, "that makes me think."

"Oh shee-it."

"You see that land out there."

Jax rolled over, looked at Leon then squinted into the sun. "Where?"

"Way down there. By the sea. That strip's known as the 'Street Without Joy.' You know that?"

"Do now."

"I got an idea. The way I see it is first we kick out the VC and then the NVA. We get the ARVNs to get the rest of the Vietnamese into refugee camps south of Hue. See? Then we resettle the place with Jews. See? We get an ally and you know the New York money won't never let this place go then. Shit,

Man. We'll call it the 'Street Without Goy.' Get it?'' Silvers laughed.

"I thought yo said it a'ready called that."

"No Man, without goy, not without joy. Don't you get it?"

"Yo brain gettin fried like spareribs, Leon. Either yo been smokin too much dew or yo got somethin from las night's screw.''

"Goy, Man, goy." Silvers shook his head. "It means gentiles. A Jewish Street Without Gentiles.''

"Oh come on na, Bro,'' Jax teased. "I knows Jews got gentiles. How else could they like pro-create?''

Silvers returned to the *Newsweek*. He read about the positive effects of the Cambodian incursion within South Vietnam and the negative effects within Cambodia, turned the page and found an article saying Secretary of Defense Melvin Laird was aiming to reduce overall US military strength from 20 divisions to 15 by mid-1972. "I know it, Jax," Silvers said waking Jax again.

"Now what?"

"I'm up for a 180-day drop. They cuttin back the size of the armed forces. They're goina let me out same day as you. You can ride on my lap all the way to the World if they don't have enough room for ya on my Freedom Bird.''

"Get serious, Man. I knows what comin down. Got the word from The Man himself. Sho did. Right from the head honcho. No Leons ever leave. They jest fade away.''

"No way, Jax. If them fuckin REMF clerkjerks mess with this kid's drop I'm callin in TAC Air on their AOs.''

Jax sat up, picked up the C-rat can and drank half the syrup. He passed the can to Silvers. Silvers drained the remainder of the juice, crushed the thin can in his hand and threw the tin into the jungle.

At the center of the defensive ring the company's command post had regrouped and the men were now sitting, discussing the exact details of the move. "Where do you think the little people are, Danny?'' Brooks asked Egan. He had asked the same question of each soldier and the consensus had been the NVA were most likely deep in the valley.

"I think they're right on the next ridge,'' Egan said clearly, pointing west.

"I think we oughta get our asses outa here,'' Tim Cahalan,

a company CP RTO, injected. "This place is goina be an asskicker. Look how steep that fucker is."

"The jungle is a neutral adversary," Lt. Caldwell quipped.

"Blow it out yer ass," Cahalan whispered behind his back.

"Hey!" Brooks said grabbing control. "Okay. It's time now to get down to business. We've had a week of slack, now it's time to move. Cahalan, have you called higher yet with the report on those two KIAs?"

"Yes Sir. Roger that."

"Okay. Call Red Rover and let him know our Rover Two element is moving out in two-five. Danny, you and Bill have your platoon ready to move. We're going to work west down that ridge. Stay in column just below the ridge down to the saddle then spread out and sweep up to that peak. We want to be there by 1300. You have two and a half hours. Second Platoon, Frank, you and Pop, you be ready to move right after 1st leaves. 3d will be back up here before you move out. They'll follow you, lag by one hour. Bill, Danny, tell your men to eat now if they haven't eaten yet and tell them to secure their rucks. We're not making any noise once we leave here. Frank, you and Pop, you make lots of noise up here while we're moving out and tell 3d to make it look like the whole company's still here until we reach that peak. CP will follow Rover Two. Where's Hoyden?"

"Right here, L-T," Lieutenant William Hoyden said from behind Brooks. Hoyden was the artillery forward observer attached to Alpha.

"FO, I want preset coordinates for that peak. I want coordinates registered for the peak, the draw and that canyon there to the November Whiskey. If I were a dink honcho I'd set up in the canyon. Let's go. I want to hear some chatter. What's everybody think?"

"L-T, I think Recon's hit the shit," Bill Brown said. Brown was the third RTO of the company CP. "They're callin for a Dust Off." Brown turned up the volume of his radio which was set on Command Net. The group paused to listen to the dialogue of metallic voices as Echo's Recon Platoon requested an urgent medical evacuation helicopter. El Paso changed the frequency of his PRC-25 radio from Alpha's internal to Recon's internal and the group monitored their sister unit's movement in the firefight. Egan rose to his knees and looked toward Recon's position. Red tracers could be seen floating down from a point on the west side of the peak. Occasionally enemy green tracers floated up toward Recon's insertion LZ. No soldiers, friendly or enemy, could be seen. There was no movement. The sound of the firefight was mostly lost in the sound of helicopter traffic and the booming of artillery batteries already laid and registered on Firebase Barnett. There was no indication of the fighting except the infrequent fireflies of red and green crossing and the crackling voices being monitored on the radio.

"That's enough of that," Brooks said shortly. "El Paso, get that radio back on our internal. Let's break it up. Get back to your people. Egan, Bill, get your men ready to move."

"Quiet Rover Four, this is Rover Two, commo check," Cherry said squeezing the transmit bar on the handset of his radio. There was no response. Cherry checked the frequency setting then repeated his call to El Paso. Again there was no response. "Quiet Rover Four, this is Rover Two. Do you read? Over."

"Two, this is Four," El Paso's voice rasped. "I got you lumpy chicken. Hotel Mike? Over," El Paso said meaning Loud and Clear. How me?

"Four, Two. Say again." There was no response. Cherry repeated his call. Again nothing.

"Two," El Paso's voice squawked in Cherry's ear. "Do you know what Mike Foxtrot Alpha is? Over."

"Four. Negative," Cherry answered.

"Two," El Paso's voice came in calm lecture-form, "it's a Romeo Tango Oscar who forgets to say 'Over' when he's completed his transmission. Mother Fuckin Asshole. Over."

"Uggh." Cherry groaned before squeezing the transmit bar. "Four. Sorry. Roger that and Wilco. Over and out." For a moment longer Cherry sat where he had been sitting all morning. Then he rose and walked toward Jax and Silvers, and Doc and Minh who had joined them. All four were eating and talking loudly.

"If they repealed the mothafuckin Gulf a Tonkin Resolution how come we still here?" Doc shouted. "Huh, Mista? Tell me that. That was the legal basis fo us bein in this bad mothafucka, woant it?"

"Not necessarily," Silvers said. "Says here 'Nixon contends that the President's power to wage war doesn't come from any particular resolution but is based on his constitutional powers as Commander-in-Chief.' "

"That crazy shee-it," Jax snapped. "They dee-cap-i-tate dick-tators, doan they? The people aint gowin stand fo it. We gowin tear him down."

"Amen, Bro. Amen," Doc said and raised a power fist salute.

"Amen," Silvers added. "But I got a problem. See, the situation here is connected to the situation in the Middle East. If we show a weak face here . . . ." Silvers paused and looked up. Cherry was standing above them, looking and listening. "What are you staring at?" Silvers asked accusingly.

"I, ah . . ." Cherry cleared his throat. He did not know what to say. He blurted out, "I was looking for Egan."

"What?" Silvers shouted.

"Hey, Man," Doc laughed. "You kin make noise now. No tellin how long we gonna have ta be quiet."

"Oh," Cherry said, a silly grin came to his face. "I ah," he wanted to join them but he was uninvited, "I, ah," his voice became louder, "ah, gotta find Egan."

Men of the 1st Plt and the company CP finished their lunches and secured their packs. Lieutenant Thomaston had told them to remain where they were until called individually. One at a time they were to circle to the north side of 848, slide into the vegetation then circle to the west ridge beneath the cover of vines and trees and begin the descent. If Alpha was being observed by NVA trailwatchers, as Brooks suspected, the tactic was designed to keep the enemy from detecting the company's movement into the canopy or at least the direction of the movement. As the first soldiers began to move unobtrusively, an unexpected helicopter approached 848, landed, released two men in fatigues, lifted off and flew away. Thomaston motioned for the first seven men to slip into the canopy under the diversion of the bird and as it left, he motioned for the men to sit and wait.

At the top of the LZ the two men were met by Lamonte. Lamonte seemed to have an almost frantic enthusiasm as he greeted the lieutenant from the 3rd Brigade Public Information Detachment and the civilian correspondent he was escorting. Cherry could not hear anything that was being said but he knew Lamonte was speaking eagerly and quickly. Man, Cherry thought. That's one cool job. I wonder what you have to do to work for Lamonte.

Sitting behind Cherry in ready order of march was Numbnuts. He threw a small stone at Cherry to get his attention. "That's Craig Caribski," Numbnuts said. "He's the guy responsible for uncovering My Lai."

"What?" Cherry whispered back.

"Yeah. I was talkin to Mister PIO. He said Caribski was comin out with us. Said he's workin for Dispatch News now. Wants ta get a story on the Ripcord fiasco."

"Really?"

"Yeah," Numbnuts said importantly. "Some of the dudes think we oughta blow him away."

"Yer kidding."

"Aw, it's just chatter. Maybe he'll take a picture of us an we'll be in all the papers."

"Hey, yeah," Cherry smiled.

"Hey, Cherry," Numbnuts said. "Did you know today's Friday the Thirteenth?" Cherry shook his head. "You superstitious?" Numbnuts asked.

"No," Cherry said. "Not really. I don't think. Are you?"

"Naw," Numbnuts said scratching at his waist then his right thigh. "Me neither. Except about some things."

"Yeah?"

"Yeah. You know. Like this hat." Numbnuts had an Australian bush hat with one side turned up.

"What about yer hat?" Cherry asked glad to be talking to someone. "Is it a good talisman?"

"Huh? Yeah. That's just it," Numbnuts said. "I aint real sure. Last time I wore it I got shot at but I didn't get hit. Does that mean it's good luck cause I didn't get hit or bad luck cause I got shot at?"

"I see what ya mean," Cherry said. His anxieties were easing with the conversation. "It may require a statistical analysis," he joked. "How many times you been out with it?"

"I only wore it once," Numbnuts said not smiling.

"A case of one is useless in statistics," Cherry tried joking again.

Numbnuts paused. He looked at Cherry, curled his upper lip and turned away.

Cherry knew that the situation he was in had changed. The men about him were different today from the way they had been last night. But he did not know why. His mind had not shifted. He did not yet possess the boonierat mentality. It was frustrating, maddening. He did not know what was happening, what was wrong with him. He felt he was no longer accepted. He was sitting in a bush, waiting, waiting again. Now he was dirty. He had been getting dirtier by the day but at least at Phu Bai, Evans and Eagle there had been places to wash. Cherry removed a canteen from his rucksack, poured some water on his OD handkerchief and wiped his face and arms. Red-brown mud smeared on his skin. He wiped and added water and washed and wiped. The mountain air had heated up and the sun beat very harshly.

I'm losing my marbles, Cherry thought. I'm losing my ability to speak. This waiting's driving me nuts. What in the hell am I doing here? I thought Silvers was going to be my friend . . . should have told him to fuck himself. I used to have a mind. Six months ago I remember being able to gross out Phil in the pizza shop and today I can't even converse with an idiot without sayin something wrong.

Daniel Egan was alone again, sitting above the northeast corner of the LZ on Hill 848 feeling very much like a platoon sergeant. He sat and stared disgustedly at Cherry who was fifty feet to his left and at the L-T who was above on the LZ talking to Lt. De Barti, Garbageman and El Paso. Egan looked east, stared into the jungle before him and beyond that jungle at the jungle on the next ridge and still beyond. Across his lap was his M-16 and around his waist was the pistol belt with two canteen pouches filled each with six magazines of ammunition. Four fragmentation grenades hung from his belt. Strapped to his left calf was a bayonet. Before him ridges fell east with the gorge of the Rach Mỹ Chãnh cutting across and through the ridgelines. Beyond the fourth ridge was a fifth where the Rach Mỹ Chãnh flowed northeastward into the Sông Thác Ma and another ridge was beyond that and then yet another.

With his left hand Egan kneaded the earth. He moved his right hand to his lap and stroked the pistol grip of his rifle. He massaged the steel of the rifle's bolt housing with his thumb, fingered the plastic pistol grip and the trigger-guard and the trigger, thumbed the safety selector, now staring east down toward the lowlands and beyond toward the sea. In his aloneness and disgust there was a sadness in vague memories that tried to force themselves to the surface of his consciousness, thoughts which he kept fully suppressed, thoughts which he supplanted with the disgust feeling and which accentuated the aloneness, which if he conjured them up would be dangerous in a bad AO. Egan hid in his disgust and loathing for what he was, for what was about him. He glared at the sun now risen high. He glared at the ridges and the valleys before him. In his mind an old sergeant was chattering. The old sergeant was saying something about the ridges which Egan did not even know he had heard the old sergeant say. Egan counted. There were four ridges down the Rach Mỹ Chãnh and two down the Sông Ô Lau. They were clear though the distance made the trees blur. He stopped counting. He put the thought out of his mind, chased it from his mind with thoughts of the gypsy girl in Australia.

"You're crazy," she had screamed at him. "Get on out of here." He'd shown up for a third day even though she'd dismissed him after the second night. It was in her apartment and she'd been listening to Isaac Hayes' "One Woman."

"Hello, Darling," he had said forcing his way in. She had been mean the night before. After 17 months in the jungle there is only one thing a soldier wants to do. Softly, violently, any way. And she had been an extreme bitch. She had tormented him. She had a lovely body and long slender legs. She had been fine in bed. Egan grinned inwardly but it went sour in his mind. Good to love but lousy to sleep with, he thought. Too restless. Stomach cramps or some shit. Everything had been a tease. She was soft passionate kisses on the ferry across the harbor to Bondi Beach; warm hugs in the hallway of the Illowra Lodge then nasty in bed. And the worst of it, Egan thought, she was totally ignorant about the world and the war. She's got a mind for bed, for love, for money, my money, and not much more. When his money began running out she had cramps. She had a talent for making men fall in love with her. Egan was disgusted with himself for having fallen. She was a poor substitute and he hated himself for having accepted her. Now she became one more thing to chase from his mind.

Egan looked again at the ridges then over at the slow progress the unit was making moving into the jungle. He got to his knees, struggled, rolled his ruck over and removed from it the letter he had begun to Stephanie. He skipped a few lines then wrote:

It's still the same day. I'm getting short. My time is almost up. I'll be back in the World in twenty five days and out of the army in a month. I'd like to see you again.

Memories of you keep floating up in my brain. Like the time in that funky Martinson Hotel when I told you you deserved better than that. I'm really feeling disconnected right now. Must be because of the start of this new operation. I should be thinking about this thing but you keep floating up before me. I don't know why but I've got this image of you and me in the Martinson right now. There was an old chair in the room and I'm lying in the bed. The lights are off but there's light coming in the window from the bar signs and street lights across the street. You're in front of the window looking out and you're naked. You are saying that I hurt you. Why did you say I hurt you?

Egan stopped writing. It did not sound right to him. He returned the letter to his ruck. The eastern ascent of 848 rose from the jungle abruptly, crested in a false peak of bomb shattered rock, merged with the debris surrounding the landing zone, rose and fell then rose to the peak. Egan was in the cover of the debris on the second rise. Again the view east hypnotized him. On the first ridge every tree, every leaf, was crisp in his vision. The second was less clear and by the fifth the vegetation was splotches of lighter and darker green. On the ridges beyond the green seemed to lose its color and become gray shaded gradations blurring and collapsing hazily into the foothills and finally piedmont. Egan counted the ridges, eleven of them. He could hear the old sergeant at the briefing hall, hear him saying, "You will be on the 12th and highest ridge with"—Egan slipped his arms into the rucksack shoulder straps, turned to the west, and rose—"with," the sergeant's voice came, "your back to the 13th valley."

CHAPTER

13

At the step-off point where White-boy entered the jungle the vegetation showed scars from the morning bombardment but only ten meters down the wilderness appeared untouched. It began with walls of green to his sides. At fifteen meters he turned left, ducked beneath several branches and found a trail west. Branches draped with vines crossed overhead. With each step the canopy thickened, the jungle became darker, the trail descended. The trail appeared to Whiteboy to have been unused in three months, perhaps even six. Palm fronds crossed the path at shoulder and waist height. Bamboo thickets, clusters of stalks clumped like pillars, rose in the midst of his downward movement. He stepped quietly, slowly, cautiously around, over and between, always looking, listening, smelling before each step. He did not smell the mortars.

When Brooks had dismissed the men from the CP conference earlier Egan had immediately searched for and found Whiteboy and had told him his squad would be point. Egan had explained to him the direction and objective of movement and then left. Lieutenant Thomaston had followed Egan to Whiteboy's position amongst the leafy brush down a trail off the northeast corner of 848. Thomaston confirmed the move and set up the diversionary step-off location and then he too had left.

"They stickin it to us ah-gain," Whiteboy had muttered to himself, his thick lips trembling imperceptibly, his great mass hunched in dread. Before him was his M-60 machine gun. He had not lowered the bi-pod legs which could be used to support the barrel but had simply rested the barrel in the crotch of a bush and generally aimed the weapon down the trail. Whiteboy had stroked the metallic side of the machine gun and had muttered to it, ''They stickin it to us ah-gain, Lit'le Boy. They au a time stickin it to us.'' He had rolled over, gotten to his knees, hefted the gun and begun organizing his squad.

There was nothing fancy about Whiteboy's organization. He had decided to walk point himself. He always walked point for his squad. Whiteboy hated it but he could not allow another boonierat in his squad to walk point. It was partially that Whiteboy believed his responsibility as squad leader carried with it a need to protect his men but it was more a matter of pride—the pride of a boonierat, of a squad leader, an M-60 gunner, a point man, a big man. That is the way he described it to himself. He could not bear that another boonierat should do his work.

With his walking point came the advantage of immediate obedience by his squad to whatever he ordered. Justin Hill, the assistant gunner and ammo bearer, would walk Whiteboy's slack. Behind Hill Whiteboy set Cookie, Bill Frye, a rifleman, then Andrews, the squad's RTO, then Harley with the M-79 grenade launcher and finally Kirtley and Mullen, both rifleman. After securing their equipment they all had risen from their positions and carried their rucks to the step-off point, where they sat and waited for Thomaston to tell them to move out.

''We're goina work west down that finger,'' Thomaston had repeated to Whiteboy for lack of anything else to say. ''If we don't find anything we're goina sweep up to that peak then maybe move southwest.''

Whiteboy had not really listened. He had sat above the step-off smoking and checking his ruck again for anything that might make a sound when he moved. A knot had grabbed his stomach, tightened, forced acidic fluid to the back of his throat. He had patted the gun, rubbed his immense hands, his thick fingers over the oily bolt carrier and feed tray. As he squeezed, the weapon seemed to push back, as he caressed, the weapon seemed to sigh and caress his hand in return.

Whiteboy had spent most of the preceding ten months in the bush, much of the time without close human contact. He had learned to speak to his weapon and to listen to it. He had learned to listen and to smell and to feel the jungle. Before entering the army Whiteboy had been a mechanic. He had always worked with his hands, always with tangible things. Whiteboy was now a mechanic with his M-60 and he was in touch with the physical world of the jungle about him. His primal instincts were accentuated in the jungle. He was in physical touch with a physical universe that required no verbal explanation or justification. Whiteboy, feeling, communicating with the physical world through his hands, was primally touching reality at a level the intellectualizing Brooks or Silvers could not feel for they cloaked reality in words as if the words were the reality and the real did not exist, could not exist, without description. Whiteboy communicated with his men in a way Brooks could never communicate, could never understand, could never feel.

"Okay," Thomaston had said. Whiteboy had risen, his giant body buried beneath an enormous rucksack. A sling ran from the M-60's front sight over Whiteboy's right shoulder then to the butt of the stock, the gun slung horizontal at Whiteboy's hip, the barrel straight forward. A belt of one hundred cartridges came from the feed tray, hung toward the ground then looped back up over the gun barrel and hung down again. Diagonally across his chest Whiteboy had two additional belts of ammo and about his waist was snapped a third. Whiteboy had glanced back at Hill to make sure he was ready then had stepped forward, down, into the first layer of jungle. Hill followed at three meters then Frye, Andrews, Harley, Kirtley and Mullen. As the descent began the helicopter with the correspondent arrived, deposited its load and departed. When it left Thomaston sent word forward to wait zero two then move out again. Whiteboy stepped quietly down.

At the step-off point Egan entered the jungle behind 3d Sqd. He was followed by Cherry and Doc McCarthy, 1st Plt's medic. Thomaston stayed at the step-off metering out soldiers at equal intervals. 1st Sqd followed the platoon CP and then 2d Sqd. Thomaston turned his post over to Lt. De Barti of the 2d Plt who metered out his men behind 1st Plt descending into the jungle.

Whiteboy set the pace for the entire column. Very slowly he moved. One pace every five or six seconds, ten paces a minute, less than 300 meters in an hour. Whiteboy picked his way downward, generally westward, turning up here, down there, as obstacles in the trail dictated. He stayed below the ridge keeping the crest always uphill to his left. He did not cut trail. He did not use a machete to straighten the path. He simply moved toward his objective along the path of least resistance as imperceptibly as possible.

Justin Hill maintained visual contact with Whiteboy. As slackman Hill paid close attention to the pointman's every motion. Hill followed Whiteboy without a sound, stepping over each root cluster, hunching beneath each low branch. Behind Hill Cookie Frye moved in slow spurts. He walked to within a meter of Hill then stopped and faced off the trail to the uphill. Frye waited there searching the jungle to the side until Andrews moved up and took his position. Then Frye moved again forward to within a meter of Hill, now stopping, looking downhill searching waiting for Andrews. Andrews moved forward when Harley assumed his position. Behind the point and slack, the squad moved forward like an inchworm on a stem, the front not moving until the rear had caught up and taken its place. Behind Mullen, the last man in 3d Sqd, Egan kept the chain unbroken and behind Egan Cherry copied the movement.

As the trail descended it became steeper and the canopy higher and thicker. Beneath the canopy the air was thick, moist, clinging. The vegetation went from dry and dusty above to wet and thick below. Light barely penetrated to the earth. The trail became muddy. As more and more men passed over the trail the mud squished and became slippery. The squishing noise was dampened by the thick air and absorbed by the jungle.

Cherry became disoriented 100 meters into the jungle. He could not hear Egan to his front. He had come up to Egan, assumed Egan's position as Egan had moved down through a hole in the green leafy wall. Dave McCarthy, the medic, moved in behind Cherry and Cherry went to move toward Egan but he had lost the trail. Cherry paused. He listened. He could neither hear nor see Egan. He stepped forward and was met by palm fronds and vines. He could not even find the path. He paused and listened again and he searched for the way to go. He glanced behind him. McCarthy was two paces back, mostly obliterated from view by the vegetation. Behind McCarthy was Numbnuts of the 1st Sqd. Cherry could not see Numbnuts at all.

"Sergeant Egan," Cherry called in a very low voice. "Sergeant Egan," he called a little louder, a bit panicky. Cherry shuffled his feet. "Sergeant Egan," he raised his voice.

McCarthy touched Cherry's shoulder. Cherry turned. Without warning, totally unexpected, a hand smacked him across the mouth. It was Egan.

"You cocksucker," Egan snarled, the sound of his voice very low yet harsh and strong. "You mothafuckin cocksuck shit fuck. What the fuck you doin?"

"I . . . ah . . ." Cherry was shocked, fearful.

Egan's eyes bulged. "Mothafucker, I'm tellin you once en only once. If I ever hear a sound from you, if I ever hear your feet touch the ground or your ruck hit a bush, I'm goina kick yer ass forever. You start concentratin, Mister. You stupid shit fuck. We got the whole fuckin column halted." Egan had hold of Cherry's fatigue shirt collar and was shaking Cherry back and forth with terrifying, rapid jerks. Then Egan disappeared through a hole in the green wall less than a foot from Cherry. Cherry stared after him as if Egan had been a spirit. Cherry did not even see the brush move.

Generally in the field boonierats established a buddy system, pairing off either by friendship or by necessity and at times by both. Whiteboy and Hill were a team. So were Pop and Garbageman, Jax and Silvers, Doc and Minh, and now Egan and Cherry.

In the CP Brooks paired off with El Paso. Those two were very close. As commander Brooks was the brain of the company and as senior RTO, El Paso was the ears and mouth. El Paso carried a PRC-25 set on the internal frequency of the company for communicating between the CP and the platoons and/or squads. Bill Brown also carried a PRC-25, his radio being set on the command network to communicate with battalion HQs which was now established with a forward TOC on Firebase Barnett. Tim Cahalan carried the Monster, a PRC-77. This radio was similar to the 25 except it was also a kryptographer, automatically scrambling or descrambling voice transmissions. The Monster was used to communicate with the rear on vital or intelligence matters such as calling in a unit's location to insure friendly artillery did not accidentally drop unfriendly explosives on them. All three radios were kept open to receive transmissions at all times. At all times the radios had to be monitored. Brown and Cahalan, along with FO, buddied-up.

The company CP entered the jungle between the 1st and 2nd Plts and inch-wormed downward with the column.

"L-T, Barnett's gettin hit," Bill Brown whispered to Brooks. Brooks did not stop nor did he acknowledge Brown's remark but the RTO knew the commander had heard and was thinking.

"They're catchin beaucoup shit," El Paso said a moment later. "Sounds like eighty-twos."

Then Brown said, "Recon's callin for another medevac."

Alpha continued to descend in column. Whiteboy was 75 meters west and below the CP. The 2d Plt was strung out behind and above the CP an equal distance. 3d Plt had returned to the LZ from patrolling and was now eating lunch, making noise and maintaining a high degree of visibility.

Along the creeping column rucksacks bore down into shoulders and backs. No matter how carefully a soldier packed his ruck, no matter how many times he tested it for comfort, when the move finally began the ruck dug in someplace. The weight from the rucks drove legs down into every fold and hole in the trail. Thigh muscles fatigued and twinged, shook from the weight and the slowness. Helmets, those being worn, felt hot and heavy and never seemed to sit just right so they strained neck muscles. Sweat from foreheads collected in eyebrows and trickled saline rivers into eyes. Weapons, always held pointing forward with both hands, the right thumb on the selector ready to flick from safe to automatic, stretched forearms and wrists and hands. Hands sweated on pistol grips and arm guards. Right hand index fingers tensed and tickled triggers.

The column moved slowly, alert, searching, the earth became steeper and more slippery and the rucks seemed to gain weight on the unsure footing. The only sound most boonierats could hear was their own breath exhausting harshly from their lungs and hissing over their teeth. Occasionally the swish of tree branches or palm fronds brushing on their helmets or clothes caused them to move even more lightly under the heavy loads. The artillery batteries on Barnett began pumping out rounds. Now explosive rumbling from the big shells rolled across the column. In the enclosure of the valley the thunder echoed and ricocheted.

At point Whiteboy slowed further. With each pace he looked twice from side to side for traces of enemy. He searched up and down for booby trap trip wires. He examined the trail for fresh human footprints.

The last of 2d Plt slipped into the overgrowth and disappeared into the jungle. The 3d Plt tightened the perimeter about the landing zone. On top of 848 the troops were still grab-assing. Rafe Ridgefield, the announcer from the Phoc Roc, was lounging back on a warm rock catching the sun's rays with John McQueen, Terry Snell and Don Nahele. Snell and Nahele were buddies from Los Angeles who had entered the army together and who had stayed together from basic through advanced training and into the boonies. All four men were smoking and laughing.

"Hey, Snell," Nahele called, "you a crusher or a folder?"

"I'm Lutheran," Snell chuckled.

"Man," Nahele drew out the word, "I just took the healthiest shit I think I ever took in my whole life."

"What a coincidence," Ridgefield laughed. "So did I."

"Jesus," Snell groaned, "I haven't shit in four days."

"I took one two nights ago that squirted out all over the place," Ridgefield said. "The anal joy was great at first but then my ass began to burn."

"That's that red pepper yer always puttin on everything," Nahele said.

"You guys don't even know what shittin's even all about," McQueen called over. "Did I ever tell you guys about Latrine F-27 down in the Delta? F-27. Defecation Sector for the 25th. Down there we used ta say, 'the larger the turd, the more efficient the shitting.' "

"Hey, Queenie," Snell called back. "When does piss become somethin separate from the body? When it's waste in the blood stream it's still part of ya, don't ya think?"

"Maybe it's when it enters the bladder," Ridgefield injected. His eyes were darting unfocused back and forth. A radio program was building quickly in his mind.

Nahele sensed Ridgefield's mind churning and he began egging him on. "Maybe it's still part a you till you piss it out," Nahele said.

"Maybe til it hits the ground," Snell added.

Ridgefield wheeled about, jumped up and announced, "I mean it. I'm goina run for Congress. I got all the problems of the world figured out. It's really very simple. I am now in possession of the solution."

"Halleelujah!" Nahele cried out. He bummed a cigarette from Snell. "Ol Rafe's goina give everybody a gallon a bourbon, a deck a Js and a piece a ass and let em drink en smoke en fuck 'emselves to death."

"Don't be crude," Rafe Ridgefield chastised. "That don't work. My opponents have been proposing exactly that for years and look just how far the Great Society has got. Nope," he said, a twinkle in his eye, "it is first and foremost a matter of the bladder. It's all obvious from there."

"Oh God," Snell snickered. "Get your entrenching tools, the shit is starting to flow."

Ridgefield stood up on the rock he had been lying on, cleared his throat, thought twice about standing on his soapbox on the LZ and crouched. "It is obviously a sign of weakness," Ridgefield addressed Snell, Nahele and McQueen and fictitious throngs in his best congressional voice, "if one urinates too often. I mean, if one urinates every time the urge presents itself, well, he'd be pissing ten to twenty times a day. He would literally be pissing his life away. And each time he urinated it would be for what, six, eight seconds. Isn't that right? I SAY THIS IS RIDICULOUS!"

"So do I," Nahele laughed.

"I'd say any urination lasting less than half a minute is a total, inexcusable waste of time. It should be illegal. Or at any rate, taxable." As Ridgefield spoke McQueen, Leahmann and several others from his squad edged over to listen. "Now, Gentlemen, the actual act of urinating and the length of time it actually takes for the fluids to be expelled are not of primary importance. However, the time it takes, the time it wastes, to find a suitable location to urinate plus the time it takes, it wastes, to get there and back and of course the time wasted zipping and unzipping, Dear Lord, if a person goes only eight times each day, he, or she, as the case may be, will spend one third of his, or her, productive time doing nothing better than peeing . . . ah . . . excuse me, relieving his, or her, bladder."

"Rafe," Snell said, "I aint had a pair of pants with a zipper in ten months."

"Now then, this is my plan," Ridgefield summoned his most articulate and deep voice. "This plan will have profound personality alterations for those upon whom it is imposed. Everyone will piss at ten o'clock in the morning. At that time they will be allowed to rid themselves of the built-up urine from the night before plus liquids from their morning coffee. The next allowable urination will be at four in the afternoon. This urination will be only for hardship cases and will require the permission of a ten-person review board. The four o'clock will enable weak individuals to relieve themselves of morning coffee break liquids, of whatever they might have consumed during lunch and of anything which might have reached the bladder since the afternoon break. Everyone will be allowed to urinate just prior to retiring for the night. This, of course, is necessitated by the need for one to get an uninterrupted night's sleep.

"Now the profound effects I anticipate this action, this legislation, to have will include a hardening of the character of the people of our beloved country, a hardening of our soft national character. It will be the first major step in disciplining the masses. Once the major population centers are pacified we will be able to advance and blanket the entire nation. No riots, no strikes, no wars. The entire world shall follow suit.

"Now then, Gentlemen," Ridgefield was virtually blasting his voice across the valley, "with the people so disciplined from holding back the urge . . ."

"What are you goina do when all the sewers explode at ten-oh-five every morning?" Snell teased.

"Maybe his old man's a plumber," Nahele said.

"Gentlemen," Ridgefield waved his arms for silence, "such trivialities. Here I squat before you . . ."

"With your dong in yer ear, Man," Nahele completed Rafe's sentence. "Hey, we gotta get goin, don't we?"

"Gentlemen, this session of the legislature shall not be adjourned until we adopt this measure now lying before us."

"Fuck it," Snell laughed. "Hey, Rafe," he said standing, "I gotta piss. You wanta time it?"

"Be careful," Nahele warned. "He may wanta hold it. Jesus H. Who's at point? Those fuckin guys sure are takin their sweetass time."

Ridgefield picked up his M-60 and he and Snell and the others slipped into their rucks and prepared to slide off the LZ and into the jungle. Ridgefield glanced quickly over the hilltop then began climbing down through the first brush and onto the now well established trail. "Sssshh," he suddenly hissed. "What's . . . oh fuck."

Whiteboy and Hill and Egan heard it too. Once, twice, phaffft. phaffft. Three, four. Now almost everyone in the column heard it. phaffft. It was an odd sound. Later Cherry would remember thinking that it sounded like a car door being closed halfway down the block on a very warm muggy summer night. It was not actually a sound. It was more a feeling at the ears as if the door closing compressed air in a sedan and the compression traveled as a shock wave. It was the sound of a mortar round leaving its firing tube somewhere in the surrounding jungle. phaffft. phaffft. Seven. Eight. Whiteboy had leaped off the trail before the second round was launched. Hill leaped when he saw Whiteboy go. Egan was on the ground, prone, beneath his rucksack, scrambling to bury himself in an indentation of earth. Up and down the line veterans were crawling, clawing for cover. Instinctively Cherry was down too. He pulled his helmet down over his ears, pulled his neck down until the helmet seemed to merge with his shoulders. PHAFFFT. PHAFFFT. No one said a word.

karrumphh. karRUMph. KARRUMP.

The first shell exploded on the ridge at the draw, the second on the ridge 20 meters up and the third 20 meters higher. The NVA were walking the mortar rounds up the ridgeline.

Whiteboy cringed with each explosion. KARRUMP. But he did not remain down. He caressed his 60. "Okay Lit'le Boy," he whispered to it. "If they gonna folla this up, we gonna be ready. God A'mighty Sweet Jesus, stop them fuckin thins."

KARRUMP. It was now very quick. Cracking echolessly. Shrapnel stones and dirt zinged from the explosions and fired into the vegetation knocking branches and leaves and vines down. KARRUMP. Another mortar shell exploded, again higher, higher than Whiteboy's location. Whiteboy raised up, pulled back, yelled to Hill, "Form a point."

KARRUMP. Mortar rounds exploded one per second, each 20 meters higher than the preceding one.

Brooks screamed to Brown, "Get ARA ASAP."

Cherry pulled his helmet down tighter. He pulled his knees to his chest, to his ears and he huddled in a tight frightened ball below his rucksack. KARRUMP. The explosions moved higher. Cherry could feel his back muscles trying to reach the earth through his chest. The hairs on his chest seemed implanted in the moist soil. As each round exploded his body experienced jolting physical fear. His eyes stared down, bulged in tight drawn skin, focused on tiny bamboo shoots and tiny bugs and then went out of focus. Beads of sweat burst from his temples. He inhaled mud, his face—mouth, nose and eyes—pressed into the trail.

Then it was silent.

"Everybody stay down," Egan's whisper yelled. "Get down and get to the right of the trail."

Whiteboy had backed up to Cherry's position and Cherry

now found himself at the center of a defensive ring set up by 3d Sqd. Egan was by his side and he had the handset from Cherry's radio. Egan twitched, jerked, whisked the handset down his left arm cursing, "Fuckin spiders." Everyone except Cherry had shed his rucksack and all were now still, hiding in the vegetation in a rounded point. Cherry wriggled from his pack.

"Quiet Rover Four, this is Rover Two. Over," Egan called El Paso.

"Two, Four," the reply was instantaneous. "Any W-I-A your location? Over."

"Negative, Four. Over." Egan snarled inwardly then said to himself, "Fuckin dinks can't hit diddlysquat."

Other squads called into the CP. Egan monitored then rose silently and vanished. Cherry was shaking. He lit a cigarette. Oh God, he thought. Three hundred and fifty days to go.

Within minutes after the last mortar round fell on Alpha Company's location ARA Cobras appeared in the sky. SSShheee— saaBAMM. The first rocket exploded against a target on the next hill. Cherry jumped. The Cobra fired two more rockets. Cherry could see the rockets leave the bird before he could hear them. Then came the explosions. Then the echoes. The echoes came from across the big valley and from intermediate ridges. A rocket left the tube at the Cobra's side, the propulsion, explosions, an immediate minute echo, pause, major echo and reverberations. SSShheee-saaBAMM bamm BAMmbammbambam. The Cobras peppered the side of the opposite hill. Rocket after rocket. The explosions were 200 to 300 meters from the defensive point where Cherry sat. He smiled. There was nothing frightening about a rocket exploding at that distance when he knew it was directed at someone else. He sighed and smiled and felt reassured. He almost rejoiced and he noticed that Hill and Harley were giggling and that Frye and Mullen and the others were lying back nonchalantly smoking. Only Whiteboy seemed tense, intent, lying prone in heavy brush with just the tip of his machine gun protruding from the leaf cover.

The two Cobras were diving in series at the targeted hill, firing two rockets each with each pass. Then the birds opened up with their mini-guns, electric Gatling guns, firing so quickly the noise ripped like a giant chain saw. Together, with rockets between, it sounded like music to Cherry. He felt pleased. Hell, he thought, this isn't so bad. Not with them birds doin most of the fighting.

There was a faint movement in the trail above Cherry. He turned. Lamonte came through taking photographs. George was behind him. They spotted Cherry, gestured hello then proceeded by. Lamonte crouched to frame Whiteboy with palm fronds. He and George discussed the best angle for the shot and the best light and depth of field settings. The Cobras made another pass. Lamonte came over to Cherry and said, "Excuse me," then aimed his camera up through a hole in the canopy where a small beam of sunlight was coming through. Lamonte waited then attempted to catch a Cobra within the small leafy frame on the next pass.

Egan reappeared. He laid his hand on Cherry's shoulder and whispered, "Come with me. Bring yer shit."

They climbed back up the path to the back of the 1st Sqd where Lt. Thomaston was monitoring the situation on Steve Hoover's PRC-25. Silvers and Jackson were sitting with him. "They're trying to blow the canopy away," Thomaston said. "They think they see something."

"Wow!" Cherry said.

"Yeah," Thomaston smiled at him. "We really brought you to the right place. Gettin your cherry busted, huh?"

Cherry smiled sheepishly.

"Those was sixty mike-mikes," Jax said. "Ef those been eighty-twos that close, they blast yo ears out."

Silvers, Jax and Hoover were concocting a mixture of C-rations and sitting back lethargically. Egan and Thomaston were still monitoring both radios, one on internal, one on command. Cherry sat a short distance below them all and said nothing yet inwardly he was smiling. He had seen his first action and he had survived it.

"Ah think we're doin just what ol Charlie wants us ta do," Whiteboy whispered to Hill. They were now lying side by side in the vegetation, concentrating on the trail below.

"Yeah. Givin Chas time ta dee-dee outa here," Hill whispered back.

"Or maneuver up heah," Whiteboy whispered.

"If we get hit, you know they got somethin down there they don't want us ta see."

"They must have sompthin down theah if they had the guts ta mortar us in daylight."

"I bet they waited for us ta come off the fuckin LZ ta drop em. They just wanted ta see what direction we'd go in."

"Ah aint gonna go down theah tonight. That's damn straight. Ah aint movin. Orders nor nothin."

"Well," Thomaston called to Cherry, "you may have missed 882 but you aint goina miss this one." Thomaston monitored the conversation between the helicopter pilots as they continued to waste the far hill.

"Those mothafuckers," Egan cursed. "Scatter'm, birds."

"Did you make Hamburger?" Thomaston turned to Hoover.

"Were you there?" Hoover replied.

"There en Blood Ridge," Thomaston said.

"That was a motherfucker, wasn't it?" Hoover said.

"Hey," Thomaston exclaimed in a normal speaking voice. The men above and below and at his side looked toward him. "They've spotted the mortar tube. They've spotted the mortar pit."

"Super," Egan chuckled. "They see the tube or just the pit?"

"They see movement down there," came the reply. "They see movement down there. Chas is dug in and got bunkers."

Cherry gulped.

C H A P T E R

14

Slowly, very slowly, Whiteboy stepped forward, down, descending toward the draw. He crept. He inched. The crest of the ridge was 25 meters uphill to his left. The draw was 50 meters ahead, to the left. He did not want to cross below the saddle of the draw in the canyon that ran down toward the big valley. He aimed at the point where the draw should be flat. He circled toward it. He would direct his squad to spread below the saddle on both sides, wait for the entire platoon to come on line behind them then begin the sweep up toward the peak.

It was becoming darker under the canopy. It was mid-afternoon, 1540 hours, but the mountain to the west already cast the pointman in shadow. Below to the right through the jungle vegetation an occasional glimpse of the Khe Ta Laou revealed the valley still cloaked beneath heavy fog.

Whiteboy proceeded deliberately. He studied each step before he made it, studied the earth, the jungle to his left and right and front. He wanted to look over his shoulder to check Hill's position yet he fought the urge and concentrated on the jungle before him. Shadows were playing in the patchwork greenness, deep black holes beneath vine draped palms aiming their muzzles toward him. It would be so easy for a sniper to be in that hole, beneath that tree, there or there or there. Fuck it, Man, Whiteboy said to himself. Doan mean nothin. But Ah aint gonna do this. This gettin worse au the time . . . If Ah had mah druthers me en Lit'le Boy'd be some place else. Fuck it. Whiteboy massaged his weapon with his large hands. He stepped forward. He planned the next step and the next and the next, like a chess player planning well in advance before moving, anticipating the locations of an enemy before him, anticipating the moves the enemy would make, the counter-moves he would have to make to survive.

Behind Whiteboy the tension in Hill was immense. He wanted to scream. It was hot, muggy. The straps of his ruck were cutting deeply into his shoulders. His mouth was dry. He did not dare make an extraneous movement.

The column had again moved out in the same order of march, Whiteboy's squad with the big infantryman at point followed by Egan and Cherry and now Thomaston then 1st Sqd, 2d Sqd, the company CP, 2d Plt and 3d Plt lagging at drag and rear security.

Whiteboy set an even slower pace than he had during the morning move. He stayed lower on the hill, below the ridge's crest. Had they been on the crest when the NVA mortars fell, the enemy would have inflicted heavy casualties but as it happened the explosions kicked shrapnel out horizontally and Alpha had been below the flying steel. No one in the column had been injured. Several of the mortar rounds had impacted on the LZ and there the shrapnel had been more serious. Carlos Fernandez, RTO of the 3d Sqd, 3d Plt, had been chatting in a clearing on the LZ when the first rounds were launched. "Man," he had said to the soldier next to him, "that sounds like mortars." With the first burst, everyone on the LZ hit the dirt. There were crater holes from the early morning bombardment and low indentations from ancient and collapsed NVA foxholes. Fernandez slithered to a shallow depression. The rounds came up the ridge, across the LZ, down the eastern side of 848. Dirt, smoke and the smell of cordite saturated the air. "Oh God," Fernandez cried. "God, you get me out of this and I do anything you ask. You know. Anything. I never do nothing wrong again. I don't touch myself. I be a monk." Within a minute it was over. There were no wounded but Fernandez' ruck was the victim of a near direct hit. It was ruined. Cans of fruit and food seeped juices onto the earth. Shrapnel had pierced three of his canteens, his poncho was shredded, his PRC-25 was scrap. And worst of all, he was going to have to salvage and carry whatever he could. No more helicopters were due at their location until resupply three days away. "For thees I say I be a monk? Me an my beeg mouth."

The mortars had stopped Alpha's progress until Major Hellman, the battalion executive officer, heard the Cobra pilots report seeing the mortar pit and then enemy movement. "Hell, yes," Major Hellman had screamed through the radio at Brooks, "I want you to go after them. What do you think you're down there for, Boy? Get off your ass and go get a body count."

"Yes Sir," Brooks said, pissed over the 'Boy' reference.

Rufus Brooks was six years old when he realized there was something different about being black. He and his older brothers had been playing stickball when the game erupted and Rufus came shooting through the family's Oakland flat chasing his brothers with the bat. The two older boys raced down the hall, cut into the parlor then stopped dead in their tracks. There, on the edge of his chair, a scowl on his face, sat their father. Rufus was last into the room. He went flying past his brothers, out of control, stumbled and pushed an end table over, knocked ashtray and ashes onto the old man.

The roar was unintelligible to the young boy but the booming noise that came from his father communicated enough message. His father rose, raged, grabbed the stickball bat and cracked it in two over the end table. "You get outa this house, Boy. I'll break every bone in your body you do a fool thing like that again." The older boys bolted; Rufus scampered at their heels thanking heaven and his sneakers to be out of the room alive.

In the hall of the flat the older boys dodged their mother but Rufus ran squash into her large soft body.

"What's matter wid you, chil'?" she cooed gently, her hand in his hair.

"Don't you go calling him child," his father shouted into the hall. "Do you want him to grow up like every other nigger on this block?"

Rufus trembled in his mother's arms. His father came out, scowled, hesitated, then apologized. He knelt in the hallway with his arm around the boy and said times were bad because he'd lost his job. "I want you and your brothers to grow to be gentlemen in the finest sense," he said. "I want you to know what is right and what is wrong. And you must always do what is right. Do you understand that, Son?"

The frightened little boy trembled, choked back a cry and with wide eyes stared at the large man.

"Rufus," his father said trying to be gentle, trying to calm the boy, "Rufus, you are black. It's not enough for you to be good. You have to be the best."

While Rufus was growing up he was surrounded by conflict both from within his family and from without. George Brooks had come from a merchant family, his own father owned and managed a small retail business in Oakland. Rufus' mother had come from a poor southern family. She was a simple unpretentious woman, unlike her husband. "We are a family of color," George Brooks would say to his son. "Of what ca-la?" his wife would shrug.

In the early fifties, after losing his job, George Brooks went to work at his father's store. At night he took classes which led to a degree. He became an electronics technician as that industry first began to boom. George so badly wanted the best for his family he pushed himself hard. For a few years things went well. He moved his young family to the new white suburb of Westgate just south of San Francisco. They had purchased the home through a white friend of his father's because at that time it was still impossible for a black man to buy in the suburbs. There were minor incidents but they passed and the Brookses settled in with their white neighbors. Until the late forties Westgate had been cabbage fields and hog farms and in the early fifties the development still had a rural atmosphere. Outwardly George Brooks was proud. His wife was excited. Inwardly George was uneasy and apprehensive.

Rufus could still recall the pride he had in his father and he could still picture the house. It had been a yellow stucco box that looked like all the other stucco boxes being constructed south of San Francisco. There had been three bedrooms, a tiled bath, a living room with a brick fireplace and a dining el and even a kitchen with a picture window that overlooked the back lawn and the newer construction beyond and the fields beyond the framed skeletons. The house was nicer than anything his cousins lived in. The families of his father's brothers lived near their grandfather's store in east Oakland. That wasn't too bad. The few cousins from his mother's side lived in run-down basement apartments where the plumbing worked sporadically and where the best entertainment during a visit was chasing the rats in the hallway.

When Rufus was nine years old his father lost his job again. Just prior to being fired George Brooks had been promoted to assistant design engineer and the whole family had celebrated.

Some of their white neighbors and some co-workers had come to their house and Rufus was shy but very proud. When George Brooks was fired no one stopped by to express their condolences. Rufus was ashamed. Years later his father told him he had been fired as part of a plot to force the blacks to move out of the neighborhood.

The Brookses went from being an oddity in Westgate to being a threat. After Brooks was without a job the neighbors spoke of the nigger family who didn't know enough or didn't care enough to finish the landscaping around their house. Incidents were infrequent at first, but the longer George Brooks was out of work the more depressed the home became and the more frequent paint or excrement or screams of "Nigger go home," splattered against the front of the house. Rufus was sheltered from the brunt of the abuse by his mother and father but he was not sheltered from his mother's tears or his father's indignation.

George Brooks instituted legal action in an attempt to get his job back. Pride forced him to accept no other employment. Rufus had not understood how or why it had happened and he thought if he could just tell someone, people would understand and they would help and everything could be set straight.

When Rufus was ten years old his family moved into a four-room apartment in the projects of east Oakland. The apartment was already occupied by the family of Rufus' uncle, and Rufus, his brothers and his parents moved into one room. The projects were rectangular rows of green and pink stucco-sided shoeboxes with caged windows and fight-for-survival, fight-for-recognition gangs.

For several years the Brooks family shifted between the poor black Fillmore district of San Francisco and the ghetto of east Oakland. George Brooks spent what little money he had attempting to rectify his employment difficulties and when the money was gone he gave up. He pumped gas. His wife became a domestic for a wealthy white family who lived in a large house in the Oakland hills. Rufus' mother would stand at the windows of the Victorian mansion and gaze out to the Bay and the Bay Bridge and across to the San Francisco skyline and south toward where her wonderful yellow stucco home had been.

On Rufus' twelfth birthday his family moved into a comfortable apartment in San Francisco's Mission District and the next year his father was again working in the electronics industry—now as an assembler. Times improved but they were never the same. George Brooks spent nights in bars and Rufus' mother withdrew and became very quiet and Rufus spent more and more time away from home, much of it roaming the streets by himself.

In high school Rufus excelled. He was accepted by the roughest street gang for his physical attributes; he became a track star and captain of the basketball team; he was liked by teachers and college-bound students. For the first time in his life he was accepted by everyone, yet he accepted no one. Each of the groups with which he associated despised all the other groups. How could he truly accept any one of them, he would ask himself, without rejecting all the others? Rufus was friendly. He listened, but he very seldom talked.

Rufus' post-high school plans were to join the Marine Corps but his father had refused to sign for him, had forced him to consider continuing his education as the only method of insuring a future. He wanted Rufus to become an attorney.

In September 1963 Rufus Brooks entered the University of San Francisco on a partial basketball scholarship. The sport became his ticket through school, his invitation to fraternities, his pass to parties and his introduction to girls, both black and white. Rufus was cool. He could play ball. To help finance his education Rufus joined the Reserve Officers' Training Corps— one month after the North Vietnamese reprisal attack on the American destroyers *C. Turner Joy* and *Maddox* in the Gulf of Tonkin.

In college Rufus maintained his quiet exterior yet he developed a harsh critical eye. People liked him. He was an intellectual and an athlete—the perfect token. He was accepted by everyone on campus though he did not allow himself to accept anyone nor would he allow anyone to know the real Rufus. He always maintained a distance. For a time Rufus dated only white girls, but then, in his junior year, he met Lila, a beautiful mocha-colored singer and painter.

"You act so BAD," Lila teased him, "but I know you. Inside you just a marshmallow. You don't fool me. You don't gotta be criticizin things for me. I love you the way you are." It was magic. He saw this woman accepting him as he saw himself, taking him as her man, without qualification, without plans, without motives.

In his senior year they were engaged. The next autumn, during his first semester of graduate school, they were married.

*   *   *

"Sir, does Red Rover wish Quiet Rover to delay until your niner element is back on station? Over," Brooks said. The reference and implication was this: the GreenMan had been flying in his C & C bird 4000 feet above the action most of the morning. The helicopter had returned to Camp Evans for refueling. In his absence Major Lothar Hellman, exec of the 7/402, sitting in the forward TOC on Firebase Barnett, was in charge. Brooks did not trust the major. He wanted to delay until the GreenMan returned.

Reports from Recon's early morn firefight indicated that the recon platoon had engaged an estimated NVA reinforced squad. Technically they were still pursuing the enemy. The GreenMan had been excited and the Old Fox had been very pleased. "Caught em with their pants down," the Old Fox had smiled. Now Alpha Company could follow it up, could seize the initiative, attack the reported bunker complex, overrun the enemy. "Goddamnit, Rover Four, you get your ass in gear," Hellman had screamed. "We got em on the run. Go get em, Boy."

Go get em, Boy, Brooks muttered to himself. I'll get em, Boy. I might just turn this element around and overrun your position. Brooks handed the krypto radio handset back to Cahalan, grabbed El Paso's handset and ordered the move to re-commence.

The motion of the point was so slow from the column's mid-point and back that most of the soldiers were sitting between steps forward. Everyone was daydreaming. Brooks had a vision of his wife. He could see Lila and the arm of another man about her waist. Fuck it. Brooks chased the image away.

This is crazy, Cherry moaned to himself. If we're goina get into it, let's get into it. Egan glared back at him everytime the radio antenna touched a twig. Fuck him, Cherry thought.

Farther back, Jackson was wondering if his child would be a boy or a girl. Girls is so pretty, he told himself, but boys is so much mo fun. William Andrew Jackson, Junior, an announcer said within Jackson's thoughts, the son of the Vietnam War hero, the great-great-great grandson of a slave, today was inaugurated as the first black President of the New United States of America.

Should Ah? Whiteboy asked himself. If Ah do an the L-T finds out, Ah'll be in a big worl a hurt. God A'mighty. If Ah do it ever gook in the AO goan know where Ah'm. Theah might even be a gook rahght theah thinkin Ah'm firin at'm an Ah can't see a godblessamerica thin. Thinkin doan always do a man

good. Sometime it's bettah ta just do it. Oh Lit'le Boy, do yo
stuff.

And in the still total silence, dispelling every thought from
every boonierat head, Whiteboy's machine gun like the first clap
of thunder in the quiet before a storm ripped—explosive
crackchattering savage spray. Not a burst. Continuous. Whiteboy
fired the big gun from his hip, spraying the black holes of
jungle, sweeping jerkily up and back. Hill jumped to his side,
emptied his own M-16 into the jungle, attached a belt to the
flapping tail of Whiteboy's ammunition, reloaded his 16 and
fired another clip. Andrews and Frye sprayed uphill, Kirtley and
Mullen downhill, Harley fired the grenade launcher over the
point. Egan jumped over Mullen, a hand grenade, pin out, spoon
depressed, in his fist, arm cocked, throw dive. Egan now prone
beside Whiteboy cutting the jungle to pieces with his M-16.
Thomaston, Jackson, Silvers and Marko jumped past Cherry.
Pop Randalph, not to be left out, up from the 2d Plt, jumped into
the middle of the growing enfilading point. Cherry was on hands
and knees, crawling forward toward Egan, his radio crackling.
"What's happenin?" El Paso demanded. He did not know if
there were fifty NVA out there or one. "Rover Two . . ."
Cherry couldn't hear. "Rover Two . . ." the radio squealed.
Suddenly it was the only sound to be heard. Everything else
ceased.

"Lobo Niner, this is Quiet Rover Four Niner," Brooks
addressed the Old Fox. The company commander now went
through a complicated explanation of the action, an action he did
not fully understand himself. He completed his transmission with
a request to withdraw to Alpha's position of earlier that afternoon and to set up for the night. He requested artillery and air
strikes devastate the peak to his west. All requests were granted.
The boonierats loved it. Brooks was dubious.

Cherry was bewildered again—excited, exhilarated, scared
and bewildered. The front of the column had backed up 100
meters, the rear had descended a short distance and the sides of
the unit had bulged, but only barely, off the trail. Word had
come down to dig in and to prepare an NDP, a night defensive
position. Air strikes and artillery were ordered. Co-ordinates
were checked and re-checked.

Cherry's exhilaration came partly from the excitement of

the day and partly because he was no longer totally petrified. So this is it, he thought. This is war. This is combat. This is what I've come so far to see and be a part of. It was a nice feeling, a satisfying accomplishment, an experience. It was scary. Well, maybe not so scary right now with all these old-timers around, he thought. Here I am, me and my young cherry ass, and here are all these cool-headed dudes. Veterans. I'm going to be okay. What little rice-propelled bastard with a little rifle is going to challenge that giant Whiteboy with his 60? And who could ever make a mistake with Egan around? Indeed, Cherry was completely surrounded by veteran boonierats. It seemed to him they were all there to protect him. The more he thought about it the more secure he felt and the more he liked them. It welled up in him as a warm happy feeling. He would do anything he could for any troop in Alpha Company, he decided. He was young, vigorous. He breathed deeply and felt the strong muscles of his chest and arms tighten. And he was in combat. It *was* wonderful, it would be wonderful. It was all that simple.

Cherry walked back to the 1st Sqd where Jackson and Lt. Thomaston were making coffee. "We're stayin here tonight," Cherry announced with a smile. "L-T says to dig in."

"Right on, Bro me," Jax said. "Want some coffee?"

"No thanks," Cherry said. Neither of the men said anything. Cherry looked around then returned down the trail and moved through the point ring to where Whiteboy was sitting.

"Ah got two months lef," Whiteboy muttered as Cherry sat. "Ah was hopin Ah could stay outa this shit." He did not take his eyes off the trail below him.

"Yeah," Cherry agreed toning down his enthusiasm.

Leon Silvers came down and joined them. He had a canteen cup with hot mocha in it. "How's it goin?" he asked handing Whiteboy the cup. Whiteboy shrugged. Silvers sat with them in silence for several minutes then rose and said, "Man, ya oughta move up and dig in."

Whiteboy looked up, nodded but just sat there. Silvers gave him a sidearm power salute, turned and climbed back up the trail and out of sight.

Cherry sat next to Whiteboy for several long minutes. He was vaguely hoping Whiteboy's stature and speed would ooze from the big soldier and into himself. They sat there with their weapons pointing down the trail. Cherry did not say anything and tried not to be too obvious yet he wanted to look at the gun Whiteboy called Lit'le Boy. He wanted to feel it, to fire it.

"Man," Whiteboy said quietly after some time, "am Ah glad they mortared us." Cherry wrinkled his forehead but said nothing. "Man," Whiteboy said, "if they'da ambushed us, Ah wouldn't even be heah." He shook his head slowly keeping his eyes on the trail and the jungle downhill.

They sat in silence. The shadow from the peak with the bunker complex was crawling up the ridge descending from 848. Clouds, at first faint and thin, were forming high above the valley. The heat of the day dissipated. The fog choking the river below them was rising.

"Where you from?" Cherry whispered. "I mean, back in the World."

"Nebraska," Whiteboy whispered back.

"Where bouts?" Cherry asked.

"A lit'le town outside a Bridgeport," Whiteboy said.

"Really?" Cherry marvelled, sounding in a very quiet voice as if he had just found a long lost brother.

"Yeah," Whiteboy turned and looked at him for the first time. "You know it?"

"No, ah . . ." Cherry stumbled. "I'm ah, I'm from Bridgeport, Connecticut."

"Um," Whiteboy moaned and turned back to the trail.

They sat in silence again. Four helicopters appeared over the hilltop where Recon had been dropped during the morning CAs. Two of the birds were Cobras which seemed to be attempting a complicated dual figure-eight movement. Off to one side a LOH, light observation helicopter (pronounced loach), hummed, hovered, darted short distances left then right, looking and behaving like a large bumblebee. Below the Cobras a Huey slick with white doors and red crosses hovered, descended, landed. Cherry was watching the helicopters through a hole in the vegetation. "More birds comin in," he whispered. Whiteboy looked over. "I wonder what's happenin," Cherry continued.

"Medevac," Whiteboy whispered.

Again they sat in silence. Finally Cherry rose, tapped the big soldier on the shoulder, nodded and walked back toward the center of the point of the defensive ring.

"We're gettin down there," Egan said to Cherry. It was dusk now. Egan was waist deep in the earth. Red-orange clay clung to his fatigues. He bent over and swung the entrenching tool, half extended like a mattock, from above his shoulder hard down into the bottom of the foxhole. He swung it hard again, keeping his hands in tight to his body. Small wedges of clay broke from the bottom. He scraped the bottom and scooped up the chips and threw them onto the ground beside the hole.

They were surrounded by the sound of ETs and machetes hacking and slashing at the ground and at roots. Men not digging were on guard. The holes being dug were two-man foxholes 30 inches in diameter, 40 inches deep. Below the thin layer of mulch and humus the ground was hard-packed clay and rock. Thick roots ran through the clay like steel reinforcement bars in concrete. The trees beside the trail were so numerous and closely packed it was difficult to find a clear 30-inch diameter surface.

"When I was a kid," Cherry said, "I thought if you dug deep enough you'd hit China. I wonder, if we dig deep enough here, will we hit the States?"

Egan looked up and laughed. "Here," he said getting out of the hole and handing Cherry the ET, "you dig. If you get there, I'll go with you."

Egan and Cherry took turns digging. The shortness of the ET and the hardness of the earth jarred Cherry's arms and hands. "This is tearin my hands apart," he complained to Egan.

Egan was not paying attention to him. Now that he was not digging he was pensive. Cherry repeated his gripe. Egan looked at him. "Ya know, I bet Nguyen's pissed the holy mothafuck off at us."

"What?"

"He took all that time siting in this trail, waiting for someone to come trickytrottin down. Then he goes riskin firin our asses up in broad daylight."

"He may think he got some of us," Cherry said, resting, rubbing his hands.

"Naw. No medevacs."

"Oh," Cherry said quizzically. "Maybe we should a had one come in as a decoy."

"Yeah," Egan agreed. "Then if he fires us up tonight maybe he'll drop em in on the same spot he missed us in this morning. Shit. Now the mothafuckers'll adjust to our location. This was a bad move stoppin here."

High above the valley a small single-engined prop-airplane appeared. It circled above Alpha's position, the sound of the small engine barely reaching the ground. The plane spiraled lower, increased the radius of its circle, descended again to an altitude perhaps only 200 meters above Company A. It made a pass over their heads from east to west and another from south to north then east to west again. Then it seemed to disappear. Several minutes later the tiny plane appeared again. It had regained much of its altitude. From the foxhole, with Egan pondering the problem of how to convince higher-higher to send in a decoy medevac, Cherry could see the small plane fire a rocket toward the opposing hillside. On the hill the rocket burst in a dense cloud of bright white-phosphorus marking smoke. Immediately the air split, a sound louder than artillery, than rockets, than bombs—a continuous roar ripping, splitting over-head and the tail of first one then immediately a second F-4 Phantom jet fighter-bomber shot past their position.

There was no warning. The fighter-bombers had come in low from the south then had dived down paralleling the descent from 848's peak, not fifty feet above the ground, not twenty feet above the treetops. Quiet, peaceful, no audible approach warning and then the entire earth shaking, rattling. In the split second it took for the F-4s to pass over the heat from their exhaust defoliated the upper tips of the trees. The heat could be felt on faces and in eyes, the sound shook men to the bone. All Cherry had seen was the second tail as it sped past, a tail looking like a three-spoke wheel with an immense hub spewing hot exhaust gases and noise and vibrating limbs out of the trees.

"Holy Fuck!" Egan yelled, smiled, crept closer to the foxhole. "Chas don't like them fast-movers. They bring in the damn-damn."

The F-4s dove down the canyon toward the valley floor then pulled up hard left sweeping in a great arc out west beyond the valley, passing out of sight out of sound range someplace to the south.

Again the air ripped instantaneously. This pass was fol-lowed by an immense concussion pressing eyeballs and eardrums in toward the centers of skulls. Cherry was standing in the foxhole when the first 250-pound bomb burst. The explosion was directly across the saddle from him, at his same elevation. The shockwave rocked the entire ridgeline. Cherry flung himself to the bottom of the hole, Egan pounced head first in on top of him, scrambling to go deeper. A second blast thundered between the two peaks.

"Holy Christ Fuck," Egan yelled. "Move them fuckers outa there."

Again the two jets screamed over. They shriekroared down the valley flying faster than sound yet at treetop level, dropping napalm canisters and finned bombs on the suspected enemy location. The jets vanished before the bombs and canisters exploded. The flash flame sucked air from the side of 848. Black smoke mushroomed, spread, cloaked the next hill. Andrews screamed. Shrapnel from the bombs smashed into trees above and about the defensive point. Egan jumped from the foxhole, scrambled to Andrews who was lying facedown holding his side. Again the Phantoms dove from atop 848. Cherry heard Egan retch loudly, then vomit.

As night approached and the jungle went from green to gray artillery worked over the NVA bunker complex on the hill west of 848. Shells exploded at irregular intervals as much as fifteen minutes apart. Free soldiers clustered in groups. Half of Alpha remained on guard.

At 1st Plt CP, which was Egan and Cherry's foxhole, Cherry and Jackson sat sharing a cup of coffee and a cigarette. Thoughts popped up in Cherry's mind like pins on an electric bowling machine. Cherry looked at each thought briefly then knocked them all down with a mental disc and let another set pop up. In all that came up there were no pins he wished to share with Jackson. Yet he wanted to talk.

Jackson also wanted to speak. He knew that within an hour they would be completely silent, would enforce their own noise discipline, and he wanted to talk before the night actually began. But to Jax Cherry was such a white boy, a condescending college white boy and every syllable that got to Jax' throat was stopped by his jaw.

"Jax," Cherry finally said, "can I, ah, ask you something?"

"Say it, Bro," Jax said back quickly, happiness in his voice.

Cherry stumbled for a moment. Then he said mechanically, "How long have you been here? I mean, ah, that's not really what I meant to say."

"Oh Man," Jax laughed. "I been here longer en yo, Cherry. Boocoo longer en yo can even imagine. I was born here. Man," Jax continued, "I can see what's happenin in yo mind. It's like written all over yo face. Yo gotta stop yo head from struttin like

yo was back on the block, cause yo strut like that heah, yo aint
never gettin back ta the block. Understand?''

"What I mean, what I meant was,'' Cherry paused, then
blurted, "I feel like a robot.'' Cherry was unable to stop himself.
He now felt committed to those words and felt he had to explain.
"I feel like a robot with things just wired into me and I don't
understand why.''

"Yo is a robot. Yo a cherry. Yo s'pose ta be like that,'' Jax
said matter-of-factly. "I remember my first time ta the field.
Here ol Jax on his first CA.'' Jackson began acting out his
words, bopping his body as he sat. "I got my helmet all buckled
down and my 16 on rock'n'roll. I jumps off the bird and hunch
over and quick like a bobcat runs inta a bush. Somebody say,
'Why yo got yo steel pot all strapped down?' An I looks around.
There're guys leanin back catchin the sun. The CO's standin up
on the LZ scratchin his balls. An I's all hunched up in this bush.
Shee-it. We was all cherry once. Man, yo jest been on yo first
CA. Yo jest been mortared. There aint nothin yo ever done
compares with CA. An, Cherry, that CA won't nothin. Wait'll
yo hit a hot one. When yo catchin all the shit Charlie can throw
an yo still in yo bird an yo bird still comin in—THAT is the
ultimate experience. Aint nothin like it. Better'n drug, better'n
Colt-45.''

Jackson motioned down the trail to Daniel Egan who was
approaching, "Even Egan was a cherry once hisself. Right,
Eg?''

"Right, Jax. What's happenin?'' Egan climbed up to them
and sat across the foxhole from them.

"Yo are, Bro,'' Jax said. "I was jest tellin yo cherry yo
was a cherry once yoself.''

"Shee-it, yeah. Hell, I was DRO at the Last Supper. You
tell'm that?'' Egan laughed a sadistic laugh.

"Sho did.''

"We nearly got him his cherry busted today.''

"We gowin get his cherry busted soon nough.''

Egan smirked to Cherry, "That was just makin out this
afternoon. Not even heavy petting.''

"I tol him that too,'' Jax laughed. "Sho did.'' It was a
strained laugh bordering on the sadistic and it strangely matched
Egan's laugh. "This one bad mofuckin AO. We gowin have us
another 714. Dinks up the ass, Dudes.'' Jax raised his left hand

and countered on his fingers. "Dinks on the LZ, Recon hittin the shit, Barnett, dinks in bunkers. There dinks everyplace."

"Fuck it. Don't mean nothin." Egan laughed again, again that strange sickening chuckle laugh.

"It's really a pretty spot," Cherry said seriously, somehow feeling guilty.

"Sho is pretty," Jax said gazing into the jungle. "Lord," Jax called in a quiet deep tone, "Lord, Yo sho done one nice job on this piece a creation but Yo sho fucked up puttin ol Jax out here. Look what these white folk done messin it up."

"Don't start that shit," Egan snarled. "I don't gotta hear that shit tonight."

"Talkin bout shit," Jax said slyly, "what stink?"

Cherry stifled a chuckle.

"Fuck it," Egan said steamed. "I don't know any other way to do what we're doin. If you can think up somethin else . . ."

"How bout we jest call this whole thing off. It dumb, Man. Dumb."

"If you can figure how," Egan challenged, "I'm willin."

"Ah, fuck it," Jax snapped. He stood, picked up his rifle and circled down toward Whiteboy who was cleaning and checking his M-60 ammo belts.

"I'd like to see this place in twenty years," Cherry said to Egan after Jackson left. "I bet there'll be a six-lane interstate coming out here."

"Yeah, and every car'll have to have an armed escort cause this war aint never gointa stop."

"I bet there'll be a small city out here in twenty years," Cherry said. "There'll be a golf course and hotels, a whole resort."

"A big tourist trap," Egan spat. "Come and search for the legs and eyes of your father."

"Ya know," Cherry said staring at Egan, feeling in this instance stronger than Egan, "you are really morbid, Man. Yer the one said we're winning."

"Cherry," Egan said cynically, "I'm a lot sicker than you'll ever know." He paused. His agreement disarmed Cherry's argument. Then he said, "But I'm a lot healthier than any mothafucker out here."

*   *   *

Lieutenant Brooks walked quietly from one end of the NDP to the other. He checked the perimeter and discussed likely routes of enemy approach, probe or attack with each platoon leader and each squad leader. They discussed fields of fire, interlocking fire and camouflage. The discussions were quick and laconic and often the words uttered had nothing to do with the situation. A squad leader would lead the company commander behind his positions. Both men could see the network of defense. It did not require words. Brooks asked every third or fourth man about his back or feet or how he felt or about what he was doing when the mortars began falling. He offered no sympathy. He expressed concern instead. He very sincerely questioned his men about their premonitions, about enemy signs they had seen, about their interpretation of the tactical situation. Brooks never stopped seeking information and feedback from his men and he gave as much information as he could to anyone sincerely interested. Tonight, though, he found he had to force himself to listen. When he discovered he was forcing himself to concentrate on the operation he thought, that bitch. That bitch. That bitch.

Brooks continued his rounds. At the forward defensive point he found Andrews nursing a bruised rib. "Hey, L-T, can I get a purple heart for this?" Andrews laughed.

"What do you have?" Brooks said, kneeling. He inspected the nasty bruise and laceration on Andrew's right side and questioned him about it. Whiteboy and Jackson broke into guffaws at hearing it again. Andrews had been defecating when the F-4s had screamed over and dropped their bombs. He had been hit by a piece of shrapnel from a bomb after the jagged piece of metal had cut in half the tree Andrews was holding to balance himself. Brooks giggled as Whiteboy re-enacted Egan's dash to help Andrews and his crawl through Andrews' shit. Brooks stopped laughing when Jackson held up a razor-sharp plate of steel eight inches across and an inch thick.

After the foxholes were dug and the weapons and ammunition were readied for the night, it was time to eat. The atmosphere at the various CPs was like that of a Boy Scout jamboree except that it was quiet.

"Hey, Man," Dave McCarthy chided Lt. Thomaston, "aint you got someplace to go? This aint no place for officers."

"Oh I thought I'd see how the war was going," Thomaston chuckled back.

"We don't have no officer's club out here. Aint no band. No donut dollies to fuck. What're you checkin us out for? Cherry ain't going ta bend over for ya."

"You got any smokes?" Thomaston said to Cherry.

To Cherry it seemed they were baiting each other strictly for his entertainment. He rummaged in his ruck for a pack but McCarthy beat him, pulling a box of Marlboros from a fatigue pocket. McCarthy passed the cigarettes around. He struck a match, lit his and Thomaston's then put the match out. He struck another match and lit Cherry's cigarette. It was darker now in the jungle, gray dark but not black dark and they did not yet worry about light discipline. The sky above the canopy had turned red and the sun was enveloped by the mountains beyond the valley.

"Didn't think I smoked," Cherry said inhaling deeply, holding the fumes, feeling the nicotine rush.

Egan returned from his constant wandering and checking of the perimeter. He also was smoking. He was very quiet. Without saying a word he removed several cans of C-rations from his rucksack. He removed a blackened, smashed, dented tin can stove and two heat tabs.

"What's for dinner?" Thomaston asked.

"Vichyssoise. Beef Bearnaise. Mocha. And, ah, pound cake with peaches. How's that sound?"

"Sounds fine to me," Thomaston said rummaging in his ruck for his can stove and canteen cup and food.

McCarthy also opened his ruck and removed various items. "Here," he said handing Egan a can of Beef Slices and Potatoes with Gravy. McCarthy also removed a one-pound stick of C-4 plastic explosive. The three clustered closer while Cherry watched. Cherry thought it was all a joke but he wasn't sure.

Egan turned back to his ruck and produced several spice bottles then turned to Cherry. "You eating?"

"Yes. I guess."

"You need a fuckin invitation?"

"No."

"I need your canteen cup. A B-2 unit. Two cans a beef slices if you got two. One beef and one ham or pork's good enough. And I need all the cream substitute you can spare."

Egan worked in a very methodical manner. He collected the cans of meat and of meat with potatoes and opened them. In a canteen cup he separated the potatoes from the beef, pouring the gravy grease in with the meat. He washed the potato chunks with a few capfuls of water and added the water to the meat. Then with the tip of his bayonet he cut and mashed the potatoes, added three packets of dried cream substitute and filled the cup with water. This he stirred and set aside. McCarthy set up two stoves and filled two canteen cups almost to the brim with water. The stoves were small C-ration cans opened on one end and with holes punched in the sides all around. Beneath the tins he placed tiny chunks of plastic explosive he had broken from the pound stick. McCarthy placed the canteen cups on the stoves and lit the explosive which ignited slowly then flared quickly to a foot-high sizzling white-hot flame and.went out. The water was boiling. To the water McCarthy added four packets of instant coffee, four packets of Cocoa Beverage Powder, three cream substitutes and three sugars. He mixed first in one cup then in the other, then he poured the mix into a third and poured the three back and forth.

The Bearnaise sauce for the beef was a mixture of two cream substitutes, four powdered crackers from a B-2 unit substituting for flour, two packets of salt, one melted tin of cheddar cheese and half a dozen shakes of tarragon leaves and onion chips from Egan's private stock.

The sauce and the meat were heated slowly over heat tabs as the mocha cups passed back and forth. Then the canteen cup of cool potato muck Egan delighted in calling Vichyssoise was handed around.

"Wow!" Cherry exclaimed quietly after Egan handed him his can of Beef Bearnaise. "This is unreal."

"What's unreal?" Egan said.

"Your food, Man," Cherry said almost giddily. He should have stopped there and he knew it immediately after he added, "Your food, this place and all the Nam."

"You dumb shit," Egan sneered. "It's only unreal if your eyes are closed. It's real, asshole. Stick yer finger inta the ground and feel it. Real. Solid. You fuckin airhead assholes give me a case of the ass."

"Hey wait, huh," Cherry said hurt. No one said anything in his defense. Cherry got up quietly, stepped the four feet to where he and Egan had smoothed the earth from the foxhole into a sleeping position and sat down. He wanted to cry. It had been a very long day. He was exhausted. His thoughts ranged wildly beyond all his earlier experiences yet produced no understanding. He loved these guys, he despised them. He had thought they were crazy, brilliant, ignorant, more sane than any people he had ever met. What did he have to do to be accepted by them?

A breeze had begun rising from the valley with the approaching darkness and now it became a wind. Soon the meeting at the company CP would commence. The Platoon RTOs had reported to El Paso that all squads were set for the night. LPs, listening posts manned by two infantrymen each, had been deployed, one 75 meters down the trail toward the draw, one on the ridge where the NVA mortars had landed and one in the canyon below the company. The LPs had waited until dark to move off from the company and into their positions. Each team had a PRC-25, their weapons, ammo, a watch and little else.

After the LPs went out MAs were set on the LZ on 848. The MAs, or mechanical ambushes, were booby traps assembled of claymore mines, detonation or det cord, blasting caps, a battery and a triggering mechanism attached to a trip wire. Two MAs were set by Don White and Don Nahele of the 3d Plt before they withdrew to the rear security position of the NDP.

Command detonated claymores were now being set in front of each fighting position. Lt. Hoyden, the forward observer whom everyone called FO (foe), completed calling in a long series of DTs and H & Is. The DTs, or defensive targets, were likely enemy approach routes or locations if they were attacking the company. FO registered the predetermined range and azimuth settings with the FDCs of the firing batteries to assure rapid and accurate delivery of artillery fire. H & I fire, harassment and interdiction, were targets of suspected or possible enemy locations or paths of movement. Artillery projectiles that screamed overhead and fell into the valley far below at seemingly random intervals were H & I. They were fired day and night but mostly at night. Their rumbling blasts remained in the hills at Khe Ta Laou, reverberating until a new explosion eradicated the lingering echo, for the entire operation.

Wind coming from the valley caused leaves high in the canopy to scrape against one another and chatter and dry palms to clash. Brooks sat with his back to the wind, purposely, so his voice would carry to those who would be before him. He sat on the ground, cross-legged, still, silent, like a distinguished Indian chieftain awaiting his war council.

Brooks had been able to produce and preserve racial harmony in his unit, in an army troubled with racial turmoil. He had heard the story of the brawl at the Phoc Roc and he had heard about Jackson and Egan quibbling during the day. There had been other incidents. Greer in the 2d Plt had refused to obey an order from Pop Randalph until Woodrow Hayes interceded. Brooks knew the racial polarization of his troops had increased during the stand-down and it was now time to put an end to it. He planned to address that situation after the business part of the meeting.

This was a difficult situation for a black lieutenant. Often when authority came from a black NCO or officer the black foot soldier felt sold-out, bitter, Uncle Tommed. "When theys E-1 to E-4," Jackson had once said, "they Bro Black. When theys E-5, they Sergeant Black. When they's E-6 or higher then they jest Sergeant and then theys lifers and it don't matter none what color a lifer is. They all OD."

Rufus Brooks was lucky. All his troops liked him. He was one of them, a boonierat. They would do almost anything for him because he would do almost anything for them. He always had, ever since he had become company commander.

The men were now assembling. It was still and dark though not completely black for the moon was full behind a partial cloud cover and not completely still for the wind was in the canopy and artillery rounds were bursting in the valley. Pop Randalph came up and sat beside Brooks. "The gooks probably moved out fer the night," Pop said handing the L-T a hot canteen cup of coffee. "Bet," he added, "they move right back in fore we get theah tomorra."

El Paso was to the L-T's other side and beside him was Cahalan then FO, Bill Brown, Minh and Doc. These eight made a tight 180° arc. The three platoon leaders, Lts. Thomaston, De Barti and Caldwell, sat together across from Brooks. Ezra Jones came down from 3d Plt, Garbageman from 2d and Egan and Jackson from 1st. They were now fully assembled in a tight circle, knees touching. Some had poncho liners, thin nylon quilted blankets the size of a poncho, wrapped around their shoulders and over the backs of their necks or even over their heads, to keep them warm. Pop handed his coffee to Jackson and started it around. Jax sipped, handed the cup to Egan and finished their earlier conversation by whispering, "Yaassir, Bro me. Like Pappy'd say, 'When I aint near the girl I love, I loves the girl I's near.' " Egan chuckled, sipped, passed the cup to

Garbageman who passed it to Jones then on to Caldwell who did not drink. He handed the cup to De Barti saying, "The euphemism I like best, I mean I really like it, is 'Armed Propaganda.' " The coffee continued around to Doc who drank and passed it to Minh whispering, "They all say that. They all say, 'if I doan see another dink the rest a my tour, I'll be happy,' but you just let somebody else get a body count, Mista, en you watch em scream, 'Why Bravo Company? Why . . .' " The coffee came full circle through the FO and the RTOs and back to the L-T who passed it back to Pop. Pop looked at him and said, "Hey, Sir, did you know today is Friday the thirteenth?" Egan overheard him and said, "Today's Thursday."

"Have your people ready and saddled up by oh-four-thirty," Brooks said to the group very quietly, the wind carrying his voice across to Thomaston but not outside the circle. "We're going to move back down that trail and spread out across the draw before first light. At first light we'll sweep up the hill. The opposition may be planning a similar move against us. I want two gun teams at point. From the draw spread south around the hill and we'll sweep up from there and from this side. Order of movement same as today. If we meet no opposition 2d Plt will recon off the peak north and northwest. 3d will recon along the ridge running southwest. 1st will rest."

"Are we going to be able to get air support at that hour, Ruf?" Caldwell asked.

"They might be socked in in the rear," Garbageman added.

"We might be socked in here," someone said.

"I'd prefer to move under cover of fog," Brooks said and added, "if we can get it. I want to get into that bunker complex undetected. No noise. We don't have to take it at once. Let's move slowly and probe it. We've got time. It doesn't have to be rushed, and we can always withdraw." Brooks let his gentle voice seep from his throat. He sounded like a cross between schoolteacher and gang leader. "Danny," Brooks addressed Egan, "you want to let us in on your contact this afternoon?"

Egan gulped. He had not been prepared for this.

"What did your pointman fire up?" Brooks pressed.

"There wasn't nothin down there," Egan said lowly. He paused. No one said anything. "My point just freaked out," Egan admitted. "He didn't see anything."

"Oh shit," Thomaston groaned. "I thought . . . I don't believe you guys."

"Who'd you have at point?" Caldwell directed the question to Thomaston.

Brooks cut them off. "It doesn't make any difference now," he said. "I've spoken with the man. We were within 30 meters of the saddle. It would probably have been better to move through there today but one man stopped us. There's no other way to go."

"Fuck it," Jones said. "Goddamnfuckit."

"That's enough," Brooks said. "Let's review what we've got. Cahalan."

"We know from the helicopter sightings," Cahalan said sounding like he was reading the minutes from the last meeting, "that there's a bunker complex over there. The fast movers destroyed five of thirty bunkers this afternoon. Earlier, there had been movement spotted and fired upon with unknown results. The opposition knows our location and direction. Recon was periodically in contact from time of insertion to 1440 hours resulting in four NVA killed by small arms fire. The NVA appeared clean, well fed and all were equipped with AKs. One US was killed and three wounded. Two of the wounded were medevacked. The C & C bird reported spotting movement a klick (kilometer) west of Firebase Barnett and on the ridge below where the Delta Darlings were inserted." Cahalan stopped.

"Oh fuck this shee-it," Jax said his eyes becoming wider and wider as Cahalan recited the day's intelligence.

"We've got to get to that next peak," Brooks said quietly. "Without it, our back's to a wall. That peak will give us room to maneuver. Questions?"

No one spoke. The business meeting came to a quick end. Everyone sat for the next few minutes in complete silence. Then Caldwell rose quietly and left. The other platoon leaders also rose and returned to their platoons. FO and Brown rolled to their sleeping position only a few feet away. The circle tightened.

"Boy, Egan," Cahalan chided him, "that cherry of yours is a real asshole."

Egan did not answer. He had been brooding and angry about Cherry ever since the CA. The damn cherry was a know-it-all, a stubborn, uncomprehending ass but no one wanted others to think his field partner was an asshole. It was a bad reflection upon himself.

Brooks took control, beginning very quietly. "I've been

watching you guys. I'm very concerned about the racial conflict I see growing in this unit."

"Conflict," Jackson jumped on the opportunity to speak, "is caused by some white mothafucka feedin lies to the people. The people, they see one thing, they told another. They told not to believe what they see. They sees land and they sees starvation and they sees some white mothafuckas sayin we can't feed them people. Fuckas say, 'See here. I own that land. I got a deed says I can do what I want with that land. Says black boys gowin kill yellow boys to protect my deed. We . . .'"

"How do you feel about that, Danny?" Brooks interrupted Jackson.

"I think he's got his head up his ass," Egan said. "What's he seein, anyway? Fifty years ago? Thirty years ago? This is 1970. Nobody in their right mind comparing America today with even twenty years ago can say that there hasn't been beaucoup progress."

"You are such a . . . a white man," Doc said slowly, pathetically. "You a good man, Eg, but you so white you blind, Mista. You come live in my neighborhood fo a year en open your eyes."

"It is to me," Minh's high distinct voice entered the night conversation, "a paradox that you fight for a land so soon after your own people have won liberation. You are just now removed from slavedom and you become imperialist warriors."

"Say again. Over," Cahalan said.

"I do not know why you, any of you, fight for my country," Minh said. "You suffer, you die and there is nothing in it for you to gain."

"Aint dat da truth," Jones said.

"What do you think, Pop?" the L-T asked.

"I don't know, Sir. I just do what I'm tol ta do. We . . . most of us are like that, I think, Sir, most of us. I don't know why. I don't know if I care why either. I don't care what you do to a American fightin man. All you got ta do is show'm a woman now en again, give him a beer and pay him on time—he'll function, Sir. Now these gooks, they're different. They only fight when they feelin good."

"We are very much like you were two hundred years ago," Minh said. He had a smile on his face but in the dark it could not be seen. "In your revolution your Continental Army was constructed of militiamen enlisted for the summer fighting season.

When their terms expired they would not re-enlist and they went to their farms for harvest time and for planting. They did not believe so strongly in your Union as did General Washington. They said it was up to him and your Congress to find replacements. We are the same. Perhaps we do not believe so strongly as President Thieu.''

"You dudes note that," El Paso said. "That's true. *Es verdad*. Minh, you always amaze me.''

"I'm goina say somethin in here about blacks," Egan said, "but I don't want it misunderstood. There is one reason and only one reason why the black man in America has not advanced at the same pace as all the other ethnic groups who came here, there, I mean, and it's not cause of the color of his skin. It's because every group that came to America except the blacks brought with them the attitude that with education and hard work they could advance to the top.''

"Shee-it," Jax sounded.

"That true," Doc agreed. "Almost true anyway. You got only one thing wrong Mista Mick. Black people came here even in their bondage with the same attitude like everybody else but they was slaves. If they tried ta learn they was punished. They was kept ignorant on purpose, Mista Mick, first as slaves then through all kinds a discrimination. That what Jax sayin. We had our chain a knowledge broken on us, over our heads. We just now weldin it back up again.''

"I think we oughta go crash, okay?" Garbageman said. He, like Pop, seldom stayed for the informal discussions. He felt uncomfortable speaking about or listening to racial problems in the presence of black troops.

"Okay," Brooks said. "Go. I think we've covered some things tonight that we can think about and talk about again later. Let me just say that conflict, whether between a man and his wife or between races or nations, follows a pattern of growth. Think about it for me, okay? We're here together. Us. All of us. Let's be tolerant of the other man's point of view. We've always helped each other. We've always pulled together. We're an unbeatable team. Perhaps someday we'll all pull together back in the World and create an unbeatable team back there. See you at 0430. I'm walking point.''

CHAPTER

15

Cherry was scared shitless. No more bewilderment. No more exhilaration. Just simple fear. Artillery rounds continued to pass overhead, sounding in the stillness of the night like freight trains rushing past. Cherry had smoothed the dirt he and Egan had pulled from the foxhole into a two-man sleeping area. He had spread his poncho out over the dirt and put his and Egan's rucks into the vegetation at the uphill end. Egan had gone to the CP meeting and left him alone. Occasionally, in the first hour after Egan left, runners from the squads came to report the LPs were out or the claymores deployed but mostly Cherry had been alone.

He surveyed his body. His arms were bruised and burned. He knew that. That had happened on the CA. But now his shins and his ass were bruised too. There were scratches on his face and the backs of his hands. Just when they occurred Cherry was not certain. Probably during the mortars, he thought. Or possibly when the jets dropped their bombs. Cherry's shoulders and back and legs were sore too. How could anyone carry a 100-pound ruck all day, climb down a mountainside with it and not be sore? The bruises added to his fear.

He lay with his eyes shut. His brain could not control his thoughts. His mind projected fractured concepts onto its inner screen and the projector was speeding out of control. He tried to slow his breathing, to relax his body, to ease the tension. His legs would not cooperate. His stomach felt as if it were full of uncured cement. His chest was taut. Rushing gulps of blood spasmodically jolted his body on the still earth. His ears were tight too, trying to listen yet not listening. The muscles and skin of his neck and scalp were taut, stretched like a drum head. He was awake yet not alert, not sensing anything beyond his own body. I am going to die, he cried inside. They are going to kill me.

"Hey, Cherry, you asleep?" It was Silvers. "Hey Cherry," Silvers nudged his shoulder, "I wanted to come over and apologize."

"What?" Cherry asked dully.

"I'm sorry if I gave you a bad time today. I just came over to say that, that's all."

"Thanks. I mean . . ."

"Tomorrow, if we get a chance, maybe I can show you how to adjust that ruck so it rides a bit higher. I'll talk to you in the morning."

"Thanks," Cherry said sitting up. He looked at where Silvers' voice had come from. There was nothing there. Cherry leaned forward and laid the side of his head upon his knees. He shut his eyes. How could things be so screwed up? He felt on the ground next to him for his rifle. At least that was there. He ran his fingers over the trigger housing assembly. It felt very cool. He lay back down keeping his hand on the M-16.

A moment later Egan materialized beneath the poncho liner next to him. Cherry didn't hear or see or feel him until Egan was already in bed with him. Egan was true infantry, true boonierat. The jungle was his home. It was no concern to him that the ground was hard or wet or cold. It only had to be defensible. Egan told Cherry that they would alternate radio watch in one-and-a-half-hour shifts. Then he was still, motionless, soundless. Cherry could not even hear him breathe. If it had not been for Egan's body warmth Cherry would have found himself doubting whether Egan was really there.

"I'm scared," Cherry said. His face was less than a foot from Egan's ear.

"That's natural," Egan said.

Cherry heard Egan's voice then nothing. On the ground everything was black. He listened very hard. His wristwatch was ticking. Air was passing in and out of his lungs. His elbows creaked. No sounds came from Egan. "I mean really," Cherry said.

"You're such a dumb fucking innocent cherry, I can't hardly believe it. You aint got no war brains at all. None. Zero."

"I'm sorry," Cherry apologized sincerely. "I really thought I'd be okay at this. I didn't think I'd be so scared."

"I don't know if you know this," Egan whispered, "but this is one good fuckin company. Dinks seldom hit good companies. They like to pick on the noisy ones where the guys aren't tryin ta stay alive. Understand? That's why you shut-up. Dinks are like wolves circlin a herd a deer. They pick off the weak and the wounded. Or the lazy. You get some of these jokers too lazy to walk around a valley ta get to the other side. Charlie stays in the valleys. We stay up on the ridges. That's our agreement. If you don't have ta go down there, don't. We don't see them. They don't see us. We're happy. They're happy."

"What about today?" Cherry asked sheepishly.

"You can't just walk in on em and expect to be invited ta dinner," Egan whispered. "We're right at their back door." Cherry groaned. Egan continued. His voice was very low and it came with so little force it barely reached Cherry's ears. "Higher-higher sent us to one bad ass AO. Fuck it. Don't mean nothin. You could get wasted steppin off a curb back in the World."

They were silent for several minutes then Egan said absent-mindedly, "I wrote a letter to Stephanie this morning. I didn't get a chance to give it to anybody. Remind me at resupply to give it to the doorgunner. I feel like he's goina have one for me."

Artillery flares began popping across the valley above the north ridge. The white phosphorus lights made a dull thud as they ignited and the parachutes were ejected. The lights drifted slowly with the wind, descending, sputtering and wheezing then burning out. Several flares popped above Alpha. They cast a strange flat illumination on the LZ where McQueen and Nahele lay behind an M-60 but only a glint of light penetrated the triple canopy to the ground where the enemy might be approaching, where Egan and Cherry were.

"You sack," Egan said to Cherry. "I'll take first radio." Egan called in the first situation report of the night to El Paso. "Sit-rep negative," is all he whispered.

"Who's Stephanie?" Cherry asked.

"Just a chick," Egan said.

*   *   *

They lay silent for several hours. A large dead tree projected scraggly branches against the sky above. The moon had moved overhead. High tangled branches looked like broken lines in a pen and ink sketch. One high limb still had leaves perhaps from a climbing vine. Egan's eyes were wide open. His right hand cradled his M-16. In his left hand he held the radio handset. His left arm crossed his chest and the handset was by his right ear. He watched a cloud slip by the moon and she was there. A broken branch spiked the cloud but the lighted edge sailed smoothly, unpenetrated. The jagged branch did not touch it. Nor did it touch the moon.

Egan closed his eyes and she was there. It made no difference whether his eyes were open or closed. A trembling tightness accentuated the quick heavy pounding in his ears and neck and spread pulsations throughout his body. He could feel her laugh, her lithe body, her small shoulders. Her large bright eyes were closed. He could not see her eyes for it was dark. The cloud continued sliding. A spear-bough drove deeply toward the glowing rim but it did not pierce the cloud's side.

Egan heard the poncho crackle. A twig snapped beside him and the jungle resonated, each vine each bamboo fiber prolonging proliferating the sound. Egan stirred imperceptibly and whispered, "What the hell are you doin?"

"Nothin," Cherry whispered.

"Motherfuck. You jerkin yer cock?"

Cherry did not answer.

"Scared, huh? Scared but not too fuckin scared ta jerk off. Okay fucker. Okay. Fuck yer hand. But do it quiet. Do it with two fingers and don't make any noise. Here," Egan passed Cherry the handset. "Don't come on it."

Slowly Egan pulled his poncho liner up about his face. She was there. Her face was dark. He could only faintly remember what she looked like. With the poncho liner over his face he could no longer see the cloud but off to the side he could see moist palm fronds vaguely glisten against the black jungle and he knew the cloud was still riding the moon's edge.

Their first meeting unrolled before him. He and Paul, a friend from college, had arranged to meet in New York City a week after summer vacation began. They planned to catch a freighter to Europe or Africa or South America. By day they would follow their quest to the piers and probe the shipping offices. At night Paul had arranged it so they could stay at Pattie and Stephanie's apartment.

Paul and Pattie and Stephanie had graduated from a small township high school in western New York State in 1964. Paul had gone to college. The girls had moved to the city for their education. They had been in the city, struggling, partying, getting by, for almost a year. Paul had gotten their address from an old high school friend a few days before he and Egan met.

They met at The Battery, drank the afternoon away then headed toward the Village. Outside, Egan could see it clearly now, the soot-blackened moldy red sandstone building rose up before him. The sidewalk was slate. It felt smooth under his feet even in his drunken condition. Decaying steps dropped beneath the building's main entrance to a basement door on which a neon sign shouted BAR.

Daniel followed Paul down. The bar opened before him. It was pleasing, quaint, a little decrepit, a sailor's tavern. The walls were lined with paintings of tall ships. Behind the bar was a model of a four-masted square-rigger. Paul and Daniel were the only customers. Paul admired the model and the tavern owner, a sea captain's widow, immediately launched into the story of a storm in the Caribbean. She said her name was Maggie.

Maggie was an old woman whose skin hung loose from jowls and arms. With her was a sailor named Witness, who confirmed and embellished the stories she told. Witness was a large angular man in his mid-fifties. Daniel was taken with the tales of his wanderings at sea. Witness bought a round. Maggie bought a round. Witness bought another. Paul and Daniel were broke but between them they raised enough for a round. Witness would not allow them to pay. He bought another. He said he was going inland to be married. "Time to plant these feet on soil," he said. Maggie chided him, cautioned him to be gentle with his new bride then added impishly, "If you ever expect to get some."

Daniel and Paul rolled up the stairs, intending to invite Pattie and Stephanie to the bar. Daniel had never met them and Paul had not seen either since graduation. They arrived at the apartment door with their bags over their shoulders, gaily laughing. They were gaily welcomed. The third floor walk-up was small, two rooms and a kitchenette. Daniel looked around drunkenly.

Pattie said she had a date and left. Stephanie refused to go to a basement bar. The college boys passed out on the floor.

"God, she is beautiful," Egan remembered thinking then. She had auburn hair that hung to her delicate shoulders. "Fragile," he had thought. "So fragile and so delicate." She became his measuring stick for every girl he met thereafter. She became his education. He could see her now that first time. She wore a flowing silk scarf as a choker around her graceful neck, a ballerina's neck. The ends of the scarf rested lightly on her breasts. "Really," she was saying so gently the words caressed the air, "I'd prefer not to go there."

Egan shifted. He pulled the poncho liner down and stared at the sky. The edge of the cloud was gone. The cloud had engulfed the moon. The jagged branch seemed limp. He felt cool. Where the moon's light penetrated the cloud, the haze glowed. Small palm spikes pricked the glow from below. She was still there. This image was much later. Maybe years. Stephanie was wearing a plum-colored poorboy sweater. She was braless and her small breasts looked soft and tantalizing. About her hips was a purple knit skirt. It drooped and clung to her slender thighs. Even her feet were pretty. He wanted to touch her feet.

Egan felt the need to move. He lay still. He had to move. Slowly he rocked forward, slowly, smoothly, so every muscle fiber of his gut pulled individually and he sat up. He drew his legs to his chest without a sound. He pulled the poncho liner around his shoulders and holding a corner in each hand wrapped his arms about his legs. Egan turned his head and lay it upon his legs. Stephanie's face still hid in the shadows but a slight glimmer lined her lips and her nose and one eye. "Why?" Egan wondered. "Why should I think of you now? Why are you with me tonight?" A heavy force pressured the back of his eyes. His throat felt thick. She did not appear this clearly during the day, during the light, but the jungle was dark and the night moved slowly.

That first New York week Egan had slept on the floor in the front room of Stephanie's apartment. He had lain on his back each morning and had watched her apply her make-up. She would rise early and spend a very long time preparing for the photographer for whom she modeled. She would sit on the floor before an aluminum ladder with one leg curled beneath her and the other bent and held just so, so she could steady her arm on her knee. On the ladder's second step there was a tiny lighted make-up mirror. On the first and third steps were bottles of cosmetics. By her right hip there was an ashtray and by her left a cup of coffee. Stephanie was never without a cigarette.

Egan could see her move clearly now, could see the room and himself. He was lying there pretending to be asleep. Watching Stephanie. She looks like a child playing, he had thought. She sang in that soft caressing voice and her thoughts seemed to frolic. He could hear her now. She braced her wrist upon her knee to apply mascara. Her hand trembled. They were thin hands with slender fingers and tiny wrists. Later Daniel's callused hands would hold them, almost engulf them.

"Take this," she whispered the fourth morning. "To read while you sit on the piers and rest from walking amongst the longshoremen." It was a copy of Gibran's *The Prophet*. That day he and Paul were rejected by twelve ships and that night they returned late. Pattie was gone for the evening and Stephanie had a friend in the second room. Paul and Daniel met him. He was older, thirty-five perhaps. To Daniel he seemed very dirty, greasy. He introduced himself as Lucifer then led Stephanie back to the second room again. Paul lay back and was snoring lightly within minutes. Daniel lay back. He listened. There are no sounds at first, then some kissing. Very soft music is put on the stereo. The kissing becomes louder. It echoes in Daniel's ears. He can feel the bastard's hands on the beautiful Stephanie. It is driving him mad. He wants to kill the greasy slimy shit. But—he cannot even stir. How can the college boy challenge the invited Lucifer? Simply because he is in love. . . .

Egan raised his head. His teeth were clenched. The mothafucker stayed the night, he thought.

During the first week Daniel did not touch Stephanie, not even so much as a handshake, not until they said good-bye. Paul got berth on a ship to Amsterdam and Daniel went to work for Kirt Sontag. Sontag ran a small tugboat and commute shuttle from Pier 15 on the East River. He was the "biggest of the little and the littlest of the big" operators from the piers. He paid poorly but he asked little and he offered Daniel a room aboard the *John J. Murphy*, a small tug that had sunk in Boston harbor in 1960, but had been raised and salvaged by Sontag. By day the *John J. Murphy* transported painting crews and supplies to the Statue of Liberty. By night the boat became Daniel's personal refuge.

For a week Daniel worked for Sontag. The second day he discovered a bar across the street from Pier 15. It was long and narrow inside. To the left of the door there was a dark wood bar and to the right against the wall were several small tables. In the far back beyond where the bar ended there were four larger tables and beyond these a small kitchen. The bar was dark and cool. Carved teak wainscoting circled the narrow hall of the bar to a five-foot height. On the upper edge of the wainscoting at ten-foot intervals there were stained prints of the sea. It could not have been more picturesque to a small town college kid. The cook was called Cookie and he actually had a wooden leg and wore a black eye patch. When Cookie found Daniel was working for Sontag he dropped the price of a glass of beer to 15¢, doubled the lunch portion and allowed Daniel to eat half a loaf of bread with butter during lunch.

It did not help.

Cherry sat up quickly causing the poncho beneath them to rustle. He handed Egan the radio handset and crunched back to the earth. Egan looked around. The jungle was very black. Everything was still. He could distinguish no sounds close by. In the distance, in the valley somewhere, artillery shells were exploding, their peaceful rumbling echo relaxed him. He lay back silently. The clouds had thickened between him and the moon and it was now difficult to distinguish individual branches against the ash sky. She was there. All of her. Her eyes. Stephanie's eyes were blue-gray, clear and deep. Egan could see her eyes and he felt elated. Suddenly the world was back to absolutes. He was in love. She was a gently flowing life and she was with him.

Egan had left New York one week after beginning with Sontag. He felt angry. Paul's ship was two days at sea. Daniel went to the apartment late, after work, and collected his few things. Pattie said good-bye and they shook hands. Stephanie was not home but as he turned to go, she arrived. Pattie left and Daniel and Stephanie talked for a few minutes. He said he must leave and he kissed her good-bye. It was the first time they touched. He could feel the warmth of her moist lips. He could feel them now. "You've got silver eyes," he had said. "No," she had laughed gently, "they're gray." "No," he corrected. "They're silver." They kissed again. His left hand was on her breast. "Good-bye," he said. And he left. He hitchhiked to Alaska, he meandered down to San Francisco, he bummed his

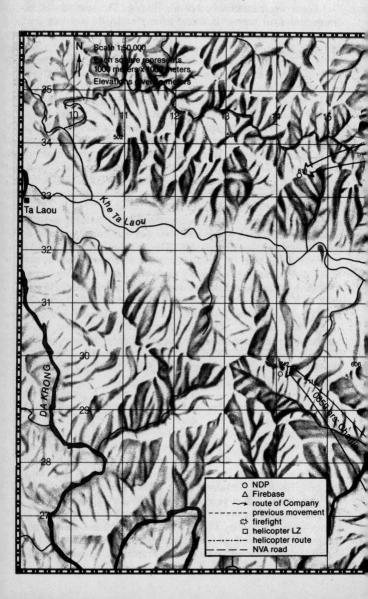

N Scale 1:50,000
Each square represents
1000 meters x 1000 meters
Elevations given in meters

○ NDP
△ Firebase
⌒➤ route of Company
- - - previous movement
✳ firefight
□ helicopter LZ
-·-·- helicopter route
— — NVA road

Grid lines are labeled using the Universal Transverse Mercator
Grid, Everest spheriod. This valley is in zone 48Q, Square YD.
To locate, read West-East then South-North. For example, ⊙ = YD 215353

17   18   19   20   21   22

Signature Delta
478

0844 hrs: Bravo

600

0845 hrs: Co. B 3/187
0845 hrs: Battery A 2/319
0905 hrs: Battery C 2/11

678
BARNETT

0840 hrs: Recon

airstrike   mortars   0840 hrs: Alpha

636

Rach My Chanh

JEROME
(ARVN)

to O'REILLY
YD 306256

way to New Orleans. He spent the summer wandering, searching. He found many things yet nothing satisfied him. He had been trapped by the mystique that was Stephanie.

The moon broke through a hole in the cloud cover. Egan was very groggy. His eyes were closed. The new glint of light penetrating the canopy ignited the nightmare which had become perversely attached to all night dreams of Stephanie. The glint rose. Egan was in the jungle in the dream. The night was very black. Sappers had penetrated the perimeter undetected. The glint rises higher. There is a sapper by his side. There is a silver machete in the enemy's hand. Moonlight sparkles on the blade as the man raises the huge knife. The machete begins its quick strike toward Egan's face.

Egan bolted upright.

SIGNIFICANT ACTIVITIES

THE FOLLOWING RESULTS FOR OPERATIONS IN THE O'REILLY/ BARNETT/JEROME AREA WERE REPORTED FOR THE 24-HOUR PERIOD ENDING 2359 13 AUGUST 70:

AMERICAN UNITS COMBAT ASSAULTED INTO THE FIREBASE BARNETT AREA AT 0840 HOURS AND RELIEVED ARVN UNITS FOR OPERATIONS IN THE FIREBASE O'REILLY AREA.

RECON, COMPANY E, 7/402 ENGAGED AN UNKNOWN SIZE EN- EMY FORCE 1500m SE OF BARNETT KILLING FOUR NVA. US CASUALTIES WERE ONE KILLED AND THREE WOUNDED. AT 0855 HOURS, VICINITY YD 198304, CO A, 7/402 DISCOVERED TWO ENEMY KILLED BY ARTILLERY. CO A WAS MORTARED AN HOUR LATER. THERE WERE NO CASUALTIES. AT 0940 HOURS BARNETT RE- CEIVED SEVEN MORTAR IMPACTIONS WITHIN THE PERIMETER. NO DAMAGE WAS REPORTED. AT 1440 HOURS RECON, CO E, 7/402 ENGAGED AN ENEMY FORCE WITH UNKNOWN RESULTS. ONE US SOLDIER RECEIVED MINOR WOUNDS.

ARVN UNITS MADE NO SIGNIFICANT CONTACT.

CHAPTER

16

14 AUGUST 1970

Everything went wrong on the 14th yet everything went right. To begin with the battalion TOC on the firebase did not make its standard wake-up calls. Brooks slept on. At 0400 El Paso, although he was awake with the radios, was dreaming about his mother. "Rafael," she called to him as she had called to him ever since his father had been killed. "Rafael, come in and stay with your mother. Today, I am very tired." "Isn't the priest with you tonight?" he snapped bitterly at her. "Rafael," she called. "I am an old woman whose husband has abandoned her. Why has he abandoned me?" She speaks Mexican-Spanish yet her speech, even in her native tongue, is poor. The boy turns and walks away from her. He passes the priest as he walks from his mother's shack. The entire world is filthy. "How is she today?" Father Raul inquires. "She is bitter," Rafael sneers. The background kaleidoscopes. They are outside the old church. Rafael says, "First she is bitter that the school takes me. Now she is bitter that the government takes me for the war." To the side in a stage whisper he adds, "She does not understand. I have not told them. I have signed up to get away." The priest is oblivious. The background becomes jungle though the old priest is still there, sitting deaf in an armchair. "They do not know," Rafael laughs, "that I have extended." It is a recurrent dream of which Rafael has told no one. During the entire dream El Paso did not look at his watch. The wake-up call from the TOC did not come. It is one of the very few times El Paso has ever faltered in his duties to Brooks and the company.

Rafael Jaoquin Pavura was raised in the torpid, sordid communal Mexican quarter of El Paso, Texas. He had been born to an old laborer and his young wife who were childless for the first ten years of their marriage. When the child was conceived the old man was well into his fifties and the impending event was not considered a blessing. Rafael was born in a jacal hut on the mesa west of Cuidad Juarez, far from the bullring and the cantinas, out on the flat arid wastelands. There the old man and the woman kept a small garden and stayed mostly to themselves. The summer of 1946 had been very hot and very dry and the plants had wilted early. In the first days after Rafael's birth and for two silent months the old man took to wandering in the barren lands. On a cool evening in early autumn the old man entered the hut, decisive, driven. He ordered his wife to pack whatever she might want to take and could carry. In the darkness they worked their way to the city and then across the Rio Bravo and north into the city of El Paso where they lost themselves in the shanties of the wetback villages.

There were no regular jobs and no place to settle and for five years the old man carried his son and the family wandered from hovel to hovel. The old man longed for the open barren lands yet the city and America offered many futures for his son that the mesa did not. It held forth the promise and anticipation of opportunity, the possibility of advancement, the promise of prosperity for future generations, the same promise America had held forth to all immigrants for over three hundred years. And the promises were very powerful in placating the old wetback. Something would happen, he told himself.

As a very young boy Rafael was allowed the freedom to wander unsupervised. At six Rafael was responsible for much of his own welfare and adept at coping with his ever-expanding world. The expanse of the Chicano community was unknown to his parents but everyone knew Rafael Jaoquin for he would dance through the streets and wander into homes. He would eat with a family he had never before seen and do it with confidence. When he would return or be returned to the shanty of his parents he would stay only long enough to tell his father of his adventures and then he would again wander off. Rafael listened to the stories of the farm workers who knew all the history of Mexico and knew all the people who had come north. He learned many of the stories and he would repeat them as though they were his. Older people loved to have him around and to listen to his stories and to laugh at his imagination but finally they would get tired and send him away. All except his papa.

A young priest once met the boy and listened, fascinated, for hours. He asked the boy about his home and the boy told the priest he was an orphan. For a week Rafael lived with Father Raul until the priest received word of a search and returned the boy to the old man and his young wife. The priest took an interest in Rafael's schooling and helped the old man obtain a night job at the canning works. At night the boy and the priest would watch the old man disappear through the wire gate and behind the chain link fence of the factory, and then the priest would bring the boy home and visit with the boy's mother while the boy was in bed.

Rafael worked for the priest, cleaning his room and sometimes the church and always delivering the messages the priest had for parishioners as he wandered through the streets telling and collecting stories. The boy loved the priest very much and he dreamed that some day he too would be a priest.

When Rafael was twelve his father died of heart failure. The old man had been moving heavy cases in the warehouse of the canning works and a high stack had toppled and trapped him. They had said he was not injured but the enclosure had frightened him and his heart had stopped. Father Raul arranged the funeral. The affair passed in near total isolation from the community. In a week the disturbance was settled, in a month forgotten. The only residual effect was a guarantee from the canning works pension that when and if the boy was ready to advance his education beyond that publicly provided, the funds would be available.

Rafael was outwardly quiet yet inwardly turbulent. His father had been destroyed by an ever closing trap which he had always hated, destroyed solely to give the boy a better future. Rafael felt cheated by the death, bitter when the mourning was so quickly over, guilty for having spent so much time with the priest and so little time with the ancient laborer.

The priest continued coming to their home for several years but Rafael's mother was now in her mid-forties and the priest too was getting old. On the nights the priest came, Rafael wandered the streets with other boys until he knew the priest would be gone. Finally the priest came no more and Rafael's mother stayed alone and complained that Rafael was not watching after her. Again he felt guilty but he knew he must wander as his father had wandered. And there was the cause.

La Raza. The Race—a revolutionary organization dedicated to returning the lands of the southwest to the brown people from whom it was stolen. In the schools it was an underground organization that initiated the young males into their first gangs and into self-righteous hatred of the Anglo oppressors.

There was a simple law in the southwest and along the border where the Anglo oligarchy controlled the lands: No man is guilty of anything unless he is a Mexican. It was the same law against which El Paso revolted many years later when it was applied by Americans to Vietnamese—the It's-Only-A-Gook Law. In the southwest the society was so structured as to continue the vicious circle of poverty, to trap the menial labor force in their mosquito-infested *barrio bajo*, a reinforced plague of illiteracy and unemployment. From this grew violence and revolutionary politics and to this Rafael was attracted. Father Raul would caution the boy with a resignation born in the carrying of a cross, "My young friend, you are going to get hurt and you are going to hurt others. I wish I knew how better to talk to you. You can work within the system to change it. You do not have to go out and do violence."

The priest had little effect yet slowly some of the boys changed. They became more political and less violent and *La Raza* became a significant political force.

Rafael had to go his own way. There was always something causing him to break from gangs and political parties and personal relationships. He always moved on toward open spaces. Someplace, sometime, in his adolescence, he was encouraged to study history, to go into law. In high school he studied hard and was influenced by two teachers who prodded him and helped him gain admission to the University of Texas at El Paso. In college he was a loner. After graduation and one year of law school he enlisted and by the spring of 1969 he was in Vietnam as an infantryman with the 7th of the 402d.

Rafael never spoke of his past or of his family. He listened to the others and he became the arbiter and the negotiator of intra-company squabbles. No one—not Jax, not Egan, not even the L-T—knew what happened in El Paso's mind, although they all knew that if El Paso said a dispute was solved then that was the decision and it stood.

* * *

On the perimeter some of the guards must have realized the time. They all had wristwatches. They could not all have been dreaming. Perhaps those who realized that the company was not yet up simply felt it was not their place to stir their sleeping brothers. Besides, most of them did not want to move at that hour.

At almost 0330 Cherry whispered to Egan, "What's that? I think I hear something."

There was a pause as Egan listened. "Like what?" he asked.

"Like, maybe a small animal. Listen. There."

"Fuck! It's one a them spiders. I hate spiders," Egan cursed lowly. There was the sound again, very close to Egan's and Cherry's heads. "Fuck," Egan's voice quivered. He very silently worked his body down, away from the sound.

"Are they poisonous?" Cherry asked, shaken.

"They're fucken big," Egan blurtwhispered.

Cherry giggled. He lifted his rifle and gently poked the brush where the sound had been. Something scampered away. Egan wiggled his body back into place.

An hour later the noise was back. Egan punched Cherry. "You hear that?"

Cherry lay very still. He reached over to Egan and placed his arm on Egan's chest. "Don't move," he said.

"Oh fuck," Egan shook. He was sweating. He felt for sure the spider was on him. He opened his eyes. Two feet above them both, there was a slender black silhouette. Egan froze. It was a banana spider, a long narrow spider body with twig-thin angular legs spread in an eight-inch ellipse against the gray-black sky. From the brush beyond their feet to the vines above their heads, filaments of silk had been woven into a parachute web. The spider twinged the taut web. Egan's heart stopped, sputtered. Cherry, one arm over Egan still, lifted his rifle. One by one he snapped the supporting threads on his side of the web. The spider charged the muzzle then retreated into the brush.

"Oh fuck. Oh fuck, oh Fuck," Egan sat up. Web clung to his face. "I hate fucken spiders," he whispered vehemently. "I can't stay here. What time is it?"

"Four thirty-five," Cherry said. He could hardly believe it. Hardass Egan afraid of spiders. He giggled silently, his whole body shook with the laugh without emitting a sound.

"What's so fucken funny?" Egan demanded but dropped it immediately. "Hey," he said, "we're supposèd ta be movin by now."

It was cold but the wind had ceased. There was a vague glow in the sky coming through the clouds. On the jungle floor nothing could be discerned in the blackness. To see a man's form the observer would have to squat and silhouette the observed against the sky. Egan radioed El Paso. Within minutes the entire company was up. They were already a half hour behind schedule.

Perimeter guards retrieved their claymores, rolled the wires about the mines and placed them in their rucks. The people who set up the MAs very cautiously disarmed them by disconnecting the batteries, then dismantling the trigger and trip wire. Radio calls went out to the LPs to return. Soldiers cleaned and oiled their weapons and cleaned their ammunition. Everyone had a cigarette going. They smoked with their hands cupped over the ember or with the ember end held in an opaque foil bag from a C-ration accessory packet.

Very carefully Egan brushed the night's dirt from his fatigues and poncho liner. He folded the liner and placed it in his ruck. Then he brushed his teeth. He used no water, simply allowing toothpaste and saliva to foam. He ejected a white stream of foam into a tiny hole and he covered the hole with dirt. Then he sucked the remaining foam from the bristles and swallowed. He carefully replaced the brush in a plastic carrying case, placed the case in a sock and placed the sock in the ammo can at the base of his rucksack. In the sock the case could not rattle against the inside of the ammo can. Egan checked his ruck carefully again for loose items. He tightened this, adjusted that. He checked his canteens. One was two-thirds full. He took a drink and passed it to Cherry who was also packing up. Cherry drank and handed it back. It was still a third full. Egan emptied the water on the ground. He did not want it to slosh as he walked.

Cherry was as imprecise with himself and his equipment as Egan was precise. He did not brush his teeth. He crushed his poncho and stuffed it into his ruck without cleaning it. He made no attempt to straighten his clothing, comb his hair or clean his face. He stuffed his poncho liner crudely about the cans in his ruck only at Egan's insistence. He cleaned his weapon but he carelessly spilled and splashed the LSA (Lubricant, Small Arms) onto his fatigues. Egan was appalled but after the thing with the spider he decided to say nothing. Doc McCarthy came by with the daily-daily (anti-malaria) pills. The column was ready to move out. It was 0509, thirty-nine minutes late.

Brooks led off. He descended by the same path that Whiteboy had taken, descended as quietly and slowly in the dark as Whiteboy had in the green-gray light below the canopy yesterday. Brooks moved steadily. He was becoming warm even in the chill of the night. He moved like an animal stalking prey, moving in the manner learned from animals and learned from the NVA and perfected through self-criticism within the company. NVA tactics in an NVA stronghold in an NVA war. Better than the NVA. Stronger. More fire support, more intrinsic fire power. Walking into a potential ambush. Brooks reached the terminus of Whiteboy's trek, the point where he had stopped the column's movement. He breathed controlled even breaths through an open mouth so as not to be heard breathing. He glanced at a trail he could not see in the blackness, his slow moving feet feeling each step down, securing each unseen foothold. The crest of the ridge was to his left. He could feel it there looming high above his left shoulder. Forward. Downward. The entire column in motion behind him.

If I were NVA, Brooks thought, I'd set up ambush on both sides of the saddle on the crest of the ridge. They know where we're going. They're going to be there. The trail steepened. Almost straight down. Like descending uneven crooked steps blindfolded with no handrail and with a hundred pounds of equipment on his back and in his hands. The draw would be at the bottom of the stairs. Down. Slowly. Down. Quietly. Brooks could hear Egan behind him. Almost imperceptible but there. A mosquito buzzed at his ear, sniffed the repellent and departed. Egan was perhaps three feet back. El Paso an additional three feet and then the gun team from 3d Sqd of Beaford and Smith—a total of ten. Brooks paused. Listened. Looked up. Either the clouds were thinning and the moonlight increasing or first light was lightening the sky. It was still black below the canopy. In another step he would be in the draw.

Behind the gun team was Cherry. Beaford carried the 60, Smith was AG. Cherry kept his left hand in constant touch with Smith's rucksack. He was like a newly blinded man being tortured. But he was trying. He tried harder than he had ever tried at anything in his life. Behind Cherry, Polanski was sporadically touching Cherry's ruck for guidance and from there back the 1st Plt descended like one continuous chain, each soldier linked to the soldier before him, forced to place complete trust in touch and in the accuracy of the touch of the men before him. Smith turned to Cherry, found his outstretched hand and pressured it down, signaling him to sit. Cherry turned and pressured Polanski to sit and up the column the signal was passed and the column halted.

Brooks was absolutely still. Behind him Egan froze. They waited. Brooks sniffed the air, opened his mouth to taste the air. Imperceptibly he inched one pace forward into the draw. He knelt. He touched the ground with his left hand. It was smooth and packed. He duck-walked across the draw keeping his left hand on the ground. It was level and smooth and packed for six or seven feet. At the other side the narrow trail snaked up the next ridge. Brooks searched the sides. Packed. He could feel ridges in the earth from thin wheels. He returned to where Egan waited motionless at the base of the descent. "Red ball," Brooks whispered. Egan nodded. The draw contained an intersecting high-speed trail which rose from the valley to the north and fell toward the valley to the south. Brooks motioned for the column to come forward.

As each man reached the red ball in the draw Brooks directed him into position. Beaford and Smith moved to the right flank along with the 2d Sqd, the M-60 machine gun team of Marko and Brunak to the left along with the 1st Sqd, Whiteboy and Hill straight ahead with the 3rd Sqd on line about them. With the twenty-seven men of the 1st Plt in place in line surrounding the base of the peak with the bunker complex Brooks ordered a pause. The pause gave 2d Plt time to move down and spread out behind 1st, and 3d Plt time to move down and spread out on the side of 848 thus being in position to cover a retreat if necessary.

The sweep up the peak west of Hill 848 was tactically perfect. It could have come straight out of an infantry manual. "Stay off the trail," Brooks directed Whiteboy. "If they're going to booby-trap us, it'll be on the trail." At first light 1st Plt moved out.

Step. Step. Climbing now. Climbing slowly. Climbing through the thick brush. The men in front waiting for the men with more difficult climbs. Staying in line. No sign of the enemy. Waiting for the first shot. Not even feeling their thighs twitching from the weight and the exertion of the climb. Not

seeing, feeling the black before them. The sky became lighter,
the floor remained dark. Not thinking. Like men with brains
removed. No judgment. Just up. Step. Step. In line. Weapons on
full automatic, aimed forward. Step. Not stopping. Step. Cherry
could feel his biceps quivering. His back aching. Step. Step.
Coming out of his rucksack and bending forward over his shoulder was his radio's antenna looking like a thin bamboo shoot. It
caught in the vegetation. His ruck was caught by a vine. He
frantically worked to extricate himself as the line advanced
without him. Step. Step. Light now penetrated through the jungle ceiling down to them. Up. Step. Step. Toward the hilltop the
canopy became thinner. Step. Step. The slope became more
gentle. They surrounded the eastern side of the peak. Up, onto,
over the top. Nothing. No one.

"Search this motherfucken hill," Thomaston cussed. "We
gotta find something."

1st Plt formed a perimeter about the north end of the peak,
dropped their rucks, removed helmets or hats and passed canteens of water around. They now lit cigarettes and smoked
without caution. Thomaston directed 1st Sqd to remain on perimeter defense and 2d and 3d to sweep the top and north and
northwest slopes. 2d Plt came up in column, dropped their
rucks, smoked and moved off to sweep the south and west
faces. Everything was quiet except for the occasional whisper,
"Mothafuck this shit."

Cherry sat with 1st Sqd. Egan and Thomaston went to the
company CP to discuss the situation with the group about Brooks.
Silvers had his journal out and was writing. He looked up at
Cherry and said, "This valley is more beautiful than I thought."

Cherry looked out from the hill. He had not noticed that it
was possible to see the valley. He had been looking at the
ground so hard and was now so tired from the climb that he had
not looked up and did not even realize day had fully arrived.
"Wow!" Cherry said softly.

Silvers' hazel eyes bulged over his protruding cheekbones.
"It's like a miniature A Shau," he said.

"It looks like the upper end of the Connecticut River Valley,"
Cherry said.

"Yeah."

Brunak turned toward them. He also had been staring at the
valley. "There's good farmland there," he said.

They all looked into the valley. The white clouds that had

persisted all day yesterday and filled the valley to the mid-level of the surrounding ridges in late afternoon had diminished considerably. Below them, the mountain wall fell to a series of rounded foothills. Across the valley, below the far mountainous ridge, the land seemed smoother. The valley center and the river were still fogged in and the mist spread into the troughs between the foothills. In a few locations the fog seemed to split without reason. There they could see what appeared to be a flat valley floor covered with lush green grass. In the center of the valley, rising out of the cloud, was a small brush-covered knoll with the immense tree rising hundreds of feet.

"Ya know," Silvers said, "I can't help but think of a bunch of peaceful villages down there. Small little towns with Scandinavian architecture, except in bamboo. Little farms. Little stores."

"Yeah," Cherry said. "I was thinking the same kind a thing. I can see where I'd put the roads."

"Yeah," Silvers said enthusiastically, "and right down there, a 72-hole golf course."

Silvers returned to his journal. Brunak and Jax were just beyond the squad leader. Cherry stared at Silvers, whose clothes were covered with dry orange clay. He already needed a shave. His hair was disheveled. He looked like a mad professor.

"What are you writing today?" Cherry asked quietly, keeping his voice only between the two of them.

"About boots," Silvers said.

"About boots?"

"Yeah, here. See?" He handed Cherry his journal. Cherry read:

'The laces on jungle boots are thick black cords which are easily tied and untied in square knots. The laces are seven or eight feet long and can be used to hold almost anything together or to make a tent with a poncho.'

Cherry looked up suspiciously. "Oh," he said.

"That's just an exercise," Silvers said quickly, justifying himself. "I try to write at least two pages every day. So I don't . . . get rusty."

"I see," Cherry said quizzically. He handed back the journal. "Rusty from what?"

"From not writing." Silvers paused. The explanation was

not enough. "Every time you write something you live a little bit longer," he said. "When you're dead you're still alive. If it's good, and it's only good if you practice, but if it's good you maybe live for six months more or maybe a year. Heck, if it's great . . . well, like Shakespeare. He died a couple a hundred years ago and he's still alive. If you can write something great you can live for thousands of years. Look at Homer."

"Maybe," Jax called over laughing, "he jest had a good agent."

"What are you going to write about next?" Cherry asked ignoring Jackson.

"Fatigues."

"Fatigues?"

"Yeah. Did you ever take a good look at em?"

"Yeah."

"What do you see?"

"Green."

"No. I mean, what? You've got to describe it."

"Like how?"

"You just put one word after the other. If you put one word after another long enough you've written a letter. Or a story. Look," Silvers' voice was rising, "let's do a description of the cloth of your fatigues."

"Ya know, Leon," Jax called again, "I a'ways know yo was a man a the cloth. Aint that so Cherry? We kin call him Mista Preacherman. The Preacher Mista Silvers."

"Hey Preacherman," Cherry joined the joke, "tell us about the Cloth."

"This," Silvers said holding up his sleeve, "is miracle fabric. These fatigues are made and designed . . ."

Suddenly outside the perimeter there was commotion. Polanski of 2d Sqd burst from the brush and rushed by shouting, "There's beaucoup shit down there." In his hands he had two mortar rounds. Smith emerged a second later with an entire arm load of 82mm mortar rounds stacked like firewood. All around men began finding things. Silvers, Cherry, Jax, all the guards clustered to examine the find then immediately spread back out on guard again. 2d Sqd brought up a total of twenty-seven mortar rounds they had found in a foxhole. Lairds from 1st Sqd found a letter written in Vietnamese on a plastic bag. He brought it to Minh for translation. Unfinished foxholes and bunkers were found on the north and west sides of the peak. A festive air of discovery erupted amongst the boonierats. Trenches were discovered connecting the bunkers into a complex. Fresh footprints were all over the soft mud in the trenches. Buried in the brush, concealed until fallen into, the North Vietnamese had constructed lean-tos of palm fronds.

Cherry went up to the CP. Minh was studying the letter Lairds had found. On the far side 2d Plt discovered a completed bunker complex. "This," Minh smiled, "is a letter from an NVA honcho. It is very beautifully written, like poetry. He writes to his mother about his coming death."

"Rufus," Lt. De Barti called immediately upon arriving at the CP. He was winded. He had run back up the hill. "Rufus, there're fifty bunkers down there. You gotta come down and see this. There's one bunker down there five feet from where they bombed yesterday, an I swear that fucker didn't cave in."

"Spread out," Thomaston yelled at the men on the peak. "Squad leaders, spread your men out. 2d Sqd, back down there. 1st, back off on the east. Now spread out. I don't want everybody clumping back up here. 3d, down that side."

"We got another eighty-two mike-mike over here," Hill called up to the peak.

"Hey! We got us another gook," Numbnuts yelled.

"Gawd A'might Sweet Jesus," Whiteboy clucked from next to Numbnuts. He bent over and grabbed the corpse. Egan and Thomaston trotted down and joined the cluster forming about the body. Cherry followed them down. "Okay," Thomaston snarled happily, "break it up. One round'd get ya all."

There were clusters of activity all over the hill. Back up on top, Moneski, squad leader 2d Sqd, brought in a badly shattered typewriter, and Murphy and Hall carried in a mimeograph machine. The soldiers still on top gathered close to inspect the strange type with the tonal marks above and below the various letters. The serial tag on the mimeograph machine was written in French. "Hey," Doc chuckled, "looks like we got their PIO. Where's Lamonte?"

"Aint that what you call an underground press?" El Paso laughed.

Letters and papers and stacks of office equipment were brought up. Minh translated a second letter. "This is a good letter to find," he told Brooks. "This one is from a private. He is writing to a friend. He complains his fellow soldiers steal his chocolate. He says they have run out of chocolate."

From the far side where 2d Plt had found the bunker complex came the sounds of chopping and slashing as boonierats set to work destroying the bunkers with machetes and entrenching tools. Half the bunkers were rooms dug deeply into the earth. The typical overhead cover consisted of two layers of logs and four layers of sandbags then a layer of dirt and finally brush for camouflage. Tunnels ran between the largest bunkers and trenches camouflaged with brush led from the bunkers up and down hill to gun positions.

"Am I glad we din't run inta gooks heah," Pop Randalph chuckled. "Dang! Ten gooks coulda held off an entire company. Ya couldn't force em out less ya was right atop em."

At 1st Plt the body of the dead NVA soldier was being stripped. Whiteboy had pulled the body from its upside-down position in the midst of broken trees. The soldier had been wearing short pants and a light shirt-jacket. He had been without shoes. Apparently he had been destroyed the previous day by mini-gun fire. Rounds had struck the soldier's head and shoulders and legs. The bones of his legs had been shattered and one arm was missing. The skin of his body appeared mashed and every blood vessel broken. Much of the body was covered by dried black blood. Where blood had not splattered to blot out the skin, the ruptured innards caused the skin to look like clear cellophane stretched over bruised meat. Splintered bones projecting through the skin mixed with surrounding splintered branches and the branches too were doused in blood. Flies swarmed above the soft marrow-filled cavities. The mangled meat was rapidly turning green-black. The man's one intact eye had fogged. Whiteboy and Bo Denhardt pulled the clothes from the body. Numbnuts pilfered the dead man's equipment and personal effects.

"Hey, Cherry," Denhardt called, "come here. I want ta show you something." Cherry went over to Denhardt who was standing by the corpse. Cherry tried not to look at the body yet he had difficulty keeping his eyes from it. "You ever see anything like this?" Denhardt asked. Denhardt lifted the corpse, sat it up and leaned the torso against a bush. Cherry was aghast. He could not conceive touching such a raunchy thing. Flies buzzed nastily at Denhardt's motions. Cherry watched Bo light a cigarette and put it in the dead man's mouth. The upper left quarter of the head was blown off. Bo lifted the one good arm and placed the man's hand on his penis. "Look at this guy,"

Denhardt laughed. "He's jerkin off. He's jerkin off," Denhardt laughed louder. "I hope I go that way."

Cherry turned and left. His stomach churned but there was nothing in it to heave. He retched dry again and then retched bile. He walked farther off swallowing the terrible taste in his mouth. He did not want anyone to know he was getting sick. They all seemed to be having a good time. Thomaston was standing in the midst of five men. He had the wallet and some papers the dead man had carried. Cherry turned and looked at the body. Egan and Denhardt were in the line of vision between him and the body but Cherry could see that the corpse had now lost its right ear also. He stepped forward. "He doesn't have any ears," Cherry whispered to Egan. Egan looked at him then walked toward the corpse.

"Oooooo-ooo! Look at this," Thomaston laughed. He had pulled a stack of eight small photographs from the wallet. They were about one inch square and apparently of the man himself and of his family. One photo of a young woman was cut in the shape of a heart. "Well, if she aint sweet." Thomaston passed the photos around. The soldiers pocketed them as souvenirs.

"Uh-hunh," someone said. "A little honey keepin the home front warm." They all laughed.

"I bet old Jody gettin a piece of that action," another voice chimed. Again they laughed.

"I wouldn't mind pokin her myself," Thomaston said.

Thomaston removed a South Vietnamese one hundred piaster bill and eleven North Vietnamese hoa then four North Vietnamese military postage stamps.

"He got it in the laigs, the chest an the haid," a voice explained to a latecomer. "He's all blowed ta shit."

Thomaston pulled a plastic envelope from the rear pocket of the NVA's pants. He opened it. There were four photographs in it. They were of an American family in front of a ranch-style suburban tract home with a Ford station wagon in the driveway. He gulped, whispered "Intelligence," and replaced the photos in the plastic.

"Hey, Lieutenant," a small voice squealed, "what you . . ."

"All right," Egan boomed from over beside the dead soldier, "who's got the mothafucker's ear? You fucken pig." Egan charged toward Denhardt. "You mothafucker. You low life cunt fuck. Put that ear back on the man's head." Denhardt tried to protest. Egan raged more furiously. "BULLSHIT!" He yelled. "Either you put that fucken ear back on that fucken dink's head or I'm goina cut yers off en nail em on him. You fucken savage." Egan spit. He grabbed Denhardt by the shoulders of his shirt, yanked him forward and threw him toward the body. "Bury that fucker before the stench makes me vomit in your mouth."

"Okay, let's . . . let's . . . let's, ah, break it up," Thomaston stuttered to the men standing around him.

Denhardt alone went back to the body. He scraped a trough of leaves and mulch from the ground and kicked the body into it. From one of the large pockets on the legs of his fatigue trousers he withdrew a deck of playing cards. He shuffled through the deck and removed the Ace of Spades. He had been waiting for this opportunity for a long time. Across the card, which Americans were told the Vietnamese held to be an evil omen, Denhardt scribbled 'SKYHAWKS.' Then he pushed an M-16 cartridge through the card and shoved the sign and post into a bullet hole in the dead man's forehead. He cursed the body and Egan. He covered the body with a thin layer of leaves.

CHAPTER

17

    Three hours before Cherry got his cherry busted, everything was peaceful, businesslike, ordinary. Atop and about the peak, at noon, the soldiers were doing their jobs and they were bored. The sun was high, the sky untainted. In the high canopy leaves caught the sun and a slight breeze and reflected the sun like glossy mirrors. Across the valley a small FAC observation Piper Cub buzzed. Closer by, two LOHs hummed and darted. Mist still cloaked the river below and the rumbling of occasional artillery rounds bursting on the western end of the Khe Ta Laou echoed and reverberated and rolled up upon the peak unnoticed.

    1st Plt had regrouped after the morning patrols and most of the soldiers sat idly, some eating C-rat lunches, some writing letters, some cleaning weapons. No one was in a hurry. The mortar rounds and office machines and rice and other odds and ends of NVA equipment had grown to a three-foot high heap. They had had to move it twice. First it was decided to evacuate the goods and they had moved them from the top of the peak to the trailhead leading back to 848. As the dump grew it was decided to blow it and everything had been moved again, now to a depression off the north crest. Boonierats from the 2d Plt had sporadically added to the dump all morning.

    The company CP directed the general movement from the south crest. Brooks conferred with De Barti and Randalph, then with FO then Thomaston then El Paso. By radio he reported to the Old Fox and the GreenMan. He returned to study the topo maps and plan his moves. The radios were squealing with new finds and more information all the time.

Brown was on the hook to the artillery on the firebase. "Ah, Armageddon Two, you had a secondary with that last dime-nickel," he called describing an explosion in the valley seemingly caused by a 105mm howitzer round detonating an enemy cache.

"Roger, Rover Four," the radio rasped.

2d Plt continued to hack at the bunker complex to the west. The slashhacking noise was considerably dampened by the vegetation but everyone in the valley knew where Alpha was. The soldiers of the 2d continued to explore and patrol deeper and lower and they continued to find additional fighting positions. "Frank," Brooks said to De Barti as he unfolded his topo map, "I want you and Pop to take a squad of your men down this ridge. Take two." Brooks traced a ridge on the map which descended to the west then looped and rose north for 600 meters to a third peak. "Be careful in the draw. Good ambush site. Don't go off the trail til you've reached that peak." He now pointed to the peak clearly visible through the thinner jungle vegetation of their own summit. "We've got a LOH coming on station to hover at your point. He'll come up on your freq." Brooks paused, turned to El Paso. "Thunder Two Six," El Paso answered without being asked. "Thanks," Brooks said and returned to De Barti. "Frank, you may hit the shit in that saddle. I think the LOH will make them dee-dee but . . . Come here and look." The two lieutenants walked off to the northwest.

Earlier in the morning 3d Plt had come down as far as the red ball in the draw just west of 848. They had set up ambush on the vertical rises on both sides of the draw and most of the men laid back, attempting to regain sleep lost on the last night of stand-down and by the 0430 wake-up. They were roused again by El Paso's message directing them to return to and secure the LZ on 848. "For a scout dog team," El Paso explained to Kinderly. No more needed be said. That was reason enough though everyone grumbled about having to retrace his steps. They had begun coming off the LZ when the mortars landed and had had to back up when the entire column pushed them up from below. They had descended into the jungle a second time when Whiteboy opened up and they had had to reclimb to the LZ. They came all the way to the draw this morning and now were going back up. And they would have to come back down again before nightfall. "What a fucked-up operation," Ridgefield lamented to Nahele.

As 3d Plt ascended east and 2d Plt descended west, a PsyOps Bird passed over, speakers blaring a *chieu hoi* message in Vietnamese. A LOH came on station, hovered at treetop level and led 2d Plt down their new trail. After a few minutes the LOH began spraying mini-gun fire all over the saddle west of the CP's peak and immediately the M-60s of the patrol opened up. Cherry froze at the first cracking shots but no one near him seemed even to hear. He monitored his radio. When Egan approached he was able to report, "Recon by fire." "Yeah," Egan nodded. Cherry walked to the west edge. The LOH was far enough down the hillside to be below him. His radio crackled with static and a report of negative results followed. 2d Plt continued the recon.

"How much water you got left?" Egan asked Cherry.

"Canteen and a half."

"You fucken cherry ass," Egan snarled. Egan was irritated. He had been thinking on and off all morning of his dream last night. He was angry about the spider incident and about having shrieked at Denhardt. That's what R&R does to ya, he kept telling himself. It freaks ya out. You can leave this shit but you can't come back. Egan set his eyes upon Cherry. "When was the last time you fired that weapon?" he asked indicating Cherry's M-16.

"I never fired this one," Cherry said. "I fired one at SERTS but we turned ours in up there. Top just gave me this one."

"Get up on the line." Egan pointed to the northeast edge of the peak where half a dozen soldiers were gathered. "Bring yer ammo. Mad minute."

"Where's that correspondent?" Numbnuts giggled when Cherry joined the group. "He oughta get a picture of me firin."

"Is he the guy," Cookie Frye asked cautiously, "ah, you know, the guy who wrote all them letters about My Lai?"

"That's the fucker," Numbnuts giggled.

"Shee-it," Happy Lairds chuckled nastily, "we oughta have him here with us. Bet he'd like some target practice. Bet I could shoot the camera from off his neck."

"You don't never see correspondents with the front troops," Numbnuts said. "He's sittin back ghostin with 3d Plt."

"Okay, fuckers," Egan snarled at them, eight all together.

Egan set his eyes on them all. He asked himself whether he should explain to this lame/lazy bunch that Caribski's letters were worth more to them than their words were worth to him but he resisted. Egan yelled at the top of his lungs, "Fire-in-the-hole . . . Fire-in-the-hole . . . Fire-in-the-hollll . . ."

All eight opened up. Beaford's M-60 led the loud bangchatter and Numbnuts' M-79 punctuated the noise. Cherry fired an entire clip on full automatic. He had never done that before. It was exciting. He ejected the magazine and reloaded and fired as fast as possible, feeling like a hero, spraying wildly at nothing. Egan grabbed his firing arm. "Put it on semi and try to hit somethin. This aint a carnival. It's practice." Cherry settled down, feeling good. Egan was right. Cherry picked out a tree 20 meters down the hill. He squeezed off a round. It missed. The others had settled down also. "About a foot to the left," Egan said from behind Cherry. Cherry tried again. "Yer way to the left," Egan said again. Cherry adjusted the rear sight and fired again. "Yer left about five inches," Egan said. Cherry adjusted the sight two more clicks. He fired and nicked the left edge. He adjusted one click, fired and hit dead center but higher than he had aimed. He lowered the front sight post a click. Right on. He picked out a twig at 25 meters and cut it in half. He turned and looked up at Egan. Egan smiled very slightly and moved off to Numbnuts, who was pumping out rounds from the hip. Egan got him to sit with the M-79, use the strap as a ranging device and pump his rounds out like a mini-mortar. Egan cut the mad minute off like turning off a tap. "Water run," he ordered.

Twelve men went on the water run, in lights, without rucksacks, nine from the 1st Plt and three from the 2d. They had collected all the empty canteens of both platoons which amounted to 137 one- and two-quart canteens. They humped down the trail between the new peak and 848. They passed through the rising pungent odor of the dead NVA soldier in his shallow mulch grave and moved down to the red ball. Up to that point it had been a piece of cake. They were loose, easy, happy, on familiar ground. Beaford and Smith were at point/slack. Then Moneski, Hall and Michaels. Cherry had gone to give the detail an RTO. Behind him was Greer, a black soldier from 2d Plt Cherry had never seen before, then Roberts and Sklar, Greer's buddies. At drag were Happy Lairds, Bo Denhardt and Polanski.

At the red ball the water run detail took a right, slowed,

tensed up, quieted and proceeded down with caution. They were
in an unpatrolled area. Beaford, Smith and the Monk were
veterans. They moved noiselessly and in slow smooth motions.
The trees about them were slashed with shrapnel from yesterday's
air strikes and from the artillery of last night and very early this
morning. All the smaller trees were splintered, many were cut in
half. At one point on the hill rising to their right there was a
large bare orange cliff where a bomb had avalanched a steep
section.

The trail was moist, smooth and clear. As it descended it
became muddier and in the mud there were fresh tracks. The
farther down they stepped the less apparent was the damage from
the shellings and the thicker the canopy. Beaford crouched down
to examine the tracks. He wasn't sure if they were yesterday's or
today's but he damn well wasn't going to stay on the red ball.
Smith and Moneski concurred. The detail paused. Moneski consulted his map. He backed up to Cherry, radioed El Paso then
led the detail right, off the trail, headed ten meters across a steep
vine-tangled face and descended until they came to the edge of a
tiny steep gorge. Water was trickling off the moss and algae-
green rock sides into a pool fifteen feet below. The pool, puddle,
was two feet long, a foot wide and perhaps eighteen inches deep.
It was filled with leaves and bugs and two tiny translucent
lizards.

Moneski signaled the detail into a loose perimeter ten to
twelve meters in diameter about the gorgehead then he and Hall
dropped down the slippery walls sliding on the moist stone and
falling to the bottom. Smith dropped halfway down and braced
himself on a small ledge. Michaels acted as runner. He collected
the empty canteens from the guards, brought them to the edge
and dropped them to Smitty who dropped them to the men in the
hole. The water men filled the canteens as quickly as possible
and tossed them back up to Smitty who tossed them to Michaels.
It was a slow process. It seemed to be taking forever. In the
gorge Monk became more and more nervous because there was
no exit. And Hall became nauseous from the air. It was like
being in the bottom of a well. Cherry sat alone by the gorgehead,
staring uphill, monitoring his radio.

3d Plt was back on 848 before the detail had filled half their
canteens. It had taken 3d less than an hour to reclimb the
familiar trail and circle the LZ. The bird with the dog team had
not arrived. The afternoon had become warm.

On the peak west of 848 a skeleton crew had been securing the perimeter. Now they all moved off below the south crest as Egan, Jackson and Silvers prepared the demolition to destroy the NVA equipment heaped on the far side.

"Hey Doc," Hill called to Doc Johnson, "you hear that music?"

"Yeah," Doc answered surprised. He looked around. Very faintly a melancholy melody seeped over the peak and down to them. "Hey," Doc called. "Hey, El Paso. Hey, tell them dumb shits ta shut off the radio."

"What radio?" El Paso called back. He had been on the hook with Calhoun of the 2d Plt monitoring 2d Plt's progress toward the next peak.

The music, Doc, Hill and El Paso were interrupted by Egan and Jackson yelling in unison at their lungs' best, "Fire-in-the-hole. Fire-in-the-hole. Fire-in-the-HOLLLlll . . ." and a tremendous concussion explosion sending dirt and fire and shrapnel and pieces of typewriter and mimeograph machine in a huge expanding cone out and up from the north face like an erupting volcano, followed immediately by at least one secondary explosion and smoke and dirt gravel rain falling noisily through the trees. Then silence. Then the forlorn crying music.

At the gorgehead Cherry had heard the music too. It was strange wailing music. Then the explosion. It shook the earth under him and he jumped up then squatted and reconcealed himself in the vegetation. Moneski rose up out of the well and grabbed him by the foot. "What the fuck was that?"

Cherry shook his head.

Moneski grabbed the radio handset grumbling he'd near shit his pants. He called El Paso. "Fire-in-the-hole," Moneski repeated handing the hook back to Cherry. "Why the fuck didn't you warn us?" Moneski mumbled and disappeared. Only half the canteens were filled.

A huey slick approached, descended and landed on the LZ on 848. A dog handler, a tracker and a German shepherd named Cherokee leaped from one side and hurried into the brush below the cleared peak. Four boonierats met the bird and with the doorgunner assisting, quickly unloaded eight cases of ammunition, explosives and supplies, a bag of mail, and a new radio and rucksack for Fernandez. A civilian photographer and his PIO escort, a cherry second lieutenant from 3d Brigade, ambled off the other side of the bird. The bird departed. It was to make several other drops about the valley then return in one hour for the photographer. This was becoming quite an operation. Not just a military correspondent, not just one civilian correspondent, but a civilian photographer with escort, two military correspondents, and Craig Caribski with escort. That was almost unheard of. The men of Company A had never seen correspondents in the boonies like this. On firebases, sure. Even forward firebases. But in the mountains? They loved it. The boonierats loved the attention.

3d Plt began breaking down the new supplies with a great show of panache. "Two cases of frags," Ridgefield called out.

"Two frags," Kinderly checked off on a fictitious list.

"Two cases Charlie-four plastic explosive," Ridgefield yelled.

"Two Charlie fours," Kinderly checked.

Snell and Nahele and McQueen got in the act, breaking the cases apart with great gusto. The photographer snapped photos like crazy or at least pretended to. They always had to spend half their time pretending to shoot the take-my-picture shots, until the men became bored and went back about their business as good soldiers must and allowed good photographers to get natural photos.

Don White, the platoon sergeant, broke down the small bag of mail, removed and distributed the letters for 3d Plt then told his 2d Sqd to hump back to the company position with the rest of the mail and as much extra ammo, frags and M-60 belts especially, as they could carry for the 1st and 2d Plts. Two squads would secure 848 until the bird returned.

Cherry had been set off by Moneski's admonition. "If the fuckers would just let you know what your job is beforehand," he cussed, "I'd be able to do it right. Do they expect me ta be a fucken mind reader?" He was pissed. He was dirty. He was hot. What am I doing here, anyway? he asked himself. I didn't even have to *be* in the army. I could have beaten the draft. Why didn't I? Cherry pondered that. Was it an act of rebellion against his parents? An assertion of independence? An opportunity for freedom from the city rut get-a-job life? Was he seeking the approval he knew parents and relatives secretly held for soldiers even if they no longer expressed it in 1970 America?

Smitty came up from the gorge. Michaels had already loaded Cherry down with ten quarts of water. Moneski and Hall came up. They looked filthy. Their fatigues were soaked with sweat. It must have been 100% humidity in the well. They saddled up, hefted their equipment and water, and moved out in almost the same order except now Cherry was behind Greer instead of Michaels. Moneski led them, directed them from behind the gun team, horizontally east from the waterhole, across a tiny crest, circling the hillside east then northeast. They stepped deliberately, placing their feet just before or just beyond twigs or leaves. Branches that crossed the narrow path were pushed aside by hand so as not to brush against one's fatigues and make noise. It was completely quiet. Branches were returned to their original position slowly, by hand, so the limbs would not snap back. Where broad brown and dry palm fans overhung the path to the height of only several feet the men gently squatted, then, on hands and knees, slid beneath the vegetation.

Cherry watched Greer closely. He tried to place his feet in Greer's footsteps. Cherry began noticing details about Greer. The man had a list of months written on the back of his helmet cover. In various shades of ink, all faded, even July, Cherry could see the first six months lined through. There was something about that that excited Cherry. Here was this soldier opening up his personal history to Cherry without being asked. Cherry decided he liked the man.

The patrol proceeded horizontally, perhaps registering a slight elevation gain, through thicker and thicker jungle. It was impossible to see five feet to either side. Tree trunks and boughs were choked by solid mats of vines. Some of the vines were as thick as human legs. Some vines had barbs that hooked onto shirts and the soldiers were continuously backing up to untangle themselves. They came through an even denser section then stopped. As Moneski had figured they had intersected the red ball. Again there were fresh signs of enemy activity. The red ball fell to the right gently and was visible for perhaps five meters. It rose to the left very steeply and was visible for perhaps three meters. The patrol froze. Moneski moved quietly to the front. He stepped out, crouched, looked up and down the leafy tunnel and stepped up. Beaford then Smith followed, maintaining an interval of six to eight feet. Between motions the riflemen sat very still on the path. "One at a time," Smitty signaled Hall. Hall paused for a minute then stepped out. Moneski was moving very slowly, staying in the brush on the left of the red ball. Michaels stepped out, signaled to Greer, "Wait. One at a time." There was no noise. Greer paused two minutes, stepped out, returned and told Cherry, "Wait one." On the red ball the detail inched forward.

Cherry sat down again. Through the vegetation he could see the red ball ascending from the right, crossing before him and disappearing up left. He waited for Greer's signal to advance. Nothing came. Greer disappeared. Cherry waited. A twig with two leaves on it was brushing Cherry's left arm. He waited. He turned slowly to the left and with the fingernails of his right hand he pinched the leaves off the twig. Things were so quiet he could hear his joints squeak as he returned his right hand to the trigger assembly of his M-16. His mind wandered. He felt impatient.

There aren't any birds out here, Cherry said to himself. I just noticed that. That really is peculiar. Lots of helicopters but no birds. Maybe they all left because they felt replaced by the mechanical flying machines. Cherry's mind wandered but his eyes were very aware of the red ball. Where the fuck did Greer go? Cherry began thinking about his brother. He thought about their motorcycles. They had once planned on running the moto-cross series at the upstate parks and tracks but then Victor had split for Canada. Cherry thought about some of the girls he knew and about McDonald's hamburgers. His mind would not stay on one thought. He began thinking about girls again. Damn, he was horny. He thought about Cathy and Judy. Then he thought about Linda. Linda. Was she still in Philadelphia? He planned his ravaging of her when he returned. Then he fantasized seducing the stewardess he'd met on the flight from New York to Seattle, seducing her while other passengers discreetly watched. What am I thinking? he thought. That's not me. I'm not like that.

Cherry looked across the trail, up the trail. He was conscious of his body and of the trail. Where the hell is Greer? They must be taking a break. Cherry turned around. The man behind him was sitting quietly, cleaning his fingernails. Cherry's mind no longer seemed to be functioning properly. He could not maintain a thought. His mind jumped and jittered impatiently. He had, it seemed, ten thoughts working at once, all struggling for dominance and failing. There was the trail. Wasn't he here to discover something about the elusive truths of the Vietnam Conflict? And Linda's body. And Victor. And his shoulders. God, they were sore. Cherry's watch was ticking. He could hear his heart pumping. He was aware of his thinking, thinking about his thinking about all these things. It was exhausting to be thinking so. He at once felt tired, physically and mentally, and yet excited, held in suspense. A twig to his right broke.

El Paso received the mail for the CP and 1st and 2d Plts from Spangler. He sorted it. He handed Brown a letter. There was a *San Francisco Chronicle* for the L-T and the July 27th issue of *Newsweek* for Silvers. He gave Cahalan the mail for 2d Plt and delivered the letters to 1st Plt personally. There was a letter for Jackson and one for Whiteboy and along with the magazine a small package for Silvers. "They didn't get it all sorted in the rear," El Paso said to Egan. "Maybe on next resupply. Ya know, fuckin REMFs can't do nothing right."

"They bring in the dogs?" Egan asked ignoring El Paso's comment.

"Just one. Brought out another civilian photographer."

"Good. That's just what the fuck we need."

"He aint stayin though. Bird's goina come back for him. Most a 3d's still up on the LZ with em."

"Can't these people ever do any fuckin thing right?"

"Who knows?" El Paso shrugged. "Hey, where's the Jew? His *mommy* sent him a package." Silvers was close by and he looked up guiltily. He knew what was coming. It came once a month. "Com'on Leon," El Paso cajoled, "let's see what *mommy* sent."

Egan and Jackson and Hoover and everybody close by were laughing and Silvers laughed too. When he had first arrived in-country it had been during the monsoon season. He had sent a description of the rains to his folks along with an explanation about immersion-foot. Immersion-foot was the army updated euphemism for trench-foot, a painful foot disorder resulting from prolonged exposure to wet in which the skin wrinkles and creases then layers begin separating leaving the foot raw. Every month since Leon's description, he had received a soft package from his mother.

"Come on, Leon," Hoover chimed in, "let's see em."

Silvers tore away the brown paper and held up two pair of bright yellow knee-high socks. He gave a half-hearted smile and sighed, "Mother!"

"Letter for Jax too," El Paso called. He enjoyed passing out the mail.

Jackson took the letter and looked at the envelope. It was from his brother-in-law. He put the letter in his helmet and returned to his perimeter position. It'll be jest like all them others, he told himself.

Brooks pretended to be studying the topo maps and the reports of contacts and enemy sightings. Things were turning up all around the valley. Charlie Company had found fighting positions with overhead cover on Hill 711 five kilometers west of Company A. Across the valley Bravo had found another red ball with signs of vehicular traffic, that could mean carriage-mounted .51 caliber machine guns or possibly 37mm anti-aircraft cannons or nothing more than a pushcart for rice. Recon was lying low, sending out patrols, not finding recent signs of enemy activity but finding old ARVN NDPs and some questionable material. Licking their wounds, Brooks thought. Only Delta had reported no sightings at all. They had come in on a peak on the north escarpment and had decided to come almost straight off the south face which was a cliff. No one, no NVA, would place positions there, Brooks thought. It would be too easily surrounded and then impossible to escape. And the GreenMan's pilot in the C & C bird with the GreenMan aboard had shot up a sampan on the river with unknown results.

Brooks stared at the maps and repeated the reports but now he was not aware he was doing it. He was thinking of Lila again, of their conflict and of conflict in general. He tried not to think about her. He attempted to supplant it with thoughts of the here and now but it didn't work. There was Lila and there was that thing bothering him and there was racial tension and there was war. They were all conflicts and he wanted to think about conflict causation but under it all there was that thing. The thing in Hawaii. Perhaps it had really begun with their first fight and with what happened afterward. Maybe, he thought, that was the origin of the Hawaii thing. It goes back a lot farther than those divorce papers, he said to himself. Farther back even than Hawaii or even than getting married. Man, he thought, so your gal's off with some Jody. So what. When you get back to the World you can slip into his AO and set up an MA. It won't mean a thing. How does Egan always say it? 'Don't mean nothin. Just say fuck it and drive on.' Yeah, it don't mean nothin. Goddamn Lila. Goddamn you. Goddamn, it's a lot easier to get into a woman's pants than it is into her head. Goddamn she knows how to hurt a person. She has the power to make me feel like shit. It's not her, Rufus, it's you. The conflict came with you. You brought it to this marriage. You bring it with you wherever you go. The causes of conflict between two people are the same as the causes of racial violence and of war. Goddamn, I wonder if that's true.

He could not get hold of his thoughts. Concepts began to crystallize then vanished. The thought production element of his brain was pumping out work faster than the analyzer element could handle it and a backup of ideas overwhelmed him. He recognized what was happening. He relaxed, took a few deep breaths. It was a perfectly beautiful day in the jungle. Well, maybe it was too warm. "Rufus," the lieutenant said to himself, "we must back up on our thoughts, back up on theory development, back up to the beginning and take this one step at a time. Think carefully. Be patient. The goal should be to develop a framework theory for conflict by careful elucidation of the concepts, correct analysis of the information available and patient resolving of the problem."

That thought made him feel very good. It gave him a clear guideline for his thinking task. *An Inquiry into Personal, Racial and International Conflict*, he titled it in his mind. Then, he said to himself, we'll get down to this Hawaii thing.

Shortly after Rufus and Lila met, he persuaded her to spend a weekend with him. She had refused to be at or near his school or with his jock friends—"like that Italian creep," she had scoffed—and that, perhaps was the real beginning. Brooks had been nearly broke. Lila was singing and painting and earning and had far more money left over after expenses than he did even with his assistance, ROTC pay and scholarship. And trying to get a date with this lady had been near impossible. She was always out with dudes with bread. "I've got two tickets to . . ." —what concert had it been—he began after finally catching her home. She said yes to it all much to his surprise. "Meet you at Keystone Korners at seven Friday," she said. And that had been that.

Dinner was delightful, the concert superb, all of it costly. Rufus had let one of his teammates reserve rooms for him. "It's gotta be cheap," he had told his friend, "but it can't look cheap." Rufus took Lila to the Kennedy Hotel down on the Embarcadero. It was the cheapest place in town. Rooms began at $7 and that was for a week. Not that his friend registered them for the cheapest room. He had paid $7 for two nights. Rufus and

Lila came in late, through the darkened lobby, a ten-foot-square room with a desk, up the dimly lighted stairs and down the dark narrow hallway. He half carried her as she nuzzled her nose into his ear. He opened the door. Without turning on the light, with only indirect lighting from the street coming through the window, he undressed her and she tore his clothes away. She was a madwoman, a crazed woman. He could not get enough of her or she of him, especially she of him. After, as he slept, tried to sleep, she stirred and moaned faintly and stimulated herself.

"This isn't a bad place," he joked and laughed the next morning, happy, cheerful, anticipating the morning, afternoon and night to come.

"This is a filthy trap," she had growled getting her first good look around. There wasn't even a shower in the bath. She hadn't noticed that before. The showers were down the hall. She went to inspect them and returned yelling, "This stinking hole's filled with bums and fags." She scurried away from his outstretched hands. "No way college boy. You bring your hookers here." She was indignant. He couldn't understand it. It caused their first fight. She called a cab and left.

Rufus had paid for the room for two nights. He stayed. Indeed the hotel proved to be infested with cockroaches and frequented by homosexuals. That night, alone, depressed, he allowed a man to pick him up. It was the first and last time. The man was a short-order cook. He invited Rufus to a birthday party at the Club 77. "Hey, I'm game," Rufus said. He could not believe what he saw. Not the guys kissing and squeezing so much, that he expected, but the food. The club was closed except to regulars and their dates. The bar was open, booze flowed freely, and in back the buffet was two eight-foot tables end-to-end stacked with mounds of food. In the center of the table there was a cake Rufus would swear was five feet in diameter and four feet high. All this just for allowing some white fag to rub his buns.

For a month after that weekend Brooks tried to get a date with Lila, even for lunch. He apologized profusely over the phone. He dated no one else. The homosexual called him several times but he refused to even talk to the man. Rufus finally arranged to see Lila but she broke the date. He tried again, then again and again. He needed her badly but every date made was broken. Finally they had it out.

"Look, you want to know what's going on," he yelled at

her. "I'll tell you what's going on. I've been trying to get a date with you for a month. That's right, Lady, a month. Every time I phone you're all booked up and you say, 'call me back.' But every time I call you you always have a sick girl friend to take care of or something. So I, like a sucker, say, 'What about the next day or the next?' and you say, 'Well I'm going sailing on Saturday and it's going to run into Sunday with the regatta and I'll be too tired Monday. Why don't you call me on Tuesday?' Lady, that's been going on all month. Lady, you just go off with your rich boyfriends. I wish you the best. That's right. I really do. I'm happy to have known you."

"My goodness," Lila said coldly, nastily. "You're jealous. You really are, aren't you? You think just because we've gone out you own me. Aren't we getting awfully possessive? Do you think you own every woman that lets you touch her? You bastards are all alike. You lay a guy once and he thinks he owns you."

"At least, Lady, I'm only out with one woman at a time. How many men do you have chasing you, hanging around cause you're in heat?"

"Why you lousy . . . lousy . . . honky's fag." That's what she said. He could hear her say it now. ". . . honky's fag. You jive with them cocksuckers in Fag Hilton." He stopped. The fight had passed. Making up from the fight had been terrific. He probably would never have thought of it again had it not been for Hawaii and then the divorce papers.

Rufus and Lila dated more and more frequently and finally exclusively. At times she bickered and complained that she was being lost in the narrowly directed course his life was taking but he was always able to overcome her arguments with an intellectual logic she could not refute. And he was so happy. That meant a lot to her. He brought enough love to their relationship for the two of them. They fought but they always made up and they had such good times. They married and soon he was on active duty.

Brooks craned his neck. Then what happened? he thought. Brooks cleared his mind. He breathed deeply and said to himself, the roots of conflict and the expansion and escalation to violence are similar whether interpersonal or international. That's the beginning of the answer. Perhaps conflicts caused by . . .

Brooks' thoughts were interrupted by the crackbarking of an M-16 close by. Then the popping of an AK, two AKs opening up. Then more 16s.

*   *   *

Cherry sat motionless for what seemed like a year. Behind him Roberts had also heard the twig snap. Cherry went rigid. The blood in his veins seemed to squeak, his tired bones and joints creaked, his watch ticked thunderously. Slowly, slower than he had ever moved in his life, he turned right. He looked behind him, moving only his eyes. Roberts had stopped cleaning his fingernails and was watching him.

Someone was coming up the trail. Cherry reached down with his left hand and silently moved the selector of his M-16 from safe through semi-automatic to automatic. Very slowly he lifted his rifle to his shoulder. He could feel his arms quivering, his stomach cramping. He examined the trail below him, scrutinizing every leaf. Again he heard something. A footstep.

His mind clicked to being a soldier. The first general order shot over his tongue. "I will guard everything within the limits of my post and quit my post only when properly relieved."

Roberts could not see the red ball from where he sat but he too heard the approach and he aimed his rifle toward the noise. The second man behind Cherry was beyond the sight of either of the two poised with their weapons.

Throw a frag, flashed through Cherry's thoughts. Throw a frag. Goddamn it, I don't have a frag. Training took over. Cherry had an instantaneous flash of an entire platoon on an infiltration exercise. The men low-crawled slowly through the woods at Ft. Dix. There were thirty men crawling and it was difficult to tell anyone was there at all.

From the depths of the trail, amidst the vines and brush, Cherry could distinguish a man's shoulder. Then a head and chest. Cherry waited. The man approached with extreme caution. He was carrying an AK-47 automatic rifle. He wore Ho Chi Minh sandals, khaki shorts and shirt and a pith helmet.

Go away! Cherry's mind ordered the soldier. Do something. Still the man approached. He was less than twenty feet away. With underhand beckoning typical of Vietnamese he motioned for someone to his rear to come forward.

Get the fuck outa there! Oh, God. Cherry was furious and frightened. Why me? If Egan were here he'd know what to do. Maybe he's South Vietnamese.

The soldier moved forward another step and all thoughts vanished from Cherry's mind. Cherry's arms steadied, the soldier's nose rested above the front sight post of Cherry's M-16. The man stepped forward into clear view. Slowly, Cherry squeezed the trigger and a volley of eight rapid shots cracked from his weapon. Instantly from below the first enemy soldier, two AK-47 rifles discharged long volleys of explosive bursts. The AK fire hit to Cherry's right and left and one round smashed into the dirt below his left foot.

Again Cherry squeezed, this time aiming only at the sound of the enemy rifles. His and Roberts' M-16s drilled the trail and jungle below them cutting branches and leaves. Cherry ejected the magazine and immediately inserted another and continued firing until the AK fire stopped. The action seemed to take minutes but Cherry knew it was only seconds. Cherry retreated toward Roberts. He dove and lay prone on his stomach. Peering from behind a tree he pointed his weapon toward the last burst of enemy fire. His breathing was deep and quick. Roberts leaped and set up beside Cherry. Sklar, Lairds, Denhardt and Polanski closed into a defensive ring, all searching the jungle.

"What'd ya see?"

"I got a dink," Cherry babbled frantically. "I saw him fall."

"Shhh," Roberts ordered. Again they waited.

"Where's everybody else?" Roberts asked quietly.

"I don't know," Cherry whispered. "They're up the hill. I've been waiting for them to . . ."

He was interrupted by Moneski's voice shouting from about forty meters up the red ball. "It's us. Don't fire. Anybody hurt? We're comin down."

CHAPTER

18

"Let's go over it again," Brooks said to Cherry, Roberts and Moneski. All four had cigarettes going.

It was late afternoon. The last of the patrols were just returning to the company position. The men who had remained behind had already dug foxholes and most had eaten. The returnees ate, rested for a few minutes, then picked and shoveled at the resisting earth. It was a repeat of the motions from the day before except this time it was more complex and more confused and they were more tired. The boonierats were back in the boonies without any vestige of REMF mentality.

"Dude from 1st Plt got'm a gook," they whispered to each other. "They sayin he blew the dink's head clean off." Even the two squads from 3d Plt which had remained on 848 were whispering it back and forth. "New cherry in 1st Plt KIAd one NVA." It excited them all.

The clearing of fields of fire and the digging in continued. Lt. Hoyden, FO, called in DT and H & I coordinates. De Barti and Thomaston checked the NDP shape to insure overlapping fire then chose the men for LPs.

"Tell me exactly what you saw," Brooks said to Cherry. Moneski had already traced the red ball's location on Brooks' map. "Which way were they heading?"

"He was coming straight up the trail," Cherry said. Cherry's eyes were like those of a deer run at night by dogs and frozen in the powerful beam of a poacher's light.

268

"He? I thought there were two. Now, try to remember," Brooks interrogated.

"There must a been two," Cherry said. "I think I saw two but I don't remember seeing the second one."

Egan and Thomaston had come to the CP and were now squatting behind Cherry. Thomaston kept touching his M-16 which he carried in his left hand. Egan massaged a frag on his belt. "I'm gettin too short for this shit," Thomaston said.

"How many days you got now?" Egan asked him.

"Twenty-seven en a wake-up," Thomaston said.

"Twenty-four en a wake-up, you cherry," Egan laughed.

"There was at least three," Roberts said.

"Did you see them?" the L-T asked.

"I didn't see nothin but I heard two AKs open up and that first dink woant firin."

"God," Cherry said. "I felt like a subject in a sensory deprivation experiment. I felt like I was hallucinating."

"Close your eyes and try to picture it," Brooks said. "What did the second man look like? What was he carrying?"

Cherry shut his eyes. "We were sitting there for about twenty minutes and I was very conscious of the sounds my, ah . . . my watch was like ticking real loud and I heard a twig snap."

"I heard it too," Roberts said.

"Try to see the second man," Brooks encouraged.

"I saw this guy. He had shorts on and he had a rifle with a wood stock. I lifted my 16. Then I brought it back down and switched the selector to automatic."

"Yeah. I watched him do that," Roberts said. "So I did the same."

"He kept coming. He's motioning like this with his left hand." Cherry waved his left hand back and forth behind and below his hip.

"Can you see his hand?" Brooks asked.

"No," Cherry said. "All I can see are his eyes." Cherry opened his eyes and jerked around quickly and started to rise.

"It's okay," Brooks stopped him. Cherry looked at Brooks, through Brooks, beyond Brooks. "It's okay," Brooks said more casually. "Look, jungle tactics are basically two-dimensional problems—time and coordinates. We've got to work things so we don't run into the enemy when he's set up. We want to come up behind him or we want him to walk into us when we're set-up. If he second-guesses us we're in a world of hurt. That's why it's important you remember every detail.''

Cherry repeated the part about two enemy rifles opening up and the hand signal the first man had made but he froze up when he tried to remember anything beyond looking into the first man's eyes.

"What happened when you went down there?" Brooks asked Moneski.

"I took half the squad down to check it out," Moneski said, "and Smitty pumped another six or eight rounds inta him."

"Was he alive?" Brooks asked.

"I don't know but he wasn't when Smitty finished. We stripped him and took his bag an weapon an skyed."

"He didn't bleed much," Roberts said. "Never saw nothin like it. First round musta stopped his heart cause he just had all these little holes in him but there wasn't much blood. They coulda been made by leeches. Cept his head."

"He was one big gook," Moneski said. "He musta stood five-ten, maybe even six foot. I bet he was Chinese. He was clean too. And he had a fresh haircut, I think. Least what was left of his head looked fresh cut. We didn't stay there long. I think the dinks dee-deed too."

"He was carryin about twenty-five pounds of rice," Egan said from outside the circle. "Rice, one lacquered gook rice bowl, two spoons, two extra uniforms, a can of AK rounds, six Chi-com frags, gas mask, sleeping blanket and a bunch of papers. That's a lotta shit for a dink dude on patrol."

"They're movin," Thomaston said.

"Maybe. Maybe not," Brooks said. "He may have been the rice bearer for his squad. They may have been a mortar squad and the men behind him might have had the tube and base plate."

"I think they're movin back in here," Thomaston said.

"Maybe they were goina mortar us," Egan said.

"Yeah. Maybe. Damn, I wish I knew what that second man was carrying. Cherry," Brooks said, "I want you to think about it. If you remember anything let me know immediately."

"Yes Sir," Cherry said meekly. He stood.

Egan rose and put his hand on Cherry's arm. "Go down to our spot," he said. "I set up behind Jax, over there. You'll see it." Cherry lit another cigarette.

* * *

The two squads from 3d Plt did not reach the NDP until 1830 hours. It was cooling and clouding up as they trudged in. The valley was thick with fog, the white mass rising steadily up the escarpments. Above, the sky was clear. The breeze rising from the valley carried wisps of the fog which tumbled about the peaks like ghosts and vanished into the drier air.

The helicopter that was to have picked up the civilian photographer from 848 had been hit by small arms fire while leaving Bravo Company and it had flown directly back to Camp Evans to have the damage assessed. The squads had no choice but to wait until the GreenMan's C & C bird landed and picked up the photographer and his escort. By then it was 1700 and the squads had had to hump to the new NDP and with double and triple ammunition loads. The trail had become more slippery with use and they struggled hard to be silent, moving at double time, trying to be off the trail before dark. When they marched in and dropped their rucks and the extra ammo they were drenched with jungle slimesweat head to foot. The green canvas of their boots was black with wet and white-ringed with salt stains. Armpits and backs and crotches were soggy. They collapsed silently about the CP.

With them were the dog handler and the dog. If the men of 3d Plt were sweat-drenched and breathing hard from the hump, the dog handler was doubly soaked and winded. He had not known which unit he would be sent to when he had packed his rucksack and, as was scout dog team procedure, he carried four days' rations for himself plus four days' for the dog. He carried extra ammo, not trusting some units to resupply him, knowing he would be at point behind the dog on most moves, on the worst moves. He also carried twenty quarts of water, another forty pounds. He sat, said not a single word, not even to report in to the company commander. The dog lay by his side, alert, relaxed, silent. The lightest ruck was carried by the civilian correspondent, Caribski, who had spent the past two days with 3d Plt but now wished to travel with the company CP. He looked weary and wet and spoke little though he listened to everything happening in and about the CP. His escort, the PIO officer from 3d Brigade, looked scared and let it be known he did not like being in the bush. The military correspondents, Lamonte and George, set up a separate sleeping position just beyond the CP. Lamonte removed the camera from his neck and went about photographing every detail of field life. George sat alone trying to overhear the CP talk and finally fell asleep.

The weird lonely music again seeped up from the valley. "What the hell is that?" Snell uttered irritably as he and Ridge-field and Nahele came to socialize at the CP.

"That is traditional Vietnamese funeral music," Minh answered. He was studying and translating the letters and documents from Cherry's KIA.

Snell looked at Ridgefield then Nahele and all three whispered in unison, "Funeral music!"

"Oh yes," Minh smiled. "It comes from 3d Brigade Psychological Operations helicopter. They try to warn the enemy that we are coming to get them."

"Well shee-it," Doc said. "Here all aftanoon I thinkin some dude got a radio. You know what I mean? Shee-it. I couldn't believe a dude be humpin a radio out here."

"Minh," Brooks called over, "just what have they been saying all afternoon?"

"They are saying SKYHAWKS is a mean battalion," Minh smiled. "They are saying Screaming Eagle soldiers are coming down from the hills to clean up the valley and that NVA soldiers should surrender."

Jackson dug a two-man foxhole and arranged a sleeping area while Silvers pulled guard ten meters below in an old NVA fighting position. When Jax finished digging he went down and relieved Silvers. It was unusual to separate the two positions by that great a distance but the slope on the perimeter forced them to move up for sleeping. Jax slipped his legs into the tiny NVA hole. He laid his M-16 across his thighs and laid out two bandoleers of magazines and four frags. Silvers had left him two claymores which they agreed should not be deployed until it became darker. Jax removed his helmet and from it took the unopened letter from his brother-in-law. The envelope was soiled and perspiration from Jackson's head had caused part of the return address to run blue-black. Jax removed his bayonet from its sheath at his left calf. He slid the blade gently below the envelope flap and split the paper.

August 4, 1970

Dear Brother Billie,

Our people have suffered too greatly for too long a time. They suffer more greatly now as a result of families being disrupted by that filthy Vietnam War. Your own lovely wife is with child as you foolishly, pathetically play soldier-slave to white men in a white man's racist imperialist war. It is impossible for you to support your family on a soldier's pay. Your wife suffers. All our women suffer. Your sweet sister suffers but not like your wife. Your sister's man is home, your wife's man is gone. Black women suffer from discrimination in jobs and education. Without their men they cannot, they are not allowed in this society, to support themselves.

Billie, the situation is critical. Your Black Brothers and Sisters in the United States are opposed to the war in Vietnam. We want our troops to return home. Nixon escalates the war. Out of one side of his foul mouth he talks peace and with a forked-tongue he orders our troops into Cambodia. American Blacks know the president does not care what we think, what we want or what we need. He's playing games with us. The military, big business, the government, they are all controlled by white racists. From us they want only our votes and our money. Nay, Brother Billie, they want one thing more—they want our beautiful Black children to fight their racist unjust war. Our Black Brothers carry a share of the Vietnam burden disproportionate to our percentage in America or our percentage in the army. Blacks sustain casualties out of all relation to their numbers. Doesn't that tell you something?

We've had it. We are tired of being used. We pay taxes so white pigs can murder our yellow Asian brothers or force them to defend themselves by slaughtering Black Americans. Fuck Nixon's War. Fuck the bombing and killing of our oppressed Asian brothers. Say No.

My brother, we are veterans, we are soldiers, we are civilians. We believe the time has come for all Blacks and Yellows and Browns to unite in our common struggle against repression. The white government of the United States orders Asians murdered, calls out troops against its own people, shoots its own students. Systematically the pig machine oppresses Black people, forces them into economic abasement and injects propaganda and prejudice into every corner of the white majority community. This pig machine has propagated a vengeful myth of its own altruism and with that myth it justifies the destruction of Vietnamese hamlets.

Nixon has played a game on the people. Congress and the courts have become unfunctional. People are fed officialese, federalese double-talk from the highest levels. And the press. What is its function? What's being reported has nothing to do with what's really happening.

Vietnam is all lies. The motherfuckers in this administration want us to believe the war can't be stopped, that the world situation is so complex if we pull out it will be like pulling the plug in a bathtub and America is the water. They say they're trying to negotiate. They say the North Vietnamese are liars. That's lies. The war can be ended now, today. You could be back here with your wife in a week. If that low-down dirty motherfucker Nixon wanted to stop the war all he has to do is call the pigs in the Pentagon and say, 'Pigs, bring the troops home.' Let the Vietnamese people rebuild their own country the way they want it, not the way we want it. That's all the fucker's got to say. And if he don't say it, Billie, then he's going to burn. He's going to burn with all them white racist pigs that keep him up there.

Think about it. Rap about it. Soon we will strike. Brother Billie, I am calling on you to join Black America. Join me, my Brother. Don't take orders. Strike! Rap with your fellow soldiers. Get them all to boycott the war from where it will hurt the white racist machine most. State-side GIs are protesting. Blacks are leading the underground. The revolution is coming. It is at hand.

                                                Marcus X

P.S. Billie, my brother-in-law and in-blood, I want you to know we all here are concerned for your safety. Also your father is ill. I think he would rest easier if his son was home. I know your sister and I would feel better with you here. And your wife is concerned for you and your child. Pap's body has been broken and worn out by slaving for

white pigs all his life. All his life he has carried the guilt
of his Blackness, ashamed and humbled wherever he went.
Do you remember crossing through the swamps to watch
he and my uncle the year they were shackled in a road
gang. They were puny and unfighting in their loathsome
Blackness, guilty and doing penance with shovels and rock
hammers for their Blackness. Billie, be proud. They will
kill you if they can. They will kill you either outright or
within your living body IF YOU ALLOW IT. If you wish
to be a soldier, be a soldier with us. Come home. Your
wife and father and your people need you.

The letter ended there. Jax quickly scanned the jungle before him then reread the postscript. That was new. Marcus
always talked about burning the government but never before
had he mentioned Pap. Jax tore the postscript from the letter and
stuck the paper in his helmet. A barely perceptible welling
choked him. He folded the letter in half and placed it on the
ground so it stood like a tent. He took a book of matches from
his pocket and burned the letter. He scattered the ashes and
reburned the few leaves of paper that had not been consumed in
the original fire. He rescattered the ashes in standard boonierat
procedure for destroying written material which might prove
somehow useful to the enemy.

Cherry sat on the ground by his rucksack, sat with his knees
drawn up to his chest, his hands tightly around his boots. He was
in the midst of shattered palm fans and branches. His rifle lay in
the brush out of reach. Egan had already dug their foxhole.
Cherry sat. A shiver ran up his spine. He closed his eyes and put
his face into the crook of his arm. He moved his face to his
knees and put his hands over his ears trying to close out the
activity around him. He let his body slump back beneath the
clutter of vegetation.

Around him men were eating or smoking. Only a few were
still digging. He closed his eyes more tightly. He could still see
that face. The man stepped forward slowly, cautiously. He moved
silently, a good jungle soldier. Cherry could see the man's eyes,
his straight black hair, his alert yet relaxed unsuspecting face.
The soldier stepped forward eliminating much of his jungle
cover. He continued to approach, up the red ball. Cherry could
see him clearly, his dark eyes clearly. Cherry could see the

soldier's face above the sight of his own weapon. "Our Father,
Who art in heaven," Cherry began mumbling, "hallowed be
Thy Name, Thy kingdom come, Thy will be done, on earth as it
is in heaven . . ."

"Hey, Cherry," Numbnuts called approaching him from
the perimeter.

"You can't call him Cherry no more," Silvers called up.

"Right on," Numbnuts said now standing just outside
Cherry's clump of brush. "What's your name?"

"We could call him Dago," Silvers said.

"That's okay," Cherry replied sitting up, "I'm kinda useta
Cherry."

"Well shee-it," Numbnuts said sticking out his hand.
"Congratulations, Cherry." He was exuberant. "Hey, how was
it down there? I heard you blew his head clean off." Numbnuts
spoke quickly, with a big smile. "Jesus, I wish I'd been there.
Maybe we coulda got another gook. Ya know, I coulda dropped
a coupla thumper rounds behind em. Bet that woulda sent those
bastards scatterin."

Cherry looked at him while he spoke. Numbnuts' hand was
still outstretched. Cherry looked into Numbnuts' eyes then he
turned away.

"I gotta dig in yet," Numbnuts shrugged. He stood waiting
for Cherry to say something, stood there nervously for half a
minute then mumbled as he left, "Jesus. If I'd only been there
with my thumper."

Numbnuts walked down to Silvers and said to the squad
leader, "What the fuck's the matter with him? What's he think
they sent him over here for, ta kiss gook ass? Man, we're s'pose
ta kill people."

Cherry lay back again. He closed his eyes again. Again he
could see the NVA soldier behind the thick vegetation. Again he
prayed.

Silvers put his hand on Cherry's leg. Cherry startled, stared
up savagely. "Take it easy, Breeze," Silvers said soothingly.
Cherry slumped back. "Take it easy, Man," Silvers repeated.
"If it'll make you feel better you probably saved a lot of our
lives. You probably busted up their party for us tonight."

Cherry took a pack of cigarettes Egan had given him from
his fatigue shirt pocket. He pulled two cigarettes from the pack,
stuck one behind his right ear and lit the other. Then he shook
his head.

"It's okay," Silvers reassured him again.

"I could a just shot him in the leg," Cherry said. "I didn't have to kill him."

"I don't know," Silvers said. "I've never been in that position. The whole time I been over here I never've seen a live gook. That's no shit. I been in the boonies seven months and I never've seen a live one." Silvers spoke slowly, soothingly. "I've seen maybe a hundred dead ones. I don't know if I ever shot any. There's a good chance I may have but I never had any in my sights. Ya know how it is during a firefight. You just fire into the brush with everybody else. When it's all over, maybe there'd be a body."

"Why are you saying this to me?" Cherry asked him quietly.

"I guess I've been watchin you," Silvers said. "I feel like I've known you for a long time. Like you were my cousin back in the World." Cherry sighed. Silvers continued. "If I'd just got here and just fired up someone I think I'd want someone to talk to."

"Thanks," Cherry said simply. He wanted to return the gesture to Silvers, felt he had to share something with him. At the same time he wanted to be left alone. He just did not wish to think or to be. He wanted to melt away.

"How far should one go to support other human beings?" Silvers asked. "How far should one go to help another striving for freedom from political or economic or religious repression?"

"I don't know," Cherry said apathetically.

"That's really what this is all about, you know?"

"Do you know what I was thinking?" Cherry asked. "I was thinking there's a meaning to all this. Maybe every man creates his own meaning. Maybe every man's his own God."

"No, I don't think so," Silvers said. "There's a balance between fighting and giving way. Between supporting others and letting others be trampled. My mother's side of the family was in Germany in the thirties and they yielded and they suffered in the forties. That was brother against brother. They were as German then as I'm American now. Everybody just sat back and appeased the Nazis. At some point a man, a people, have to stand up and fight."

Silvers left. Egan was sitting next to Cherry. Somehow he had arrived, seated himself and removed a can of Cs from his

ruck and begun eating, all completely silent and undetected.
"Don't mean a fuckin thing," Egan said nodding toward Silvers.

Cherry startled again. "Where'd you come from?"

"CP."

"When?"

"Couple minutes ago." It was becoming dark under the
canopy. Cherry could still see the perimeter guards but all color
had faded and now everything was gray—Light and noise discipline automatically went into effect—boonierats cupped their
cigarettes as they smoked, the digging stopped, voices lowered.
Egan continued eating something from the C-rat can. He had not
heated it. When he finished he cut the bottom from the can and
crushed the tin. Then he checked Cherry's radio. He said nothing.
That increased Cherry's jitters. Cherry had even waited for Egan
before eating, expecting to help prepare a meal. Now Egan was
finished.

Egan removed from his rucksack the letter he had been
writing to Stephanie. He read the last lines and began writing
again. As he wrote it became darker and darker. Cherry sat still
beside him and in the advancing darkness Egan seemed to fade,
dissolve, until his only presence was the faint sound of his
writing.

"How can you do that?" Cherry whispered.

"Do what?" Egan whispered back.

"Write. I can't see a thing." Cherry was very cautious
about the volume of his voice.

"Why do you have to see it?" Egan said. He sounded very
relaxed.

"How can you write without seeing it?" Cherry asked
again.

"I know what it looks like," Egan answered. "I know
where the paper is and where my hand is so I know what it looks
like."

"You got all the answers to this place, don't you?"

"What?" Egan said.

"You got all the fuckin answers, don't you?" Cherry accused.
"What would you a done where I was today?"

"Ssshhh. Keep it down. You mean on the water run?"

"Yeah."

"I don't know. I wasn't there."

"I could a shot him in the leg. I didn't have to kill him."

"You could be dead too."

"I could a just nicked him. I killed him. I killed a man today."

"You killed a soldier," Egan said softly. "Since when is a soldier a man?"

"By comin here," Cherry lamented, "I said I wanted to kill a man. That not only do I condone killing but that I actively support . . . wanted to kill. I think I always knew that too. I just fooled myself into thinking I came here to observe this."

"You tryin ta be the good guy?" Egan said snidely.

"I didn't have to kill him. I think I must of wanted to kill."

"You're gettin flaky."

"I don't have the right to play God over another man. Nobody's got that right. I actively supported this killing today. This genocide."

"Where'd you say you were from?" Egan interrupted.

"Connecticut. Bridgeport." Cherry said the words deliberately, slowly. He had been working himself toward a frenzy.

"Northeast? Industrial city?"

"Yeah."

"Arms?"

"Ah . . . I think so. Yeah, sure. Sikorsky Helicopter. Avco Lycoming. They make the engines for the Hueys."

"Colt? M-16s?"

"No. That's in Hartford."

"Lots a war industry jobs in Bridgeport and in Connecticut though?"

"Yeah."

"Is building weapons actively supporting and wanting to kill?"

"I don't know. That's different."

"Ever know anyone who said no to doin their job?"

"Yeah. My brother Vic split for Canada when they tried to draft him."

"Give the fucker my regards. I can respect that. I can't respect the fuckers makin weapons then callin us baby burners. They eat my shit."

"I killed a man in cold blood. I coulda screamed. I coulda fired high."

"You'd be dead. Look asshole, this is a clean war out here. There's no villes, no women, no children. No civilians. You got friendly forces and enemy forces. There's no My Lais up here. When someone's killed he's a combatant. And whether he wanted to be here or not he decided to condone the rules of the game and he best ass goina abide by the consequences.''

·"Shee-it.''

"That's the way it is, Breeze. Nice-en-clean. Nobody here but soldiers. Man-to-man. You beat your man today. Maybe he'll beat you tomorrow.''

"Fuck you.''

"Ha. Can't see gettin blown away for a piece a land nobody wants, huh?''

"That's right.''

"Well, get yer fuckin weapon then.''

"Lamonte,'' Brooks whispered. In the dark he had left the CP and walked the six or seven meters to Lamonte and George's sleeping position.

"Yes Sir,'' Lamonte answered. George was surprised the commander knew their position.

"Lamonte, are you and George on the clearance record at the TOC?''

"Hell yes.''

"With 3d Brigade?'' Brooks questioned.

"Hell no,'' Lamonte muttered. "1st Brigade.''

"We've been opconned to 3d. They can't find a copy of your security clearance. The Old Fox wants me to confiscate your film and send you in with first resupply.''

"Confiscate my film? What's that asshole think we're doin out here? You gotta be kiddin.''

"Nope. That's what they told me.''

"Aw, L-T. You know me. Can't you tell them to check it out with Division PIO? We're on record with Division.''

"They said they did. Division didn't know you were out with a 3d Brigade unit, they said. I told them you travel with us all the time. They said not in 3d Brigade's AO.''

"Aw fer Chrissake.''

"Lamonte, it's nothing to worry about. 3d Brigade's just pulling a power play because they think you'll scoop their story.''

"Oh, fuck this shit. I been humpin two days out here. Come in on the CA. Workin my ass off to get some decent shots and they want to confiscate my film.'' Caribski, the correspondent, crept closer to get the story. Brooks returned to the CP, and Lamonte and George and Caribski and the PIO escort from 3d Brigade discussed the situation and Caribski and Lamonte agreed to meet in the rear to discuss censorship. Then they all crept over to the CP for the nightly meeting.

The ground mist was thickening and in lungs the heavy moisture combined with cigarette smoke residue. Tiny muffled coughs sporadically broke the stillness at the CP. It was dark and impossible to see. The moon had just begun rising. Behind the dense cloud cover the moon was gray-yellow, amorphous. With the exception of Egan, Jackson and Thomaston, all the platoon leaders and platoon sergeants and the regulars were assembled. Cahalan recited a review of the day's intelligence. "At 0640 we discovered a bunker complex comprised of approximately 50 bunkers with overhead cover and 150 fighting positions," Cahalan said. "The complex appeared to be complete on only three sides of the hill. All bunkers with overhead cover were destroyed along with significant amounts of enemy ammunition and equipment.

"Intelligence reports from battalion say we are about sitting in the middle of the 5th Infantry Battalion of the 812th NVA Regiment." Cahalan paused. There was a round of muffled coughs. "Brigade reports a definite troop flow between this valley and the Firebase O'Reilly area. They say they're not sure which way the major flow is going."

"That figures," Egan said from outside the circle. He, Thomaston and Jax had approached undetected in the darkness. "They don't know their ass from a hole in the ground."

"Shut up, Sergeant," Caldwell ordered.

Cahalan continued. "Brigade figures the dink we got today was part of the flow. A LOH fired up a sampan on the river at 131324, that's about a klick en a half downriver from that big tree that sticks up. Aircraft from 2d of the 17th spotted an estimated two companies of opposition three klicks west of here. Air strikes and artillery were employed with unknown results. Bravo engaged three gooks. They followed blood trails until dusk with unknown results."

"Sir," Pop Randalph whispered in his high hoarse voice. "Sir, I bet they goan hit us tonight."

"Probe us," Egan said. "They'll probe us first. They don't know enough about us yet. They'll probe us to figure out our setup and number."

"It's my feeling," Brooks said quietly, "they're withdrawing right now because we're an unknown element."

"Yeah," Egan agreed. "They'll want to probe us first."

"We've had a lot of air activity," FO inserted. "And you've been patrolling all over the place at once and still maintaining people here in their complex. They may think there's more of us than there is. They know we had people here today and over at the LZ and on that peak to the november whiskey. My guess is they think we've got two companies right here. We've had enough birds to bring in two companies."

"So they're pulling back," Brooks said. "Pulling back to pick at us, nibble on our flanks, then dig in later."

"If that was a mortar squad the water run shot up this afternoon," Thomaston spoke slowly, "they're probably from that infantry battalion. Nguyen's being pushed. He's being pushed down and concentrated. He's making a strategic withdrawal. He's going to stop and fight someplace."

Caldwell coughed. "Why don't they just bring in the B-52s and cave the valley in?"

"Hey," Brooks said. "Listen. We'll work west down this ridge first then go down there, maybe cross the river and work the other side of the valley coming east. We'll be real cool and spiral down toward that knoll in the valley floor and take a look. GreenMan's made that our ultimate objective."

"That's one fuck of a hump, Mista," Doc warned.

"We don't have to jump right in there," Brooks said, "but we're going to move quick. We will move a lot. I don't want to get bogged down on tee-tee caches while they snipe us to pieces. Let's try to keep up the illusion that there's two hundred of us here."

While the meeting was in progress Minh had been analyzing the documents taken from the NVA soldier Cherry had killed. Minh had been just outside the CP circle. When darkness came he covered himself with two ponchos and continued reading and translating by flashlight. Two men had been stationed beside him to insure that no light escaped from the poncho hootch. Minh emerged into the meeting. "Lieutenant," Minh called softly to Brooks.

"Minh," Brooks looked toward the sound of the tonal voice in the dark, "have you found anything in those docs?"

"Oh, yes Sir," Minh said. "Lieutenant, I believe this man to be an important honcho. He was to carry instructions from the 7th NVA Front to the K-19 Sapper Battalion. The documents speak highly of the K-19 Battalion. They say K-19 is part of the

304th NVA Division and is now opconned to the 812th which is same-same 5th Infantry. K-19 is part of an elite homeguard unit from Hanoi. They say K-19 guide carries battle streamers from the battle of Dien Bien Phu."

"They're going to hit O'Reilly," Lt. Caldwell said. "My guess is they're going to use the sappers to overrun O'Reilly."

"What else do they say, Minh?" Brooks asked.

"The documents say it is important to the liberation effort for the 7th Front to combine with the siege of Firebase O'Reilly also many American deaths. They say this is very important for public reaction to hasten American withdrawals. They say the American assistance here is a blessing."

There was a long pause. It was very quiet and no one even dared to cough a muffled cough. The ground mist was becoming thicker. The moon was slightly higher though still murky behind clouds. The jungle floor was intensely dark. Everyone was waiting for Brooks. He broke the silence. He spoke quietly yet very firmly. "Get back to your people," he said. "We're moving out in zero-five."

SIGNIFICANT ACTIVITIES

THE FOLLOWING RESULTS FOR OPERATIONS IN THE O'REILLY/ BARNETT/JEROME AREA WERE REPORTED FOR THE 24-HOUR PERIOD ENDING 2359 13 AUGUST 70:

AT 0640 HOURS COMPANY A, 7/402 ENTERED AN NVA BUNKER COMPLEX AT YD 193304. THE COMPLEX COMPRISED OF 50 BUNKERS WITH OVERHEAD COVER AND 150 FIGHTING POSITIONS. CO A UNCOVERED A CACHE OF OFFICE EQUIPMENT AND PRINTING FACILITIES ALONG WITH SIGNIFICANT AMOUNTS OF SMALL ARMS AND MORTAR AMMUNITION. THE EQUIPMENT AND BUNKERS WERE DESTROYED. CO C OF THE SAME BATTALION DISCOVERED FIGHTING POSITIONS WITH OVERHEAD COVER ON HILL 711 AT YD 145296. THE POSITIONS WERE DESTROYED. AT 1117 HOURS TWO KILOMETERS WEST OF FIREBASE BARNETT CO B, 7/402 ENGAGED THREE ENEMY WITH UNKNOWN RESULTS.

ELEMENTS OF THE 1ST INFANTRY DIVISION (ARVN) SPOTTED TWO COMPANIES OF NVA REGULARS 800 METERS WEST OF FIREBASE O'REILLY. ARTILLERY WAS EMPLOYED WITH UNKNOWN RESULTS. THE 4TH BN, 1ST REGT (ARVN) CAPTURED AN NVA SOLDIER TWO KILOMETERS EAST OF FIREBASE JEROME.

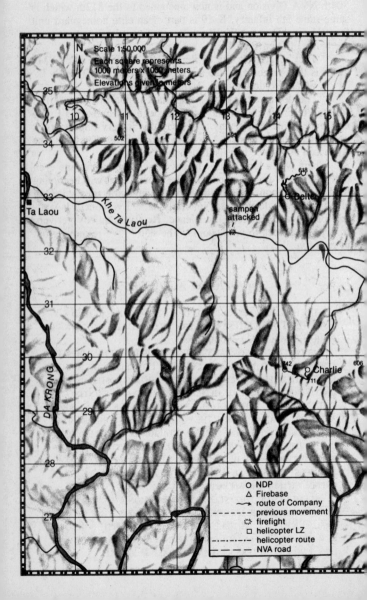

Grid lines are labeled using the Universal Transverse Mercator Grid, Everest spheriod. This valley is in zone 48Q, Square YD. To locate read West-East then South-North. For example, • = YD 215353

17   18   19   20   21   22

478

603

Bravo

678
BARNETT

Recon

Alpha
346

150 NVA
spotted

O
636

NVA ambushed

water
hole

Rach My Chenh

JEROME
(ARVN)

O'REILLY
YD 306256

AT 1430 HOURS THE C & C SHIP FROM THE 7/402 SPOTTED A SAMPAN BENEATH THE FOG OVER THE KHE TA LAOU RIVER. THE PILOT ENGAGED THE TARGET WITH ORGANIC WEAPONS FIRE WITH UNKNOWN RESULTS.

AIRCRAFT FROM THE 2D BN, 17TH CAV SPOTTED APPROXIMATELY 150 NVA SOLDIERS ON THE SIDE OF HILL 636 FOUR KILOMETERS SOUTHWEST OF FIREBASE BARNETT. AIR STRIKES AND ARTILLERY WERE EMPLOYED WITH UNKNOWN RESULTS.

CO A, 7/402 AMBUSHED AN NVA SQUAD THREE KILOMETERS SOUTH OF FIREBASE BARNETT AT APPROXIMATELY 1540 HOURS RESULTING IN ONE ENEMY KILLED.

THERE WERE NO SIGNIFICANT US OR ARVN CASUALTIES.

CHAPTER

19

15 AUGUST 1970

It was two hours past midnight. The moon was rising behind fast tumbling clouds and the sky was illuminated with eerie turbulence. The ground fog was thick and sticky. Alpha was in column, moving, stumbling, bitching. They had humped off the east side of the peak, then, following a compass course, they circled the peak to the south then west and finally northwest where they picked up the trail along the flat ridge down through the shallow draw and up toward the isolated peak that 2d Plt had reconned with helicopter at point the previous afternoon. From there until they reached their objective eleven days away the inertia of their forward motion would keep them in motion, never stopping, never slowing, gradually accelerating in their spiral descent into hell.

The path of Alpha's movement was very dark because of the ground mist. The soldiers felt insecure moving in the blackness, feeling their way toward a possible ambush. They bitched. They were tired. They had been working since before dawn. They had stopped long enough to dig in and set up and now they were moving through the unknown.

Night vision is a gift but a gift which each receiver must develop. Brooks had excellent night vision as did Jackson and Numbnuts Willis, who never let anyone know. Part of the ambient knowledge within the infantry was how to exploit the gift. To see at night it is necessary to look NOT directly at the object of sight but to look left or right of it about 15°. That way the image passing through the eye's lens hits the side of the retina where the rods, black/white receptors, are concentrated and not the center of the retina where the cones, color receptors, are clustered. Cherry knew all this but he had never practiced it before and on the night march he was nearly blind. Oh God. Oh God. This is fucked. Oh God, this is fucked. He was shaking.

As important as night vision is kinesthesis, the ability to comprehend the signals of the muscles, tendons and joints and to know the precise location and movement of one's body and bodily components. It is through the understanding of those sensory experiences one knows one's environment and one's position in it. Cherry knew this also. He had had enough psychology and physiology classes to know in detail the theories and even the history of their development. But the knowledge without practice was nearly useless.

Egan had scant knowledge of the theory of night vision and only slightly more knowledge of kinesthesis. But Egan was a mole. He had an immense amount of practice in night moving and he took considerable pride in his ability. He asked, volunteered, cajoled and forced the L-T to allow him to walk point. Behind him was Pop Randalph and behind them the bitching was universal.

The column was in a black cave of unknowns. They groped for the contours of the trail, the slope, the holes, the protruding roots. They stumbled forward in a long line, trying to be silent, listening to the swishing soundlessness of the good infantrymen, listening to the quick slip, topple—"Ooooophs, oh shit! Fuck this, Man"—of the bad. They followed Egan into dips and over crests, generally downward toward the valley then generally upward toward the peak.

As they moved in column Egan thought of the NVA soldiers who would also be moving now. Bitching, he thought, just like these assholes. Every army's made up of assholes. They're the only fuckers dumb enough to fight. It gave him strength because he was not bitching. It made him feel secure and superior and happy. Egan thought about the NVA sergeants and lieutenants who surely had to be leading equally unwilling, lazy, scared NVA soldiers. They're just like us. Egan felt warm. He felt warmth for the bitching assholes he was leading and warmth for the NVA assholes being lead toward him. Only one thing ruined Egan's night march, spider webs. Spider webs seemed to cross his path a hundred times.

Pop Randalph at Egan's slack was oblivious to everything. His body behaved perfectly, mechanically, without his consciousness. His eyes saw nothing but black void and only if the void were disturbed would his mind register. 2d Plt followed, then the company CP, 3d Plt and 1st at rear security. In the middle of 1st Cherry stumbled along swearing, one hand on Lt. Thomaston's ruck before him, one holding his M-16. He could feel the edginess of the others about him, the fear of being ambushed.

Behind Cherry Jackson was raging pissed. What that fuckin Marcus think I ken do? Jax snarled wildly in the dark. He think I ken jest git up an walk away. Where to? Fucka. An who gowin listen ta me if I says, 'Throw down yo weapons Brotha Boonierats. The word has come, Marcus has declared this war ended.' Mothafuckin dinks id love it. Walk right up en fuck everyone a us up. Then whut I got to be proud a? Pap sick, huh? Dat too bad. Aint my fault. Fucka tryin make me feel guilt. Can't that mothafucka Marcus see? Can't he see? Hey! I's somebody. I aint no nigger-slave soldier. I's somebody out here. He jest aint seen them people in Hue or Phu Luong. I am here fightin for freedom an justice an I's somebody. That the difference, Mista Marcus. I's really important here, dig? This the first time I ever been somebody. Every fucka here depend on me, depend on Jax keepin the gooks from comin through his side a the perimeter. That aint no shit. And when I comes home, stand back! That's right Mista. Pap'll be proud. He proud now. I know. An ef the revolution do come, I am ready. I am trained. I am experienced. I am ready to lead my company fo my people gainst any mothafuckin white honky pig.

Cherry entered a tiny clearing. The velvet dark below the canopy was a void: no light, no brush, no breeze, no sound. The column had stopped. The bitching had stopped. He had lost hand contact with Thomaston's ruck. No one was holding him from behind. He stood still, exhausted, too tired to be frightened anymore, too tired to make the effort to sit. Everything had vanished. The men of Company A had melted into the mist and moist humus of the trail.

"We're NDPing here," Egan's whisper oozed from the void. "Settle down right there. I'm goina check the squads. Make sure we got everybody."

Cherry nodded. He walked forward several steps and bumped into Thomaston. He stepped back, set his ruck down quietly, removed his helmet and sat down. Egan's whisper oozed from the void again. "Just rest. I got first radio watch. We're set up in a straight line on the trail." Egan grabbed Cherry's right arm, shook it gently. "There's our people behind you"—he pushed Cherry's body—"and up that way." He rocked Cherry back and forth. "This way here or that way there, if you see somebody, shoot em. I'll be back in one-five."

Cherry sat very still. He was very tired and the thick mist had condensed to make him soggy. He was too tired to fear an enemy probe yet a chill ran over his shoulders and across his neck. He closed his eyes. He could see the face of the enemy soldier he had shot. The face would not leave him alone. The soldier moved cautiously, slowly. Cherry stared into the man's dark eyes. Cherry shook his head, looked elsewhere. The eyes stayed before him. The soldier was looking directly back at Cherry. Surely he could see Cherry behind the brush aiming his M-16 directly at the soldier's face. The face came forward, the eyes twinkled, a smile came to the man's lips. The image of the black post of the M-16 sight covered the man's mouth. The man laughed. He laughed uproariously. He laughed at Cherry and stepped forward. The face enlarged, the eyes were wild, frenzied. Cherry stared back, growled, slowly squeezed the trigger of his weapon. The gun barked explosively, the muzzle flashing, the soldier's head . . .

"Hey! Cherry!" It was Egan. "Come with me. Bring the radio. L-T wants your radio to the CP."

How can one explain the anticipation, the tremendous suspense and expectation of R&R. It affects every move, every thought. Perhaps the old system of being in for the duration is better. Brooks had been a platoon leader with Bravo Company, 7/402, for five months when he left the boonies for R&R. In those last days of December 1969 it had been for him as if every effort, every night in the monsoon slime, every incoming round was endured solely for the reward of spending six nights away from Nam, six nights with Lila. Brooks had not had any specific expectations before he left, just the general anticipation of his sweet lady in a Hawaiian wonderland.

It began as he expected. He savored the very first passionate kiss in ten months, savored her lips as they embraced. They neither noticed nor would they have cared that the scene was repeated a hundred times about them by a hundred soldiers and soldiers' wives. Brooks was speechless. God, she was warm.

They kissed and embraced and kissed and embraced and in the taxi leaving the airport for their hotel they devoured each other, not even noticing the demonstrators greeting the arrivals from Vietnam with their shouted chant:

HEY, BABYKILLER, PLEASE
SHOOT YOURSELF, NOT VIETNAMESE.

But in all the anticipation, all the expectation, there is no thought, no preparation. That comes later, after the return to Nam, comes while trying to piece together what happened. For Lieutenant Rufus Brooks it was a dreaded thought with dream-like qualities but not truly a dream for he would be conscious and he could run from the thoughts and hide in his work. During the night march the thoughts of R&R overpowered the concerns of work, overran the fleeting intellectualizations on conflict. The thought condensed to one day, a repetition of one day of his life as if time were a record with a scratch and on each revolution the needle jumped back to the same day, the same horrid day.

The beginning of that day was glorious. When they finally broke away from each other long enough to speak, Rufus held Lila at arm's length and softly cooed, "Let me look at you." She giggled and breathed back, "And you. You've lost so much weight. Aren't they taking care of you?"

"I'm fine," Rufus said squeezing her again. He wanted to sprint upstairs to their room. He squeezed her tightly and she squeezed him back. He could feel the soft firmness of her breasts through his uniform, the warmth of her thighs against his legs. Rufus had always had a strong hard body but the months of field duty had made his legs tighter, harder, had flattened his belly and made his chest more solid. Lila stroked his arms, his back, his neck. He felt alive again, vibrant.

He held her at arm's length again. "Hey, what's this?" he asked. "What'd you do to your eyes?"

"Do you like them?"

"Hey, they're green. What'd you do? You don't have green eyes."

Lila raised her eyebrows flashing her sparkling eyes at him, smiling, teasing and tempting him. "Colored contacts," she grinned. Rufus pulled her to him, squeezed, then held her at arm's length again and covered her shoulders with his huge hands, massaging gently, lightly feeling the tops of her breasts with his thumbs. Lila's eyes were beautiful but they made him feel uneasy, as if he did not know her.

"Should we, ah, get a drink or something?" he asked anxiously. "Tell me everything that's been happening to you."

"Let's just go upstairs," she whispered coyly. "Let's go upstairs." He ran his hand down her back to her small solid round buttocks. "Ooooh, Rufus! Please! Not here. People are looking. Let's go upstairs and get you out of that uniform. I bought you some clothes this morning."

Upstairs they leaped to the bed. Rufus pulled at Lila's clothes wildly, festively, feverishly. Lila twisted and turned helping him. She covered her breasts with her hands. She stroked her nipples. He ripped at his own shirt exposing the strong shoulders and chest, the powerful neck and arms. She ran her hands down her thighs, hungry for him, wanting to feel his weight on her. He pulled at her panties and she raised her thighs, brought her knees up allowing him to whisk the last stitch of cloth away. She covered her body coquettishly, eyes sparkling, smiling, giggling as he tore his pants off. She squealed and squiggled and feinted squeamish shock at his exposure. And they made love. They loved each other over and over.

To her, he had never felt so wonderful, so warm, so light yet so firm. He had never moved so smoothly. He had never touched her in so many places simultaneously. To him her mouth had never been so sweet, her tongue so sensual. Her excitement rose higher, higher, faster, tauter.

"Oooooo," she groaned. "Oooh Rufus, Rufus, Rufus. Oooh Rufus. Make me pregnant." Love exploded from her. "Make me pregnant. Oooh Rufus, I want all of you."

"Oh my sweet Lila, I love you so. I love you so much. I've missed you so much. Lila. Lila."

Rufus had never been so excited, Lila never so exciting. The nearness of her wonderful glowing body, the newness, renewedness of their love was overwhelming. They relaxed, kissed, lay in the bed. She teased him, tickled his side, kissed his scrotum. Nibbling at him she watched his excitement rise. He ran his fingers down her back onto her ass. He followed his fingers with his tongue. Lila lay on her back and he kissed her body, her proud body. She arched her back as he mouthed her breasts, licked and rolled the nipples with his tongue. Their passion had never known the variety. They loved again and again and then they relaxed.

"It's going to be wonderful," Lila said. "There's so much to see and to do. Let's not waste any time doing nothing."

Rufus agreed fully. It was wonderful. It was wonderful having her to make the decisions. He gave himself to her totally, trustingly. "Lila," he confessed, "I've thought about you so much. All the time. You're on my mind all the time." It was as if he needed her to carry him now. "You're everything to me," he said. With the last sentence he felt he had made a mistake, had given too much, even to a wife. Lila did not return his loneliness confession with one of her own.

"It's going to be wonderful," she said laying her head on his chest. They did not say anything for several minutes. Rufus felt pleasantly tired. Yet he was anxious. He thought about his platoon, about each of the men in his platoon. He chose his words carefully, trying to be lighthearted, "I wonder," he said, "where those poor bastards are sleeping tonight?" Lila rose up on her forearms on his chest and looked into his eyes. He avoided her gaze. "This is the first real bed," he chuckled, "I've been in in ten months. I've slept on the ground or on a cot every night for ten months. I've slept in my clothes on the ground ever since July when I went to the Oh-deuce."

"Is it bad?" Lila asked sympathetically.

"No. That part's not bad," Rufus said. "I was just wondering where they were. It's raining there now and we're in the mountains." He changed his tone to sound more cheerful. "It's wonderful to be here with you."

"Rufus," she asked. He knew what was coming. Every one in Nam who had returned from R&R said wives always asked it on the first night. "Rufus," Lila asked. She put her head down on his chest again. "Have you killed anyone?"

He paused and sighed. He took a deep breath. "Why don't you ask me if I've saved anyone's life?" he said.

"L-T. Bravo's gettin hit." It was El Paso. He had been monitoring all three CP radios while Cahalan and Brown slept. A light rain had begun falling. It was very cool and a shiver ran up Brooks' back. Sporadic rifle shots cracked from across the valley. Bravo Company had been inserted on the north escarpment of the Khe Ta Laou on the 13th, had moved north, uphill and NDPed. On the 14th they had engaged three NVA soldiers in a brief firefight and had pursued them south across their insertion LZ toward the valley. The Bravo troops had lost the NVA trail and had returned to the LZ for their NDP. They were now north northwest of Alpha by 2½ kilometers with only lower hills and the valley between. More rifles chattered. The NVA were probing Bravo first from one side then another. A few frags exploded.

"Put everyone on alert," Brooks directed El Paso. "Monitor Bravo's internal and have Egan's cherry bring his radio up here."

An illumination flare popped above Bravo's position. Then another and another. Several popped over the center of the valley. The light pierced the canopy and fell eerily upon the boonierats of Company A. Brooks hated calling for illumination. The light fell indiscriminately, silhouetting enemy and friendly forces alike. Usually US forces NDPed on high ground and the illumination actually helped the NVA kill more Americans then vice versa.

El Paso, Cahalan and Brown along with Doc, Minh and FO clustered low close about Brooks. "We're going to run into a lot of shit in this AO," FO said quietly to the RTOs.

"I hope we don't get hit by mortars again," Brown said. "I hate those fucken things."

"Anything comin at you is bad shit," El Paso said. Artillery from Barnett began firing Bravo's DTs.

"Down south," FO said getting everyone's attention, "we used to use a doughnut. We'd use a full brigade to encircle the enemy just before dark. All night long they'd pour in artillery and air strikes. The dinks'd try to move out. In the morning we'd go in and mop up."

Egan and Cherry joined the CP circle. Egan had led Cherry to the CP during a break from the illumination. Cherry slapped at a mosquito. Egan grabbed his hand. "Keep the fuckin noise down," he snarled. Doc handed Cherry a small plastic bottle of insect repellent. Cherry squirted some into his hands and wiped it on his face and neck and passed it back. It passed around the circle. The mosquitos had come out with the rain.

Nine men with four radios sat quietly listening to the valley noises and to the faint rushing air sound of the radios. The probe of Bravo had slackened. It had lasted less than ten minutes. The artillery crews on Barnett ceased shooting illumination and DTs for Bravo and returned to the random H & I fire, the blasts rumbling and echoing in the dark. It seemed peaceful. Cherry had not slept when the column stopped. He had not rested before the night move. With the security of being at the center of the company and surrounded by eight others he tried to close his eyes. It was peaceful.

A new sound entered the night. It was that most horrible of sounds, that light concussion of air non-sound, a mortar being fired. And everyone of them knew it was not friendly mortars. They had no sister units that close, in that direction, below them east in the valley. FO, Egan and Brooks instinctively pulled out lensmatic compasses and fixed on the sound. Everyone else froze. There was no place to move. No holes had been dug. Along the column men, already on the ground, lay flatter, condensed their bodies. Sweat sprouted in beads on foreheads. phaffft. Hearts slowing, eyes widening, balls clinging climbing, rectums constricting and sphincters clamping down in anticipation. phaffft. phaffft. Ten times. Twelve times. Ears like radar searching the sky. Then lightning bursts in the mist and karrumph . . . karrumph . . . Flashes across the valley. karrumph. karrumph.

Radios crackled lowly. Panicked voices could be heard. "Bravo's FO is hit," Cahalan reported. Rounds continued to explode at Bravo's location. Twelve, sixteen, twenty times. "They got three dudes hit." Then rifles chattered. AKs, RPD machine guns clattered and were answered by M-16s and M-60s. The fire intensified. Hand grenades and RPGs and thumpers exchanged percussion. The howitzers on Barnett reacted firing Bravo's DTs. "Drop one hundred, left fifty." The caller was working the howitzer rounds around his perimeter.

Amid the explosions and the continuous small arms cacophony came the popping sounds of the NVA mortar tube below Company A. The enemy mortar team was firing furiously. Brooks grabbed Cahalan's handset, threw it back and scrambled for Brown's. He keyed the handset bar furiously, interrupting Bravo's artillery adjustments. "Armageddon Two, Armageddon Two, this is Quiet Rover Four, over." He unkeyed. "Come on you bastard, I got a fix on the tube." Brooks keyed again. "Armageddon . . ." He paused. Everyone else had frozen. The twelve howitzers on Barnett were all firing. The booming from Barnett and the explosions across the valley increased. Brooks violently shoved the handset into FO's hand. "Get Arty. Tell em you hear the tube. Tell em you'll adjust by sound." El Paso covered Brooks with a poncho and Egan produced a flashlight and topo map. They could still hear the NVA mortar rounds being launched. "We are receiving in-coming mortars at our sierra," an RTO in the TOC bunker on Barnett reported. "Firebase gettin hit," FO reported to the group. FO reached the FDC at Barnett. He calmly explained the situation. "Armageddon Two, Rover Four. Fire mission. Over." FO gave the direction and approximate location of the target as Egan and Brooks deciphered the coordinates from the map. FO casually suggested the type of projectile and fuse action and adjustment. Then he added, "Now fo Gawd sakes fire the Gawddamned thang."

"Stand by for shot," the radio rasped.

"Standin by," FO said coolly.

The popping sound had stopped. It now began popping again, popping over and over. Again the boonierats of Alpha clung to the earth. Had the NVA mortar team adjusted to their, Alpha's, position? The small arms fire from Bravo never ceased.

"Shot out," the radio rasped.

"Shot out," FO repeated.

FLASH!KARRUMP! The first NVA mortar rounds exploded, the noise following the flash by half a breath. Flash!KARRUMP! Flash! KARRUMP! Flash!KARRUMP!

"Shee-it," Doc smiled.

The howitzer round from Barnett exploded near to where the sound of the popping tube had come. "Right fifty," FO called. "Yo on the money. Fire for effect."

KARRUMP! The NVA mortar rounds were exploding on Alpha's old NDP, on their location of three hours earlier. "Shee-it," Doc laughed. He turned to Minh and punched him on the shoulder. Up and down the column troops were breathing easier.

KARABABOOMBOOMBOOMBOOM! Six US 105mm howitzer rounds exploded in the valley very close below Company A. The entire peak rocked. KARABABOOMBOOMBOOMBOOM! Another volley exploded. "Get em, Arty." Another volley. The earth shook. Rifle fire was still clattering from Bravo's position. KARABABOOMBOOMBOOMBOOM! Silent cheers arose, imaginary banners waved. Silent bands played. The cavalry rode across ninety unseeable TV screens. The pioneers were saved.

The frequency of artillery explosions in the valley increased. The 105s from Barnett were joined by huge 175mm and eight-inch howitzers from distant firebases. The small arms chatter at Bravo ceased, then erupted, then ceased again. It settled down to sporadic crackings in the wet drizzle night sky.

"Bravo's requesting an emergency Dust-Off," Cahalan reported to the group.

"No fucken way, Man," Brown said.

"How in fuck they gonna get them dudes out?" Doc whispered angrily. "How they gonna get a bird inta the middle a dis mothafuck?"

"Their FO's dead," Cahalan said. "They got three urgent, one priority, one tactical urgent. And their FO."

"Oh this fucken valley," El Paso said. "It's socked in tighter en shit in yer ass when hell's rainin down."

Cherry's hands and legs were quivering. He had his radio on company internal freq and monitored the routine sit-reps from his squads and the other platoon CPs. His whole body shook. Oh God. Don't let any of us get blown away. Please God.

The sounds of the valley diminished. The small arms fire at Bravo's location ceased. The NVA mortar tube was silent. US artillery slowed but continued to erupt in the valley. Waiting dragged heavily.

"How will they get the wounded out?" Cherry whispered to Egan.

"They'll get em," Egan said. "Medevac pilots got big brass balls."

Doc Johnson was sick, nauseous. The inability to help, to affect the situation at all, always made him ill with frustration and anger. You trah, trah, trah, Doc thought, an what it get you? You trah bein good, doin right, an it doan change a fucken thing, Mista. Not a fucken thing. It was the same in the rear and the lowlands as it was in the boonies. It was even the same back in the World.

Doc was a large dark brown man, large and heavy for an infantryman. He had a large head and fuzzy black coarse hair and a scant fuzzy moustache that came to the corners of his mouth and curled back into itself. His chin was covered with coarse stubble. Over his left eye there was a deep scar, pink against his deep brown skin, that ran to the bridge of his nose and obliterated the eyebrow. In all, Doc had a heavy thick look which many people automatically associated with slowness, dullness and dumbness.

Doc, Sergeant Alexander Vernon Johnson, was a city black. He was born and raised in New York, Manhattan, up at 143d Street with a turf extending from the Hudson River east across all of Harlem, mixed neighborhoods, mixed ghetto of Puerto Ricans and blacks, some whites, old Irish and Jewish remnants. Doc's family had been lured from the South in the 1920s by the prospect of high-paying employment in the factories of the northeast, lured with tens of thousands of southern blacks migrating for a better life. Long before he was born, in 1949, his people had settled into a pattern of male nomadic job searching and broken matriarchal families. Alexander was raised by a woman who was not his mother in a family where the siblings were not blood brothers and sisters in a street culture which was more tribal than cognatic. Alexander had no father but many fathers, no mother but many mothers and no siblings but brothers and sisters everywhere on the turf.

For a boy growing up in the city, the street was a good place, the best place. Inside it was dull, dingy gray close and dirty with age, the kind of dirt cleaning does not affect. Inside was where the winos laid in the hallways, where the roaches spawned in the moisture beneath sinks and behind tipping commodes. Inside the paint had all yellowed and cracked and chipped, and the plaster walls and ceilings had cracks running like veins in science book pictures of the human body. In the street there was handball and stickball and stoopball, and over at the school there was basketball. On the street the buildings had color and the walls carried ads for skin bleach and hair straightener. On the street there was music and dance. The street never, never was completely dark.

Street life connotates a harsh nastiness to the uninitiated but to a boy who knew the street it was communal, pleasant. Alexander knew from very early on that someone or thing would watch out for his welfare by forcing him to school or by rapping with him when he needed a man to talk to or by protecting him when a rival gang invaded his turf. He was an inner-city poor black child who did not know he was poor and who scoffed at the social worker's condescension. For a time he was a city cowboy, a small time street hustler, good friend, bad enemy.

Alexander was the kind of teenager his country calls first when it needs men for war, the kind of man his country, even its military, rejects when there is no need for strong hands to carry rifles and strong backs to carry the dead.

So it was with Alexander Johnson in 1966. At seventeen, his country decided it would like to use his services. Perhaps he was lucky to have had a brother advise him to enlist for a school instead of simply being drafted or perhaps he was wise enough to accept the advice or perhaps it was the vein-cracked walls and the science book diagram, for Alexander signed up for four years and a guarantee of medical corps training. Perhaps that was not luck at all.

When Alexander left New York for basic training in early '67, he thought New York would be an easy place to forget, the kind of place a man turns from easily. But almost immediately he missed his home, his siblings and his sister who was not his sister at all: his delightful little sister Marlena, three months apart in age and always together.

When Alexander came home after basic training and before he was shipped to Texas for twenty-six weeks of medical training, he spent his week's leave on the streets with old friends, but mostly he spent time with Marlena. One evening they had come through the streets and upon a street meeting. There were lots of young children running about and older people on the stoops sitting and talking and some older men sitting together drinking wine and several hard-looking women standing by the curb watching the street. It was late March and it was warm for the first time since the January thaw. Down the block, away from the meeting, Puerto Rican punks were playing stickball with stones, trying to clear the street and hit the windows in the buildings on the far side with their triples and homers.

On the center stoop there were two sisters and three brothers. One sister raised up her arms and started to sing and the others joined in. Marlena's eyes lit as she watched and listened and Alexander watched her as she watched the meeting.

A white couple approached, crossed the street and passed, then recrossed the street and continued on their way. "Look at them folk," Marlena sighed, "all dressed up in their white skin and their threads just so. That make me sad."

"That jus crazy," Alexander said. "White folk is crazy. I'll tell you bout them in Basic. Lena, white folk is a crazy cluster."

Marlena slipped her arm around Alexander's waist and he put his arm about her shoulder and they looked at each other and gave each other a squeeze and she said, "Let's go listen to some sounds and maybe do some boogyin."

The schools for army medics in San Antonio lasted from twelve to forty weeks depending upon the specialty. Draftees with two year commitments generally were run through a short course that concentrated on basic combat first aid—traumatic amputation, sucking chest wounds, shock. Enlistees, Regular Army personnel with more promising service length, were trained in all the various medical fields from operating room technicians to physical therapists. For most, when their schooling was over, their first duty assignment placed them with medical detachments attached to combat units; they became grunt medics. It was thus with Alexander, twenty-six weeks of intensive medical training followed by a month's leave and a year with the First Cavalry Division, November '67 to November '68, in I Corps, the Republic of Vietnam, as a grunt with a big bag of medical supplies.

During the time of his paramedical training it was discovered that Marlena was suffering from a blood disease of the sickle-cell syndrome, a lethal disease where increasing numbers of red blood cells deform, become excessively fragile and finally burst in great numbers releasing toxins into the victim's system. Treating the symptoms can elongate a victim's life but the disease is painful, unstoppable and incurable.

After a year with the Cav, Doc was assigned to the RNV training school at Fort Riley, Kansas, an assignment stimulating at first but terribly isolated and finally completely unacceptable.

In July of '69 Marlena died from untreated internal lung ulcerations and the complications of pneumonia. She died as much from lack of treatment as from the disease. "Died, Mothafucka," Doc had screamed in drunken nauseous vomiting when he'd heard, "cause she was a beautiful black lady inheritin bad genes from some badass fucka seven thousand years ago. Died cause them people, my people, don't yet know that they don't have ta die." On request, Doc was transferred back to Vietnam and in December of '69 he was assigned to the 326th Medical Battalion Detachment attached to the First Brigade of the 101st Airborne Division (Airmobile).

During the early months of his second tour Doc was in charge of the Oh-deuce MEDCAPs, Medical Civil Assistance Program. He and another medic and an interpreter and usually one or two boonierats temporarily in from the bush would go from hamlet to hamlet on a scheduled route. They tried to visit each of their eleven assigned hamlets once every week to ten days. At first that had given Doc Johnson a great deal of satisfaction but then the despair, the depression, the nausea set in. Doc Johnson once described it to El Paso.

"There one thing, Mista, you gotta know first," Doc had said. "It's old age that hold traditional Vietnamese society together. You remember Quay, one fine Marvin de ARVN? Quay was my interpreter fo three months. He tell me how the Buddhist and the Taoist and the Confucianist all hold there to be a proper order in the universe. Like that's their religion. Ya know what I mean? Everybody gotta respect the old cause that's their proper place. You doan never be sarcastic to a old papa-san. He is like the man, the key of their social structure.

"We go to a ville like Luong Vinh. There'd be dogs layin outside and baby-sans runnin round naked amongst the grass shacks. We go up to the school buildin which our own engineers built a corrugated steel in the center of the ville and Quay'd look for the village chief.

"Mista, people'd jam inta that tin shack ta see me. They be round the corner standin in line. All a em barefoot. Quay'd go out, explain to em that I'd see all the baby-sans first, then the mamas with small children and then the old. People be standin on tiptoes ta see what I doin. Be jus like a circus tent. I'm maybe about done. Some old lady come up an I know she got TB or pneumonia an she gonna die. So I give her maybe some vitamins or somethin cause I know I can't do nothin fo her. Or an old man come up and talk to Quay and Quay, he say to me, 'Doc, you give this man some medicine. He an old man. He have no money. He need something to trade fo food.' Like that.

"Then I realized it, Mista. You understand what I'm sayin? There a reign a terror in them villes. It aint the Cong. It aint the NVA. It's the cowboys. All these young bucks who aint been drafted yet. They like a gang back on the block cept worse. They approach, little kids dee-dee. Mama-sans run. I give this one old man some *Sing tô*, vitamins, and some nitrofurizone fo ringworm. He leave the school house an four wiseass cowboys take half a what I give'm. They rough him up tee-tee then let'm go. Like a protection racket, Mista. The old man whimper his shit ta some baby-sans but he powerless.

"Cowboys. That's pure Americanization. They take half a everybody's shit an sell it on the black market. All the middle-aged men been drafted. Or killed. They the link between the young and the old. These kids grow up without discipline. They're like animals. The whole social structure fallin apart, Mista. An you know why? You know why, Mista? Nixon pushed Saigon inta passin one hundred percent mobilization an they draft every dude from eighteen to thirty-eight. And they put the seventeen and the thirty-nine ta forty-three-year-olds in the popular forces. Aint nobody left home ta mind the ville and the ville probably a refugee camp tha's overcrowded anyway. Break my heart, Man. It break my fuckin heart.''

It was the same feeling Doc Johnson had now, that same feeling he suffered when he had a boonierat brother lying with his intestines on the ground and blood flowing from a dozen holes in his body and the valley's socked in and he could not get a medevac. It made him sick. The frustration went very deep. It went back to his sister's death. Poor Marlena. She could have been helped but he could not, did not, help. It came from being black, from being low class ghetto, from speaking low ghetto English. You trah, Man. You trah, trah, trah. If only I could be a doctor, a real doctor. If only I could go to school, I could be a researcher or a doctor.

Cherry could not stop shaking. His arms and back were quivering with the cold and his teeth chattered. ''Maybe I'm coming down with malaria,'' he whispered to himself. ''Oh God, please let us get out of here.'' Cherry had not been to church in over four years. He had been raised Roman Catholic, been baptized and confirmed and then he had broken away. Before coming to the boonies he had not prayed in years. Now he prayed hard. He thought of every prayer he had ever memorized as a child and he mouthed them. He said *Hail Marys* and *The Lord's Prayer* and the *Act of Contrition*.

''GreenMan's on the horn to Bravo's niner,'' Cahalan's voice slid into the wet blackness. ''They got a Dust-Off comin out.'' Cahalan reported in short low bursts, listening then speaking then listening.

''Bout fuckin time,'' Egan said.

''They tried earlier,'' Cahalan said. ''First bird got lost comin up the Sông Bo. Ran low on fuel and returned.''

Random artillery had been exploding in the valley. It stopped as the helicopters approached. For a moment everything was completely silent. Then the soft thwack of rotor blades reached the valley and quickly the noise level rose. The birds either had come out without lights on or the rainmist obscured and diffused the light completely. To Alpha they were only noise.

''Little people gonna lay-n-wait fo the evac,'' FO said.

''They goina want that bird,'' Egan agreed.

"Oh God," Cherry said aloud.

The sound of the rotor blades slapping the night air caused an eerie sensation. It was difficult to distinguish what had arrived. There were at least two Cobras, one very large bird, possibly a Chinook, and three, maybe four Hueys.

Bravo's Senior RTO, Joe Escalato, was directing the birds to his location by sound. Escalato was well known to the oldtimers of Alpha. He had been Lt. Brooks' RTO when the L-T was a platoon leader with Bravo, and Escalato was a good friend of El Paso's. "You can do it, Babe," El Paso quietly cheered him. El Paso monitored Escalato's net. Bravo troops popped two green star clusters, handheld flares that fired vertically a hundred feet then burst like small skyrockets.

"I've two lime stars." The Dust-Off commander identified Bravo's signal. The medical evacuation helicopter began its descent toward Bravo company. The large helicopter circling above began dropping parachute flares. Dozens of them. The burning white phosphorus splashed brightness throughout the valley and sent flat white light down through the canopy to the wet jungle floor. "I've my LZ marked with four reds at the corners," Escalato informed the pilot. The flare ship circled Bravo again, dropping a second ring of flares. The lights rocked gently beneath the parachutes, descended, sputtered and went out. The flare ship renewed the lights with each pass. Alpha troops froze. "Bird's makin a pass," El Paso reported. "The center of my LZ is marked with a strobe," Escalato's voice came from the radio. "Bird's comin in," El Paso informed the group. With all the light from the flares it was still not possible for Alpha to see Bravo. The sky glowed like the inside of a frosted light bulb.

When the medevac helicopter was still about 100 meters in the air Bravo company opened up like a mad minute, 16s, 60s, 79s, frags. They showered the jungle with suppressive fire. The intensity slowed as they reloaded. "Bird's in," El Paso said. Loud exploding pops from AKs intermingled with the blasting chatter of the friendly fire. "They're loadin up," El Paso reported. "Bird's comin out." The suppressive fire continued the entire time the helicopter was on the ground and as it lifted, the firing intensified. Sporadic fire came from AKs, as if the NVA were toying with Bravo, simply letting them know their mad minute was a joke. The medevac was up. The helicopters retreated from the valley. The flares sank and went out.

The night was peaceful again. Only the exploding H & I rounds disrupted the black velvet mistdrizzle. At the CP they passed the time softly discussing whatever came to mind. FO told several stories of units he had been with in the Mekong Delta on an earlier tour. El Paso jumped on an opportunity to tell Cherry about the history of Vietnam and Egan added his views of the present political situation. Doc spoke a little about the proper treatment for various wounds he suspected Bravo troops had sustained. No one mentioned Bravo's dead FO. At one point the L-T said a few lines about the causes of war and violence and Cherry said he believed it was genetically predestined by the structure of the brain. "I want to hear more about that," Brooks said. In their exhaustion none of them went into much detail. The GreenMan radioed Brooks and told him to speed up Alpha's movement and get into the valley. "You gotta get in there and hurt those little people," he said. He also congratulated Brooks on evading the NVA mortars. It was Cherry's first CP rap session. He enjoyed it immensely. For the others it was a repeat of many previous nights. Cahalan, Brown, Doc and Minh slept. At 0455 the NVA began a full scale assault on Bravo Company.

"Oh them fuckas," Doc said waking.

CHAPTER
20

It had been a very long night and now they were moving again, moving in the lightless cavern beneath the canopy, moving back down the ridge they had ascended to their wet and sleepless NDP, moving closer and closer to their central valley objective. At least the rain's stopped, they consoled each other. "At least we didn't get hit," Cherry said to Silvers who followed him in the chain of tired soldiers. The boonierats of Alpha walked somnambulant, unaware of their motion. Their steps were cautious and tentative. No longer were their legs sure enough, strong enough, to be trusted when extended over the unsure, unseen footing. Thighs twinged from the weight carried, from the exertion of the climb, from the undissolved stiffness and chill of the night before and from the demand to move silently.

Bravo and the NVA were still firing it up across the valley. The rifle cracking had nagged Alpha for almost an hour before they moved out and it persisted while they descended south from their NDP. Cherry had monitored the fight for the CP. Bravo had seven more wounded. Barnett was mortared again. They reported no casualties. Delta reported a suspected probe. "They wouldn't know a probe from a firecracker fart," Egan sneered contemptuously. And Alpha, Quiet Rover Alpha, damn the L-T, Alpha was moving again, in the dark again, bitching cussing stumbling again. The scout dog team was at point followed by 3d Plt, the company CP, 1st Plt and 2d.

Egan was pleased with the way the operation was rolling,

with the excitement of the cache finds and the contacts. He felt
strong and to him the cool night air was invigorating. The fact
that he had slept less than four hours in two days or that he
would probably not sleep more than three hours any day of the
operation did not bother him. Nor did the lack of adequate food
and water, nor the danger of descending into a valley. He looked
forward to it. He thrived on it. He had prepared himself for it in
every act he had ever made in Vietnam. He was a good soldier.
He loved tactics. He loved playing the game. That the stake was
his life only heightened his zeal and anticipation. There was only
one inconsistent gelding emotion; he had twenty-three and a
wake-up days remaining on his extended tour and in twenty-four
he would seek out Stephanie. He would find her, be with her.
Stephanie. She was the antithesis of Nam. She was the good, the
peaceful, the loving. Stephanie was tenderness. Stephanie was
truth packaged perfectly. She did not have to be intellectualized,
rationalized, analyzed. To perceive her was to understand, without doubt, without complication. How he had managed to mess
up their relationship so completely he could not imagine. After
Egan's summer of wandering and after he had returned to school,
he had called her. There had been no answer. He had nightmared
that she had gained thirty pounds, that she was fat and ugly and
that his imagination had created a Venus di Milo from a blank
casing. He hitchhiked to New York. He found her more perfect
than he could possibly have imagined.

The thoughts of Stephanie ignited a craving in Egan, strong,
exciting, agitating. It was the unfulfilled want, the wanting so
hard and the not having. The craving surmounted even the
conjured image of Stephanie and became a nebulous encompass-
ing desire. He wanted it so bad he could taste it but the *it* had no
definition. He wanted it so strong and had not had it in so long
the desire turned his mouth sour and dry. He felt very alone not
having it and that caused him to desire it more. He could not,
would not settle for anything less. He wanted it all or nothing.
He had wanted it so bad, during his R&R to Sydney, he had
almost made something that was not it into it in his mind.

In Phu Bai Egan had told the Murf about the ladies in
Australia, he had told his boonierat brothers in the Phoc Roc
how he and the young one had eaten and drunk and danced and
partied and how they had balled. When Egan had told the stories
to Murphy he felt they were successful enough to tell to the L-T
and the boonierats of Alpha, to share with them, with the guys

who had been on R&R and who had told and retold stories about their ladies in Bangkok and Hong Kong and Taipei. Egan had had a good time and his stories were good, as good as anybody's. But it had been less than he had wanted, less fulfilling, less consuming.

As he silently walked along the dark trail he thought about the *it* that he and Stephanie had shared. There is nothing like spending a night with a woman you have no feeling for, he thought, to make you cherish all the more the moments you had with the woman you loved.

It had been October in New York. A day of drizzle like the night of drizzle just past. Egan had dreamt of Stephanie's caressing voice and her graceful arms as she applied make-up and of her silver eyes. She welcomed him lightly, smiling, seeming to caress his presence without touching him, seeming to bathe everything about her in radiating warmth. They spoke briefly, small talk, and kissed hello. She was very happy to see him. He noticed one major difference in her. Oh, there were other differences; her auburn hair was cut short and close. She had fine hair cut now in sharp jagged edges that curved down about her ears and pointed to her eyes, that split and curled and that glistened like spun glass. But that was minor. There was something else. The trembling in her hands had worsened. From that moment on Egan would always be aware of Stephanie's quivering hands. It was such a small thing, subtle flutters, yet it seemed immense.

The quivering became a part of the mystique of Stephanie. To Egan it was an amorous tremor. The trembling somehow melted Fgan to his soul. When he watched her he became fragile and insignificant, when she watched him he was unconquerable. And yet Egan knew, was sure, Stephanie was unaware of the powers she possessed, of how she possessed him.

As the column passed through the dark saddle Egan could picture Stephanie's eyes perfectly. The deep blue silver irises contained distinctive flecks of blue and brown and black. The large irises were perforated by large deep black pupils and surrounded by unblemished crystalline white.

She had been taken by surprise when Daniel arrived that wet October afternoon. She had not worked that day and she was not wearing make-up. Her natural radiance was so potent Daniel had found it difficult to keep his eyes upon her, yet he had been unable to look away. Stephanie was wearing a floor length red

flannel robe with long sleeves. The cloak was open at her throat.
He could see that under the robe she wore nothing. They remi-
nisced about the early summer weeks and he told her tales of his
journey. She invited him to dine with her and he rambled about
fishing for graylings in Alaska, drinking and shooting pool with
Indians in Washington State and finally of getting his face kicked
in at a party in Florida. Stephanie made a salad and broiled
steaks. Each time she bent, the flannel robe parted from her body
and Daniel could see her lovely breasts and nipples. He became
very excited and it excited her that he beamed so innocently.

They ate and talked then sat on the floor listening to records
and talked some more. Gradually they moved closer and closer
until they touched and kissed. She led him to the studio bed.
They kissed and hugged and petted until Stephanie opened his
shirt, removed it. She gleefully opened his pants, helped him
strip and helped him remove her robe. He was nineteen and
innocent. Somehow, in the masculine world of sports and school
he had never learned, experienced, a woman. Now he did. In the
jungle, Egan's recollection of that first experience was of perfectly blended tenderness and bliss, physical and spiritual. It
drove him mad thinking about it. After they loved he had felt
very pleased, pleased with himself. In the bathroom while he
dressed he looked at his penis then at himself in the mirror. He
smiled and said to himself, now it's been in.

But what next? He did not know. He did not understand his
own feelings. He told Stephanie he had to be back at school and
he left. He did not have to leave but he left because he had to
move, to think. It became a pattern for his side of their relationship.
Always he had to leave, to experience something new, to see
more of the world. Charged with her love he had energy bursting
his insides and he channeled it into leaving. He would leave and
return many times over the course of the next four years. This
time it would be a year before he saw Stephanie again.

In the dark, in motion with the CP, Brooks raised an
important personal question from the depths of his mind. He had
successfully chased this thought away by losing himself in his
work or in his theory development or even in thoughts of his life
with Lila. But now decision-time was approaching. He had to
address it. Should Rufus Brooks extend his tour in Vietnam and
exit the army a free man or should he DEROS in thirteen days
and accept the fate of ten months World duty? Brooks tried to

look at the question in a logical manner but logic was of no help. Where logic breaks down, Brooks mumbled in his head as he followed in column, is not within its own system but without. It breaks down at the origin of argumentation. It breaks apart when we attempt to verbalize a unity and divide that unity into cause and effect to fit our logical framework. Yet the cause and effect exist only in our words. They are, in fact, one and the same.

Do I split or do I stay? Brooks brooded as he stepped through the dark. In his mind he decided to score his argument by giving a point to DEROS or to EXTEND for each factor affecting his decision. Hawaii, he thought. One to EXTEND. Maybe not. One to DEROS. Lila, one to EXTEND. No, Lila, one to DEROS. War, one to DEROS. Wait one. He rethought that point. He had to admit he enjoyed the romance of small unit maneuvers, points and platoons, rover elements and squads. He liked being an infantry commander. Hell, not the killing. He was no sadist. But he liked commanding and attempting to outfox the NVA. War, one to EXTEND. Let's admit it all. He liked the time afforded for deep meditation. Firefights occupied a very small percentage of his time, of any army's time. There was a very high percentage of empty time, time without a complicated commercial world blaring its hundred thousand daily messages each demanding a thought. War, one more to EXTEND. Of course, I might get myself killed. Score one to DEROS. Now simply getting out of the army has to register one to EXTEND because there's a 150-day drop included with EXTEND. Yet returning to the World ASAP may be essential if I'm to save this marriage. Time, one to DEROS. Running score—tied up.

The point of the column was through the saddle and climbing southwest, approaching a peak a klick from the night's NDP, when Cherokee alerted. The dog froze then agitated into a point, then whined. The dog handler froze, squatted. In compressing wave action the entire column ceased moving. The sky was graying. Below the canopy it was still night. The dog handler called Cherokee back and ordered him to silence. He signaled to the men behind him.

Ridgefield's squad moved forward with Nahele and his machine gun leading. Terry Snell radioed Kinderly of the alert. Kinderly radioed El Paso. Cherry monitored the call and immediately panic nausea seized him. The column stood silent. The

hand message to sit and take five passed forward and back from
the CP.

"No. No. Please no," Cherry whimpered nervously. Oh
God. Oh please God, he cried silently. He has not prepared for
an action right now. He was too tired. It was too dark. He could
not accept the possibility of having to fight now, of being shot.

From behind him came a nudge. Cherry turned and heard
Silvers sigh, "Man, am I glad we're stoppin. Man, am I tired."

"Silvers?" Cherry whispered.

"Yeah."

"Oh God. Man, I know we're goina hit the shit. I just
know it."

"Naw."

"Oh God. I'm shakin like a leaf. Man, you gotta do
somethin for me." Cherry's voice was full of panic and infec-
tious fear.

"What is it?"

"Dog's alerted."

"Oh," Silvers relaxed as if saying, is that all. "Where?"

"How the fuck should I know? Wherever he's at. Oh God,
I don't want this to happen."

"Sshhh," Silvers sounded. He moved closer to Cherry.
Cherry fumbled frantically in his fatigue jacket for a pen and
piece of paper. "You okay?" Silvers asked.

"If anything happens to me"—Cherry paused. He was
holding Silvers' wrist and shaking. He had thought of doing this
several times during the night but he was afraid of being ostracized.
"If something happens to me, write to my brother. He's in
Canada. Let him know. The army won't do that." In the dark
Cherry wrote Vic's address on a scrap of paper. He recalled
Egan's speech about writing in the dark.

"Okay," Silvers whispered. Cherry was calmer now but he
still was nervous and shaking. "Hey," Silvers whispered. He
too wrote something in the dark. "Hey, with me, if anything
happens, gather all my notes and send them to this address. It's
my sister and brother-in-law. They'll know what to do with
em."

Cherry and Silvers and the entire column less the 1st and 2d
Sqds of 3d Plt sat silently and Cherry prayed. He prayed that no
one in his unit be hurt. He prayed that none get blown away.
That calmed him some more and the advancing first light added
to his feeling of security. Above the canopy it was gray, dark

gray but no longer black. I don't want anyone to end up like that gook, Cherry thought. In the excitement of the night his apparition had not returned. I don't want to end up like that. God, don't let that happen to me. Cherry's mind cleared as his nervousness subsided. He thought about his prayers. Then he thought about his food. He was hungry. I've got enough for two days, he told himself, and I've enough water too. I think. I've twenty magazines of ammo, four hundred rounds. Is that enough? Damn, I'm hungry. Except for the one hot meal Egan had prepared on 848 Cherry had eaten only cold food directly from the C-rat cans. He returned to thoughts of prayer, now quite calm and intellectual. So there aren't any atheists in foxholes, he mused. Well, what am I praying to. He had succeeded in embarrassing himself to himself. I don't have a God, he thought. I got skin and bones and gray matter. Cherry ruminated on that for several moments. The sky was becoming lighter and lighter. "I better stop praying," Cherry whispered into the morning air, "and start using my brain to get my young ass through this shit."

The radio crackled lowly. Alpha's column rose and began moving again. Light now penetrated the canopy. In the treetops on the peak to the west the first sun splashed and dazzled. The column was shadowed by the mountain to the east and by the canopy. Cherry could just see Egan before him. Cherry had not slept a wink all night but the rising sun excited him. At the next take-five break Cherry tapped Egan on the shoulder and greeted him like a lost brother. He was delighted to see Egan. Hey! Hey! Cherry's face tried to beam to Egan. Hey, you got me through last night, you and the L-T. You guys really got your shit together. I'll follow you anywhere.

Egan smiled back suspiciously. "You monitor Bravo's first light search?" Egan asked.

"No," Cherry answered. He did not know when the firing from across the valley had stopped.

"They got one dead, eleven wounded. Got thirty-four dinks piled up and lots more blood trails."

There was little time between first light and dawn and the heat buildup. Whatever Cherokee had alerted on, the boonierats of Alpha had not found. Two squads from 3d Plt had swept the peak and reconned the flanks. They had returned to the column and the move continued. It became warmer with each step. The clouds vanished. As Cherry crossed the first peak he could see the valley. The fog had already receded from the walls and now sat thin above the floor and over the river.

Alpha moved quickly in the gray light, increasing their intervals. As the sun ascended they slowed and began the cautious inchworm movement. They moved west along the ridge of the south escarpment of the Khe Ta Laqu. They descended 50 meters then climbed 100 to the next peak. Every fifteen minutes they paused and sat for one or two. They lit cigarettes and inhaled deeply feeling the wonderful exhilaration and relief of the day's first nicotine. The wetness evaporated from their fatigues, the chill of their bodies warmed, the stiffness stretched and loosened.

Alpha continued west. They came down a 330-meter vertical descent while moving only 600 meters horizontal. The slope down from the second peak was steep and rocky and it was nearly impossible to keep from stumbling. Alpha moved and paused and moved and paused. The fatigues that had dried from the early heat were wet with sweat. At pauses the boonierats removed fatigue shirts. They popped salt tablets and drank their water and then moved and sweated. Their bodily fluids soaked their armpits and crotches and their skin burned. Cherry guzzled a full quart of water. The sun seemed to have leaped from the eastern horizon to the center of heaven and then to have stopped. It burned straight down. The jungle leaves trapped and reflected the radiant heat and baked the soldiers as they marched. The heat and the slope and the heavy vegetation began to take a toll. To Whiteboy and to Egan and to many of the others there was satisfaction in the pain, pain properly borne. Arms and legs, hands and feet tingled from the exertion. The stiffness of the night which had been relaxed by the early warmth now returned as joints swelled from the heat and early stages of dehydration.

"Quiet Rover Four, this is Red Rover," the GreenMan radioed Brooks from his now high circling C & C bird. "What are you doing? Goddamnit! Move! I want you in that low feature. Check out that sighting then get down there. Get down there and hurt those little people."

Alpha moved. At the bottom of the descent there was a stream. 3d Plt fanned out above and below a ford then quickly sent one squad across to establish a stream bankhead. 1st Lt. Larry Caldwell led. "Boy Asshole on the charge," Ridgefield mocked. 3d set security on both sides and 1st moved through. Cherry stopped to refill a canteen. He had again been down to

one quart. He bent over and splashed cool water on his face and
drank from his hands. The water was sweet and clear and had
neither the chlorine odor of REMF water nor the musky stale taste
of the gorge water. Others bent and drank and filled canteens.
Moneski and Roberts sought Cherry out. They found him replac-
ing his canteen, his M-16 in his left hand, a cigarette in his
mouth. They quietly exchanged greetings and friendly slaps.

1st Plt moved out at point, 3d Sqd, 2d 1st. The company
CP followed. 2d Plt washed and drank in the stream then fell in
behind the CP. 3d Plt withdrew security and came at drag. The
recharge from the stream lasted only moments. They now were
climbing, sweating, baking in the muggy jungle oven. They
struggled up vertical banks, over vine choked boulders, under
resisting bamboo clusters. Thorns tore at their arms, grasses
slashed their faces. Up, slowly up the side of Hill 636. Exhaustion overtook many. Fatigue in quadraceps caused legs to buckle
and they fell forward, uphill to their knees. In the dips hamstring
muscles gave out and they fell back onto their rucks and onto
their asses. Each time they attempted to fall quietly. Muscles
twitched as they climbed, crawled, scratched their way up. At
one point the trail became so steep the point squad had to cut
vines and jerryrig ropes for the boonierats to pull themselves up.
The point squad set security at the top of the earthen bank and
had each succeeding soldier hand up his weapon. Then the man
grabbed the vines and clawed at the dirt and dragged himself up
only to have to continue. As each man passed the bank became
barer and more slippery. Each succeeding soldier took longer,
often falling back to the bottom and having to drag himself back
to try again.

"Aw, fuck. I can't do it," Numbnuts whined after falling
twice.

"Come on, Man. You can do it," Silvers encouraged him.

"How far we gotta go?"

"I don't know. Come on, now."

Numbnuts tried again. Bo Denhardt pushed him from below,
allowed him to step on his shoulders. Numbnuts pulled feebly at
the vine, his hands stiff and weak from the heat. He held on,
worked his knees up, pushed his body forward, gave up and
collapsed crashing down onto Denhardt.

"You motherfucker. Get the goddamn fuck up there."

"I can't."

"Goddamnit, you slimy sonofabitch. Go."

"I can't. Leave me here."

"Go."

"I gotta stop. I can't make it."

"What the fuck's goin on here?" Egan came back down.

"That slimy prick's skatin on us," Denhardt spit.

"I can't do it," Numbnuts began crying. He was breathing shallow quick breaths. Doc Johnson came forward from the CP.

"I'm dyin, Doc," Numbnuts cried pathetically, miserably. "I can't go any farther. I gotta drop out. I got heat frustration."

"Prostration," Doc corrected, pursing his thick lips. He looked closely at Numbnuts. The man was covered with sweat like all of them. Doc shook his head knowing Numbnuts was physically okay. Doc stepped to Numbnuts, squatted, felt his forehead. It was wet and dirty and warm. "You're okay," Doc said officially to Numbnuts and to Egan. Egan grabbed Numbnuts' ruck and scampered up the bank without a word. Numbnuts tried again. Disgust saturated the air about him. He was a slacker and Alpha Company did not condone slackers. Denhardt pushed and cussed. Silvers pulled from the top. They were not gentle. They got him up. Alpha never left a man behind.

The climb continued. They humped hard, force marched. The sun bore down as if it were a weight. They stopped for five then climbed. They stopped again. "Get that raggedyass outfit movin," the GreenMan screamed. "Move. Get them little people." And they moved. The peak of Hill 636 was 900 map meters west of the stream, 380 meters elevation gain. The jungle closed in tighter and tighter, vines and palms and tree branches crossed the trail at every step.

The column meandered north south east west around over under obstacles. Alpha did not cut trail, not if they could avoid cutting. The sound of a single machete slashing at the jungle could be heard for hundreds of meters. It gave away position and invited enemy ambush or an enemy mortar barrage, and Alpha was on the side of the hill where aircraft from the 2d of the 17th had spotted one hundred and fifty enemy only twenty-four hours earlier. Even in their exhaustion they were aware of danger.

The 900 meters stretched to over 2000. Most of the boonierats were young men with strong bodies. Many had been athletes in high school or college or street athletes on the block. The L-T had played basketball and Egan football. Cherry had been a swimmer and had run moto-cross. Doc had played streetball every warm day. There is a pleasure that physical men derive from using their bodies, a pleasure in achievement and a pleasure from simple hard use. By noon, halfway to the summit of 636, even the physical were exhausted.

When Numbnuts had originally been assigned to Alpha he had been an assistant gunner but he had decided it was safer to carry an M-79 because as a thumperman he would always be far behind the point, behind the front of a firefight. Thumpermen pump grenades up and over the M-60s and 16s. With a 79 one could not walk point. One could not walk slack. But M-79 rounds are heavy and Numbnuts was now carrying 58 HE and three buckshot rounds, twenty-seven pounds of ammunition. "This is kickin my ass," he whispered to himself. "I'll die here. I'm goina die of heat frustration." At each stop after the incident at the steep bank, Numbnuts discarded rounds of ammunition. He hid them. Two in a small crevice, three beneath a rock, six in a cathole beneath his defecation. He bailed out anything he could, discarded over half his ammunition, and he justified it telling himself, "It's not like I'm droppin my claymore. There aint no way I'd turn over my claymore."

Alpha continued climbing. The sun, the hot mugginess, the tremendous exertion now produced serious casualties. Larsen Catt, Catman, squad leader 3d Sqd, 2d Plt, collapsed hot, dry and twitching. Bowerman in 3d Plt, dizzy and disoriented, vomited uncontrollably. Even Egan, hardass Egan, found he was barely sweating. His burnt lips and skin were dry and cracking and bleeding. Cahalan, in the CP, retched. Still they moved. Six men collapsed. No one, not even the strongest, was immune.

Doc Johnson grabbed the L-T. He had treated three of the heat victims and he had consulted with the platoon medics via radio about the others. "We stoppin, Mista. That is it. You tell that mothafucka in that Charlie-Charlie bird fuck hisself. Let him come down here an hump. I says we stop." And they stopped. With the point less than 50 vertical meters from the summit of 636, they stopped and hid from the sun.

During the hump that took Alpha to the side of 636 Bravo, Charlie and Recon all made contact with elements of the North Vietnamese force. At 0715 Bravo, while following blood trails left from their night-long battle, sighted, engaged and killed eight North Vietnamese soldiers. They had been working west parallel to Alpha, toward the valley. At 1030 hours Recon, moving toward Hill 848 from the north, was ambushed. Their

Vietnamese scout was wounded. At 1100 hours one platoon of
Charlie Company was extracted from the south escarpment ridge
and was re-inserted on the valley floor 1800 meters due west of
the knoll with the high tree. The insertion LZ was hot. Two GIs
were wounded and medevacked. One NVA soldier was killed
and one wounded and captured. The NVA evidently did not plan
to evacuate the Khe Ta Laou without a fight.

When Alpha stopped the column was stretched out over 250
meters. Slowly the L-T and the platoon leaders and platoon
sergeants and the boonierats themselves reorganized the sprawling ranks. The less weary soldiers were sent off to the sides as
LPs and OPs. The exhausted were allowed to collapse and rest
and eat. All drank heavily, replenishing their bodily fluids.
Stragglers from the front platoons who had fallen back stumbled
forward, back to their proper order. Silvers had given Jackson
responsibility for Numbnuts and long after the column was settled Jackson was still struggling to get Numbnuts back to their
squad.

"Cocksuckin cocksuck fuck chuck dude," Jax complained
after depositing his limp charge. "I's had it. I's had it with Mista
Rude. Tell Jewboy tell Mista Jewd, Jackson's fuckin up that
dude. Sucka's crude." Jax hunted up Doc Johnson. "Over heah,
Black," Jax whispered to the medic.

"What's happenin, Bro?" Doc greeted Jax with an abbreviated field dap.

"It is oh-vah. It is oh-vah. I am no babysit-tar. I am callin
this done. Throw down yo gun." Jax spoke frantically accentuat-
ing the rhyme, punctuating the beats with flailing hands and
swinging M-16.

"Whatsamatta?" Doc asked in one word.

"We have suffered. Our people suffer. Vietnam is jest a
buffer. It keep minds off revolution. But bet yo ass, Jax got the
solution. They killin Brothas one two three, they gowin kill yo,
they gowin kill me. Whut fo Mista Black, fo a whiteman's
money sack."

Doc was taken aback. He had been a million miles from
Jax' thoughts. When Jax found him, Doc was checking his big
black bag, counting his camouflaged field dressings and syringes
of morphine, checking his supply of anti-malaria pills and checking all the other paraphernalia he had carefully packed, packed
as always in the identical location in the aid bag. Doc counted

his supplies by feel. If he needed the bag in the dark he was prepared. "Slow down," Doc said sizing Jax up. "Now, whatsamatta?"

"Does yo realize," Jax' eyes were sizzling mad, "does yo realize whut we dowin. We sup-portin a regime. We sup-portin a gov'ment that murders. We dowin the murderin heah fo whitey so he ken do the murderin of our people there."

"Jax, you aint makin no sense."

"It is time fo the revolution. It is at hand. Join me, my brotha, join my stand."

"Gainst who?" Doc whispered harshly.

"Gainst the fucka runnin this machine."

"Gainst the L-T? He a Brotha."

"No fuckin way. Doan feed me no shit. He a puppetman. He part a it. Dat man a Oreo. Yo got whut I mean. He killin Black men, that we all seen."

"Man," Doc said scrutinizing Jax, "has your brain got fried. Come here." Doc grabbed Jax and felt his skin. It was dry. Doc broke out his own canteen and splashed Jax in the face then ordered, "Drink."

"Yo doan understand," Jax said suspiciously. "Yo becomin one a them. They killin my Pap. They gowin kill me. I am droppin out. Doan yo see? It oh-vah. Why should I waste my time fuckin with a dink? This jest stink." Jax huffed, pulled out his hair pick and rammed it into his scalp, then added, "It's time ta git oh-vah on the machine. I's down Doc, I's real low. Tell em I's crazy. Send me in, Bro."

"You know," Doc said very slowly, rubbing his chin, "a long time ago I met a man stopped me from hustlin. Convinced me ta get off the street. Taught me stuff. Told me ta get my shit inta a tight little ball. I been down. I been all the way down. Aint nothin there. A man taught me how ta get up. Thas where I at. Man taught me ya can't get oh-vah on nothin."

"What man teach yo that?"

"Bad man, Bro. Baaaad. Man named Mista Jungle."

CHAPTER

21

Whiteboy was alone on OP when he heard digging. He had concealed himself beneath a bush on a small rise, south, above the exhausted column on the trail. He glanced behind him, down, back toward the column. The sound was faint. It stopped. He looked forward. The digging began again. Whiteboy poked his head out. The sound persisted. The usual jungle sounds of helicopters and artillery masked the faint scraping. He was not certain he heard digging noises at all yet he was sure someone was digging very near him. He felt it. He looked to his right. He sat very still. The sound ceased. He looked forward. It began once more. He looked down, between his legs, under his ass. It felt as if someone were digging beneath him. He turned again, he massaged the warm metal of Lit'le Boy's trigger mechanism. The sound stopped. He did not have the faintest idea what he was hearing. He relaxed. The sound became louder, nearer.

"Ssssst." Whiteboy tried to get somebody's attention. No one responded. "SSSSST," he hissed loudly aiming his signal toward the column. Still no one responded.

In the column fifteen meters below Whiteboy, Frye and Harley were lounging back intensely studying the exposed curves of a recent *Playboy* centerfold. "Goddamn," Frye sighed holding the page lengthwise, "I'd crawl through a klick a claymores pushin my ruck with my nose just ta hear her fart over the Monster net."

318

Harley drooled at Frye's shoulder. "Man, Cookie," he whistled, "I'd go two klicks."

"SSSSSTTT!" Whiteboy near screamed. He slipped away from his post and came charging down toward the column. "Gawd A'mighty Sweet Jesus," Whiteboy raged at Frye and Harley, "you aint got enough brains ta plug up an ant's ass. Caint you hear me? Go git Egan." Whiteboy spun around and charged back up the hill. As he approached his OP he slowed. He moved Lit'le Boy's selector from safe to fire. He walked around the position cautiously, curiously. There was a four-inch diameter hole where he had been sitting.

Egan, El Paso, the L-T, Cherry and Cahalan were sitting clustered together in a shadow cave of palm fans topped by a tall vine-clogged tree. They monitored the radios. "That shouldn'ta happened, Man," El Paso moaned to Egan. "It shouldn'ta happened. Somebody fucked up."

"It's always somebody fucked up," Cahalan said quickly, sadly. There was anger in his voice, slight, but there. He was a man who seldom showed emotion. Those that knew him, El Paso, Egan, the L-T, they could feel it. To Cherry it was undetectable. "You guys always say that. It's not somebody fucked up. It's this place is fucked."

"It's BULLSHIT!" Egan snapped. He was pissed. "It's bullshit. Them mothafuckin dinks are bullshit. Wastin Escalato. Wastin him like that. We'll get em. Mothafuck. Sure as I'm sittin here, we are goina get them fuckin dinks."

Brooks was very quiet. He did not want to talk. All the old-timers knew Escalato. El Paso recalled with a sad smile, "Fucker was always smilin." El Paso shook his head. "Dumb fucker always had a good word for everybody." Escalato and El Paso had been closest friends outside their companies. Both were chicanos from the southwest. Both had become their company's senior RTO. On operations where Alpha and Bravo had maneuvered together the two RTOs radioed back and forth in Spanish. They loved to do that. If the NVA were monitoring them the likelihood of being interpreted was significantly less. Besides, the colonel didn't understand a word of Spanish and they could speak without fear of reprisal. After a pause El Paso moaned and shook his head again, "Oh Man," he said. He threw an empty C-rat tin into the brush. "He was too good. That should never a happened."

Egan picked at the spreading sun sores and jungle rot on his arm. He was filled with indignation and hate and he wanted action. He wanted to be moving.

Cherry was between Egan and the L-T. "What's that matter," he whispered flatly to Egan. "What's the matter with you? Don't you know, 'War is good. It's wonderful.' "

Egan looked at him in blank disgust. Egan rolled his tongue and jaw then spat a stream of thick saliva and C-rat juice which hit Cherry in the chin. He stared into Cherry's face waiting for Cherry to move, to swing.

"I'm sorry," Cherry whispered. "I guess that was a low shot. Ah, ya know, I didn't know Escalato."

"Aaaah, fuckit. Don't mean nothin." Egan jerked up quickly and walked off.

"War," Brooks said after another pause. "War." He was tapping his fingers on the ground. "It is important to understand how war occurs if mankind is going to avoid it in the future. If we are going to avoid having our Escalatos blown away . . ."

"Hey! Where's Egan?" Harley interrupted. It had taken him six or seven minutes to find the CP. Brooks motioned with his thumb down the trail. "Whiteboy found somethin, I think," Harley smiled.

By the time the L-T, Egan and the others reached Whiteboy the opening in the earth had increased to a foot around. Whiteboy was squatting ten feet from the crumbling edge. He held Lit'le Boy in one hand aimed at the hole and a frag in the other. As the group arrived Whiteboy held up the frag hand to slow their approach. Then he pointed to the hole.

"Whatcha got?" Harley whispered.

"What took ya so fucken long?" Whiteboy whispered back. Ignoring the others he turned to the L-T and Egan, shook his head in disbelief and said, "It just keeps a gittin bigger. Ah heard this diggin. Gawd A'mighty. Ah run down en git Harley. Tell him ta git Egan, an it sure does take that man some time."

They all stared at the hole. The edge continued crumbling. "You frag it yet?" Egan gleamed. Whiteboy shrugged and shook his head. "Get security out," Egan directed. He grabbed Whiteboy's hand grenade, straightened the pin and clutched his hand about the tiny steel bomb. A smile came to his face. He looked at the L-T. Brooks nodded. Egan knelt and crawled quickly toward the hole. Two feet away he stopped. He could see into the hole only a yard. He lay flat, extended his arm, released the grenade spoon, counted one-two, dropped the grenade into the hole and chuckled, ''Catch.'' The others backed up several steps and squatted. Egan rolled to his right and stayed down. From very deep there came a muffled explosion. Egan reached into an ammo pouch on his belt, removed another grenade, straightened the pin. Then he rolled to the hole. He stuck his head over the opening then quickly snapped it back. He had not seen anything significant. Gradually he edged back over the opening and peered in. He saw nothing except the dirt insides of the shaft. He could not see the bottom. The shaft was about two feet in diameter and it dropped down, out of sight, at a 30° or 40° angle. Egan dropped the second grenade into the tunnel, this time staying over the opening for several seconds, listening to the bomb fall, before spinning away.

''Hey. We got somethin here,'' Egan said getting up after the second explosion. ''That fucker's deep. I think we found the opening to a tunnel complex.''

''Well, check it out,'' El Paso grinned. He walked over and inspected the hole. ''This looks like the one we found by Maureen in July.''

''This one's deep, Man,'' Egan assured him. ''We gotta get inta this. Nice work, Whiteboy. We gotta open this up.''

Little by little Alpha moved all its attention to what became known amongst them as Whiteboy's Hole. Brooks directed De Barti and 2d Plt to climb up past 1st Plt and spread out in a wide perimeter. He had 1st Plt expand the perimeter south of Whiteboy's Hole and he had 3d move up and seal off the downhill.

''Red Rover, Red Rover,'' Brooks called the GreenMan. He had a controllable urge to say 'Red Rover, Red Rover, let the GreenMan come over.' He chuckled to himself.

''Quiet, Rover Four, this is Red Rover, over,'' came the sober reply.

Brooks explained in detail what Alpha had found and he requested permission to remain at their present location to dig into the situation. His speculation, along with the others', was running wild.

''Fifteen minutes,'' the GreenMan steamed. The battalion commander had his master plan, a plan unseen by the men on the ground, and this hole was not part of it. ''The hell with that hole, dammit. There were a hundred and fifty enemy soldiers a quarter klick west of your position less than twenty-four hours ago. Arty blasted the hell out of them. Go find . . ."

"Red Rover," Brooks attempted to interrupt by keying the handset.

The GreenMan's stride was unbroken. ". . . some blood trails. Find some bodies. What in hell do you think you're down there for? Over."

"Red Rover. They could have come from the earth. Over."

"Fifteen minutes. Then check out that sighting. Then get moving. Get down there and hurt those people. We're looking for a fight, dammit, not a sandbox. What's happening to you down there? Over. Out."

"We're going to have to do this quickly," Brooks told El Paso and Lt. Thomaston. "GreenMan wants us moving in fifteen."

Egan, Cherry and Whiteboy had already opened up the top of the tunnel with their entrenching tools. They had peered into the hole as deeply as their flashlight beams would penetrate. Still they could not see the bottom. Egan donned a gas mask, borrowed Doc's .45 and descended head first into the tunnel. The fit was tight. Ten feet in his shoulders hit on both sides. Egan slinked downward. He pulled himself downward with his forearms. The tunnel dropped steeply and at thirty feet Egan was hit with a strong foreboding and claustrophobic reaction. Dumb Mick, he yelled at himself. Do it right. Get the fuck outa here and do it right. He edged backwards, upwards pushing with his forearms. It was difficult to climb in reverse in the tunnel and the exertion caused him to breathe very hard into the mask. The eye lenses fogged raising his paranoia and increasing his feeling of being trapped. He strained harder. His heart rate jumped. Someone grabbed him from behind. He attempted to swing around, to aim the .45 at . . .

"See anything down there?" Cherry said smiling. He had hold of Egan's ankles and was pulling him up and out the last few feet.

Egan ripped off the mask. He inhaled one large breath. "It's too fucken steep. We need a rope."

"How deep could you see, Danny?" Brooks asked. "This thing's gotta be fifty feet deep at least," Egan said. His breathing had normalized, the claustrophobic reaction receded. He became excited again. "Ya can't tell how deep it is cause ya can't judge the distance in there. But, Man, we gotta check this out. We can't leave this. They got somethin down there. Nobody digs a tunnel fifty feet deep for nothin. We gotta get into it. We need a rope. Ya can't get back out without a rope.''

All around the hole people were talking, peering in, then returning to their conversations. Guard teams alternated watch giving every man a few minutes to inspect the find. Escalato was forgotten. Brooks called the GreenMan again and requested time enough to ascertain the parameters of the tunnel. He explained the depth to which his tunnel rat had descended and he described and perhaps embellished the view Egan had seen. He also requested a kick-out of two hundred feet of rope. The GreenMan asked a dozen questions then told Brooks he would call him back. Could the tunnel fit into his plan?

Brooks waited. Alpha rested. The reprieve from the climb was welcomed yet stopping caused a queasiness amongst the old-timers. ''Gawd dang dinks goan climb right up on us,'' Pop Randalph complained to Lt. De Barti. ''Hell, we're foolin with their air vent. They know where it's at, dang it, and they know Alpha of the Oh-deuce is fuckin with it.''

''How they going to know that, Pop,'' De Barti mocked the old boonierat.

''Well, hell, Sir. They dug it. They goan drop some mortar rounds right atop o' us.''

Still Alpha waited. They ate, smoked, fidgeted. They talked about the tunnel. Everyone had heard a tunnel story. They repeated them. They speculated. They imagined a vast complex. The sun had shifted imperceptibly from east to west. It continued to burn down. Every other boonierat tried to sleep. Each platoon sent out one squad in lights, weapons and ammo sans rucks, to recon the hillside about their perimeter and to search for other possible outlets for the complex.

After fifty minutes the GreenMan called. He told Brooks to expect a kick-out of rope, demolition supplies, a mity-mite blower, smudge pots and CS canisters. ''You're due romeo sierra in twenty,'' GreenMan radioed. ''Blow a lema zulu on the high feature.'' The battalion commander reasoned that Alpha, due to resupply the next morning, could send an element up to the peak of 636 to cut a landing zone and still have a contingent of troops delving into the tunnel. In that way they would do tomorrow's work today plus excavate the hole, and by tomorrow afternoon he would have them in the valley. Before the GreenMan finished delivering his order, Bravo Company broke in and reported being pinned down by .51 caliber machine gun fire.

They requested immediate aerial and artillery support and their third medevac in twelve hours. Within two minutes the rumbling of artillery from across the valley echoed over Alpha. Five minutes later a Huey was hovering ten feet above Alpha's now partially cleared attraction. The crew chief threw down the rope first, then crates of C-4 explosive, smudge pots and CS tear gas canisters, two five-gallon jerry cans of gasoline, and finally, shoving with his boot, a heavy wooden crate containing a motorized blower.

"I'm goin back down first," Egan told Brooks. "Doc," Egan went over to McCarthy, "let me borrow your .45 too." Now Egan had two pistols. He borrowed a second flashlight from Lt. Thomaston. He tied the rope about his waist and arranged rope signals with Whiteboy and Cherry and he dove back in.

"That fucker's crazy," Harley laughed to Frye. "You couldn't get my ass down there for all the pussy in Saigon."

Frye pulled out his dog-eared *Playboy* Playmate. "How bout for a night with this," he laughed.

"No fuckin way," Harley chuckled. "Not for a month with that."

Easy, Mick. Egan slowed himself at fifteen feet. He proceeded with extreme caution. He yanked once on the rope signaling he was okay. Whiteboy jerked once back signaling receipt of the message. Doc Johnson, Cherry, Brooks, Thomaston and El Paso had rigged a poncho tent over the opening of the tunnel so as to reduce Egan's silhouette if there were enemy below him. Whiteboy sat within the blackout. Egan descended. His feet were above his head and he could feel blood pulsating at the back of his neck. He slid downward, inching forward under control, holding himself back, feeling if he let himself go he would fall tumble down to . . . to where? His shoulders were fatigued from holding himself back. It was like doing push-ups with feet elevated. He went deeper, pushed forward by curiosity and by his desire to find and destroy the enemy and by his need to show the boonierats how it was done. He could hear his own breathing into the mask. The mask smelled like rubber. At various levels the tunnel widened to perhaps two and a half feet, at other spots it narrowed to a tight squeeze through. Egan slipped deeper. He checked the sides carefully for closed or covered connecting tunnels. He found none. He jerked the rope once and edged down. The walls were the hard clay and shale stone mixture of deep foxholes and bunkers. They appeared to have been scraped with pointed sticks for the upper side of the tube was raked with inch-wide scratch marks. The bottom was smooth from having been crawled on. The entire radial surface was fresh. As Egan snaked down checking for booby trap wires he could not help but admire the work the little people had done.

Egan held one .45 in his right hand and with it he tapped the tube's walls. He kept the second .45 in his belt at his back, the barrel stuck down between his cheeks. He was now more than one hundred feet in, fifty feet deep. He felt a slight breeze rising to him. It stopped, then began again, then stopped. Doors, he thought. Cherry relieved Whiteboy at the orifice. Egan tugged. Cherry tugged back. Egan continued. At seventy-five feet down, with one hundred and forty-five feet of line stretched behind him, Egan came to a small room large enough for two men to sit in. In the floor of the room there was a hole about eight inches in diameter. Egan pushed a flashlight into it. A shaft dropped straight down for eight to ten feet, then stopped. The shaft was definitely too narrow for any man, even the tiniest Vietnamese, to pass through. Egan lifted the mask carefully, sniffed carefully as he broke the air seal on one side. Okay, he thought. He removed the mask. He looked down into the narrow shaft. How in the fuck . . . ?

On the surface above Brooks was back on the hook, now with the brigade commander, Old Fox. Lamonte and George were photographing the hole, the poncho hootch and the soldiers working. Andrews, Hill and Whiteboy dislodged the mity-mite from its crate, gassed it up and prepared the smudge pots. "Yes Sir," Brooks said in exasperation. "Yes Sir . . . No Sir . . . That's a negative, Sir. Sir, the man is not an unauthorized citizen . . . Sir? . . . That's affirm, Sir. I have their film . . . Yes Sir, I'll have them report directly to you . . . Yes Sir, the civilian is still with us . . . With 3d Plt. He's being escorted by Lieutenant Carrie from the 3d Brigade PIO . . . I'll give Carrie the film, Sir."

Doc came up to Brooks while he was on the radio. "I doan like it, L-T," he interrupted. "Eg's down there too long. He doan have good air in there and he doan have the good sense ta come up til he droppin."

"Tell him," Brooks snapped unkeying the radio handset, "to get the fuck up then. He's exposing all my men."

"Huh?" Doc backed away. He was surprised by the quickness of the L-T's response. He turned and walked toward the blackout tent.

"Yes Sir. Over." Brooks snarled at the handset and threw it down. "That asshole," he muttered. "Doesn't he have any goddamned better thing to worry about than PIO's fuckin film?"

"Sir," Lamonte had overheard the L-T speaking.

"Do what you have to do, Lamonte," Brooks said.

"Thanks, L-T," Lamonte said. "Sir, did you know 90 percent of all American males finish high school and 55 percent at least begin college?"

"No. I didn't know that," Brooks said.

"Makes ya wonder," Lamonte said, "how a dumb shit like Old Fox became a brigade commander with all the smart people around."

"He's comin up," Cherry called from inside the poncho tent. "Give me a hand."

Cherry, Whiteboy and Doc Johnson pulled steadily on the rope. They kept enough pressure on the line to power-assist Egan up but not so much pressure as to hamper the climber's own actions. In three minutes Egan crawled out head first. He was covered with brown-orange clay. Lamonte and George snapped pictures. "I need an E-T," Egan said immediately upon removing the gas mask. Six questions sprang at him. Then six more. If the soldiers had had microphones it would have looked like a newsmen's mob of a heavyweight challenger after he had KOed the champ. Everyone wanted his question answered first. Everyone wanted to get near the hero.

Egan excitedly gave a detailed account of the tunnel but there were few details. He speculated about where the tunnel was going and to what it connected, how far and how extensive the system. "If it's that far down it could go right through the mountain or even under the valley." He wanted to go back down. Over and over soldiers asked, how, if the only opening to the tunnel was a small shaft at the bottom, did the NVA dig it from inside? "That's what I mean to find out," Egan said.

Brooks cut them all off. He had a bad feeling about the hole. "We're going to pump it full of smoke," Brooks said. "Get that blower on top of the hole and light the smudge pots."

"Aw, L-T!" Egan's enthusiasm dampened.

"El Paso, alert the platoons. Have them on the lookout for smoke rising from other air shafts."

"Gawd damn," Whiteboy shook his head in awe. "You could drop a whole air strike load a bombs rahght atop em heah and you wouldn't even cause em a headache nor nothin."

"Hell," Harley rasped, "they'd be impervious to B-52s."

"You can't even attack em," Frye added. "You can't make a ground assault on em. You can't make a underground assault."

Andrews and Hill started the mity-mite. The small gasoline engine sounded like a lawnmower. Hill lit the first smudge pot. Black smoke billowed up as it caught. He grabbed the pot, placed it at the top of the hole and, with Andrews' help, he sealed the blower tube to the hole and the pumping began.

"This is great, L-T," Egan exuded exhilaration from every fiber of his body once he had accepted not returning to the hole. "L-T, this could reveal a hundred secret connections. If they're that deep, this thing could go all the way to Laos. We gotta bring in a bigger blower. We oughta get the biggest blower the army has and pump this land full of smoke until it comes up somewhere."

Brooks agreed. So did El Paso and Doc and Thomaston. Their enthusiasm was contagious. Cherry caught it and spread it to the 1st Sqd when he went over to tell Silvers the details. Cahalan radioed all of Alpha's sister units using the krypto net, explained the find and asked them to be on the lookout for rising smoke. The excitement spread like an epidemic. Brooks conferred with the GreenMan in his C & C bird and he, in turn, had instructions passed to all the helicopters in the Khe Ta Laou area and to those working as far south as Firebase O'Reilly. "Look for smoke."

Alpha threw in another smudge pot. Then another. They tossed in smoke grenades of different colors. They searched for rising smoke. They checked the tunnel to see if it had been sealed off below but there was no smoke back-up. They refilled the gas tank on the motor and kept the mity-mite blowing.

At 1700 hours the Old Fox ordered them to move. Brooks argued that they should stay. The GreenMan arbitrated and compromised the two sides to the plan made earlier. He directed Brooks to have two platoons continue up Hill 636. He ordered them to cut the LZ at the peak then to continue past it toward Hill 606, a full kilometer further west. "Just more bullshit," Alpha troopers cussed. If they were looking for NVA, here they had something. The enemy would not be where aircraft had spotted them yesterday. They never stayed still above ground.

3d Plt rucked up and humped toward Hill 606 to search for blood trails. 2d Plt rucked up, took two of the cases of C-4, and headed for 636 to blow an LZ. The company CP and 1st Plt tightened the perimeter about Whiteboy's Hole and prepared to NDP about the noise of the mity-mite. They lit another smudge pot and dumped it down the tunnel. They opened a canister of crystal CS tear gas and added that to the plunging fumes. The hole accepted it all.

The afternoon droned slowly on for the 1st Plt of Alpha while all about them sporadic actions flared. The .51 caliber machine gun that had pinned Bravo down earlier and wounded one American had been destroyed by rockets from a Cobra. Bravo had barely regrouped and moved out when they were mortared. They took five rounds, had three more casualties, none serious enough for immediate evacuation. They rose and moved forward, farther west. Forty minutes after being mortared they stumbled into an NVA hospital bunker complex. It had been evacuated only moments before. Warm food was found in the first underground room. Tunnels led from there in three directions. The hospital contained a ward room with nineteen jungle beds, plus other bunkers and tunnels the leery Bravo troops refused to explore with the onset of darkness. They would return tomorrow. At 1855 hours Firebase Barnett was mortared, sixteen rounds impacting within the perimeter. They reported no casualties though a supply helicopter was badly damaged. With the approaching night it was too late to rig and sling it out beneath a Chinook. That would be first priority on 16 August. 2d Plt of Alpha reached the peak of 636 at 1900 hours and by 1930, working like madmen, they had blown down all the larger trees. They moved a hundred yards north in late dusk and settled into a circular NDP. 3d Plt crossed the top of 636 and descended west 210 meters into a steep canyon. At the bottom of the chasm the dog, Cherokee, at point, alerted. The dog handler wanted to stop and have the boonierats recon the trail ahead and to the flanks. Lt. Caldwell didn't want to be caught in the canyon at dark. He wanted to reach the peak of 606 and NDP there. He ordered the column forward. Twenty meters up the far side, just at sunset, Cherokee was shot through the head by a sniper. 3d Plt retreated east and settled into an L-shaped ambush/NDP on the down slope of 636.

Night closed upon the valley and hillsides with the suddenness common in mountain regions. In the last few minutes of gray light, all the boonierats of 1st Plt shifted south, uphill. They situated themselves as far as possible from the droning mity-mite while still keeping the hole and the machine tangentially in touch with the perimeter. Whiteboy manned the position closest to the hole. Gawd, he thought. You only have ta be lucky nough ta sit on somethin lahk that ta be-come famous. Ever'body in battalion knows that Ah discovered the secret openin ta all the North Vietnamese Army's supply routes inta I Corps. Shee-it, Ah hope that picture Mr. PIO took comes out. In the last minutes before blackness Whiteboy picked a board from the mity-mite crate and carved a crude plaque:

WHITEBOY'S MINE

C. JANOFF—DISCOVERER—A/7.402

With the dropping of the sun the temperature went from broil to cool. FO established new DTs and called in a series of H & I targets. "Hey, L-T," he said softly to an uneasy Brooks, "look at it this way; at least we're still keepin up the illusion there are two hundred of us out here. Nobody in their right mind would secure a noise maker like that in an AO like this with only thirty-four men. The dinks are bound ta think there's a hundred of us here."

Indeed the CP and 1st Plt consisted of only thirty-four men. Lamonte, George, Carrie, Caribski and the dog team had all left with 3d Plt. Brooks, his three RTOs, Doc, Minh, Cherry and Egan were at the center of the NDP, leaving twenty-six for guard. Thomaston and FO moved down and manned a position between 2d and 3d Sqds. Doc McCarthy teamed with Whiteboy. The thirteen positions with overlapping fields of fire nestled tightly in amongst the trees and brush. Each position put out two claymore mines. Up and down the trail, Egan and El Paso set two mechanical ambushes. Jax and Silvers set an MA on the ridge above the platoon. All of them silently cussed the mity-mite, cussed the noise, cussed the smell of gasoline and smoke, the acidic taste the air had acquired from the CS crystals, and Whiteboy for finding the hole in the first place.

The men in the CP circle, joined now by Jackson, were acutely aware of their precarious position. They sat in a knee-touching circle, the four radios at the center hissing an almost imperceptible white noise. Brooks sat at the highest point against

the tree, with El Paso to his right and Cahalan to his left. Brown
was next to Cahalan. Jax was next. He had crawled up for the
meeting, intending to make an announcement. Egan was to his
left, then Cherry, Doc and Minh. They spoke in voices so low,
had it not been that they anticipated many of each other's
comments they would never have understood the conversation.
Cherry, as the newest member, found it difficult to follow the
words in the dark.

"Hey, Bro Jax," El Paso whispered across the circle,
"give me some teeth. I can't see you."

"Yo bes not be able to see this duke," Jax smiled. "Ef yo
see em, then so ken a gook."

"We got somethin big here, L-T," Egan whispered. "You
goina stay here and see it through?"

"You oughta split," Doc said toward Brooks. "You gettin
too short for this shit."

"How many days, L-T?" Brown whispered.

"Thirteen en a wake-up if I decide to DEROS," Brooks
said. "I haven't decided yet."

"You should dee-dee," El Paso said. "You owe it ta
yerself."

"I feel like we are on the heels of a major victory," Brooks
said.

"We on the heels of a pipe dream," Doc countered. "That
aint nothin but a hole. If it's more, dinks aint neva gonna let ya
in there."

They were all silent for several minutes. The mity-mite
droned on. The radios hissed. Brooks had the uneasy thought
that he had extended the last time for the wrong reason. He did
not wish to repeat the mistake yet there was a gut feeling of
being needed. These men were his men. They liked him, knew
he was not just their commander but their friend. It meant a lot
to Brooks. Yet still he could not decide. He said nothing.

Cahalan broke the silence. "Hey, Eg, is it true you're goina
write a book?" Egan and the others faced the darkness that
emitted Cahalan's voice. "Doc says you're goina write the diary
of a tunnel rat . . . call it, *The Grotto-Canal Diary*." They all
chuckled.

Jax rose to a squatting position. He rocked forward and
back on his feet. He had been debating inwardly whether or not
to express his prepared remarks. He let go. "We gowin seize
power by force a arms," his voice lamented in the darkness.

"By war we gowin get our solution. Our task is to kill the world's pigs, an ol Jax gowin lead the revolution." Jax remained with the group only one second more. No one answered him. He felt very alone in his disgust with the war and in his belief that it was racially directed and inspired. The silence of his friends, he felt, was driving him away. He crawled back to his guard position.

Still they remained silent. Brooks grabbed his forehead and massaged his temples. Somehow, he thought, before I leave, I've got to help straighten that man out. "Hey," Brooks whispered, "let's get into it. Cahalan."

"It's a long report tonight," Cahalan said and without hesitation he listed the day's events, chronologically, statistically. He mentioned Bravo's location on each contact and the estimated size of the enemy force. Wherever possible he named the enemy unit and added what its usual structure should contain. He ran down the list of SKYHAWK companies, then the firebase bombardments, the activities of an enemy engaged by aircraft and finally his fragmented information about ARVN engagements in the AO south of the Khe Ta Laou.

"How you keep all that in your head?" Doc whispered.

Brooks cut him off. "Doc," he said.

"I got two items," Doc said slowly, sounding more professional than Cherry had ever heard him. "First, resupply tomorrow. I've requested plasma. I need plasma." Doc's speech began quickening. "I want fifty bags. I want evera other sucka humpin a bag a blood en I want evera medic humpin five. Dig? McCarthy. Where you at?"

"He's over with Whiteboy," Egan said.

"You tell him five. Got that? Five."

"I'll tell him," Egan assured Doc.

"Second," Doc whispered firmly at Brooks. "They all dehydrated. Everaone a em. You can't push a man so hard he droppin then expect him ta fight. What we gonna do today if we'd run inta a hun'red-fifty dinks? Huh? You tell that mothafucka GreenMan he gonna have him eighty-fo V-S-I infantrymen from Alpha bein evacked, he aint careful. You gimme da mothafuckin hook. I'll tell im."

Cherry smiled from ear to ear. He was sitting next to Doc, touching him, feeling him punctuate his speech with jabbing arms. He wanted to say, you tell him, Doc, but he remained quiet.

Without answering Doc, Brooks called, "Danny."

"I just want to say, I'm goin back in that hole tomorrow. I want ta go back down with an E-T. We're on ta somethin big. I don't know if the dinks'll let us in or not but I think it's imperative we try."

"Concerning the hole," Brooks said, "we're going to have to wait to see what GreenMan and Old Fox want us to do. We're going to resupply second tomorrow behind Delta. I think we'll have to be up on six-three-six by ten-hundred hours. He wants us in that valley with a passion."

"That mothafucka," Doc cussed, "he gonna burn these men up. It fo klicks minimum to that valley."

"Hey," Brooks said. "First we'll have to see if there's any smoke. We may have to follow and find the rest of this complex."

Cherry wanted to join the conversation but he did not wish to force himself upon them. "How extensive do you think this tunnel is?" he asked.

"That mothafucka go all the way ta China," Doc snarled.

"Some people," Minh whispered, "believe the tunnels go from the Ho Chi Minh Trail all the way to lowlands."

Cherry whistled soundlessly.

"We've never been able to break into the tunnels," El Paso said. "Intelligence reports claim the dinks got an elaborate network."

"The trails of the Ho Chi Minh," Cahalan recited, "appear to be an almost endless series of well-engineered dirt roads. They are highly maintained by coolie labor and often tunnels cut through mountains." No one questioned Cahalan as to where or how he knew. Cahalan always knew these things. "Throughout the maze of interlacing routes," he continued, "are numerous underground transfer points and supply depots where weapons, ammunition and food are unloaded and broken down for redistribution to units within the south. We are most likely on a branch line."

Brooks rubbed his scalp. Cahalan, he thought. That man is indispensable. Brooks attempted to picture Cahalan's description superimposed on a topo map of the Khe Ta Laou. Where and how should he move his men?

"They say," Brown intruded, "the dinks got everything we got. They got trucks, they got howitzers. They even got helicopters."

"No way," Doc challenged him.

"Yes Sir. I shit you not."

Cahalan's voice again entered the darkness. "Intelligence teams have reported spotting several helicopters painted all black and without identification. No one has ever confirmed or denied the reports. The birds are either the NVA's or the CIA's."

"Do you really think this tunnel might go all the way to Laos?" Cherry asked.

"It's not that far," Egan whispered. "We're not even fifteen klicks from Laos."

Cherry was impressed. He had not pictured them being that near the Ho Chi Minh Trail.

"I do not think we can ever get into these tunnels," Minh whispered. "I do not think we should try. If we find they are so extensive as you say, your government will withdraw. They will say Vietnam is a lost cause."

"I thought you wanted us out," Cherry said.

"Yes," Minh answered. "Out. Your army, your people out. But we must always have your friendship, your moral support and your materiel."

"Five years ago," Egan said contemptuously, "they said the dinks owned the countryside and everything but the center cities. Now most of it is ours. Two years ago they said the dinks owned the night. Now we own it. Now they say the dinks own the underground. We'll get in there. We'll own that too before long."

"No, I think not," Minh said softly. "I fight along your side as a brother but I do not like what I see. I do not like what you do to my country. Your money makes us poor. The more of your money that comes into my country, the more are my people forced into poverty."

"That don't ee-ven make sense," Brown said.

"Oh yes," Minh answered. "Before a man could make 1000 piasters a month and feed his family. Your money comes and prices go up. Now he makes 10,000 piasters a month and he must steal to even feed himself."

"Well, we'd be pretty incredibly naive to believe we haven't fucked with the economy here," Egan conceded for Brown.

"You see," Minh continued, "you cannot win this war for us." His voice was very soft. "If you win then we are conquered. We have been conquered many times before. Each time we rise up and drive out the foreign army. It is in our blood. And you will be driven out. After you are here a very long time, you will find we are a poor country. There will be nothing to keep you here and you will want to leave. Then we will rise up and drive you out.''

"What the hell do you think we're doin here?" Brown whispered angrily. "We don't want your country."

"We're here to establish peace," Egan said. "We're not here puttin up permanent bases. We aint even tryin to defeat North Vietnam.''

"Yeah," Brown carried on. "We don't care what you guys do. You can be free to do whatever you like. Soon as we stop the dinks.''

Minh was overwhelmed by their retorts. Cherry attempted to come to his rescue. "Fighting for peace is like fucking for virginity,'' he said. It had been a cliché at college and everyone in the peace movement agreed it was valid.

"No it's not," Egan said. No one else commented. Egan's words were final. Now Cherry felt shunned from the group.

"I mean . . .'' Cherry began after a pause.

"No it's not," Egan repeated flatly. "That's a lamebrain's over-simplification and the analogy doesn't hold. And it doesn't hold because you don't know what peace is. It is possible to fight for peace, to defend oneself, to deter or stop an aggressor. Fuck your pat little phrases.''

"We've made a commitment to your country, Minh, and to your people," Brooks added. "We've committed ourselves to guarantee you the right to choose your own government. My government claims your country is under attack by forces organized, trained and equipped by another country. How do you feel about that?''

"You Americans," Minh said softly, respectfully, "sometimes you are blind.''

"Yeah," Cherry chimed in. "They're not under attack by another country. It's their own country that's attacking em. Ah, I mean . . .''

"Look around shithead," Egan growled. "Who the fuck you think we're fightin? ARVNs?''

"Well," Cherry came right back repeating another idea he had heard earlier, "their way of life is a lot closer to communism than it is to our way anyway. Maybe we should let the communists have this place.''

"What do you base that on?" Egan said.

"You know. The way they live, kind of all on top of each

other sharing everything and their religions and all. It stresses the group more than the individual.''

"Would you say communism is more in style with their living style than is western democracy?'' Egan baited him.

"Yeah, I would,'' Cherry said.

"Would you say that federalism, you know, a powerful central government, stresses the individual more than the society or the society more than the individual?''

"The society.'' Cherry said cautiously, feeling Egan preparing a semantic trap.

"I think so too,'' Egan said. "El Paso?''

"Generally the larger the population a government controls, the more it must deal with the people as a mass than as individuals. And the more powerful a government is the more it controls the people governed.''

"Do you agree with that?'' Egan asked Cherry.

"Yes, I would, but . . .''

"Do western multi-party governments tend to control their people more or less than one-party systems such as in Russia or China?''

"Less.''

"And the party in power,'' Egan continued, "can it be toppled more easily in a multi-party system or in a one-party cell-system?''

"Multi-party.''

"Then the government in a multi-party system must not have as great control over the people as does the government in a single party communist system. True?''

"True.''

"Now, in Vietnam's cultural tradition, do the people like to have the central government direct their village affairs?''

"No,'' Minh answered the question. "It is not good for the national government to control the village.''

"Then our way must be closer to their traditional way than would be communism,'' Egan concluded.

"But they're all Vietnamese,'' Cherry protested. "They're Vietnamese just like the ARVNs.''

"Eg, *mi hermano*,'' El Paso said calmly. "Your argument is good but flawed. When people say the traditional culture here is more adaptable to communism than to something else, that something else is not democracy but capitalism. Perhaps, Cherry, what you propose is a socialist system. It is not quite true, also, that these people are all Vietnamese.''

In his many months in the jungle El Paso had found hundreds of hours to read. He read Vietnamese histories and he read the current events affecting Vietnam. He now launched into a detailed historical account of how various peoples arrived in Vietnam and from where the population came. El Paso told how some nomadic tribes descended from China to settle the regions about Hanoi and Haipong and how other peoples migrated east from south central Asia to settle the areas of Cambodia and the Mekong Delta. Still others drifted west from Polynesia. "Never," El Paso stated emphatically, "have the people of the North and the people of the South been one people. They have always fought each other. The early unifications of Vietnam invariably refer to the uniting of segments above the 17th parallel. Hell, there weren't hardly any people south of the 17th until the 14th century. This land was empty, emptier than America when the white man came.''

Cherry was surprised by how thoroughly El Paso knew the subject. El Paso continued for a short time, then said, "We often call our opponents Viet Cong and we think of them as independent rebellious South Vietnamese. I do not think this is the case. All our contacts are with North Vietnamese regulars. This is part of the confusion and political myth of the war. It is part of the propaganda the North produces to justify their invasion of the South.''

Minh remained silent through El Paso's remarks. Cherry acknowledged it with a quiet, "I see." Doc wearily asked, "What all that got ta do with anythin?" They were all very tired. The droning of the mity-mite did not allow them for even one moment to believe their position was uncompromised. The excitement of discovering and speculating on the tunnel had dissipated and apprehension filled the void.

Moonlight seeped into the black above as the moon began its late ascent. Thin clouds were forming at a very high altitude and the moonlight reflected off their earth facing surfaces.

"Hey," Brooks said, "it's getting late. Get some sleep. We'll have other times to discuss these things.''

Cherry lay on his back in the dirt, his face flushed, feverish. The night had become cold and damp. Doc and Minh lay next to each other to Cherry's left. Egan was shoulder to shoulder with him on the right. At his feet El Paso and the L-T and Brown snuggled into the crotch of a stubby tree. All shivered with cold and their compromised position. Beneath a thin poncho liner Cahalan monitored the radios, checking 1st Plt squads, the other platoon CPs and reporting to the battalion forward TOC on Firebase Barnett.

Cherry shivered severely. "Oh God. No," his whisper demanded. "Go Away!" The soldier had returned. Cherry's thoughts sped. He was completely exhausted. His arms and legs ached. The burns and scratches were not healing, but festering, inflamed and slowly oozing sticky thick liquid. Cherry shut his eyes. The NVA soldier moved quickly in Cherry's imagination. He moved quickly, determined to get his face into the sight of Cherry's M-16, determined to look straight up the barrel, through the sights, into Cherry's eyes. The enemy's head enlarged, his eyes, set deep in hollow haunted sockets, gleamed. A smirk rolled across the man's mouth. The mouth opened large, larger than the entire growing head, all teeth and tongue flashing. Cherry tensed about the trigger, began squeezing, squeezing with both hands, ten fingers, the headmouth became larger, the tongue whipping madly, saliva splashing Cherry squeezing the rifle exploding, flashing . . .

Oh fuck. I gotta get that man outa my head. Please Dear Lord, please . . . Cherry had sat up without being aware of having moved. The jungle rule—Always Be Quiet—had seeped into his subconscious. He had not even awakened Egan.

Cherry tightened the poncho liner about his neck and shoulders. His face remained hot. God. God? What god? He forced himself to think of something other than the dead NVA. Use your brain, he told himself. It can get you through. He searched his mind. He thought of Linda but the thought would not stick. He thought about school. Images dashed through his mind, a classroom, a lecture hall. Cherry forced the thought on. He wanted to sleep. So badly he wished for peaceful, unthinking sleep.

He recalled a picture his eyes had recorded several years before he had arrived in Nam. It was autumn in Vermont, the peak of the foliage-seeker season. The sun had set and the sky was very dark and clear. Vic was driving the pickup truck with their moto-cross motorcycles in the back. Jim, Cherry paused, Jim he thought, that was me: I rode shotgun. They had been returning from a backhills course, coming down a twisting side

road. From the crest of a mountain peak they looked down for
several miles to Interstate 91. The roadway and numerous adjacent capillaries were jammed with automobiles. The reds of
taillights and the beams from headlights illuminated arteries and
veins on the blackness. Cherry could see the image clearly in his
mind, could see all the tiny cells traveling through the organism,
giving the body life.

The organism is a parasite, Cherry thought, forced the
thought to expand. The earth is a parasite sucking life from a far
more complex animal which in its turn lives in a small cage in a
small shed on a small plot of the surface of a very immense
planet, a planet which is tiny and insignificant in its own universe.
God, Cherry smiled to himself, to have a thought to play with
without that fucken gook stickin his head into it. Cherry pursued
the idea. Someone on that immense insignificant planet has
captured the animal in which the earth is a parasite. It is a doctor
or scientist. Cherry could see the scientist working in his white
lab coat. He could see it all now. It opened like *The Book of
Revelations* before him. The scientist was operating on the animal to find the cause of its sickness. To the scientist the earth is
the size of a molecule. To the earth the pathologist shall be
forever unknown. After all, Cherry smiled, we have not yet
explored even neighboring molecules much less the organ within
which the earth feeds. The perspective from earth to intestinal
wall is unimaginably vast. If there is a wall at the outer boundary
of the universe, what lies beyond the wall? Stomach? Rectum?
Skin? Air? A surgeon? Cherry laughed to himself. If I can
imagine all this, he asked himself, is not my imagination larger
than all of it?

Cherry was sitting upright, still shivering. The moon crested
the mountain ridges and flooded the upper canopy. It was full.
Flat colorless light fell into the valley and diffused in ground
mist. The jungle floor on the side of Hill 636 remained black.
Cherry looked around. The sound of the mity-mite throbbed in
his ears. A guard on the perimeter coughed.

Gotta stop thinkin. I gotta sleep. I oughta jerk off. I wish I
was with Linda. Oh please stop. World stand still. That's a
fuckin order. Oh God, I wish I could plug my brain into a tape
recorder and look at the results after I DEROS. Maybe it would
make sense then.

*   *   *

As the moon rose a thin shaft of light penetrated the canopy. A glint triggered Egan's nightmare. A sapper was by his side. The silver machete was in his hand. Moon beams sparkled upon the blade as the dark foe raised the huge knife higher, aiming, cocking, striking down toward his eyes . . .

Egan snapped up, spun and landed on his fingertips and toes, like a cat, ready to leap. Adrenaline fired him awake alert paranoid. He smelled the night, listened to the night, swept a paw into the night. To let the machete fall would be to accept his own death.

"Somebody said if you ate it, you'd either get high as a kite or sick as a dog. So I ate it."

"Just blow the fucken claymore. You got movement out there? Blow the fucken claymore."

"I can't. There aint no C-4 in it."

"Numbnuts, where the motherfuck is the C-4?" Steve Hoover quietly removed another grenade from his gear. He couldn't believe what he was hearing and he was pissed.

"I ate it. I ate it. I figured I'd get high. After today's hump, Man, I had ta do somethin. Maybe I'd get sick see? Then Doc'd have ta medevac me. I'd get medevacked see? That's good. Or I'd get high. That's good. Either way it had to come out good."

"Fuck you. Just fuck you. Go out there and blow yerself. When did you eat the fuckin C-4?"

"This afternoon."

"Did you get high?"

"No."

"Are you sick?"

"No."

"Fuck you. You whore sonavabitch," Hoover whispered seething, staring into the jungle.

"Well at least I put out my claymore. Where the hell's yours?" Numbnuts whined.

"I'm goina stick mine up your ass. You hear anything more?"

"No."

"Go over an tell the L-T we got movement and that our claymores are fucked up and won't blow."

"Maybe it was just the wind."

"Fuck you."

"Fuck you too. Of all the guys in this fuckin platoon, I

gotta get stuck with some dude who's got a three word vocabulary."

" 'Fuck you' is two words bat shit. Now go over and check out the L-T and see if Jax heard anything and don't make any noise."

"Where's the CP?"

"Wait here. I'll go." Hoover began crawling away from Numbnuts.

"Hey, a . . ."

"What?"

"I aint really sure I heard anything. Maybe we should just wait."

"Listen mothafucker, you either heard somethin or you didn't."

"I don't know."

"What time is it?"

"Three-thirty."

"You fucken bat shit." Hoover shook his head and crawled back to his position. He lay alert and strained his ears trying to differentiate the night sounds. The mity-mite and artillery rumbling came from behind them. A slight breeze rustled the vegetation all around. "Okay, mothafucker," he snarled after eight or ten minutes. "You listen close. I'm sackin. You don't fuck with me unless you hear somethin. You hear somethin or even think you hear somethin, get me up. Get a fix on the direction. Keep your fuckin eyes pinned open and if I get killed cause a you, so help me I'll come back an haunt you till the day I die. How much C-4 did you eat?"

"Just a little. Tee-tee. I didn't want to get too high or too sick. I got the rest in my ruck."

"How long you been in the Nam, Man?"

"Four . . . over four months. I got held up at Cam Ranh for a while cause they didn't have a unit for me."

"Four months in Nam and yer already eatin your claymores. Man, that stuff aint good for you. An Jack, you don't go gettin high up here. You aint in Saigon, bat shit, you up the Sông Bo. There's dinks out there. You so fuckin dumb, I can't . . . What was that?"

"I didn't hear nuthin."

"Shut up. Somethin's out there."

"You see . . ."

"Shut up." Hoover keyed his radio handset breaking squelch

on all the radios. He did not speak. He rolled slowly to his left. In his right hand he grasped a frag. Very slowly he worked the pin out. Very gradually he slid from his position and moved to alert Silvers and Jax.

Numbnuts was petrified. He cocked his M-79. He squeezed the claquer firing device on his defunct claymore. Even the blasting cap did not explode. Sweat ran down his face. He shook nervously. Hoover did not return. Numbnuts fired his thumper. Whooaaccck, the round blew from the barrel. Then KaBuaccck, the small grenade exploded. Numbnuts was sure he could hear the enemy scatter. The mechanical ambush up the trail triggered and exploded, a violent thunderclap. To his right and left boonierats tossed frags. Claymore mines exploded before half-a-dozen positions. Boonierats could hear NVA dragging bodies through the heavy growth. They fired at the noises. Brown at the CP called the firebase and within minutes pre-arranged DTs were flattening and burning the vegetation in a wide circumference about 1st Plt. The fusillade gradually died, exhausted, numbed by a lack of return fire.

SIGNIFICANT ACTIVITIES

THE FOLLOWING RESULTS FOR OPERATIONS IN THE O'REILLY/ BARNETT/JEROME AREA WERE REPORTED FOR THE 24-HOUR PERIOD ENDING 2359 15 AUGUST 70:

IN A NIGHT-LONG BATTLE CO B, 7/402 ENGAGED AN ESTI-MATED COMPANY-SIZED NVA FORCE IN THE VICINITY OF YD 173329, THREE KILOMETERS WSW OF FIREBASE BARNETT. A FIRST LIGHT SEARCH REVEALED 34 ENEMY KILLED AND NUMEROUS BLOOD TRAILS. CO B CAPTURED 16 INDIVIDUAL WEAPONS AND SIGNIFI-CANT AMOUNTS OF OTHER ENEMY EQUIPMENT. US CASUALTIES WERE ONE KIA AND 11 WIA.

AT 0340 HOURS FIREBASE BARNETT WAS MORTARED. NO DAMAGE OR CASUALTIES WERE REPORTED.

AT 0715 HOURS, A SQUAD FROM CO B, 7/402 WHILE FOLLOW-ING A BLOOD TRAIL, ENGAGED A REINFORCED SQUAD OF NVA KILLING EIGHT.

THE RECON PLT OF CO E, 7/402 WAS AMBUSHED ON HILL 848 BY AN UNKNOWN SIZE ENEMY FORCE. THE UNIT RETURNED OR-GANIC WEAPONS FIRE AND THE NVA BROKE CONTACT. CASUAL-TIES WERE ONE KCS WIA. AT 1100 HOURS, ONE PLATOON OF CO C,

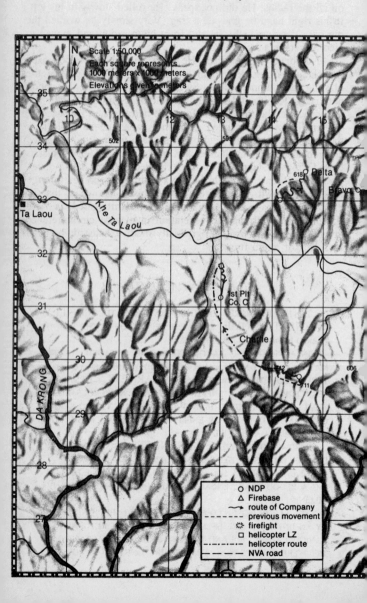

N
Scale 1:50,000
Each square represents
1000 meters x 1000 meters
Elevations given in meters

Ta Laou

Khe Ta Laou

DA KRONG

618 Delta
Bravo

1st Plt
Co. C

Charlie

711
606

O   NDP
△   Firebase
⌒   route of Company
- - - -   previous movement
※   firefight
□   helicopter LZ
-·-·-   helicopter route
- - -   NVA road

Grid lines are labeled using the Universal Transverse Mercator Grid, Everest Spheriod. This valley is in zone 48Q, Square YD. To locate, read West-East then South-North. For example, • = YD 215353

17   18   19   20   21   22

478
NVA
hospital
complex

600

678
BARNETT

false NDP   Recon

2d Plt
1st Plt

Alpha   Rach My Chanh

Whiteboy's
Mine

JEROME
(ARVN)

o O'REILLY
YD 506258

7/402 WAS EXTRACTED FROM THE MOUNTAIN RIDGE SOUTH OF THE KHE TA LAOU AND WAS REINSERTED ON THE VALLEY FLOOR VICINITY YD 130317. THE LANDING ZONE RECEIVED FIRE FROM THE NORTH AND EAST RESULTING IN TWO US WIA. NVA CASUALTIES WERE ONE KIA AND ONE POW CAPTURED.

AT 1145 HOURS ONE KILOMETER SOUTH OF FIREBASE O'REILLY THE 1ST REGT (ARVN) RECEIVED 82MM MORTAR, RPG AND SMALL ARMS FIRE FROM A COMPANY-SIZE ENEMY FORCE. THE ELEMENT RETURNED ORGANIC WEAPONS FIRE AND WAS SUPPORTED BY AIRCRAFT FROM THE 2/17 CAV (US) AND 4/77 ARA (US). A SEARCH OF THE CONTACT AREA REVEALED 15 NVA KIA AND THREE CREW-SERVED WEAPONS CAPTURED.

A GROUND BDA BY ELEMENTS OF THE 2/17 CAV AND THE HAC BAO COMPANY FOUR KILOMETERS NORTHEAST OF FIREBASE RANGER RESULTED IN THE DISCOVERY OF 12 BUNKERS, EIGHT HUTS, 60 NVA UNIFORMS, 14 MEDICAL KITS, 2640 POUNDS OF RICE, 100 122MM ROCKETS AND MISC DOCUMENTS. ADDITIONAL ELEMENTS OF THE 1ST INF DIV (ARVN) KILLED 27 ENEMY IN THE VICINITY OF FIREBASE O'REILLY.

AT 1330 HOURS CO B, 7/402 WAS ENGAGED BY AN NVA SQUAD USING A .51 CALIBER MACHINE GUN. CO B CALLED IN ARA AND THE MACHINE GUN EMPLACEMENT WAS DESTROYED. AT 1430 HOURS, B/7/402 WAS AGAIN MORTARED AS THEY DISCOVERED THE ENTRANCE TO AN NVA FIELD HOSPITAL BUNKER COMPLEX. A FULL REPORT ON THIS ACTION IS CONSOLIDATED UNDER SIGNIFICANT ACTIVITIES 16 AUGUST 70.

1ST PLT OF CO A, 7/402 DISCOVERED A TUNNEL AIR SHAFT FOUR KILOMETERS SW OF FIREBASE BARNETT AT 1520 HOURS. THE UNIT PROBED THE SHAFT THROUGHOUT THE AFTERNOON AND EVENING WITH NO RESULTS.

AT 1855 HOURS FIREBASE BARNETT CAME UNDER ATTACK. THE ATTACK WAS REPULSED USING ORGANIC WEAPONS FIRE. ONE HUEY UH-1D HELICOPTER WAS DAMAGED.

AT SUNSET, VICINITY YD 160295, AN ELEMENT OF CO A, 7/402 WAS ENGAGED BY AN UNKNOWN SIZE ENEMY FORCE RESULTING IN THE DEATH OF ONE SCOUT DOG.

CHAPTER

22

16 AUGUST 1970

Egan and Whiteboy cussed bitterly when the ground collapsed. Brooks and El Paso shrugged their shoulders dejectedly and walked away. They had argued their best. Cherry did not fully understand. Generally, 1st Plt believed it was a mistake, felt they were victimized into committing an error. The entire day had been erroneous and demoralizing. It had been the kind of day champions lose to cellar dwellers and honor students fail easy exams. When the 1st Plt of Alpha blew the tunnel at 1300 hours and all that ground caved in the situation seemed perfectly normal—all fucked up.

No one had fallen asleep before first light. After the Numbnuts-initiated mad minute, the perimeter went on 100 percent alert. Cherry and Egan crawled outward and reinforced Whiteboy's squad. The night became colder. Ground mist rising, flooding the dark crevices between already black jungle, drained heat from boonierat bodies and dampened clothes and poncho liners. All pairs cuddled, side-to-side, back-to-back, shivering, awake, miserable, exhausted.

Throughout the night the mity-mite and distant omnipresent artillery bursts rumbled and echoed. Black mist changed to gray. The jungle remained dark. The leaf-vine canopy silhouetted menacingly against the dull sky. First light dispelled the night. Half of 1st Plt fell asleep. They slept past sunrise at 0639 and they slept through a spectacular show as the sun broke over the east ridges and peaks and splashed and refracted in the sky turning the clouds red and the sky purple. "Only in Nam," Egan smiled at the sky. Half the platoon slept on through routine morning activities, slept until the sun burned away the mist and clouds.

The other half did not sleep. Egan rose at the earliest sign of light and silently prepared his web gear for morning patrols. There was a feeling of relief and happiness amongst the waking, relief that day had arrived. During Nam nights boonierats often feared someone somehow would devise a method of eliminating daylight and daytime would never again arrive. It was always a relief when the sky changed and a boonierat could see his brothers still there.

Doc Johnson and El Paso moved silently through the dis-persed squads checking and accounting for the L-T. ''How'd the night go?'' Doc asked here and there. A thumbs-up sign or a nod were the only responses. Doc McCarthy delivered a daily-daily pill to every soldier, a tiny white pill designed to inhibit *falicipreum* and *volvax malaria*. Everyone accepted a pill but half the pills found their way, with a wish, over shoulders. It would be better to be medevacked out with malaria than to get wasted in the valley.

Egan gathered a small team for a first light check. They disassembled the down-trail mechanical ambush, then patrolled west, uphill. The higher MA had blown. Artillery rounds had smashed small craters into the jungle. There were no bodies, no blood trails, no signs. It was as if no one had been there last night. The patrol returned.

''Oh, Man,'' Hoover chuckled to Jax and Silvers. ''You shoulda seen Numbnuts last night. That fucker says he ate the C-4 from his claymore so he'd get sick. Then he says he hears somethin. I tell him he's full a shit. I think he pissed his pants. Man, you shoulda seen that dumb fuck. Scared shitless. When I skyed he was near cryin. I know there aint nothin there and I knew what that dumb fuckin shit was goina do.''

Egan returned to his and Cherry's position. He broke out his C-rat can stove, a canteen cup, water, a piece of C-4 and coffee packets. Cherry woke, shook his head, looked at Egan through bleary eyes. ''Twenty-two and a wake-up,'' Egan announced cheerfully.

Egan washed as best he could using the corner of a towel and a C-rat tin of water. He concocted a breakfast of virtually inedible C-rat ham and eggs, doctoring the yellowish muck with peach jam, a dash of Tabasco sauce and several splashes of coffee. Egan mixed the mush with his bayonet then ate it with a plastic spoon. The sight of it being eaten turned Cherry's stomach. Cherry ate a cold can of pork slices, a tin of crackers with cheese spread, eating first the cheese and then the crackers, and his last can of fruit cocktail. Egan cleaned and packed his ruck carefully checking the tightness of every strap. Cherry crammed his gear into the pocket of his pack, as before, then sat on it. Egan re-tied and tightened his bootlaces, checked his web gear, cleaned his ammo and weapon and then brushed his teeth. Cherry dusted the cover of his M-16 with his hand and sat waiting, expecting word to come to move in zero five.

"Man," Egan shook his head. "You're a mess. Look at you. I never seen a dude get so filthy in so short a time. You need a shave."

"What's this lifer crap?" Cherry barked back snidely. "Want me to spit-shine my boots too?"

"I want you to be clean, Asshole," Egan snarled.

All about them boonierats were moving now. Moneski led 2d Sqd out on patrol. Brooks talked with the GreenMan, and FO called the FDC on Barnett with more coordinates. None of Alpha's three platoons had found a sign of the one hundred and fifty NVA soldiers seen by aircraft two days earlier. The mity-mite continued pumping and the hole continued accepting the smoke. Above the valley and as far west as the Laotian border helicopters searched for smoke rising. None was spotted. Brown called forward supply with a coded, up-dated request list. ". . . charlie-charlie-uniform one, delta-delta-juliet one, alpha-alpha-foxtrot eight, delta . . ." He spoke on and on into the handset. On the firebase a supply clerk translated the message into mean-ingful figures on a cage-sheet, a list to which only the quantity needed to be added. Brooks talked to the Old Fox about the hole. He radioed 2d and 3d Plts and instructed them to return to the LZ on Hill 636 for resupply. He told them the CP and 1st would rendezvous with them at 1300. Routine activity continued and most of the boonierats became bored and simply rested in the shade.

"Jax," Egan said excitedly, "let me take yer E-T, okay?" He grabbed Jax' entrenching tool.

"Bro, yo aint gowin back down there, is yo?" Jax asked, incredulous shock beaming from his tired eyes.

"Right on, Jax," Egan gleamed, spun and trotted toward the tunnel opening.

"Oh, Man," Jax shook his head. "Dat fucka crazy."

"Better en havin em tell either you or me ta go down there," Silvers whispered.

At the opening Egan stood in a cluster of CP soldiers, Whiteboy, Thomaston and Cherry. He had tied off his pants legs at the crotch and knees and bloused them tightly about his ankles. Over his torso he wore a T-shirt, a long-sleeve jungle sweater and a fatigue blouse. As additional protection against the tear gas crystals in the hole he wore gloves and a hat. Like the day before he donned a gas mask and carried two flashlights and two .45s. Cherry secured the rope about his waist and Egan plunged in.

The trip down was identical to the earlier one except now smoke residue shortened the effective length of the flashlight beam. Egan turned it off and proceeded in the dark. Slowly down. Deeper. Deeper. It was almost routine. Whiteboy gave three sharp tugs on the line indicating Egan was 100 feet out. Egan pulled once. He forced himself left against the tunnel wall, held the flashlight in his right hand, extended it to the opposite wall. He paused a moment, aimed a .45 down the tunnel and clicked the beam on, one two, off. His eyes registered an empty tunnel. Egan proceeded repeating the lighting at fifteen- to twenty-foot intervals. At 145 feet Whiteboy jerked the line four times. Egan yanked back. He should be in the small room. He turned the light on. The tunnel continued down. Egan inched lower, flicking the light at random. No room. At 170 feet he was stopped by a 250-pound bomb. He could hear digging sounds on the other side.

3d Plt had spent a restless night also. They had backed themselves into a small gorge after retreating from the sniper. Caldwell had placed an ambush team at the top, LPs on the flanks and three fighting positions across the front. He placed his platoon CP at the center in a thin natural trench. The dog handler and the tracker spent the night with the ambush team as far from Lt. Caldwell as possible. "That mothafucka's dead," the handler passed sentence on the platoon leader. "He gonna wish he nevah saw the light a day. What kinda man let a dog die? Just let him whimper en die en not even send a squad afta the dink who done it. Just turn around en run. What kinda man is that? I'll tell you. A daid one." His feeling penetrated almost every boonierat in 3d. A feeling of total disbelief and disgust had grabbed them all.

"Boy Asshole done it again," they cussed. "Where we gonna move to if we hit. That coward's fuckin us." The hate had not been easy to sleep with.

The sun was high and hot when 3d Plt finally moved out. Rafe Ridgefield walked point. Nahele with his M-60 was at slack. They moved out of the small gorge and onto a little used trail, perhaps an animal trail, Rafe thought. He led them south-west around behind Hill 636. Still they found no indication of the one hundred and fifty NVA. They began climbing toward the peak. Ridgefield moved slowly, cautiously, pausing for a break every ten to fifteen minutes. Various thoughts were accumulating in his head, assembling themselves into a . . . Da-da! DA-DA! NEW AND UPROARIOUS RADIO PROGRAM FOR ALL MY MARVELOUS LISTENERS OUT THERE IN RADIOLAND.

Ridgefield paused in very heavy vegetation to assess how to proceed. Behind him Nahele sat down and lit a cigarette. Ridge-field studied his map and checked his compass. He climbed forward three paces and mounted the prone carcass of a thick dead teak tree. He stood on the trunk and stared into the erratic green leaf wall of the jungle with the thousand irregular black shadows under palm fronds and behind branches. The trail had completely disappeared. Rafe stared into the dark holes in the vine masses, into the pockets where all light was excluded, blocked by moist living vegetation high above and layer upon layer of dead rotting support entanglement below. Older life supporting new life, he thought. The dead supporting the living in ever increasing heights of jungle, old trees dying, smothered and strangled beneath ever newer covers of green, spreading, reaching for the sun, climbing over the decaying structure, weigh-ing heavily upon disintegrating branches, dying and decompos-ing as each new layer smothered the one below until the substructure weakened and the weight increased to the point of collapse. Ridgefield stared at the vegetation. A supporting limb snapped. A slow-motion avalanche of green crashed as a section of canopy imploded. He jumped down, squatted. Behind him others sought cover. He stared into the vegetation. It shook as if the earth below had opened its jaws and eaten a huge chunk of life. Ridgefield looked into the new wall, into the new life growing from the old, and he understood it all. He laughed delighted with the revelation and he jumped back onto the tree trunk and searched the black voids and the greenness for a trail to make the climb to the peak easier. As he stared directly into one black nothingness its center flashed bluewhite, a perfect circle, a blinding muzzle flash from within the depths of the void. He never saw anything again.

"How the fuck did a bomb get down there?" El Paso questioned.

"How the fuck do I know?" Egan shrugged.

"Danny, are you sure it's a bomb?" Brooks asked breaking from his radio report to the GreenMan.

"You fuckin guys think I'm makin it up? Fuck it. Go down and look for yourselves."

"What happened to the room?" Whiteboy asked.

"I don't fuckin know," Egan growled.

"Well Gawd A'mighty, a room caint just dis-ay-pear."

"Well the fuckin thing just dis-ay-peared."

"GreenMan wants us moving," Brooks stopped the questioning. "He wants us to blow it."

"No way," Egan shouted.

"Ya caint blow mah hole," Whiteboy protested.

"We gotta dig it out," Egan said. "Send three of us down to dig a room before the bomb. Then we can dig the bomb out."

"Ah couldint fit in thaht hole," Whiteboy lamented. "If Ah could Ah'd go down there with ya, Eg."

El Paso took the hook back from Brooks. He radioed GreenMan's RTO and explained the situation and said they had three volunteers to go back down. He explained what they wanted to do and what they believed, speculated, the tunnel would lead to. Brooks took the hook and talked to GreenMan again. He asked for a day. Denied. Six hours. Denied. Two hours. Denied.

"Aw, they stickin it to us ah-gain," Whiteboy grumbled walking off and kicking a burnt-out smudge pot.

"We're gettin fucked, L-T," Egan complained.

"Blow the fucker," Brooks ordered.

Towing a reel of wire and two cases of C-4, Egan re-entered the shaft. He was in about fifty feet when word of Ridgefield's death reached the CP. On the ground above, 1st Plt packed up and prepared to move out. Egan and the hole were the only things keeping them from going.

"Can't they signal him to hurry up?" Numbnuts whined to Cherry. "We'll be the last ones to resupply."

"So what?" Cherry said. He was very tense. Numbnuts' whine irritated him.

"So what?!" Numbnuts cried. "We'll get all the leftovers. Them others'll go through all the Cs and take all the good meals. We'll be stuck with Ham and Lima Beans."

"Wow, Dude! Here a man from the company gets wasted and all you think about is lima beans."

Egan's progress was slowed by the encumbrance of the explosives. He crawled forward, tired of the tunnel now that it would be blown, caved in, never excavated, its secrets never revealed. Now it was just a hole in the ground. He casually searched the sides for sealed junctions and found none. When he reached 170 feet the bomb stopped him again. He scraped and dug about it and packed both cases of explosives in pockets between the bomb and the dirt. He implanted two electrical blasting caps, wired them and unreeled as he backed out. At the top he was greeted by Brooks who told him about Ridgefield. No matter how many times it happened the death of a boonierat seized his stomach and twisted it. "Fuck it," he whispered. "Don't mean nothin."

2d Plt had reached and secured the LZ. The first resupply helicopter was landing on the peak only 150 meters west. Brooks, Whiteboy and Egan ran the wire across 1st Plt's NDP and up the ridge. Moneski and the 2d Sqd had already begun the hump west, uphill, toward the LZ when the demolition trio shouted, "Fire-in-the-hole. Fire-in-the-hole. Fire-in-the-ho . . ." Egan squeezed the claquer firing device. The C-4 exploded muffled. The earth shook violently. It was impossible to tell if the bomb exploded. The earth continued to rumble sending tremors throughout 636, then a 20 × 25 foot rectangular area of surface, including a section of the trail they had ascended yesterday and defended last night, collapsed, sunk straight down twelve feet, filling a subterranean room almost eighty feet below the surface.

Normally resupply day was a skate, a day the command cut the boonierats some slack. Resupply day meant mail and packages and news items and time to relax and reorganize. Normally there was time to prepare a meal and eat something other than cold C-rations, time to clean up and possibly change clothes, time—between helicopter comings and goings—to be noisy. There had been times when Old Zarno, the battalion sergeant major, had come out to the field with an entire kitchen force and the boonierats of Alpha were served a hot meal on the LZ. One time, up by Firebase Maureen, the resupply after Lt. Kamamara DEROSed, the old forward observer had sent out six cases of ice cream cups packed in dry ice. That was an exceptional resupply. Then there was the resupply during the monsoon operation in the southern A Shau, when no helicopters could fly for seven days because of dense fog and Alpha was totally out of food. No extras arrived. Just food and batteries kicked out the back of a C-130 cargo plane and parachuted down. The boonierats had had to search the jungle for the pallets for twelve hours. It was torture but life was at stake and resupply was blessed and life saving. The resupply on the 16th of August was neither a skate nor an emergency.

2d Plt had arrived at the summit of Hill 636 after a short hump from their NDP. Immediately they set to work, one squad cutting and clearing the LZ while the other two squads provided security. Small trees, brush and bamboo were hacked apart with machetes, and these, along with the loose branches and shattered debris from blowing down the larger trees with C-4 the day before, were hauled off the peak and away from the LZ to insure they would not be swept up into the helicopter rotors. Tree trunks and heavy limbs were tugged aside. The security squads busied themselves clearing fields of fire about the perimeter. Hands blistered. The sun peaked. The temperature rose. The sun baked down on the cleared hilltop and the exposed earth dried and became dusty. Boonierats shed their shirts and continued working. The first two log birds arrived, one behind the other. The boonierats unloaded seventy cases of C-rations, batteries for the company's fifteen radios and heavy loads of M-60 belts, fragmentation grenades and new M-16 magazines and cartridges. No mail. "Shee-it," Alex Mohnsen cussed. The supplies were stacked beside the landing zone and the clearing squad became the breakdown squad. Quickly they resupplied, confiscating extra canned fruit and meat slices and tins of pound cake. Grudgingly they broke down and arranged distribution of the supplies. The temperature continued to climb.

3d Plt arrived after having carried Ridgefield's body and gear up the south slope of 636. A detail from 3d brought the body and extra ruck and weapon to the edge of the LZ. The body was wrapped in a poncho and the legs from the knees down hung out. "That ol mothafucker," Nahele said lamely to Snell and McQueen, "he sure's hell heavy." "The fucker'd a done the same for you," Snell babbled back. Ridgefield's detail became 3d Plt's breakdown squad. The others expanded and secured the perimeter.

Lieutenant Caldwell watched and directed his platoon's detail as he talked cheerfully to the civilian correspondent, Caribski, and the PIO escort officer, Lt. Carrie. "Ah, you know," Caldwell said officially, "it's a terrible thing when one of your men gets zapped." Carrie pretended to listen but actually he was concentrating on four men standing about fifteen feet behind and to one side of Caldwell. They were Lamonte, George, the dog handler and McQueen. Lamonte seemed to be helping the dog handler prepare a letter or some documents. "They're good men," Caldwell said. "Sometimes they can't always see the reasoning behind command decisions but they're a good bunch."

Caribski also paid Caldwell only partial attention. Several of the soldiers from 2d Plt's detail were wisecracking about his muttonchop sideburns and his hair which was long and completely covered his ears. He was a large man, heavier than most boonierats. He looked strong. Most soldiers considered civilian journalists to be a weird lot. So few went to the field they were always an object of curiosity. For many, flying from Saigon to Camp Eagle was going to the boonies. Very seldom did a civilian actually stay in the bush for days and of those who did only a small percent sat and listened. Most journalists had strong political leanings and tended to lead conversations, tended to get the boonierats to say what they themselves wanted to hear. Caribski was different. He was a cross of both worlds. He was an ex-GI, ex-Viet Vet. He had humped a ruck before. There was a romantic aura about him and about what he was doing. Some soldiers despised him for My Lai but in Alpha he earned general respect. He had talked and listened and humped. When the third log bird came in with clothes from the company fund and sundry materials but still no mail and then left with Lt. Carrie and Caribski and Ridgefield's body, the disgust thickened.

1st Plt and the company CP reached the LZ on 636 by mid-afternoon, hot, sluggish, disgusted like the rest. They had one hour to resupply before the back bird, the helicopter which would come to remove all the unused and returnable items, came in and resupply was over. Hastily they removed C-ration meals from cases then cans from boxes. They sorted through the meals grabbing ten then discarding those disliked if a suitable replacement could be found. "Ham and Limas! Ham and Limas!"

Numbnuts shouted. "I hate ham and lima beans. Hey, Cherry,
I'll trade ya three ham and limas for one can of fruit. Aw, come
on. How bout . . . oh, Man, just give me somethin other than
mothers en beans . . . Aw no, I a'ready got three meatballs en
beans."

The company fund clothes had been picked over too before
1st Plt arrived. Only forty sets had come out and all forty sets,
clean though worn, had been distributed. Forty sets of filthy
fatigues lay piled ready for back bird withdrawal. The supply
teams had not sent out any clean socks.

Egan secluded himself on one side of the LZ. He had
rummaged through the filthy fatigues and removed an untorn set
about the right size. Anything was better than his CS crystal-
infested clothes from the tunnel. His skin burned in hundreds of
places. Egan changed quickly, powdered his feet, put on a clean
pair of socks he had had in his ruck, sat back and pulled out the
letter he had been writing to Stephanie.

> 8-16—I'm going to have to give this to the doorgunner
> in half an hour so I'll be brief. You've been on my mind a
> lot. I'm due to leave here in twenty-two days and can
> realistically expect to be out of the army in three or four
> more. I want to see you. I never knew how deeply you
> touched me, how much you'd come to mean to me until
> now. The thought of seeing you again is driving me mad.
> We had a lot of good times and some bad. I don't know
> why I always had to be leaving but I think my desire to
> wander has been satiated by my time here. I feel funny
> writing you now, again, after so long, but how could I
> have written before when I didn't know how long it would
> be before I was out. Stephanie, if you can, please say I
> may come to see you.

> All my love,
> Daniel

Egan folded the letter, slid it into the envelope, sealed it,
addressed it and wrote FREE on the stamp corner. He strode
toward 1st Plt's CP, found Cherry and said, "Hey, when the
bird comes in, go up and see if we got any mail. Get the mail for
1st Plt. And, ah, give this to the doorgunner with the outgoing
mail, okay?"

"Why yo ask the man ta do that fo?" Jax said from behind Egan. "Of all us wid interest, aint none got mo interest then yo. Yo the platoon sergeant, yo fine. Maybe she wrote yo, this time." Egan pulled the letter back from Cherry and walked away. "Problem wid that man," Jax said to Cherry, "wid his woman, he doan know where he stan."

On the other side of the LZ Doc and El Paso were listening to Lamonte and George describe their day with 3d Plt. "I can see why they call him Boy Asshole," Lamonte said. "Man, he wouldn't even let the dog handler go up an put the dog out of its misery."

"I think they shoulda had a medevac come in for it," George said.

"He's a fucker, Man," Lamonte continued. "You guys better watch out for him."

"He do Rafe?" Doc asked intensely.

"Naw, I don't think that was his fault," Lamonte answered. "Kinderly said Ridgefield was on the wrong trail. Got crossed up someplace. White wanted ta have a bird come in with a hoist so we wouldn't have ta carry him but Boy Asshole wouldn't even request one. He just turned the platoon around just like he did when the dog got it and he had us runnin away. I thought Nahele'd blow his ass off."

"He's an asshole, Man," George said. "I think you're goina have trouble ever gettin another scout dog team ta work with this company."

Brooks came over to the group, excused himself and very apologetically told Lamonte he had to confiscate his film. "L-T, I already gave it to Lt. Carrie," Lamonte said. Brooks pursed his lips. "I know Sir, it wasn't your doing. That 3d Brigade commander, he sure's got his head up his ass."

Brooks shook his head slowly, shrugged his shoulders and winked, "Doesn't mean anything," he said. "Hey, both of you. Thanks very much for coming out with us. It makes a lot of us feel good to have you here."

When Brooks returned to the CP Lamonte said, "He's one in a million. That man's got his shit together."

"Right on, Bro," El Paso said. "Where you going now?"

"I don't know," Lamonte said. "We'll be in for two days to write our stories then maybe we'll go out with 2d of the three-two-seventh."

"You really give the film to Carrie?" George asked Lamonte.

"Fuck no! I told him you gave it to the L-T."

Cherry, Egan and Thomaston grouped together with Brooks
and his RTOs and FO to discuss the afternoon move. There
would be three hours of light remaining after the back bird left
and the GreenMan was repeating his shrill order: "Get down
there and hurt those little people."

"We aint walkin inta the middle a that valley in the middle
of the fucken night," Egan warned flatly.

"No," Brooks agreed. "We won't move down there yet. I
think we should set up some ambushes up here. Move out and
leave some ambush teams. Can we get some volunteers?"

"Give us ten," Thomaston answered. He and Egan rose
and circled the peak asking for ambush team volunteers. Cherry
sat by the CP listening as the others prepared for the continuing
move. He brushed a mosquito from his face and felt a small sore
bump. He rubbed his fingers over his forehead and down by the
side of his nose. "Oh God," he muttered. "Pimples!" Cherry
checked and examined his body. His face had broken out and
had several cuts, his arms were cut and bruised and the burns he
had received on the CA were sore and oozing. His back and leg
muscles were sore and his shoulders hurt from where the rucksack straps cut. Now he had a full ruck again and the straps
would cut deeper. He slipped a hand under his shirt and felt his
shoulders. There too the skin was breaking out. Just like being
thirteen again, he thought. He sat forward and felt the cloth of
his pants tighten against his crotch. He was sore there also. His
pants, the dirt and sweat, and the night mist were combining to
irritate his inner thigh skin. Cherry got up, found Egan. "Hey,"
he asked, "is the ambush team goina have ta hump very far?"

"Negative," Egan replied.

"Are they goina need an RTO?" Cherry asked.

"That's affirm," Egan smiled. Oh to get rid of this dude
for a day, he thought.

"Could I volunteer?" Cherry persisted expecting Egan to say no.

"Right on," Egan beamed.

When the back bird came in, Egan grabbed Cherry and
pulled him toward the LZ. "Come on," he shouted. "I got
somethin for ya." The bird sat down, Egan ran forward, gave
the doorgunner his letter and spoke to him for several seconds.
Then he ran back to Cherry. The detail from 2d Plt loaded the
material being sent back. "Scream," Egan shouted into the

noise of the rotorslap and engineroar. Cherry looked at him incredulously. "Yeah, SCREAM," Egan yelled and he screamed as loud as he could. "AAAAAAAAAAAAAAAaaaaaa . . . Try it."

Brooks stood on one of the helicopter skids talking to the pilot, the last of the leftovers were being packed.

"Try it," Egan shouted into the noise of the helicopter and he screamed again jumping and shaking and laughing.

Cherry attempted a yell, "AAaaaa . . ."

"Really yell," Egan demanded laughing, tears coming to his eyes from facing into the gale rotor wash.

"AAAEeeeik," Cherry shouted. He laughed.

"AAAAAAAAAAAaaaahh," Egan screamed laughing and shaking.

"AAAAAAAaaaeeeikk," Cherry screamed and laughed out of control. Egan was holding his wrist and shaking it up and back. They were like two sport fanatics watching their team win in the last second.

"AAAAAAAAaaaahh . . ." They screamed together. Then the helicopter lifted and left and again they had to be silent.

It was 1700 hours when Alpha finally began moving again, west again. The GreenMan's pushing and shouting had reversed the slowdown of resupply. The call of the Khe Ta Laou accelerated their hump. Alpha moved out at a killer pace. They moved in column, 3d Plt, the CP, 2d and 1st. They moved quickly down the west side of 636 to a rivulet gorge between that peak and the peak of Hill 606. Nahele walked point, Snell slack. Their disgust had changed to hatred. Nahele led the column along the gorge, cut above the rivulet, looking for a crossing. He refused to cross where Caldwell directed, nor would he cross where they had crossed the day before, where, on the other side, Cherokee was killed.

Nahele led the column 100 meters parallel with the trickling water to just above a tiny waterfall. There, after sending security upstream, he crossed. The vegetation at the gorge crossing was thick and lush and dark. The canopy created an almost opaque roof and Nahele and Snell followed by the column slipped across in the darkness. Nine men remained at the crossing. They would return to 636 to ambush the LZ. Nahele worked the gorge cut back along the west side then turned due west and picked a steep climb toward 606's peak. He moved slowly, jungle patrol cautious,

yet steadily. He covered the one map kilometer, perhaps two
surface klicks, in under an hour. Everyone behind the point was
panting. The unit circled the peak, rested for five minutes then
moved out again, again Nahele at point. Alpha continued its
murderous march. They descended west off 606 into another
steep-sided ravine, crossed another stream at the bottom and
climbed another hill. Every 200 meters they paused for a five-
minute break to allow the column to close up.

At times the trail became so steep they had to crawl and dig
in with their fingers and knees to ascend. They climbed to a
position just below the next peak west, Hill 711, broke for five,
spread out on line and swept up and over the top. On top they
rediscovered the NVA bunkers Charlie Company had found and
destroyed on the 13th. Half the bunkers had been rebuilt. The
enemy was nowhere to be seen. Alpha set up a full company
perimeter in the enemy fighting complex. It was almost sunset.
Brooks directed patrols, FO called DTs to the firebase, Doc
checked and taped a turned ankle of a boonierat in 2d Plt. Men
were directed urgently in every direction. A hasty CP meeting
was called. Brooks, with the concurrence of all the platoon
leaders and sergeants, directed 2d and 3d Plts to move out at
gray dusk for an NDP 300 meters northeast, downhill. It would
mark the beginning of Alpha's plunge into the valley. Brooks
directed 1st Plt, accompanied by the company CP, to follow 2d
and 3d to the new NDP, then to leave their rucks and return east
in lights. They would move back to Hill 606 and set up as a
reaction force for the ambush team.

They waited for the proper degree of grayness in the advancing dusk. It would be only a matter of minutes. From the summit
of Hill 711 the soldiers could see west down the Khe Ta Laou
and across the Da Krong and the narrow plain and into the
foothills of Laos. The sun splashed a reverse pattern of the day's
first light, splashed and refracted against the base of accumulating high clouds. The sky glowed momentarily then became gray.
The clouds above the Laotian hills grew thick and began to roll
east.

The boonierats watched the front approach, watched the sky
seemingly fold in upon itself and upon them. Everything became
still and quiet.

"You decide what you'll do yet, Ruf?" Lt. Thomaston
asked Lt. Brooks as they waited.

"What would you do . . . Bill?" Brooks responded. He had almost called him Lila. Be here, he ordered his mind.

"I'd DEROS," Thomaston said. "Of course, I can't make up your mind. But if you go, I get the company, I think. I think the GreenMan'd give it to me."

"You don't have much time left yourself," Brooks said.

"Twenty-five and a wake-up. He might give it to Wurzback but I think I'd be acting CO at least."

"Let's ruck up," Brooks said standing. He helped Thomaston up then asked, "Do you really want it?"

"Can't look bad on my record," Thomaston said.

"I'll let you know within a day or two," Brooks said.

The ambush team that had dropped off at the ravine between Hills 636 and 606 consisted of the 1st Sqd of the 1st Plt minus Steve Hoover, plus Cherry and Doc McCarthy. They had set up a tiny defensive ring on the east bank of the gorge above the crossing. Ambush had its benefits and its drawbacks. The volunteers did not have to hump. They sat, rested, relaxed. Two at a time they crawled to the stream to fill their canteens and wash. The drawbacks would begin after dark.

"Gettin useta boonie life?" Silvers whispered to Cherry when their turn in the stream came.

"Mostly," Cherry whispered back. Cherry was nervous and tight. The gorge crossing reminded him of the red ball from the water run. Cherry's eyes examined the jungle west of the water and the stream above. He could feel the NVA soldier out there, feel his first KIA watching him.

Silvers removed his clothes and sat in the water. He washed himself attempting to make as few motions as possible. He had brought a bar of soap and he lathered himself and rinsed part by part, foot to head, slowly. Cherry's head snapped up frequently while he filled his canteens. His eyes searched the stream bank and jungle.

"Here," Silvers whispered flipping Cherry the bar of soap. "Ya owe it to yerself." Silvers dressed quietly. He stood guard while Cherry undressed.

Undressing made Cherry feel more aware of his body and more vulnerable. He was coated with dirt. Oh God, my pits stink, he thought. The water was cool and clear though it felt somehow grainy as if it had picked up and suspended immense quantities of clear sand. The coolness felt wonderful. Cherry squatted by the stream and washed quickly, cupping water upon himself with his hands, soaping then rinsing by cupping again.

"Ya oughta get in," Silvers whispered. "That'll keep the jungle rot from gettin ya."

"This reminds me of a stream at Pomparaug," Cherry said stepping into the stream timidly, straining to maintain control. He did not want to step too far from his rifle.

"Where?" Silvers whispered.

"A Boy Scout camp I went to."

"Oh."

"This is really a nice spot," Cherry said. "I wish I could stop thinkin about dinks for just one fucken moment."

"Yeah," Silvers whispered. They were standing very close to each other. "I know whatcha mean."

"Leon," Cherry said very quietly. He stepped from the water and dried himself with his filthy towel. "I've been havin some terrible nightmares." Silvers shrugged sympathetically. "I keep seein that guy," Cherry said. Silvers dropped his head and did not speak. "I keep thinkin he'll go away," Cherry explained. "Then we get to a spot like this and I can feel him out there watchin me."

Silvers nodded his head in agreement. He was not sure how to respond. "It was either you or him," he said finally.

"Leon, I'm goina see that guy every night for the rest of my life."

"It'll go away, Man."

"Leon," Cherry said trying to stress the intensity of the emotion that had gripped him, "he didn't just die." Cherry shook like a naked frightened child. "He didn't just die, Leon."

"It don't do any good to think about it," Silvers said. Cherry's emotional display unsettled him. "Man, the first rule out here is survive. That means kill em before they kill you."

"Leon, when he fell," Cherry's eyes were glazing over and he was inducing a trance as if he wanted to force the NVA soldier's spirit to appear, "he . . . he was kickin. I wanted to go over and stop him but the AKs were firin. I was like a robot. I just fired at the noise and he kept kickin and twitchin."

"Come on," Silvers said grasping Cherry hard by the arm. "Get dressed. Just say fuck it and drive on. Don't mean nothin. Where's my soap?"

Silvers' jolt knocked Cherry out of his trance. He dressed

quickly, grabbed his rifle and Silvers' soap. "Here," he said
returning the soap. "Thanks."

"Oh shit. Goddamn."

"What?"

"Look at this, Mothafucker."

"What?"

"There. On my soap. You fucken pig. Yer pubies." Silvers
held the bar of soap by his fingertips and wiped it against a rock
scratching off a few curly black hairs.

"Oh shee-it," Cherry gurgled beneath his breath.

"Mothafucker. You expect me to use that soap!"

The ravine became still and dark. Everyone had washed.
The jungle about them seemed to be tightening down, closing in.
The ambush team discussed their plan. Lairds and Denhardt said
they should move out now. Silvers paused and told them to wait
five more minutes. They all squirmed. "Call Quiet Rover,"
Silvers directed Cherry. "Tell em we're movin up." They moved
out. Silvers led with Jax at slack then the gun team of Marko and
Brunak, Lairds, Denhardt, Numbnuts, Cherry and Doc McCarthy at drag. They climbed straight but slowly, pausing often to
insure they were not observed.

The ambush team stopped their ascent 200 meters from the
LZ on the summit of 636. With each step up the canopy had
thinned and it had become lighter. Silvers was apprehensive.
Had he left the ravine too soon? It had been very dark by the
stream but it was now far too light to move into ambush position.
The team sat in line on the trail, in complete silence. With only
nine men they did not dare even cough.

Without warning a wind gusted from the west. Just a single
gust, then calm. It had come suddenly and it caused the vegetation to shudder. Good, Silvers thought. With a wind we'll be
able to move in undetected. The team's plan was to slip in from
below and set up behind the blown trees just off the LZ. This
would give them clear fire across the crest. With luck, North
Vietnamese troops would come scavenging. It was common for
soldiers of the rich American army to discard unwanted cans of
food or even for some, like Numbnuts, to discard extra
ammunition. The poorer NVA thrived on American LZs and old
NDP sites. The better the American unit the less they left but
Americans, unaccustomed to want, able to call in resupply
helicopters, nearly always left something for NVA foragers.

A second gust of wind shook the canopy. Keep it up,

Silvers thought. He looked west into the wind. The gusts came
in force now. The soldiers could see the clouds behind the wind,
high towering clouds closing upon them from the west, enveloping the valley and the ridges. They could see the line of the
approaching rain, the rain curtain reaching 711, 606, the ravine
below them.

Wind shook the jungle above them. The rushing seemed to
vibrate the hill. Steadily the curtain advanced, harsh parallel
streaking water, not drops but lines crashing, resonating the
foliage. Doc McCarthy at the rear of the team got hit first. One
gigantic splat then total inundation swept across them all and the
rain and ricocheting mist became as ambient as the subdued
light. Numbnuts, Cherry and McCarthy at the team's tail pulled
their shirts tight in useless protection. Numbnuts unstrapped his
helmet from his ruck and put it on his head. Cherry watched him
and did the same. The noise of the rain on the helmets and in the
canopy was very loud.

"Rover Two Two, Quiet Rover Four, security check. Over."
El Paso radioed Cherry. Cherry scrunched down over the handset
and listened as El Paso repeated the call. Then Cherry keyed the
handset twice, indicating they were secure.

With the rain came darkness. What luck, Silvers thought.
He stood. He was totally soaked. The trail became a mudbrown
stream. Man, what luck, he thought. When the boonierats were
moving they liked the rain because it was difficult to be heard.
When they were set up they hated the rain for then it was cold
and it masked the sounds of the moving enemy. Great, Silvers
thought. He stirred Jackson. "Let's go." Jax grabbed Marko's
shoulder and gave a tug. Marko grabbed Brunak's, Brunak
Lairds', Lairds Denhardt's, and Denhardt Numbnuts'. There the
signal broke. Numbnuts did not respond. The wind tore into
him, opening his shirt even as he struggled to keep it shut. He
did not want to move. He simply sat. The first six team members
squirmed up toward the LZ in complete blackness, unaware of
the last three sitting quietly.

The squall further eroded Alpha's morale. It had been a
miserable day and now there was this tremendous torrent. From
the first stinging splash it had saturated them to the skin. The
platoons had humped off 711 in the initial onslaught. They had
slid and slipped and fallen on the trail. The weight of their
rucksacks toppled them. Their boot soles clogged with mud and

their feet shot out from under them a dozen times each. 2d and 3d Plts set up a hasty NDP and sent out patrols. 1st and the CP left their rucks and quickly descended then climbed back to Hill 606. At their new NDP they huddled in pockets under the palms but the rain was so thick and the wind so fierce, they felt totally exposed. In the midst of the assembling CP group Brooks sat. Water puddled on his thighs. It ran from his face into his mouth. It trickled in streams beneath his shirt. The burden of command had become heavier. His company was too spread out for such a hostile AO and his troops were disgusted with the day's events. Their fear was increasing, their confidence waning. The noise of the rain obliterated any possibility of hearing enemy movement. To add to the injustices their NDP site was so steep they could not lie down without rolling or sliding downhill. The guards found trees or shrubs to lie against or to straddle but gravity pushed them into the trees with all their weight and every few minutes they had to shift positions. It would be a miserable, restless night.

The CP group was joined by Thomaston and Egan and the meeting began. It lasted only a few minutes. Cahalan reviewed the day's activities about the valley. Recon had killed one NVA in a brief encounter. Bravo had engaged an unknown-sized enemy force with unknown results. Egan bitched about the tunnel. "God mothafuckin whore damn," he cussed. "We're practically still right there. We're jumpin back and forth, not goin anywhere, not doin anything where we're at." El Paso agreed and said that's what killed Ridgefield. That dampened their spirits even more.

"Where ma plasma?" Doc questioned. "They was supposed ta send out a hun'red bag."

No one answered him. They all seemed to be in a stupor. Their eyes had sunk into deepening sockets. Since leaving the tunnel they had covered 3000 map meters, perhaps six kilometers climbing up and down, each carrying refilled rucks and equipment, all on full alert, in either tropical heat or in harsh cold rain.

"Tomorrow," Brooks said a little too loud, loud enough to inject command energy into his weary soldiers, "tomorrow we get out of here. We cross the valley. El Paso, get De Barti and Caldwell on the hook. Cahalan get Red Rover. Any questions? No? Good. Tomorrow we get the ambush team back in at first light, then rendezvous with 2d and 3d. Then we cross the valley."

* * *

Cherry shuddered. The wind was harsher now. He had crossed and wrapped his arms about his chest. His rifle was muzzle up between his legs, his thighs pressed it as if for warmth. The jungle was pitch black. Cherry could not even see McCarthy who was sitting less than a meter from his feet. The trail had become a river and the water surged against Cherry's ruck and his ass. The water streamed right through the material of his pants. Cherry's teeth chattered. With this wind and rain, he thought, I could probably scream and not be heard. El Paso called again checking security. Cherry keyed the transmit bar. He rolled to his left, to his knees, and crawled forward a foot. Numbnuts was right there.

"Hey," Cherry hissed. "Hey, find out when we're . . ." Cherry reached out and grabbed the thumperman.

"What?" Numbnuts said, startled.

"Cool it. Hey, when we goina move? Were you sleepin?"

"I wasn't sleepin," Numbnuts snapped.

"When we goina move out?" Cherry asked.

McCarthy tapped Cherry from behind. "We movin? I'm fuckin freezin. When we . . ."

It took three or four minutes in the dark for them to determine they had broken contact, had become separated, were alone. "Hey, nobody signaled me," Numbnuts defended himself.

"You mothafucker," McCarthy spit at Numbnuts' face. "I can't believe you did that."

"I wasn't sleepin," Numbnuts snapped again. "Maybe you was sleepin."

The urge to smash Numbnuts in the face seethed in McCarthy. It seethed in Cherry too. Cherry forced his brain back into control. What should I do? he thought. What's got to be done? He knew he could not call out, 'Hey, where are you guys?' though that was his first impulse. He hesitated to use the radio. He could call back to the CP but he could not call the ambush team. He had the team's only radio.

"Willis," Cherry addressed Numbnuts using the thumperman's surname to establish his own authority, "move up the trail about ten feet. See if you can find Denhardt. Doc, you watch below us. I'm goina call Rover Two and get Egan. We gotta link back up with the team."

"I aint goin up there," Numbnuts protested. "I can't see."

"Shut the fuck up," Cherry whispered violently. A natural

command instinct had surfaced in him. "When you speak, you speak quiet, Fucker."

"You go up there," Numbnuts whined irritably. "Why should I listen to you? Huh? It wasn't my fault . . . Auughh . . ." He screamed as Cherry jerked him up by his shirt then slammed him down into the mud. Cherry grasped him by the throat, held him with his left hand. Numbnuts squirmed. Cherry cocked his right arm, squeezed his fist, aimed at Numbnuts' head . . .

"What the fuck are you doin?" Someone grabbed Cherry. "Where the fuck you been?" It was Silvers. "Get up. Get up there. Get up there. What the fuck's wrong with you?"

Silvers grabbed Cherry, spun him uphill and pushed him. Numbnuts jumped up about to protest but Silvers was already at the head of the little column. Numbnuts ran a few furious steps to catch up. Cherry was vibrating with rage at the injustice of Silvers' accusing him. He stepped more lightly than he had ever stepped. Rain or no rain, he was a good soldier and he wasn't going to take the rap for Numbnuts' fuck-up. Cherry stepped where Silvers stepped except smoother, quieter. As they approached the summit LZ the slope leveled and they slowed. All of a sudden the howl and roar of the wind was engulfed in three successive explosions BOOM!BOOM!BOOM! and a fusillade of firing.

Cherry and Silvers dropped. The firing was 30 meters away. Silvers rose and crept quickly cautiously forward. Cherry, McCarthy and Numbnuts followed. Jax, Lairds and Denhardt were all firing their 16s and Marko the 60 as Brunak fed. They sprayed fire across the entire LZ.

"Over there," Denhardt yelled. "Out there," he screamed. Silvers reached him. "There's gooks over there. I seen em." He continued firing. Silvers tossed a grenade and fired. Cherry squeezed off a burst on full automatic. Then everything became quiet. There had been no return fire.

They paused. The team huddled together to discuss what to do next. The rain was still coming down hard and making noise in the canopy. The NVA could be maneuvering up to their sides, around behind them, maybe even in front of them. "We blew it, Man," Marko said. "We gotta go back."

"Call the CP," Jax said. "Tell em we done blowed our position. Ef anybody out here, they know right where we at."

They all agreed. No one, including Silvers, wanted to remain. They had fired too much at too little.

Silvers grabbed the hook. "Quiet Rover Four, this is Rover Two Two. Over," Silvers called. At the CP El Paso answered and passed the hook to the L-T. "We're comin back in," Silvers informed Brooks. Brooks asked questions. He listened. He thought it would be more dangerous for the team to move than to stay and rearrange themselves. Silvers argued for returning. Brooks denied his request again. Their conversation ended there.

"Let's go," Silvers said. And without permission the ambush team backed out of its position behind the blown trees, returned to the trail and descended toward the ravine. Very quietly they descended in column, all of them very alert now, holding the rucksacks to their front in an unbroken chain.

Egan and Thomaston had crawled away from the CP meeting and had dragged themselves through the mud to a guard/ sleeping position at the side of a foot-thick tree. It could not have been more uncomfortable. Because of the slope, they slid into each other, pressed each other against the tree. On top of all else, where the tree's roots spread, rising from the ground like an inverted fan, the tiny cavities and recesses were filled with spider webs. Egan felt wretched. Finally he got up, moved up the hill several meters, found a thin tree trunk and tied himself to it. He settled back wrapped in a poncho liner and poncho and closed his eyes. Stephanie came to him immediately. Like magic she eased the discomfort and anguish. She floated into the jungle and the rain ceased, the wind became a gentle breeze.

After that October afternoon in New York Daniel Egan lost contact with Stephanie. He called a few times without receiving an answer and finally found the phone disconnected. It must have been at least a month between calls and in those months he found a new Daniel, a man sexually attractive to women. All this time, he thought, I thought you had to be something special to get a girl. I thought they had to love you. In the course of a semester Daniel moved from naive small town boy to campus stud. He kept score, laughing about it with his football friends, and flaunting his prowess at fraternity parties. He fell in love a dozen times and forgot a dozen names. And he found he hated it. Something was missing.

On a cold snowy night in February Daniel was in bed with Little Fannie, a fraternity sweetheart. They had just made love or at least balled. He had just come. He was still atop her, still in her, semi-flaccid. For this, he had said to himself, for this I didn't pull it for two days. He lay there thinking. Then he rolled off. "Fannie," he said. "Ah, I got a big exam tomorrow. I got to study." She said go ahead and pulled the blanket tightly about herself. "Ya can't stay while I'm studying," he said.

"You got to be kidding," she had said. In the end he threw her out. After she left he lay alone for a long time. Then he rose, went to his desk and wrote a note to Stephanie.

Now in the vacuum of darkness, on that empty fetid hillside morass where he had tied himself, her image warming his enslaved soul solidified and she spoke the soliloquy of her reply, a reply which did not arrive until early June.

Dear Daniel,
    I'll bet you're wondering what's happened to me. Things have happened quickly and have been very complicated but I'll try to explain as best I can.
    The last time we talked I told you I didn't know where I was going. I had to leave NYC, so, I went home. I'm skipping around. I've been having trouble with my step-father because he thinks what I did was a terrible sin. I'll get to that. One night, shortly after I moved back in, he and mother were arguing about my being here and I overheard and went downstairs to tell him to leave mother alone and that I would leave. Before I knew it I was telling him how he had never shown me any love. The idea that he had failed as a father and that therefore had contributed to my sin surprised him. He's always been such a success at everything.
    Anyway, I'm married, getting divorced, and I've had an abortion. Actually, you're not going to believe this, but I had two. I've been through quite a lot since I last saw you. The first abortion didn't work. I don't know if you know anything about them. They certainly are not fun. I became very ill after my second D & C which is a scraping of the uterus. I only got out of the hospital yesterday. When I get up and around I'm planning to get a job and save some money so I can go to school. I want to work with children. I have definitely decided not to go into art.
    As far as the divorce is concerned that will be happening very soon. Not a definite date now but soon. As soon

as possible. I hesitate to write you, Daniel, because I've been so sick and because I really don't know if it is the right thing to do. I respect you so much and I don't want you to get involved in anything ugly. This is really hard for me to put into words but it is how I feel. I wasn't going to write then I started thinking about how much I wanted to hear more from you and that you would know yourself just how much to get involved. I don't understand exactly how I feel. The whole time I was living with my husband I couldn't stand it and I thought of you constantly. I wanted to call you so badly. Daniel, please write. Write me a long letter. You're such a wonderful writer, so precise and beautiful with words.

　　Please don't be afraid of my feelings. I'll never press you. Could you send me a sketch too? I know someday you'll be a superb architect. It's very late but I don't want this letter to end. It's almost like I'm talking to you. I guess I should get to bed.

　　　　　　　　　　　　　　　　　Love,
　　　　　　　　　　　　　　　　　Stephanie

　　Two Fridays after the letter arrived, Daniel left school. He hitchhiked to her, arrived on her doorstep at three Saturday morning and allowed the long sleepless night to torture him in an attempt to atone for his lapse. "I brought you something," he smiled when she opened the door six hours later.

　　"Daniel," she screamed with glee. She rushed to him and they embraced and held each other tightly and then her mother was there saying hello and making them breakfast.

　　Saturday was beautiful. She took him to a lake and they hiked to the secluded far shore. Stephanie had never been lovelier. The air remained crisp all day, the sunshine warm and clean.

　　"Daniel," she said. God, he thought, how much I love to hear you say my name. "Why are you so quiet? Talk to me. I've told you all about my past eight months and you've told me nothing."

　　He wanted to speak but he couldn't. How could he confess to her that he had been on a fuckathon. He looked into those beautiful eyes and he thought of himself and he felt like dirt.

　　"I love your sketch," Stephanie said. She kissed him then

raised her sweater and exposed her breasts and gently pulled Daniel's face to her.

Egan lying tied to a tree on the wet jungle hillside rolled to his side and pushed the poncho liner up higher about his neck. He felt pleasantly warm. The image before him shifted. There were two lovers alone and in darkness. He recognized himself. "I've designed some of the world's most wonderful homes in my head," his image said.

She laughed. "I've painted some of the greatest pictures in my mind."

They both laughed. Then they stopped and were silent and they shared a sorrow. What if I never really design them? he shuddered. What if they are not the most wonderful when they are on paper? She too shuddered, then breaking their silence Stephanie said, "Please. Let's go someplace."

"Yes," Daniel said. "Let's go."

"Where?"

"Nowhere. Let's just go." They rose and stood for a dizzy moment and looked at each other. Stephanie sat back down. "Get up," Daniel pleaded gently. "We will go . . . somewhere."

"Where?" Stephanie cried. "You're going to go back to school or to a job. Leaving me again."

In the cold jungle the memory now agitated Egan. Perhaps he had been too close to it then. Perhaps he could understand it better now, from this distance in time and space. Much of what Daniel Egan remembered of Stephanie was not her at all but was only him when he was with her. Perhaps I wasn't sensitive enough to perceive more than just me, he thought. I never asked her how she felt or what she thought. *I didn't really know her.* She is not really here at all, he thought. The wind blew colder. He wanted to know her so much more.

His dream convoluted. The warmth vanished. The fragrance became the odor of jungle rot and dead men. The sky's glow dimmed, became dark and ugly. A harsh glint chased Stephanie's image from the screen of his mind. Egan was petrified. He was tied down, staked out, unable to react. The sapper squatted by his side. The silver machete was in his right hand. Egan tried to move. The rope restraints cut into his wrists, his ankles. He arched his back, lifted his belly. Moonlight sparkled upon the blade and in the sapper's eyes as the dark foe raised the knife. The enemy cocked his wrist, aimed the blade for Egan's eyes, began the downward killing stroke. Egan craned his neck to

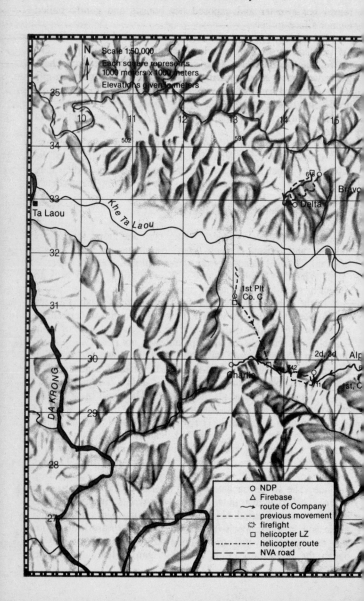

N
Scale 1:50,000
Each square represents
1000 meters x 1000 meters
Elevations given in meters

○ NDP
△ Firebase
⌒ route of Company
--- previous movement
❉ firefight
□ helicopter LZ
-·-·- helicopter route
-- NVA road

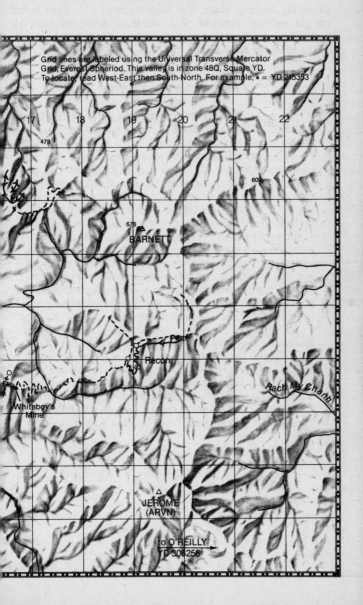

Grid lines are labeled using the Universal Transverse Mercator
Grid, Everest Spheriod. This valley is in zone 48Q, Square YD.
To locate, read West-East then South-North. For example, • = YD 215353

17   18   19   20   21   22

478

609

678
BARNETT

Recon

Rach My Chanh

Whiteboy's
Mine

JEROME
(ARVN)

To O'REILLY
YD 306258

avoid the slashing blade. The blade touched . . . Egan bolted upright panting, paranoid. Rain streamed down his face. He grabbed his forehead, his nose, his cheeks. He tasted the stream to insure it was not blood.

SIGNIFICANT ACTIVITIES

THE FOLLOWING RESULTS OF OPERATIONS IN THE O'REILLY/ BARNETT/JEROME AREA WERE REPORTED FOR THE 24-HOUR PERIOD ENDING 2359 16 AUGUST 70:

AT 0950 HOURS, VICINITY YD 191298, RECON, CO E, 7/402 EN-GAGED AN UNKNOWN SIZE ENEMY FORCE KILLING ONE NVA. CO B, 7/402 CONTINUED TO EXPLORE THE NVA HOSPITAL COMPLEX THEY UNCOVERED 15 AUGUST. THE COMPLEX CONTAINED A TO-TAL OF 18 BUNKERS SCATTERED OVER A SQUARE KILOMETER. SEVERAL OF THE BUNKERS WERE INTERCONNECTED BY A TUNNEL NETWORK CUT DEEPLY INTO THE MOUNTAINOUS TERRAIN. THIRTY-FOUR MEDICAL KITS AND 1100 POUNDS OF MEDICAL SUPPLIES WERE EVACUATED. A CACHE CONTAINING 100 NVA UNIFORMS AND 2400 POUNDS OF RICE WAS DESTROYED. IN AN EVIDENT IN-TENSIVE CARE INFIRMARY BUNKER A BODY WAS DISCOVERED ALONG WITH ONE VERY SERIOUSLY WOUNDED ENEMY SOLDIER. THE PRISONER WAS EVACUATED TO PHU BAI.

AT YD 193273, THE 1ST BN, 3D REGT (ARVN) RECEIVED RPG AND SMALL ARMS FIRE FROM AN ESTIMATED ENEMY BATTALION SURROUNDING THEIR POSITION. THE ARVN ELEMENT RETURNED ORGANIC WEAPONS FIRE RESULTING IN 38 NVA KIA AND ONE POW CAPTURED. 13 ARVN SOLDIERS WERE WOUNDED IN THE ACTION.

AT MIDDAY, FOUR KILOMETERS SOUTHWEST OF FIREBASE BARNETT, ONE US SOLDIER FROM CO A, 7/402 WAS KILLED BY A SNIPER. THE UNIT RETURNED FIRE WITH UNKNOWN RESULTS.

C H A P T E R

▮▮▮▮ 23 ▮▮▮▮

1 7   A U G U S T   1 9 7 0

Cherry had changed, had been changing. He had begun changing long before but now the alteration accelerated. He had changed from play-soldier to trainee, then from state-side soldier to REMF soldier and then to cherry soldier. They were changes which happened to him, not changes of him, changes which occurred because the army had moved him. Those changes were not great. On 17 August he changed greatly, he changed to just plain soldier.

"We're startin back," Cherry radioed Quiet Rover. It was not yet first light. "We're on our way back," he lied.

"Ah, roger that Two Two," El Paso replied. At the CP El Paso was on radio watch again. He rolled and woke Brooks. "Ambush team comin back in."

"Uh! What time is it?"

"Oh five-four-eight," El Paso said.

First light was approaching. Cahalan stirred beside El Paso. Above them Doc was going through his aid bag. The sky's blackness softened. It was still raining. Brooks got up and relieved himself against a tree below their position.

"We're at the blue feature," Cherry radioed in a fictitious progress report fifteen minutes after his first call. All the soldiers at the CP were up, folding ponchos, cleaning weapons, brushing teeth. The guards were up too. They had humped to the NDP in lights which meant they had not brought food. Some of them bitched about being hungry. Doc Johnson passed amongst them handing each man a Monday Pill, a large orange quinine anti-malaria tablet. Everyone swallowed one. The Monday Pill was very seldom discarded. It was a big bright orange pill, it looked important, and it marked the passing of another week. That gave it ritual significance.

At 0625 Cherry radioed the CP again to give his position and determine theirs. They were very close. In fact they were less than fifty meters from 1st Plt.

After the ambush squad had blown its cover by engaging suspected enemy movement on the LZ, they had backed off Hill 636 and, in the dark, had wormed back down to the ravine. "Fuck the L-T," Silvers had said. "We aint stayin here. That'd be suicide." They all agreed. At the ravine they crossed the stream, discussed setting up but decided to move up. Silvers had followed the trail down but he had not known where to go up. He had simply set a compass course and stumbled in one general direction mumbling to himself the entire time, "God don't let the gooks be here. God don't let the gooks be here." Quite by accident they had found a small indentation in the hill, which was partially protected from the elements and in the dark appeared very defensible. They had devised a guard/radio watch schedule—two awake, seven asleep—and, exhausted from the day's work, had slept. Every two hours the guards changed. Every hour the CP called for a situation report. For Cherry, for all of 1st Sqd except Silvers who bore the responsibility of their move, it had been the best night of sleep since stand-down.

The ambush team stood up and marched in silently.

Whiteboy, Egan and Thomaston greeted them. "What'd you guys fire up?" Egan asked.

"Gooks," Lairds laughed.

"Let's go over it," Thomaston said. He pumped them with questions, received vague answers about movement and asked them if they would like to return for a first light check, "Which you shoulda done before you left."

"Augh, Man," Silvers groaned, "we just humped back."

"I'll go," Egan volunteered. "Who wants to tricky-trot up there with me?"

In lights the recon element, Egan, Whiteboy, Moneski and his gun team and Hoover with the radio, moved very quickly. They were to the LZ and back in forty minutes.

"Hey," Egan laughed when they returned. "Hey Silvers. Here's your gook. Here's the gook you got last night." On the end of his rifle Egan had an American fatigue shirt that had been blown to hell. Half the platoon clustered close to see. They were all laughing.

Whiteboy guffawed. "Yer squad finally got a body count." Whiteboy threw the shirt up into a tree. "It was just a dang-a-lin lahk that," he laughed.

"Ah, that don't prove nothin," Numbnuts protested. Everyone laughed at him.

Egan grabbed the shirt and tossed it at Silvers playfully. "Here's your gook, Leon."

They were uncharacteristically loud. Cherry laughed along with them all, not saying a word.

1st Plt and the company CP retraced their steps across the ridge, into the ravine and up, and rendezvoused with 2d and 3d Plts. The unit's field force now stood at eighty-three, down from ninety on the morning of 16 August if the PIOs and correspondent and the dog team and Ridgefield were included: eighty-three men with the mission of descending into the Khe Ta Laou to assault the suspected Headquarters of the 7th NVA Front, eighty-three soldiers assigned to search out and destroy a suspected, long occupied, extensively developed and heavily defended supply base and staging area.

The company moved in column down a finger toward the valley. 2d Plt led followed by the CP and then 3d. 1st Plt hung back as rear security. The column moved quickly at first; then, as the point element hit thicker and thicker vegetation, the column barely edged forward. The terrain became steeper. Standing was exhausting. Rucks dug deeply into shoulders. The straps pulled at shoulder skin made resistant by the continuing rain. The skin distorted from the pressure and felt as if it were ripping. Arms became weary from holding weapons, from grasping small trees for handholds to keep from sliding, from pushing and lifting bodies and rucks back up after they had fallen. The point pulled his machete and selectively sliced a trail. Behind point one hundred and sixty-six boots mulched the cuttings into the mud and sections of the trail became slides. Alpha came to a series of cliffs. 1st Plt sent forward the ropes Egan had used at the tunnel. The point rigged them for rappeling and the column descended.

From the top of the first cliff Cherry glared down at the valley. It was the closest he had come. He, all the boonierats, had been looking at it for four days, glimpsing it through breaks in the vegetation, through a waxing and waning fog shroud. Cherry glared down upon it. Beneath the fog there would be a different world. Over he went, rappeled.

The column continued to descend. The morning was quiet except for the rain and the noise of men slipping and falling, and the bursting of artillery far to the northeast. By noon the point element of the column reached the first rolling hills, mounds, between the steep slope of the finger and the valley floor. The boonierats set up a defensive perimeter and rested. The 1st Sqd of the 1st Plt, the farthest extreme of the column, was only halfway down the finger, still in the cliffs. For them the trail had become so mushed by the preceding troops, they had to crawl backward and dig their fingers into the thick slop to keep from tumbling off the trail and into the jungle below.

The column expanded into an elongated egg about the first mound as the troops at the rear completed the steep descent. Alpha was half-in, half-above the valley fog, a thick sticky-feeling mist through which the rain continued to fall but through which no one could see. The vegetation about them was as different from the trees and vines of the ridge as it would have been if they had crossed space to another planet. It was gray scraggle brush, low, only five to ten feet high, and it was so incredibly dense, except on paths, it was impossible to even shove an arm deeply into it. With the mist it made the boonierats uneasy and frightened. It was another world, the NVA's world. Hand signals passed unnecessarily: maintain strict noise discipline, keep movement to a minimum. Egan moved a thumb toward his open mouth signaling to Cherry, eat. Cherry passed the signal to Doc McCarthy behind him and slipped from his ruck.

Along with all his other aches and stiffness, Cherry found the skin of his thighs was raw. Shit, Man, he said to himself, what if I got a case of the black syph. Oh shit. Maybe I got it from movin them barrels of shit down at Cam Ranh. Cherry glanced about him then unbuttoned his pant fly. He looked at his legs. Patches of skin on his inner thighs from his testicles down about four inches were brightly inflamed. The rainwater dripping from his hands onto the chafed skin burned. "Oh God," Cherry moaned. He did not want to tell anyone because he was embarrassed by the location of the sofes and also because he feared it might be something serious. He had heard stories about strains of venereal disease immune to penicillin and all other modern drugs. There were rumors of an American colony on Guam of

infected men from Vietnam that the government would not allow
to return to the States. He looked at the rash again. It was on his
balls too. Oh shit. Oh shit, oh shit. Cherry tried to recall from
his biology classes what the incubation period for syphilis was.
He looked down. Goddamn, each day it gets worse, he thought.
He thought about how it had progressed, spoke it to himself as if
he were telling a medic. "Doc," he said to himself, "it's really
gettin bad. I don't know where I could a got it. I aint even sure
what it is but I can hardly walk with it."

Lt. Brooks had been working his way around Alpha's
perimeter. He very quietly asked questions and advice. When he
reached Egan he squatted. Egan was sitting in a puddle. He
appeared comfortable. The L-T and Egan tapped fists. "If you
were a little people," Brooks asked, "where would you be?"

"If I knew somebody was comin after me?" Egan asked.

"Yeah," Brooks said.

"Are you rulin out the tunnels in the hills?"

"Yep. Down here. Where?"

"I'd be leavin a trail so you'd follow me to my battleground."

"Where?"

"Away from my headquarters."

"Where would you put your headquarters?"

"Away from the trail I'd want you to follow."

Brooks pulled out his topo map. "Show me."

Egan looked at the map. He studied it. "Not in the foothills,
we might come down on them. Not on the flat, too easy for the
birds to fire em up. Ah, unless they got some Russian tanks in
here, ya know, L-T . . ."

"What?"

". . . I'd be at the high feature on the river. There's the
ridge comin out toward it from both sides. Not a lot of room for
fast movers to work."

"Thanks."

"Right on."

Brooks moved back to Cherry, asked him how he was
holding up, and moved on as Cherry nodded okay. Cherry
waited until the commander had passed Doc McCarthy then he
crept back to the medic. Egan turned and watched. Fuck Egan,
Cherry thought.

"Ah Doc, ah, can I ask you somethin?"

"Yeah. What is it?"

"I got this, ah, problem."

"What is it?" McCarthy asked. He looked at Cherry very sympathetically and asked him, "Where is it?"

Thanks, Cherry thought. This guy's got a talent for making it easy. "It's my groin. I think I got the syph."

"You got burnin?"

"Yeah."

"Really bad, I mean."

"I can hardly walk," Cherry said.

"Walk? I mean when you piss."

"No Doc. When I walk."

"Let me see," Doc said.

Cherry unbuttoned his pants. Goddamn Egan, watchin, Cherry thought. Cherry dropped his fatigue trousers and pulled up the inside of his OD boxer trunks exposing the chafed hot skin.

"Ooooo! You got it bad," McCarthy said. "You shouldn't a let it get that bad." Egan had come back to look. Doc winked at him. "Got it bad."

"What is it?" Cherry said turning away from Egan.

Egan pulled his bayonet from the sheath at his calf and smiled sadistically. "Ah ha, gotta cut it off."

Cherry's eyes widened. He began pulling his pants up. "Well what the fuck is it?" he demanded.

In one quick motion Egan slipped the blade of his bayonet into Cherry's boxer trunks and cut the cloth up the side.

"Crotch rot," McCarthy said. "Jungle rot of the crotch."

Egan kept Cherry off-balance tugging at the waistband of his underwear as he slipped the bayonet blade into the other side and cut the material. Then he whipped the tattered cloth away and flicked it into the jungle brush. "You can't wear underwear here," Egan chuckled. "It'll rot yer balls off."

"Here," McCarthy said handing Cherry a tube of salve. "Rub some of this on it."

Suddenly from behind them 60s and 16s erupted. Cherry hit the dirt pulling his pants up. Egan charged toward the firing. Grenades exploded. Snell, Nahele and McQueen from 3d Plt came racing through, running to the fight. The initial firing lasted less than ten seconds. Jackson, Marko, Brunak, Lairds and Denhardt had fired simultaneously down the slope of the mound. They were at the very rear of the column. They had descended the cliffs last, had crossed the small draw to the mound and had been sitting quietly when they heard the chatter. They all turned slowly and looked through the tangle of dense brush and they saw an NVA squad. The enemy soldiers were walking casually, talking, their rifles slung over their shoulders. The initial blast felled four.

Egan, Brooks, Silvers, Nahele, a whole group of them lay on the ground, whispered back and forth. "Silvers, take six men down there," Brooks directed pointing to the right. "Danny, Don, Queenie," Brooks pointed to the left. Brooks, Thomaston and Whiteboy dropped down straight. Above, at the spot where 1st Sqd had been when they fired, Moneski's squad covered the advancing recon and all around the perimeter men shifted to fill gaps.

"Holy fucken Christ!" Egan uttered. In the hollow below the mound there was a red ball but it was unlike any red ball Egan had ever seen. The trail was five feet wide with an all-weather surface. The ground had been leveled and reinforced with bamboo. The canopy above had been woven into living semi-solid mats. Egan's group followed the trail only half-a-dozen meters then stopped. In the opposite direction Silvers' squad followed the trail a few meters to where it turned to the hill. Here a culvert allowed a stream to pass beneath the trail without washing it out. Where Brooks descended his group found blood puddles, blood trails, a small rucksack and nothing more. There were no bodies. The boonierats retreated back to the mound.

"There's gotta been at least a dozen," Thomaston said.

"You think you hit four, maybe five?" Brooks asked.

"At least," Marko whispered and Silvers and Jax agreed.

"They had to have at least a dozen to carry those bodies out a there that quick," Thomaston said. "I don't think if there were only seven or eight they could a done that."

"Look at this shit," Egan whistled. He was pilfering the NVA ruck. Along with a bag of rice and a bowl there was black licorice candy, a C-ration B-2 Unit, US matches and various odds and ends Alpha had left at their resupply site.

"So," Silvers said punching Egan's shoulder and chuckling, "there's my gook."

Alpha moved out again almost immediately. They remained in the same order, 2d Plt, CP, 3d and 1st. Their fight was not for the road, and they had no intention of following it to a certain ambush. They called the action in to the TOC and found that Bravo Company was again engaged in a major battle. The

Bravos had left the hospital complex and had returned toward their original insertion LZ. At the same location where they had been assaulted on the night of the 14th, they cornered a well entrenched NVA company. Artillery was attempting to soften their objective. The rain and fog prohibited Tac Air or helicopter support. Alpha monitored the fight. Recon too was in a skirmish.

The column humped north and slightly west moving from mound to mound of ever decreasing size, descending to the flat valley floor. Alpha humped steadily, cautiously. They crossed another red ball and this one too had an all-weather surface. At a pause Brooks studied his topo map. None of the trails were indicative. Alpha continued toward the river, aiming northwest now, downstream. The mist thickened. The vegetation changed again as they descended, the dense scragglebrush giving way to dense bamboo and elephant grass. In places the bamboo was over fifteen feet high. The point man felt as if he were breaking trail through knife blades of spring steel. His arms were soon slashed and bloody and his face had multiple tiny lacerations. The grass cut fine and quick and a boonierat did not know until after he was cut that a blade had touched him. The blood trickled and microscopic barbs stung in the wounds. The point alternated with his slack and finally every man in the lead squad had experienced the agony of breaking trail.

The valley floor was even more eerie than the mounds. The rain continued. It was nearly impossible for Alpha to establish their precise position. Surrounded by fog and high grass they could not sight landmarks. The flat valley floor revealed no clues. They knew the location of the first mound below the cliffs and their own approximate direction. The distance they moved was vague. When Brooks believed, guessed, his point element was 100 meters from the river, he called a halt. The column sat.

"El Paso, call De Barti," Brooks directed. "Tell him to move his gunteams to point. Call Snell and get Nahele and McQueen up here. Have Thomaston send up Whiteboy."

When the two machine gun teams from behind the CP reached Brooks, they and the entire CP moved forward. They walked quietly up the trail stepping over and around seated men. At 2d Plt's command post Brooks and De Barti planned Alpha's sweep to the river.

Leon Silvers was at the rear of the column. To his front was Brunak, then Marko and Jax and the rest of 1st Sqd ending with

Numbnuts. 1st Plt's CP had dropped back to between 1st and 2d Sqds. The boonierats were sitting at six to eight foot intervals. Thomaston, facing Egan, held up two fingers on his right hand and four on his left. He smiled and mouthed, "Twenty-four and a wake-up."

"Twenty-one, you cherry," Egan smiled back.

The column began to move again then it stopped. It moved a little then stopped again. Cherry came up behind Egan and whispered, "They're at the river."

Egan nodded, moved up several feet and sat down.

Cherry sat where he had been standing. One by one the men to his rear situated themselves on the wet ground. A cool breeze swayed the tall grass. Cherry examined his fingers. The skin was puffed and white and wrinkled from the long exposure to the wet. He began to meditate, to ponder the loneliness he was experiencing. For extended hours they all humped without speaking. For hours he marched seeing only the one man before him and at times not even seeing him. Cherry longed for a CP meeting. He looked to his rear. McCarthy was lying back on his ruck. From behind the medic, Numbnuts' whisper seeped into the quiet. That guy won't ever learn, Cherry said to himself. An uneasy feeling came upon Cherry. He looked left then right. Somebody was watching. He looked over his shoulder again at McCarthy. The mist was so thick it blurred his image. Cherry could feel eyes on the back of his neck. He glanced around anxiously. He could see nothing but dense walls of elephant grass. Maybe it's better not to look, he thought. He tried to ignore it. His stomach tightened. He felt as if something was about to reach out and grab him. "Fuck it," he whispered. The breeze swayed the top of the grass again. He fidgeted apprehensively. Trail watchers? Timidly he turned left gaping into the grass. Slowly he looked right. His hand played with the trigger mechanism of his weapon. He shortened his neck. His helmet touched his ruck. He waited for the spell to break, for the column to move. Maybe I oughta tell McCarthy, he thought. He hesitated. It's too unfounded. I haven't seen anything. He tried to relax but still he could feel eyes focusing on the back of his neck. Again he turned. He was very low on the ground. The eyes were still behind him. His arms trembled, his fists clenched, his mind lost awareness. He stared vacantly at his fatigue pants— wet and filthy. His boots were coated with slime and splinters of grass. Cherry shut his eyes, shrunk lower for protection. Colors, all shades of green, swirled in strange geometric kaleidoscope clouds. Forms precipitated. At the base he could see ankles congealing, his ankles, his knees. He was suspended in blackness with only his legs illuminated by the geometric green glow. Slowly the kaleidoscope turned. The vision focused. Baggy green fatigue pant legs unclouded. The image cleared upward to his waist. He was not sure if his eyes were open or shut. He could see his shirt, his shoulders. Every minute segment, every stitch, was in perfect focus. Cherry could see his neck. Then the head appeared. It was large. Too large. Then the face. It was not Cherry's face. It was the face of the enemy soldier. It stared at Cherry. It had Cherry's body. The face contorted. Cherry's body took one cautious step forward, stepped right through Cherry lying on the trail. Behind him eyes bore down on his back, burned hate into his neck. It was not a man. It was a bird, some sort of hawk. Falcon. Cherry's heart pounded. His eyes crushed tight. The falcon hovered unseen behind him—invisible and waiting, waiting to strike, waiting to split the air with lightning speed, to swoop down invisible—The Talons of God!

The man stood between Cherry and God. He glared into Cherry's eyes from atop Cherry's own body.

We got to move. I can't sit here. Cherry was frozen. Thoughts flashed through his head but they could not penetrate the image before his eyes. Don't let the talons get me, he prayed. Cherry cowered lower into the foul muck. Oh God. Oh God. I'm sorry. I had to do it. Titanic wings beat creating wind in the valley, gusts bending the wretched grass. God, you could have turned him around. He was coming at me. Tears welled to Cherry's eyes. The valley blackened and for protracted seconds Cherry's heart ceased to beat.

The soldier took shape again, smiling laughing behind thick vegetation. He snarled and stepped forward. Cherry could see the head, the soldier's taunting face above the sight of Cherry's own weapon. The face became Cherry's face. Cherry squeezed his weapon, he tried not to squeeze, he squeezed, the muzzle flashed, the rifle kicked, the face erupted, the forehead burst red, exploding. The body dropped into the darkness twitching in violent spasms. Crimson gore dissolved to chalky-pale hollow, then to sallow complexed bone, an emaciated skull. The skull's eyes glared green, glared into Cherry's soul.

Cherry's body twitched. He opened his eyes. He looked around. He stood. He clenched his teeth. "Fuck it," he cussed bitterly. "Don't mean nothin.'' Cherry moved up to Egan. "Let's get this God fucken show on the road."

Brooks orchestrated the river crossing. He sent 2d Plt's 3d Sqd upriver thirty meters and directed them to stay ten meters away from the riverbank. 2d Sqd he sent downriver. 1st Sqd he held to be sent straight ahead. Between the squads he sent the extra gunteams. "Don't approach the water," he emphasized to every squad, every rifle team. The squads worked to their positions then sat and watched and waited. Brooks made them sit and observe for a full fifteen minutes.

"Move up," El Paso radioed on Brooks' command. All elements moved to within viewing distance of the water and sat again, still concealed by valley floor vegetation. Again, for fifteen minutes they observed. They watched the river, the near bank and the far. Fog hung about them, over them, in the grass. But it did not lie on the water's surface. The water was dark and appeared still, almost stagnant. Rain textured the surface with thousands of minute expanding ringwaves. On both sides the riverbank rose as vertical black muck rims topped with cowlicks of green grass. Elephant grass and bamboo encroached to the water's edge and variously overhung the river where the bank was collapsing. At the point where Alpha intersected the river, the Khe Ta Laou was about twenty-five meters wide.

The security squads up and down river set up half-arc perimeters with the machine guns facing the river and the back of the arcs open to the column. The machine gunners opened and extended the bi-pod legs of the 60s and laid their ammo out in preparation for a fight. Behind them thumpermen mock registered their grenade launchers. Riflemen opened tiny holes in the grass to aim through.

"Let's go," Brooks motioned. 1st Sqd and the company CP and all of 2d Plt moved to the river's edge. The column moved up behind them. Old Pop Randalph climbed down and into the deceptive current. Even at the very edge it caused him to stagger as the black water suddenly gurgled and surged against his legs. Pop retreated, slipped out of his ruck, removed his boonie hat and web gear and laid his weapon down. Again he waded into the water, cautious, aware that there might be enemy gunners on the far side. The water was running very fast. Four paces out the bottom dropped and Pop was over his head, paddling back toward shore. He was 10 meters below where he had slipped by the time he could stand. He returned to point. He consulted with the L-T and with De Barti and with Camillo Baiez. Pop removed his boots and his shirt and climbed back into the water. He took two steps out, dove in and began stroking with all his strength, kicking and splashing like a miniature paddlewheel riverboat. The current grabbed him and swept him downstream at twice the speed he was swimming across. He was swept past the downstream security team before he was halfway. Mohnsen, Jones, Smith and Garbageman set out after him, noisily, nervously trampling the vegetation as they raced along the bank.

When he finally hit the far side Pop was seventy-five meters below point. He stayed low, pulled himself out of the water, signaled thumbs-up okay to the troops chasing him, and disappeared into the grass beyond the far bank. Five minutes later he reappeared directly across from Brooks. "Goddamn," De Barti sighed. "That ol drunk. I thought alcohol and water mixed. He had me nearly pissin."

"This is fucked, Mista," Doc Johnson said toward both lieutenants. FO stood beside Doc. He nodded his head in agreement. He was not impressed.

Brooks glanced at them then turned back to the river. Baiez had a coil of light nylon cord to which he had attached a weight. He looked across at Pop, hunched over, ground his feet into the mud, went into his wind-up and let his pitch fly. The coil backlashed and flew after the weight in a clump snapping stopped out ten meters and kerplunking into the river. Baiez reeled it in and tried again. Then again and again.

"Bravo got three casualties," Brown interrupted Brooks with a report of action up the valley. "They're really in it deep. They're gettin inta that complex."

Brooks snarled angry and disgusted. Here Bravo was being chewed to pieces and he could not even get Alpha across a goddamned water obstacle. Brooks grabbed Baiez. "Give me that fuckin thing," he snapped. Brooks jerked the cord and weight from the squad leader's hands. He recoiled the line loosely on the ground then threw the weight across the river.

Pop retrieved it. On the company's side they attached the heavier rope they had used in the tunnel and at the cliffs. Pop pulled the line across, anchored it to himself and signaled for the troops to come. One at a time, in full gear, the men waded in, treaded as best as possible, hung on to the rope, pulled hand-over-hand to the far side. "Fucked, Man, fucked," Doc shook his head. The weight of their equipment forced each soldier under. After six had crossed, after Shaw had nearly drowned when he lost the rope, several boonierats stripped and recrossed and acted as lifeguards and guides. On the north side each man opened his weapon to drain the barrel of water, then disappeared into the grass enlarging the ever increasing perimeter. 3d Plt crossed after one squad of 2d. Then the CP crossed, then 1st Plt and finally the security teams. They reorganized themselves, emptied and squeezed water from their gear. It had all been soaked by the rain and most of it was not much wetter. But almost everyone's cigarettes had been saturated. This was a crisis. Cigarettes were carried in two-piece plastic boxes; boxes that kept out rain but they were not waterproof.

Alpha moved out in disgust. Ten minutes later they were forced into another delay. The valley north of the river was infested with a moist-land leech which seemed to thrive everywhere except in running water. The boonierats had unsuspectingly been assaulted by the leeches as soon as they had crossed. The leeches crawled like inchworms and attached themselves, boring painlessly into wet boonierat skin. Unless seen, a leech could suck its head a quarter inch deep before the area began to burn. After the tenth complaint, Doc Johnson ordered Brooks to halt the company. "Have em pair off," Doc said. "Have the fuckas check each other out."

Oh Christ, Brooks thought. What the hell next? Their progress had been very slow. He did not want to sit in the valley unnecessarily. He was embarrassed by the sloppiness of the river crossing. Several of the troops had lost gear in the river and the whole thing, though it began perfectly, lacked discipline. This wasn't his Alpha. He was sick. He checked El Paso's back and found a leech near the RTO's armpit. It was already late afternoon. Brooks wanted to get up to a high feature to NDP. "Goddamn leeches," he whispered to El Paso as he snapped the tiny slimy body then dug in with his fingernails for the head. Get a hold of yourself, Rufus, he told himself. You can't lose it now. Fuck that bitch. You can pull this back together. "Augh no," he sighed. He reached down into his pants. He could feel the cool clammy body of a sucker on his abdomen just above his groin. He opened his pants. The leech squirmed behind its sucking head. Brooks reached for his cigarettes instinctively. He opened the box. Brown tobacco juice water sloshed over his fingers.

It was still raining when the column reached the abrupt face of the north escarpment. They had come 400 meters from the river through elephant grass and bamboo without feeling any apparent elevation change and then they hit the road and the mountain cliff.

"Oh my Holy Mother," Garbageman gasped seeing the road. 2d Plt had led off again after everyone had tightened and tied off clothing against the leech invasion. The point squad had changed from Catt's to Mohnsen's. Garbageman was at point, Smith, with his 60, at slack. Where they hit the road at the base of the mountain there was a ten foot wide all-weather road, not only reinforced with bamboo but solidified with gravel. It was adjacent to the cliff and ran as far as Garbageman could see in the fog in both directions. Elephant grass formed a cleanly trimmed wall along the valley side of the road, the cliff had been evenly cleaved on the other shoulder. Again, grass and bamboo had been woven into living nets to form a natural-looking roof. From the air the roof would appear to be unbroken jungle valley floor and it would conceal all road traffic. To Garbageman standing in the vegetation ogling the road, it was evident that NVA honchos had established the road here because of the difficulty helicopters would have molesting troop or munitions traffic. Garbageman had never seen an enemy road so wide, wide enough for two-way cart traffic, wide enough for trucks. It made the red balls look like animal trails. The surface was rutted with recent signs of activity yet showed signs of continuous care and maintenance.

Smitty up, Garbageman signaled. Smith came forward. "Go back and get De Barti and Pop," Garbageman whispered. "They gotta check this the fuck out, Man." Word passed back. Pop Randalph came forward, then Lt. De Barti. "L-T gonna have to see this," they agreed and they radioed the CP. The boonierats of the lead squad fanned out in the grass forming a T at the columnhead. The column halted.

Brooks, his three RTOs and FO worked their way to point. From the depths of the grass they all examined the road.

"What do you think, Ruf?" De Barti asked the L-T very quietly. They were separated from the others by six or seven feet. De Barti did not want to expose his deep apprehension to the troops. "I don't think we oughta use it."

Brooks pulled out his topo map without answering and the two lieutenants studied it. "If we can find a way up the cliff . . ." Brooks began.

"No way we're goin up that shit," De Barti said. "It's vertical."

"It can't be vertical for very far," Brooks said. The two mused over the map and peered out of the grass at the road. They could see only a small strip. Brooks removed his hat and scratched his scalp. Go back through the leeches and recross the river, go up the road, down the road, try to climb the cliff. All about him the boonierats were becoming more and more restless. It was getting near dusk. With a road like this, he thought, the NVA could have thousands of troops in here. Brooks went to Cahalan. "Get me Red Rover," he said. "Bill," he turned to FO, "have you ever come across a road like this?"

"No, L-T, can't say I have."

"Can you get arty on it?"

"Yes Sir. Can do."

"Good. Call in targets all along this contour."

"L-T," Cahalan whispered, "I've got the GreenMan."

The GreenMan was at the forward TOC on Firebase Barnett. For him the day had held several torturous decisions, the most difficult having been whether or not to commit Bravo Company to a full-scale assault against the NVA bunker complex. Rain and fog had socked in the valley and the rear and all helicopter support except emergency medical evacuation had been cancelled. Bravo could retreat and attack tomorrow although they would run the risk of being hit tonight or Bravo could attack without helicopter support. Bravo attacked. When Cahalan reached the GreenMan, Bravo had overrun the bunker complex, killed seventeen enemy soldiers and suffered five wounded. The medevac bird from Eagle Dust-Off, along with four escort Cobras and a chase ship, a Huey on station to pick up the medevac crew should that helicopter be shot down, was approaching Bravo's location.

"Quiet Rover, this is Red Rover," the GreenMan snarled after Brooks had reported briefly about the enemy road, "proceed to your echo by november echo ASAP. Caution your papa Sky Devil Six is to your november one kilo. Play ball with Sky Devil.''

"Who's Sky Devil?" De Barti asked Cahalan.

"Ah, that'd be Delta Company, Sir," Cahalan answered.

"Oh fuck," De Barti groaned. "Not that clusterfuck."

Brooks described the road in greater detail, hoping the GreenMan would be able to assist him. He did not want to have his company march down the enemy road. It appeared impossible to cross the road and ascend the cliffs at that point, yet he felt he had to get off the valley floor. As he conversed on the radio the sound of helicopters above the valley pulsated the wet air.

"Get me a full reconnaissance of that feature," the GreenMan directed. "And, play ball with Sky Devil. Out."

Oh shit, Brooks thought. "Roger that, niner. Wilco. Out." Brooks looked around. He directed Cahalan to establish communication with Delta Company to determine Delta's exact position and to see if the Delta Darlings had found a way up and down the cliff face. "Tell them," Brooks said, "Red Rover wants us to rendezvous. It'll be a hell of a lot better if we can get up to them on the ridge than to have them come down here." Brooks turned to FO again and asked, "Where do you think this road goes?"

"I don't really know," FO said. "Like you figure, it probably follows the contours pretty close. If the dinks are moving heavy material, they'd a built the road as level as possible."

"After we get out of range, have arty seal this thing off behind us. See if they'll drop some rounds west of here right now."

It was 1800 hours when Alpha began moving again. Garbageman was still at point, Smitty and Pop walked a double slack. Slowly, apprehensively, Garbageman stepped onto the road and into the dark corridor formed by the grass wall and the cliff. He scanned up and back. Fog limited visibility to under twenty meters. The pointman turned right and began moving. Carefully he checked the mountain wall which rose to his left. The slacks emerged from the grass eight feet behind point, they split and walked one on each side of the road. Mohnsen and Jones emerged next continuing the double pattern set by the slacks, then Greer and Roberts, Sklar and De Barti, and El Paso and Brooks.

Oh Man, I don't like this one fucken bit, Garbageman whispered to himself. He stopped and crouched. Both slacks moved up and squatted by the point. "This is a Goddamned highway," Garbageman whispered. "Man I don't dig this shit one fucken bit. This don't even make sense."

"Want me ta walk point?" Pop asked, his eyes twinkling.

That was the ultimate affront, the most severe attack on the Garbageman's manhood and pride. "Naw," he whispered. "I can do it."

"Maybe we oughta both do it," Pop gave him an alternative that he could accept without losing face.

"Ah, yeah," Garbageman seized the chance. They rose and with one at each edge proceeded in double point with a single slack.

2d Plt was followed onto the road by the remainder of the CP. All the RTOs had folded their flexible radio antennas that protruded from their rucks and labeled them as valuable communication targets. El Paso had slid his antenna into his belt, Cahalan stuck his into a hole in his shirt, Brown rolled his in a loop and forced it back down into the ruck. 3d Plt followed the CP and 1st followed 3d. They moved very slowly, very quietly. It took almost half an hour for the entire column to turn the corner from the narrow jungle grass passage onto the enemy supply road. The boonierats continued the double column. They remained on the road, heading east, looking for an opening in the cliff they might ascend up to the ridge. They maintained wide intervals. By the time Silvers, at drag, finally stepped onto the road, Alpha was spread 125 meters long.

Silvers came onto the road behind Brunak. He stood at the intersection for several minutes, staring to the rear, allowing the column to progress away from him. An artillery round burst 700 meters west, the concussion rumbling up the road and echoing in from the south escarpment a fraction of a second apart. Silvers turned and quickly marched to catch up. As he reached a point 30 meters from where he had left the grass he turned to look back. A single explosive pop cracked the air. Silvers dropped in the center of the road. Every man in Alpha dove for cover. There was another crack. Boonierats dove into the grass, scrambled for concealment, searched for a target. Brunak had been hit by the second round. "Bravo Bravo," a squashed tight-chest scream for a medic escaped from his throat. Boonierats raced through

the grass toward him. No one had found a target. No one fired.
Marko, Jax and Lairds surrounded Brunak. They expected
follow-up fire. None came. Marko aimed his 60 down the road.
There was nothing there. He aimed the weapon over Silvers'
body which had collapsed backward onto the rucksack it had
been carrying. Silvers' helmet had fallen off and rolled away.
His legs had doubled beneath his body before the body had
toppled backward and spread across the pack. The head slumped
back over the ruck, the eyes stared upside-down motionless
down the vacant road upon which Alpha had trespassed.

"Bravo," Jax yelled from beside Brunak.

Egan, Whiteboy and Doc McCarthy came crashing through
the grass. Others were coming back. Most had shed their rucks.
Brunak screamed. McCarthy squatted by his side. 1st Sqd with
Egan and several others maneuvered down through the grass past
Silvers and formed a perimeter.

Cherry, Thomaston and Moneski's squad reacted second,
rushing back and reinforcing the soldiers about Brunak. Doc
Johnson sprinted down the center of the road running like a
madman, his aid bag in one hand, a .45 in the other. Doc
dove into the mud behind Silvers. He got to his knees and
hunched over the body. There was a splat of blood in the
center of Silvers' throat. Working quickly yet gently Doc
lifted Leon's head. The neck no longer had a back. The bullet
had entered through the soft flesh below Silvers' chin then
tumbled and ripped its way out the nape of the neck carrying
most of the cervical vertebrae, the surrounding muscle tissue,
the trachea, esophagus, arteries, veins and a tremendous amount
of blood.

In the grass McCarthy worked on Brunak. Brunak had
caught a round in the right side. It was difficult to determine how
badly he had been hit but McCarthy was sure it was bad. Brunak
was laughing, then tensing, cramping his entire body, then laughing again, flowing from consciousness, pain and spasms, to
empty shock. McCarthy applied a field dressing to the hole in
Brunak's side and jabbed him with a syringe of morphine. From
his aid bag he took a 500ml plastic bag labeled Plasma Protein
Fraction (Human). The plasma solution came in a kit complete
with IV needle and airway cannula. McCarthy pumped Brunak's
arm then jammed the needle in. He knew he was missing as
soon as the needle broke the skin. He yanked it out. Brunak

flinched. Then he laughed. McCarthy stuck him again and began the IV flow.

On the trail Doc Johnson had closed Silvers' eyes. The medic methodically wrapped a large sterile dressing about the dead man's neck so no one would see the extent of the damage. Doc pulled a towel from Silvers' ruck and placed part of it behind Leon's head. He brought the remainder over the sallow face. Then, holding his aid bag, Doc rolled off the trail into the grass.

Cherry squatted in the grass beside Thomaston. He awaited directions. Egan came back to them. He grabbed the handset, radioed El Paso, explained the situation, and requested a priority medevac. He tossed the hook back to Cherry and snapped, "Git down. I don't want ta call in a bird for you too."

Hoover crawled over to the group about Brunak. Thomaston grabbed his hook and radioed the CP. "We're movin back into the grass fifty meters," he said after talking to Brooks. "We'll get the Dust-Off out there."

Thomaston and Egan directed the perimeter to move further down while they, with Jax' help, pulled Silvers' body from the road. With the others breaking a trail and then crushing a tiny clearing toward the valley center, Egan and Jax jumped back onto the road and pulled Silvers' body, ruck and weapon into the grass. Jax separated the ruck from the body of his dead field partner. He lifted the body gently and carried it to the clearing. "Yo gowin be alright now, Leon, my friend," Jax whispered soothingly. "Yo kin relax an fo'get this place." Cherry followed carrying the blood-soaked ruck. Lairds brought the extra weapon and helmet. Brunak, McCarthy and 2d Sqd had already reached and secured the clearing. 3d Plt pulled back to reinforce the evac site, 2d Plt and the CP circled the perimeter in recon patrols, pushing to points 100 meters from the designated pick-up zone.

"Hey," Egan said to Cherry. "You need some good shit?"

"What shit?"

"Here," Egan said rustling through Silvers' equipment. He tossed Cherry a two-quart canteen.

Cherry looked at it, then walked over to the ruck. Across the top, blood drenched but unharmed, was a five-quart water blivet. Cherry untied it. The blivet was a double-layered plastic bladder enclosed in a strong nylon bag, the three bags joined at the top with a canteen neck and screw cap. Water blivets were less cumbersome than canteens and they could be used as pillows. They were in very short supply. "I'd like to take this," Cherry said.

"You got it," Egan answered.

"And his bayonet."

"Take it."

Numbnuts let Cherry and Egan leave the ruck before he went over and scavenged all C-rat meals that were not Ham and Lima Beans. Denhardt scavenged Brunak's ruck.

It was after sunset, late dusk, when the medical evacuation helicopter finally found Alpha. The thick mist prevented the Dust-Off commander from seeing marking smoke and it was not dark enough to use the mini-strobes. The birds even had difficulty finding the valley for all of northern I Corps lay in thick fog and rain. The Dust-Off had first to locate Barnett, then follow a vector path 268°, almost due west.

Cherry directed the bird's approach by ear. "You're passing to our sierra maybe two hundred meters," he called. Then again, "You're approaching us. You're passing over us right, right . . . now."

The helicopter made a half-dozen passes, at first so high it could not be seen through the fog, then lower and lower. Finally it hovered 15 meters over their position. From the ground Cherry could see the crew chief standing on the left skid and the medic standing on the right. Huge red crosses were painted on white squares on the bird's bottom and sides. The rotor wash from the bird made the rain slam down and sting on upturned faces. Escort ships could be heard circling though they could not be seen. From the right side of the helicopter stuck a three-foot arm and from that dropped a small torpedo-shaped object on a steel cable. The torpedo dropped evenly and in seconds it was on the ground. Doc Johnson, Doc McCarthy, Thomaston and Jax grabbed the torpedo and unfolded it.

"What's that thing?" Cherry questioned.

"Jungle penetrator," Egan answered.

The four men lifted Brunak and his gear and strapped him into a sitting position on the now unfolded, tri-pronged, anchor-like seat. They strapped his gear across from him. Thomaston stretched his arms up over his head and extended his thumbs signaling the crew chief to take him away. The hoist cranked and Brunak rose, swayed beneath the bird, and ascended. The medic reached out and pulled him in. The bird departed, circled and returned. The procedure was repeated with the body and gear of Leon Silvers. Then the medevac departed for good. No trace of the dead or the wounded remained except for blood and neck tissue in the midst of the enemy road and the blood stain on Cherry's water blivet.

C H A P T E R

██████████████ 24 ██████████████

Bug repellent was also used to repel leeches. Typically boonierats carried several plastic bottles of the fluid. By 2300 hours every soldier in Alpha had run out. That night's position came to be known amongst them as NDP on Leech Reef. They called the night Bloodsucker's Bitterness. The bloodsuckers were not all leeches.

It had been nearly dark when the medevac departed and Alpha had formed up again, in column again, on the road again. Brooks had opted for a quick 200-meter hump east up the roadway. He had hoped to find a passage up the cliffs to the north ridge. Tension amongst the men was high. With every step every man searched the corridor walls left and right, top and bottom. At drag Marko, Jax, Egan and Cherry walked backward. Fifty meters behind Whiteboy and his squad followed. They had dropped off in hopes of catching NVA trail watchers popping up after the column.

At point Garbageman, Pop, Smitty and Mohnsen walked a staggered lead sweep, each scrutinizing one parameter of the corridor. Innumerable sites along the road indicated signs of enemy troops moving into the elephant grass. Footprints in the mud filled with water as the point element approached. At two points where minute trails exited the road, Pop was certain the grass of the wall swayed not from wind but from having been brushed. He saw nothing. Where trails intersected with the road, riflemen stood guard for the column, 16s or 60s aimed up the secondary routes. All weapons were off safe, on automatic. This

was unusual for the normal unsure footing demanded the precau-
tion of keeping weapons on safe. An index finger was kept on
the trigger and a thumb on the safety lever. The two could be
squeezed simultaneously taking no more time than only squeezing the trigger. An unofficial agreement had passed through
Alpha when the boonierats had moved out. That they moved out
at all was a testament to the faith they had in Brooks. Brooks
was aware of their faith and loyalty. He gritted his teeth and told
himself it was the only way. Mohnsen had glanced conspiratori-
ally at Smith then clicked to full automatic, Smith turned to
Jones, Jones to Garbageman. In back Egan nodded to Cherry. At
middle El Paso nodded to FO and FO to the L-T. The nods,
glances and clicking began at numerous foci and expanded to
encompass the entire column. All weapons were aimed outward
from the advancing double column.

The rain had subsided, abated to a drizzlemist and the
temperature had fallen from cool to cold to very cold. In the
lushly vegetated mountains of the Annamite Range rainy season
temperatures of 30° F were neither incongruous nor unknown
and nights below 40° were common. But in August, temperatures seldom fell below 50° and the boonierats of Alpha were not
dressed for the cold. Coupled with the wet, the cold chilled them
to miserable teeth chattering. Being on the roads with night's
edge on the sky increased their inner trembling. Their eyes
played tricks as they stared up the cliffs or up the road or into the
grass. Shadows darted about, poked up in peripheral vision then
vanished under direct scrutiny.

"Keep pushing," Brooks radioed forward. "Keep it moving.
Find a passage up the cliffs."

But there was no passage. The wall to their left rose vertically as a single monolith without gully, without break. When
visibility neared zero Brooks ordered the unit to halt. Whiteboy's
squad caught up, the column squeezed together, closed intervals
from ten feet to three. On command the soldiers turned right 90°
and dissolved into the grass. They swept in like a silent wave,
breaking after 100 meters. The flanks contracted and with the
instinct of well-disciplined troops the boonierats formed an irregular oval perimeter. Quietly the perimeter guards laid down and
arranged guard schedules. The leech assault began immediately.

At Alpha's center the CP formed a tight nucleus. "Don't
dig in," Brooks whispered to El Paso. "No noise, no movement,
no lights. Get that word out. We're going to hide here. I don't

want to hear the sound of digging.'' Then to El Paso Brooks said unofficially, ''Every time we dig I feel like I'm digging my own grave.''

Beside the company commander FO and Brown had buried themselves beneath two ponchos. By flashlight FO studied the topo map and plotted his targets. Tonight, he thought, I'm goina bring in arty all over that road. FO called the FDC on Barnett and gave a long list of coordinates. First he called in DTs for Alpha, then he called in the road. He discussed the target with the artillery commander. Without being able to observe the impactions it would be impossible to ascertain the extent of damage the rounds were causing or, indeed, if the rounds were even hitting the target. Five meters too far to the north and the rounds would land up the cliff, perhaps caving sections of cliff in upon the road. That would be of little use. The NVA would use the loose dirt and rock to improve the road surface. Rounds landing five meters too far south would impact in the elephant grass and not affect the road at all. Only direct hits at road center would cause the NVA to slow. The craters would fill with water and vehicular traffic would bog down in the quagmire. With luck, arty would blow the ceiling off the corridor and expose the road to air attack. FO described the road in detail. And he described the cliffs. The battery commander asked FO to wait one. He checked with the forward TOC on the firebase and with the main TOC at Evans. He radioed FO back. The road would receive H & I fire, later, maybe. From Barnett he did not believe he could drop rounds onto the road. His guns were north of the cliffs and the road was protected. But possibly, the eight-inchers at Firebase Bastogne far to the south, if they had time and if they had no higher priority missions, might drop a few rounds in the vicinity of the road. That was the best he could do.

Cherry and Egan slithered to the CP for the nightly meeting. ''Do you guys have any extra bug repellent?'' Brooks asked.

''Aw fuck,'' Egan growled quietly. He had soaked his fatigues with every drop of repellent he had had. ''I was hopin you had some. These mothafuckers are suckin me dry.''

''Doc had one in his ear,'' El Paso whispered matter-of-factly.

''Numbnuts got one in his ass,'' Cherry chuckled.

''Musta had ta share the space with his head,'' Brown whispered laughing.

They bantered back and forth very quietly and moved closer and closer. They sat together in a cluster with Brooks at the center. There were thirteen of them, the seven from the CP, Egan, Cherry and Jax from 1st Plt, De Barti and Garbageman from 2d, and Caldwell from 3d. Each man was wrapped in a poncho liner for warmth and over that in a poncho to keep the leeches out. Had it been light enough to see, the cluster would have looked like thirteen crumpled dirty bags of trash tossed atop one another in a muck snot swamp. In the blackness they were nothing but thirteen quivering voices. Some chattered from the wet and cold. Some shivered feeling the crawling cool clamminess of endless legions of leeches inching ever closer to their flesh.

Ah, for a smoke, Egan thought. To smoke and burn the suckers off. To watch the mother whores squirm. Fucken night. Fucken light discipline. Can't light up. Most of these assholes don't have a goddamn dry cigarette. Assholes. How many times do ya have ta tell em to keep their smokes in their ammo cans.

Jax moaned. "Oh Man, these mothafuckas eatin me up. Up the side my head, they done whup. These mothafuckas eatin good tanight. On that road, friends, they eatin right."

"Ssshhh," Brooks hushed Jax. "Cahalan, report."

Cahalan reported. He went into detail about Bravo's action at what they now called Comeback Ridge. Then he described Recon's skirmish. Cahalan had questioned the TOC RTOs about the various actions by US and ARVN forces in and around Khe Ta Laou. He reiterated all he had learned and then he recounted Alpha's own day formally concluding with a Lessons Learned section based on discussions Brooks had had with FO and Thomaston and others about the river crossing and about how Silvers was killed and how it could have been avoided, and how 1st Plt adjusted rear security for the second road march.

Only now did the reality of Silvers' death begin to hit Cherry. He had gone into shock, functioning perfectly yet not recognizing the meaning of the events about him. It was a perfect soldier's reaction and though it made Cherry sorrowful, it also made him happy. Now, in the dark quiet, he could ponder. What'd I do with that address he gave me? Cherry asked himself. I told him I'd send his stuff to somebody. What stuff. They took it all away with his body. Cherry pondered the death itself. But it was difficult for Cherry to think about death. He did not have words and concepts to build his thoughts. There had been his Christian upbringing and his biological science courses and each had provided him with a set of theoretical constructs to frame his thoughts but he had rejected the first and tonight the second seemed inadequate. Cherry put his hand to his right calf. The new bayonet was there. It felt good. Like Egan's, Cherry thought. He smiled. All around him the others chatted softly.

"Hey, Doc," Brown whispered.

"Yeah," Doc answered.

"Oooo, Doc! Lieutenant Caldwell's got the funniest red mark on his ass."

"What that?"

"I aint sure," Brown chuckled. "I think maybe it's lipstick."

"Bullshit," Caldwell said seriously offended. "Cut that chatter."

Disgust with Caldwell had passed among all the EM of Alpha. "When the dinks opened up," Brown laughed more quietly, "I saw him kiss his ass good-bye."

Brooks stifled a snicker. "Hey," he stopped the peripheral talk, "listen up. There are times," he said very solemnly altering the mood, "when a man or men follow another man simply because the other man is in a position of authority. If you all followed me unquestioningly and you didn't give me advice, we'd all be dead. I want to hear what you're thinking. Tomorrow, we're sending a platoon to rendezvous with Delta and the rest of us are going to probe all over this valley. Maybe we'll cross back over to the other side."

"We aint goin back on that road?" Garbageman asked.

"I think we ought to stay off it, Ruf," De Barti agreed with Garbageman. "At least as much as possible."

"GreenMan wants us to find a way up the cliff and mark it," Brooks said. "We might need it later. Besides, we have to find it to meet with Delta."

"This is fucked down here, Mista," Doc said disgustedly. "We stay in this valley, we gonna rot."

"I don't like it either," FO said. "That dink this afternoon. He must have counted every man in our column. I just know he did. He counted every 60, every radio. You can forget trying to keep up any illusion about two companies. They know everything about us. You can bet yer ass that dink gets a gold star for today."

"Those fuckers," Garbageman cursed. "Them shithead bastards. It seems like they always know where we're at. They're goina snipe the shit outa us."

"They gowin suck us in," Jax said. "They gowin leave us signs like an in-vi-tation. Then they gowin shut the door. This pig shit. This white man's war."

"Come on, Man," Egan said quietly. "Haven't we had enough of that crap."

Before the meeting Egan had had to quiet Jax and Marko. Silvers had been Jackson's field partner and Brunak as AG had been Marko's. Jax and Marko buddied up as soon as the medevac bird departed. Then Egan and Thomaston had come and appointed Jackson squad leader. Marko thought the promotion should have been his.

When they moved into the new NDP the two had huddled and pointed their weapons outward. In the cold wetness Marko had asked, "Jax, you got a chick?"

"Shee-it Man," Jax answered jiving quietly, "I got all kinda chicks. Black en white. They loves my ass."

"Man, what I wouldn't give to see a round-eye right now," Marko said.

"Roun-eye!?" Jax exclaimed. This man need some educatin, he thought. "Doan give me none that roun-eye shit. Eyes aint roun. Roun-eye? Ma-aann. Yo white fuckas always screamin roun-eye when yo mean white."

"I don't give a rat's ass what color she is long's she pink inside," Marko countered. "I'd ball a black bitch ta be outta here right now."

"Yo honkey mothafucka," Jax seethed. "Yo mean yo'd ee-ven stick yo golden dick in black pussy. Yo'd even lower yoself that far ta get out a heah. We here cause a white fucken pigs."

"Augh you fucken son of a nigger cunt," Marko spun and grabbed Jackson's shirt. "When you goina see this aint white America's war fought by his nigger slaves. What the fuck do you think I am? White dudes like me get blown away more often than niggers like you. You fucken black bastards sold your souls. Your people sold their yellow Bros down the fucken drain, Boy, just so they could be like us whites. This aint whitey's war, nigger. It's *our* war."

Jax was ready to kill Marko. No one called Jackson a nigger. Jax began a suffocated scream. Egan had come down and grabbed them both and had drained the fury. He had talked to them quietly and had asked them both to come to the CP meeting to bring up their debate. Jax had come alone.

"Yo ask me up here yoself," Jax reminded Egan.

"Hey," Brooks said. "First let's settle the local problems. Then we can work on the world situation." They returned to the discussion of their plans with Brooks saying, "Our ultimate objective is the high feature by the river. That knoll with the big tree. Our ultimate mission is to clear the NVA from the center of the valley. Those goals establish the parameters of our actions."

"Our ultimate goal," Doc said, "is ta remain alive." Doc had been unusually quiet ever since the medevac. Silvers had not been the first dead man he had evacuated and he would not be the last. And Brunak would not be the last of the wounded. Somehow, their shootings affected Doc more deeply than any before. Perhaps it was because 1st Sqd, 1st Plt was, except for that Numbnuts character, among the best squads Doc had ever seen. They were always alert, vigilant. If they were so easily sniped wasn't he all the more vulnerable?

Doc's usual speech was a mixture of city-black street dialect and army/boonierat jargon. Now he spoke with an almost professional eloquence. "Leon Silvers died instantly," Doc said. "He died from the traumatic amputation of his head. That's quick. Brunak is gonna be different. That man has a long struggle ahead of him, if he makes it. When they hoisted him this afternoon he was in deep hypovolemic shock. He was losing a lot of blood and it wasn't coming out. That means edema, the effusion of serous fluids into intracellular space. McCarthy hadn't inserted the IV properly and Brunak's vascular system was draining. Dig? There won't enough blood left in him for his heart to pump. He gone into tachycardia."

"What's that mean, Doc?" De Barti asked.

"His heart beating at an excessive rate," Doc said. "It was tryin ta pump up the pressure in a system that was full a holes."

"He's goina make it, aint he, Doc?"

"I talked to the TOC bout an hour ago," Doc answered. "They doan have no word yet." No one spoke so Doc Johnson continued. "I got one question, Mista," he said sliding to his less formal speech. "One question. How many mo mothafuckas we gonna git blown away fo we reach that ultimate objective? We got men here sufferin from immersion foot, from jungle rot. Half the company's got colds and half gonna catch pneumonia. What the fuck fo, Mista?"

"We bein Judas Goats fo a whiteman's operation," Jax said. "They sendin us down here ta git slaughtered so they know right where ta drop the bombs. That way they doan have ta spend so much money on bombs cause they ken drop less.''

"No company of mine is going to be slaughtered," Brooks said firmly. He had heard enough of their complaints. "It pisses me off to hear you guys talk like that, like . . ."

El Paso interrupted him. "Yes," he said, "but we can talk about it, can't we?"

Brooks looked through the darkness toward El Paso's voice. He paused attempting to think of a response. No one else spoke. Brooks could not think of an alternative. He was trapped. Later he would think to himself, I should have said, 'Yes, you can talk, but let's talk tactics first.' Now he could not think. He wanted their opinions but he wanted them to agree with his own.

"Maybe," Lt. Caldwell said, "you men should think more about killing dinks than about turning chicken and running."

"Fuck that shit," Egan snapped angrily at Caldwell.

"Wait a minute," Brooks said tenuously. "This meeting is open. El Paso's right. We can talk."

They spoke quickly now, all except Caldwell without anger. Each man was firmly entrenched in his own convictions yet each was willing to sway, to lean, just a little because the other men were boonierats. From that base they spoke and listened to each other respectively.

"I'd like to know something," Cherry asserted himself. "I'd like to know what the hell we're doin here."

El Paso took him by as much surprise as Doc had earlier even though he had heard El Paso's scholarly speech before. "The problem," El Paso began, "problems, encountered in trying to resolve which historical antecedents caused our intervention and what the historical morality of that intervention is, are complicated by our inability to withdraw to a greater perspective and also by the ongoing occurrence of events." That, Cherry thought, has got to be a prepared speech. "It is as if historical perspective were depth," El Paso said. "And that depth is a cone. The greater the depth the greater also the diameter. Every year we descend into history we find not simply greater lineal understanding of today's events but we also find these events inseparably tied to other events. Looking at today is like looking at the point of the cone. Looking at historical antecedents is looking into the cone. To get an accurate understanding of today we must work toward the base understanding, seeing everything in each expanding strata below. At a certain point the known details and connections begin to diminish and the cone reverses and becomes smaller until it points out and there we are in pre-history.''

"Wow!" De Barti exclaimed. "That's beautiful."

"Well, what's that all mean?" Garbageman asked.

"What do you call that?" De Barti asked.

"I understand what you're saying," Cherry said, "but that doesn't answer why we're here."

"That," El Paso chuckled to De Barti, "is El Paso's biconoid theory of history."

"Biconoid? Biconoid?" Egan repeated to himself. "Two cones," he said.

"Joined at the base," El Paso added. He was pleased.

"So what?" Caldwell said.

"So," El Paso said moving on, "it depends on how far back and how wide you want to go to justify or explain or understand what the fuck's happenin here now."

"We've been over a lot of that before," Brooks said.

"You ever hear of the Oxford Oath?" Egan asked El Paso.

"About 1935?" El Paso replied.

"Yep," Egan said. He had thought he would catch El Paso with that one. He had tried many times and only rarely succeeded.

"Well, what is it?" Cherry asked.

"It was a sworn statement," Egan said. "And a slogan. It was somewhat the equivalent of chanting 'Stop the War in Vietnam.' "

"Huh?"

"It was a movement in England," El Paso explained. "About '35 or '36. It was an oath where students resolved never to bear arms for king or country. The oath was agreed to by a majority of Oxford Union members. The Oxford Union was a nationwide student organization. They say Hitler used to quote it to his general staff to lessen their anxiety when he'd want to make another move toward world conquest. Hitler said it was evidence the British were rotten to the core and that his staff was exaggerating the risk of his moves."

"It allowed Hitler to advance unchallenged," Egan said. "That's just what the NVA are thriving on too. Vo Nguyen Giap uses student dissent in the World to dupe his dinks into thinking we're weak. And that's only where it begins. China and Russia use it too. Ya know, maybe we're here simply as a show of strength and will. And that show is a deterrent. It keeps the

Commies in check so they don't blunder us into a thermo-nuclear holocaust. That won't happen if Tricky Dick keeps a shit load of us here. We become a safety valve for world tension."

"That's a bunch a shit," FO countered quietly. "We're more apt to blunder us into World War Three by being here than by withdrawing."

"What about the Middle East?" Egan said. "Egypt's got Russkie advisors, Russkie technicians, Russkie troops manning SAM missiles. We back down here what's goina keep the Kremlin from pushin inta Israel? That would blow up the earth. We can't just say we aint goina defend our allies. Be just like the '30s. Mao'd take Taiwan. Russia'd take Berlin. The communists'd move in everywhere."

"You Americans," Minh said softly. He did not want to speak with so many GIs clustered for he felt very much alienated when they had these discussions, but he could no longer allow them to prattle without injecting his thoughts. "You Americans," he repeated, "you are most blind. You do not see my country or my people. All you see are your words. We were reduced to ignorant child-slaves under the yoke of colonialism. It is not communism you most protect us from. Communism is not a threat to us. We need your support to keep out a foreign enemy. Soon we will not need that. But you should not fear us if we become communist. It will be communism for us, not against you. We must be the ones to have power over ourselves."

"Amen, Brother," Jax whispered enthusiastically. "Vietnamese Power to Vietnamese People. Black Power to Black People."

"And White Power to White People," Brown added.

"Amen," Doc said.

"If you view the world," El Paso began, "as Western and Eastern power centers and vast power voids, the expansion of communism since, well, 1917, is a simple swinging back of the slow moving power pendulum pushed to one extreme by colonialism. The Europeans expanded outward from the 1400s to like 1945. Communism is a backlash movement for a lot of countries that were once colonies. If it's strong today that's because colonialism was strong earlier."

"I'm not sure I follow that," De Barti said.

"During the colonial period western European nations sought to impose their religions and cultures on native population, savages as they called everyone except themselves, all over the globe—including America.''

"Oh yes,'' Minh spoke again. "But America is not a good example of colonialism. Europe did not colonize a native population in America.''

"Well, yeah,'' El Paso agreed but also disagreed. He did not wish to discuss America. He said, "They did in South and Central America. In North America the Europeans simply exterminated the Indians.''

"Yes, that is what I mean,'' Minh said. "Your Indians were replaced by American Europeans. America never experienced the cultural shock of being colonized.''

"That's very true,'' El Paso conceded. He moved on quickly trying to maintain his momentum but was cut off.

"Unless you were black,'' Brooks said.

"Or Indian, Mexican, Eskimo or some other intrinsic minority,'' El Paso regained control. "But that's the thing with communism in ex-colonies. You see, it's a backlash to the cultural shock of colonialism. The Europeans destroyed native political organizations, family foundations, religions, and economies. They converted the native culture to Western, tried to anyway. Entire value systems were disrupted. That caused tremendous stress which continues today.''

"Oh yes,'' Minh said. "And your technology also disrupts my culture.''

"That disrupts our own culture too, Minh,'' De Barti said.

"But why communism?'' Egan asked. "There hasn't been a society in history in which Marxist collectivization has been popular. Communist states are always police states. Commie economic policies always destroy their own economy. No one, once it's been accomplished, likes it. Minh, it'll be either you join the collective farm or factory or they'll kill you. It's that simple.''

"They've got to try it,'' El Paso said. "Coming out of colonialism is like coming out of childhood, like going through adolescence. They've got to experience it all in order to decide in which direction to go. It won't last long. Communism has a moral ring if you read the doctrines. It really sounds wonderful. It demands justice for the exploited.''

"Yeah, but in reality it doubles the exploitation,'' Egan said.

"It always denies freedoms," Brown added.

"Yeah, it coerces people to keep from falling on its face," Cahalan said.

"So did colonialism," El Paso answered.

"What we must have," Minh said, "is a Vietnamese government which takes the best of all foreign worlds. It must eat and digest the good and let it help us grow as a Vietnamese nation."

"I'd still like to know what we're doin here," Cherry said.

"We're stopping the North Vietnamese from invading South Vietnam," Caldwell said bluntly. Cherry's inability to perceive the obvious, along with Brooks' and the others' infuriated him. They don't have to understand it, he thought. It is simply fact. God, does it have to be rammed down their throats? "What the hell's the matter with you all?" Caldwell whispered severely. "Why are we here? What do we want?" He mocked them. He aimed his voice at Cherry. "We want the fighting to stop, the opposing forces to disengage and withdraw. We're ready to negotiate a peaceful solution." Caldwell directed his voice toward Minh. "We'll support you. Guarantee you free elections, give you democracy. If you go . . . ah . . . if your people want to unify with the dinks, that's their prerogative. We're only here to make sure it's not shoved down your throats by foreign invaders."

"You can't give anyone democracy," El Paso said maliciously. "Not what you mean. Democracy like you mean is a western cultural thing. You're trying to cram American standards down the throats of a culture that doesn't hold that standard and you're demanding they fight for it. Man, that's straight Nixon logic. You're tellin them to fight so they can lose their own culture and be like you Anglos."

"You going to tell me these people'd be better off under that henchman Ho Chi Minh?"

El Paso did not answer.

"Well, come on," Caldwell taunted. "Let me tell you something. The Ho Chi Minh government at the time of our initial involvement didn't represent even fifteen percent of the people of the North and not two percent of the people in the South. It wasn't a legal representative of the country. The government we back down here had as much support as that bitch did in the North. There were two main differences. The North was a closed and repressive society and Ho usurped complete control.

Anybody not liking it was killed. Down here it was an open society, open to world view and criticism, and to opposition political factions. Maybe there's corruption keeping the factions limited but factions are allowed. Now, perhaps because of American aid, the government here has fifty percent popular support. How can anyone claim the ARVN government isn't a legal government?''

"I must ask you," Minh said, "what you believe made Ho Chi Minh? Or a Hitler? Or any dictator? Ho, he was pushed to power because the Japanese and Chinese feared America. We feared America would make us a French colony again. What do you believe consolidated his power? Was it not America's over-zealous manner of being helpful? To many of my countrymen your assistance appears to be aggression and imperialism. Yes, my friend, your solution may be better than a northern solution, but it can only be better if it is without you.''

"That's a lot of shit, Minh," Caldwell said defending his statements. "You've got a closed society in the North. You've got a repressive government there. Look how far you've come. When Westy took command of MACV in '64 terrorists were bombing right inside Saigon with ease and regularity. Nobody believed in a republic here in the South. We gave you time and space to grow and you've grown. Your government's working. Your military's become decent. Your country is going places.''

Brooks interceded. "I have to agree with Lt. Caldwell," he said to the shock of El Paso and Doc and Jax. Even Egan could hardly believe it. How could anyone side with Boy Asshole? "I think he's right," Brooks said. "We've given a nation time to settle and grow.''

"Yo bein sucked in by that line, L-T," Jax said.

"Perhaps," Brooks agreed, "but if that line is the truth, I'm willing to be sucked in by it." Another man's words haunted the back of Brooks' consciousness. He had not thought about them since he had first heard them. Nor had he placed much importance on them when they were spoken. Now their meaning crystalized. 'If you believe in what you are fighting for,' the Old Fox had said at the staging area, you are more apt to risk your life. You are more apt to win. You will not fight badly, thus you are less apt to die. The more you risk death the less apt you are to die. Your men, Lieutenant, must believe in what they are doing.' Brooks said, "Jax, don't you believe we're helping the

South Vietnamese to maintain a free society? If the North conquers the South they'll establish a slave state. Hey?''

"I agree with the L-T," Cahalan said.

"So do I," said Brown.

"That's simplistic bullshit," Egan whispered to Cherry so only Cherry could hear.

"See," Lt. Caldwell said. "I tell ya, I'm right."

"I tell ya," Egan snarled, "yer an asshole."

"You best remember your manners, Troop," Caldwell said.

"In a leech's ass," Egan challenged.

"Stop it," Brooks said firmly.

"How come Boy Asshole never walks point?" Egan seethed.

"Or slack?" Garbageman whispered. "Thomaston, De Barti, L-T, you all take your turn."

"That is not . . ."

Brooks stopped them all. "We will not proceed with this line of thought," he said.

"I'd like ta say something," Egan began in a different tone. "Ya know that red ball, that first one this mornin? I bet that fucker led to an entrance at the base of the hill where Whiteboy's Hole was. They might have bunkers and tunnels all through these hills. We might be better off down here hidin in the grass. If it wasn't for the leeches this wouldn't be so bad." Then he said, "I was also thinkin bout Ridgefield and our token Jew. Ridge . . ."

"How come yer always such a prick?" Cherry shot the question at Egan. "You're so fucken obnoxious you're unreal."

"Don't mean nothin," Egan laughed. "It's all academic anyway. Aint nobody here but us and the dinks an there aint no place else ta go."

"That token Jew was a friend a mine," Cherry said. He touched his hand to his calf and felt the bayonet and felt a pang of guilt.

"You think he wasn't a friend of mine?" Egan snapped. "You're such a fucken cherry."

"Stop," Brooks said. "We don't meet to call each other names."

"Sorry," Cherry whispered.

"Yeah. Me too," Egan said.

"That's it. Break it up," Brooks said.

The meeting broke quickly with the platoon people returning to their perimeter areas. Doc and El Paso accompanied Jax,

Egan and Cherry to 1st Plt's location leaving Brooks wondering if he was losing his ability to command his company.

"That white sonavabitch Nixon," Jax said when he and the others settled, "he aint nothin but a plague on mankind. Man, that dude sly. He one cagey mothafucka. They makin money off us. They makin money off Israel. Sure they's concerned. This place fall, it like sewin up their pockets. I says, Save Our Blood. Doan do my ol lady no good I get blow'd way fo some ARVN here o fo some Jew there, Lord let Leon rest in peace. We got brothers en sisters in jail, Man. In jail in the World. I'd rather git scattered stormin the prison that got Bobby Seale chained up then in some fucken valley aint nobody give a shit bout."

"Amen, Bro," El Paso said. They were all speaking very calmly now. "Peace marches, they got their place. Everybody standin round flippin each other peace signs. But that aint where it's at."

"That right," Jax said. "Things is rotten to the core. We gotta git down, deal on em, overthrow the government."

"Black people have known the enemy fo hundreds a years," Doc said in his deep voice. "You white people, you just now catchin on."

"They suckin our blood," Jax said. "They the baddest bloodsuckers."

"Amen," El Paso sighed.

"Goddamn Jews own half a Harlem," Doc said. "They keep my brothers en sisters in the ghetto. They sic the fuzz on us, keep us down. They take all the money out a our neighborhoods so our schools are bad so we can't never learn an get out. That outside interference, Mista. Black people gotta have Black Power. We gotta run our own schools. Have our own doctors, our own police, our own judges. You understand what I'm sayin?"

"Ah, don't be duped, Man," Egan said. "They do it in white neighborhoods too. A pig's a pig."

They talked on. The night was very dark and very wet and very cold. Leeches crawled into their pants and shirts. At one point, as Egan was catnapping, the cool slime of a crawling bloodsucker on his lips woke him. "Eech," he coughed, spit, shaking his head as the leech dropped into his mouth. Periodically each man wiped his hands over his body, extra carefully about his privates, checking for leeches. Sometimes a small leech would be found unattached and it would be squished between thumb and forefinger. Sometimes a large leech would be found attached. All Alpha was out of repellent and even those with dry cigarettes did not dare light up. With fingernails they dug into their own flesh and pinched away at the buried head, usually snapping the leech at the neck and leaving the mouth. After the leech died, the wound burned.

"You know that poster," Cherry whispered to El Paso late in the night, "ya know that one, 'WHAT IF THEY GAVE A WAR AND NO ONE SHOWED UP?' What if we didn't come and the NVA didn't come? There'd be nobody to kill."

El Paso smiled in the dark. Cherry still did not understand, he thought. Maybe he's even regressing. El Paso sighed weakly and thought Cherry would need a long time to crawl out from under his thick layers of campus propaganda and government indoctrination. Neither side has the answer, he thought.

"What if they gave a war and only one side showed up?" El Paso asked him.

"Huh?"

"That has happened, you know," El Paso said gently. They were sitting very close to each other wrapped like five enchiladas in their ponchos and poncho liners. They spoke very quietly, speaking directly into one another's ears. "It happened in Russia under Stalin and in China under Mao. They called it a purge."

"Aw, you know what I mean," Cherry said.

"Yes," El Paso said. "But it's dangerous to talk in slogans like that." He spoke very easily. He wanted to talk, to tell stories, to pass the night. "Would you like to hear more Vietnamese history, Brother?"

"Yes," Cherry said. "I'd like to know it all."

"Just a little, eh? Then we'll give Egan the radios and we'll cut some Zs. Maybe you would like to hear of Nguyen Ai Quoc. That is Ho Chi Minh's real name. He once led a war where only one side showed up. What would you like to know? About exploitation perhaps? Perhaps representation?"

"Both," Cherry said. El Paso's voice in his ear was both soothing and interesting. Cherry flashed on Silvers each time the night became quiet and he longed to keep El Paso speaking.

"Okay, Brother. Did you know Uncle Ho had many of his political enemies put to death while he was coming to power in the 1940s. He once said, 'All those who do not follow the line which I have laid down will be broken.' In '45 and '46 he purged the anti-communist nationalists, the Dai Viet, and the

Catholics and he directed the Viet Minh in the South. Diem was a popular nationalist back then. Uncle Ho tried to have him assassinated. He wasn't successful but he was in having Ta Tu Thau rubbed out because Ta was head of a rival communist faction. The Viet Minh almost took over the South at that time but the British stopped them."

"The British?"

"Ah, you didn't know the British fucked around over here?"

"No."

"Oh yes," El Paso said lazily. "Right after World War Two. The Japanese had Nam during the war. The Germans had crushed the French in Europe and the French lost their colony here to the Japs. When the Japs were defeated Britain and America tried to force the Vietnamese back into the French Empire. Boy Asshole did not have it entirely wrong and, of course, Minh is very astute. Most of the British were from India and only led by Anglo officers. All that happened while both England and the United States were proclaiming the Atlantic Charter and the principles of equality and independence for all pre-war colonies. The Anglos turned their backs on Nam out of sympathy for the defeated French, and for money too."

"How come you didn't say that earlier tonight?" Cherry asked.

"Oh, you know," El Paso shrugged. "No matter how hard you tell a man something he will not believe it unless he already believes it. *Es verdad*. Our first blunder here was to support the French. Roosevelt committed us to that. FDR not only condoned the French move but he sold them $160 million of war materiel. Truman kept it going. Eisenhower brought in the advisors, Kennedy the ground troops. The American public has always been one president behind. Johnson was not the one to begin the American combat role. He just escalated it."

"Wait a minute," Cherry stopped him. "Didn't FDR die before World War Two was over?"

"Yes. But he made the commitment. Tricky Dick inherited the entire mess. Now he is winding it down, withdrawing everyone. People think we are still escalating."

"He's an asshole."

"Yes. But they all are. Is there a politician anywhere you can trust?"

"I don't know. Hey, what about Nixon's Vietnamization and pacification and what about the Paris Peace Talks?"

"Those are very old programs. You should know the Vietnamese are very gentle and very polite and they love war. They must love war. They have been fighting non-stop for two thousand years. If you put two friendly papa-sans in a room for twenty-four hours, one will emerge victorious."

"Hey, that's good." Cherry laughed. "Ha. Put two . . ."

"Pacification," El Paso continued gently, "is a French phrase going back to the late 1850s. The French wanted to mollify the natives, 'for humanity.' They wanted the natives to be peaceful and to accept French rule. Dien Bien Phu showed what one hundred years of Pacification earned for the French. The American who coined that term was stupid. It was an insult to all Vietnamese." El Paso spat. Cherry could feel his body jerk as he spit. "We moved peasants off their rice farms and into camps on the coast. Then we keep the NVA from rocketing the camps. So what? ¡Estupido! Pacification is a term for newspapers and official reports. The only 'hearts and minds' it wins are the ones making big profits off the war."

"God, Man! You oughta talk to somebody. Maybe you should write the president."

"No one listens, Cherry. No matter how hard you tell a man something he will not believe it unless he is inclined to believe it. Pacification began as a protection for French missionaries. The emperor, Tu Duc, he was trying to keep western imperialism out of Nam and he blew away a few missionaries. Sometimes I think every man wants to get rid of a priest here or there.

"One more parallel, Cherry. Did you know the French only wanted Vietnam so the British wouldn't have it? That was the game of colonialization. It was like saying, 'So it don't go communist.' That's a stupid reason. It is very much like it was before, only now we have some new names for it."

"Where'd you learn all this, Man?" Cherry asked.

"It is all in the history books. I don't have a monopoly on it. Do you want to know about negotiations?"

"I'd very much like to hear."

"It will be like it was before. The French ratified a treaty with Tu Duc in 1863. In exchange for French backing the emperor gave the French Saigon. The people hated the French and they hated Tu Duc. Tu Duc wanted to slaughter the Catholics. The French said, okay, as long as we can have Saigon. The people went to guerrilla tactics to fight them both. To the people the treaty meant nothing. Over the next four years France suppressed the resistance in the South. The Vietnamese people were wild about losing Saigon by 'negotiation.' One night, legend says, Tu Duc smelled an evil wind so he moved into league with Napoleon and renegotiated a return of Cochin China, the southern third of Nam. In return he opened the entire country to the French and he agreed to become a vassal and his country would become a French protectorate. The Vietnamese attacked Tu Duc and French trade went bad. The businessmen got pissed at Napoleon for not conquering and Napoleon reneged on the treaty. Treaties mean nothing. If we sign a treaty tomorrow that will not stop the war."

"Were the French that bad?" Cherry asked.

"Yes," Egan said joining the conversation. He had sat up to check for leeches again. One was stuck to his right eyelid. He dug his fingers into his eyelid and squeezed. The leech burst and watery blood and slime ran down his face. "Fucken French starved the peasants," Egan said.

"What're you doin, Bro?"

"Goddamn fucken leech in my eye."

"Wake Doc up."

"Fuck it. Don't mean nothin."

Doc had silently risen and was now on his knees by Egan gently checking Egan's eye by touch. "Bloodsuckers, Mista. The whole world full of em. Get under yer poncho and let me look at that with a light."

"How'd the French starve the peasants?" Cherry asked.

"They did stuff like force them to build railroads instead of lettin em raise rice. They died of famine because so many worked on the railroad and so few worked in the paddies. Twenty-five thousand starved to death."

"Hey," Egan said—he and Doc emerged from under the poncho—"let me ask, if you coulda come here back then and, say, killed the fucker who ran the railroad . . ."

"Doumer," El Paso said.

"Okay," Egan said, "killed Doumer to keep those twenty-five thousand peasants from being murdered, would you have done it?" No one answered. Egan pressed. "Huh? Would that have been right? The Jew use ta ask me that. He use ta say, would we have been justified in killing Hitler in '37 or '38 and thus stopping World War Two? Stopping the slaughter of six million Jews? Of twenty-five million Russians? Of maybe a total of fifty million people? I didn't come here to kill. I came here to stop killing. So did you. How could anybody in good conscience refuse to come. It was people sticking their heads in the sand who let fifty million people be slaughtered in six years. El Paso, Doc, Jax, you awake . . ."

"I listenin."

". . . Cherry, you came to save, not to destroy. Brothers, your hearts are pure. It's the bloodsuckin politicians who've fucked us. Me, you, all of us."

At the CP Brooks lay semi-conscious, cold, trembling. He lay between Cahalan and Brown but their body heat was not enough to keep him warm. He trembled into that state between sleep and wakefulness where dreams flow and are sometimes controlled. He fell through a black hole into nothingness and the void filled with the gentle fragrance of Hawaiian flowers, bloomed with soft splashes of color, warmed with the touch of Lila. Those first moments repeated and sped by. If R&R's beginning had been a wonder, the next days held no wonder at all. The tiny crack between Rufus and Lila spread gradually, steadily, a hundred minute inuendos forcing them apart until the invisible crack became a chasm.

After they had loved for the nth time and he had lain back satisfied, warm and secure, Lila had said, "Oh Rufus. It's going to be so wonderful. It is wonderful."

Rufus was anxious about seeing Lila again after so long but he had not expected her to be anxious too. He had simply not thought of it from her perspective. "Yes, it is wonderful," he said.

"Let's go out," Lila said. "Let's not waste any time. Okay?"

"Okay," he said smiling. She looked so pretty and so young.

"We don't have a lot of time," Lila said. "There isn't going to be enough time to see all the things I want to see. I just know it. Let's go eat then let's go to the beach. Oh my, we've been here almost six hours and we haven't even seen the beach."

Rufus had to shower first. He had washed beneath the cold showers at Eagle, then again in warm showers at Da Nang and at Ton Son Nhut but he still had not felt clean. He could not dislodge months of jungle dirt in minutes of showers. Rufus showered with Lila. She got out and dressed. He continued washing. He scrubbed his feet for ten minutes and his balls for five. He scraped at his body with his fingernails removing layers of dead and calloused skin. Come on, Lila groaned to herself. We don't have forever.

Lila had dressed in colorful native African dress, her head wrapped in a high turban, her shoulders naked. She had accentuated her green eyes with cobalt blue eyeshadow and raised the arch of the brows. She was stunning. Rufus just finished showering. "Oh Rufus," she said, "don't wear that uniform."

"I'm not ashamed of it," Rufus said simply, not defensively.

"Oh, of course not, Silly. I only meant, well, you know, we're here among civilians."

"Okay." He smiled but it hurt him. A tiny chip had been made in the polished lacquer of his pride.

"Come here, Silly." Lila smiled warmly after he had dressed in the clothes she had bought for him. He obeyed and embraced her. Lila laughed and ran her fingers through his hair. She vigorously massaged his scalp.

Why are you doing that? Rufus asked himself. Does my short hair give me away? Does it offend you?

Rufus and Lila dined at a very fancy restaurant on the first night of R&R, the night of the day of their most wonderful love spree.

Look at these rich sons of bitches in here picking at their food, Rufus said to himself disgustedly. God, even she's doing it. Rufus did not mention his thoughts. His irritation and frustration grew.

"I wonder what those guys are eating right now." Rufus laughed as he plunged a thick juicy hunk of meat into his mouth and swallowed it after chewing only twice.

"My fish is wonderful." Lila smiled. "This sauce is just . . . just, scrumptious. How's your steak?"

"Good." He winked at her. "We call ourselves boonierats," he said with pride.

"What?" She laughed at the name.

"Boonierats," he repeated and thought maybe that name does sound silly.

"What's a boonierat?" she asked laughing.

"Just an infantry soldier." Rufus smiled. "A grunt."

"A grunt?"

"Well, more than a grunt. Marines are grunts. Soldiers

from the Big Red One are grunts. We're boonierats. We live in the boonies, we don't just visit. The jungle is our home.''

"Let's not talk about Vietnam," Lila said. "Let's talk about Hawaii and about you and me.''

I'm nothing right now but Vietnam, he thought. "All right," Rufus said. "Hey," he said cheerfully, loudly, "let's order a bottle of champagne. I'd love a fucking bottle of champagne.'' The word *fucking* had come out so easily, so naturally, he had not even noticed it until he saw the appalled look on Lila's face and the side-glance of the waiter. Well fuck them, he thought bitterly.

After eating they took a taxi to a secluded beach. Three taxis had passed them up and finally the furious doorman had halted the fourth. The streets near the restaurant had been crowded with bustling people. Someone knocked into Rufus. He spun and violently shoved the man back, "Watch it, Mothafucka.''

"Oh, so sorry, Sir,'' an old oriental bowed slightly and scurried away. Other people on the sidewalk stared at him and Lila. Rufus breathed deeply. He could feel the ambient prejudice, the thick unwelcome Hawaii reserves for blacks. Or is it just that I'm a soldier? he asked himself.

"God," Lila seethed in the taxi. "Did you have to make a scene?''

"Aw fuck em;'' Rufus snapped. "Fuck them phony people. They don't even know what the fuck's happening.''

"Please don't talk that way, Rufus,'' Lila ordered.

"These fucking people don't even know there's a war going on. Rich, innocent mothafuckas.''

"Rufus!''

"Hey, you too.''

They walked the beach in silence. The night was moonlit and beautiful and Lila wanted to skip and wade barefoot. Rufus wanted to return to their room and have room service bring up more champagne. Don't let one bad pitch destroy your whole ballgame, he said to himself. "Look," Rufus said stopping. "I'm sorry. It takes some time to adjust to this. Hey, you know?''

"Rufus, I'm sorry too,'' Lila said. "I guess I haven't let you tell me much about what's happened to you.''

"Hey, okay. There's not much to tell. I treat my men as my equals over there. They're men. I'm a man. I respect them for what they are and they return that respect.''

Lila pressed the palm of her hand to her cheek and stood before him. "I'm not sure I understand."

Rufus ran through explanations in his mind but he rejected each. He knew Lila was not interested in or capable of comprehending what his infantry unit was, what it meant to him. There was an *esprit de corps* among his men built on the deep concern each had for every other. They worked together, they fought together, they shared life and death. How can those words mean anything to someone who has not experienced it? Yet Rufus wanted to talk, wanted Lila to understand. But he could not talk. He put his arms out to her and drew her to him and they embraced. Lila kept her head buried in his chest. He did not belong to her any longer, nor did she any longer belong to him. They had come from different worlds, had merged, and had been separated by the army. They came together again in Hawaii and again they were from different worlds. They embraced a good-bye embrace. They both felt it but neither said it. That would take much longer. "Hey, let's go back and get a few drinks at the hotel," he suggested and she quietly agreed.

Over the next few days Rufus and Lila went through the motions of a returning soldier and a faithful wife on vacation. They went to Diamond Head, to Pearl Harbor, to a hotel sponsored luau. They surfed, paddled an outrigger, played tennis. Rufus told Lila a little about his men, a little about tactics, a little about the gore of modern warfare. And they drank. Both drank heavily. Rufus passed out the next two nights. He could not relax.

And in the morning, in bed, "How the hell can you say that?" he demanded.

"You stink. You never used to sweat like that," she accused.

"Hey," he was furious. "Look! Three things. One, men sweat. Okay, you're a fine lady and you don't sweat. Well, men sweat. Two, blacks sweat. Okay, you're a fine black lady and you don't sweat but blacks sweat. And three, black men sweat. Why do you think whites call us shines? It's because we sweat. I'm a black man and I sweat like a black man and I smell like a black man. I don't know how you plug up your pores so effectively but I'll tell you this—I can't do it. I won't do it. I'm going to wet stink like the black man I am."

"Rufus," she cooed. "White men sweat too."

He jumped out of bed and stamped off to the bath.

During the days and nights, a dozen times, Rufus flashed upon evening operations on hillsides in Nam, on morning fights on ridges, on night probes in valleys. Again he tried to tell Lila about his men, about heroism he had witnessed, about hours he had endured. And again he felt her lack of interest, her apathy at best, her deliberate rejection, her distaste and hatred. Rufus attempted a different approach. Once he said, "Power is not simply what fire power you have. It's not what you have. It's what the enemy thinks you have." She did not understand. He tried another vein, something that should mean much to the artist in her black body. "There is a wholeness in black culture which has been disembodied in much of white, especially Anglo-white, culture. The disembodying of the culture is both the cause and the effect of perceptions which divide everything into components and then attempts to explain everything as complex constructions of those components. When I say everything, I mean everything. I mean seeing a man as a composite of molecules and a poem as a composite of words or a culture as a composite of people and not seeing the energies which run through the forms, the molecules, the words, the people, the energy which ties the elements together into what the thing is. It's that energy which our blackness is losing by becoming white."

She shook her head without hearing.

He dove deeper.

She stopped him. "Brooks," Lila said, "you're an ass. Can't you stop thinking of war and politics and race? Can't you be normal?" She looked at him and she saw he was shaking. "Please be normal," she said. "Please be here. Please," Lila pleaded. She began to cry. "Be here with me. There's a world here that is not just your words."

"I don't understand you anymore," he said. "What happened to that lady that I knew that really cared for us. That wanted so many things for us. The same things that I wanted for the two of us together. You used to believe in me. You didn't want to be only you."

"I still want those things, Rufus. It's you who's changed. I still want happiness and joy for us. I still want kids for us. I want to be much more than I am now for us. And I know it's for us because I don't care about any of that just for me. I want to share it with you. Oh, Rufus." Her tears were running wild. He was like a total stranger.

Brooks lay back thinking, dreaming. He watched that cou-

ple that he was certain he knew yet that he did not know at all.
He watched them at night on the beach or in bed not touching.
Brooks watched the woman talk to the man. She was very upset.
"Love doesn't have to hurt," she cried. "Don't you see? Can't
you see? You don't have to hurt me. I'll love you without the
hurt. Can't you see that, Rufus?"

Brooks rolled over and shivered against Brown. "It doesn't
have to hurt," he muttered. Lila's crying dried up and she turned
hard.

"Not tonight," she said when they were in their room.
"Hell, you're so drunk, you couldn't if I wanted you to."

Brooks sat up. His armpit was burning. He reached into his
shirt and felt the leech and retched empty stomach acid, hot and
bitter at the back of his mouth. He swallowed. He wanted to
chase all thoughts from his head. He needed sleep. Perhaps
Thomaston was right, he told himself. Perhaps if he told the
GreenMan he wanted out, wanted to DEROS and cancel his
extension, perhaps he would be out of the boonies come next
resupply. He could do that much for Thomaston. Let him have
the company. Not for himself. Not for Lila. He was tired, so
tired. So tense. Cahalan was asleep next to him. Brooks could
feel his rhythmic breathing. On the other side Brown was awake
with the radios, noiselessly adjusting the frequencies, monitoring
other companies and Alpha's platoons. Twice he called a security check to each LP, to each platoon CP. Twice each one
responded with negative keying. I've slept with these guys more
than I have with my wife, Brooks thought. A pang of self-pity
hit him. A single sharp arrow of pain driving down from between his eyes, down to his throat, down his chest and out his
gut. It was as if he had been skewered with a giant fishhook. He
clenched his fists and said to himself, "Anxiety must be converted to achievement not to frustration or depression." He said
the words very formally, very evenly. "One must burn stress out
of one's system," he continued. "Convert anxiety. Do not
believe in failure. Analyze every situation to maximize the benefits and minimize the detriments." Ah. It was working. He was
successful in talking away the pain, the anxiety. Now, he said to
himself, if only I could decide what to do.

SIGNIFICANT ACTIVITIES

THE FOLLOWING RESULTS FOR OPERATIONS IN THE O'REILLY/ BARNETT/JEROME AREA WERE REPORTED FOR THE 24-HOUR PERIOD ENDING 2359 17 AUGUST 70:

INCLEMENT WEATHER LIMITED AIRMOBILE OPERATIONS ON THE 17TH. OPERATIONS BY THE 2D SQDN 17TH CAVALRY (AMBL) IN SUPPORT OF THE 1ST INF DIV (ARVN) IN THE VICINITY OF FIREBASES O'REILLY, RIPCORD AND JEROME WERE DELAYED OR CANCELLED, AND ONE COMPANY-SIZE ASSAULT WAS CANCELLED.

CONTACT IN THE BARNETT AREA WAS HEAVY THROUGHOUT THE DAY WITH CO B, 7/402 CLEARING AN ENEMY COMPANY FROM THE SAME RIDGELINE WHERE IT HAD FOUGHT SEVERAL DAYS EARLIER (YD 173329). THE UNIT, SUPPORTED BY ARTILLERY, ASSAULTED THE POSITION THREE TIMES AND SECURED THE HILL MASS AT 1530 HOURS. SEVEN US SOLDIERS WERE WOUNDED IN THE ACTION. 11 ENEMY WERE KILLED BY SMALL ARMS FIRE AND FIVE WERE KILLED BY ARTILLERY. CAPTURED WEAPONS INCLUDED ONE RPD MACHINE GUN, TWO B-40 ROCKET LAUNCHERS, TEN AK-47S, ONE 82MM MORTAR TUBE AND ONE 9MM PISTOL. IN OTHER ACTION, CO A, 7/402 SUSTAINED ONE KILLED AND ONE WOUNDED.

Scale 1:50,000
Each square represents
1000 meters x 1000 meters
Elevations given in meters

Ta Laou

Khe Ta Laou

Delta

sniper attack

Alpha
Dust Off

Charlie

cliffs

1st, CP

2d, 3d

Ambush Team

DA KRONG

○	NDP
△	Firebase
⌒→	route of Company
---	previous movement
✳	firefight
☐	helicopter LZ
-·-·-	helicopter route
— —	NVA road

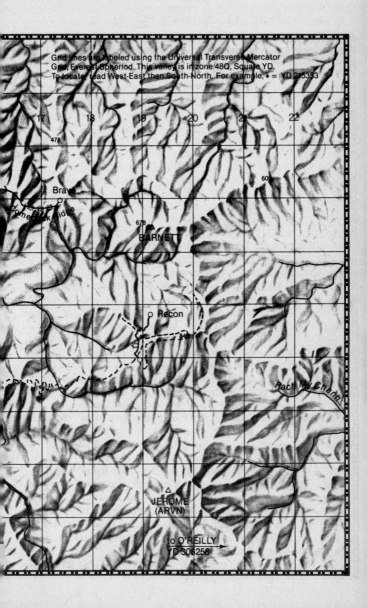

Grid lines are labeled using the Universal Transverse Mercator
Grid, Everest Spheriod. This valley is in zone 48Q, Square YD.
To locate, read West-East then South-North. For example, • = YD 215353

CHAPTER

25

First light broke upon the valley as ugly gray mist. The drizzle had not ceased during the night. Alpha was awakened by a horrible roar as if they lay beneath a speeding freight train, then a boom, then the explosion. Jax jolted up. It was still dark on the ground. The top of the grass was just distinguishable from the moist sky. SSSSSEEEECKK-boom-BOOOOMM split the air above him. "Motha! They firin dat thing too mothafucken close." The roar split the sky again. "Shee-it." Jax lay back down and tried to sleep. Another round passed over. An eight-inch howitzer from Firebase Bastogne far to the south had begun the road mission. Alpha was on the GTL, gun-target line, a straight line from the gun to the target. They heard two explosions for each projectile, the small sonic boom of the shell traveling faster than the speed of sound, then the explosion of the round. As each round passed over Jax could feel his back trying to grab the ground, trying to mix his molecules with those of the dirt. The howitzer fired twelve rounds over a half-hour period and then ceased.

Jax pulled his poncho and poncho liner tighter over his head. The drizzle became rain. Grayness penetrated into the grass. A single large drop of water worked its way under Jax' poncho and onto the skin of his back. A chill ran up his neck and down his arms and legs to his fingers and toes. Quietly Jax rolled over and went back to sleep. A minute later another drop squeezed past the poncho and fell into his ear.

"Okay, okay," he muttered. "I's gettin up." Jax threw off

his poncho. His fatigues were soggy and his skin felt as gray as the sky. Jax removed packets of cocoa, sugar and cream, and a piece of C-4 from his ruck. He grasped his canteen cup which had filled with clean rainwater during the night and put it on his C-rat can stove. He lit the C-4, it flared white hot and died out. The water boiled. Jax mixed the packets and sipped the steaming brew. His breath formed a cloud before him as he blew the cocoa to cool it. Around him no one else was stirring. Jax scrounged in his ruck for a clean pair of socks and the foot powder Doc had given him. He sat down and removed his boots and socks. The skin of his feet was clammy gray and swollen. The constant moisture was causing the surface tissue to peel. Jax looked at his feet for a moment then said, "Hello, feet. Remember me? I's the dude got yo dowin all the dancin. I jest want ta let yo know Jax ree-lee a-preciates the job yo ol boys down der dowin fo me up here. Guess whut? I brought yo somethin. Got yo dudes some powder an a pair a socks that like new. There"—Jax sprinkled the powder on his feet and rubbed it in—"how dat feel? Fix yo dudes right up. Yo jest take it easy now. Yo hear da news? Yo pappy's a squad leader. How bout dat? Hey, hey. L-T say we gowin sit here today. Gowin take it easy. First thing I gowin do, feet, is get yo back in yo stinkin home. Then we gowin clear this AO a leeches, then we gowin rest."

The fog cloak over the valley floor rose with the dawn. It now lay ten to twelve feet above Alpha. Visibility below the fog would have been perhaps an eighth mile had the thick grass permitted it. Boonierats woke cautiously, quietly. Egan was up, sitting on his ruck, writing. Cherry was awake though he had not yet moved. He looked at Egan. Egan's face was swollen and his right eye was swollen half-shut from the leech bite. Cherry lay motionless. It had not been a good night. He had lain awake long after the conversation had ceased and when he did finally sleep, he dreamed.

Cherry had had first radio watch. During the watch he had thought about Silvers, about how he died. He analyzed every detail and he thought about alternative ways to carry his radio so it would not announce to snipers or trail watchers his important communication function. During his vigil he did not close his eyes. He lay back. His body tense. It was as if all his nerves were one long thin filament stretched taut. And it was in motion, vibrating, like a piano wire. It was as if someone had started a wave action in the wire and the waves oscillated and moved up the wire quickly, hit the end and bounded back through new waves zinging up. He had lain there jangled and taut, not in fear of death or of being hit, but in fear of not acting, not knowing how to act. His face burned as if all his energies were being forced into his head.

Cherry reviewed everything he could recall about jungle warfare. He recalled basic training and AIT, RVN training and SERTS. There had been night-fire classes, quick-fire drills, first aid and ambush classes. Cherry wanted to be good, had to be good, he decided, if he was to survive. In his mind he rehearsed what he should do if he were in column and they were ambushed from the left. He imagined his body reacting left. Then to the right. Front, rear. If someone near him were hit he placed himself mentally in the situation. Then he thought about calling in artillery support. He could do it—if he had to. Of that he was certain. He said to himself, if you think about a situation happening and you think about the proper response, when it happens you will respond properly without having to think. What did Silvers do? How does El Paso sound? Egan. How does Egan move so quietly? What does he do? How does he look? see? smell? feel? Cherry tried to assimilate all their lessons.

Then Cherry had passed the radio to Egan and had lain back and closed his eyes. A picture of Leon Silvers burned on his mind. Wrapped about Cherry, his water-soaked poncho liner became a blanket of sticky warm blood. He opened his eyes. He thought of turning to Egan, of offering to allow Egan to sleep while he took another watch. He decided against it. When the single shot felled Leon on the road Cherry had not jumped from the noise. His mind had been wandering and though the AK pop had startled him, it was the sight of others diving into the grass which brought the awareness of danger to him. I was probably the last fuckin guy off the road, he said to himself.

Cherry quivered. His insides pounded hot, pulsed painfully. His brain ached. He could barely breathe. He forced himself to allow the nightmare to begin. He forced himself to observe his mind in terror.

Half of him was on the enemy road. Everybody had scattered. Leon lay crumpled in a massive bloody heap at Cherry's feet. The sweet smell of blood rushed to Cherry's nose. The image was entirely still except for Cherry's own motion as if Cherry stood in a color photograph. He screamed. "That bullet. That was mine. That was meant for me. For my neck."

From out of the trail, rising ghost-like from the earth, through the vehicle marred road, rose a figure. The figure wavered as though seen through heat. It was dressed in US jungle fatigues and it was soaked in blood. The image of Cherry's body beneath its ruck shook. Its chest tightened as Cherry's chest tightened on the ground where he lay. Breathing became difficult. Cherry allowed the image to run. He realized he had control over it, could stop it now, whenever he wished. He watched his image watch the horror of the sordid scene on the road. In the photo Cherry froze now as the figure on the trail continued to rise and once at full height the rippling mirage solidified. It was that face again, a firm face, tight yellow-tan skin stretched over delicate bones, deep brown eyes laughing. The figure took one step forward and the face burst in deep red gush splatter. Cherry laughed.

The picture shifted. It came alive. The bloody Silvers at Cherry's feet became an angered, wounded, filthy rat clawing toward the grass shrieking and dragging its shattered gory abdomen. In the grass a hundred foul creatures scurried aimlessly in interlocking circles. Then the ghost figure before Cherry dropped. The head became a skull and glowed iridescent green. It approached. It came closer. It became larger and larger and winds swirled about the green glow until they whisked Cherry's weapon from his hand and blew his helmet from his head. Cherry spun and fled and laughed madly. He ran with every atom of energy in his being. The glowing skull became larger. The frozen wind lashed at Cherry's back. "You're not God," Cherry's image teased, tormented the spirit. "You're not God. You're Satan. Fuck you. You can't touch me. I'm God."

"Hey," Egan woke Cherry. "What the fuck you laughing at?"

Cherry did not fall back to sleep or to dream. He thought about Leon. Hadn't he and Leon exchanged addresses only a few days before? Didn't Cherry agree to write to Leon's sister and brother-in-law? Yes, now he recalled that clearly. How could he write? What could he say? He still did not know what he had done with the address. Tears welled up in Cherry's eyes. He just got blown away. Just like that. Oh God, I can hardly believe it. Thinking about Silvers made Cherry feel very alone and very vulnerable. Them mothafuckers. Them mothafuckin dinks. I'm goina kill every mothafuckin gook slope I see. For you, Leon, you poor bastard.

Cherry's thoughts wandered aimlessly through the darkest night hours. He thought of Linda. He masturbated, quietly shooting his juices into the cold muck outside his poncho. He thought about food, about eating. Eating is a very social behavior, he said to himself as if he were reading a study for a psychology class. It's very important to boonierats. It's the only time we kinda socialize. It's the only time we talk. Man, there aint no social life here in the boonies except that twice or three times a day when we eat. Cherry felt a flash of guilt from his first days in the army, from his very first KP. He had not yet even been assigned to a basic training brigade. He was in the transfer center at Ft. Dix. They had awakened him at 0330 that morning to pull KP. All day he washed dishes and pots and pans and washed the dining hall floor between meals and at four in the afternoon he and three other KPs were ordered to cut up carrots and celery for the evening soup. Tiredly they chopped and sliced, carelessly cutting the vegetables, dropping them on the floor, stepping on them, picking up squished pieces and dropping them into the giant pots, laughing and joking.

Later he had been inserted into the serving line and he had ladled out the soup and had felt nauseous and guilty watching the other recruits and he felt even sicker when he thought about what others might do to the food he ate. Since that time he had always held a rigid standard about teamwork of army units, the communal eating, living, the communal everything, the total communistic society, the societal ideal so opposed by the military minds. And here in the army, he thought, who is the most vehement opposition to authoritarian communalism? It is the same political left draftee who comes very close, some indeed go beyond, proposing that all society should be communal. Not militaristic but communal just the same, communal but for the strongest advocates who would replace the old order with the new, and who would be at the top of the new order. And who would be exempt from the common communal life which they see everyone else living happily. The Great White Father in Washington looking after his boys wherever they are, wherever he sends them. What wonderful control, what complete authority. "Fuck it," Cherry laughed. "Just say fuck it. Don't mean nothin. Drive on."

It was now light. Cherry watched Egan writing for several more minutes, then he got up. He sat on his ruck and brushed his hands through his hair and pushed out pieces of vegetation. His

scalp was crusted with sweat and dirt. He had never been so
dirty. Cherry felt his forehead, his nose. They were covered with
pimples. On his cheeks his beard was a splotchy stubble which
itched. His arm sores had become worse. He pressed about
them. The wet scabs broke easily and oozed pus. His crotch rot
was worse. The skin of his scrotum and inner thighs was red sore
and white sore.

Cherry watched Egan. They did not speak. Egan carefully
put his writing tablet and pens in the waterproof can at the base
of his ruck. He removed a razor and soap and toothpaste. Cherry
watched Egan shave in a puddle, watched how attentive Egan
was to his cleanliness, even in the boonies. Cherry decided to
emulate the platoon sergeant. He washed. With the corner of his
towel he scrubbed his face and torso. He borrowed Egan's razor
and shaved. He shaved in his own puddle, leaving on only the
sprouts of a moustache. Cherry scrubbed his arms. The scabs
broke and the soap stung in the open sores. He brushed his teeth.
He tightened his boots. He repacked his ruck leaving out coffee,
cocoa, pound cake and fruit cocktail for breakfast. Instead of
repacking his toothbrush he placed it in his fatigue shirt pocket
so that the bristled end stuck through the pen slit in the pocket
flap. Egan kept his toothbrush in his shirt pocket like that.
Cherry wanted to emulate everything.

Now Cherry was eager to move out. He did not want to lie
in the muck any longer. He fidgeted and adjusted his ruck straps
again. He looked around. No one else was up. Cherry, you en
your cherry ass, he assured himself, you're getting it down.

He decided to write a letter. He rose, then squatted by his
ruck. He extracted a plastic bag containing pens and writing
paper. The paper was damp. Cherry sat back on the ruck. I
should write to Silvers' sister, he thought. I should. Cherry
stared at the black paper. He thumbed the edge of the page then
began, "Dear Vic," he wrote. I'll write to the Silverses next, he
told himself. "There must be a few things in the world more
boring than sitting with an infantry company when they have
nothing to do." How can you write that? he asked himself.
Twelve hours of quiet and you're bored. Something is fuckin
with my mind. He began again. "Don't believe anything you
read in the papers about Nam. In twenty days I know more about
this place than in four years of concern back in the World."

Cherry stopped again. Now how can I say that? Before I
knew exactly where the government stood and I knew just what

was happening. Now I don't have any idea what we're doing and everything the government said seems either to mean nothing or to be a lie.

He began a third time. "My mind came very close to total collapse these past few days. In five days in the field I have shot a man and I have seen my best friend killed. Yesterday I felt like vomiting. Today, immunity, sweet immunity is setting in and I'm finally crawling out from under my shell as the apathy and insensitivity take hold."

A slap jolted Cherry's shoulder and he leaped, grabbed for his rifle and swung around. Egan lurched for his 16 when Cherry jumped. Jax was in the grass between their rucks. "Rovers," he whispered quickly to identify himself as a member of Alpha. "Doan shoot me Bros. It me, Jax." He had a huge sheepish smile.

"Oh fuckin Christ," Egan sighed. "Cherry, you make me jumpy as shit. Jax, what you come sneakin up on us for?"

"Yo guys up, huh?"

"Yeah," Egan hissed.

"Marko on watch," Jax explained as he wiggled his ass onto Cherry's ruck and shared the seat. "I could not sleep," Jax orated, his eyes twinkling. "I's there all tucked up in my poncho an one big ol drop a rain squeeze hisself inside with me en join me bout the neck. I get cold, Man. Chills run up my pretty black neck, down my pretty black back. My toes get colder en yesterday's cow flop." Jax' voice was in its best rhythmic gait. Egan laughed and tapped his feet in the muck in which he had slept. Here was Jax, after their words of the past few days, back to his old style. Egan felt warmed by Jax' gesture.

"I looks up," Jax continued. "An the sky comin almost light nough so yo know it there. I pulls my poncho over my head an rolls back over an tries ta sleep again. 'Jest one minute,' say Ol Mista Rain. 'I's cold out here too. Yo let me come in there with yo an warm up.' I says, 'Aint no way, Mista Rain.' But he doan listen an he squeeze in again an this time he saunter his sillyass inta my ear. 'Okay, okay,' I says. 'I gettin up.' Then I peers out en see Ol Mista Rain, he aint cuttin nobody no slack. I get up. I says, 'body a Jackson, how yo this mornin?' Ol bod say, 'Beautiful cept my feet is faauuukkupp.' So I says, 'Why doan we go up en see Eg en Cherry? Yo know Eg aint never asleep.' An sho nough, here Ol Jax right wid ya now."

Egan held his right fist out and Jackson met it lightly with his own right fist as they dapped. The two fists tapped knuckles-to-knuckles and back-to-back. Open hands passed over each other in sensual caresses of brotherhood. Left hands came forward and touched and passed open over clasped rights and slid up right arms to shoulders then pulled across to the center of each man's chest and clenched into fists. "I'm glad you're here," Egan said.

Cherry watched silently then got up suddenly, very quickly said, "Excuse me," and rushed for the perimeter. A loose warm rush swept down into his bowels. He stopped, opened his pants, squatted. A watery brown gush sloshed onto the jungle floor muck. Feces splashed onto his boots. "Oh God, no," Cherry groaned. "Not the shits."

"Sky Devil Niner, Quiet Rover Four," Brooks radioed Delta Company's commander. At 1100 hours, after a lethargic morning, Alpha's CP and 2d Plt began moving north in column back toward the road. 1st and 3d Plts had patrols reconning to the south, east and west. At the NDP the remaining boonierats continued silent restful guard.

"Rover Four, this is Sky Devil," the radio rasped in jocular reply. "Your wish is my command. Over."

"What the hell?" Brooks muttered to El Paso. El Paso shrugged. "Devil," Brooks transmitted, "my papa element is in your ballpark six zero zero mike to your sierra. We would like to play ball and will jump the red rope on your comic book to close in one hotel. Over."

"Roger dodger, Rover. Check it out. Rendezvous with Sky Devils echo tango alpha one hotel. My team is ready to play ball and wilco. Over."

"Thanks much, Niner," Brooks said. "Out."

Delta Company had been moving back and forth on the north ridge for five days, being careful never to progress too far from their first secured LZ. Since daybreak they were to have been moving down the mountain toward the road and toward the rendezvous with Alpha. In reality only their CP had moved from a fixed position Delta's 3d Plt had established atop the ridge to a fixed position Delta's 1st Plt had 400 meters down a rocky finger. Alpha's rendezvous element would do most of the humping.

Brooks signaled with both hands, thumbs jerked outward. 2d Plt and the CP quietly spread out through the grass forming a long line. Again on signal they moved now sweeping forward, slowly, approaching to within two meters of the road. There they halted. They stood completely still for several minutes then one by one squatted or sat to observe. In the midday light and with the higher fog ceiling the corridor was yet more awesome. The surface was composed of rock and gravel and the drainage system was elaborate. On the walls signs of natural material marked junctions and turnaround points. One eight-inch round from the pre-dawn barrage had impacted directly on the road. The explosion had cratered the road surface and destroyed a thirty-foot section of roof. The crater had filled with water. There was no other evidence of damage from the artillery. Brooks radioed the TOC with a new road description and the arty results. Then he cautiously moved forward. The flank gunners also moved to the road's shoulder. They searched the far stretches. Through the hole blown in the roof Brooks could see a small cut in the cliff and a passageway up to Delta. He walked in the grass down the line, observing from various angles.

At Alex Mohnsen's squad Brooks stopped and stood still. The squad leader came to him. "L-T," Mohnsen whispered, "we aint goina NDP with Delta, are we?" Brooks did not look at him. "They're the noisiest dudes in battalion, L-T."

"I know," Brooks whispered back not taking his eyes from the north ridge wall.

They were all silent again. They waited. The road remained empty. Halfway down the line Garbageman tapped one finger against his rifle in time with a silent song being played by a rock group in his head. Toward the far end, Hackworth muffled a cough in the crook of his arm, trapping the sound completely. He stifled the next urge to cough. And the next. Brooks stood rigid. Like everyone else's, his uniform blended well with the grass. Mohnsen looked up at him several times. Brooks, motionless, was difficult to discern from even this short an interval. "Patience," Brooks muttered beneath his breath. He was very aware of the suppressed restlessness of his men. Still they waited and observed.

After forty minutes Brooks moved. He returned to the CP. They rose. In both directions boonierats slowly stood, one by one. Brooks led off. He stepped from the concealment of the grass onto the road, crossed to the narrow cut and began climbing. He climbed slowly yet steadily. A stream fell through the cut. The water felt cold flowing in his boots. Behind the commander others crossed and climbed. Flank security remained out until almost the last man had crossed the road; then the flanks collapsed, crossed and followed. When the entire rendezvous element was on the mountain slope, Brooks paused. He was winded. The passage was steep, the climb exhausting. Pop Randalph crawled past him to take point. Lt. De Barti moved to slack. 3d Sqd slid in behind, then the CP, 1st and 2d. They climbed in column north, then northeast, always up, always toward Delta.

The vegetation on the north escarpment of the Khe Ta Laou was sparse and offered very little cover. Pop stayed low and stayed in gullies as he climbed. Behind him boonierats stepped into his footsteps. At just under fifty meters up the wall, Pop broke through the fog. High above the sky had a broken cloud cover. To the east there were patches of blue so bright Pop could not look at them. To the west over the Laotian foothills, the horizon was heavy dark and foreboding. Pop continued up. He climbed for half an hour reaching an area where the land leveled and thick jungle congestion concealed their advance.

"Tim," Brooks whispered, "call Delta. See if they've got us visual."

"Yes Sir," Cahalan answered. The column continued. "Sky Devil, this is Quiet Rover," Cahalan began.

"We see ya, Good Buddy," came the flippant reply. "Just yall stand right up and walk on in. Ol Delta got you covered. We're just thirty mikes up the high feature."

Company D's CP and 1st Plt were situated amongst a multi-peaked rock outcropping that overlooked the valley on three sides. On the fourth, the finger ridge ran perpendicular up to the main north ridgeline. The outcropping looked like a bartizan battlement on a castle wall, the sheered off south face aiming directly toward the knoll at the center of the valley. Alpha's rendezvous element circled the position. The 2d Plt boonierats stopped outside the perimeter. Brooks, his RTOs, FO and Doc Johnson entered the perimeter and walked silently toward the center. From all sides came jeers. "Man, look what just dragged in." "Hey, Hardcore, don't go givin the old man any ideas." "Aint that them crazy fuckers from Alpha?" "Break out the dew. Them dudes need a toke."

Brooks walked erect, eyes forward, oblivious to the Delta troops. FO followed the L-Ts example, as did El Paso and Doc. Brown nodded to several of the men he knew. Cahalan paused to talk to an old friend. At the center of the NDP Delta's CP had erected a poncho hootch large enough for six men to sleep beneath. Throughout the outcropping ponchos were stretched over bootlaces to make pup tents, or tied to rock walls to form lean-tos. No one had made any attempt to camouflage the shelters. Under every shelter there were men sleeping or reading. All of them appeared dry.

"Hi," shouted Captain O'Hare from within the CP hootch. The Delta commander was a stout jovial man with a bushy moustache. His uniform was clean. His hands were clean. "Glad you could make it," he called. "You're just in time for coffee."

"Hello, Peter," Brooks said formally, softly. He squatted outside the hootch and looked in. Delta's commander and RTOs had been playing poker.

"Come in, come in," O'Hare persisted. "Sit down and grab a cup of coffee. Geez, this operation sure's turned into a giant clusterfuck, huh? Why don't you have your men come in and join me and my boys? Do you believe all this rain?"

"They're okay where they are," Brooks said coolly. "GreenMan give you anything for me?"

"I'll say he did," O'Hare said, "but first let me get you that coffee." O'Hare rolled to his knees and crawled to the edge of the hootch where a ten-cup pot was steaming. "All the comforts of home," he chuckled as he poured rich black liquid into a canteen cup. "Here."

"Thanks," Brooks said. He took the cup, sipped the coffee and passed it out to El Paso. O'Hare sighed. "Peter, I need all the bug juice you and your men can spare. My men are being eaten alive by the leeches in that valley."

"Yeah, I was surprised to find you guys crossed the river." O'Hare avoided Brooks' eyes. "How is it down there?"

"Peter," Brooks said, "I need insect repellent and I want to know what the GreenMan said."

"Well, Ruf. Let me first say I'm sure glad the old man didn't pick my company to go tricky-trottin down inta that. You guys just marched right through the middle of Gookville like you was comin down the middle a Main Street. I bet that scared them gooks halfway to hell."

Brooks stood and backed away from the hootch a few steps, hoping to draw O'Hare out. "Shit, L-T. Look at that," El Paso whispered from behind him. Several Delta troops on the perimeter were smoking and passing their smoke back and forth. The butt popped sending sparks flying. The soldiers laughed. "Holy

Mother of God,'' El Paso whispered. ''They're blowin dew out here.''

The personality of Delta Company was as different from Alpha as Brooks was from O'Hare. The companies were like brothers who had grown apart. On the surface Alpha was quiet, pensive, cautious yet daring. Delta was loud, boisterous, macho. In many ways Delta was a throwback to an earlier American personality in Vietnam which exuded bravado and faith in the American military way, while Alpha was the younger brother, taught tactics primarily by the NVA. Yet both companies came from the same parentage, the same battalion, division, country. The same technology was behind both, and the same can-do spirit, and the same ugly withdrawal symptoms sent from a country turned sour on war and demanding the return of its soldiers. Oh God, Brooks thought. Just let up a little, just relax and let them relax, and this is what you'll have.

O'Hare came out from beneath the poncho roof. He had put on a rain jacket. ''Did you hear, Bravo got another POW? They got em an NVA honcho.''

''When?'' Brooks asked. He stepped away from O'Hare coaxing the other commander into open neutral ground.

''Earlier this morning. They killed another gook and got this honcho, and an AK and two RPGs. Can you believe it? Taking a prisoner in this shit.''

''Where'd they get them?''

''Another bunker complex. Those bastards are dug in all over this valley.''

''They weren't moving?''

''Nope. Not from what I monitored anyway. They said both gooks were clean and healthy.''

Brooks signaled to Cahalan. The RTO approached immediately. ''Get a full sit-rep on Bravo's action,'' he whispered then walked off pulling O'Hare with him. Alpha's CP contingent followed at a distance. ''How much bug juice did your men come up with?'' Brooks asked O'Hare quietly.

''I'm sorry, Ruf,'' O'Hare said sheepishly. ''My boys don't seem to be carrying much at all. I got three or four vials you can take.''

''That's it?''

''Yeah. Like I said, we weren't carrying much. If you'd radioed earlier I could have asked the GreenMan to bring some out. He dropped in yesterday and talked to me for about thirty minutes. Then his bird came back and he left. Can you believe, flyin in weather like this? Crazy, huh?''

Brooks had continued walking while they talked. Now he was at the edge of the cliff overlooking the valley. O'Hare stopped a few feet back. FO, El Paso, Brown, Cahalan and Doc stopped fifteen feet away. There were no Delta troops at the edge and indeed no perimeter positions along the cliff at all. Brooks seemed mesmerized by the view. He stared silently. O'Hare shuffled his feet. The valley was multiple shades of gray, the floor and Alpha's lower element covered by a dirty thick gray fluff. Above was lighter gray, to the west very dark, the hills almost black, in the distant east unexpected patches of blue sparkling like jewels.

"Every time I see that mother," Brooks said nastily, nodding toward the lone tree protruding above the valley fog, "it gets bigger. That's one colossal tree. Look at that thing. Look at the size of that. Peter''—Brooks turned to O'Hare then turned back—"how far do you think that tree is from here?"

"About a klick," O'Hare said.

"If you were up there you could see the whole valley," Brooks said.

"Ah, Ruf," O'Hare stammered, "do you want to know about the GreenMan?"

"Yes," Brooks answered. He turned again and leaned casually against a rock at the cliff edge.

O'Hare began in alarm, "He wanted me to tell, ah, to offer you one of my platoons." Brooks shifted. O'Hare stepped back another foot. "It'll be op-conned to you while you're down there. Ah, he, ah, thought you might need some more bodies."

Brooks set his gaze on O'Hare's eyes. Even leaning Brooks was taller than the stocky commander. Brooks did not move a muscle, his breathing was imperceptible. That's why I don't DEROS, he thought. That's why. My men might get stuck with a man like O'Hare. I wouldn't give any of them a fifty-fifty chance in the valley with O'Hare. "Peter," Brooks said.

"Yes, Rufus," O'Hare jumped nervously.

"Do you like small unit tactics? Harassment and attack?"

"Huh? Yeah. Of course."

"So do I."

"Oh. Yeah."

"You'll be up here—won't you—if we get in trouble?"

"Yeah, Ruf. You know you can count on us."

"You could probably be down to us in two or three hours if we were this side of the river."

"Yeah. I'm sure we could. Ah, well. You know. It would depend."

"Let's just leave it that way," Brooks said gently. "Okay?"

O'Hare laughed. "That's what GreenMan said you'd do," he said. "You know, Ruf, it's good talking to you. You're the only other commander I've spoken with in the bush in I can't remember how long. We got to talk more often, ya know? We got to stick together."

"Right on, Bro," Brooks gave O'Hare a power salute.

O'Hare nodded furiously. "Sometimes it gets lonely out here, being in command. It's good to talk to another commander. We understand each other."

"Captain," Brooks let the disgust come through, "if you need understanding, look to your men."

Brooks rejoined his CP group and led them through the tiny hootch-city of Delta's NDP. On their way out the calls came again, friendlier this time, "Go get em, Alpha." "Do em a job, Man." "Kick ass. Don't take no names."

Outside the perimeter, regrouped with 2d Plt, Brooks relaxed. He turned to FO, pointed and asked, "Bill, how far is that tree from here?"

FO glanced to the valley center. "Fourteen hundred meters," he said. "Maybe fourteen fifty."

Brooks nodded. "We're going to circle that mother," he said. "I want to go clear around it before we hit it." The men around him nodded agreement.

They began the descent. Halfway down to the road the fog enveloped them. They paused. Brooks whispered very quietly to El Paso, "If you ever get a commander like O'Hare, waste him."

At the road an eerie feeling swept through the rendezvous element. No one said a word. They crossed quickly and blended into the elephant grass. The crater which the eight-incher had blown in the road had been drained and partially filled. The hole that had been blasted in the roof was already less than half the size it had been when Alpha had crossed to climb to Delta. No one was around.

At dusk, forty minutes after 2d Plt and the CP reunited with Alpha, Alpha moved out. They moved in column, generally east, staying on the valley floor between the road and the river. 1st Plt humped between 3d at point and 2d at drag. Cherry quietly followed Egan. He was weary. Other than the few words with Jax and Egan at dawn Cherry had not spoken to anyone in twenty hours. When 2d Plt left for Delta, Cherry had manned 1st Plt's CP alone. Egan had gone out on patrol, Thomaston set up a separate two-platoon CP where the company CP had been, Mc-Carthy went with Hoover. Late in the afternoon Cherry had broken squelch on his radio and whispered, "Sit-rep negative," in response to a call from El Paso. At that point he had realized those were the first sounds he had made in nine hours though he had been carrying on conversations in his imagination with himself, with his brother and with Egan. When Egan returned he had immediately waved Cherry into silence, pointed a finger in the air and circled. We're surrounded, Cherry speculated. He began to indicate his puzzlement when the rush hit his bowels again and he sprinted for the perimeter. It was his seventh trip since daybreak.

While Cherry squatted, Whiteboy went running by, his pants half down, his hand on his penis. Doc McCarthy was chasing him with at least three cigarettes burning. Behind McCarthy, Hill, Harley and Andrews were all giggling, trying to keep silent, trying to keep up with the medic. Whiteboy circled back and Hill and Harley cornered him.

"Aw, Gawd A'mighty. Whut am Ah gonna do?" Whiteboy whispered. He was still holding his penis.

"Shoot it with Little Boy," Harley laughed staring at Whiteboy's groin.

"Here, Whiteboy," McCarthy whispered catching up. He held up the cigarettes. "I'll get rid of it for ya." And the medic descended upon Whiteboy who let him get to within a foot then jumped back.

"Ah got to figger," Whiteboy said. He half giggled at McCarthy approaching like that but he was obviously afraid and in pain. Cherry pulled up his own pants and approached. He looked at everyone's object of concern. Hanging out of Whiteboy's urethra was the tail end of a leech.

"Come on," McCarthy chuckled. "I won't burn off more than an inch. You got plenty ta spare and you aint usin that thing here, anyhow."

Egan appeared, as always, seemingly out of nowhere. He immediately perceived the situation and produced, to everyone's astonishment, a small bottle of bug repellent. Without a word he walked to Whiteboy, removed the bottle top and dropped half a dozen drops on the leech. It squirmed and began to withdraw. Egan squeezed several more drops on. "Hold still," he ordered.

Whiteboy was nearly in tears of joy. "More, Eg," he pleaded. Egan squeezed another drop. The leech seemed to back out further. "Whut are you, Eg? A junkie? More. Please." Egan squeezed, another drop fell then the bottle deflated empty. Egan tossed it over his shoulder and smiled, shrugged and left. The others stood silently around staring at Whiteboy and the leech, stifling their laughs. Cherry ran back to his perimeter spot, pulled his pants down and squatted. Then he snapped upward and looked back for leeches.

Alpha forded several wide though shallow streams on the move east. They crossed all without ropes. Each time they crossed they proceeded in similar manner to the crossing of the day before, sweeping, pausing, observing before entering the open space. Each time Brooks felt the maneuver went smoother and quicker. With each stream crossing the vegetation changed. Alpha left the brutal elephant grass for the congestion of bamboo and then for a scary sparse low brush and sand meadow.

The valley floor here was a series of rolling swells. "Hold them up," Brooks told El Paso when the CP reached the meadow edge. "Who's at point?"

"3d Sqd, 3d Plt," El Paso answered. He radioed the halt forward.

That dumb son of a bitch Caldwell, Brooks thought. He pulled out his topo map, made note of the location's coordinates, looked up and ordered a slow withdrawal from the sparsely vegetated area. 3d Plt withdrew and the point headed south then east again skirting the meadow. Half a kilometer beyond the meadow, the point called a halt.

"What do they have?" Brooks asked El Paso.

"Cornfield," El Paso said.

The CP moved forward. Before and beside the point there stood tall cornstalks in a well-cultivated field. Silently Brooks directed elements to flank the field. The column advanced from behind filling the voids created by the circling troops. Almost immediately 3d Plt found the field's parameters. It was barely six meters wide and thirty meters long. Brooks led a sweep up the center. El Paso picked an ear of corn. He peeled back the husk. The kernels looked ripe and juicy. He cautiously licked the

ear. No taste. He took a small bite. Sweet. He picked another ear
and gave it to the L-T. Taste it, he signaled. Brooks did. Doc
watched, picked, tasted, then picked several. Soon every man on
the center sweep was harvesting the corn. Pick it but keep
moving, Brooks signaled.

Alpha left the cornfield, reformed in column and climbed
up and over the next swell east. Brooks called a halt. Brown and
FO worked their way to the back of the unit and into a position
to observe the enemy food supply.

"Fire mission, over," FO whispered into the handset. The
radio responded. To FO the handset felt alive. His words spoken
into the small plastic and metal apparatus set the FDC and the
gun bunnies scurrying. He was the eyes of the artillery unit.

"Rover Four, Two. Stand by for shot," the radio rasped.

"Roger Two," FO radioed. To Brown he said, "Pass the
word, stand by for shot."

"Shot out," the radio sounded.

"Shot out," FO repeated. Then he counted to himself,
". . . one thousand five, one thousand six . . ." Twenty meters above the valley floor a white cloud popped into existence.
It was fifty meters right of the field. "Left fifty," FO called.
"Fire for effect." Three HE rounds impacted across the near end
of the field. Then three more. "Oh, oh. Boys, yo on the
money," FO cheered the arty unit via radio. The rounds passing
over Alpha and exploding at FO's command, even so near,
sounded friendly. Up and down the line boonierats felt warmed
by the violent eruptions. "Add fifty," FO called. The field was
progressively decimated. Half of Alpha's boonierats crunched
joyously into the sweet raw corn.

The rain became heavier as darkness closed about Alpha
and the fog again descended to ground level. The unit moved
cautiously through high discontinuous brush, moved generally
eastward, the land slowly rising, the vegetation slowly thickening.
When it was very dark the unit stopped, the column shortened
and widened, the boonierats sat, covered themselves with poncho and poncho liner, ate, and set up LPs and guard watches.
The CP meeting was concise and only Thomaston and Caldwell
and the CP group attended. Cahalan's report was also short.
Bravo and Recon had both made contact, both in bunker
complexes, both at the eastern edge of the valley. Bravo's
contact had taken forty minutes. They killed one NVA and

captured one who wore first lieutenant insignias. Recon's engagement lasted less than a minute. They also killed one NVA and captured one. Recon's prisoner was half-dead, blown to pieces. Both prisoners were evacuated by medical helicopters. Except for Delta, all the other SKYHAWK companies were tightening their grip around the Khe Ta Laou. The gaps between the units were receiving continuous artillery H & I fire and constant high level electronic and infrared surveillance. There was no evidence of major enemy movements into or out of the Khe Ta Laou and intelligence teams suspected they had overrated the valley's significance.

Cahalan's report was followed by a brief discussion. Then Brooks said, "Tomorrow, we cross the river and check out the south bank." The meeting ended. It was early, dark, quiet and cool. The night promised to drag by slowly. Half of Alpha slept, the other half fidgeted. Brooks too was uncomfortable. At 2300 hours he radioed 2d Plt and requested Pop Randalph to bring six volunteers to the CP. Ten minutes later Pop crawled into the CP circle followed by all of Mohnsen's squad except Roberts and Sklar.

"Yes Sir," Pop reported.

"3d's got an LP due east fifty meters," Brooks said to the assembled team. "I want you to go out to them, leave them there, move 150 meters farther east and set up an ambush site."

"Aye aye, Sir," Pop said. "I know just the spot."

Brooks whispered a few questions checking out the team. He had Ezra Jones, Mohnsen's RTO, contact the LP and inform them of the move. "Plenty of time, Pop," Brooks patted the old boonierat on the shoulder. "Take your time."

The team departed but still Brooks felt uneasy. He lay back and tried to sleep. El Paso was on radio watch. Cahalan was breathing easily. Minh and Doc were whispering a few feet away. Brooks crawled to them. Then Egan showed up. Then Jax. Then Cherry. The men formed a tight cluster. The discussion began almost as if it had not ceased the night before.

"Do you know who was the first American to die for freedom?" Doc asked.

"You mean here?" Cherry asked.

"I mean ever, Mista. I mean the very first."

"Who?"

"Crispus Attucks," Doc said proudly. "Killed in the Boston Massacre in 1770. That man won't even free yet he died so your great-grandpappy could own mine. That man was a black slave.''

"Right on," Jax laughed. "A black begun the first revolution an it was over blacks the second was fought. Now this black gowin begin the third. Let whitey eat my turd.''

"Oh, eat my asshole," Egan snapped.

"The revolution is at hand," Jax giggled. He was having a good time. "Come wid me, Bro, join our band. A new gov'ment we'll give the land.''

"Look around, Man," Egan said. "Is this what you want ta do back in the World? You want ta hump a 60 back there?''

"How are you going to overthrow the government?" Cherry asked seriously.

"We shall unite the people," Jax said. "People of the world unite! Fight imperialist dogs! Stand up, be courageous! Advance! Wave upon wave of my people will descend upon the filthy butchers. We gowin form a platoon.''

"If one shot is fired," Egan took Jax' bait, "your revolution'll create a monster.''

Jax just laughed.

"You mothafucker," Egan laughed back bitterly. "You mothafuckers talkin revolution. You just want to steal what other men created. Color only gives you an excuse.''

"They been doin it to us forever," Doc said. "There aint no Brothers doin it out here. We all pullin our weight.''

Jax reached out and grabbed Cherry's arm. "Bro, why doan you join us? Yo get back Jax gowin need a good RTO.''

"I got a long time to go," Cherry avoided answering.

"You're just tryin ta get over," Egan sighed.

"Like au yo white granddaddies did on mine," Jax said.

"Not mine, Man," Cherry said.

"All the whites did," Doc said.

"Fuck that," Cherry whispered firmly. "My ancestors were serfs in Italy while yours were slaves here. Hey, Man, my grandparents came to this country in 1896 and at that time most of the Italians lived in crowded city tenements and worked in mills. Back then only twenty percent of all Americans lived in cities. My people were trapped there just like yours. But they didn't go cryin to the governmeñt, 'bus my kids to the WASP countryside.' ''

"Course not, Bro," Jax laughed. "They won't no buses in 1896. Yo'd have ta walked.''

"Ha," Cherry huffed. "But my people didn't stay there either."

"Right on Little Bro," Jax said. "Yo learnin. That jest what I's sayin. We doan condone the pigs. Ef yo dowin whut they wantin yo ta do, yo helpin ta perpetuate their system. The revolution is at hand. Join us."

"People are dumb," Egan injected. "They're dumb and they're apathetic and they like to be used. They don't like to make decisions or to be responsible. Even for themselves. They want to be led. They want to be exploited."

"Do you really think so?" Brooks asked softly. He was enjoying the conversation, and now too, the night.

Egan looked through the blackness toward Brooks. He was aware of the L-T's debating skills and he proceeded cautiously. He had already committed himself. "Yes, I do. Look around. You have to beg people to be platoon sergeants, even. There's a dozen guys in 1st qualified to be platoon sergeant who are satisfied sitting back puttin in their time."

"Jax," Brooks' soft whisper floated in the black mist. "Why do you think the people allowed themselves to be exploited by a . . . an elite?"

"That whut I's sayin, L-T. We doan condone it no mo."

"But blacks did before?"

"They had to."

"Could it be as Danny said. They were too lazy or simply did not care?"

"Lazy and shiftless, L-T?" Doc whispered nastily.

"What do you think, Minh? Your country was exploited for a very long time. Could the people secretly have wished to be members of the elite and thus wanted it to remain?"

"Oh no, L-T," Minh's whisper was high and thin. "I do not think this is so. But it may be so. To have an elite you must have the masses, yes? Perhaps they are a unity. Perhaps one cannot be eliminated without eliminating both. And then who remains?"

"Huh?" Cherry uttered.

"Thank you, Minh," Brooks said. "Maybe we should think about that. Perhaps many blacks in the World no longer want to be used. Perhaps they now refuse to condone being automatically relegated to society's lowest levels. But they're not, no matter what they say, on the road to destroying the country. Perhaps they are securing the perpetuation of the system by fighting to be the elite. Perhaps they are out to build a better country."

"Like they built a better Watts?" Egan suggested sarcastically. "Or maybe a better Detroit? By rioting and burning the place down? By forming guerrilla platoons, secret armies, to overthrow the government?"

"Guerrilla groups doan just happen, Mista," Doc said. "Riots doan just happen. You know that. They produced. They produced in a kind a society where there's hopelessness." Doc paused. He flashed on hot summers in Harlem, heat wave days when the TV crews showed up to film eggs frying on car hoods and black children playing in the gushing water of fire hydrants. It always looked like so much fun. Like an amusement park. Inside the tenements, unfilmed, men lay sprawled, near naked, gasping for breath. Only the putrid air seemed more listless than the jobless old women who sat unable to move. Very old people died in their rooms unnoticed until evening when they were carried out. The evening brought little relief from the heat. Doc remembered the summer when Marlena, a tiny child, was nearly killed by roof rats in her makeshift bed. For a month the wounds on her legs seeped. Doc cleared his throat. The others were silent. "Riots doan just happen," he repeated sadly. "They come from despair, Mista. You know what I mean? They doan come from repression. They come from crushed expectations. It aint far from hopelessness to riots."

"Doc, I don't understand. I don't see things as hopeless," Cherry said easily, trying to sound sympathetic yet encouraging. "I see opportunity everywhere."

"You brought up that way, Mista. You see people makin it. Where I come from, I see people wastin way. Hopeless, Man. You can say what you want but nobody listens. Like you. You can't hear me. They pass laws, they say they spendin money. Nothin happen. Jax right, Bros. The government gonna fall. It's the government who decide who live, who die. The government decide who drafted, who shipped to Nam, who a boonierat, who get jobs, who starve."

"It's not that way for everyone," Cherry said.

"The revolution is comin," Doc said very sadly. "It comin an the government can't stop it. They can't stop it cause the guerrilla is the heart of the people. The heart of the people that the government discards."

"Maybe you dudes are right," Egan said. This time he had

really listened. What was being said went against much of what he believed but he could not deny it. "It's right to say the government's in control. They got the guns. All political legitimacy comes out of the barrel of a gun. All human rights, speech rights, property rights. If you really don't have them maybe you do have to revolt. I take back a lot of what I said. If the government tries to take your freedoms you got to revolt. That's power out of the barrel of a gun. Americans have traditionally had a low flash point. That's why we know such great freedoms. And you're right. We are losin it. We're losin it little by little to the Nixon machine and to the bureaucratic machine. But you know somethin? We're askin to lose it. We're sellin our freedoms one by one to that bastard. We're sellin it to be taken care of by a paternalistic government. And that's cause people are lazy and they don't care. Yeah. If you gotta revolt, that means you care."

"Right on, Bro," Jax whispered.

After a pause Brooks said, "It is important for us to understand how racial violence occurs if it is to be avoided in the future. Doc, you said something just now that really hit me. Race riots don't just happen. Wars do not just happen. Would you do me a favor and ponder that? I want to talk some more, but later."

The little group broke up and the men returned to their positions. Brooks went to his ruck and silently removed a stenographer's pad from the waterproof ammo can at its base. The time had come. He would write down his observations and thoughts about conflict. In the dark he wrote carefully, large and cryptic. On the cover he printed, AN INQUIRY INTO PERSONAL, RACIAL AND INTERNATIONAL CONFLICT. On the first page he wrote: Conflict does not just happen. Wars do not just happen. Divorce does not just happen.

Then he put the notebook away. To himself he said, I must DEROS now. I must write my dissertation. I'll radio GreenMan in the morning. Should I tell anyone else?

Why do I always come out sounding like a bigot? Egan asked himself. He and Cherry were back amongst 1st Plt. Egan mulled over the argument with Jackson and reviewed the other conversation at the CP. He did not, could not, believe he was a racist. He would not even describe himself as right wing. He believed he was very open minded, very much a man who weighs all sides of an argument.

Cherry's whisper disrupted his thoughts. "What?" he said.

"How do you think Jax and Doc and the L-T feel about you comin down on blacks?" Cherry repeated.

Holy Shit, Egan thought. Was I that bad? Egan spoke softly in that jungle-night voice developed in veteran boonierats, a firm voice with almost no sound. "Boonierats is a race," he said. "We can say things like that. Nobody takes it personal."

"Not even you callin Silvers a token Jew?"

"You don't understand yet," Egan said. "Takin it personal is for people back in the World. We got a separate culture out here. And in some respects it's better. Fuck Man, an AK round don't care what color your paint job is."

Cherry took a deep breath and exhaled slowly. "You got no feelings, Eg," he said. It was the very first time Cherry had ever used the nickname. He felt slightly apprehensive yet it brought him to Egan's plane.

"You don't understand, Man," Egan said. "You're goina have to experience it all for yourself first. I got feelings."

"Goddamnit," Cherry grunted. "I don't understand you. I think you just hide in that hardass role you're always playin."

"What?"

"Silvers gets blown away. Brunak gets wounded. You either don't care or you hide it awfully well."

"Man, you're bein an asshole."

"Silvers got blown away. I'll never see him again. He's dead, Man."

"What difference does that make to you? Or to me?" Egan was feeling quite heated. "He's dead. You want me to write his folks and say, 'Ah, I knew yer kid. He didn't die bad. There wasn't time for pain cause he caught it in the neck.' Maybe you'd have me go easy. Say, 'He got it fuckin a sleeze in the ville at the height of orgasm.' What the fuck do you want from me, Man?"

"Nothin," Cherry said. Their conversation wasn't going as he had expected.

"Look, Cherry," Egan calmed. "If I'm goina mourn for a dude, I gotta do it in my way, in my time. Man, boonierats are different kinds of people. You want to think about Silvers, think about why he got blown away. For me, I gotta think about what to do. I had to replace him, make Jax squad leader. That wasn't easy. Marko and Denhardt both could a been made squad leader.''

"You didn't do that cause Jax is black, did you?''

"Fuck no. Denhardt's got no brains at all and Marko couldn't lead his grandmother through a supermarket without antagonizing her. I mean it when I say boonierats is a race. Look, I love these guys out here. I know I can depend on em.''

Cherry did not answer.

"One night on 882 we had twenty-eight wounded,'' Egan said. "Everybody seemed to be bleedin. Black, white, yellow. None of the docs said, 'Go find a medic yer own color. I only treat my kind.' The docs treat everybody. Pointmen lead everybody. When some of those dudes died everybody felt bad. Jax felt for his white boonierat brothers just like I felt for my black ones. It don't always show. And I hate to see fucken blacks riot in the World. Fuck it. I don't think it's s'pose ta show.''

Cherry and Egan lay back. Cherry was on radio watch. Egan passed quickly from awake to semi-consciousness. His mind zigged and zagged in agitation. Stephanie appeared and calmed him. He watched her form, the image solidify. The sun came out. It was spring and warm and the air was sweet with the smell of fresh cut grass. How had he ever let her slip away? Perhaps he hadn't. Perhaps she would be there when he returned. The closer he came to his DEROS and ETS the more he thought of her.

Daniel Egan visited Stephanie often during the summer of her divorce and through the following autumn and winter. His memory exploded with small anecdotes of those days. His entire body burned with desire for her. The soft sleepy neck of Stephanie rose from a woeful droop and swung back tossing her hair in a gleeful, careless arc. Her eyes glistened. Her moist lips trembled with laughter. Come, her image beckoned to him. Come with me. On the jungle floor Egan's body quivered in resistance. Come, she beckoned. His body shook. He felt at peace. Smoothly, silently, pleasantly, his spirit slipped from his body and joined Stephanie in the image in his mind. For a moment Daniel glanced back at the soldierly figure, the cold filthy miserable body crumpled on a hundred-pound pack, then the spirit turned its back and smiled at Stephanie. They strolled in a glistening world by a small stream. Before them a stone bridge arched.

They walked to it and crossed and walked on to a pond. The day was warm. Fat-leafed maples reflected in the water. Daniel broke pieces of bread from a loaf he was carrying and tossed the pieces to the ducks swimming nearby. The colorful birds paddled closer, a few even came out of the water to feed near their feet. The ducks fought one another aggressively yet they remained timid and watchful as Daniel tossed the food to them. Stephanie knelt down by the water's edge and the ducks came to her and took the bread from her hand. She sat back and the ducks stretched their necks across her lap. She stroked them tenderly and they ate. Daniel inched nearer to pet one. They all scattered. We're all like that, he had thought. Anyone can come to her without fear, yet she herself is so timid. She's so strong yet so timid.

"Do you remember the book you left me in New York?" she asked.

"Yes," he said lying back.

"When you came back I told you I hadn't read it."

"I remember."

"You said, 'I knew you wouldn't.' "

"I didn't say that, did I?"

"Um-hum, you did. If you bring me *The Sun Also Rises*, I promise I'll read it. I started *Hawaii* two weeks ago."

"How do you like it?" he asked.

"I'm really enjoying it," Stephanie laughed, "but I must admit big books kind of scare me."

The image flowed. The physical being on the jungle valley floor pushed it, trying to force it, to speed it up as if time were running out and the body wished to relive as many episodes as possible. "I received your book today," Stephanie's voice came to Daniel over the phone. He was back at school. He had sent her his battered copy of *The Sun Also Rises*. "It's a beautiful book," she said. "I haven't started it yet but I like to touch it and to look at it. It's beautiful.

"I'm sending you my Sandy Bull album, *Fantasia*. I think it's more me than any others I have or anything else I have, except my eyes. Which I can't give you though I'd like to." Stephanie laughed gleefully for a time and Daniel laughed though no sound came from him. "I'm reading *The Fountainhead* by Ayn Rand," she said. "You've probably read it but if not I'll send it to you. I really like it and Howard Roark reminds me of you. How is the Alaska house coming? Please don't forget how much I want to see your drawings.''

On some plane in between, Daniel Egan was aware he never showed Stephanie the Alaska house drawings. Now, in another image, she let him have it. They were in a small upstate bar, Stephanie was sad and serious and so delightful. ''I told myself I wasn't going to do this but I am. You know, Daniel, in some ways you're very selfish. I know you know it. Talk to me, Daniel. I know it's there but you won't give it to me. I love you and hate you for doing it.

''Daniel,'' she pleaded, ''I want, and I am trying, to come to your level. Oh, that sitting back level, that observing confident level. I want it. I'm getting it. But Christ, Daniel, will you talk to me? Are you doing it purposely? I bet you are. I can meet you there. TALK TO ME! You bastard. You beautiful bastard.''

''Stephanie,'' Daniel answered her now an answer he had never given. ''I care. I care for you more than for anything else I've ever known. I just don't know how to say it.''

His thoughts sped on. Stephanie, I'm striving to gain your level, the level of natural humanity uncluttered with mass produced technology. I care for you . . . I care . . . I love . . . I love you.

''I've been volunteering at the daycare center.'' Stephanie smiled. They were lying together. The day had been exquisite and the night was warm. Stephanie was happy and sorrowful and troubled. ''I've been working in a room with eleven children, seven of which are Negro. The first day I walked in all I had to do was smile and there were six children hanging around my neck and on my legs. They seemed so starved for affection. This one little boy named Jeremiah is one of my favorites. Daniel, he is just darling. I want to adopt him. His mom is on relief and she's an alcoholic. Jeremiah comes to the center with no underwear, pants five sizes to big with the zipper broken and the pants pinned to his shirt so they won't fall down. I went to a rummage sale and bought him underwear and shirts and sent them home with him. The next day his mom sent a note with him saying she didn't mind Jeremiah coming to the center but she did not approve of us trying to buy his love with clothes. Wow, Daniel, I was really hurt. I guess I've got a lot to learn.

''Oh, Daniel, there are some sad moments but mostly we really have fun. I could go on and on about the funny things the children do. I wish you could see them. You'd love them too.''

Daniel sat and listened and loved her for being so enthusiastic and so sensitive and for loving the children. But he said nothing except to ask her if she'd given up art completely. She responded in a way he never understood. "Daniel, no one will ever really know, will they? No one will ever know what's inside you. They can get an idea but they'll never really know. That makes me sad."

"I've always believed," Daniel's image sounded very far off, "that a person is what he does. A person is what he accomplishes, what he creates. An artist, for example, is a person who creates art. It's not one who fosters the image to others that he creates art when in fact he creates nothing. That's a pseudo-artist. A person who takes care of children is a child care specialist. That's who they are. Do you see? If you are what you do then identity crises are caused by not knowing what to do or by not doing. An identity must be constructed by doing, creating, building . . ."

"How about by reading and thinking and dreaming?"

He heard her say that now. He saw the hurt on her face now. *Why wouldn't I allow myself to hear her?* he asked now. I was a bastard.

Again, tumbling through weightless voids and into another scene. His body no longer wanted to push the fantasy. He no longer wished to re-experience all their times yet he was out of control. The picture flowed at its own speed, its own discretion, on its own energy. It was the same scene he had remembered the day of the CA but this time it was clearer and their positions were reversed. They were in a room in the old Martinson Hotel which looked out across the railroad tracks to a dully lit cobblestone street. It was raining. Daniel was standing by the only window in the room. The empty eyes of the stores across the tracks, across the street, reflected mud-ash earth and debris. On the corner up the street a tavern sign flashed *Iron-City Beer—On Tap*.

The window sill and frame of the hotel room were partially lighted from the light of the street. The room was dark with the exception of a single candle burning in the corner. Stephanie lay in the bed looking at Daniel's back. The room was old and dingy. Stephanie rose, circled the bed and put her arms around Daniel's shoulders. She lay her cheek against his back. Daniel turned and she let go. She was still naked. She stretched her hands gracefully toward him, he took them softly and held them then brought her to him.

"I'm sorry, Steph," he said. "I didn't understand." It was his spirit speaking. It was not his image. He had hurt her while they made love. During his campus exploits he had developed a harsh dominant athletic style which did not suit Stephanie at all. Harshness hurt her. The abortion had left scar tissue at her cervix which caused her pain on deep thrusts. "I'm sorry," Egan's spirit said. "I'm sorry for all of this. Someday, I'll make it up to you."

After that time he did not see Stephanie for many months. Now watching the lone mirage he thought how insensitive he was to all the things Stephanie said. That is the tragedy of his life. He was not sensitive to Stephanie when it had been possible. He had not even been sensitive to his own feelings. The hallucination rolled and shook violently. He was above his own body, his cold wet sleeping body wrapped in poncho and poncho liner. Squatting beside him was the sapper. The enemy smiled—his teeth glistened. I've got you this time, the soldier seemed to say to the hovering spirit. Slowly the machete lifted. In slow motion the dark foe whipped the silver blade in a circle then powerfully brought the blade down toward Egan's face. "I've got to get back," the spirit cried. "I've got to get back into my body. I've got to help him." The spirit was frantic, the body on the ruck cowed, the enemy blade descended in slow motion. The razor sharp edge pierced the bridge of Egan's nose. Slowly the blade, driven by the might of the enemy's powerful hand, cleaved into Egan's eyes dividing the orbs. The spirit slipped back into Egan physically expanding his cringing viscera. A series of small explosions shook his ears. Then an M-60 opened up far to the north.

"What's that," Cherry whispered.

Egan grabbed his face. He was silently crying.

In the dark, in the rain, two NVA sapper teams noiselessly crawled up the cliffs of the north escarpment to the rock outcropping which held Delta's NDP. Below, half of Alpha was asleep, half was on vigilant watch. Egan was in the midst of dream. The sappers slid silently to the perimeter edge then froze and observed. For two days the NVA had been watching the Americans from above. Delta barely altered their alignment from the moment they set up and they quickly established a routine movement pattern. The sapper unit studied Delta's fighting positions, the positioning of the poncho hootches and the behavior habits of Delta's troops. They carefully conceived and detailed their attack. At dusk they began to execute the plan.

The two teams climbed straight up the cliff, one settled among the rocks at the cliff edge, the other veered and followed the path which Alpha's rendezvous element had used during the afternoon. For three hours the sapper teams motionlessly watched as Delta troops fidgeted and fussed and divulged their positions. Then the team at the cliff edge penetrated the perimeter. The sapper team leader found two Delta soldiers asleep with their M-60 machine gun on bi-pod between them. Noiselessly the sapper thrust a thin-bladed bayonet into the first soldier's throat. He drove the blade upward toward the back of the head, twisted and withdrew. The body twitched then relaxed. Next to him his buddy slept on. The sapper cautiously circled the dead man. The second guard awoke, startled. He tried to sit up to scream. The sapper smashed stiff fingers into his Adam's apple knocking the man back, stifling his scream. Then, quickly, he bayoneted the man's throat. The team infiltrated the NDP, worked to predetermined points among the rocks and brush and became rigid. At Delta's CP two men were smoking.

The second sapper team remained outside the perimeter. Slowly, soundlessly, they crawled about Delta's claymore mines. As they found each one, they turned it around and aimed it in upon the defenders. Then they all lay quietly. After a pause of fifteen minutes the outside sapper team again began to move. They made a little noise. Delta did not react. The sappers moved again making more noise.

"Sir," a Delta perimeter guard came to the CP. "I think we got movement inside the claymores."

"You see anything?" O'Hare asked. He was up. He put out his cigarette.

"Whatcha got, Bobby?" an RTO asked.

"I aint sure. Bat Man thought he heard somethin."

"Throw a frag at it," the RTO said.

"No, wait a minute," O'Hare said. "Call the firebase," he directed the RTO. "Tell em we want some illum."

The guard returned to his position and several minutes later a mortar-launched illumination flare popped over Delta casting the rocks and vegetation in a queer flat light. The sappers remained low and motionless. More flares popped and floated gently downwind on their parachutes. The sapper team within Delta's perimeter eyed their foes. The illum glimmered on the wet poncho-hootches. More flares popped. The mortar team kept the area lighted for twenty minutes until O'Hare cancelled the mission. Delta went back to sleep.

Two hours passed. The sappers had not moved a hair. Delta twisted beneath their poncho tents. "Let's keep it down," O'Hare called out to a perimeter position at one point.

"Augh, Sir, it's Willie," a troop called back. "The fucker keeps snorin.'"

A third voice called out, "Bullshit. Now shut up."

From another position a man giggled. Then the chatter subsided and Delta slept again. The sappers moved. The outside team infiltrated between two sleeping guard positions. The inside team spread out. On a single click-signal all the sappers unloaded and fused their sachel charges. Then deftly they placed the charges by and where possible between the heads of the sleeping Americans. Immediately they began their withdrawal. The first team in crawled back to their cliff entrance and grabbed the M-60 and the ammunition. The second team crawled out. The first sachel charge exploded. Then another and another. All the GIs were up. People were running, screaming. More sachel charges exploded. O'Hare's RTO found one between him and the captain and flung it out of their hootch. It exploded wounding a perimeter guard who had run for the CP as the blasts began. Someone yelled, "SAPPERS!" An M-60 opened up firing into the NDP. Other soldiers fired at their own men. Several Delta troops began running, shouting, trying to organize the unit. The M-60 fired upon the running troops. There was mass confusion. Delta did not know who was who. Then came a quick succession of small explosions.

Explosions vary in length of time depending upon the amount and type of explosive. A quick explosion makes a sharp sound. Slower, longer burning materials cause a deeper sound, more of a roar. The sachel charges were slow and of relatively little power. The first few blew heads apart but most at best only blew out eardrums or eyes. At Alpha, a kilometer away, the old-timers recognized the sound. Four months earlier, on Hill 714, the NVA had killed five Alpha boonierats using similar tactics. Now the NVA were throwing sachel charges into Delta's perimeter to increase the chaos, get the GIs up and running so they could be shot by their own men.

The unmistakable crackblast of a claymore resounded from Delta. Everyone in Alpha was up then down. Alpha lay perfectly still, prone, in the mud. On 100 percent alert. At Delta a perimeter guard had squeezed his claymore claquer firing device. The claymore removed his face.

"What's that?" Cherry whispered to Egan.

"Sappers. Nobody up there firin. See if you can monitor."

"I don't know their freq."

A call came from El Paso. "Pass the word. Sit tight."

Egan slithered off to check his platoon. "Lie quiet," he repeated to each position. "Ambush team and LPs comin in. Watch for em. Don't fire em up." At Jax and Marko's location Egan found the two talking. "Stop the chattering. Keep it down."

Jax rolled over. "Oh Man. Cut it out. If yo was a dink, would yo come tricky-trottin inta our AO? Theys fuckin wid Delta, Man. They aint even gowin fuck with us after they woke everybody up."

El Paso radioed the platoon RTOs. "L-T says we're movin when the Dust-Offs come. Have em packed up."

When the medical evacuation helicopters reached the Khe Ta Laou they repeated the night medevac procedure they had used when Bravo had been hit five days earlier. A flare ship circled high above dropping flares and illuminating the entire sky. Four Cobras and two LOHs escorted the four Dust-Off Hueys. Above the flock of birds was the charlie-charlie of the GreenMan. The noise was tremendous after the silence of the night.

On the valley floor Egan led off. Jax walked his slack. The LPs and the ambush team, all accounted for, formed a rear drag. The light above the medevac site glowed in the fog over the valley but on the ground it was dark. Egan bulled his way through the vegetation. He did not cut a path. He moved slowly. Sometimes he crawled, sometimes he sidestepped, but he never stopped. He used a lensmatic compass for direction and he led Alpha east. He walked as if he knew the terrain, as if he had been expecting to lead the column on this exact move, as if he had practiced it. The medical evacuation from Delta took over an hour. The birds did not extract all the dead or the routine wounded. They would be evacuated during daylight. The birds removed only the eleven seriously wounded.

Alpha had moved almost 200 meters east by the time the

last medevac and the escort fleet left the valley. Egan stopped. He sat down and waited as Brooks had instructed. Behind him the entire company sat. And sat quietly for the rest of the night. The next day would begin their fight.

SIGNIFICANT ACTIVITIES

THE FOLLOWING RESULTS FOR OPERATIONS IN THE O'REILLY/ BARNETT/JEROME AREA WERE REPORTED FOR THE 24-HOUR PERIOD ENDING 2359 18 AUGUST 70:

RAIN CONTINUED ON THIS DATE THROUGHOUT THE OPERATIONAL AREA CAUSING THE CANCELLATION OF 18 TAC AIR SORTIES AND THE POSTPONEMENT OF ONE COMPANY-SIZE ASSAULT.

ONE KILOMETER WEST OF FIREBASE BARNETT, AN ELEMENT OF CO B, 7/402 ENGAGED AN UNKNOWN SIZE ENEMY FORCE IN A BUNKER COMPLEX KILLING ONE NVA AND CAPTURING AN NVA 1ST LIEUTENANT. THE POW WAS EVACUATED FOR INTERROGATION. THE UNIT ALSO CAPTURED ONE AK-47 AND TWO RPG LAUNCHERS.

LATER IN THE MORNING, RECON, CO E, 7/402 WAS AMBUSHED BY AN UNKNOWN SIZE ENEMY FORCE IN THE VICINITY OF HILL 848 AT YD 193303. THE UNIT RETURNED ORGANIC WEAPONS FIRE KILLING ONE NVA AND CAPTURING ONE POW. THE POW WAS EVACUATED FOR MEDICAL TREATMENT.

AT 1805 HOURS CO A, 7/402 DISCOVERED A CULTIVATED CORNFIELD VICINITY YD 158320. THE FIELD WAS DESTROYED BY ARTILLERY FROM FIREBASE BARNETT.

ARVN UNITS MADE NO SIGNIFICANT CONTACTS ON THIS DATE.

Grid lines are labeled using the Universal Transverse Mercator
Grid, Everest Spheriod. This valley is in zone 48Q, Square YD.
To locate, read West-East then South-North. For example, • = YD 215353

17   18   19   20   21   22

478

609

Bravo

678
BARNETT

ornfield
o Alpha
alse
NDP

836   Recon

536

Rach My Chanh

△
JEROME
(ARVN)

to O'REILLY
(YD 30.258)

CHAPTER

26

19 AUGUST 1970

In the gray yet dark Egan rose. He rose from the exact place he had sat hours earlier. He had not moved all night. Nor had he slept. Jax fell in behind Egan. They did not speak. Next back, Cherry was on the radio. He keyed the handset and whispered almost inaudibly, "Four, Two. Moving. Out." He did not wait for a response.

Behind the point Alpha rose, moving now in three silent, unequal, parallel columns. 1st Plt and the Co CP led down the center. The formation looked like a wide based bi-pod. 2d Plt moved south 50 meters toward the river then turned and followed 1st, lagging back 150 to 200 meters on the right flank. 3d Plt moved left 50 meters toward the road and followed 1st by 100 meters. The formation gave Alpha partial sweep advantages plus surprise drags to catch enemy followers and flanking and maneuver elements should they run head-on into the enemy. Egan led the head column eastward over successive undulating rolls through brush then bamboo and brush again. The valley floor rose toward the headwaters. Rain fell. The mist thinned.

In column formation action usually happens at point, sometimes at drag, seldom in the middle. To middle-soldiers days passed as endless meaningless humps, walking, carrying a ruck and a weapon, following the man in front. Many middle-soldiers neither knew nor cared to know where they were going. Some did not care to know why. Some men gravitated to the middle. That was how they wanted it. To Cherry, it was maddening. He had spent most of six days at middle. Now as third man back he was eager almost zealous. His passions were boiling. He did not know why. Twice Jax motioned him to back away, to keep his interval. He calmed himself by singing marching songs within his mind. *I don't know but I been told,* Cherry as march leader sang out. *I don't know but I been told,* his fictitious platoon answered back all in cadence. *That her pussy's made o gold,* he sang. *That her pussy's made o gold,* they answered. Cherry yelled, *Sound Off!* The platoon, *One Two.* Cherry, *Sound Off!* The platoon, *Three Four.* Cherry, *Cadence count.* They, *One two three four, Onetwo—threefour.* He began another verse. *Had a girl from North Korea . . .*

Egan led Alpha east then south then east again. The valley floor swelled and fell yet each rise was higher than each fall. By dawn Alpha had crossed a kilometer of jungle and risen 100 meters. It was still raining. The mist was below them. Egan climbed slowly up the first real hill in the valley floor. At the crest he stopped and squatted. He motioned Jax down and Cherry forward. From the crest they could see the river to the right and rolling hills before them. On the side of a mound, perhaps 170 meters away, there was a squad of NVA soldiers. They were walking in column, spaced, swinging their arms freely, seemingly oblivious to everything. Egan flattened. Cherry squatted slightly below him. Egan counted: eleven soldiers, eight with rifles, three unarmed. Every enemy soldier wore a pack. Egan immediately, instinctively, estimated their rucks to weigh forty pounds. They were traveling heavy, east, uphill. Maybe toward Bravo, Egan thought. He grabbed Cherry's radio. He called Brooks, reported quickly. The flank columns stopped. Egan called the battalion TOC directly. Simultaneously he produced a small set of binoculars from his ruck and a topo map from a fatigue leg pocket. Egan handed Cherry the binoculars. "Watch em," he whispered. Cherry's excitement doubled.

"Rover Two, Red Rover One," the radio responded. It was Major Hellman, the battalion executive officer. The GreenMan must be sleeping after last night, Egan thought. Quickly Egan explained the target. "Can you adjust fire from your location? Over," Hellman asked.

"That's affirmative," Egan answered. The NVA squad was approaching hilltop. Cherry wanted Egan to hurry. "Armageddon Two, Rover Two," Egan now radioed the artillery unit on Barnett.

"Roger, Rover Two. This is Armageddon Two. Over."

Egan read off the coordinates. He spoke very quickly yet paced and distinctive and to Cherry it seemed slow. "Dinks in the open," Egan said. He knew the cannon-cockers loved that call. "Lotsa dinks," Egan encouraged them.

Cherry followed the enemy's progress through the binoculars. At the distance they appeared small and unreal. A second squad appeared and began climbing after the first. If they're supposed to be so good, Cherry thought, how come they're in the open?

"Whole battery. Hotel Echo. Airbursts at five zero," Egan whispered. This was no time for test rounds.

"Shot out," Cherry heard the radio rasp.

"Shot out," Egan repeated gleefully.

Then came a horrible rushing sound. Cherry's heart was pumping massive surges of blood. Six rounds screamed down. Cherry's eyes were pasted to the binoculars. He could see the horror on the faces of the enemy. The rounds exploded. Four NVA soldiers were blown down. The NVA dropped, scattered. A second salvo screamed down. The rounds seemed to explode on the ground but in reality they were bursting a hundred-sixty feet above the earth and exploding a hot metal shower downward.

"Drop fifty." Egan smiled.

Cherry could see soldiers wriggling. Others limped. One seemed blown to bits. Another ran without arms. One body dragged itself without legs. At the distance, in the dawn light, it seemed colorless and unreal. "Man, they're still there," Cherry began. "We got seven. Seven hit bad. Least two dead. Keep em firing. There's some to the left. They ran left into that clump of trees. Some below."

Egan called in the adjustments. He was no longer watching the action. He watched Cherry. Egan smiled, chuckled at Cherry's enthusiasm. His Cherry was going nuts. Egan loved it. "Here," he said to Cherry. "You call in the adjustments." Cherry took the hook. "Work em back en forth."

Now Cherry transmitted. "Left fifty, add one hundred."

The rounds screamed in and exploded uncomfortably close to Alpha. "Jesus Christ, watch it," Egan laughed. "You're s'pose ta get them, not us."

Cherry laughed, muted and hysterical. Jax laughed at them both from below. Brooks had reached the point now. He laughed with them too. They all laughed viewing the enemy carnage on the hill before them. "Let's go mop up," Brooks said pleased.

Alpha approached the site of the NVA dead cautiously.

They were still in three columns, now spread farther apart, the two flanks forward, 1st Plt lagging in the center. They closed in upon the site. The flanks halted, 1st Plt swept up the middle. There were no bodies. No weapons. No equipment. There were a half-dozen blood trails and Polanski in 2d Sqd found a hand. Alpha pursued the blood trails south and west to the river's edge. The trails vanished.

Cherry was pissed. "Why do you expect them to leave the bodies of their comrades behind on the battlefield?" Minh asked Cherry after Alpha had retreated to a thickly vegetated rise. They had set up a quick perimeter and were now eating breakfast and resting. At 1st Plt CP, Jax, Moneski, Doc Johnson and Lt. Thomaston were listening to Minh and Cherry. "In American units," Minh said seriously, "you pride yourselves on never leaving an American soldier's body behind. We Vietnamese are not different. The enemy is not different. It is not mysterious that they should take their dead and wounded. All armies do exactly the same."

"I don't know," Cherry said. "We saw about twenty dinks and I saw at least ten of em get greased. They musta had ah . . . there musta been like thirty or forty of em to sky like that."

"Hellman don't believe we got em," Monk said. "He was chewin out the L-T royal, Man. He didn't ee-ven need a radio. We coulda heard him right from the firebase."

"Why he on the L-T's ass?" Jax questioned.

"Man, you know," Doc said.

Thomaston injected, "It don't count unless you can verify the bodies."

"What?" Cherry squealed.

"That's right, Bro," Doc said. "Hey, you okay?" Doc stood up. Cherry indicated he was okay. Doc motioned him away from the others. "You doan look right, Mista," Doc said.

"I'm okay, Doc," Cherry said. "Really." Doc looked at him unbelieving. "I, ah, got some cuts en some jock rot. That's all." Doc still looked at him. "And, ah, the ah . . . the shits."

"McCarthy give you anything?"

"Naw, Doc. It's okay. It's goin away."

"Gonna get worse," Doc said. "Mista, I ken smell ya. How long you had it?" Doc questioned Cherry on every detail to Cherry's embarrassment. "Listen, Mista," Doc said finally, "that shit is dysentery. That caused by a flagellated protozoan. Dig? Under adverse conditions they can form a cyst. Not form it themselves but cause it. Right now you jus built up a concentration which is causin irritation in your intestines. That triggers the peristaltic action which gives you the shits. You know what I mean?''

"Wow!" Cherry said. Again the black medic with his Harlem street dialect had completely amazed him. He thought for a moment then asked, "What should I do?"

Doc pulled a vial from his pocket. "F-S-N 6505-074-4702," he read off the label. "Lomotil. Two pills, four times a day. Slows intestinal motility. Doan go O-Din on em." He handed the bottle to Cherry. Then Doc shook his head. He gave Cherry that unbelieving look again. "Man," Doc whispered, "you still a cherry. I wasn't gonna say this but you gotta learn faster'n you is doin, Bro. You aint gonna be able to depend on Egan ta tell me somethin wrong with you. He DEROSin in two weeks."

"Egan?!"

Doc looked at Cherry again, shook his head and walked away.

"I'm a pretty fair swimmer," Cherry said to Lt. Brooks.

Alpha was at the river. They had backed off the rise where they had eaten breakfast, again using the unequal three-pronged formation, and had moved west, downstream 200 meters. Egan had walked point, Jax slack. They had crossed five trails running from the river toward the north escarpment. Three of the trails were narrow and old. Foliage had closed over them and small yellow grass shoots choked their middles. Two were red balls. Both showed signs of recent heavy use. Alpha had moved quietly, slowly, until the sounds of a helicopter fleet broke upon the valley. At that point Brooks had directed them to move to the river. The maneuver was similar to the first river crossing except using three prongs eliminated the need to establish flank security. Alpha had sat just back from the river's edge, observing. The helicopters were CAing Recon from Hill 848 to Delta's position on the north escarpment. Even in the rain the helicopters flew. They would be in the air nearly all day.

Brooks looked at Cherry. "How fair?" he asked.

"I use ta be on the swim team," Cherry said.

"Do you know what you're volunteering for?" Brooks asked.

"Yes Sir."

Brooks studied his face. Cahalan crawled up to them. "L-T."

"Hey?" Brooks whispered. He was still watching Cherry.

"I just got word on Brunak." Cherry and Brooks turned and looked at Cahalan. "They're going to medevac him to Japan," Cahalan reported. "They say he's going to make it, they think."

"Good," Brooks nodded. "Send FO up here."

Brunak, Cherry thought. Jesus H., I'd forgotten all about him and . . . and Silvers. Cherry looked through the grass and brush. Fifteen feet away the Khe Ta Laou was shimmering dark. Silvers, Cherry thought. I gotta write his folks.

Lt. Hoyden approached noiselessly and nodded to Brooks. "FO," Brooks asked, "can we get some arty about 300 meters downriver and maybe some on the knoll and some up behind us?"

"Can do," FO said. He pulled out his map and asked, "Where do you want it?"

"Someplace to distract the little people," Brooks said. "Something to make them keep their heads down."

"When?"

"Now."

FO grabbed Brown's handset and radioed Armageddon Two. He talked to the FDC officer giving coordinates and explanations. "In one five," FO whispered to Brooks. "Behind us and across only. Too much bird traffic downstream."

Brooks nodded. He turned to Cherry. "Be ready. Go when the first round falls."

Cherry moved a few feet to the left. Cahalan and Hoyden disappeared into the vegetation away from the river. Lt. Caldwell appeared next to Brooks. Without trying Cherry overheard their conversation.

"Larry," Brooks asked. He sounded pissed. "Whatever possessed you to go straight through that meadow?"

"Lieutenant Brooks," Caldwell said sarcastically, defensively, "my mission was to take my force east as best and as quickly as I could."

"Your primary mission, Lieutenant Caldwell, is to insure the safety of your people. Moving east was secondary. You needlessly exposed yourself and your platoon in that meadow."

"I did what I thought best, Sir," Caldwell said tauntingly.

"Well, fuck it. You'd better start thinking differently, because, that was not the best."

Cherry moved down to just above the river's edge. 1st Plt was behind him preparing themselves for the crossing. Cherry stripped naked. His crotch was still sore and inflamed. The infections on his arms were about the same. His asshole burned. The skin of his feet was mushy and convoluted. For all the cleaning he had tried to do in the last two days, he still stank. Being naked felt wonderful, even though it was cold. Cherry took an end of the heavy crossing rope from Egan. He wrapped it about his waist and Egan tied it. "Ask em ta call the weatherman," Cherry whispered to Egan. "Ask em to turn on some sun."

"Shee-it," Egan laughed. "I don't think we know his freq."

"Maybe we can call God," Cherry suggested. "This weather sucks."

Jax was there helping Egan coil the line. "God's freq on the high band," Jax laughed. He went over to Cherry's gear and fiddled with the frequency settings on the PRC-25. "I think it 72/95," Jax chuckled, "but I doan know his call sign." Cherry and Egan chuckled too. "Augh fug," Jax continued. He returned the dials to the proper settings, "Yo caint git Him on this set. You need a monster set."

"Man," Cherry whispered laughing, "maybe we can build a fire. I'm freezin my balls off."

"Don't mean nothin," Egan whispered. "They aint doin you no good out here."

Two rounds freighttrained across the sky then exploded to Alpha's south. A third exploded upriver. Cherry crawled to the water and slipped silently in. More artillery rounds exploded. Cherry breast-stroked at an angle into the current. He swam smoothly, quickly, silently, a very strong swimmer. In twenty seconds he was on the opposite bank. He crawled from the river, scampered up the bank, backed into some brush, grasped the rope and motioned for someone to come across. Egan slipped into the water in lights with both his and Cherry's rifles. Even the minimal equipment sunk him. Cherry strained on the rope trying to keep Egan up but Egan and the line went under. Cherry strained harder. Egan's head broke the surface at mid-stream then down again. A minute later he emerged gasping at the far side. He stormed up the bank into cover, drained the barrel of both M-16s and searched the jungle. Jax was on his way over. Then Thomaston. Then Marko. Egan directed the south bank.

Thomaston and Marko secured the rope. Jax began the defensive ring. Egan stripped. He and Cherry slipped back into the water and became guides and life guards as the others crossed. Alpha's move went quickly and no equipment was lost. On each crossing Cherry dove under and washed a bit of his body, mostly his arms. This is blessed water, he thought. On the bank Brooks caught himself staring at the two naked soldiers. He became upset with himself.

"Fuckin gooks is aw'right," Pop Randalph chuckled. "Look at them thangs, Sir." Pop, Garbageman and Lt. De Barti had come to the CP with half a dozen traps.

"I'll be dipped in shit," Garbageman giggled. "There got to be at least a dozen of em so far."

Where Alpha had emerged from the river, the bank was littered with bamboo scraps as if someone had had a small mill by the water. There were numerous footpaths leading up and down the river's edge. 1st Plt had moved due south, 2d had gone west downstream, 3d east upriver. Fifty meters downstream 2d found the fishing camp. Then 3d Plt found the marijuana fields. Minutes later 1st found the ruins of an old village. It was like nothing any of them had ever seen before in the mountains.

De Barti held out two of the fish-traps to Brooks. "There's fresh tracks all over the place down there," the platoon leader said to the company commander. "It looks like they got maybe a platoon of *dan cong* (civilian coolies) doing nothing but catching fish for their troops. We've got ten traps so far and we've only swept a small stretch of bank."

Brooks lifted one of the traps and inspected it. The trap was a cylindrical bamboo cage closed at one end and having a bamboo cone opening at the other. The traps were simple yet the workmanship was elegant. Brooks sighed. "How's your security?" he asked.

Before De Barti could respond El Paso interrupted them with Caldwell's report of the marijuana field. Then fields. Two, then a third and finally a fourth. Then Paul Calhoun called from 2d Plt to report that they could not collect any more traps because they couldn't carry them all. "We're in their fishin grounds," Calhoun reported. "They got enough traps here ta feed a regiment. We got a few small animal snares too." A queer feeling ran up Garbageman's neck to the base of his skull as the report came in. He no longer felt like giggling.

"Destroy what you have," Brooks directed De Barti. "Stop the search and get out of there. Mark it for arty. We're moving south-twenty-west." Brooks turned to his RTOs. "Cahalan, call in the report. We're going over to 3d."

A quarter of Caldwell's men were busy harvesting the crop they had found. Everyone else was on security. The four fields were in a square. Each patch was approximately 15 × 25 meters. The marijuana plants ranged from three to seven feet high. Before Brooks could inspect the fields, Thomaston radioed saying that 1st Plt had discovered the ruins of an ancient village. "It can't be too ancient if you're finding old thatch," Brooks radioed.

"It's all rotting. Rotten," Thomaston transmitted. "It musta been a Montegnard ville but it's collapsed and there's new growth over it all. Over."

"Any indications of it on your funny papers? Over."

"Negative that. There's an abandoned ville indicated four kilos to the whiskey. Over."

"How many hootches? Over."

"Six for sure. Maybe eight. They're just lumps on the floor. There's a new red ball running right through the ville. Five, six feet wide with overhead cover. *Beaucoup* signs recent activity. Carts . . . doesn't seem to go anyplace."

Major Hellman cut in on Alpha's internal. "Quiet Rover Four, this is Red Rover One. Do you read? Over."

"Red Rover One, Four Niner," Brooks responded. "I've got you lumpy chicken. Over."

Hellman said he had been monitoring Alpha and that he wanted the fields of marijuana cut and burned, the fishing traps collected for evacuation and the red ball monitored for enemy traffic. "UUUh," Brooks grunted. He thought, that guy, some-day he is going to get everybody killed. Brooks did not answer Hellman's order. Hellman repeated his order and Brooks snarled into the handset, "Just how in the fuck are we going to burn a fucken half-acre of grass out here, Red Rover? It's been raining down here for a thousand years."

"Rover Four Niner, do you know who this is?"

"I am not going to compromise my position for a few fucking fishing traps and a field of dew. You got the coordinates. You want to destroy it, fine. Go ahead. Over. Out." Brooks seethed. He rammed the handset back into El Paso's hand and told him to get the unit moving.

* * *

Alpha continued their three pronged formation moving south away from the river 100 meters then arching southwest and finally west. There were signs of enemy activity everywhere. The North Vietnamese seemed to have an almost endless series of well engineered dirt roads and trails snaking south from the valley center toward the mountains. All routes had overhead cover. Egan was more apprehensive than he had ever been. Every step put them on a potential ambush site. They crossed from brush to elephant grass again as they descended. Egan stayed off the established trails except for crossing them. Then he approached slowly, stopped, observed and crossed quickly. At one point Egan thought 3d Plt was crowding 1st on the left flank. Nahele was at point there. Egan paused, brought Cherry up, radioed Kinderly. "I can hear you assholes," Egan whispered. "Aint no way," Kinderly answered. 3d was 100 meters back. Egan squatted and called a general halt.

Recon's airlift to reinforce Delta was completed. Bravo, three klicks northeast of Alpha, was resupplying. Those pilots, Egan thought. They do incredible things. We should have a LOH on station. Jax had moved past Egan. Egan sat with Cherry. He called Brooks. "Feeling. Trail watchers to sierra." They sat soundlessly. Whiteboy and 3d Sqd advanced to point. The column rose. Egan stopped Whiteboy and led off again himself, the big squad leader at slack, then Cherry. While they sat Cherry had plucked pieces of grass and stuck them into his helmetcover and ruck to break up the smooth lines of the radio and his head. Others had watched him and copied. Behind Cherry 3d Sqd followed, then the Co and Plt CPs, 2d Sqd and 1st now at drag. The other columns advanced also. All three were being watched.

A disconnected thought vision came to Cherry. Disconnected from Nam. He did not know why or how the thought began. Perhaps the grass or being able to see the hills again triggered it or perhaps the sense of power he had from the morning artillery raid or perhaps the cleansing action of the riverwater. The triggering stimulus made no difference to him, but the meaning of the vision seemed all important. As he walked, Cherry saw himself gliding above a rugged stretch of California coast. The sun was out. It was a magnificent day, his second day as a soarer, a hang glider. Cherry had never attempted hang-gliding, had never been to California, had indeed no knowledge of soaring at all, yet in the vision every detail was perfect. He could see himself above the bluffs before the Pacific,

could feel the cool ocean breeze. Three days earlier he had been
to the doctor. He knew the history in the vision without having
to see it or think it. Somehow, he had strained himself very
badly and he had ignored it for a long time. Finally he had gone
to see a specialist and the doctor told him he had poisoned his
system. The condition is irreversible, the doctor explained. You
will be dead within five days. Cherry, the man in the vision, had
fallen into deep depression. Before he had met with the specialist
he had known what the man would say. The depression seeped
from the vision to the soldier on the valley floor in Vietnam.
Cherry felt very sad. Yet physically he felt strong. His muscles
were in fine shape. The doctor had acknowledged that. Cherry
decided to become a soarer as his last earthly feat. He also
decided this would be the best way to end his life. He told no
one.

On his first day of soaring he was an excellent student. His
instructor was a wing salesman and Cherry had the latest gear. It
gave the soarer an incredible amount of control. They practiced,
the salesman instructed and Cherry learned. Day two found them
on the cliffs and bluffs just south of Mendocino. Perhaps Cherry
had seen a TV special. How could he know these things? How
could it be so real? It was a beautiful day with a crisp September
wind gusting in crystal blue sky. Off Cherry leaped and then
returned. He was ready now. His secret plan was to marry his
physical being with the Pacific coastline—that exact spot where
it is neither land nor sea but sometimes either and sometimes
both. A wavewashed rock-sand beach.

He soared, first a bit awkwardly, then more and more
gracefully. First just a bit above the bluff and then higher and
higher over the ocean. Into dives then out to barrel rolls and
loops. The new wing was more maneuverable than any earlier
design. Higher. The wing was incredible. From three hundred
feet over the bluff he could see the coast for one hundred miles
and the endless ocean. Freedom, elation, higher.

It is time, he said to himself. Cherry looked straight down.
It was late afternoon. He had been in the air for three hours.
Slowly he nosed over and folded the wing back into a missile,
gravity shooting him ever faster toward the earth. The speed was
terrific. The pressure of the wind on his eyes seemed to be
ripping them apart. Tears squished out and shot across his face
and temples and lost themselves in the wind. Faster. Darting to
the coastline. I don't want it, Cherry thought. I can't do it.

Violently he forced the bars to expand the wing. He was still crashing. I can't do it to myself, he screamed. The wing grabbed a tiny fluff of rising air and whipped, thrashed, and a few vertical feet from the coast leveled and began ascending.

Then the vision was gone. Cherry thought about it. He smiled. That's like saying I can't kill myself, he thought. He felt very happy. The vision seemed to have taken only a minute. Cherry looked forward smiling broadly. Goddamn, he thought, Egan sure is moving slow this time. He had not advanced twenty steps during the dream. Dream? It seemed so real.

Suddenly the air erupts—Egan opens up with his 16 and falls flat—Whiteboy's 60 barkbuzzes through a hundred rounds— four men jump from vegetation to the left—Cherry lunges forward—Hill jumps over him—Egan is up firing again. He fires a burst which cuts one man in half. AK fire is coming from their front, left and right. All of 3d Sqd charges the ambush. Whiteboy is standing, machine-gunning from the waist, firing his ass off. Cherry runs into the fire with the surging boonierats—he is spraying rounds to the right. He falls sprawled flat believing for a moment he is still upright sprinting—MOVE! MOVE! MOVE! Thomaston screaming—Cherry's legs pumping though he is prone then he is up sprinting—rifles crackbarking popping, grenade explosion—Rover Five, Rover Four, they're breaking your way, El Paso—Cherry doesn't realize he is up. He sprints forward hurtling bushes and prone reloading boonierats. The NVA are running, retreating. Cherry heaves a grenade then another without consciously aiming. Behind him Egan blasts a wounded NVA. More NVA open up from down the trail. Harley, Frye, Mullen reloading, Cherry still charging—BOOM—more explosions. Tracers zing up through the grass and brush. A fireball erupts to Cherry's left, the concussion knocks him down—a wounded enemy soldier lifts an AK toward Cherry's head—Cherry spinning bringing his 16 around—the soldier's eyes flaring open with amazement or fear—Egan has unloaded six rounds into his chest—no cry of pain—amazement—the eyes rolling up the body sagging, collapsing. They fucked up, Egan thinking laughing. They blew it too early. Grenade! Brooks screams—he is in the middle firing with them, he leaps away—Egan down reloading— the noise incredible—the grenade has landed behind, at Egan's feet. He is unaware. Cherry sees it smack, splatting in the mud. He shouts but no sound leaves his throat. He lunges for the handbomb, a swimmer's dive thrusting out flat with both legs, arms stretched forward, eyes on the grenade. He grabs it, his body still in the air, squeezing it in his hand his body crashing in the mud rolling like a shortstop and throwing the grenade back toward the enemy, the bomb exploding in the air. Whiteboy sees enemy in brush uptrail. He drills one. The body caves in. Marko up. Chops brush to debris with his 60. In back Numbnuts is flat on the ground. He hasn't raised his head since the first volley erupted. He hasn't fired. Egan grabs Cherry's radio to call Armageddon, the firebase artillery. FO is already calling in support.

The firing decreases. The NVA retreated left and right. 2d and 3d Plts had maneuvered to the flanks of 1st. Shots and explosions came first from 3d's position then from 2d's. Denhardt and Lairds slit the throats of five NVA insuring they were dead. Alpha regrouped almost instantly, three prongs turning south. The action had exploded suddenly, flashed like powder and died in less than two minutes. One NVA soldier had made a slight last movement as his unit, having followed 1st Plt's approach, setup a hasty L-shaped ambush. Egan had seen him and surprised the ambushers a moment before they were ready. 1st Plt killed five at the ambush site. 3d Plt caught three fleeing and killed them. 2d gunned down one. Whiteboy received Alpha's only wound, a piece of grass slit his eyelid. The grudge stake for the Khe Ta Laou was being raised.

"How many do you think got away?" Brooks asked the group.

Alpha was now set up together on an earthen swell at the base of the south escarpment. They had moved very quickly not allowing the NVA time to reorganize. "Them raggedy-ass mothafuckas neva knew what was comin down," Harley whispered to Whiteboy.

"Gawd A'mighty Sweet Jesus," Whiteboy whispered back. "Ya ken say that fer me too. Sure as shit stinks."

"You en Little Boy was doin a J-O-B," Egan chuckled. "We shoulda had the photogs here today."

"Fuckin God," Frye said. "Ever since the dinks stole that 60 from Delta I been expectin ta walk inta an ambush where they'd be usin the likes a Little Boy on us."

"Hey," Brooks called softly. "One meeting, huh?"

"I'd estimate there were fifteen at most," Thomaston said.

"We know at least two got by us," De Barti added.

"None escaped through 3d," Caldwell said.

Brooks leaned forward then rocked back. He was sitting cross-legged, a topo map on his lap, his rifle beneath it. Close about him were his platoon leaders and advisers. They were well concealed in a briar thicket. Alpha's perimeter circled the CP at a ten to fifteen meter radius. The men were still excited. And happy. They had hit the enemy behind his own lines, hit him hard, then run. Now Brooks had to figure a way to get them back down there, even deeper in, without being ambushed. The NVA won't make that mistake again, he thought. And we better not use the tri-fork formation again. They'll be onto it. Brooks rocked back and forth slowly, studying the map, pondering his situation, mentally moving his unit and the enemy and trying to perceive the outcome. Each time the NVA had hit Alpha, Alpha had been moving toward the center of the valley. When they were moving either toward the mountains or beyond the valley center toward the open plain to the west, the NVA had not touched them. Was that a matter of coincidence?

On the perimeter Cherry was jubilant. He had reacted well and he knew it. It had been his first experience of the freedom of a firefight, the anything goes rage of a battle. He felt young and strong. He had been free to perform. He could have laid in the muck like Numbnuts or a few of the others who said they were pinned down, but he hadn't. He was ebullient. He had been able to protect himself, to save Egan and to be saved by Egan. Goddamn, we carry a vicious personal arsenal, he thought. Had it lasted longer, I could have called in artillery, Cobras, the fast movers. Cherry sat smug, snug, buried in foliage. The heft of his M-16 felt good in his hands. He was so happy. They all had reacted well, he decided. This was man-to-man friendship. A gutsy bond. Combat camaraderie. They shared discomfort and death and victory. If you get killed, he told himself, that's not so bad. Didn't El Paso say it right? Everybody has to die sometime. It's if you get maimed, that's when it's bad. That would suck. Going home maimed would be rotten. Wounded, he thought, wounded but not badly wounded, that would be okay. That'd pass. Getting killed'd pass too. Really, the only bad part about getting killed would be not having gotten to do all those things I always wanted to do. I got places to go, girls to know. Hell, I aint tired of livin this life yet. Cherry looked into the field before him. He was aware of his responsibility, ability, to kill anything out there that moved. I am a mangod, he said to himself. Every man is part god; every man who knows his soul belongs only to himself.

It was up there again. High over the valley. The music, the PsyOps bird with its loudspeakers blaring. Minh looked up but he could not see the bird. It is probably above the range of .51 cals, he thought. Minh did not like hearing the music. He tried to shut it out. The PsyOps people were playing the same tape they had played on the first and second days of the operation. The bird descended slowly, spiralling down, playing the music first near the firebase then over the north escarpment, now over the valley center. Minh could not help but listen. The sorrowful funeral music brought back many memories, memories of a war that had rocked his land all his life and much more. Minh had heard the music played for brothers and cousins and friends. He remembered how his cousin's body had been delivered to his family in 1965. The body came in an opaque black plastic bag. When the bag was opened the family found the body just as it had been at the moment of death. Minh's cousin was still in uniform. The blood was still sticky on the newly cold flesh. Above the valley the tune changed. Minh knew the new song also. It was said to be a popular song in the North. A girl sang woefully of her first lover who was far away. A metal drum beat the melancholy rhythm. When the song was over a third began. This one Minh found very saddening also for it was about a young boy who had left his love and gone off to combat. The melody began slowly. A lonely soldier sang the words. The PsyOps bird was directly over Alpha. The mist and fog had thinned but the helicopter was so high it could not be seen from the ground. With it two Cobras could be heard. Then all sounds of the birds left. Minh and Doc were seated just outside the CP circle.

"Funeral music again?" Doc asked quietly.

"Yes," Minh whispered.

They sat quietly for several minutes. Suddenly they could hear helicopters again, many helicopters sounding as if they were diving directly for Alpha. All of Alpha looked up. A Huey was diving off the south ridge down toward the valley floor. Behind it to its left and right were Cobras. Behind them two more Cobras chased. From the Huey a spray of leaflets gushed, thousands of leaflets falling, being caught in the rotor wash of the helicopters and splaying then fluttering, falling gently with the rain. "Them crazy fuckas," Doc whispered. "Trying ta draw fire so the snakes can shoot em up. Crazy, Man. Crazy." The birds pulled out of their dive, gained altitude and the Huey began a new broadcast. The loudspeakers crackled. The tape recorded message in Vietnamese blared.

"Dear Comrades of the 812th Regiment, can you identify me?" Minh translated sentence by sentence for Doc. "I am Lieutenant Le Xuan Que, Political Commissar from the 812th. I have rallied to the Free World Forces."

"That the POW?" Doc whispered quickly between sentences.

"Yes," Minh said concentrating on the broadcast.

"Po fucka," Doc said.

Minh continued translating. "For years I was with Battalion K-34. I served with KI/6 Company on 652 Mountain. Then I served with the K-19 Sapper Battalion. Three days ago I was captured. Now I am a free man with the People of the Republic of Vietnam. I appeal to all my friends to rally before you are killed by Free World Forces. Do you remember Battalion Commander, Duong, and Political Commissar, Co Rang Vau, told us many times about plans to encircle the enemy? After many days of fighting what have you accomplished? Do you see our comrades who fought with us? What has happened? I hope survivors of 652 Mountain and of Khe Ta Laou become clear-headed enough to understand the hollow promises of our cadre. I advise you to allow yourselves the opportunity to rally to the Government of Vietnam. Be like me. Or go back home. Leave the battlefield. Do you know that no one buried Phi, Link, Chieu or Song of the K-19 who died during our assault against the Americans? In the past week companies of Americans and South Vietnamese have killed hundreds of our comrades. Already this morning twenty of your friends have been killed. Much of your ammunition has been discovered and destroyed. The Americans have terrifying helicopters. They are coming to get you. You have a choice. Pick up the leaflets we are dropping. Hold them up to the Allies as they come for you. Do not hold your weapons. You will not be shot. Comrades, the Allies have treated me well and they have taken care of my health. Soldiers of the 7th Front, You Do Not Have To Die!"

The helicopter repeated the message down the valley, the message no longer intelligible to Minh at Alpha. Listening, squatting beside Minh, were Brooks, El Paso and Egan. Minh

looked at them. Then he said, imitating Jax, "Shee-it. Aint no ·
fucken way we aint gowin shoot em." They all laughed.

At 1600 hours Alpha was ambushed again. They had moved
back down toward the river, this time with two recon squads
eighty meters forward of the main column. 2d Plt had led off
with Baiez' and Mohnsen's squads reconning and Catt's squad at
column point. Behind Catt's came the Co CP then 1st Plt and 3d
at drag. The exhilaration of the earlier firefight had waned. The
boonierats were again tired. They did not wish to descend again
into the valley. Yet into the valley they went. Brooks had
directed the unit in a spiral off the earthen swell, uphill, then
east, then north and finally west again. The vegetation was
patchy and discontinuous, elephant grass then secondary scrub
brush, then bamboo. Five hundred meters from where they
started hell broke loose slowly.

It began with Mohnsen's squad. Smith was at point,
Garbageman at slack, then Mohnsen, Jones (RTO), Greer, Roberts and Sklar. A single AK round broke the air. Sniper? Trail
watcher? It seemed like a warning shot fired high. They stopped.
Squatted. Jones radioed El Paso. There was movement in the
brush twenty meters ahead. Mohnsen moved up to Smith, kept
him from firing. The squad leader motioned Smith and Garbageman
right. The squad moved forward. Roberts and Sklar to the left.
Mohnsen, Jones and Greer straight in. Jones radioed their position and situation to the other recon squad. They moved out.
Another sniper round cracked, slashed through the high vegetation.
They all wanted to open up but the sound was somehow muffled,
its location blurred. They pursued quietly, hearts pumping faster,
adrenaline flowing. Three AKs opened up at them. Mohnsen's
squad exploded in a charging fusillade. They attacked the noise,
firing, meeting the challenge of an unseen enemy, breaking an
unknown ambush, attempting to gain fire superiority. Again the
NVA fired, lower now, more continuous yet still retreating.
Garbageman saw one. He unloaded half a magazine at the
fleeing soldier. The rounds slammed into the NVA's legs,
ass, lower back and the body collapsed running forward—
Mothafuckers, Garbageman screaming—Mohnsen, Jones charging—
got em runnin, kick ass, take no names. Then from three sides
the entire jungle explodes, rocking—grenades, RPGs, RPDs and
AKs. The ground shakes and thunders deafening all of Mohnsen's
people. Quickly, quickly, everything happening instantaneously,

a long instantaneousness, last forever in a flash. Then slowly, the reality congealing and time again pacing—Got to get out, Mohnsen. Got to get my people out. Jones screaming, crying. He is down yet still he returns fire. Armageddon Two, he screams into the radio, the noise about him too loud for him to hear any response—a series of rounds catches Greer's right thigh ripping the flesh and shattering bone, the leg disintegrates, he falls contorted, the leg twitching violently. Rockets whiz over Mohnsen, explode. Tracers zinging, then fireballs and thunder and smoke, powder, odor, pinned down, fear. The earth about them erupts, the air above becomes a fire tempest. Four boonierats are hit. All seven lay flat trying to creep into the earth, burying themselves in the rotting vegetation hugging the swamp floor muck. Smith bellows loud from pain, hit in the neck and shoulder and arm—Save us, God, save us—Mohnsen crawling to Jones grabbing blood-sticky radio. No American fire now, the NVA settling back to a controlled second-by-second torturous rifle fire methodically pecking at every square inch of their ambush kill zone, life seeping out of Greer, out of Smith. NVA gloating but not closing overrunning the site. Boonierats sad remorseful run to death from stupidity of falling into a trap at least two thousand years old. NVA in a U-shaped ambush clockwork pelting the killzone unseen.

From fifty meters away Baiez maneuvers his squad to behind the NVA position. The enemy have trenched-in beneath thick bamboo, their firing heard but not seen. Within two minutes the left flank recon squad is atop the NVA rear firing at noise, not seeing, just firing trying to break the NVA hold over Mohnsen. Another minute later the main column flanking right and coming frontally—the NVA opening up again with all their force, now inward, now outward. Brooks screaming into the radio, screaming at boonierats, "Keep your fire low. Keep it low."

"Come on, Man," Mohnsen whispers to Jones. "Come on. Hang on to me." Mohnsen works Jones' body on top of his own then begins crawling, retreating. Roberts pushes his bloody stumped torso after Mohnsen. Garbageman pulls Greer, wraps his arm over Greer's chest like a lifeguard pulling a drowning victim. Sklar helps Smith. Crawling, all crawling, retreating, faces in the mud, slime oozing into their eyes and mouths, blood, fluids oozing out.

"Get em back," Brooks calls, "Get em back."

FO calling in artillery behind the NVA position. Cahalan calling for a medevac. El Paso monitoring each squad's position, directing, passing the L-T's orders. Withdrawing, withdrawing. Disengaged.

"Mark it," Brooks directs. At Alpha's flanks and from center three red smoke-grenades are detonated. They billow thick plumes. From high above the valley the GreenMan directs attack. Two Cobras swoop down firing rockets toward the concealed enemy fighting position.

"Where's Greer? Where's Garbageman?" Mohnsen asked.

"Hit." Jones gurgles sputum blood.

"Where?"

Jones pointing toward the inferno.

"Stop the birds. Stop the birds. Stop the fire."

The helicopter barrage ceases, the birds circle. A rear element administers to the wounded. There are no cries of pain. Medics and soldiers helping. Cherry watching disattached as if not comprehending yet completely comprehending. "Medevac," Cahalan screams into the handset. "M-E-D-E-V-A-C. You dumb mother. Got that." Fear and bile surge to his throat, into his mouth, burning. The odor of explosions, gunsmoke, cordite and burned flesh is incredible and disgusting. He vomits. He does not care. "Get me a Dust-Off, here. Now . . . Fuck you, don't tell me not to cuss on your freq . . . you crazy . . . crazy son of a bitch. Get off this freq . . . get me Mercy Eagle. Fuck the colonel. Get me Dust-Off or this company's comin back in an looking you up. Over." Cahalan shaking uncontrollably, crying. Doc Johnson working on Roberts. Both of his arms are torn apart at the shoulders. Fragments of bone and bamboo stick to the raw tissue, Doc Johnson works over the body like a highly trained mechanic. He works quickly, systematically, having Minh and Brown assist. Doc removes Roberts' left boot and begins an IV of plasmatine in the foot. He shoots Roberts with a syringe of morphine, then returns to the mangled stumps retying them off, quickly cleaning and wrapping the meaty shreds.

Simultaneously Brooks maneuvers 1st Plt and the remains of 2d back to the ambush site while 3d Plt retreats to an open space 250 meters east to establish a perimeter and an evacuation LZ. Egan directs the frontal assault. "Jax, take your squad around right," he speaks with complete confidence and authority. "Cherry, Bill, we'll go left. Take it easy. 3d Sqd out farther right. Monk, you bring 2d straight in easy. Don't no one push it too hard. We all cover each other.''

Cherry looks at Lt. Thomaston. It is obvious Thomaston will follow Egan, will let Egan direct everything. All 1st Plt knows who commands 1st Plt. Thomaston had long ago put his rank and authority behind Egan and followed.

"Right on," Jax says leading his squad right.

The flank elements waddle forward. 2d Sqd eases up the center. The Cobra rockets had blown chunks out of the jungle exposing two NVA bunkers and a vacated lateral fighting position. 1st Plt moves in, then stops. The bodies of Greer and Garbageman, a mangled mix of blood, mush and jungle, are splattered and nearly unrecognizable as human.

"Cover me," Egan whispers to Cherry. He crosses to the fighting position, slides in, freezes, waits, then inches forward. His 16 is in his left hand, a grenade in his right. Jax tightens 1st Sqd on the right. Whiteboy closes the far right. To the far left Baiez' squad pinches in. Egan slithers from the foxhole toward the bunker, rolls, lays up next to the opening, rolls tosses in the grenade and rolls back. The concussion seems tame compared to the earlier hell. Cherry slithers to the fighting position and sets up cover for Egan. Brooks appears next to him from nowhere. Egan crawls to the second bunker and blows it. Then he dives in. Brooks jumps up and dives into the first. A second later they each reappear. Brooks has a shattered AK-47 rifle. Egan a sachel of grenades and two cans of AK ammunition. There are no NVA bodies. Alpha sweeps through the miniature bunker complex and fifty meters beyond. There are signs of enemy activity everywhere but no NVA and no blood trails.

Twenty minutes after blowing the bunkers Alpha retreated to where 3d Plt had cleared the evac LZ. The bunkers had exuded ghosts upon Alpha. They were not on a trail. The recon squad was in the middle of thick brush away from all trails. The ghosts followed the boonierats, infectiously passed from one to the next until a plague of skittish panic seized all but the doped wounded and dead.

The Dust-Off bird arrived and circled high above waiting for Alpha to bring its casualties to the LZ. Then the helicopter descended, set down. Medics helped the wounded, boonierats loaded the dead, the bird rose, sped off. It was late afternoon. Mist fumed from the sodden thickets building to fog. The jungle closed, pressed in. Alpha had to escape.

* * *

Egan did not stop to analyze any of the numerous trails he crossed. He did not study the tracks in the mud. It was clear, too clear. They had crossed into the midst of the long established enemy area. That madman Brooks, Egan thought. Mad. Flee behind their perimeter. It's beautiful. Sweat poured from Egan's armpits. Beads formed on his forehead, broke and streamed down his face. The salt burned in jungle sores on his face. He paid it no attention. He walked carefully, quietly, looking left right up down. He sniffed the air with each step. He saw no movement. Only fetid valley odor registered in his brain.

The column followed Egan, each man taking mental notes. Pop Randalph at column drag couldn't believe his eyes. In his three Vietnam tours he had never seen such an elaborate and extensive enemy area. Fishing grounds, game snares, cultivated fields, roads, bunkers connected by trenches and commo-wire, tunnels, most everything dug in and underground. "This aint no place fer yall ta be," he repeated again and again.

Cherry had fallen in behind Egan and now walked slack. His vision tunnelled, he lost all peripheral perception, he focused on Egan. I thought we weren't goina march in and knock on Charlie's back door, his mind chattered. That's what the L-T said.

Hide, Brooks thought. Hide where they won't look. Hide between them, amongst them. Use their bunkers. They build them everywhere to use in emergencies but they don't occupy even a fraction of them. Hide. If they can't see you, they can't hit you.

At point Egan came upon a road as wide as the road beneath the north ridge. Across the road was a bamboo thicket looking like an impenetrable wall. Egan looked up and down the road. No movement. He sniffed. No smell. He listened. No sound. The road showed fresh tracks. Egan motioned for Cherry to cover him and to sit. He shed his ruck, crossed the road to the thicket, crawled into a hole in the wall and disappeared. A minute later he reappeared and came back to Cherry. He radioed Brooks. Alpha rose and followed.

The vegetation was very thick and it was difficult to see. Egan was at point, on hands and knees, crawling inward, penetrating the thicket. Cherry crawled behind Egan. One by one the boonierats scampered from the brush on one side of the road to the hole in the bamboo wall on the other. They crawled after the point. They cussed and bitched silently, afraid to make a sound. Dumb! Fucken Dumb! L-T's gone mad. GreenMan's behind this. No boonierat'd ever choose this way. They cussed themselves for snapping bamboo stalks and making noise. The bamboo made a tunnel about them. There was no place to look, no cautious observation, just follow the tunnel and the heels of the boonierat in front. At point Egan found the brush to be thickening. He crawled, then rested, looking, listening, then crawled again. The vegetation caught on his ruck and he had to strain to break through. The entire company crawled behind him. At drag Pop and Doc Hayes attempted to obliterate the signs of seventy-six pairs of GI jungle boots crossing the road. Then they attempted to seal the bamboo tunnel.

After 200 meters the thicket gave way to brush and elephant grass. Alpha crawled to the edge, circled to form a perimeter and stopped. Everyone was exhausted, filthy, yet purged of the ghosts from the bunkers.

At what time he had fallen into lonely sleepless dreaming Brooks did not know. He was not sure when the valley had socked in beneath the fogmist and darkness, nor when the dreaming stopped and his consciousness controlled his thoughts. He was only aware of a sickening taste in his mouth and the cold drizzle.

For two days he and Lila acted the parts of a soldier and his lover. They did the tourist things, they ate at another luau, they drank heavily, they pawed each other. Yet they spoke little. Nam was constantly on his mind yet he had agreed not to talk about the war. The hardships the war had caused her were on Lila's mind but she dared not talk of that. She never told anyone she was married to a soldier. How could she tell him that? In her stateside life she denied him in a hundred silent ways. It almost seemed the patriotic thing to do. How was she to now be the army wife? They had toured Oahu in the morning then gone sail-surfing then returned to the hotel. Just how or why it had happened he did not know. It confused him and it tormented him to this night. The image of him and Lila washed over him like a cold wave.

"I'm not going to end up like her," Lila said defensively while removing her bathing suit. He watched longingly and she pretended she didn't see him watching. "I'm not going to let you do that to me."

"I don't know what you're talking about," Rufus said turning his back to her.

"My mother was a smart woman," Lila said. "She had it all together." Rufus turned back and looked at her. He was confused and did not know what to do. This is something she's been thinking about for a long time, he told himself. Lila was slightly drunk and she slurred her words, but as Rufus suspected, the thoughts were not new thoughts. "After she do all the stuff, washing, cooking, like that, for the family, she don't have no time for her own thing. The old man come home criticizing, tearing her down. Little things."

"Are you telling me I do that to you?"

"Old man say he don't like the way she dressed, or the food aint right, aint done enough. Like that. Always tearing her down."

There was an aggression and hate in Lila's manner Rufus had not seen since their first fights. Rufus tried to soothe and pass over the rough edge. "Hey, come here, now," he said pulling her to him, toward the bed. They were both now naked.

"That's not happening to me," Lila said allowing herself to be wrapped in his arms. "You all the time expecting me to be just what you expect me to be. No way."

"Lila, come on," he said sitting, rubbing his hands on her body, pulling her down to the bed. Her body relaxed but her head raced on. "Sweet, sweet Lila," he said nuzzling her in a practiced way.

"Another thing," Lila said. "Your old man. I can't believe him. He living back in the '20s or someplace." Rufus removed his hands from Lila. He was excited yet anxious. "You know what he said to me before I left?" Rufus bent back and hugged Lila. He flicked his tongue across her nipples, alternating from breast to breast. His hand slipped between her thighs and she squirmed. "He said, 'We are not Blacks. We are not Negroes.' He said, 'We are of color.' He's crazy. What the hell are you doing?" Lila pushed him away and sat up. She rose from the bed, turned on the radio, took her time finding a station and returned to the bed. During the physical break, perhaps because of a flash radio news item as Lila turned the dial, Rufus' concentration leaped back to Nam. He saw a scene of six dead enemy soldiers and one wounded American. Firing smashed into the trees. Someone screamed. Rufus wilted, lowered his body gently to the bed as if hiding from possible enemies in the walls.

Lila returned to the bed and, acting bored, as if she had nothing better to do, she stroked-squeezed Rufus' flaccid manhood. It stayed limp. She smothered a laugh. "That the best you can do, Stud?" Lila rolled over and lay facing away from him.

Rufus looked at Lila's ass and then at his penis. His penis drooped across his muscular thigh. He could not feel it. He sat up, rolled to his knees and on hands and knees hovered over her, kissing her body up and down, aware always that his penis was still limp and hanging dead between his legs. Rufus caressed, massaged, titillated Lila and she purred softly, her eyes closed, thinking about someone else, he thought, she lying on her belly now, breathing a little quicker, a little harder, undulating her pelvis slowly with the caress of Rufus' large hand, the stimulation of his thick finger. Rufus lay forward and pressed his chest to Lila's back, supporting his body with his knees and chest, fingering Lila with one hand and squeezing his limp penis with the other. It stiffened slightly. He thought of her warmth and it stiffened more. He moved behind her and his penis touched her and shrank. Fear, embarrassment, overcame him. Come on, he coaxed himself. Come on. Rufus continued caressing Lila. She reached down and adjusted his hand to give herself more pleasure. He pulled harder on himself hoping she would not roll over. "Oh, Rufus," Lila moaned. "You should do this all the time. You always want to get in me so fast. I feel so hot and juicy. Don't stop." Rufus inserted his finger deeper, he let himself lie on her and he curled his other arm about her and stroked her forehead. He kissed her back. Lila grabbed his hand from her head and brought it to her mouth. She kissed his fingers. Then she began sucking his middle finger rhythmically, undulating her groin in time. "Come in me," she cried. "Oh, I'm ready," she gurgled, she rolled under him. Rufus continued stimulating her vagina with his hand. He closed his eyes and pretended—pretended another man was with them—was behind Lila—was behind him. His penis became rigid. He slid atop Lila, between her thighs, he opened his eyes and wilted. "Fuck me," she cried. "Fuck me. Give it to me . . . give . . . what's the matter with you?"

After they got up she repeated it, nastily, trying to hurt him, repeated it again and again. "What's the matter with you?"

"Look, ah, I just flashed on, ah, something. That's all."

"Oh good. You get me all jacked up then go thinking about your boys again."

"What the fuck are you saying?"

"Here he is, Mr. Fagman. You can have him. Mr. Stud. A one-ton bomb with a half-inch wick. But don't worry. He's not dangerous."

"Wait a minute, Bitch. All you gotta do is spread them thighs. It's me that's gotta do the work."

"The WORK!? Is that what you call it?"

It did not get better between them. She was hurt and she wanted to hurt him. They drank more heavily. "You think it easy for me?" she asked the next day. "You know how many nights I spend alone? I'm out singing, working with all these really right dudes, out in really fine company, and I go home alone. I may not always do that, Stud."

Rufus, the ex-athlete, felt as if his body had betrayed him. The fifth night of R&R they tried again to make love and again he could not keep hard. They sat, not looking at each other, not speaking, each wondering how to get through the time remaining until they would return to their own worlds, each disgusted with the other, hurt by the other, disappointed with the other and with their own selves.

On the sixth and last night of R&R Rufus said to Lila, "I don't know what it is, or why. I thought we could make it. I don't know or maybe I do. I think maybe I really do. You think because I've told you I love you, you've unlocked all the mystery of me and there isn't anything left to find. You think there's no room to look at me anymore and it's time to move on. Lady, I don't think you've even scratched the surface."

"Maybe," Lila answered softly, they had ceased shouting that morning, "that's because you won't let me. You've got this coating of words so wrapped around you you can't even see yourself. How do you expect me to know you?"

On the second night she had said, "Not tonight, Honey." On the sixth night it became his turn and he did not even try. All my life, he told himself, I've been good at whatever I've attempted. I'm not going to start failing now. He gawked at her. She grinned at him, nastily, crudely, destructively. "I hate you," Lila said and they passed the night in polite silence.

At noon the next day, Lieutenant Brooks, in uniform, said good-bye to Mrs. Brooks. They spoke formally. Around them other soldiers were politely saying good-bye to their wives also. There was no frantic passion as there had been when that planeload had arrived from Vietnam. There were only a few tears.

"It wasn't supposed to be this way, Rufus," Lila said softly not looking at him.

"No," he answered. "It wasn't."

"Good-bye." Tears welled then streamed.

"Good-bye," he said simply, watching her crack. She turned and ran from him, ran from the loading gate, from the terminal, from Hawaii. He turned and walked up the ramp. In his throat he sang:

> *Walk like a man, Fast as I can,*
> *Walk like a man from you.*
> *I'll tell the world, forget about a girl,*
> *and walk like a man from you.*

The Hawaii torment followed him, chased him for months. There was a side of the conflict he never saw, never imagined. Had he seen it he would not have understood it. Lila continued to spend lonely nights and anguished days. When she had left for Hawaii she had wanted something to call her own, a baby, a family, yet the dream had soured. Upon returning she tried to get a steady job. She had to become self-sufficient again and learn not to depend on his allotment. She asked herself a thousand times if she could leave him. She did not want another man. Men became repulsive. Should she divorce him? In March she wrote him a note which said only, "I didn't want to be pregnant and I'm not." Could she send it? Could she? She did and with it she decided irreversibly to divorce and she set about building her support system which jelled in July. In early August she filed the papers.

In his mind Brooks entered the bedroom of a penthouse bachelor's pad. He crept in slowly, noiselessly, in the best boonierat fashion. She did not know he had returned. It was his first day back. They were giggling on the bed. The lights were low. Lila, her sensuous mocha-colored body naked on the Jody's legs, her mouth on his large penis. The Jody laying back, eyes stoned-closed dreaming. Brooks snapped his right hand toward the bed. The spoon flew from the grenade with a metallic ting. No wait. His mind stopped the scene. The image switched. He and Lila were on the bed making love. He watched her so lovingly lick and suck him. It excited him beyond description. It excited him as he lay on the cold valley floor. With the excitement there nagged a secret thoughtimage which he tried to chase away, which disgusted him. It was a mental picture he watched begin a hundred times since Hawaii yet never allowed it to run on. If Lila could enjoy it so, if she could bring him so much pleasure, if he could love it so, would he be able to bring that pleasure to another man? He wanted to suck a cock. Yes. He wanted to feel the head in his mouth, to lick the ridge. He wanted to suck his own cock but he couldn't. He was in bed with the Jody. The Jody was Egan. Oh, that beautiful cock Egan had plunged into that gypsy bitch in Australia. What would it be like to be eating her pussy and then have Egan step from the shadows and begin to fuck her while he ate her? His mouth on her lips, on her juiciness and on Egan's hot shaft simultaneously. He could feel her back off. It was Lila. Egan had been fucking his wife. Egan was his Jody. Lila kissed Rufus passionately. She stuck her tongue deeply into his mouth, licked her own juices from his chin. Then Egan began rubbing his giant cock against her face. She turned and licked it. She turned back and kissed Rufus deeply pulling him to Egan. Egan's erectness was between them, between their lips as they kissed and licked. Then the cock slid into his mouth. Lila held Rufus' face to it. Egan pumped back and forth. Brooks squirmed on the jungle floor. Stop. Not that. He pushed Egan out of the picture and brought Lila's head down to his groin. Suck me. That's how it should be. His mind shot spiralling into a void. He felt the darkness, the emptiness expanding. He was losing everything. The emptiness grew forcing his entire life away. Everything became a black void, expanding, expanding like a giant bubble of nothingness, like a gigantic balloon with only a speck of dust at center. Expanding—a helium-filled balloon—ever expanding, its walls becoming fainter, more fragile. Emptiness expanding, concentrating tension and pressure at the walls, the outer edge of the void. Pressure more severe than those at the ocean's greatest depths, pressure within and without. The darkness of his closed lids expanding beyond his body, beyond his mind, and the tension and static balanced forces escalating, threatening to collapse, threatening a tremendous implosion destined to destroy the center where his eyes are shut. Hold it together, he demanded of his mind. Hold it together. It hasn't all collapsed yet. It doesn't have to.

SIGNIFICANT ACTIVITIES

THE FOLLOWING RESULTS OF OPERATIONS IN THE O'REILLY/ BARNETT/JEROME AREA WERE REPORTED FOR THE 24-HOUR PERIOD ENDING 2359 19 AUGUST 70:

AT 0310 HOURS COMPANY D, 7/402 RECEIVED A SAPPER AT-TACK IN THEIR NDP IN THE VICINITY OF YD 143328 RESULTING IN SEVEN US KIA AND 17 US WIA OF WHICH 11 REQUIRED MEDICAL EVACUATION. ENEMY CASUALTIES WERE UNKNOWN.

FOUR SEPARATE ATROCITIES WERE PERPETRATED BY THE EN-EMY AGAINST VILLAGE POPULACES OF THUA THIEN PROVINCE PRIOR TO DAYBREAK RESULTING IN NINE CIVILIAN CASUALTIES. DETACHMENT 4, 7TH PSYOPS BN IN COORDINATION WITH DIS-TRICT LEADERS AND THE VIETNAMESE INFORMATION SERVICE COLLECTED ANTI-GOVERNMENT AND ANTI-FREE WORLD MILITARY ASSISTANCE FORCE LEAFLETS WHICH THE ENEMY HAD DISTRI-BUTED. GROUND LOUDSPEAKER TEAMS WERE DEPLOYED AND IM-MEDIATELY BEGAN BROADCASTING PRO-GVN MESSAGES. THE EF-FECT OF THE NVA PROPAGANDA WAS EFFECTIVELY NEGATED. PHOTOGRAPHS AND TAPE RECORDED INTERVIEWS WERE MADE FOR POSSIBLE FUTURE USE.

AT 0737 HOURS, COMPANY A, 7/402 SPOTTED TWO NVA SQUADS IN THE OPEN THREE KILOMETERS WEST SOUTHWEST OF FIREBASE BARNETT. ARTILLERY WAS EMPLOYED. A SEARCH OF THE AREA REVEALED NUMEROUS BLOOD TRAILS.

DURING A LATE MORNING SWEEP, 2D PLT, CO A, 7/402 DISCOV-ERED AN NVA FISHING CAMP, VICINITY YD 165311, WITH NUMER-OUS BAMBOO FISH TRAPS AND SEVERAL SMALL ANIMAL SNARES. THE TRAPS AND SNARES WERE DESTROYED. AT 1215 HOURS 3D PLT OF CO A REPORTED FINDING FOUR MARIJUANA PATCHES VI-CINITY YD 168309. WHITE PHOSPHORUS ARTILLERY ROUNDS WERE EMPLOYED TO DESTROY THE CROP.

AT 1330 HOURS ON A SWEEP SOUTH OF THE KHE TA LAOU RIVER CO A WAS AMBUSHED BY AN ESTIMATED REINFORCED NVA SQUAD. THE UNIT RETURNED ORGANIC WEAPONS FIRE AND WAS SUPPORTED BY ARTILLERY RESULTING IN NINE ENEMY KILLED AND FOUR INDIVIDUAL WEAPONS CAPTURED. NO US CASUALTIES WERE REPORTED.

IN A MASS GRAVE APPROXIMATELY THREE KILOMETERS NORTHWEST OF FIREBASE RIPCORD, THE 3D CO, 3D BN, 1ST

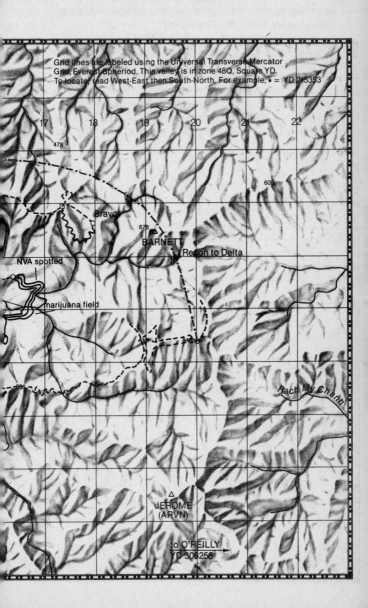

Grid lines are labeled using the Universal Transverse Mercator
Grid, Everest Spheriod. This valley is in zone 48Q, Square YD.
To locate, read West-East then South-North. For example, • = YD 215353

17   18   19   20   21   22

478

609

Bravo

678

BARNETT

Recon to Delta

NVA spotted

marijuana field

846

996

Rach My Chanh

△
JEROME
(ARVN)

to O'REILLY
YD 306258

REGT (ARVN) DISCOVERED 20 ENEMY KILLED DURING THE PREVIOUS WEEK BY TACTICAL AIR STRIKES.

WHILE RECONNING AN ENEMY BASE AREA VICINITY YD 155307, A SQUAD OF CO A, 7/402 WAS AMBUSHED BY AN UNKNOWN SIZED ENEMY FORCE. THE SQUAD RETURNED ORGANIC WEAPONS FIRE AND WAS SUPPORTED BY ARA AND REINFORCED BY TWO PLATOONS OF CO A. TWO US WERE KIA, THREE US WERE WOUNDED AND EVACUATED. ENEMY CASUALTIES WERE UNKNOWN.

FIREBASE BARNETT RECEIVED 13 ROUNDS OF 82MM MORTAR FIRE AT 1819 HOURS. NO CASUALTIES WERE REPORTED.

CHAPTER

27

2 0 A U G U S T 1 9 7 0

By first light the raindrizzle had ceased. Alpha was socked in beneath thick valley mist. The boonierats hardly moved. For an hour the only noise was the RTOs calling in situation reports and resupply requests and Brown calling in the altered supply order for now seventy-five men. Doc Johnson had convinced the L-T to send Whiteboy to the rear because of the big soldier's eye wound. Melvin Harley would act as squad leader until Whiteboy returned.

Alpha rested. Today would be resupply day and they anticipated none of the complications of the last resupply. Brooks cut them as much slack as he dared. He sent out only three five-man patrols, one from each platoon, and they were instructed to stay relatively close. "Just have a look around," he had told the platoon leaders. "Get us some targets for arty, collect intelligence, but avoid engaging the enemy if possible." Everyone had agreed enthusiastically and had left Brooks alone in the dawning while he called the GreenMan.

"Red Rover One, this is Quiet Rover Four," he radioed. He was not sure how to proceed. He had a personal request.

Brooks spoke with the TOC RTO and finally got the GreenMan. "Four, this is One Niner. Over."

"One," Brooks addressed the GreenMan. How could he say it other than just saying it? He could not think of a way. "One, Quiet Rover Four Niner requests to delta echo romeo oscar sierra on two eight August. Over." There! Finally he had said it. There was a long pause. He wanted to DEROS in eight days. He would be out of the field in five days or less. His decision was made. Now it would be up to the GreenMan to approve it and up to Personnel to implement it.

"Four," the GreenMan's voice came from the handset, "that's a rodge. That's affirm. I have you deltaechoromeooscarsierra on two eight August—providing Texas Star reaches termination. Four, I need you. Over. Out."

There had been no CP meeting the previous night because of the fleeing and hiding. In the unreal security of dawn the usual boonierats gathered at the CP. They felt extra tired, extra irritable, yet they generally maintained the macho, though dampened, facade of young soldiers.

Cherry sat quietly monitoring the various companies' internals about the valley. Doc, Minh and Whiteboy spoke quietly among themselves. Brown and Cahalan shared a cold can of Spaghetti and Meatballs. El Paso monitored the reconning patrols and he and FO plotted targets. Egan painstakingly cleaned his weapon. Thomaston, Caldwell and De Barti savored the smoke of a single last cigarette.

"Hey, Eg," Thomaston called lowly, "how many today?"

"Eighteen en a wake-up," Egan answered. "What about you?"

"Twenty-one."

"You cherries," Brooks laughed. "EIGHT!" he announced.

"Is that fucken right?" Thomaston said astounded.

"You finally decided," Egan added.

"You owe it to yerself," Doc said. "Right on."

"I didn't think you'd ever leave," El Paso smiled.

"But I still have eight days," Brooks said. He was happy and they were happy for him. "Let's get down to business."

The boonierats closed in about their commander. They whispered one-to-one the clichés they always whispered when a boonierat brother left. "Get some for me." "Look out, Mama, Daddy been holdin it so long, it gonna explode." "I bet he shoots his load before he ee-ven enters the door and still blows her eyes out." "Bet yer ass he will."

"Well," Pop Randalph smiled at them all, quieted them as he leaned into the center of the circle, "when yer twenty you can send a squirt right across the room. When yer twenty-five you still got enough muzzle velocity to fire from the hip. But, I gotta let yall know, when yer thirty-seven, goddammitall, it'll still come out with a bit a coaxin but you best have a bucket under it. How old are you, Sir?"

"Old enough to reach halfway across the room," Brooks chuckled.

"Why, hell. Here all this time I thought you was seventeen."

They all laughed then Brooks put a damper on the meeting. They discussed yesterday's ambush of Mohnsen's squad. What happened, why it happened, how it could have been avoided. "Recon elements should not pursue ambushers," Brooks said. "It's the same damn thing that happened to Bravo down on the Sông Bo. They sucked them in then blew them away."

"L-T, I don't think you can say that," Lt. De Barti challenged him.

"I agree, Sir," Pop said. "You gotta return fire, suppress their fire, an gain fire superiority. Otherwise they goan eat you up."

"Not a seven-man recon element," Brooks said. "When they began taking fire they should have held their position until maneuver elements could have flanked them."

"No Sir," Pop said. "I disagree. Most times you can't wait for nobody. You gotta break the back of a ambush."

"That's true," Egan said.

"Yes," El Paso agreed then tried for a compromise, "but I think what Mohnsen did was run through his ambush. They should have stopped the second they realized there were enemy on their sides. They could still have disengaged."

"Hey," Brooks said. "Listen. As long as I'm in command here, recon elements are to return fire but to disengage as rapidly as possible. They are to wait for reinforcements or for arty or ARA. That's it. Any questions?" No one answered. Egan bit down and tightened his jaw. Pop examined his fingers. The weariness that was in them all seemed to seep to the surface. Brooks removed his odd baseball-style hat and scratched his scalp. "We're going to have plenty of opportunities over the next few days to mix it up with Charlie," Brooks said. "Don't worry about that. GreenMan still wants us to clean out this valley. After resupply we're coming back here. We're going for their heart."

Before Alpha moved out Brooks walked to each platoon. He wanted to tell as many of his men as was possible. He especially wanted to tell the old-timers. He wanted to say he was

leaving them but not abandoning them. That was always bullshit.
It seemed everyone always said that in one form or another just
before they DEROSed. Then they would leave and perhaps send
a letter or maybe even a package. But soon that ceased and they
were out of touch; the old unit was filled with cherries and the
vet was surrounded by a different and demanding world. But
Brooks believed he would be different. He would not forget. He
wanted them to know that. Slowly he moved to 1st Plt's area. He
carried only his weapon and a notebook. Yes, he thought. It is
also time to write down their views and perceptions on conflict.
Perhaps, in the next five days, I can make enough notes to lay
the foundation for a thesis. And yes, one thing more, he felt it,
knew it without verbalizing it, to write these things down and to
speak them out would calm his troubled mind. It had been near
impossible for him to look at Egan this morning. Perhaps he
would tell Egan his dream. Not explicitly, generally. Egan had
lady problems too. They all knew that even if no one said it. It
would be easy to talk to him.

"Sssssssttt. Jax."

"Here, L-T."

"How you doing, Little Brother?" Brooks asked. It was
going to be harder than he had thought.

"Like a uncorked jug upside-down. Drained, Man."

"You've already heard?"

"Right on."

"How do you feel about it?"

"Doan mean nothin," Jax said softly. "Only yo din't have
ta do it like that. I never thought yo do it like that. Yo aint one a
em."

"Jax, it's my time to go."

"That aint it, L-T. Shee-it. Yo owe it to yerself. I's happy
fo yo but I aint believin yo din't know. Jest spring it on us like
locust attackin."

"I'm sorry, Jax," Brooks said. Jax sounded very depressed
and it saddened Brooks.

"Who gowin get the company?" Jax asked. "Yo aint
gowin give it to that mothafucken honky Thomaston, is yo?"

"That's not my decision. The GreenMan decides that.
Thomaston's pretty good though."

"That honky fucka doan know his weapon from his ass wid
out Eg point it out to'm. An Eg leavin in two weeks. We gowin
get our asses kicked seven ways ta hell."

"Jax, it's going to work out." Brooks felt a little disgusted. Goddamn, he had the right to leave. "Hey, what are you going to do?" Brooks shrugged and tried to sound carefree.

"Gowin start a war," Jax said very factually.

"No, Jax. Now listen. You'll lose everything you ever worked for if you do that."

"Aint gowin miss somethin I aint never had."

Doc and El Paso approached Jax' perimeter position, whispered the password and came forward. They sat, one to each side of Jax and the L-T, and aimed their weapons outward. "Doc," Brooks whispered, "when I'm gone I want you to keep an eye on Jax here. Watch over him, okay? El Paso, you too."

"He okay," Doc said. "He'll be watchin over us. What's happenin, Jackson?"

"War," Jax said. "War in our homeland."

"Can't fight with that," Doc said.

"You guys be careful, huh? Please." Brooks pulled out his notebook. "Hey," he said. "I want to give you guys my address. Look me up when you get back." He wrote his name and address several times and tore the bottom from the page. "Here," he said. "Give me your addresses too."

"There aint gowin be no address when I get back," Jax said. "I's gowin be roamin. Sabotagin. Blowin up the cities, creatin terror. We gowin hold a million people hostage. Trade their lives for King Richard's."

"Take the countryside first," El Paso said. "Then the cities'll fall."

"Not this time, Bro. We got the cities already. We jest gowin hafta squeeze. Then the country'll fall."

"What about your kid, Jax?" Brooks said softly.

"I'm gowin do it fo my kid!" Jax snapped emphatically. "Whut yo think I's talkin bout?"

Egan and Cherry slid into the thicket beside El Paso. The vegetation was so dense they could not see Doc on the other end. Doc rolled to his knees and crawled to the other end. He exchanged abbreviated daps with Egan and Cherry. "Jax pissed about L-T skyin," Doc whispered.

"They killin our fucken people, they killin Pap, and they takin the best man away from me," Jax continued. He launched into a quiet tirade of name calling and complaints. He quoted Eldridge Cleaver, "The oppressor has no right which the oppressed is bound to respect." And he added his own invectives.

"They all a time inventin programs to help minorities which all a time helps keep em down. You hear bout affirmative action. I got affirmative action. Right here in my 16."

"What do you think about all this, Danny?" Brooks asked Egan. Egan shrugged and said nothing. He did not want to get into it.

"What about you, Doc?" Brooks asked.

Doc shook his head. He looked at Egan. Egan always had something to say. "Doan you care about us no mo, Eg?" Doc said.

"What?"

"Doan you care about Jax no mo? We gotta hear from you. L-T leavin. We gonna be lookin to you ta carry us inta the new honcho. Keep him cool. You dig, Mista? You always got somethin ta say cause you always sayin somethin. What you think?"

"Well, I think there are alternatives to racially administered programs or racially interpreted legislation. And I think they might be more effective because they won't stink and there won't be any racial backlash." Brooks was listening intently to Egan. He began to take notes on his steno pad. Jax glared at Egan, looked at the L-T unsure, interested. Egan continued. "We might call it communityism or something. We could base the action taken to equalize opportunities on communities and not on race. Each community might be defined as this thousand or maybe twenty-five hundred people, no larger. That way it couldn't be corrupted like if you had one community for a city of one hundred thousand or something."

"That's an interesting idea, Danny," Brooks said.

"Yeah," Egan agreed. "It could get around all the racism bullshit. You know, why should a black doctor's kid have preference in a job or in getting admitted to school or something over a white laborer's kid. That's not the problem we're trying to solve. I think if a poor community, and there'd be lots that'd be all black or all Chicano or all Indian or something, if they were treated specially so the poor did not stay poor, the whole idea of equalizing opportunity, ah, hum . . . what am I trying ta say? You know, you could break the poor produce poor and the illiterate produce illiterate syndrome. And that's what we're trying to do. Break down the ghettos but not because they are race ghettos, because they are jails which imprison people and don't let them get out. Let's make sure everyone who wants to get out has the opportunity to get out but not simply because they

are black. And don't nobody stress race so there'd be no backlash and no hate. Poor could be mixed with rich and vice versa
by busing or somethin. But not blacks with whites simply because blacks are black and whites are white. That only keeps the
emphasis on race. It institutionalizes race and it institutionalizes
the ghettos. That shit keeps blacks down no matter how many
programs you got.''

Alpha moved out of the bamboo thicket, across paths,
trails, roads. They moved generally south, generally up, ascending toward a knoll on the side of Hill 636. FO called in a random
pattern artillery barrage in the path of their advance, clearing
their way, and a sweep of rounds exploding in the trail behind
them to close off their rear. They moved slowly, climbed cautiously yet steadily. Under no circumstance did the L-T or any of
them want to delay resupply. They pushed on without stopping.
They crossed through elephant grass and into brush. Over the
mounds they went and to the base of the cliffs. They were two
kilometers farther east in the valley than they had been on their
original descent. The cliffs here were bluffs and with their
half-empty rucks they climbed easily. With each step up the fog
thinned, each foot higher the sky lightened. The scrub brush
became jungle forest and suddenly the pointman was blinded by
the bright searing sun. Alpha rose like a column of dead out of
the mist and into the sundappled jungle. Like moles the boonierats
squinted, blinded by the sun. And then they were there, on a
large vegetated hump on the side of 636. They worked like
madmen, two platoons on security, one chopping, slashing with
machetes, clearing an LZ. A bird, the first unfogged view of a
helicopter in many days, passed over, returned, hovered, kicked
out two cases of TNT and left. The demo crew set about blowing
the larger trees down. "Cheap fuckers," the demo team members cussed, "dynamite stead a C-4. Shee-it." Then, "Fire-in-
the-hole. Fireinthehole . . . fireinthehoooo . . ."

Cherry looked around at the men he had been with. Their
eyes were hollow, haunted. The weariness of the valley showed
on their skin, their drawn cheeks, mostly in their eyes. Could I
possibly look that bad? he thought. No way, Breeze. No way.

The sun seared and dried the newly exposed jungle floor
and the surface turned to dust. The boonierats stripped off their
shirts to expose their skin and it too dried, flaked and peeled. In
the jungle the security teams hung their fatigues on branches and

opened their rucks and spread their equipment. The sun filtered through the canopy and the dancing shadows accentuated the gaunt faces, the ghoulish stares which possessed half of Alpha.

Brooks sat alone below the LZ workers, above the perimeter guards, sat alone obsessed with the view of the valley before him. Marshmallow Lake, he thought. It looks like a marshmallow lake. From above the mist again looked soft and clean and white yet it was not beautiful anymore. It was ugly. Brooks glared at the valley, at the rising cliffs and at the ridges and fingers, at the gorges and the undulating foothillmounds all hidden beneath triple canopy. Brooks snarled at the valley floor cloaked by bamboo forests and elephant grass and that blessed terrible ever-present mist. Entire NVA divisions were concealed in those landforms. Enemy, enemy everywhere. Perhaps the valley itself was a malicious adversary. And there in the middle above the mist ugliness, above it all, alone, stood that immense tree. Brooks sat still, hypnotized by the tree. He cursed it in his mind. What must be at the tree's base? Brooks removed the topo map of the valley from the large pocket on his fatigue pant thigh. He traced the river, located various high features and aligned the tree. There, right there, he thought, right there on the river. On a knoll on the river. All signs, all intuition pulled him toward the knoll and the tree. That was his mission. Alpha had circumvented the knoll on their first descent into the valley, now they would spiral back down, in tighter. Seize the knoll. Why not? Why not just go direct? Why not walk right up to it? Follow an arty raid on in. No. One more time around. One more time through Leech Row. Then we'll cross the river and hit it.

"L-T," Doc Johnson approached the commander from the LZ.

"Hey," Brooks called up, coming from his trance.

"Dry em out."

"What?"

"Let me see your feet," Doc said. "Take off them boots." Doc did not raise his voice but he spoke with absolute authority. Brooks grumbled as he unlaced first one boot, then the other. "Socks too," Doc said. "We got trouble."

Brooks peeled his OD issue socks from his ankles and feet as if they were a second skin. "Uuuumm," he groaned. He wiggled his toes. The skin was gray and ulcerated.

Doc grabbed one of the L-T's feet and inspected it. Brooks

winced. "You lucky you ken walk, Mista," Doc said disgustedly. "Half your company sufferin from immersion foot. You expectin these dudes ta walk any place you best get em dried out."

Brooks stood up barefoot and twisted in small spasms of agony as twigs ripped at the soft convoluted flesh of his feet. "Let's inspect them all," he said to Doc and the two set off on a slow circuit of the perimeter inspecting that prize asset of the infantry—feet.

Half the company was suffering from the onset of immersion foot. Doc and the L-T looked at foot after foot. Every foot was wrinkled and gray. A quarter of Alpha's feet were swollen. A tenth had progressed to being convoluted. The two worst cases, both in 3d Plt, were Arasim in 2d Sqd and Roseville in 3d. With both of these men the immersion foot had progressed to the point where the skin cracked and fungal infections had begun. The outer skin layer of Roseville's left foot had completely died and was peeling off in putrid chunks. Below, the tissue was raw.

"Evac those two," Brooks agreed with Doc. "Get them out of here on the first log bird." Arasim was delighted. He was packed in a minute.

On the opposite side of the perimeter Whiteboy was also all packed and ready to leave. His eye was worse than it had been when originally cut. The eye watered constantly now and Whiteboy said it felt . . . "lahk someone throwed a shovel full a ground glass in theah."

"Whiteboy," Brooks said, "do you really feel like I should medevac you? We need your firepower."

"L-T, Ah caint keep mah eye open."

"Really?"

"L-T, Ah'd stay out heah. Haven't Ah always done mah part? Ah'll be back, L-T, in no time a'tall."

"Okay, get up to the LZ with Roseville. But listen, we *do* need you. Get back as soon as possible. Okay?"

"Yes Sir, L-T."

Brooks completed the circuit and sat down again below the LZ. How, he thought, can I tell a man to get back here as soon as possible, that we need him, when I'm leaving? About him now half his company was not only barefoot but naked. To his left Cherry lay in the sun, his pants at his ankles. His legs spread wide apart, his penis flopped up upon his belly, his red raw thighs, burning ass and crotch rot drying and baking in the sun.

"Hey," Brooks called to Cherry. Cherry looked over. They were not cautious about noise. What with the machete hacking and the blowing down of trees, everyone in the valley knew exactly where Alpha was. With the LZ completed much of Alpha was in the open. They knew it was unlikely the NVA would hit them. The sky was full of helicopters and FAC planes. Ownership of the night may have been in dispute but the day very much belonged to the Screaming Eagles. The perimeter guards still camouflaged themselves. There were three two-man OPs hidden 100 meters out. The security guards rotated hourly with soldiers loafing about the LZ. The slicks which were to resupply them at 1100 hours had been called off for an emergency CA of ARVN infantry nine kilometers to the south. Resupply was rescheduled for 1330 hours. Alpha lay back in the sun.

"Hey," Brooks said again getting up and reseating himself a few feet from Cherry. "Several weeks back we were talking about war and you said something about it being biologically determined. Would you tell me something about it?"

Cherry twisted his body to look at the L-T while keeping his legs spread for the sun. "Yeah, I guess," he said. "What kind a thing did you want to hear?"

"You know," Brooks said not looking at Cherry, "theories maybe. Are there biological theories about war?"

"Yeah, sure," Cherry said. "Kinda." His mind had been far from biological theories.

"You're a biologist, aren't you?"

"No," Cherry said. He sat up yet still kept his legs open to the sun. "I got a BA in psych."

"Where's the biology come in?"

"I did a lot of reading and research into physiological correlates to behavior," Cherry said. "After I decided to go into psych I found I thought most of it was bullshit. Almost all of it except the material based on neurological or physiological data."

"Oh," Brooks said. He was disappointed.

"But wait a minute," Cherry said. He wanted to tell Brooks his views. Cherry felt eager to impress the L-T and talking, thinking about his subject brought him a step back toward reality, toward a world he was quickly forgetting. "Ya see, L-T, what you're talking about is behavior, human behavior. That's the realm of psychology. It's just that so much of psychology has been individual conjecture that it turned me off. There are physiological correlates to all behavior. When I was a student my interests were about what happens in the central nervous system when a person does something, or what happens there before he does something. What makes him do it, behave? War is a kind of behavior."

Brooks changed his position and became more attentive. "Are there books on the biological, ah, on psychological or physiological, ah . . . connected to war?"

"Well . . . well there are some." Cherry hesitated. "Not exactly like that but . . . well . . . you might want to read *The Territorial Imperative*. I forget who it's by."

"Wait a minute." Brooks pulled a ballpoint from his pocket and the steno pad from his pants. "*The . . . Territorial . . . Imperative*," he said slowly writing the name down.

"Yeah, and ah, *African Genesis*," Cherry added. "I'm sure they both contain bibliographies."

"Good," Brooks said.

"L-T, the crux of their position is that man is an animal. It gets a little complicated but it's possible to extrapolate from the known data to relatively sophisticated ideas or maybe theories, hypotheses anyway, about war."

"Tell me more," Brooks said moving closer.

"Okay," Cherry said settling back and attempting to recall segments of his formal education. Brooks was poised to take notes. "I'm goina throw some facts and figures to start with to help me think. Okay?"

"Yeah. Okay."

"Okay. First, mankind is like three million years old. Maybe older. He's been evolving the whole time." Cherry frowned, paused, rolled to his side and continued. "Man a long time back was a hunter. As an animal he either hunted game or he gathered food. He didn't cultivate crops or raise animals for slaughter until something like ten or fifteen thousand years ago. Long time back he had a very tiny brain. Try to picture these pre-men men. They lived in small packs and hunted. They ran game. And they were evolving. But during evolution they never lost their hunter-brain. Instead, what happened was, they developed new layers over the old brain. Not really layers like you'd pack a snowball or something but like you'd take a snowball then add another ball to it here, and another there and over hundreds of generations the new balls became larger and larger and wrapped themselves about the original ball which we'll call the brain stem.

Can you see that?'' Cherry began sketching his image in the earth.

"Okay," Brooks said. "So?"

"Well," Cherry jumped the conversation forward, "these two balls are the neocortex. They're maybe five hundred thousand years old. Now it's been shown through neurological experiments and . . . ah, there's another guy you should read, Wilder Penfield. I think one of his books was something like *Mechanisms of the Brain*. Something like that. He and others did a lot of work on functional mapping of the brain. Do you know what that means?"

"Like separating the brain into parts by function?"

"Yeah. Exactly," Cherry smiled. "Into functional areas instead of anatomical parts. For example they found that there is a specific area for reading, another for memory of words while you're reading. There's an area for writing which has its own word memory area which is why a person's vocabulary for reading or writing or speaking is all different. There are specific areas for specific motor movements. Specific areas for things even as specific as remembering a tune. There are mechanisms for integrating memory with new information being received to form concepts. The way our neural pathways are structured has a lot to do with the way we think or behave."

"That's fascinating," Brooks said. He was taking sketchy notes. A word here or there.

"Wait a minute," Cherry said. "I'll get back to this but first let me say that emotions, fear, aggressive behavior, territorial behavior, the strong emotions, they seem to be located in the brain stem or are at least activated by stimulating the brain stem. The higher cortex is the location of abstract thought and complex concepts and planning and worry. Stuff like that." Cherry was becoming wound up. It was like taking his oral comprehensive examinations prior to graduating from college except that this time it was fun. He was surprised at the avalanche of thoughts and facts, of figures and ideas that crashed down upon his speech center all trying to be communicated to the L-T at one moment. "You see," Cherry said, "our brains are built on an ancient brain stem and our brain stem dates back to when we were animals, maybe back to when we were reptiles. You can't understand human behavior in the present without looking at man's evolutionary history. We were built, muscles, heart, skeleton, maybe mind, to run or to attack. Physiologically we want to do these things. We bring a lot of our past to the present in the anatomical and functional makeup of our bodies and brains. Humans were aggressive territorial animals. We still are today but now we're more refined and we're capable of building and using helicopters and fighter-bombers to express our ancient physiological emotions.''

Brooks was now writing feverishly. It was a new approach for him and it fit in with his other beliefs about war. The concept excited him. He put to the back of his mind the LZ and the valley and everything else about him. There was something significant in what Cherry was saying. Something that went deeper than even Cherry knew.

"The brain stem still functions," Cherry began again when the L-T's pen slowed. "When people are under stress they revert or regress to earlier forms of behavior. The neocortex is, ah, the brain kind of short circuits and bypasses the neocortex. Let me back up a moment. I said before physiologically we want to run. It's more basic than that. The most basic need of any organism, the most basic drive, is for stimulation or information from its environment. That's what's behind man's drive to explore the reaches of space. If we want to understand the complex behaviors, first we have to understand the most basic, and that is the drive to acquire information from the environment. The acquisition may be equated with stimulation, so it may be said that man requires or has a drive for stimulation. Follow that to its extreme, daredevil sports are almost maximum stimulation. The only thing more stimulating is war.''

"That seems a bit farfetched," Brooks said.

"Maybe," Cherry said. "Maybe the last part but in combination with our evolutionary makeup, the idea of a drive for stimulation and the fact that if we're stimulated in a stressful way we'll regress to our animal instincts . . . see? Combined, they push us to fight.''

"Hum. Yeah," Brooks said cautiously. He found it easy to accept Cherry's statements but difficult to accept his conclusions. "I'm not sure . . ." Brooks began.

"We should have a course on bio-knowledge or bio-culture," Cherry interrupted him. "One of the questions no one's been able to answer is how much information we're born with. How much of our present do we organize because of information we possess within our cells? In our DNA or RNA? How much knowledge is passed genetically from generation to generation?''

"Hum," Brooks mused. "If that were true . . ."

"Yeah," Cherry said. "Do you know there have been birds hatched in incubators and raised completely alone and yet in a planetarium these birds can navigate the course they've got to fly to migrate with their species? It's as if they have a complete map of the stars in their genetic structure and a complete understanding of how to use it. They don't learn it. They're born with it. How much knowledge do you think man's born with?"

"If that's true," Brooks said quickly trying to get a word in edgewise, "I wonder if different races maybe have slightly different organizations of their brain structures and maybe even of the information passed from . . ."

"It's true," Cherry said. He was feeling very good.

"Hey," Brooks said softly, "talking about evolution, there's physical evolution and there's also cultural evolution."

"I'm not sure I understand."

"Well, a culture passes knowledge from one generation to the next and that body of information grows. The culture evolves to a higher form, a more complex society."

"Yeah, of course."

"I've got some questions," Brooks said. "Why must every man make the same mistakes in his life that his father and his grandfather made in theirs? Why must every generation have its war? Each year our weapons systems evolve to a higher and higher state but mankind just repeats itself again and again and all the time with larger weapons and with larger consequences. Why can't the mind of man evolve?"

"It does, L-T. Well . . ." Cherry stopped. He was thinking that it does because of the higher layers and that it doesn't because the brain stem continues to repeat itself. Cherry's face contorted and showed his conflicting thoughts. "Evolution isn't really clean," he said finally. "Like, did you know that Neanderthal man had a larger brain than present-day man. Anthropologists say that we have superior verbal abilities but maybe he just didn't . . . ah . . . maybe he lost his brain stem. Like he wasn't aggressive enough. Homo sapiens destroyed him."

"Maybe we talked him to death," Brooks laughed. Cherry laughed too. The two of them talked on and on as Alpha dried out, rested, rejuvenated.

Brooks continued taking notes. He was skeptical but now was the time to find ideas—later he could validate or discard them. At one point he wrote: It would be arrogant to believe that man is the last creature of creation. Will the Creator stop here or will He create something superior to us? Brooks read that to Cherry to get his reaction.

Cherry looked at him oddly then said, "God created man in his own image. Then God became man. Do you know why? It's because Man is God."

At 1330 hours El Paso and Doc interrupted the conversation telling them the log birds would be on station in one five.

The first resupply bird delivered what Alpha had come to call the *très bien* resupply. Doc had heard Minh use the term and he thought it was Vietnamese for 'Three Bs' as in beans, bullets and batteries. Jax had picked it up from Doc and from those two it had spread and become universal company jargon. With the *très bien* resupply, amongst the cases of C-rats, ammunition and radio batteries packed onto the helicopter, was Spec 4 Molino.

"Hey Man," Molino screamed to Whiteboy, the two passing in the roar of the helicopter rotorwash, "they stickin it ta me, too."

Then the bird and Whiteboy, Arasim and Roseville were gone. Molino stood on the silent LZ in starched, tailored REMF fatigues. He squinted at the Alpha troops near him. He stood stock-still shocked. He had seen them all on stand-down only eight days past. They had been drunk and cheerful and healthy-looking. They had transformed to vacant shells, to wraiths, to apparitions. Yet they did not know it. They lugged cases of C-rats off the LZ and broke them down, they cleaned their weapons, they resolutely worked at their tasks, attempting to appear like living soldiers. On all of them Molino saw death. He shuddered.

"Hey, Egan," Molino called spotting the barefoot platoon sergeant in the shade of a palm frond lean-to.

Egan looked at him. "Three Buds and three Millers," he mocked.

"Comin right up," Molino laughed. He could not keep his eyes on Egan. Egan's feet were gray and smelled dead, even at ten paces. Scabs and sores crusted his arms. His lips were cracked, blistered, peeling. "Hey, the Murf was by. He come over the other day to see ya."

"Fuckin Murf," Egan smiled. "How he doin?"

"Man, he couldn't believe you went back out. Man, he said ta tell ya about Mama-san. Said, Man, that you'd wanta know."

"Which mama-san?" Egan snarled suspiciously.

"You know, Man. The one the Murf always goes up to."

"What about Mama-san?" Egan asked.

"She been blown away, Man. She an three of her gook kids. All her daughters, I think. They tryina say the VC done it but the Murf thinks it was GIs. Some dude the old bitch fucked. Maybe give him some bad dew . . . Hey, where ya goin, Man?"

To Molino, El Paso looked much healthier than Egan. Tough brown skin, Molino thought, like Dago skin. The ex-bartender/librarian cornered the barefoot senior RTO in amongst the CP's ruck pile. "Hey, ¿que pasa, Señor?"

"You are, Bro," El Paso said quietly.

"I brought ya somethin, Man," Molino said. He slipped shoulders and arms from the unfamiliar straps of his ruck and let the weight crash to the ground. "Fucken things," he cussed. He dug through the jumbled contents and pulled out a thick paperback. "Here," he said handing El Paso the book. It was a copy of *Vietnam: A Political History* by Joseph Buttinger. "It come in just before the GreenMan stuck it to me," Molino explained. "I know you read this stuff so I checked it out for ya."

"Well," El Paso said accepting the book, "check it out, Bro. Check . . . It . . . Out! Thanks."

"Yeah, I was sure you'd want it."

"Hum," El Paso moaned reading the backcover then the table of contents.

"Hey," Molino said trying to maintain a mellowcool voice, "this . . . they say this is a bad AO."

"Could be worse," El Paso said detached, leafing through the book.

"Gotta be a bad AO. They tell me Rapper Rafe got clean scattered to the breeze."

"You mean Ridgefield?"

"They said you couldn't even find his chest or arms and that you guys just put the pieces in a bodybag."

"I wasn't there," El Paso said eyeing Molino. Molino was staring off toward the valley. "I wasn't there but that's not how it happened. Sniper got him. Only one round. Maybe two."

"That's not what I heard," Molino said lowly. "Shit. Him an Escalato in the same week. That's fucked, Man."

"Yeah, it's fucked," El Paso agreed matter-of-factly.

"No fuckin way I wanted to come out here, Man," Molino said. El Paso did not answer. "Don't nobody expect me to accept my own execution. That's for fools and Mama didn't raise no fools. I'm gonna fight it every mothafuckin step of the way. You'd do that, right?''

"Yeah," El Paso said.

"Hey," Molino said. "Hey Bro, would you do me a favor?"

"What do ya need?"

"Oh, it's nothin, Man. Maybe I shouldn't even ask." Molino squirmed pretending discomfort.

"What is it?"

"Well, I . . . ah . . . I was wonderin . . . ah . . . if you could, you know . . ."

"Know what, Man," El Paso let him squirm.

"If you could talk to the L-T, Bro," Molino pleaded. "I'd like to get inta the CP. Man, I can't even picture myself down with a squad. I'd probably get half of em killed if I ever had ta walk point."

"Naw, you'd be good, Bro." El Paso smiled to himself. "*Es verdad*. I know. You are a cagey person. You'd be very good to have at point."

"Oh no, no, no. Not me Bro. Hey . . . ah . . . I'm . . . ah . . . outa practice at that sort a thing. Bro, I know you could set it up for me. Man, I'd hump yer books if you get me into the CP."

"Ah, my friend . . ."

"El Paso," Molino was becoming frantic, "I'll hump yer batteries." El Paso looked down and shook his head. "Man, yer water. That's half the weight of yer ruck."

"I caint do, my friend," El Paso said sliding into a deep chicano accent. He threw up his hands. "L-T, he say, send Molino to Mohnsen. You go there. 2d Sqd, 2d Platoon. There, there is only Mohnsen and Sklar left. You caint kill half a squad when there are only three people."

The GreenMan burst upon Alpha bringing more enthusiasm than Alpha's ascension to the sun. Along with his radiant smile and praise he brought dry cigarettes and lighters, bug repellent, foot powder and a crate of XM-203s. He also had with him the battalion executive officer, Major Hellman, and Command Sergeant Major Zarnochuk. He had ordered them both to smile. All three looked pink against the grayness of Alpha. Pink and clean and spit-shined.

"Lieutenant," the GreenMan's voice was clear and strong, "you're doing one helluva fine job. One helluva fine job. You and your men have been wreaking havoc down there." The GreenMan raised his voice so the entire LZ crew could not help but hear him. "Your kind of success calls for rewards," the commander beamed, "and I've got a bunch coming your way. Major. Break out that first box. We'll get to the other one later."

Half a dozen troops had approached to a respectful distance. They squeezed closer. The GreenMan played to his audience. Major Hellman bent over slowly. He slit the cardboard with his knife and peeled back the lid. The GreenMan stepped forward. His eyes twinkled like a boy playing ringmaster beneath the bigtop. He reached into the box and pulled out five shiny chrome Zippo lighters and he tossed them to the infantrymen standing staring acting no different from the Vietnamese peasant children when they themselves tossed cigarettes or gum to the kids in a ville.

"Oh wow, Man! Look at this," the children-soldiers squealed. The lighters were engraved on one side with a map of Vietnam and on the other:

BOONIERAT

A / 7 / 402
101ST AIRBORNE
AUGUST '70
WAS A BITCH.

"There's one for every man here," the GreenMan beamed.

"Let's keep this orderly," Brooks said as a second half dozen soldiers clustered forward. "El Paso. Call the platoons. Have them send up one man from each squad for the lighters and cigarettes." Brooks bent and grabbed a lighter and smiled. The Zippo had a nice feel, a nice heft. "Thank you Sir," he said to the Green-Man and the GreenMan beamed brighter. In minutes every Alpha troop was smoking a firm dry cigarette lit with his new Zippo.

Then the smiles stopped. At one end of the LZ Old Zarno cussed out Jax for the hair pic stuck in his growing fuzzy 'fro. Hellman indiscreetly jumped on a sleepy FO for the sloppy example the forward observer was setting. FO was naked, ". . . in full view of enlisted troops." The GreenMan shook his head and hustled Brooks away from everyone with a 'Let's-have-a-look-around' gesture.

"Tell me about Delta," the GreenMan said when they were alone. "How were they set up? What were they doing when you were there? How did they act? Were they quiet?"

Brooks told him what he and the others had observed. The GreenMan seemed concerned, sincerely concerned and hurt. "How am I supposed to help these men?" the GreenMan whispered. "Lieutenant, if no one informs me about how badly one of my units is performing, I cannot correct it. That was a massacre, Lieutenant. And I've half a mind to have you court-martialed for not reporting O'Hare's incompetence to me." The GreenMan did not speak in anger. Not yet. He seemed very saddened by the event at Delta two nights previous. Then he burst out, "What the fuck was the motherfucker doing?" The GreenMan cussed like a trooper. "That sadass got his fucking self and five others killed. Seventeen wounded. If he hadn't got himself killed, I'd of killed him myself." He paused to take several deep breaths. Brooks had never seen the GreenMan upset. "Lieutenant, a lot of people in America are screaming about our ground forces still pursuing the enemy." The GreenMan's voice became bitter. "They're asking why we don't stay in our bases and let them come to us. Those people do not understand the first thing about war. If we sit in fixed defensive installations they'd murder us all in three months. We must constantly be searching for the enemy, finding him, hitting him before he can hit us. The moment we set up, the NVA moves. If we do not pursue he can resupply at will, advance at will. He can choose the time, the place, the method of attack. That's why we're out here. If you set up some hideous semi-permanent base here, like O'Hare, I promise you, the enemy will know and he will maul you. Get these men moving. Keep them moving. All my companies will be moving.

"That Delta thing, that was strictly a leadership failure," the GreenMan continued. "Lieutenant, O'Hare failed his men. Perhaps I failed O'Hare. I'm not going to fail you. You," the GreenMan called to a troop they were passing as they walked, "come here." Cherry approached the colonel. He was not sure if he should salute or not. "Why hasn't this man shaved?" the GreenMan growled at Brooks. "Look at his rucksack. It's filthy. A mess like that makes enough noise to let the entire valley know where you are. Get that man squared away. Lieutenant, follow me. I want to inspect every one of your troops."

Cherry sighed soundlessly watching the GreenMan stomp off.

"This entire battalion's too fat, too lazy." the GreenMan was now ranting with anger. "This is the 101st. This is SKYHAWKS, Seventh of the Four-oh-Deuce. I've stripped every possible man from the rear. You got Molino, that worthless candyass. Running a goddamned club when there's nobody in the rear except clerks and jerks. I've sent nine men to Delta, three to Bravo. All the cooks are on Barnett. We're going to lean-out this unit, Lieutenant. Every able-bodied man in the bush. You have two men in the rear on charges, don't you?"

"No Sir. That's another company."

"If you get any, they can wait for their trials out here."

"Yes Sir."

"I need leaders, Lieutenant. Any officer who can't do the job is . . . is not going to be transferred. He's going to become a rifleman. I'll make sergeants acting platoon leaders before I'll let a piss-poor lieutenant kill any of my men. If you have problems with your leaders, let me know. Right now. We'll shuffle them around this afternoon. I've got the authority to do that. What do you need?"

The GreenMan's rage had taken Brooks by surprise. "Nothing, Sir," he said without thinking.

As they passed through the 3d Plt CP set-up the GreenMan switched back to his salesmanager voice. "Rufus," he said, "I'm impressed with your moves so far. I think Alpha is doing a fantastic job. Truly fantastic. I know you've been plagued by the weather but the intelligence information alone that you have amassed has been enough to sufficiently alter the balance of force in this valley. The Old Fox said that to me himself. The NVA will never again be able to run through here unmolested."

The two commanders completed their circuit of the perimeter and were now back beside the LZ. The GreenMan again showed disappointment. He had taken in tremendous detail. As they stood the GreenMan listed every improperly discarded tin can, every unconcealed soldier, every weapon lying on the ground and not ready in the hands of a boonierat. Then they stood in the shade of vine-choked trees and peered into the valley and discussed intelligence reports and tactics. Brooks retold him of Leech Row and of the enemy roads and the thickets and fog. "You go back down there and finish the job, Lieutenant," the GreenMan said. "You can do it. It won't take much longer. There's two less enemy there now than there was this morning. My pilot and I got two on our way over here."

"Yes Sir. I heard," Brooks smiled. He paused then said, "Sir, about my request to DEROS . . ."

"You go back there, Lieutenant. Finish the job and you can go home knowing you left this country safer. You should be able to clean this place up in two or three days. Go back down there, Lieutenant. Become a guerrilla behind the guerrilla lines. Can you do that?"

"Yes Sir," Brooks said. The GreenMan seemed to be expecting him to say more so he added, "I can hide down there, Sir. In the thickets. Among them. We can pick them apart, piece by piece."

"Good," the GreenMan smiled. He was satisfied. "Follow me," he beamed loudly marching to the unopened crate he had brought to the LZ with the cigarettes and lighters. "Break that one open, Major. Lieutenant, bring up all your thumpermen."

Major Hellman broke open the crate and lifted from it the first new XM-203. The XM-203 was a replacement for the M-79. It was an over/under, an M-16 rifle on top mated to an M-79 grenade launcher on the bottom, all on an M-16 stock. Hellman handed one to Old Zarno then reached in and lifted another. "Look at these beauties," he said smiling. And indeed the men who received them considered them beauties.

"You'll be a one man army with that," the GreenMan said to one smiling troop. "What's your name?"

"Willis, Sir," Numbnuts said smartly snapping the new weapon to his shoulder.

"That's the first one of its kind in all I Corps," the GreenMan said to Numbnuts. "You've got the first, Alpha's got the first nine." The sound of the C & C bird could be heard as it approached Alpha's location. "Good luck with those," the GreenMan beamed to all of the company's thumpermen. "And good hunting." The C & C bird hovered, set down. The GreenMan saluted Brooks. "Find em. Fix em. Fight em. Finish em. For the glory of the Infantry, Lieutenant."

Brooks returned the salute. "SKYHAWKS, Sir," he said sharply.

The third bird in brought mail, clothes, two members of the 7/402 battalion kitchen staff and mermite cans of Kool-Aid and chipped beef.

"What the fuck is this?" Molino moaned to Mohnsen when the kitchen orderly slopped a ladleful of the brownred mush atop a soggy piece of toast and handed it to him on a paper plate.

"What the fuck do you care?" the orderly laughed.

"It aint Cs," Mohnsen smiled.

"Shit-on-a-shingle," Molino shook his head. "Christ, last time we had this was when Zarno threw that correspondent out of the mess hall."

"What correspondent?" De Barti asked from behind Molino.

"Didn't you guys hear?" Molino asked.

"Naw," said Calhoun. "We never hear nothin."

"That dude, Caribski," Molino laughed. "Lamonte brought him down to battalion mess. You shoulda seen Zarno. He turned red as a beet. Begins screamin at this guy. Ya know, this dude's got muttonchop sideburns and hair about this long." Molino motioned with his hand just above his shoulder. " 'Get outa here,' Zarno screams. 'We don't want no bums in our mess hall. Get out.' I mean Zarno's screamin at him. PIO is there tryin ta calm Zarno down. 'Sergeant Major,' he says, 'this man is a civilian news correspondent.' 'I don't give a shit,' Zarno yells. 'Get that long-haired hippie bum outa my mess hall.' I thought Zarno was goina hit him. Instead he shoves Lamonte. You shoulda seen it."

"Well, what happened?" Mohnsen asked. Five of them had worked their way through the chow line and now sat clustered in the sun on the LZ.

"The guy got up and left," Molino laughed. "He got up and walked out and everybody got up and gave him a standing ovation. Man, you shoulda seen Zarno. His whole face turned purple. I thought he'd blow a blood vessel right there on the spot."

"Man, I wish I was there," Calhoun said.

"What for?" De Barti laughed. "This food's worse than Cs." They all laughed.

"You know what they do at division?" Molino said. He was enjoying being the center of attention.

"Tell us, Man," Mohnsen said. Mohnsen had clung to Molino ever since the ex-bartender had been assigned to him. Molino somehow filled the vacancies in Mohnsen's mind, the vacancies of the dead and wounded from his squad.

"Man, you wouldn't believe it," Molino said. "But I shit you not, this is the God's honest truth."

"Come on," De Barti prodded him.

"You know," Molino said, "like at the general's mess. He has, like, thirty people to dinner every night."

"Bet they don't eat this shit," Hayes laughed.

"Man, like they eat steak or lobster tail every night. Every night, Man. They get a choice of three entrees. And, they get served immediately. Steak, lobster tails and one other every night. Rabbit or chicken or duck. That's the third. You know how they do it?"

"Oh wow. I wish I could eat there just one night a month," Calhoun said.

"How?" De Barti asked.

"You know how they can serve everybody immediately?"

"How?"

"They cook up three times as many entrees as people they got comin. Then if everybody orders lobster they got thirty lobsters cooked up. They dump the rest of it."

"Naw. No way."

"I shit you not. Dudes on KP got it set up so they always throw the leftover entrees inta one garbage can. Then at night the dudes from the headquarters companies, they sneak down and eat the general's garbage."

"Mail for Choo-lee-nee," El Paso called out as he came toward 1st Plt. "Sorry, Bro," he whispered to Egan. "Nother letter for Choo-lee-nee. Nother letter for Choo-lee-nee. Oooo! This one smells nice. Postcard for Choo-lee-nee."

Cherry blushed. A postcard and three letters. Half the mail for 1st Plt and all for him. El Paso read the card aloud. " 'Dear Jimmy, We always think of you and I pray for you every night. Uncle Tony said CYA—you'd understand. Much love, Aunt Millie.' Aaww, aint that sweet! Oooo-ooo! Smell this one." El Paso handed the letter to Doc McCarthy who sniffed it and passed it to Cherry.

Cherry got up all smiles. He moved a short distance away and opened the letter from Linda. As he began reading he heard El Paso say, "Anyone want Leon's *Newsweek*? Here's some good shit. Listen, '. . . five years of warfare against the US have so badly depleted Viet Cong ranks that today an estimated 75% of the communist troops in main-force units are North Vietnamese . . . barred by a lack of popular support from reverting entirely to guerrilla warfare, the communists are limited in what they can accomplish . . .' "

"Hey, El Paso," Thomaston chuckled. "Who the fuck are the other twenty-five percent?"

Cherry shuffled the pages of Linda's letter, looked at them for a moment without reading as if the shape or color might tell him what she would say. Then he read.

Hi Jim!

Guess what? I got a new job in downtown Norwalk. I'm a secretary to two men who sold their business about eight years ago and bought a whole bunch of properties which they manage. It's a real small office—the two owners, a bookkeeper, an accountant and me. I'm the only girl. I know I couldn't have stood working in a big office with all the catty women so I found something more me. I bet you thought by now I'd be off somewhere carousing, huh? Well, I was a little confused as to what I wanted but things are a little better now. Not that I'm settling in, I'm just content for now.

My sister got engaged about a week ago and is getting married in October. She hardly knows the guy. He isn't exactly welcomed into the family either but if she wants to marry a darkie (he's not black, just dark) that's her business.

My Dad got a new car. It's white. I already don't like it because the first time I got into it I hit my head. I'll probably hold this grudge against it until I smash it up. Dad wants me to get one of my own but I say I don't need a car. There's always one available here if I want it.

Oh, what else has happened? I made it to Boston last month and I love it there. If things work out as I hope they will, next January I may take an apartment up there with a friend who goes to college in Boston. I'll work. I really love Boston. The people are very friendly.

If my money situation works out I'll have enough for a car and an apartment. My parents won't say too much. What can they say? If they say no, I'll go anyway and they know it. I know they wouldn't hold me back from doing anything. I made it to NYC a few days since you left. I've a friend at Columbia, so I stay there for freesies. I don't really like New York too much, but for a lack of anything else better to do, I go there.

Time out to eat. I'm still a skinny little bitch! One night I went for a ride because I was bored. I stopped at a

gas station and asked where I was just out of curiosity.
Massachusetts. Nice little ride I had.

Well, Jim, have a happy. I'll be thinking about you.

Love,
Linda

"God, Mista. Oh God!" Doc was sobbing.

"What's the matter, Doc?" Egan asked. They were at the
CP. The radio message had arrived just before Egan came up to
talk to Brooks about their move back into the valley. "What is
it?" Egan asked perplexed. He could not imagine anything that
had happened to Alpha or to any of the battalion units that would
cause Doc to cry now.

"It's Whiteboy, Eg. Aw Eg. They got Whiteboy. They got
his bird wid a .51 cal, Mista, they done got his mothafucken bird
comin outa Barnett. In the chest, Eg. A .51 cal in the chest."

Egan stopped. Everything in him stopped. He looked at Doc
then turned without saying a word and walked away.

Whiteboy had boarded a helicopter on the firebase which
would take him to Camp Eagle. The forward supply crew had
razzed him about his minor eye wound and he had laughed with
them. Then as the bird left the peak and sped down the mountainside an NVA fire team had opened up with a .51 caliber machine
gun. Several rounds impacted in the bird doing minor damage.
One round hit Whiteboy in the lower left abdomen. The round
smashed upward at an angle moving through his diaphragm and
stomach, shattering ribs and exiting through his right front chest.
It took the helicopter sixteen minutes to have him at the 326th
Medical Detachment at Camp Evans. He received immediate aid
and was flown to Phu Bai and operated on. He was then evacuated to Da Nang. The next day Clayton Janoff would be evacuated farther, this time to Zama, Japan, where he would die
seventeen days after having been wounded.

In late afternoon the back bird arrived to take out the
kitchen staff and mermite cans, all the unclaimed food and
weapons and anything else Alpha wanted to DX but did not want
to fall into enemy hands. The sun was still hot like a white fever
blister in the sky. Alpha was packed and ready to move. The LZ
was spotless. Brooks had screamed at every troop within range
after the GreenMan had left and after the shock of Whiteboy's
wounding had jolted him. "Clean this site," he had snapped. "I

don't want to see an uncrushed can, a usable piece of cardboard or a usable fighting position. Don't leave a fucking thing the dinks can use. And if I hear a sound from a soul, every man here's going to pay."

And Alpha had cleaned. They cleaned their weapons and themselves and they cleaned the LZ. Even in their filthy ragged fatigues every troop looked sharp. Everything was tightened, trimmed. Ammunition was cleaned, almost polished. Alpha knew it was going to fight. Alpha wanted a fight. And in their fight the last thing they wanted was a weapon jammed with mud-caked ammo. They cleaned with hate, prepared with hatred. Fuck up Whiteboy, huh? Have the colonel yell at our L-T, huh? Well, fuck em. We'll show em.

Then the back bird arrived. Alpha had received almost no clean fatigues from the company clothes fund during resupply but now they received one-hundred-fifty pair of clean dry boot socks. They had received seventy-five tiny bottles of insect repellent. Now they received two-hundred-fifty bottles more. Doc hustled around distributing the goods and Alpha sat, changed socks and cooled down.

Alpha moved out, up around down, back onto the valley floor. They leap-frogged down and west. 3d Plt led then 2d with the Co CP and finally 1st. As the others left the high ground, 1st Plt dug and chopped pretending to be digging in for the night. 3d Plt moved slowly, in column, through the discontinuous brush and on into thickets of bamboo. They halted and formed a tiny perimeter. 2d Plt followed 3d by twenty minutes. They reached 3d's position and worked through and beyond by 200 meters. Then they too halted. 1st Plt left the LZ and followed. They moved through 3d, then through 2d and finally beyond, west 200 meters.

During the descent to the valley floor Brooks was plagued with doubt. "Step by step," he whispered to himself trying to dispel the uncertainty. "Step by step. Down into a tiny hell I struggle to go. May the gods pardon me for leading seventy-five men into this inferno." Then he stopped whispering and just thought. Why do I do this bidding for others? Why do I ask these soldiers to do bidding for me? Stop it. Don't question it. Not now. Step by step. Down. One step at a time. One thought at a time. One tree, one blade of elephant grass. An endless progression of life goes before me. One by one. Steps, trees, thoughts, lives.

Twenty minutes after 1st Plt had stopped, 3d rose. 3d leap-frogged 2d then 1st and moved 200 meters beyond. At each set-up Alpha hoped to catch the NVA moving. They spotted no movement. They slipped back under the valley's mistblanket and the mist sapped the sun's residual warmth from their bodies. The trail was thickslick mud. The valley stench clogged their throats like sputum in the throat of a derelict. Old fears surrounded them like the mist, dampening their hatred and bravado. They fought the fears.

"Hey, Cherry," Egan whispered, "aint we about on the 18th hole of yer golf course."

"Yeah," Cherry laughed, fidgeted. "I'm goina put the green right under yer ass."

"You leave my ass alone," Egan winked. "Play with yer own putter."

Beneath the mist it had become dark. The platoons continued leap-frogging. Now west, now north. One klick. Two klicks. They were in it deep, in thick vegetation, in enemy territory. The knoll would be only 500 meters north of them. Brooks called a halt. No one made a sound. No one ate. FO radioed in DT and H & I coordinates so quietly that Brown next to him couldn't hear. And Alpha sat. It became darker.

"Hey, Cherry." It was Thomaston. "Company's staying here tonight," he whispered. "You got LP. Go out—to the north about fifty meters. Take Willis with you."

"With Numbnuts?!" Cherry blurted.

"Ssshhh. Yeah."

"No way, Sir."

"What?"

"No fucken way, Sir."

"It's your turn," Thomaston said.

"I'll go," Cherry said, "but if Numbnuts is goin, I aint. No way."

"What do you mean you're not going?"

"Hey, that noisy fucker falls asleep every night," Cherry whispered.

"I do not," Numbnuts' voice came from behind Thomaston.

"I aint goin with him," Cherry said firmly but quietly.

"I didn't fall asleep that night . . ." Numbnuts began then his voice muffled and Cherry could hear Egan on top of Numbnuts whispering shut-up and cursing.

"Me en Cherry'll go," Egan whispered to Thomaston. Numbnuts disappeared in the darkness.

Cherry crawled behind Egan, crawled, duck-walked, slithered, down a narrow path and then into a thicket. They moved very little yet managed to open a tiny two-man cave in the growth. Then Egan left. He set out two claymore mines beside the path then returned to the cave. They positioned the radio between them, their rifles across their legs, frags spread before them, they sat for a long time without speaking. Both were awake, alert, listening.

Egan broke the silence after two hours. "How's your lady?" he asked very quietly.

Cherry paused before answering, taking time to listen to the darkness. "Okay," he answered. Then, "She's a spoiled bitch."

They spoke now very quietly, leaving long gaps between phrases to listen. "Good lookin?" Egan asked.

"Beautiful," Cherry whispered.

"I'm a fucken fool when it comes to beautiful women," Egan confessed.

"I've done some pretty dumb things myself," Cherry admitted.

They sat silent again for a long time then Egan told Cherry an anecdote from his high school days. Because of the pauses the story took an hour. "I had a crush on this one lady," Egan said. "She was captain of the cheerleaders and, Man, she had the greatest legs in the world . . . and I was a shy mothafucker . . . One time I take one of the other cheerleaders to a dance and we go parking afterward and I play all sorts of games so I can grab her tits and stick my hand on her pussy . . . feel her all over . . . had a great time. Word gets out I'm fast . . . shy me, fast. I aint never been a fast dude in my life but I don't give a shit about this one so I grab her all over. Annie with the great legs lets it be known that she wants to go out with me and the next dance is after our last football game . . . I work up the nerve to ask her. I could talk to her but I couldn't ask her out . . . finally I ask her . . . she's let everyone know she wants to go with me so of course she accepts. I'm trippin. I don't know if this is gettin across to ya. I had a crush on her . . . she was the prettiest girl in my school and I was a funny lookin Irish kid who tripped over his tongue. Annie says she'd go. I almost cream my fatigues on the spot." Egan paused for a long time. He was not sure if Cherry was listening or if he could even hear him. He was not really sure he was speaking at all. "I take her to the dance and she's got to sit up on some podium because she's Queen of the Victory Parade . . . somethin like that. I'm gettin frustrated . . . can't say anything cause I'm shy. After the dance we go out . . . we're doublin with this dude who's our star tailback. We go out to the bluffs . . . that's where we always go parkin. He and his honey are gettin it on in the front seat while this lady and I, I'm terrified, we're talkin in the back seat and I don't know what to do. Then Annie leans over and begins kissin me and Man, I'm in number-ten shock. Like I can't respond . . . Fucked up, huh?"

Cherry laughed very quietly, so quietly Egan did not hear. He said nothing for perhaps twenty minutes. Then he said, "I did that once too." Long pause. "Once I had a crush on this chick. I useta walk by her house late at night . . . shit like that."

"I useta do that with Annie," Egan whispered.

Ten-minute pause. "One time I'm out cleanin the yard," Cherry said. "She walked by . . . she said hi and I turned red. She walked on. Man, I waited til she was outa sight then I ran behind the stores, circled back up the block and came walkin down the sidewalk toward her . . . like three blocks away. All I could do was smile . . . she laughs and we walk by each other . . . Then I circle the buildings again. I think I gotta say somethin to her. I run up the backstreet to her street . . . sit against a tree and wait for her and she comes walkin up and she looks scared and runs by. I never talked to her once and I was always ashamed when I saw her after that."

"Fucked up, huh?" Egan laughed.

"Yeah," Cherry said.

Doc and Minh had gone to sleep on a tiny mound on the valley floor. It was not much of a mound but it had felt drier and softer than the surrounding mud and they had covered it with one poncho, covered themselves with the other and had gone to sleep. Suddenly they both woke and both were burning all over. They felt as if someone were lighting matches on their skin. Doc jumped and jerked. Minh rubbed himself all over. They both jumped up. They were on top an anthill and both of them were covered with ants. The ants bit their legs and backs and stomachs and scalps. The bites burned. There were ants in their boots. It was almost as if the ants had covered them cautiously then on

command all began biting at once. It was pitch black. Doc and
Minh tried to be silent but the ants were eating them. They
pulled their gear away from the mound and stumbled on bushes
in the dark. "Au, au," Minh squealed quietly. "Mothafucka,"
Doc cried grabbing his armpits and falling to his knees. They
shook out their ponchos. Cahalan and Brooks rose and questioned them and helped them but they couldn't get away from the
ants. Doc sprayed a full bottle of insect repellent on himself. He
covered his face. There were ants hiding in the kinks of his hair.
He ripped at his scalp. He rubbed repellent into his hair and got
it in his eyes and it stung. Minh splashed the repellent on his
clothes but that did no good. They could not see the ants to brush
them off. They stripped and washed themselves in repellent.

Sporadically through the night a single ant would sting one
or the other.

The talk of their ladies had set Egan consciously to thinking
of Stephanie. He would write her one more time, he decided.
One short letter. He would write her in the morning, he decided,
but he would think now about what he would say. Relaxing now,
he penned in his mind. Can't get enthusiastic about this war or
this country anymore, he imagined writing. It isn't a good war to
stay at or to watch for very long. I've been here too long. Shit. I
can't write her that. He closed his eyes and tried to make her
appear. He could feel her burning within him. Deep inside all
good things burn, he told himself. All things of enough good for
one to recognize their existence. Any feeling, if it is strong
enough, if it works its way from the mind down to the viscera, is
good. That's where you are, Steph. You are strong enough in me
to exist, to move me, to obsess me. Saying those words, saying
her name, made him feel very clear-headed and peaceful.

Egan looked about in the silent blackness. He leaned against
the radio and felt Cherry's arm on the box. "I'm sackin," he
whispered.

"Roger that," Cherry answered.

Now Egan dreamed of Stephanie. He could see her. They
were in the park. When? It must have been very late. Pigeons
cooed. Small birds tweeked. He laughed and danced and laughed
again. The boughs of the trees swooshed with the wind in
rhythm to his jig. Leaves swirled on the walks in miniature
tornadoes. The sun felt warm. She sat there cold. She laughed at
his jig. "Come on now," he sang out. "Aren't you alive? Can't

you feel the joy of this beautiful planet?'' Stephanie sat and smiled and looked pretty. Perhaps she was angry. He had not interpreted it that way then. It's nice to be free with the breeze, he had thought. To be high with the wind is wonderful but for her it is impossible. What's the matter with her? What's going on? Her blood seems to run too thickly through her brain for her to move. Perhaps it is her precision, her preciseness, that won't allow her to move, to dance, to sing. That's crazy, he now thought. She had such beauty of movement.

"Come here," his image ordered her. She did not move. "Come here," he pleaded. "Come and love with me."

"You're a fool," Stephanie said graciously. Daniel heard her say it, heard her now. It had been a bitter thing to say and she looked away sorry for having said it but he had not been aware of her then, except that she seemed unable to move.

Perhaps he had known it. They both knew he had been too lax this time. He hadn't written. He hadn't called. How much time had he allowed to pass, he could not recall. It must have been too much. He had not even answered her letters. I got bogged down in my studies, he told himself. His memory of those last letters was hazy yet he could see excerpts of Stephanie's beautiful handwriting.

I feel like you're right here with me. Oh Daniel, I wish you were here. I really want to kiss you. When are you coming. I'm so anxious. I so want to see you and hear you.

One letter was a series of overlapping and interlocking sketches. They were exquisite. Faces of children, still lifes of pillows and wine bottles and candles in long slender candelabrums. And eyes. Very fine lines catching every detail of soft and harsh eyes.

The short letter arrived. This one burned deeply when the words passed through Egan's mind.

Dear Daniel,
    I don't know what your opinion will be but I feel I must tell you what's been happening to me these past months. Up until today I thought I was very much pregnant. I have been terribly upset—Oh Christ! I don't even want to talk about it, but everything from suicide to running away has been clogging my head. Trying to make plans to go

back to school but not knowing if I could see them through. I suppose you can imagine. I went to a doctor a few weeks ago and he said it was too early to tell. The relief of mind I had today was amazing.

I am going to school. Looked all day for a room but didn't find one. It's 1:30. I should be asleep but I had to write you. I tried writing before but I just couldn't. You know, Daniel, I think you're more trouble than you're worth. I've been very much alone. It was bad throwing around the thought of pregnancy again.

Daniel, when trust goes out of love, then love has lost its meaning and is no more. Trust is part of love and freedom and friendship. As trust runs down relationships strain and the habitants become jailed by their fears of each other. Trust is not built on words or pleasantries. It has to be a mutual pact built on sharing and on responsibility. One must give as one receives. One must respect the life of another, and must have that respect returned for trust and love to grow and for one to say and have said of him, "Him I trust. Him I love."

I'm sorry about this letter but it's late—I'm tired—but I knew I couldn't sleep until I wrote.

Sometimes I wonder where my mind, my heart and my soul are. Or if they even are. I'm sure they are but blissfulness makes them love to hide.

> Love,
> Stephanie

I was crazy about you, Daniel said to her in his mind as he lay in the muck of the valley floor. Don't you see, he tried to explain. I had to go. We were caught up by a world that ran us. That ran over us. I remember saying good-bye to you. You always made me so happy. I think I said to you, 'Neither you nor I wish to have the things having each other would bring. You'd never have security with me and I'd never feel free with you.' Oh Steph, I remember saying that. I remember the song that was playing in the car the day I left.

> *We sang in the sunshine,*
> *We laughed every day,*
> *We sang in the sunshine,*
> *Til I went on my way.*

Stephanie, now my year is over. Oh shit. I'm sorry. I remember you said I hurt you. I don't think it ever sunk in until maybe just now. Oh God, I'm such a dumb Mick. How long is that? Three years? I'm pretty slow. You'll have to help me. Can I say it now—I'm sorry if I hurt you.

SIGNIFICANT ACTIVITIES

THE FOLLOWING RESULTS FOR OPERATIONS IN THE O'REILLY/ BARNETT/JEROME AREA WERE REPORTED FOR THE 24-HOUR PERIOD ENDING 2359 20 AUGUST 70:

DURING THE ENTIRE DAY SPORADIC FIGHTING WAS REPORTED BY THE 2D AND 4TH BNS, 1ST REGT (ARVN) IN THE FIREBASE O'REILLY AREA. ENEMY LOSSES INCLUDED 250 ONE-HALF POUND SACHEL CHARGES, 100 82MM MORTAR ROUNDS AND FIVE CREW SERVED WEAPONS. ARVN CASUALTIES WERE TWO KIA AND NINE WIA.

THE 7TH BN, 402D INF CONTINUED OPERATIONS IN THE VICIN-ITY OF FIREBASE BARNETT ON THIS DATE WITH ONLY LIGHT CONTACT. AT 1427 HOURS THE BATTALION COMMANDER'S C & C HELICOPTER SPOTTED FOUR NVA IN THE OPEN. ARTILLERY WAS EMPLOYED RESULTING IN TWO NVA KIA. AT 1710 HOURS A HELI-COPTER FROM D COMPANY, 101ST AVIATION BN RECEIVED .51 CALIBER MACHINE GUN FIRE WHILE DEPARTING FROM FIREBASE BARNETT. ONE US SOLDIER WAS WOUNDED. THE AIRCRAFT RECEIVED MINOR DAMAGE.

AT 1830 HOURS FIREBASE BARNETT RECEIVED 19 ROUNDS OF 61MM MORTAR FIRE, SEVEN IMPACTING WITHIN THE PERIMETER. ONE US SOLDIER WAS WOUNDED. COUNTER BATTERY FIRE WAS EMPLOYED WITH UNKNOWN RESULTS.

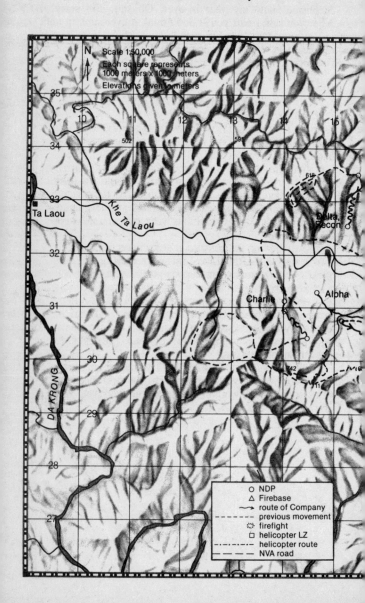

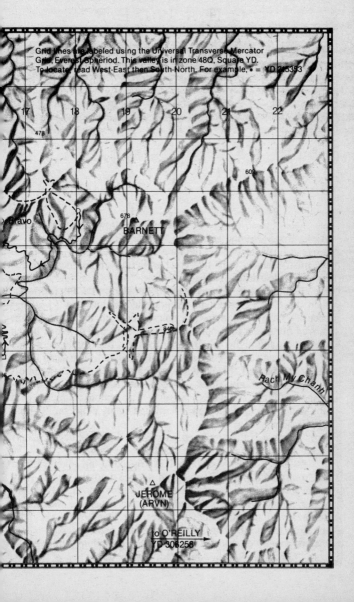

Grid lines are labeled using the Universal Transverse Mercator
Grid, Everest Spheriod. This valley is in zone 48Q, Square YD.
To locate, read West-East then South-North. For example, ● = YD 215353

17   18   19   20   21   22

478

605

678
BARNETT

Bravo

840

Rach My Chanh

JEROME
(ARVN)

to O'REILLY
YD 306258

CHAPTER

████ 28 ████

21-23 AUGUST 1970
CAMPOBASSO

The sky yellowed and stood still. Alpha froze. No one seemed to breathe. Then the mist began to move, to roll, to twist. Lightning split the heavens, flashbulbed the mist. Thunder burst like great artillery. Rain fell heavy, hard, in close thick drops. Alpha moved.

Egan led off. Cherry walked his slack. 1st Plt followed, then the Co CP, 2d Plt in the protected middle and 3d at rear security. The column moved quickly beneath the dawn storm, moved northwest then north to the river's edge. The move began three days and nights which lost Alpha in a blurring haze of time and space and rain. The recent past dissolved. The near future never approached. Black nights passed to dark gray days almost without distinction. Alpha scrapped with the NVA—small running firefights, ambushes, pursuits. The actions mingled with non-action, became encased in hardened empty dullness, in glass-eyed madness.

"Fuck it," they repeated a thousand times. "Fuck it. Don't mean nothin. Drive on." The mantra of the infantry.

"Got it," Cherry said. He had stripped in the cold rain, tied the rope about his waist and had slipped into the river. They were 800 meters west of the knoll at valley center. The frigid water chilled him and softened his oozing sores. He was barely cognizant of the chill and the sores. He focused his eyes and mind on the north shore. Artillery rounds exploded 200 to 500 meters downriver. Mortar rounds impacted randomly upriver.

"Go for it," Egan whispered. Cherry dove.

1st Plt was spread on line at the river's edge, a meter inside the vegetation. All eyes were on Cherry breast stroking silently against the rainswell waters, or on the north bank shrub mist searching for movement. Asses were in three inches of cold rain mud.

"This is fucked," Jax whispered to Doc. "This mofuck division fucked up."

"What he pushin fo?" Doc shook his head woefully. "What fo, Mista?"

"L-T gettin fucked up," Jax said.

"He pushin too hard," Doc said. "He becomin a lifer. I can't believe it, Bro. He aint nevah goan leave."

"We's all gowin die here," Jax said painfully. "We's all gowin die."

"Why, Mista? Why?"

"Asshole." Egan joined Doc and Jax in the grass. He raged quietly not perceiving their mood.

"What's happenin, Bro?" Doc asked.

"Rope's goina drown Little Brother in the blue feature. Assholes. Shoulda never sent him across. Nobody could swim that shit." Cherry was approaching mid-stream, pulling, snapping into a short glide, pulling, working like mad, making no discernible progress through the main current.

"Dis fucked," Jax repeated.

"Fuck it," Egan snarled.

Cherry exerted, inched toward the north bank. The current was forcing him downstream, the rope holding him in the on-rush. He reached, pulled, extended, pulled. All of 1st Plt watched. Pull, they cheered him silently. Pull. Cherry's frogkick clapped, his arms pulled, he shot forward a foot, glided, the current pushed him back ten inches, he stroked again. Past mid-stream, toward the north bank, the current fell off. He reached, pulled, reached the bank. Up. Out. Disappeared into the land of Leech Row. Egan stripped off everything except his fatigue pants. He plunged into the river with his and Cherry's M-16s and pulled himself across on the rope. Mechanically 1st Plt converged on the rope, waded into the river and pulled. Cherry returned to the water as lifeguard and guide, then Egan assisted and then Brooks.

"I didn't know black men could swim," Egan nudged Cherry over Brooks' back, all three fighting cold riverwater swell to stay in place.

"They can't," Brooks laughed looking quickly from Egan to Cherry. "I've got Dago blood in me. The oil keeps me up."

Then they were up and out and Alpha was again moving quickly, moving, spraying insect repellent on the leeches, rain diluting the repellent, leeches sucking, boonierats bitching. "Fuck it. Don't mean nothin. Drive on."

Alpha followed a streambed north. It was hardly more than a watery shallow gutter in the valley floor yet it afforded two advantages. It was lower than the surrounding earth giving them a natural protective, concealing trench. And it made the going easier. Woody brush and vegetation choked both streambanks. Branches bridged the narrow trench at three, four, five feet. Only grass grew in the streambed, grass and leeches. Thighs and legs swished through the grass re-saturating fatigues and boots with every step. Moneski lead Alpha north 150 meters through the tunnel then emerged east into a thicket. Alpha inched across the valley floor crossing trail after trail, red balls, and an engineered road with traffic signs that Minh said warned enemy logistic and supply troops against loitering. Alpha moved east 700 meters to another dense thicket, a thicket across the river from the knoll, 150 meters north of the swollen river.

"Man, this is so thick, we could stay right here," Egan told Brooks. "Nobody could touch us. They couldn't attack into this shit. With a half-dozen OPs en LPs, we could wreak havoc down here."

"No way, Man," Bill Brown shook his head.

Brooks smiled. Egan asked Brown, "Why not? Think about it. If they were set up in a thicket as thick as this shit, could we attack them? Ya can't walk in here. Ya can't move up on anybody in force."

"Like Br'er Rabbit," Doc chuckled nastily from behind. "Doan throw me in the briar patch. L-T, doan throw me up in them hills."

"It may be possible," Brooks said. He had already decided. He called a halt.

Alpha was in the middle of an elongated network of NVA supply trails. Brooks ordered them to circle up, slip in and hide. Let the morning and the rain come.

Alpha hid. Morning came. The rain continued. The position was a low area, a large shallow pit, surrounded by a natural earthen berm and cloaked beneath a variety of very dense vegetation. The CP set up near the center of the pit and the platoons manned the berm. Brooks had the word passed, "We're staying until tomorrow." The boonierats dug in quietly. They carved small hollows and trenches under the thickest brambles or bamboo clusters. Quarters were close. Two of every three men slept, slept soggy, rested, prepared for the day and night to come.

Like all Americans they could not resist giving their location a name. Their base NDP came to be known amongst them as Campobasso. It was Cherry who came up with the name. In Italian Campobasso meant low field or possibly base camp. Cherry did not tell the L-T or Egan or any of his boonierat brothers that Campobasso was his maternal grandparents' hometown. He simply suggested the name and it stuck. The name fit. It was easy radio-ese. Alpha used it. Cherry loved it.

"What do you think, Pop?" Brooks whispered to Pop Randalph.

"Don't know, Sir," Pop answered in his high hoarse whisper.

Brooks sat cross-legged, draped with a poncho, his notebook and his maps across his lap. "Three tours? Why Pop? What makes you keep coming back for more?" The L-T's voice was barely audible.

"You know why I'm heah, Sir?" Pop rasped. "I'm heah, Sir, because I am a soldier. An I'm a good soldier. I'm a better platoon sergeant than you'll find anywhere. Except for that dumb son of a bitch, Mohnsen, I'd have a near perfect record."

"But what keeps you here?" Brooks asked. "What keeps you as a soldier here?"

"Sir," Pop's face twitched. "We have a mission. An I can accomplish that mission better'n anyone else. Better en with less loss of life."

"Do you really believe that, Pop?" Brooks asked. He asked it sincerely without the slightest skepticism.

"Yes Sir," Pop answered.

"Good," Brooks said. "Who's going with you?"

"Sergeant Egan en his cherry."

"Good," Brooks said.

Pop, Egan and Cherry had volunteered for the first MA mission. From Campobasso Brooks had already sent out six LP/OPs. Recon patrols were being organized. Ambush teams would come later. Brooks called them all Rover Teams and the

name excited the boonierats. At dusk they would go out in every
direction to determine the enemy situation and feed information
to the commander for the planned assault on the headquarters
complex, if they could find it, if it existed. But first, Brooks
decided, we must disrupt NVA movement all about us. We'll set
MAs on the red balls.

The three men of the first team emptied their pockets. They
removed all excess equipment. Using only light webbing Cherry
strapped his radio tightly against his back. Egan carried five
claymore mines in a towel. Pop carried a used radio battery, rolls
of det cord and trip wire, a slide-type trigger mechanism and
blasting caps. All three carried their 16s, bandoleers of magazines and four fragmentation grenades each.

"Break squelch twice," El Paso instructed Cherry. "Then
all's cool. Three times you sittin tight waitin for trouble to pass.
Four, you comin back in. We'll notify the perimeter."

"Right on, Bro," Cherry whispered.

Rover Team Stephanie departed north, moving quickly beyond
the perimeter, out beyond the LP/OP toward the enemy road
below the north escarpment. Wind and rain covered their movement and the sound of their footfalls. Pop led them unmercifully
under the heaviest thickets, through the most vile muck, into the
stench of sewer-decay humus, a path the NVA would never
choose, would never expect Americans to attempt. Much of the
time they crawled. Between each motion they lay flat, listening.
They moved more and more slowly, crossing trails only when
necessary, skirting them when possible. They lay motionless,
face-in-the-muck prone for ever-increasing periods. Then they
crawled again. The road/red ball was north, they had only to
avoid enemy and head generally north and they would hit it. "If
they can't see you, they can't shoot you," Egan had said to
Cherry before they had left. "They aint goan see us," Pop
winked.

Now they lay before the road, in a foul quagmire. They lay
prone beneath brambles. They observed. They listened. Their
ears were stimulated just below their threshold of recognition.
Had an enemy squad just passed? Had they almost been stepped
on? It reminded Cherry of summer night hide-and-seek when he
was young. His favorite place to hide had been in the thick grass
below the quince trees. There he would watch his brother Vic
walk by, almost step on him. Cherry laughed silently to himself.
Can't find me, mothafuckas. His body trembled.

* * *

Egan looked at Cherry. That dumb mothafucker, he thought. He's got to experience it all. Can't tell him a fuckin thing. Egan wanted to shake him. Cherry, he wanted to say, for godchristsakes can't you listen and learn? Can't you see all I'm tryin ta do is teach you, speed up your learning so you don't have to make the same mistakes I made? It's a wonder mankind's gotten as far as it has, Egan thought. It's a wonder we're not all still learning and relearning that fire burns. Fuck it. Maybe we are.

L-T's goan nuts, Pop thought, though he could not describe it to himself. Tactically their maneuver was perfect. He had never seen such an AO and he had never known a commander to direct and execute an infiltration so superbly. Yet something was not right. L-T en his questions, Pop scrunched up his face thinking. L-T goan nuts.

Cherry's thoughts skipped. We could talk about our home lives and our upbringing. I could tell Jax or Doc about my family and they could tell me about theirs. I'd say, 'I never had a black friend. I mean, like, I never truly knew a black person.' I could say, 'I grew up with blacks. You know, we went to school together, played together. Every once in a while we went to each other's homes. But it was always like another world to me, as if I didn't understand the language or wasn't allowed. It was as if there was a law against getting to know a black.' And then his imagination filled with Doc saying, 'Fo blacks, it is a law.' Squelch broke twice on Cherry's radio, El Paso signaling for a situation report. Cherry keyed his handset twice and stared at the road. All was still except the rain and the wind.

Pop stealthily slipped from the muck and slid to the road. Egan signaled Cherry to stay put. He followed Pop onto the road. Without an utterance they commenced to deploy the ambush. Egan set one claymore two feet off the road, below brush, ten feet up the road. He angled the mine slightly upward, up and across the road. Pop unscrewed the plastic fastener used to secure a blasting cap, inserted an end of det cord and screwed the fastener back in place. Then he unrolled the cord and brought it across the road to where Egan was aiming a second claymore. Pop measured the cord, cut it and returned to the road. Carefully he camouflaged the cord, burying it in the road mud, being extra careful to reconstruct the cartwheel grooves after burying the cord. Egan waited until Pop was finished. The two worked methodically, steadily. Egan inserted and secured the cord to one side of the second claymore connecting the first two mines. Pop took over and secured the new end of the det cord roll to the second insert on the mine and unrolled and weaved the cord through the brush down the trail to where Egan was aiming a third claymore directly across toward Cherry. Pop connected this mine to the second. Egan set up a fourth and fifth down the road, one on each side. Pop daisy-chained the remaining mines to the first three. At the center of the MA, opposite Cherry, Egan stretched a monofilament trip wire line across, three inches above, the road. He fastened the trip wire to one side of a slide trigger. Egan secured the other side of the trigger to a rigid brush stump and camouflaged it. From one side of the trigger he ran a blasting cap wire to one terminal of the battery. Pop removed an electrical blasting cap from his shirt pocket, unwound the wires, attached one to the trigger slide and inserted the cap into the first claymore. Egan checked the slide mechanism, checked the trip wire and camouflage for the mines and the battery. Then he retreated to Cherry. Cherry watched fascinated, a smile on his face, twinkles in his eyes. Pop signaled for them both to withdraw. He quickly visually rechecked the booby trap then armed it by attaching the second blasting cap wire to the second terminal of the battery.

While Pop, Egan and Cherry were north on the road, Rover Team Claudia—Snell, Nahele and McQueen of 3d Plt—worked their way south to the river then upstream 200 meters. They sat immobile observing the river and across to the knoll. Within twenty minutes of set-up they spotted an NVA squad on the south riverbank. The enemy squad began unloading materials for a long wooden sampan. Snell radioed El Paso, spoke with Brooks, then called Armageddon Two. "Fire mission. Over."

Rounds landed in the river and on the swamp valley floor geysering riverwater and valleymud up with the flash and cordite smoke. The next three salvos were airbursts and geysered down showers of explosion-propelled shrapnel. The arty raid killed, all members of Rover Team Claudia agreed, at least five NVA. They were credited with a body count of four.

"¿Que pasa?" Brooks asked El Paso.

"You are, L-T," El Paso smiled.

"What are you thinking?" Brooks asked staring intensely at his senior RTO.

"I was thinking of my mother," El Paso answered. "You know, L-T, she used to say to me, 'Rafael, come in and stay with your mother. Today, I am very tired.' She used to say that to me all of the time." Brooks rubbed his hand up under his baseball cap, wiped rain from his forehead, and continued searching El Paso's face. "I should have taken her advice," El Paso said.

Brooks smiled. He and El Paso were the very center of Alpha and he liked that. He liked his RTO. Here they sat together on one poncho, under one poncho, wet together, in control together. They had spoken very little for days. Most of their interaction had been official. Earlier this day they had briefly discussed left-right politics but each time they began they had been interrupted by demands of the mission. Brooks opened his notebook carefully under the poncho.

"What were you telling me about Spanish?" Brooks asked after a pause.

"You mean the *con*?" El Paso asked.

"Yes," Brooks said eagerly.

"It is like this," El Paso began in a voice easy to listen to, as if he were telling a story. "You see, a Chicano is *with* something. Anglos, they are *for* something. We do not say I am *for* this or *for* that, we say *con*, *with* this or *with* that. When you say you are for something you disassociate yourself from it. You and it are different. Don't you agree? But Spanish-speaking people, we are with an idea or an issue. We say I am with this candidate or with this policy. It is we and we are it. It does not exist by itself as it does for the Anglos. When my people talk about the government it is not to be an entity by itself that we must serve. It is us and it must serve us."

Brooks made a few notes then said, "I hear you yet I don't see that in reality."

"Maybe you do not know enough about Spanish-speaking people. It is the *con*, why we are so passionate."

"The *con*," Brooks repeated to himself attempting to assimilate the concept. He repeated it again.

"Before we were talking about right and left governments," El Paso said, "and right or left factions. I don't think that is a realistic representation of American politics. L-T, you are interested in words as symbols and how they affect our thoughts. If we continually use right-left dichotomies to describe a particular polarization, does the description become part of the cause for the polarization?''

"I don't know," Brooks said writing the question down.

"This is what I think. Politics are not lineal. The left-center-right line is a poor descriptive symbol. Let's put a policy decision, a topic like this war, in the center. The right demands that we remain here, that we redouble our effort. And the right criticizes the government for not following a rightist course. From the left there are others pulling at the government. They want all American troops withdrawn now. They criticize the government not following a leftist course. And we only have two alternatives. Maybe that is because that is the rules we set up for ourselves. But it is not the real situation.

"What we, the government and the people of the United States, do could be better represented by a sphere with a dot at the center. The dot is our policy. On the surface of the sphere are all the interested parties. There's Dow Chemical with a big line to the dot and there's Irma Dinky-dau from Lost City, Nevada, with a thread, and there are a hundred million others. Everybody's pulling the dot in different directions and it's staying pretty close to center.''

"Hey," Brooks smiled. "And true polarization occurs only when the surface participants are pushed to the poles. Perhaps when you have heavy concentrations of interest groups. Or maybe one side polarizing forces the other side to polarize.''

"Yes," El Paso agreed. "But in a free society you do not get complete polarization because the interest groups are capable of wandering around anywhere on the surface of the sphere.''

"If they know it a sphere," Doc said sliding under their poncho. He had overheard fragments of their conversation from his wet hole only an arm's reach away. "What happen, Mista, when somebody come long an purge an entire pole? Huh? Then your dot gonna be way outa whack.''

Egan and Cherry materialized silently from the mistblur. "Rover Team Stephanie reports," Cherry whispered.

"Yeah," El Paso said attempting to disarm Doc's argument, ignoring the return of the rover team. El Paso liked his model and he wanted to defend it. "However, we don't have purges in our society. Not great purges like they've had in Russia or China. See, there people are forced off the sphere. There people can't stabilize the policy dots in the center because they aint allowed to wander about and pressure and pull the dot from all angles.''

"What you mean we don't got great purges? What happened to the red race, Mista? You fogettin somethin. White fuckas always have purges."

"Hey," Egan jumped right in, "we got repression of minorities and we got some purged people but it's not like in the Soviet Union or in China or even in North Vietnam. Asian fuckas," Egan mocked Doc's voice, "always have purges. You can't name a great American purge."

"We couldn't have one now," Cherry said. "Too many people would stand up and object."

"Exactly," El Paso stated firmly. "Free criticism is good. It keeps government honest and stable."

The conversation turned away from racial problems and back to war. El Paso delivered a lecture on the legality of the war. "There are very sound arguments holding this war to be unconstitutional," El Paso said. "Like when Nixon decided to send troops into Cambodia. That was not legal. He reigns over our lives, he reigns over the country. He makes decisions by himself without regard to anyone else pulling on the policy dot, almost as if he were a dictator. It simply cannot be legal. Not under these circumstances. The president can order invasions if our country is threatened. The Constitution says that that is okay. And there are legal precedents for similar action. FDR sent Americans into North Africa and then into Europe without congressional approval but the power to declare war does not rest with the president. That power is in the hands of Congress. Congress must declare war and the president must approve.

"There are many precedents in our history which extend the president's original war powers. President Polk attacked Mexico in 1845 without congressional approval. Only after the fact did Congress declare war. President Wilson, he had the navy bombard Vera Cruz and he sent American troops into Mexico after Pancho Villa. But no earlier president ever stretched his powers like Johnson in 1965. He completely usurped all the war-declaring power from Congress."

"Hey, what about the Gulf of Tonkin Resolution?" Brooks asked.

"That only authorized the president to retaliate to that one attack. It can't be used to justify half a million men and full-scale war. Besides, under the Constitution, Congress cannot give its powers away."

"What about the SEATO treaty?" Cherry asked.

"That treaty states that all countries involved must act in accordance with their constitutional processes. A treaty cannot supercede the constitution."

"Then why are you here?" Brooks asked.

"L-T, if I did not come, I'd be in jail," El Paso said.

During the discussion Brooks had been watching first El Paso, then Egan, then Cherry, then Doc. His mind jumped back to earlier statements. "Do we each have within us," Brooks asked, "a dot which we pull in many directions, a dot which determines our personal policy and course?"

There was contact to the south. A single burst of fire, a silent second, then answering fire and mingling fire. Then all was quiet. At Campobasso Brooks and El Paso waited for the report while the others prepared themselves. The report seemed a long time coming. Then Rover Team Danielle, four boonierats from 1st Plt, 2d Sqd led by Moneski, radioed its report. They had made Alpha's first direct contact since the river crossing. It had been short, small, sweet. Danielle ambushed a two-man NVA trail watcher unit. The Americans had set up moments before in an NVA position off one trail. The NVA had come from behind, unsuspecting, ready to move into their own position. One enemy soldier had been killed instantly. The other was hit and had fled. Rover Team Danielle pursued, caught the wounded man, took and returned fire, blowing the NVA soldier to pieces. The team sustained no casualties.

The nightly CP meeting on the 21st took place before dusk. Rain had fallen all day, the monotonous pattering drops being sporadically disrupted by cloudbursts. The sky had again settled back, it seemed in response to Brooks' meeting, to the dark gray of steady rain. The meeting was brief. Eighteen platoon members attended, all the platoon sergeants and leaders and the platoon CP RTOs and all of the squad leaders or a stand-in for those on patrol. The soldiers sat close together, almost in each other's laps, to hear Brooks give the operational orders for the next two days.

The NVA were not accustomed to American units working at night, moving at night and setting up during the day. They were not accustomed to it because so few American units did it. Brooks had been consulting his advisers individually since resupply and he was now convinced Alpha was in position and could pull it off. "We're going to pick them apart from right here," Brooks said. "Hide and hit. Melt into the mud and ambush them. If this is as important a supply area as S-2 says it is, they've got to be moving. It'll be no different than our usual nightly ambushes except that we're going to have twelve ambush teams out at once. This time, you're not ambush teams. You'll be Rover Teams. And you'll be out for two days." Brooks detailed the operation. Half of every squad would go; half would stay in or near Campobasso. The company and platoon CPs would provide men for three teams and radios for four. Brooks assigned each Rover Team a specific Area of Operation. He suggested ambush locations in each area. He rose and climbed among his men, pointing out to each leader, on the individual's map, the spots he thought looked promising, the trails in each area he had marked on his map from the first circuit they had made about the knoll. "Hide and hit," Brooks said coldly. "Hit and run. Evade detection. Don't engage more than you can kill immediately. Ambush."

"Ambush," Moneski repeated. "Just like earlier today. It's a dream."

"Snipe," Brooks said. "We've got three Starlight scopes. Use them."

"Snipe," Snell nodded. "And call in arty."

"Let arty get some." Brooks smiled. The group was psyching up. Cold blood lust, contempt for the enemy, spewed from one then another. "Use your MAs," Brooks said.

"Blow em away," Catt cooed.

"Kill the fuckers," Cherry giggled venomously.

"Kill the fuckers," Mohnsen cried, wept bitter tears.

Brooks let them seethe then purposefully settled them back down with a few cautions and a few questions. "Field ingenuity," he whispered. "Every boonierat must think for himself, adjust himself to the situation he finds himself in. You guys have to be more versatile, more flexible than the dinks. And you have to be smarter. Think about what you are going to do before you do it. Plan. Out-fox them. Don't go out of your own AOs without clearance. Don't ambush each other. No chatter on the nets. Rovers!"

"Aye, L-T," they whispered.

"Kill em, kill em, kill em," Mohnsen beat his rifle butt against the ground.

"Teams Cindy, Joan, Ellen and Laurie," Brooks whispered, "you leave at 1900 hours. Teams Claudia, Beth, Irene and Mary, you leave at 1915 hours. Teams Danielle, Suzie, Jill and Stephanie—1930."

Before the first boonierat could rise an ear-splitting concussion rocked Alpha. The MA on the road below the north escarpment had detonated.

As Rover Team Stephanie—now Egan, Cherry and Bo Denhardt—rucked up, Brooks collared Egan. "I want to ask you some questions before you sky, Danny," Brooks said. He was a man now completely different from the one who had led the briefing, rally, only minutes before. He spoke in his graduate student voice, concerned, contemplative, the exact opposite of the previous passion. And he seemed unaware of the change. Indeed Egan noted what seemed to him to be a complete repression or denial of the commander role. It made Egan uncomfortable.

"Danny," Brooks said meekly, "what causes conflict?"

Egan dropped his ruck and sat atop it. "I'll tell ya what I know," he said. "I been thinkin about this for ya. You'll have ta check it out for yourself but here's some shit I remember from school. And some shit I just think."

Brooks smiled softly in the rain, silently begging Egan's indulgence as he uncovered his notebook and covered it and himself with his poncho.

"I had an engineering prof, guy named Tom Wheeler, who did his thesis on the effects of technological advances on population demographics. Something like that. Basically what he said was every major advance in technology is followed by a period of prosperity, then a population explosion. Works like this. A technological advance alleviates the pressure of population but then the pressure builds up again except now to a higher level. Follow me?"

"Kinda," Brooks whispered, writing.

"Look," Egan said. "Go way back. Hunter/gatherer mankind learns how to herd animals. He stabilizes his life following pastures. For a while everyone has food and prospers. Then there's a population explosion followed by overcrowding, disease and famine."

"And war?"

"Yeah, I guess. Anyway, now nomadic mankind learns how to cultivate crops. He settles down on fertile lands and he becomes more stabilized but at a more complex level. For a while everyone prospers, has food, the whole thing. Then there's a population explosion followed by overcrowding, disease, famine and probably war and migration. Mankind then learns how to store food against famine, how to irrigate against drought. For a while everyone prospers, again at a more complex level. With no pressure man seems to be more fertile. The population explodes and puts the pressure back on and the same problems occur."

"Are you saying," Brooks asked softly, "that war is a means of limiting population?"

"Wait a minute," Egan said. "I don't know if I got there yet."

"Excuse me," Brooks apologized.

Egan's concentration on his thoughts deepened. "Each advance brings greater stability yet with a higher, more complex structure supporting it. Each period of stability brings a population explosion. That can be documented. If you plot the growth of human population before every major increase you'll find a major technological advance. After each major increase you find population pressure and war. Pressure is conflict, L-T. Want to stop the pressure? After the next advance, stop people from fuckin each other."

"Sew up all the cunts of the Third World, huh?" Brooks joked, laughed, trying to lessen Egan's intensity, and also trying to reduce Egan's last statement to the absurd because to Brooks it smacked of racism.

"The whole world," Egan said sharply, defensively. "Fuck it, Man. You listenin? There aint no chance about this. There aint no such thing as chance. Only ignorance of natural laws."

"I didn't mean to put your theory down," Brooks said. "I've been writing what you've been saying. How does it fit though, in a world where some nations are rich and some poor? Some advanced, some not?"

"Advances in technology don't just happen, L-T," Egan said calmer. "Technology grows. It has prerequisites." Brooks shifted beneath his poncho. Egan slid lower on his ruck, then slid off the ruck and onto the ground next to the lieutenant. "Look, in what are today's industrial nations, before they were industrial, certain conditions existed. The advanced societies today were the early machine societies. And those societies changed to accept new styles of living. And they gave up a lot to do it."

"What did they . . ."

"Wait a minute. In places like England there was a belief in rational thought, in natural sciences and in mathematics. They prized analytical thinking. They had to give up more comfortable religions for ones that would accommodate their science. Maybe they gave up their souls. But see, L-T," Egan was concentrating hard again, burning his words out quietly, "those things led to a high degree of technology built on a substructure of technology. The less complex fed the more complex. Technology, with only minor lapses, stayed ahead of their population pressures. If the pressure ever catches up and undermines the substructure all developed countries have a long way to fall."

"Well, why can't Vietnam use the technology too?" Brooks asked. "If they could use it to stay ahead of their population pressures there'd be no war."

"No base. Development is not a matter of the industrialized nations giving equipment and advice to the Third World. That just doesn't do it." Egan was trying to pull old thoughts from areas of his mind that he had not used in a long time. "It just hasn't worked that way," Egan said. "These people can blame America or western Europe for conspiring to keep them down, for keeping the price of their raw materials low while selling high-priced finished goods to them but the fact is there's no conspiracy. The conspiracy is in the minds of communists who want to control these people. It's really a matter of no base structure."

"Then what you're saying," Brooks whispered, "is that Third World societies just haven't accepted the pain of giving up their old cultures and building the base for new westernized forms."

"Well, yeah. There it is, L-T. These people got something we lost. To gain economic prosperity you got to want to work, you got to want that wealth bad enough to work at boring dehumanized work, highly technical work. You got to love machines like papa-san loves his water-bo. Cause that's what technological advances are."

"We think ourselves into what we are and our thought patterns are determined by the culture of our upbringing," Brooks repeated a statement of his own theory which he wanted to tie to Egan's.

"Oh. Okay," Egan said. "Now I read you lumpy chicken. That's what you meant when you said we think ourselves into war."

"Yeah," Brooks said. "That's what I meant. So, industrialism is based on a people whose culture identifies with strong causative forces, with logical cause and effect patterns of thought. And western culture is based on logical thought patterns. And to get that we gave up something."

"Yep," Egan agreed. "Or at least we accepted something along with it that isn't positive."

"War," Brooks said.

"It's inevitable," Egan said.

"We think ourselves into it and our minds don't have an alternative. We're a war-or-peace culture." Brooks wrote that down.

The two of them sat silently in the rain, in the gray darkness, feeling close again. For some moments neither spoke. The valley seemed quiet. Artillery rounds were bursting far away. The noise of the rain had become so normal they did not notice it. Campobasso held only twenty-five soldiers and in the thicket none could be seen.

"Do you think war is against human nature?" Brooks asked just as Egan was about to rise to leave.

"No way," Egan said settling back down. "People are always sayin it's against human nature for man to war against man." Egan spoke with contempt for the idea. "They say any advocate of war is against mankind. You can make just as good an argument for war being man's nature. If you want the truth all you gotta say is man's nature is intermittently warlike. War and peace. They have a continuous, maybe sine-like, maybe erratic, function. Did you know that on any given day there's an average of twelve wars goin on on earth? There's been over a hundred wars since World War Two. You don't gotta justify war. Fuck the pansyass politicians and the pantywaist left. War's its own justification."

"That's sad," Brooks said.

"Why?" Egan demanded.

"We're here and that justifies our being here?" Brooks made it sound ridiculous.

"The only justification you need for Nam is we're doin it. It is, thus it is right. That goes for everything. If it is, so it is."

"That's crazy, Danny."

"Don't worry, L-T. It's supposed to be. The stupider the war, the more the blunders, the better for mankind. Shit, if we ever become one hundred percent proficient at killing each other, then we'll kill one hundred percent of us minus one. Like if we have thermo-nuclear war. We're a lot better off runnin around with 16s than if we begin tossin ICBMs at each other."

"Why can't we change mankind and eliminate the need for conflict yet still remain different and flexible. It would only require tolerance."

"Never happen."

"Why?"

"You'd have ta change it all—every last man, woman and child—if you wanted ta break the cycle of peace-war-peace-war. You'd have ta build a new base. If you can't change the system that produces war there's one thing you best mothafuckin do —you better win them fuckin wars."

"Amen," Brooks said.

Egan began rising. "We gotta get to our AO," he said to Brooks. "I gotta find what happened to the MA."

"Wait a minute," Brooks said. "I want to ask you just ah . . . about something else."

"Yeah."

"I want to switch to personal conflict. Like," Brooks hesitated then nearly blurted it out loud instead of whispering it in his field voice, "like between my wife and me. You know the situation?"

"Yeah. I know."

"You ever not been able to get it up?" Brooks asked.

"You mean like . . ."

"Yeah."

"When drinkin," Egan admitted.

"What about, you know, like when perfectly sober?" Brooks asked.

"I never had that problem," Egan said, "but I think it's common. Temporary impotence they call it. Like if you're nervous. *Playboy*, I think, they had an article on it. I think it said it happens to fifty percent of all dudes at one time or another."

"Really?" Brooks was amazed.

"Yeah."

"Ah . . ." Brooks began slowly again, "have you ever fantasized about another man being with your lady?" He now had almost no voice at all. "I mean, like seeing an image of another dude and your lady making love?"

"Oh yeah," Egan answered robustly. "All the time. I think

everybody does that.'' Suddenly to Egan, Brooks seemed transparent.

"It doesn't mean, ah, like ah . . .''

"This is really botherin you, huh?''

"Yeah. I guess so.''

"Happen in Hawaii? Begin there?''

"Yeah. How'd you know?''

"Same thing happened to Hughes. Happened to Rattler too.''

"Really?'' Again Brooks was amazed. "What about, like seeing you and another guy and your lady? Three of you?''

"Yeah. Sometimes,'' Egan said. "I don't think a guy can get it on with a lady who he knows has had other dudes and at some point not think when he's eatin her he's gettin some other dude's cum or when she's stickin her tongue in his mouth thinkin like she'd wrapped that same tongue around somebody else's meat. It's almost like he was blowin the other dude.''

Brooks looked at Egan, shocked. Then subdued he said, "Yeah. I guess so.''

"Yeah,'' Egan continued. "Rattler said the Doc . . . not Doc but the shrink at Division . . . he called it the Nam Syndrome.''

"Really?''

"Yeah. Rattler thought he was turnin fag. He was really shook up, L-T. You didn't know him then. He was really nuts. That's why he went to the shrink.''

"I thought that was because of what happened on 714 and 882?''

"Well, he couldn't come out en say somethin like that.''

"Yeah, I guess not,'' Brooks agreed. "Hey, Danny, ah, either of those guys tell you what happened, ah, what kind of thoughts . . .''

"Yeah, that's what I mean,'' Egan said. "Rattler said he kept jerkin off fantasizin he was gettin butt-fucked.''

A single shot cracked the air. Nothing more. It came from south and west of the CP. In the rain splattered valley night the exact direction and distance of a single shot was impossible to determine. An aerial diagram of Alpha's set up would have looked like the cross-section of an orange cut perpendicular to the axis. The very center would be almost empty. Only a skeleton CP remained. The first circle out would be formed by the apex of the sections. This would be the thinned though still tightly packed berm perimeter of Campobasso. Farther out, spaced almost evenly about the center, are six dots, seeds, LP/OPs protecting the center. Expanding beyond and filling the circle are twelve sections, the AOs of the rover teams. To the south is the river. To the north is the road. The teams with sections to the southwest were Mary, Claudia and Laurie. There was no report. Then the squelch on El Paso's radio was broken three slow times. Sitting tight. Nothing more happened.

At the CP Cahalan monitored a krypto call that excited Brooks and FO. Bravo Company's honcho POW from several days earlier had agreed to lead that company to a headquarters bunker complex he maintained they had swept over twice without discovering.

"There it is," FO said, smiling, relieved.

"Thank God," Cahalan said. "They're goina send Bravo back up that ridge."

"Least it aint us," El Paso said.

"I still think there might be a bunker complex on that knoll," Brooks said cautiously.

"You heard the man, L-T," Cahalan said wanting to believe the call. "Their hotel quebec is down by Bravo."

"Don't get your hopes up too high," Brooks said. "Bravo still hasn't found it."

After an hour the squelch on El Paso's radio was broken twice. Rover Team Laurie reported laconically, "Kilo india alpha one november victor alpha. Counted two seven moving november. Out."

Cherry and Egan and Denhardt left Campobasso well after dark. The rain had not ceased. It was very dark. Egan led them at a slow walk. The move even to the close perimeter of their NDP was hard. They cleared themselves with the guards, radioed the LP and walked out erect. They made no sound. They moved slowly, Egan leading, Cherry laying one hand on Egan's ruck following in the middle, Denhardt holding Cherry's ruck at drag. No one spoke. No one coughed. No equipment rattled. Egan kept one eye on the luminous dial of his compass. Cherry counted their steps. Every few meters they froze and listened. Then they moved on. Twenty meters, forty, sixty. They froze. The LP should be to their left. Cherry keyed his handset three quick clicks to break the natural static of the radio at the LP. The

LP acknowledged by repeating the signal. Rover Team Stephanie moved on. And on.

They came to a trail Pop had skirted earlier when he had led Egan and Cherry to the road. Egan dropped slowly to his knees. He felt the ground for a thin, rigid piece of grass. He found one. He lifted it to his face and brushed it across his nose. He brushed it against his pant leg, over the compass, on the ground. Egan hefted the grass blade in his right hand then spread prone, on his stomach in the trail. Cherry followed Egan down kneeling behind him in the muck of the trail, grabbed Egan's left foot with his left hand. Denhardt slowly squatted behind Cherry. The team inched forward.

Egan brushed the ground before him with the grass blade before each movement. Very slowly he extended his right hand with the grass checking each inch of trail for booby trap trip wires. There was no rush. He had all night to cover only a few hundred meters. He retracted his hand then pulled himself forward the cleared one-third meter. Cherry and Denhardt crawled forward with him. Egan repeated the sweep. The trail was bare of growth because of heavy traffic. The mud was three-inch thick slime. It seeped into every opening in Egan's fatigues, into all their boots. Somehow it was not uncomfortable. It was soft. It was no wetter than they already were. It even felt warm. Cherry felt very relaxed.

Where puddles inundated the trail Egan put the grass stalk between his lips and walked his fingers slowly through the water. Then he slid into the puddle and checked the next arm's length of dark territory. Cherry continued counting. After every fifty movements he shook Egan's left foot. After three hundred and fifty movements they ceased moving. The road, the smell of cordite, was directly ahead.

Jax' skin was almost rotted through. Of that he was sure. His muscles were cramping from the cold and the hours of stillness. He was sure he would die of exposure. "Au this fucken way," he whispered to Hoover. "Au this way ta die a nee-moan-ya."

"My pecker's freezin off," Marko whispered over.

Earlier Jax had been more enthusiastic. When the L-T had asked him for the name of his Rover Team, Jax had cooed, "I's be Jax, they's my Jills; Jax en Jills goes up the hills ta fetch nine pail a mud; Jax come back, the Jills got sack; carryin nine pail wid gook blood.''

Rover Team Jill was the farthest east of any Alpha element and long into the night they seemed to be in the quietest locale. They had set up in a hollow in a bamboo thicket three meters from a narrow trail. They had left Campobasso on schedule at 1930 hours and had reached, found, their night position by 2100. For five hours they had sat still, cold, waiting. They had gone out with great anticipation and enthusiasm for the tactic, had gone with the expectation of a first-time fisherman, and with the same patience.

Jax could no longer control his arms, legs and chest from shaking. He was wet, had been wet for what seemed like forever. The hot dry interlude at resupply was forgotten. Jax' teeth began to chatter. Hoover snuggled up to him on one side, Marko on the other. They each wrapped an arm over Jax' back. The warmth felt good but it was not enough.

''Fuck it,'' Marko said. ''Just say fuck it. Don't . . .''

''The fuck it doan,'' Jax whispered wildly, standing up. ''We gotta . . .''

At that there was an explosion perhaps thirty feet away. They froze, solidified like statues. Jax' chillchatter vanished. The sound had been a loud pop, a giant explosive cork blasting from a bottle. POUAHK. A second mortar round was launched. Jax turned to Marko then siezed a grenade from his belt. ''Frags,'' he whispered. Hoover and Marko immediately grabbed two each. Jax stepped forward, one pace, two, three, to the edge of the trail. Hoover was to one side, Marko to the other. The sound of the mortar team chattering in Vietnamese came from their close right front. ''Throw two, then hit it,'' Jax whispered. ''On go.'' He paused to give them time. Then he whispered, ''Go.'' They cocked and threw.

Another mortar round was launched.

Jax, Marko and Hoover each immediately depinned and threw their second fragmentation grenade. Then they hit the ground. Marko's first frag went beyond the NVA, Jax' to the left, Hoover's also behind. All exploded simultaneously. An enemy soldier screamed. The second three frags exploded. There was scurrying in the brush, there was the sound of a body being dragged. Then all was silent. Rover Team Jill lay perfectly still until first light. Jax smiled the rest of the night.

*　　　*　　　*

In the center of the Khe Ta Laou River valley nothing moved before first light. The NVA had called a halt to routine early morning moves. During the preceding afternoon and night they had been in contact five times with unknown elements of the American battalion that was stamping around in the hills and most probably sending a coordinated series of ambush teams into the valley on a one-shot attempt. All five contacts had resulted in North Vietnamese losses with no apparent American losses. The situation could not be serious. Americans never stayed in one area for long without building an outpost. They had not built one so they must leave soon. Sit tight, the NVA command ordered. Sit tight until tonight.

During that same pre-dawn Cherry had his last rational thoughts. Rover Team Stephanie had moved from the trail they had crawled up, into a tangle of debris, vines and bamboo. They spoke not a word. They breathed the smell of burnt explosive and the smell of blood hour after blackrain hour. Chill set into every bone. Egan took it in stride. He always did. His sense of easiness, almost casualness, permeated the others and they too relaxed. Denhardt breathed slowly, deeply. The war odor was pleasant to him. Stuck in that remote rotting valley of death one had either to accept the smell and be pleased with it or accept the smell and abhor it. Either way, sanity fled.

Earlier at Campobasso Cherry had been nearby while Brooks questioned the platoon sergeant. He had heard snatches of speech and had wanted to comment but he had not been invited into their circle. In his mind he now pictured Egan and him in serious discussion. Suddenly he found himself with Egan. They were at a CP, chatting softly, almost intimately.

Every day since they first encountered each other at Phu Bai Cherry and Egan spent more and more time together. They were now almost older brother, younger brother. Hadn't Egan even called him Little Brother earlier that very day?

"Yer such a cherry," Egan's image laughed to the image of Cherry.

"I thought you were on the other side of that," the Cherry-image answered firmly.

"A man's got a right to have more than one opinion," Egan whispered. "Goddamn, if I believed everything I've ever said I'd be so mixed up I'd be crazy."

"Sometimes, yer such an ass," Cherry joked.

"And yer such a cherry," Egan retorted and he grabbed Cherry's head and mussed his hair playfully. Then he said seriously, "Ya know, Cherry, all my life everybody's been tellin me how nice I am and that kinda shit. And all my life I been tellin myself what an ass I am. Then I came to Nam. And I discovered I wasn't a fuckhead. I discovered I was okay. Now everybody tells me I'm an ass. Cherry, yer a cherry ta life. People want you ta be an asshole so they tell ya when yer being an ass how good ya are and when yer bein okay what an ass ya are. It makes em feel superior. Fuck em. Fuck it an drive on, Breeze. It don't mean nothin."

"Eg," the Cherry-image said lightly, good-naturedly, the way only the closest of friends can laugh during serious conversations, "Eg, you gotta live with people."

"Fuck em all," Egan said.

"Man. Man, you are doomed. Man, you are doomed to being a lonely person. Shee-it, when a dude can do everything for himself, when he don't need anybody, he's goina be lonely. Nobody can please you, Mister Egan. Nobody's good enough for you. You gotta do it all yourself and that's lonely, Eg. Lonely."

"Yeah," Egan's image agreed. "But here, in Nam, here it's alive too. You can't trust somebody else with your security cause aint nobody goina look out for you as well as you. You remember that when I'm gone."

Cherry dozed. He awoke in despair, in agony. Something from the very depths of his body was screaming. The sky hinted at becoming light. Cherry snapped his head toward Egan. The platoon sergeant was there where he should be. Egan nodded to the trail. Cherry looked. Something in his mind snapped. Cherry stared at the darkened rain-blurred scene. He stared at the carnage only feet away. Egan motioned for Denhardt to recon the trail to their east. Egan snaked through the grass west. Cherry continued staring. The sky lightened in imperceptible stages. Cherry's body twisted. He snarled then laughed to himself. "Fuck it. Really don't mean nothin. Drive on."

Cherry rose slowly. He rose to full height and stretched. He threw his shoulders back, stretching out the night cramps. He arched his back, he wiggled his toes and fingers. He felt for his frags. They were in a pouch on his belt as was right. His rifle was in his left hand. He ran his fingers over it. He aimed the muzzle downward and slowly withdrew the bolt carrier halfway, draining any water which might have entered the barrel during the night. Noiselessly he let the bolt slide back closed and he shoved hard to insure it seated completely. Then he looked up again. They, it, was still there.

Cherry took a half step forward. He advanced without his ruck. He looked left for Egan, right for Denhardt, then stepped among it on the road. He laughed quietly, apprehensively. He looked up and down the road and he looked straight up at the woven canopy, beyond into the rain into the lighting sky into heaven. He half-stepped forward and he stepped on a half head, a half face. He jolted back nervously and giggled. An eye was looking at him from the mud. Cherry stared back. The eye looked at him. Cherry's leg snapped out reflexively. He felt the eye pop beneath his heel. There were at least five bodies, perhaps six, strewn over forty feet of road. Cherry smiled. How could Egan have placed the claymores so perfectly? How had he known the first man would miss the trip wire allowing the squad to completely enter the kill zone? That cunning mothafucker. Mangled them all. Must have gotten em all, too, Cherry thought. No one left to collect their weapons. Cherry bent down and lifted a Soviet AK-47 assault rifle from the mud. A hand came up with it. A hand and four tattered inches of wrist and arm. He carefully pulled the fingers from the trigger guard. The skin was cold, stiff, slimy. The stock of the rifle was splintered. Cherry dropped it back onto the piece of hand and arm and maybe a chunk of abdomen.

That raggedy-ass mothafucker don't look so bad, Cherry thought advancing to the next body. He unsheathed his bayonet and removed two NVA ears. As he hacked off the second there was movement at the corner of his eye. He spun and sprawled flat amongst the dead, aimed his 16 up the road, flipped to automatic and began to squeeze on an advancing blur.

"SKYHAWKS," came an immediate whispered call. Cherry toyed with the idea of squeezing the trigger anyway. "SKY-HAWKS," Denhardt's whispered call came again.

Cherry relaxed. "SKYHAWKS," he whispered as Denhardt materialized from the mistdarkness. Cherry returned to the NVA corpse and retrieved the ears. "These are for Whiteboy and Silvers," he whispered to Denhardt. Then he went back to the half head and cut the ear from it. "Here," Cherry said. "This one's for you."

*   *   *

When Egan returned from his recon west he directed Rover Team Stephanie to police up the MA site. There were four AK-47s and an RPG launcher, ammunition, letters and documents. The boonierats split the load, Egan retrieved the trigger mechanism for the MA. Then they dissolved into the thickets to hide and to eat and to wait for dawn. "Wait til Pop hears of this," Cherry said happily to Egan. "Pop'll be just so proud." Egan looked at Cherry and nodded.

Cherry ate a C-ration meal of Spaghetti and Meatballs in Tomato Sauce. He ate it ravenously. His stomach was still empty. He opened another can. This one was pork slices. Cherry plucked a thick firm slice from the can with his mud-crusted fingers. He jammed the slice into his mouth. He chewed twice, swallowed, jammed in another slice. He drained the juice from the can into his mouth then dropped the can beside the spaghetti tin.

Egan reached over and picked the cans up and signaled for Cherry to put them into his ruck. No signs of American presence were to be left by the rover teams. "Pack it back here to Campobasso," Brooks had directed the team leaders. "Pack everything out that you pack in," he had said. "Except your shit. Bury that deep and camouflage the spot."

Cherry ate a B-2 unit tin of Crackers and Cheese and washed it down with water from the blood-stained blivet that had been Leon Silvers'. The pimples that had formed days earlier on his arms and legs and face and back and had then turned to sores and then oozing ulcerations were now filth-covered jungle rot. The sun and drying at the LZ on Hill 636 had accomplished little. The treatment had been too short and the patient had returned too quickly to the wet rotting valley floor.

Cherry did not care. He aped Egan, washing carefully in a puddle but it was for show, for camaraderie, not for cleanliness. He wasn't concerned about the sores. They were beyond the point of hurting. "Like my shoulders," Cherry would have said had he even thought of it. "My shoulders hurt like hell from the ruck at first but they toughened up. Now they don't hurt at all. My skin's the same. It's getting tougher." Indeed, Cherry was becoming callused hands, shoulders and mind. The wetness softened the calluses on his hands and shoulders and they rubbed off. The wetness had no effect on the calluses of his mind except to make them thicker.

Combining with the toughening of his mind were new

abilities, the new keenness of ears, sharpness of eyes, the education of his nose to jungle smells. Cherry developed a new acuteness of these senses which allowed him to know the primitive world which extended all about him, to know it more quickly and more fully, he was certain, than any other boonierat, even Egan.

But Cherry did not think of these things now. They did not really matter. Cherry only thought of two things. He thought of eating and he thought of killing. "Let's go," he pleaded to Egan when Egan dawdled over his morning coffee. "Let's set up another one. I got an idea just where."

The MA Cherry set up under Egan's watchful direction was similar to the first booby-trapping of the road beneath the cliffs except that it used only three claymores. It did not need more and they did not have an unlimited supply. Cherry picked the site. It was beneath the woven canopy of the road at a spot where the ceiling needed repair. "This'll be a riot," he told Denhardt. "Wait'll they try to fix this one."

Cherry worked as methodically as Egan and Pop had worked setting the first MA. He set and aimed the claymores from one point, in three directions. He hid the mines on the road corridor wall aiming across, up and down the trail. He imagined the enemy crew carelessly approaching the site, their security out, their work about to begin. Cherry set the trip wire in the canopy so it would be triggered when the repair team began reconstructing the roof. "Let em get in a good close clusterfuck," he laughed.

"Oing douk mann cowy?" Doc tried.

"*Ông duoc mahn khoe?*" Minh repeated.

"*Ông* douk *manh* cowee?" Doc tried again.

"*Da, Cãm on,*" Minh said.

"Ya, cam urn," Doc repeated.

"Oh, that is very good," Minh said. *"Tôi lã Minh."*

"*Tôi lã* Alexander," Doc said.

"Oh yes, very good," Minh said. "Now, *môt, hai, ba, bôn, nam, sáu, bay, tám, chin, múoî.*"

"Mot, hi, ba, bon, nam, sow-oo, bay . . ."

"No, no, no. *Môt, hai, ba. Ba,*" Minh intonated. "Not baa. *Ba.*"

"Hey Man, I aint never gonna learn it. You say ba not ba. There aint no difference."

"Yes, yes. Listen. *Ba*. Here, we shall write it and then say it."

"Minh," Doc said. "I gotta get these dudes up. Lazy fuckas. Half em still crashed."

"We should write. *Viêt, dó lá môt cách nói không bi ngat lái.*"

"What'd you say?"

"That is a quote from Renad. 'Writing is a way of speaking without interruption.' "

"No shit." Doc chuckled. "Minh, you my main man. Here, eat this."

"Daily-daily?"

"Daily-daily."

Doc slithered from beneath the poncho he and Minh had strung eighteen inches above the earth the afternoon before. They had covered the sides of the hootch and one end with palm and bamboo scraps and had camouflaged the top with a tangle of bramble branches. After they had set up they had simply crawled in and rested and let the valley, the rover teams and the war go on about them. The whole idea of hiding an infantry company in a valley and breaking it into ambush teams was, to both Doc and Minh, insane. With the sounds of each explosion reaching their hootch Doc had squirmed out into the rain and had edged over to El Paso to find out what was happening and if he was needed. El Paso and the L-T had set up a similar though smaller rain shelter less than five feet away. Brown and Cahalan's hootch made a triangle of the three. Each time Doc found El Paso, El Paso had nothing to report and Doc had returned to his hootch and rested. Restlessness came with first light. Minh and Doc traded words, English for Vietnamese, for half an hour. Then Minh began in earnest to try to teach Doc Vietnamese.

Doc looked at the sky in disgust. Rain. Fog and rain. His boonierats were melting. Doc shook his head. He stepped lightly to the rear of his hootch, relieved himself, then went to check in with El Paso and Brooks.

"Daily-daily," Doc whispered cheerfully handing in two tiny white anti-malaria pills. "Up ya go, L-T. Hey, your boys soundin like they done a J-O-B las night. What the score?"

"We got at least ten," El Paso beamed. "It's like shootin tacos in a barrel a refried beans."

"No shit?"

"No shit."

"Nooo shee-it?"

"No shit, Man. I shit you not."

"Shee-it!"

"No shit."

"Shit, Man. I think you shittin me."

"I shit you not, Bro."

"Will you guys cut that shit out?" Brooks laughed and the three of them giggled. Doc shimmied in beneath their poncho with them and the three lay on their backs looking up at the damp plastic coated ceiling less than an arm's reach above.

They were silent for a moment then Doc said, "No shit," very quickly and the three of them burst into giggles again. "I gotta get Minh," Doc said sliding back out into the rain. He stood up and walked the two paces to his hootch then returned and ducked his head in and whispered, "Sshheeee-yit."

Soon there were four beneath the single poncho. They lay like packed sardines, not moving, not talking. Brooks was half outside on one side and Doc was half out on the other. After perhaps four or five minutes Doc and Brooks and El Paso whispered, starting very low and building to a whispered crescendo, "ssshheeEEE-YYITT."

They found it hilarious and forced fingers into their mouths to keep from laughing loudly. Minh did not get it and they found that even funnier. "What is so funny about shit?" Minh asked seriously, a smile coming to his face.

"Don'tcha get it?" El Paso chuckled.

"No," Minh said.

"No Shit," Doc said and the four of them giggled.

"Hey," Brooks called a pause to the laughter. "I want to ask you some shit . . ." The laughter became uncontrollable again. "Come on," Brooks said. He was feeling better this day than he had for many days past. "Come on," he repeated. "No shit." Giggles, suppressed giggles. "Anybody want some mocha? I got a hot cupful."

"Ooooh shit, that is hot," Doc laughed grabbing the cup, spilling the hot liquid on Minh.

"Ouch!" Minh screamed suppressed, bolting upright, hitting the top of the poncho, snapping a line on the roof and caving in the head end which held a puddle in a sway. The water splashed onto El Paso's laughing face.

"Augh fuck," El Paso said shaking his head violently.

"Oh, now we goan from shit ta fuck," Doc teased him but he did not laugh. The laughing was over.

Brooks, Minh and Doc moved to Doc's hootch for the discussion. As he had with the others Brooks opened with the question, "What causes conflict?"

"Life is motion," Minh said. "Life sways between plus and minus. You view this as conflict. Why?"

"I'm not imagining conflict," Brooks defended his thoughts, his thesis. "It's there. Personal, interracial, international. Jesus, Minh! We're in the midst of a war and you ask me why I view it as conflict?"

"You have asked for weeks everyone the same thing. Everyone gives you an answer. You still ask. Perhaps you do not seek the answer. Perhaps you are more satisfied with the question. It is a good question."

"Perhaps." Brooks was thinking furiously, trying to make a connection.

"Yes, perhaps," Minh said. "The ultimate reality is not static matter but the motion of physical existence."

"Say that again," Brooks said.

"Reality ultimately is not static matter but the motion of physical existence," Minh said. "The most essential thing about life is that it is not static. If it does not flow, if you place emphasis on having instead of doing, you will miss the essence of life."

"Wow!" Doc said rolling on his side to look at Minh. "Wow! That's heavy Mista."

"I have learned very much with Americans," Minh said. "I have learned much by watching you and thinking about you." Minh was gazing at the roof of the hootch, looking as though through it to a very distant point. "You Americans," Minh said. "You have so much. You think you can do everything. You think you can control nature with your words and your theories. I think sometimes you miss the point."

"Words are important to me," Brooks confessed. "I want to find out, if, first, our thoughts control our actions. Then, if our thoughts are determined by the language we learn and finally, are the determinants of conflict, of war, built into the structure of our language. Can't you see? If all that is true, we would be able to restructure human languages to eradicate war."

"Oh, L-T," Minh sighed. "You are more intelligent than most Americans but that only makes your plans more complex. You are like them all. You think you can do anything."

"It can be done, Minh."

"L-T Brooks, man does not control nature with his scientific theory or with his engineering principles or with his history or with words of any kind. All he does is seek to explain nature. We seek to know how it works. Perhaps to be able to forecast the future from the past. We can arrange elements but we are one with nature and perhaps nature has simply had us arrange the elements for her. Things happen. People die. That is the flow of reality."

"Do you accept war, Minh?" Brooks was agitated. He tried to hide it by speaking even more softly than usual. He still sounded accusing. "Do you accept a war that has ripped your country apart for thirty years?"

"I can do nothing else but accept it. It is. Perhaps it is not all evil. We go to war. America sends her technology to my country and we learn and we will never again be so backward. Maybe this war is good."

"Egan said something about that. He said technology only thrives in cultures where the religion and . . . what did he say? Wait one. Let me look." Brooks flipped back through several pages of his notebook and scanned his writing. "He said some cultures are passive and believe a man must bend with the wind and flow with nature while other cultures are active. Active cultures have active religions and beliefs and think they can control their own fate. Industrialism only grows in active cultures for it requires those active thoughts as a base."

Minh did not say anything for what seemed like a long time. Brooks and Doc remained silent. They listened to the spattering rain on the poncho above them and to the slight breeze in the vegetation. At a far distance, perhaps at the firebase, a lone helicopter was landing. Earlier Brooks had received the report and forecast. A storm had come in from Laos. The rain would last forty-eight to seventy-two hours. Then it would clear. The valley would remain in intermittent fog.

Minh broke the pause by asking Brooks what he meant by activist culture and activist religion. They discussed this lethargically for some time.

"No L-T," Minh said. "You make a mistake. I am Taoist and Zen but they are not my religion. They are not religion in

your western use of the word. Maybe my Tao is more close to
being principles of consciousness. It is what I live by. How I see
myself and people around me and nature around people. Occiden-
tals have no knowledge of their principles. Your principles are
based only on not dying. The most terrible thing ever to an
occidental is to die. You will do anything to live a day longer.
What may be worse than dying is living without dignity or
without . . . I do not know how to say it in English . . .
without Tao. You have moral codes and religious laws and civil
laws imposed on you but it is unusual to find an American with
principles of living inside him. All Vietnamese know this. There
is nothing in your culture to lead you to develop your inside
principles. That is why you require outside laws. We are just the
reverse. Then Europeans came and conquered our land and
brought us their true religions and their true gods and their
god-made laws. Now we have that too.

"The problem with your active church," Minh continued,
still staring up through the poncho, "is that you propose to have
all the answers. All you really have is a systematic format on
which to pose the questions. Your answers are rhetorically achieved
and predetermined from the format and thus are only true within
the framework of your system. Your religion has no more meaning,
no more real answers, than the Tao did twenty-five hundred
years ago. And the Tao did not then and does not now have a
rigid format or a firm construction so its answers were not and
are not conceived in the asking. Do you understand, Sir?"

"That's exactly it," Brooks said. "That's what I've been
saying about war. War is predetermined from the format of
languages and culture. If we could unstructure the language then
restructure it on a less rigid format . . . see? War would not be
conceived in our speech."

They talked for hours. Brooks left several times. For two
hours he was gone—over to FO's lowslung hootch to study the
maps of the valley and to piece together the intelligence reports
from the rover teams and from battalion and brigade. Brooks
consulted with El Paso and Cahalan. After each tactical consulta-
tion he returned to Minh and Doc. They talked to the hour
where, beneath a rainsky, day and night are indiscernible.

Doc Johnson had been becoming more melancholy and
contemplative all afternoon. *"Yea, though I walk through this
valley of the shadow of darkness and death,"* he quoted the 23d
Psalm, *"I shall not fear, for thou art with me."* Doc looked at

Minh and the L-T. "That mean somethin to me, Mista," Doc said.

"Nor shall I fear," Brooks said, adding a common boonierat paraphrase of the psalm, "for thy arty and thy B-52s are on call to comfort me."

"That fucked Mista," Doc said sadly.

"Yeah, I guess so," Brooks said. "But we're only a tiny part. Somebody else is running the show."

"A man should control himself," Minh said. "It is not the rightful pursuit of any man to try to control the life of another. And each village must be responsible for its own internal affairs. The provincial government must stop at the village gate and the national government should control only interprovince relations. No nation should control another."

"You both educated men," Doc said. "This makes me feel sad. I feel sad, Mista. My country fuckin with yours. I don't know why. You tell me why?" Neither Minh nor Brooks answered. They had been over it many times before. "You know somethin, Mista? We can do most anything. In fifty years we increased life expectancy in America by fifty percent. That's right. If we keep goin, average dude in the World in fifty years gonna live to one hundred twenty years old. We wipe out typhus, smallpox, polio, diphtheria. Why, Mista? Why? Like the L-T wanta know. Why caint we wipe out war?"

"I have a solution for my country," Minh said.

"Well, what the fuck you doin here?" Doc asked harshly. "You belong in Saigon."

"What is your solution, Minh?" Brooks whispered.

"No one," Minh said staring straight up again, "no one will accept a national election of the North and the South with the winner-take-all result. But we could reunite at a very high level similar to your federal government over your state governments. We could still maintain a government in Saigon and a government in Hanoi. Then we would have a neutral federal national government in Hue. That government would stop at the next level down. We would have our harmony restored."

At 0200 hours Rover Team Danielle spotted an enemy force approaching their position. The NVA were moving slowly up a medium-use trail. The point and slack each carried American rucksacks. The third soldier carried an American PRC-25 radio.

They all had rifles which they carried in tight against their bodies. The pointman advanced cautiously, raising and lowering a bulky tube to and from his face between each movement. It appeared to be a scope of some kind. Five meters behind the lead element were four soldiers, two pushing two pulling a small cart. The cart looked much like the market place carts of Da Nang or Hue with their bicycle wheels at the sides and their wooden traces. It was overflowing with supplies but in the dark neither Moneski nor Beaford could distinguish what comprised the load. They woke Gorwitz and Smith silently and pointed out the advancing enemy. The NVA were perhaps ten meters down the path. Rover Team Danielle had occupied an old NVA fighting position a meter off the trail. They waited. Moneski wanted the cart. He wanted to engage the unprepared cartmen with their weapons in the cart. Danielle waited. The NVA approached. Beaford's hands sweated on his machine gun. The enemy squad used five minutes to cover ten meters. When the point was opposite Moneski he stopped. He put his weapon down and turned to the slackman and said something very quietly. There was a pause then they laughed quietly and proceeded. Beaford urinated in his pants. The cart passed. The laborers were breathing hard, forcing the wheels through the mud of the trail. Moneski waited until they were up the trail to a point where it bent. Rover Team Danielle opened up with two M-16s and Beaford's 60. All four cartmen were shot and killed. The other enemy soldiers fled. They did not return fire. The rover team decided to abandon the cart. They backed out of their position and retreated to a secondary position they had chosen earlier.

An hour later Paul Calhoun of Rover Team Ellen killed a lone NVA soldier as the enemy rose from a riverwatcher position not ten meters from Calhoun, Pop Randalph and Jim Woods. Then Rover Team Laurie ambushed and killed three enemy soldiers next to the river. Pop Randalph's second MA, set up between RTs Laurie and Ellen, killed two soldiers fleeing Laurie's ambush. The night had settled down for only a short time when Cherry's MA exploded.

"Get em all," Cherry pleaded from his hidden muck-filled trench. "One for the Garbageman and one for Ridgefield. Get one for Silvers and . . . oh shit . . . get em for anybody." Cherry moved to rise. He wanted to count the dead. Egan grabbed him, held him still. "I gotta see," Cherry whined.

"I don't wanta put ya in for a Purple Heart," Egan answered.

They waited. They waited until half an hour after first light. Cherry fidgeted. His eyes were glassy. He had not slept. He rolled over and with his back to Denhardt and Egan he fondled himself. He thought of the stewardess on the flight from New York to Seattle who had been pleasant and he imagined her naked. Then he thought about Linda. His girl. Not anyone's girl. She made him angry. Off to Boston. Off to New York. Philadelphia. They had never made love yet he could picture her naked too. He could see her fine legs and her soft muff. Cherry rolled his tongue inside his mouth and imagined it in Linda's vagina. That bitch, he thought. I bet she's screwin like a rabbit. I bet she always has. Been screwin guys left and right even when we were goin out. Never gave me none. Bitch. Cherry's anger raised his excitement. Christ, he thought. I need a girl. I need someone to fuck. I got so much jizz stored up if I fucked right now I'd shoot so hard I'd blast her ovaries up to her sinuses. Oh, get em all.

Egan allowed Cherry to recon the MA site while he and Denhardt pulled security. They had killed three NVA soldiers. All three had been carrying rifles. One had had an old infrared-night scope. Later, when Cherry packed it back to Campobasso, FO identified it as French, vintage 1954. The scope amazed everyone in Alpha because they had all been led to believe the US Starlight scopes, technically and in concept, were very recent developments.

Brooks' mind had been working all night. By first light he believed the NVA knew Alpha was on the valley floor and within range of the knoll and NVA guns, but he also believed the enemy did not know Alpha's specific location any better than Alpha knew the enemy's. No enemy troops harassed Alpha's base, nor did mortar rounds impact on or near Campobasso. Bravo and Delta companies had both been hit. Firebase Barnett was mortared. Two Americans were killed, three wounded.

Brooks spent the day of 23 August much as he had spent the day before except that instead of talking he wrote. Occasionally he left his hootch. He spent an hour with FO and several shorter periods with each Doc, Minh, El Paso, Cahalan and Brown. Brooks spoke via krypto radio with the GreenMan. The operation was going well, and the GreenMan encouraged and advised him. When Lt. De Barti returned with Rover Team Joan Brooks briefed and debriefed him thoroughly yet he always returned to his notebooks. He wrote for the best part of ten hours and in that period he completed the rough draft of his thesis on conflict.

AN INQUIRY INTO PERSONAL, RACIAL AND INTERNATIONAL
CONFLICT—RUFUS BROOKS—AUGUST 1970

We think ourselves into war. The antecedents are in our minds.

Conflict, major conflict, does not just happen. It evolves. It may explode over a particular incident but the tension evolves leading gradually to the incident and the explosion. The elements of any conflict, whether it be between individuals or between nations, must form, grow, approach, collide and ignite. Let us here explore the causes and dynamics of conflict and of ultimate conflict—WAR.

Our world is coming apart and it is imperative that we go one step farther and develop a new perspective about, and response to, conflict. Conflicts are actions. Conflict is active disagreement, in its final stage violent disagreement, fights, riots, wars. Here we must set a premise— action, all human action, is preceded by thought. The argument can then be drawn, if thought precedes action then thought precedes conflict. Let us explore the thoughts, and the origins and dynamics of those thoughts, which lead to conflict.

EXPLORATION ONE: The roots of conflict and the expansion and escalation to violence grow from our competitive instincts and are accentuated by our language patterns. When we get into a conflict-compete situation we accentuate the differences in order to strengthen our position. Why? Is this innate in man or is it a part of our mythos, a culturally transferred response handed down from generation to generation? Is the mechanism for transfer language? Written and spoken? What elements in human languages cause us to think ourselves into war? What causes us to perceive a given situation as a conflict situation? What forms our character? What passes xenophobic responses?

LANGUAGE: Thought structured by language. And whose language? English. The white man's language.

Language is a verbal network developed over eons. Written language developed from concrete pictographs to lineal abstract ideography. In language, words, as symbols of reality, are connected one to the next to develop thoughts and concepts. Words evoke other words at a measurable frequency. Given a specific word the word which follows it has a pre-determined tendency to be another specific word. In linguistics this is known as a frequency response. This word to word response frequency is the structure of our language. It has been, to a great extent, formalized. Nouns as subjects of sentences are followed by verbs as predicates. Infants are taught the language of their fathers and later pass the same language to their sons. This is the mechanism for the transfer of acceptable behavior and knowledge from generation to generation. This vast body of a society's knowledge and responses is its mythos. The mechanism for socializing an infant to his culture has a specific though complex structure and that structure controls a human being's potential thoughts. That learned structure determines how a human perceives the world about him. It controls his actions.

The verbal network of western cultures (White) to which we (Black Americans) find ourselves prescribing, accepting, assimilating, has and is proliferating from its western base (America & Western Europe) and has encompassed nearly the entire globe with the possible exceptions of the Asian countries which still maintain pictographic languages. Western verbal structure interprets interpeoples' differences as problems. This, Western Culture teaches, leads to the need for a solution. In Western Cultures solutions may be forced upon situations. This is confrontation and conflict, and this, we are taught, leads to a higher level structure.

This network is built on a view of reality as thesis-antithesis clash resulting in synthesis—a network which forces polarization of entities, which forces, by definition, the entities to contrast, which leads to verbalization of threats, military threats, which heightens our insecurity and raises our defensiveness, which makes us ever more threatening to others and causes them to raise their defensiveness, which leads finally to warfare.

White America would do well to study Eastern thought where synthesis is perceived as the undesirable limiting of natural circles, a thought pattern where every thesis must have an antithesis for it to exist and in which the elimination of either eliminates both. It is a matter of attempting to describe hot while denying the existence of cold. They are not simply opposites. They are varying quantities of one quality and to wipe out one means not to raise by synthesis both to a higher level but to destroy the entity, the quality, itself.

Perhaps we should look to see where language has come from, what road it has traveled to arrive at its present structure. Formal language, like history, is created, established and passed on by the victorious. The winners throughout history are the ones who have passed on language forms and frequencies, patterns which structure our perceptions and thoughts. The way the defeated thought, the structure of their speech and the frequency of their words, has been lost with their military losses. Perhaps it would be more accurate to say the structure of their thought has been repressed with their losses. Victors are allowed to speak, to write, and to publish.

In English-speaking cultures we have a language tradition in which people voice their exposure and contact with other cultures in xenophobic patterns. We are not taught to rejoice in meeting strangers. We are taught to beware, to be fearful. This language also provides a set of cognitive models and expectations which guide our cultural response to publicly articulated threats, threats often posed by politicians with self-

serving motives, politicians threatening us with the supremacy or domination of us by another nation. A man says, "Do you want your children to live under the domination of Red Russia?" One must answer, "No." The "No" is built into our language system. The question is a yes or no question. You're going out of the system if you say anything else. If you say something else you're a radical. Then the Man says, "If South Vietnam falls, it will topple all the staggering unstable dominos we support. If they fall your children will be in forced labor camps and communal farms with Red Guards. Do you want that?" Our response is built into our language structure. The politicians and the news media are very aware of the predetermined patterns (though for different reasons—one for direct control, one for sales, equals $ equals a power of sorts).

I am proposing we break that conformity with a re-thinking, a total restructuring of our semantic network in a manner that the popular rhetoric of inter-peoples differences and tensions reconstructs the experience of those tensions and then directs our responses into alternate manners of eliminating tension. No more rhetorical questions. No more 'Yes-No' questions. Only questions which recreate reality, not lies, and ask us to answer in manners as complex as the reality.

Perhaps part of the problem is that words are only lineal. Western languages have lineal structure. Reality is not lineal. Therefore, words are inadequate to describe reality. According to Cherry visual imagery and spatial relationships are controlled by the right hemisphere of the brain while language is an exclusive property of the left hemisphere. Is it possible Western and Eastern cultures differ so greatly in perspective because the Chinese language is pictorial, is a non-lineal language in which symbols are built to portray reality instead of strung together to describe reality? Is it possible the inscrutableness of the Chinese is due to Western language-thought being founded in the left hemisphere and Eastern language-thought being founded in the right? Neurologically the right hemisphere (again according to Cherry) is the location of what we call the subconscious and also dream and spatial relationships. It is difficult for a man to communicate between his own conscious and subconscious. It must be near impossible for understanding to pass between Western and Eastern minds because it must be like one man's conscious attempting to communicate with another man's subconscious.

Western language tradition analyzes phenomena by breaking them down into components, into separately strung together parts. Preceding parts are considered to cause following parts. Everything is broken into cause-effect dichotomies. Is it possible our political tradition of left-right dichotomy is caused by our language tradition and that by using this descriptive model we structure our perception of reality and affect our reality by forcing it to polarize? (Ref. El Paso.)

Our perception of our political world role is affected by our language tradition. If our language-determined role model is skewed to-

ward dichotomy, toward perceiving and establishing opposing parts, is that not the same as saying, the model causes tension? Our response to tension is also predetermined in our political rhetoric. Our language and thought patterns cause us to react to insecurities both aggressively and defensively. Our actions then cause others to react to us defensively and aggressively. The severity of conflict is heightened. This psychotic behavior propels us into divorce courts, into race riots and into war. Internationally this behavior is military threats and arms escalation. Why do we believe these will lessen tension? They increase it. Is it any wonder that the Soviet Union (its leaders also under the Western language tradition) maintains that if America builds a Safeguard system to protect its Minuteman ICBM force from destruction by Soviet SS-9 missiles, then they, the Soviets, must build a system that will destroy Safeguard. If they do not, the argument goes, they will be unprepared to deter an American assault. Then America says if we do not build a Safeguard system the Soviets may make a first strike against us and with it wipe out our ability to strike back. That will heighten their desire to strike. Each side says it desires to make nuclear war so devastating it will be unthinkable. No one would start such a war. America says do it by limiting your defensives. Russia says do it by expanding your offensive. Either way all the people die. It is a paradox—the more insecure we feel the more defensive we become. The more defensive we become the more we force those about us to be defensive. We thus increase the tension in an unintentional psychotic spiraling manner because of our inability to respond in any other way. Things often are not what they seem. (Minh.)

EXPLORATION TWO: Politicians, Political Rhetoric—How the system works. From the perception of the world in thesis-antithesis terms, more simply an us-vs-them mentality, rises the politician. In America, the pattern of government separated into branches with checks and balances is both an expression of conflict mentality and a cause of future conflict (institutionalizes the pattern—Egan). The political party system is an expression of the same thing. The politician is the tie between the two. It is he who elevates differences, purposefully creating conflict whether conflict exists or not.

It happens this way. A man saying he is the representative of many men about him declares his ideology and he declares his policy and he says his are the best for everyone. In order to defend his stand he must note the differences between him and others. In so doing he establishes conflict where only differences before existed. (There is nothing intrinsically wrong or conflicting about differences.) The man's philosophy is self-serving to both him and the men supporting him. It must be. Politicians are a psychotic form unto themselves. They must gain power to serve. They live on power, by power, for power. They greedily accept it but it must be 'sold' to the masses. An effective 'sales tool' is fear, fear of differences the politician has just established and will now focus on selectively and accentuate. The policy becomes In The National

Interest, or Manifest Destiny, or The Red Menace. The differences become conflicts, the conflicts are accentuated, the response to the heightened conflict is defensive and self-righteous. The interest of one man for the benefit of a select group of men has come to be the party or the nation's policy. The party or the nation becomes aggressively defensive and forces the group who has become the 'bad guys' or the 'political opposition' into a defensive posture. The mutual perception of each other's aggressive/defensive posture, the fear for one's own security, results in a crystallization of differences, the establishment of obstacles to creative thought and finally to actions to eliminate the threat.

It begins with a dichotomy structure of rationality in our language, spreads to polarization of opinions with ever increasing tension. What we lack is a structure to drain off the tension. A country prepares for war and war is very unreal to those who prepare for it and who have never fought. Politicians make it noble to do your best for the men there. For the soldier it becomes his 'Duty' or his 'Mission.' (Ref. Pop R.) The men are often confused.

I enjoy some of the word games we play at war. Pacification. Vietnamization. Mechanical Ambush. Do I enjoy these because they stimulate me? Do I seek stimulation thusly? (Ref. Cherry.) Those are the little word games the military machine has come up with. Perhaps there are others which are so buried in our language tradition we never notice them. Some are big ones. By recognizing just what language is, we immediately recognize some of the more poorly camouflaged, some of the poor substitutes for reality. These are the words and phrases with extended connotations and denotations politicians and other leaders love to use. BEWARE: Servant-of-the-people; communist takeover; human rights; civil rights; self-determination; freedom. If someone threatens you with one of these or promises you one of these, beware. Beware. Governments do not give freedoms anymore than they give taxes. Governments are in the business of restricting human action from unlimited freedom to parameters the people will find acceptable.

THE PEOPLE: That's a good one. Who are the people? Why is it that whoever uses that phrase is referring to himself and the people he wants to control?

Let us develop a new mode of thinking which is more closely tied to reality than our present mode. A mode where every man is independent because his language allows him alternatives. This new way to think, to speak, will, should, allow greater freedom to participate in our culture's therapy. Beware: political rhetoric is self-serving and self-limiting. In many instances it is, at best, irrelevant. The outcome of inter-peoples contacts often depends on factors totally detached from spoken words.

Using this manner of thinking in ref. to international conflict gives the individual person, the man-in-the-street, a new freedom to participate in the flow of history, in the direction of his nation's policies, in the humanity of mankind. He need not have one voice with the president and only be able to express opposition in the form of a vote, one vote every forty-eight months. We can learn to become more independent of external pressures from politicians telling us that X people is trying to destroy us, from business trying to tell us we are not whole without their product, from race leaders telling us that every man from that other race is prejudiced against us and thus we best defend ourselves.

A common adverse effect of every organized system of thought, religious or governmental, is the encouragement of dependence. Governments make us feel that international and indeed even interpersonal relationships are beyond our comprehension and ability. Correct relations can be achieved only through the augmentation of their system powered by our supportive backing. People today consider it impossible not to leave international affairs to the government. They consider it normal for the government to establish goals and quotas for racial and sexual harmony, equal-opportunity reinforcement. We have become victims of the establishment even as we have become part of it.

People who understand that conflict in interpersonal relations is a normal event, that it tends to come and go in cycles, that they are capable of dealing with others themselves without a rigid set of regulations directing them, these people will not wind up as victims, as automatons of the machine. They will not become dependent upon external sources for their security therefore they will not become defensive, then aggressively defensive forcing others into aggressive-defensive postures simply because X leader from Y country or B leader from C race says their security is threatened—says that because he needs that to keep him in power. People who understand will not become dependent on external sources for their security because they will be confident of their own competence to interrelate, to relate with all people of the world. They may consult professionals for information and advice when a problem seems beyond their own competence but they will accept responsibility for the routine management of their own relationships and extend them as far as they may go.

EXPLORATION THREE: Thoughts of Friends.

El Paso: With the exception of oil, world primary commodity prices dropped in relationship to the price of manufactured goods during the past several decades. The United States is partly to blame. During the 1950s the US produced vast quantities of inexpensive, exportable rice through a farm subsidy program. This resulted in an oversupply on the world market and it destroyed the export market for Vietnam and it caused increased poverty in this land. (Incredible, how we are all tied together.) The industrialized West controls the price of manufactured goods because it alone is capable of producing such goods and it has the ability and wealth to control the price of raw materials. Poverty, need, causes conflict.

Egan: There are two ways to solve the problem of poverty and wealth between the haves and the have-nots. One, the poor can increase their wealth through increased production so that simply there is more wealth and everybody lives better and has a better standard of living; or two, wealth can be redistributed so the rich don't have so much and the poor don't have so little. Here the amount of wealth stays the same.

The first view is capitalistic, the second communistic or socialistic. Now, I ask you, under what systems in the world do we see people having the best standard of living? (Note rhetorical Q? Eg asks.) Empirically, is there any doubt?

Doc: The wars of the 20th century may be due to population pressures caused by longer life expectancy. In Vietnam, the introduction of Western medical practices caused the population to increase from sixteen million in 1900 to twenty-eight million in 1950. A 56% increase. Doc says he is not sure of his figures but that is what they tell new medics in San Antonio.

FO: If you think our society is sick maybe it's because we are catering to the illness instead of promoting good health.

Cahalan: Critics and English teachers tend to see all stories as conflicts between antagonists and protagonists. In reality your best stories are written with the characters being people doing things people do. In good literature each character has good and bad qualities which interact with the good and bad qualities of the other characters. They intertwine, not oppose. That's how it should be. That's how life is.

Jax: All wars are expressions by suppressed people of their desires to rule themselves.

Cherry: Maslow once said, "If the only tool you have is a hammer, you tend to see every problem as a nail." If you're a soldier, I guess you tend to see every problem as a target.

Brown: Sports are war. You'd kill a man to beat him on a basketball court if it were for the NCAA championship. Man, I love the game. I love the competition. But, we got to realize it's part of our society which helps a crazy man like Nixon control the people.

Minh: Nothing happens by itself. Everything is unity. Though you may seem isolated from the rest of the world, everything you do is interconnected with the universe. You are not here alone.

The state does not exist apart from the individuals who comprise its citizenry.

There is no such thing as inconsistency. Inconsistencies are a product of a static view of life. (To me this rings true. I have heard and expressed these views before myself, in a slightly different slant. Minh, sometimes I think you are inside my head.) Life is a balance. For everything we acquire, we lose something. To dam a river to generate electrical power you must be willing to accept the loss of the river. You say love is inconsistent with hate. I say they are one. To eliminate hate is also to destroy love. (Perhaps he means to destroy the capacity to hate is also to destroy the capacity to love.) Perhaps that may be taken some steps further. I do not know. Is peace a quality of war? Can one be eliminated without eliminating both?

EXPLORATION FOUR: *Personal Conflict—Marriage.*

Conflict at all levels follows a pattern. At all levels it has seeds, it grows, evolves and finally explodes or perhaps the final level is, it dies. We liked each other, respected each other and perhaps loved each other. Or perhaps we only loved the image we each held of the other. Did our learned language control our perception of each other? Were our ideals of marriage and mates limited, controlled by that language? Were our responses within that marriage, our responses to each other, pre-established by language and thus predestined for conflict? I believe our respect for each other forbade us from stepping over pre-determined bounds and the limiting of our responses to each other destroyed us. These limits, these restrictions were both qualitative and quantitative. They confined our acceptable behavior to a mass-produced, language-induced, artificial rut. If we could graph emotions, ours would have been flat lines with no peaks of elation nor dips to despair. We became excessive only in our limitations and our boundaries were closing on the center. The limits on our emotions became a progressively steeper descent, a self-enhancing restrictiveness ever concentrating until we had no acceptable responses left and had to explode. The more thwarted I, and now I realize, she, became, the more we allowed ourselves to die. Suffocation was evident in physical and sexual as well as psychological and social events in our lives. We had locked ourselves together in a decaying relationship. All this I believe was due to our accepting pre-established frequency responses in our language and they controlled our thoughts. Hawaii was an effect. It began like a movie script—every word and motion perfectly culturally acceptable, perfectly played. Oh, how well we knew our roles without even realizing we were playing them. The perception of differences we did not know how to accept led to irritation we could not diffuse. The irritation led us to entrench, to build false securities, to build walls. We sought and built separate support systems and we prepared for war. The walls heightened our fears and insecurities. We passed from defensive to offensive. We exploded. Perhaps divorce is the death of conflict.

EXPLORATION FIVE: *The American Ideal in Vietnam.*

We came not to conquer. We came to help. We came to insure security and independence. We came to end conflict. We said and we showed that we would selflessly lay down our lives to end this conflict. And yet our altruism has corrupted itself until we can only be satisfied with annihilation. We define everything about is in terms of conflict. As long as there are two sides there will be conflict and we have said we will not tolerate conflict. We will stamp it out. It is the same as sentencing Vietnam to total destruction and annihilation. Perhaps they do not need us. Perhaps without us they will annihilate themselves for they too are determined to end the conflict.

EXPLORATION SIX: Proposals and Solutions—A Proposal for Disarmament.

War is an end result of a series of happenings that occur or which begin when two cultures find they have real or imagined differences and they react in accordance with pre-established behavior patterns. In order to eliminate confrontation behavior and tactics we must substitute for it mutual analysis of the differences, undertaken with mutual respect. We must develop structures which drain away tension. Those structures must be in our thought patterns, in our language, for if we succeed in achieving peace without changing the thought patterns which produced the war we will simply find those same patterns producing wars in the future.

Our language must not speak of power but of people, not of buildings but of lives. We must remove the plastic wrap of fear, domination and status quo *and let reality breathe freely.*

We must alter our perceptions of reality, alter the language structure which contains the mechanism and forms which teach the raw human, the infant, how to perceive, how to interpret what is perceived, and how to act upon those interpretations, so that war is more difficult than peace. It must become easier for mankind to disengage from conflicts than to either engage in or maintain conflicts. And these things we must do without forcing the conflict inside individuals, races, nations— for that is repression and repression compresses tension into a bomb casing and it soon must explode.

This will require time. I doubt it can be legislated. It will eventually require every man to be a leader of himself. Is that possible? Where do we begin? Pre-industrialization, were all men leaders? Is that what a culture gives up to become modern?

Let us treat all people as individuals and all individuals fairly. Let us each believe and teach our young—first, I am an individual human being and then I am a human being. From that basis, I am male. Then Black. Then a soldier. But before all, I am a human individual supporting myself and the unity of humanity.

A more specific proposal. If peace is our long-range objective then armament and deterrence are not the ultimate courses to follow. They do not lead to long-term peace. They are short-range, stop-gap procedures and must be viewed as such. Long-term peace can only be achieved in the absence of 15% GNP military budgets and giant arms stockpiles. We must accomplish the following very soon or the world will cease to exist for humanity. No one is willing to disarm unilaterally. Minh's approach to unifying Vietnam may serve as a model for universal disarmament. Every nation on earth—all will be UN members—will, through their own internally administered mechanism, supply the UN army with, let's begin with one tenth of one percent and work up to ? percent of its men, ages 18 to 25, for 2½ years. Each nation will reduce its armed forces by the number of men contributed. Each UN soldier will learn to speak two languages: possibly Chinese, English or Spanish, beyond his native tongue. Each country will be taxed for this army's upkeep equivalent to what it would pay to support these soldiers at home. All units will be totally integrated by nationality. Gradually all arms will be turned over to the world government and then, once accomplished, gradually the arms will be reduced. The World Army will never be completely disbanded for it will become the security instrument for the people of the world.

Some possibilities: All multi-national corporations shall pay an income tax [deductible from their present national income taxes (perhaps)] to the world government.

If the UN is to serve as the world government it must be restructured to have real inter-national power while maintaining little or no intra-national power.

The day passed. Night arrived. Brooks was elated and exhausted. He conversed via krypto radio with Major Hellman, the XO, in the GreenMan's absence. The Major was not elated. "What in hell are you doing?" he demanded. "You're sitting on your asses while everybody else is humping their tails off. What's wrong with you, Lieutenant?"

"We're getting results, Sir," Brooks answered. He wanted to add, Isn't that what we're here for?

"Get the lead out, Lieutenant. Get moving. Do you want to be another Delta?"

"Oh, yes Sir," Brooks answered. "I had forgotten all about Delta, Sir. How dumb of me. Yes Sir, we're being just like Sky Devil."

Brooks rolled toward El Paso and told him to call the rover teams. "Have them work their way in," he said. "Bring them in slowly. At their pace."

Hellman was still raving on the other radio. El Paso began his call but Brooks stopped him. "This guy's fucked," Brooks said suddenly, uncharacteristically. "Wait one." He paused to think. "Call in the following," he said. "Call in Rover Teams Ellen, Claudia and Stephanie. Tell them I want them here by 0300. They can do anything they want until then. We'll call the others in tomorrow. When you're finished, get the advisers together."

A semblance of CP advisers assembled about the commander. There was fighting to the east. From the sound it could have been either Rover Team Cindy or Jill. To the southwest artillery explosions, first a single round, then a salvo of six, then another and another exploding above the river. Laurie was calling in the raid. They had spotted three or four sampans on the river. In the fog they were not certain. The artillery sunk at least two boats.

Doc, the three CP RTOs, FO and Minh sat in a semi-circle before Brooks. Lt. De Barti and Molino and Lt. Caldwell made a second row. Good God, Brooks thought to himself. Where are all my best troops? No Pop, no Egan, no Jax, Monk, Baiez, Snell, Jenkins, White. Those present were his middle-troops, comfort zone troops. Brooks slid a hand beneath his odd-style cap and scratched his scalp. He was tired from all the writing yet happy about his rough draft. It would have to be revised, he knew, but it was a start. He looked around. FO's tactical opinion was good. El Paso's good. De Barti's fair. Brooks did not really trust Minh. After all this time he had to admit to himself he did not trust Minh with tactics. The rest were worthless, he thought. He did not include Cahalan in any category. Cahalan was his secretary, his guy-Friday. Cahalan knew everything; he just didn't know how to put it together.

Brooks began by re-debriefing De Barti on RT Joan's success. The commander pumped De Barti for every detail. How and where had they set up? Who first spotted the NVA? What were the enemy soldiers doing? How long had the rovers been in position? The questions and answers were informative and the procedure instructive to anyone who might find himself someday in charge. As usual the better soldiers listened carefully. The poorer had no idea why the L-T bothered. Caldwell was lost in his own thoughts a thousand miles away. The question period gave Brooks time to ponder. Should he or should he not throw open the tactical discussion to this group. He decided he must.

"Hey," Brooks said. "Let's hear it. We've got an objective that we've skirted. We've got to hit it. How do you guys think we ought to work it?"

"We got any options?" Lt. Caldwell asked.

"Let's get the fuck outa here," Molino said.

"We've got seventy-five men times four directions of options," Brooks said.

"Couldn't we run for a ridgeline and call in air strikes?" Molino asked quietly.

"Sounds good to me," Caldwell pressed.

"Okay," Brooks snarled. "Option one. I don't think the GreenMan'll agree but we can get fast movers here ourselves. Option two? Anybody?"

"Perhaps," Minh suggested, "if we call in enough artillery tonight, the enemy will leave this valley by tomorrow."

"No way, José," El Paso chuckled.

"We're going after the knoll, aren't we, L-T?" FO asked.

"That's right."

Molino injected, "Maybe you could get the artillery to level it, huh, Sir?"

"We'll have artillery support," FO assured them.

"We're goina resupply tomorrow, aren't we?" De Barti asked.

"Major Hellman wants us to resupply up by Delta," Brooks threw the information out.

"En let evera gook in the valley know where we is?" a voice said from behind the circle. "Are you kiddin? Rover Team Ellen reports, Sir." It was Pop. No one had heard him arrive.

"When we hittin that knoll?" Calhoun asked very quietly.

"They one giant clusterfuck ovah theah, Sir," Woods added. "We seen em. In an outa the fog. Couldn't get no bead on em most a the time cause a the fog, Sir."

Brooks was overjoyed. "Welcome back," he said. Before the group Brooks briefed and debriefed Rover Team Ellen. Pop was tight-lipped about their actions though talkative about his observations of the enemy. Woods wanted to talk. It had been three days since he had been able to speak more than a whisper and telling this group about their contacts made him a hero. Calhoun was much the same except he was quieter and more technical.

"How much extra food do your men have, Pop?" Brooks asked leaving the RT actions.

"We all carry a four-day resupply, Sir," Pop said.

"What about 3d, Larry?"

"The same, L-T," Caldwell answered stiffly.

"And 1st?"

"They always got a four-day," El Paso said.

"Then we're okay through tomorrow?" Brooks asked rhetorically. They all agreed or remained quiet. "I know we're okay through tomorrow," Brooks said peevishly. "I want to know how much *extra* food your men have. If we resupply tomorrow we give our position away. If we don't . . ." He did not finish.

"L-T," Calhoun said after a pause, "most everybody carries a extra day's food."

"Okay," Brooks said.

"My platoon'll be okay too," Caldwell volunteered.

"What about ammo?" Brooks asked. "And batteries?"

"Batteries better be okay through tomorrow and the next day," El Paso said.

"Fuck," Calhoun said. "We've had the radios on near continuous for the past two days. Four batteries per set. That's only eighty hours. You talkin another maybe forty, fifty hours. Aint no way."

"Can we conserve them if we get everybody in?" Brooks asked.

"L-T," Calhoun continued, "you got every set out with the rovers or with the LPs. Hell, you even got Brown's out with somebody. We're just about out of time now."

"We're low on claymores, Sir," Pop said. "But, hell, we got a mission. That's what we come here for."

"We won't need claymores to assault that knoll," Brooks said. "We're going to recon it tomorrow, hit it before dawn the next day. Delta and Recon will be on call. They'll be our reaction force. They'll be moving all around up there tomorrow. El Paso, get the rest of the rovers in. Have them turn their radios off. Fuck resupply."

The GreenMan's maneuvering and guidance of the 7th of the 402d was paying off not just for Alpha but for all his line companies. On the morning of 22 August Bravo swept back over the ridge and through the hospital complex where they had previously engaged the enemy three times. This time they were led by the NVA honcho POW they had captured. The POW led a platoon of Bravo into a second bunker complex that was concealed by the first. The boonierats of Bravo engaged a small element of enemy troops. The NVA could hardly believe that an American unit would hit them there again. The Bravos killed seven NVA and captured over three tons of rice which was destroyed in place by saturating it with gasoline and herbicides. Bravo sustained no casualties. At 1415 hours the NVA POW attempted to escape and was killed by organic weapons fire. Bravo rested and resupplied on the 23d. On the 24th they would move down to seal off the northeast corner of the Khe Ta Laou.

Charlie Company had been in the western end of the valley trudging back and forth for seven days. On the eve of 21 August, feeling secure that they had discovered every path, trail and road leading into the Khe Ta Laou, they began mining, booby-trapping and ambushing the routes. That night three of their traps caught NVA supply teams. Charlie policed up 700 pounds of ammunition and rice and three carts and they found a series of blood trails. The night of the 22d produced three more clashes. This time Charlie got bodies. Six. And a truck. The 23d was their most successful day. NVA supply teams detonated four widow-makers making eight new widows.

Echo's recon platoon was separated from Delta on the 22d and CAed back to Hill 848. That night they were probed by an NVA company coming into the Khe Ta Laou. Six Americans were wounded in the ensuing battle. All were medevacked. Two died. One was evacuated to Da Nang and then to Japan and three were returned to duty. Fourteen enemy were killed, thirteen new AK-47 rifles were captured along with one 9mm pistol and numerous documents. An analysis of the documents revealed that the enemy force was one of five newly arrived replacement units for the NVA 5th Infantry Battalion. The replacements had orders to reinforce the NVA 7th Front Headquarters situated in the Khe Ta Laou.

Delta company, under its new commander, Captain Ernie Masgary, managed to kill three enemy soldiers on the 22d. The Delta troops decapitated the enemy bodies and displayed the heads on poles. On the 23d they found two of their troops who had been on an LP fifty meters from the perimeter. These men also were decapitated. Their heads were found placed on poles where they had been killed. Their bodies had been removed and were never recovered.

SIGNIFICANT ACTIVITIES

THE FOLLOWING RESULTS FOR OPERATIONS IN THE O'REILLY/ BARNETT/JEROME AREA WERE REPORTED FOR THE THREE-DAY PERIOD ENDING 2359 23 AUGUST 1970:

THIS THREE-DAY PERIOD WAS CHARACTERIZED BY A WELL COORDINATED SERIES OF RAIDS AND AMBUSHES BY THE 7TH BATTALION, 402D INFANTRY AGAINST THE 7TH NVA FRONT IN THE KHE TA LAOU RIVER VALLEY.

A SQUAD OF 3D PLT, CO A, 7/402 SPOTTED AN NVA SQUAD IN THE VICINITY OF YD 150320 AT ABOUT NOON ON THE 21ST. ARTILLERY WAS EMPLOYED RESULTING IN FOUR NVA KILLED. AN HOUR

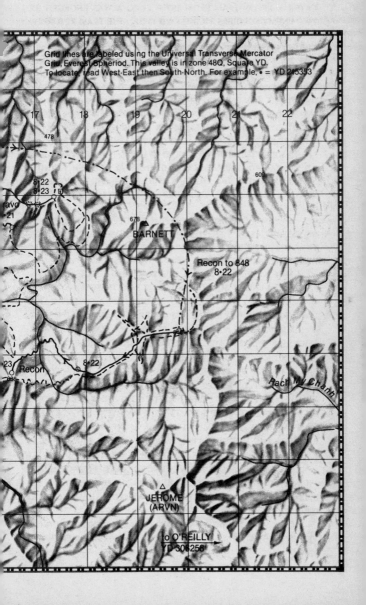

Grid lines are labeled using the Universal Transverse Mercator Grid, Everest Spheriod. This valley is in zone 48Q, Square YD. To locate: read West-East then South-North. For example, • = YD 215353

17   18   19   20   21   22

478

609

8·22
8·23

avo
21

678
BARNETT

Recon to 848
8·22

23
Recon
886

8·22

Rach My Chanh

JEROME
(ARVN)

to O'REILLY
YD 306258

LATER A RECON TEAM FROM 1ST PLT, CO A WAS ENGAGED BY TWO ENEMY SOLDIERS VICINITY YD 147322. THE TEAM RETURNED ORGANIC WEAPONS FIRE KILLING BOTH ENEMY. COMPANY A CONTINUED MAKING CONTACT WITH SMALL ELEMENTS OF THE ENEMY UNIT ALL DURING THE NIGHT OF THE 21ST. RESULTS WERE AS FOLLOWS: VICINITY YD 147320, ONE NVA KILLED BY CO A SNIPER AT 2045 HOURS. AT 0200 HOURS ON THE 22D AN ELEMENT OF 1ST PLT, CO A DISCOVERED AN NVA MORTAR SQUAD AT YD 155323. THE ENEMY HAD JUST FIRED TWO 82MM ROUNDS WHICH IMPACTED OUTSIDE THE PERIMETER AT FIREBASE BARNETT. THE ELEMENT ENGAGED THE ENEMY WITH FRAGMENTATION GRENADES KILLING THREE NVA AND DAMAGING THE MORTAR TUBE. AN NVA SQUAD TRIPPED A CO A MECHANICAL AMBUSH VICINITY YD 151325 DURING THE NIGHT. A FIRST LIGHT CHECK REVEALED FIVE NVA KIA. FOUR AK-47 RIFLES AND ONE RPG LAUNCHER WERE CAPTURED.

CO C, 7/402 CAUGHT THREE ELEMENTS OF NVA IN AMBUSHES. NO ENEMY CASUALTIES WERE REPORTED THOUGH THE UNIT CAPTURED 700 POUNDS OF RICE AND THREE CARTS. THE CARTS AND RICE WERE DESTROYED.

ON 22 AUGUST CO A CONTINUED TO MAKE SPORADIC CONTACT WITH ENEMY SQUADS. IN FIVE SEPARATE ACTIONS NORTH OF THE KHE TA LAOU RIVER CO A KILLED 14 NVA SOLDIERS AND CAPTURED NINE AK-47S, ONE SKS CARBINE, AN INFRARED SCOPE, 16 82MM MORTAR ROUNDS, SIX RUCKSACKS (AMERICAN), ONE PERSONAL RADIO COMBAT (AMERICAN) AND VARIOUS LETTERS AND DOCUMENTS. THE EQUIPMENT WAS DESTROYED ON THE 24TH.

AT 1058 HOURS VICINITY YD 171328 CO B, 7/402 DISCOVERED A BUNKER COMPLEX HIDDEN BENEATH A COMPLEX THEY HAD DESTROYED SEVERAL DAYS EARLIER. THE COMPLEX WAS DEFENDED BY AN NVA REINFORCED SQUAD WHICH WAS WELL ENTRENCHED. CO B ENGAGED THE ENEMY WITH ORGANIC WEAPONS FIRE OVERRUNNING THE POSITION AT 1325 HOURS. SEVEN ENEMY WERE KILLED AND THREE TONS OF RICE WERE DESTROYED.

CO C, 7/402 KILLED SIX NVA IN TWO SEPARATE ENGAGEMENTS VICINITY YD 122326. A FIREFIGHT ENSUING ONE OF THE CONTACTS LED CO C TO A SOVIET-BUILT MEDIUM WEIGHT UTILITY VEHICLE (TRUCK).

CO D, 7/402 ENGAGED AN UNKNOWN SIZE ENEMY PATROL VICINITY YD 147332 AT 2025 HOURS KILLING THREE ENEMY WITH SAF.

IN THE FIREBASE O'REILLY AREA ON 22 AUGUST AN ELEMENT OF THE 3D BN, 1ST REGT (ARVN) ENGAGED A LARGE ENEMY FORCE. ARTILLERY, ARA AND TACTICAL AIR STRIKES SUPPORTED THE GROUND FORCES WHICH WERE IN CONTACT FROM 0930 HOURS UNTIL SUNSET. A SEARCH OF THE CONTACT AREA REVEALED 42 NVA KIA, 26 BY ARA FROM THE 4TH BN, 77TH ARTY (AMBL), 101ST. THREE ARVN SOLDIERS WERE KILLED AND NINE WOUNDED.

AT 0240 HOURS ON 23 AUGUST RECON PLT, CO E, 7/402 WAS PROBED IN THEIR NDP. THE UNIT WAS PROBED AGAIN AT 0345 HOURS AND AT 0435 HOURS AN UNKNOWN SIZE ELEMENT OF ENEMY ASSAULTED THE UNIT'S POSITION FROM THE SOUTHEAST WOUNDING SIX AMERICANS. ALL WERE EVACUATED AT FIRST LIGHT. A FIRST LIGHT CHECK OF THE PERIMETER REVEALED 14 ENEMY KILLED, FIVE BY SAF AND NINE BY ARTILLERY. 13 INDIVIDUAL WEAPONS WERE CAPTURED ALONG WITH LETTERS AND DOCUMENTS.

AN LP OF CO D, 7/402 WAS OVERRUN BY AN UNKNOWN SIZE ENEMY FORCE RESULTING IN TWO US SOLDIERS KILLED IN ACTION.

IN FOUR SEPARATE ACTIONS, CO C, 7/402 KILLED EIGHT ENEMY SOLDIERS VICINITY YD 129317. SIX INDIVIDUAL WEAPONS WERE CAPTURED.

28 ENEMY WERE KILLED IN THE FIREBASE O'REILLY AREA BY ELEMENTS OF THE 1ST AND 3D REGTS (ARVN) SUPPORTED BY ARA AND TACTICAL AIR STRIKES IN DAY LONG ACTIONS. ARVN CASUALTIES WERE FIVE WOUNDED AND TWO KILLED.

CHAPTER

29

24 AUGUST 1970

They did not see the river until they were in it. The night was black beneath the mist. The entire valley floor was wet swamp. Egan led the small group east from Campobasso then south. No one spoke. They sloshed through the bog. The rain and its camouflaging noise had ceased. They moved slowly though there was little time.

Behind Egan was Cherry and behind him, Pop. Further back were Snell, Nahele and McQueen, then Denhardt, Doc Johnson and Minh and finally Woods and Calhoun. Essentially the patrol consisted of Alpha's best boonierats, best medic and only scout. Their mission would require the best. They moved with the stealth of a lone cat until Egan fell into the river with a noisy, ear-splitting splash.

Rover Teams Claudia and Stephanie had returned to Campobasso shortly past midnight. The others would return between dawn and dusk on the 24th. Brooks, FO and El Paso spent the night debriefing Claudia and Stephanie along with Pop's team, Ellen, and then briefing them all on the next mission. "We need a physical recon of the knoll," Brooks had said. He asked for volunteers which was his style. When he wanted a man to do something he made the man want to do it. He made his boonierats feel good, feel special. All nine volunteered. They were hungry for more action. It showed in their eyes. Doc too volunteered though he did so because he was afraid for these crazy men, afraid they would need his services. And Minh volunteered because he wished to stay with Doc. Brooks accepted them all.

As they discussed the mission a series of engagements progressed slowly up the west side of their AO. First RT Mary's MA detonated. Jenkins radioed the results almost immediately. Three NVA killed or wounded and now dead, and two rifles captured. A few minutes later RT Irene sniped and killed an enemy soldier and sent half a dozen fleeing north. They did not pursue. The same enemy squad ran into RT Beth set up across the trail. In the ensuing firefight Beth killed two. Juan Rodriguez was wounded though not seriously. Alpha's four-day total now stood at forty-seven NVA KIA versus one US WIA.

The briefing continued while the fighting went on to the west. The recon team would move east then south to the river. Three men would cross traveling as lightly as possible. They would recon the knoll as much as possible, before dawn, then recross the river and return. They could decide among themselves who would go, Brooks said, though he suggested they pick the strongest swimmers. They should leave Campobasso by 0330, in ten minutes.

Brooks was concentrating well now. He did not think of conflict. Nor did he think of Lila. And the DEROS/Extend question also had dissolved. He would DEROS when the GreenMan was through with him which should be in as little as four days. Now he did not have to think of those things. He had only to think of Alpha, the valley, the knoll and the NVA. Brooks concentrated on the topo map, buried himself beneath a poncho and with a flashlight stared at the map until it engraved itself on his mind, until it told him what the land already knew, what the enemy must do. He moved Alpha on the gameboard in his head and he saw the NVA counter his move. He tried his unit there and saw the pitfalls. He moved the NVA. No, they would not do that. I wouldn't do that if I were them. That's a bad move. He moved them again. He attempted alternative after alternative and he countered each. They would be out for Alpha. He knew that. Alpha had been their nemesis. They would play extra hard to destroy it.

Major Hellman radioed. "Where in the name of hell are your resupply lists?" he demanded. "Charlie, Delta and Recon are ready for resupply but Alpha hasn't even checked in with S-4. What the hell are you doing, Lieutenant?"

Brooks kept cool. Hellman was only the XO. The GreenMan

would be, might be, flexible enough to allow Alpha to postpone resupply and carry out Brooks' plan. Brooks had Cahalan compile the lists. They needed food for seventy-four men, clothing, socks, dozens of personal items. They needed radio batteries. Not just the normal replacement number but enough to replace the reserve they carried unknown and unexpected by the command. And they needed ammo. Claymores, frags, 60 and 16 rounds and 79 rounds for the new XM 203 over/unders.

"Call it in," Brooks said. "Tell them we'll resupply last."

The recon team moved fifty meters upriver from where Egan had splashed in. They set up a small perimeter and ambush five meters from a red ball/river intersection. They had spent an hour moving 800 meters. It was 0430 and they were behind schedule. Egan, Cherry and McQueen stripped off all excess gear. They would not attempt to engage the enemy. They had, at best, two hours to cross, to observe, and then to get the hell out. They carried no rifles, no radio. Each man carried three frags and a bayonet. They removed their boots and tied them to their waists then eased into the dark current. False dawn lightened the sky but the knoll, indeed even the south bank, was invisible through the fog. They swam. Cherry led, breaststroking quickly, quietly. He reached the far bank, crouched in the shallow water and awaited the others. McQueen swam into him. Then Egan. They put their boots on, crawled up the bank and waited soundlessly. Then they moved very slowly, very quietly away from the river. They listened to the river current babbling over tiny snags at the bank. The sound faded as they dissolved inland. With each step they paused. They crossed first one trail, then another, then a red ball. They headed south, then west until they were behind the knoll. To that point the valley floor had been about like the valley floor everywhere they had walked: grass, discontinuous brush, secondary scrub and bamboo. Now it changed. It rose steeply, almost a cliff. Egan led the group farther west across the base of the peninsula of the knoll. All the while they climbed. Not so steeply now. The vegetation changed. It resembled the ridge foliage and it was silhouetted against the clearing sky. At mid-peninsula they discovered two parallel trails. The paths were narrow and ran toward the top. Beyond the second trail there was a trench. It also ran toward the top. They crossed it and burrowed into the undergrowth and sat. Egan checked his compass. He checked his watch. It was 0520.

* * *

On the far side of the river Minh, Doc and Snell sat next to each other trying to stay warm. Snell had camouflaged his radio by sticking to it six pieces of grass, just enough to break up its square appearance, and he had pushed the set as far from himself as the handset cord would allow. He sat and waited too.

To Minh the wait was terrifying. The Americans were becoming restless, too restless with him. They had begun looking at him as if he were a gook. Even Brooks had changed. Oh yes, Minh thought. He had felt it. He could feel the hungry eyes on him, the cold breath of these crazy men. Doc is my only friend, Minh told himself. If it were not for Doc they would destroy me. Minh thought about the North Vietnamese. They had developed greatly from the time three years ago when Minh knew them.

They will kill all these Americans, Minh thought. And they will kill me too. It is as Doc said, a suicide mission. Perhaps I should slip off into the jungle. They would love to capture me. How easily I could rid myself of these American fatigues and become one with them. Oh, what am I thinking? They too would murder me. They would torture me as they did my City of Hue. It is only with Doc that I am safe.

At Campobasso they waited too. Night was passing. Had the recon got off all right? Brooks wondered. From the ambush vantage point Snell had reported watching the three vanish into the fog and dark at mid-stream. That's balls, Brooks thought. Egan, Cherry, McQueen. Balls. The goddamned biggest brass balls in the Nam. No company should be without boonierats like those.

False dawn had come and gone. First light was approaching quickly. The scattered rover teams were becoming restless. For days they had lost themselves in thorn thickets and beneath mist. For days they had paid no attention to time. They had become disoriented. Time had lost its sequential pace. Beneath the mist day and night lost contrast. The boonierats slept when the sky was coal black and when it was slate gray. They moved with equal ease day or night. Within their sections they pulled guard in shifts, ate in shifts, slept in shifts. Each shift lasted no more than two hours. Had they been on a spaceship with no night or far beneath the sea with no day they would have been equally time disoriented. Only one thing kept them from total insanity, saved them from the burden of being lost in time: to most of

them it meant nothing. Time was not measured in sunrises and
sunsets, not in days. It was measured in shifts and resupplies and
operations and tours. For the rovers the operation would not end
until they conquered the knoll or were destroyed trying.

As the sky lightened the knoll materialized above them.
They had ascended to a height where the fog was thin. Below
them ground mist and blackness obscured even the closest foliage.
But above, above there was a shadow, a black blur against a
gray fog sky, an immense black blur which seemed to envelop
them. The sky became brighter. The top of the blur was a single
tree so immense it seemed to dwarf them and the knoll.

Cherry heard them first. There seemed to be only a few.
They moved quietly though casually. Cherry hefted a grenade
and stared through the brush at them, at them approaching. Egan
laid his hand lightly on Cherry's, then more firmly. He motioned
downhill and froze. Cherry dared not turn to look. Now he heard
the second group too. He heard McQueen breathe. The groups
met on the trails before them. Those descending yawned. They
handed something, scopes, to those climbing. They chatted softly,
easily, then parted, those climbing, continuing up, those
descending, continuing down. Then one stopped. He walked to
the side of the trail and looked into the trench. He squatted,
looked at the trail edge, then at the trench again. He called softly
to the others but they had gone. Quickly the soldier picked up a
handful of dead leaves and scattered them over the spot he had
scrutinized. Then he relieved himself. Cherry could see his urine
steaming. He was nearly urinating on McQueen. When he finished he strolled down into the mist and darkness.

Rover Team Jill arrived at Campobasso at 0620 hours, just
after first light. They were restless, hungry, exhausted. Jax was
wired. For ten minutes neither Brooks nor FO was able to ask a
question. Finally Jax shut up long enough for the debriefing to
begin. What had they seen since their contact with the mortar
teams? Who, what, when, where? Details. Details. Brooks wanted
more pieces of the gameboard. He and Jax reviewed the topo
map. He noted every trail, every enemy sighting. He noted the
times. Then Brooks, FO and El Paso connected the dots again.
Where were the little people? Where do they come from? Where
do they go? What would they know about Alpha from the
contacts? Could they pin down Alpha's location? With the earlier

morning contacts the engagements of the last four days made a box around Alpha. Could the NVA still think, did they ever think, that the contacts were made by elements of Delta coming down the cliffs and Charlie coming up the valley? Very unlikely, Brooks thought. It was time to go.

"Brown," Brooks called his command net RTO.

"Yes L-T."

"Take these three to the berm. Let them sleep for the next six. You pull guard for them. Okay?"

"Roger that, L-T."

"Make them sleep," Brooks said. "If you need anything send a runner. Conserve your batteries."

"L-T," Cahalan called. Brooks looked at the krypto RTO. "It's Major Hellman on the hook. He says he can have log birds at our station at dawn plus thirty."

"What?"

"The resupply, L-T. Hellman's got our shit already to fly."

"Augh fuck. FUCK resupply! When's the GreenMan coming back?"

"I don't know, L-T."

"Tell that assh . . . , tell the major we've got too many men out on X-rays. Tell him better than half the company is out humping and won't be in before, ah, noon."

Cherry emerged from the water onto the river's north bank alone. He was winded from the swim. About his waist he had the end of a heavy rope. He crawled into the vegetation and put his boots on. It was 0720, thirty-one minutes after sunrise. The river and the valley floor were still cloaked in mist but it was thin and above was light. The sun was out.

"Sssstt. SKYHAWKS," Cherry called.

"SKYHAWKS yer cherry ass," Pop whispered back. "Where in hell's Egan en Queenie?"

"Here," Cherry said quickly. "On the other end a this." He untied the rope from his waist. Urgently he said, "We're goina need everybody to haul it in."

"They daid?"

"Goddamnit, Pop! No. Course not. They're guiding the cart. Now get em over here. The dinks are goina be madder'n hell when they wake up."

"What?"

"Git."

Pop scrambled back into the brush and in seconds had Snell, Denhardt, Calhoun, Doc and Minh heaving on the rope. Nahele and Woods moved up the trails to pull security.

"Pull," Cherry began a soft cadence. "Pull. Pull. Pull." The rope came toward them.

"What the fuck is it?" Calhoun asked.

"You'll see," Cherry gasped. "Pull. Pull."

They pulled. The mist was too thick for them to see the far bank but they heard the clatter and the splash and the tension on the rope quadrupled almost pulling them all into the river.

"Pull. Pull. Pull." Cherry continued the cadence.

They pulled, they strained. The rope came toward them steadily now. They grabbed forward, pulled back. Then, about mid-stream, it appeared, or *they* appeared. McQueen and Egan seemed to be hanging on, guiding it, keeping it from capsizing. The damn thing was half-boat, half-cart. An amphibious cart with a bow rope. There were double bicycle wheels on each side, half-out of the water. The inside appeared full. The cargo was heaped high though it was covered with a tarp. The recon squad pulled harder. Cherry quickened the cadence.

"I'll be dipped in shit," Snell laughed. All of them began chuckling.

The cart wheels hit bottom on the near side. McQueen and Egan lurched for the bank and scrambled into the covering vegetation. "Get it up and get out," McQueen spurted the words out.

"They'll be here, there," Egan pointed across the river, "any minute."

They rushed. Four of them slid down the bank and surrounded the cart. They pushed and lifted. The others pulled on the rope. The cart seemed to weigh tons. The wheels lodged against the bank. The cart wouldn't climb the steep mud wall. Three more boonierats slid into the current. Seven lifted. Pop and Minh pulled with all their might from the top. All strained. The wheels dislodged from the muck. Boonierat feet sunk in deep. "Up," Cherry whispered. "Up. Up." Up they surged. Up rose the cart, up over the lip. On its wheels it shot forward, nearly running Minh over. The boonierats clambered up the bank. They caught the cart and rolled it away from the river, up a narrow trail, then in under cover. Cherry whipped the tarp off the cargo. There were seven 122mm rockets, four rocket boosters, four vehicle mount radios and an envelope of documents.

*   *   *

"What's that one say, Minh?" Doc asked.

Snell had radioed the haul to the CP immediately after they had set up a perimeter. "You got a what?" El Paso had asked.

"An amphibious cart loaded with one-two-twos and radios," Snell reiterated.

No one in Alpha, no one in the battalion, no one in the entire brigade, had ever seen an amphibious cart. The concept of it gave the NVA greater logistical flexibility than anyone dreamed they had. A cart like that would eliminate the need for bridges or ferries or boats, Brooks realized. Brooks radioed the GreenMan. He was still away from the station. "Say again, Over," Major Hellman had Brooks repeat the description a third time. Then he ordered Brooks to have his men rig the cart for extraction. He would come in with the GreenMan's bird himself and lift the cart out.

Pop and Egan attached the bow rope to the cart's stern corners jerryrigging a sling for the extraction. Then they filled in at the perimeter allowing Doc and Minh the freedom to translate at least a few of the documents before the envelope was taken away with the cart.

"What's that one say?" Doc repeated.

"This says," Minh translated as he read, " 'the great American people are behind us and against their own army. The firebase they call O'Reilly is already making American newspapers. The people of the United States are up in arms against their Imperialist War Lords. We should take strength from the proletariat, our comrades in America. If we are strong we can repeat the effectiveness of Firebase Ripcord on the American people and their Congress.' "

"This is fucked," Brooks moaned to himself. "Why in hell didn't they just look at it? Report it? Fucken Hellman. He's going to bring a bird in here. That's it. It's over. They know our exact location, our exact plan." Brooks called in El Paso and FO and Monk, Moneski, who had just arrived with RT Danielle. He settled himself down before he addressed them. Then he fed them his thoughts and apprehension.

El Paso acted frustrated and angry and sympathetic. This time he was no help. FO plotted the recon river crossing and suggested an immediate barrage on and about the river's south bank. Brooks agreed and had FO call Armageddon Two to lay it on. The Monk, weary from his rover team ordeal, shrugged. "Aint no problem," he said. "Have em push the cart upstream a klick."

"Of course," Brooks agreed. He lit up. "Hey, sure, of course. Monk, that's genius. El Paso, get Pop on the hook."

Alpha's recon team moved reluctantly. The ground mist was thinning with every passing minute. It was no longer dark or gray on the valley floor although visibility beneath the fog was still less than twenty meters. Pop led the patrol. Egan and Cherry walked a double slack. In order to move the cart they had to stay on a trail and expose themselves to the potential of booby traps, ambushes and snipers. They moved slowly, laboriously. They took turns pushing and pulling. The cart rolled easily but the exposure was terrifying. Each of them bitched separately. Sometimes they bitched in twos.

"Pop smoke. Over," Hellman radioed.

"Pop smoke," Snell whispered to Egan. Egan set off a deep green smoke grenade and the smoke billowed and mixed with the mist. "Smoke out. Over," Snell radioed back.

"I see Lucky Lime. Over," Hellman called.

"That's affirm," Snell verified the color. He could hear the helicopter making its passes. First high, then low.

"Pop smoke," Hellman ordered again.

"What the fuck," Snell cussed. He tossed out a purple canister. "Smoke out. Over."

"I see Goofy Grape. Over."

"Roger that, Red Rover. Goofy Grape. Over." Then aside, "Goofy Fucker."

The helicopter hovered over their location, the rotor wash pushed the ground mist away creating a hole in the fog. The sun was blinding. The pilot rocked the ship side-to-side enlarging the hole, giving Major Hellman a chance to see the ground and the cart and the troops below. Egan stood atop the cart. He was holding up a loop in the rigging. The crew chief stood on one skid directing the pilot down. Major Hellman stood on the opposite skid. "Great job," he screamed into the roar of the helicopter engine. On the ground Doc and Minh watched him. The other boonierats had set up a wide, loose security perimeter. Doc signaled Egan that the lines below him were okay. "Great job," Hellman screamed again. He threw a half-full mail sack toward Doc and waved. Egan secured the rope loop to the hook

on the belly of the Huey and signaled the crew chief. The bird
rose slightly, then more. The lines became taut. Egan jumped
from the cart and grabbed his M-16. The bird lifted, rotated. The
cart rose and swung. The bird gained altitude. The ground mist
closed back in. Doc had grabbed and opened the mail bag. He
had seen it purely by accident. On the very top there was a letter
for Egan. He reached in and pulled it out. The squad reformed
quickly. Doc stared at the letter. Pop urged the squad to leave
quickly. "To the north and then west," he said.

"South to the river," Egan said. "Better cover."

Doc smiled. He grabbed Egan and handed him the letter.
Doc was grinning broadly, happy for Egan. The return address
simply said Stephanie.

Mortar rounds began falling and exploding.

Brooks had completed the debriefing of RT Cindy and was
almost finished with Suzie when the recon team took its first
casualty. RT Suzie had made no contacts in the four days of
hide-n-hit. They were the only team who not only had no kills
but also had no sightings. Why? What had they been doing?
How had they operated? The team consisted of Harley, Andrews
and Hill, all good soldiers from Whiteboy's old squad. Brooks
pried. He found no irregularities. Perhaps Egan's team, which
had been to Harley's east, had halted the traffic before it reached
RT Suzie. Brooks did not push it too far. He did not reprimand,
did not show disappointment. Brooks himself was critical of
other commanders he called "body-count mad." He did not
want to be categorized with them. He dropped the subject,
briefed the three boonierats on the upcoming mission and dismissed them with "Good job. Thanks. Get some rest. Conserve
your batteries." He would, however, watch them more closely.
Had it not been Whiteboy opening up with his machine gun on
nothing who halted the move off Hill 848? The sound of mortar
rounds exploding upriver halted his thoughts.

Minh was the first one hit. The first mortar rounds exploded
very close and the boonierats hit the dirt. The second and third
rounds exploded among them. And Minh was hit. He was hit in
the back of the head and neck and up his left side. Blood gushed
from his head. Doc was on him immediately. Inaccurate automatic weapons fire raked their general area from a distance.

Mortar rounds began exploding again. Metal sliced into Snell's legs. He had been on the radio to Brooks with the first explosion. He groaned, grunted. Then it did not hurt at all. He checked his legs. He could see splinters of tangled feet but he could not believe they were his feet. Pop was next to him with his compass out. More rounds exploded on them.

"Augh fuck," Snell moaned. "I'm sorry, Pop. Oh shit, I'm sorry."

"Quiet Rover Four, X-ray. Over," Pop called.

"X-ray, Four. Over."

"We dashin november. Enemy fire coming from our sierra fifty-five degree whiskey. Range maybe five hundred meters. Over. Out."

From Campobasso Brooks radioed the GreenMan. FO radioed Armageddon Two.

Doc tied three camouflaged battle-dressings to Minh's head. Blood was coming from Minh's nose and running over his face in wide bright streams. "Get em on my back," Doc told Denhardt. He lifted the small Vietnamese scout and fell in behind McQueen. Egan was leading them due north almost at a run. They hunched low and ran through the grass and brush. Cherry and Pop helped Snell in a kind of double three-legged race. Mortar rounds continued exploding all about them.

"Fucken gooks," Egan hissed. Fucken gooks en fucken Hellman en his fucken bird. Egan's mind raced as he broke through the vegetation like a mad fullback. We shoulda blown the fucken thing. They're aimin in on the extraction spot. Can't see us. Can't have one a their units here, right here. Egan slowed before an area of low brush. His thoughts caught up to him. They wouldn't mortar their own people. Egan had been pumping his thighs high, breaking through brambles, leaving a mashed clearing behind him. The others had followed blindly in his wake. The NVA mortars moved east, then west. Now they were being walked north. They were falling behind the squad. Armageddon, the 105 howitzer battery on Barnett, shot out a salvo of counter-battery fire. Then another. Armageddon worked rounds quickly back and forth over the area Pop had designated to Brooks. Then the howitzers fired at coordinates FO had called in earlier. The mortars ceased with Armageddon's third salvo.

Doc had Minh on the ground. He knelt at his side and ripped the small scout's shirt open. Minh's back was a blotted mass of blood. Doc put his ear to Minh's chest. Egan rushed down to help. Cherry raised Minh's legs. Behind them Calhoun and Pop radioed Dust-Off. Nahele and McQueen cut Snell's pants and boots off and tied tourniquets at the tops of his thighs. Denhardt and Woods spread out for security. Doc raised up onto his knees. For half a second he stared blankly at Egan then at Minh's tiny chest. Doc cocked his right arm and smashed Minh's chest with his fist, smashed down hard jolting the ceased heart. He ran a finger up Minh's abdomen to the sternum, moved up two finger widths, set the heel of his hand and compressed. "Breathe em," Doc ordered Egan who was already around to Minh's head. Egan checked Minh's mouth and cleared rice vomit from the airway. Gently, trying to stay clear of the wounds, he lifted Minh's neck and pushed his head back, then rechecked the mouth and airway. Egan covered Minh's mouth, squeezed Minh's nostrils, and blew quick hard breaths. He could feel the air inflate Minh's lungs. Doc continued pumping on Minh's chest, compressing, releasing, sixty times a minute. Egan settled down to inflating Minh's lungs every five seconds. They got their rhythms and settled in. "Check them dressings," Doc ordered Cherry. "Come on," he snapped when Cherry hesitated.

The medical evacuation helicopter was in the air within three minutes of notification. It headed inland from Camp Evans and rendezvoused with two escort Cobras above the Rach Mỹ Chành River. The artillery unit on Firebase Barnett fired half-battery harassment salvos once each minute until the Dust-Off reached the valley. Pop handled the Dust-Off systematically. He established direct radio contact with the medevac pilot and gave him an approximate 265° vector from the firebase. A firebase RTO came on the net and informed the pilot, "We have winds at 90°, five to seven knots." Pop took over again. He briefed the pilot on the tactical situation. "There aint a friendly in a klick radius. Over."

"Roger that," the pilot answered. He asked several questions about the LZ and about the wounded.

"Low brush area to our november," Pop said. "Ground fog burning off. It's still maybe ten feet thick. When your skids hit the fog you'll be right atop us." Pop kept up constant directions. Nahele took Snell to the south edge of the pick-up site. McQueen, Denhardt and Woods secured the north side. Calhoun relinquished the radio to Pop and moved east. Pop moved into the low brush area. All the time Doc and Egan rhythmically worked over Minh's body.

"You can quit," Cherry said. "He's dead."

Neither answered. Neither stopped. Cherry lit a cigarette, took a deep drag and let it out. He took another drag then held the smoke for Doc. Doc scowled and shook his head.

"Doc," Cherry said matter-of-factly. "He's dead. I can see his brains. They spillin out all over." Cherry reached over to Minh's head. He flicked up the edge of the field dressings. A blood pocket beneath released. The blood flowed thickly onto the earth. A mass of bloody gray-pink-white sponge-like tissue followed it. Cherry lifted the dressing higher exposing the opened side and back of the head and neck. Egan stopped the inflations. He stared at Cherry. Cherry's eyes were intense, crazy.

Doc continued the compressions. His eyes were shut. He was crying. Cherry looked closely at Minh's head. He poked a finger into the cavity. "That's the cerebrum," he said. He leaned closer. "That's the area of the brain stem. That there must be the medulla oblongata. And this back here is the cerebellum."

The sound of helicopters returned to the Khe Ta Laou as it had not been since the operation's sixth day. Charlie, Delta and Recon were all resupplying. Chinooks resupplied the firebase. The day became hot. The sky cleared. Only a vestige of ground mist remained about the valley, mostly along the river and at valley center. Alpha was together, all seventy-two boonierats at Campobasso. The last of the rover teams had arrived at noon. The recon team returned at 1230 hours. Brooks continued to tell Hellman and the GreenMan that Alpha was split up all over. "But on their way back in . . . right now," he said. If they'll just stay out of here until we debrief, he thought, then we'll have the munition to delay resupply.

"This I want to hear step-by-step, minute-by-minute," Brooks said when he had them together. He and FO and El Paso along with all three platoon lieutenants debriefed the recon team. Pop looked very weary. Doc did not speak. McQueen was glassy-eyed, Cherry indifferent. He had bruises on his face, "from slamming his face into the ground when the mortars fell," he said. Egan's hands were bandaged. "Maybe from the cart," he told Brooks. In his pocket was the letter from Stephanie. He

wanted to get away to read it in private but Brooks wanted to
debrief. At first the debriefers had to drag details from them.
Slowly they all came around, came to, and began to tell and
retell what they saw. Egan went into great detail about watching
the changing of the guard or the observers at the knoll. He told
them about the two parallel trails a meter apart and about the
trench. "Before we skyed we checked out the trench," Egan
explained. "They got land-lines running up the side. That's what
the dude who pissed on McQueen was coverin." The questions
continued. Numerous inquiries were directed to the subject of the
scopes. McQueen had had the best view but he still had not seen
them clearly. They all speculated and FO said he was certain if
the dinks had nightscopes for patrols, they would have nightscopes
for the observers on the knoll.

More details. Where did the trails and trench go down to?
The recondos were not sure. "We circled back goin downhill
and a little farther west," Egan explained. "Then we hit the red
ball. That thing had so many cart tracks, Man, I can't tell you.
My guess is it feeds a bunker complex and my guess is the
complex is at the bottom of that knoll. They aint goina have shit
up top except the OP."

More questions. The shape of the slope? The steepness of
its sides? Again the team could not say for sure. "Map looks
right to me," Cherry ventured. He spoke awkwardly, working
his jaw with great effort to control the words. "It's maybe
steeper than the map indicates."

"Yeah," Egan agreed. "The whole thing seems higher too.
Map's got its top at two hundred meters, only sixty meters
higher than the river. I'd guess it's more like a hundred. Those
trails and the trench were almost exactly on a north-south line."

Back they went to the trails, to the guards. McQueen said
he guessed only half the guards changed at a time. Four came
down, four went up. "Bet they had four more up there," he
said. "They changed at 0530," he added. "If we hit em we
should hit em at the end of their shift when they're gettin ready
to quit. 0500 or 0515."

"I love it when you guys are thinking," Brooks smiled.
"They must have an incredible vantage point from up there
when the valley's clear." He scratched his scalp. "They could
see the entire valley. They could . . . with scopes, they could
have seen us when we came off 848."

The debriefing continued. Egan told them all the story of the cart. It had been so simple, he said, that it made him feel silly. "It was like a college prank," he said. They had followed the first red ball away from the knoll to where it intersected a second road that seemed to head upriver. They followed the second for 400 meters and found the cart parked, just parked, at the edge of the trail.

They looked around and found four soldiers asleep nearby. Egan and Cherry watched them as McQueen pushed the cart up the trail. It rolled very easily. When he was what they estimated a hundred meters away, they left the enemy and caught up to McQueen. Then they simply rolled it to the river and Cherry had swum across with the bow rope. It had been the easiest part of the recon, the easiest mission he had ever had. They had all laughed about it until Hellman decided he wanted to extract the damned thing. "You know the story from there," Egan said glumly.

During the afternoon Campobasso turned into a hot fetid swamp. The boonierats who had been rovers attempted to sleep. They were weary, wet, as odorous as the swamp itself. Their eyes had sunk deeper into the sallow hollow sockets of their faces. Tongues swelled in dry mouths. They were out of decent water. They were filthy. The slack period gave them the time to realize it and the heat highlighted it. CP soldiers pulled LP/OP, platoon personnel who had remained at Campobasso pulled berm guard. Mosquitos rose in swarms by early evening. The place, like the entire north valley floor, was infested with land leeches. And the insect repellent had again run out. The sleeping boonierats wrapped ponchos around their heads and over their hands. The mosquitos and the leeches found their way in. The entire company was nauseous and spent. Everyone, that is, except Egan.

Egan had his letter from Stephanie. And what a letter. He wanted to scream, to holler in joy. He took her picture from his wallet. He had not looked at the picture in months. Now he caressed it, ran a gentle finger down her cheek. The photo had cracked and faded. It had been wet for so long, mildew grew on the back and on the edges. Egan wiped the paper carefully. God, she is beautiful.

My Daniel (the letter began. It was dated August 13th, 1970. It had crossed his in the mail.) Do you know what a

soul looks like? It looks like a tree with branches, a
sapling but with many branches that extend throughout
one's body. To some people you show an extremity, a
leaf. To others you let them lie in the branches. Well,
when you came along I let you look at the whole thing.
You asked me if you could take it for a day or so and
examine it. You had seen the whole thing so I said, sure
and you plucked my soul leaving only the roots behind.
But before you returned the next day something must have
happened and you did not come back. I didn't get my soul
back and I've been without one ever since. I thought I
might grow a new one from the old roots but that takes so
much time. It would be easier if you would bring my soul
back. Oh Daniel, I've been thinking of you so much. I
worry about you. Please write to me. Tell me you're all
right. I know your time there is almost over. When will
you be home? Can I meet you at the airport? I'm dying to
see you again.

Love,
Stephanie

At 1640 hours on the 24th of August sixteen mortar rounds
landed within the perimeter of Firebase Barnett. Two American
soldiers were killed and three wounded. At 1730 hours the
NVA hit Delta wounding five Americans. One enemy soldier
was killed. Through it all Brooks continued to be hassled by
Major Hellman, then by the GreenMan. It took four calls
but finally he convinced the command his plan was sound.
He spoke with them only over the krypto radio and still he
spoke in code.

"Red Rover, Red Rover. The game is to be played on the
Ides plus ten on the home court. The spectators should arrive by
five. Goodyear over the stadium standby. Left forward driving to
the hoop, center feeding. Over."

"Quiet Rover this is Red Rover," the GreenMan answered.
"The Star-Spangled Banner is over. Play ball. Over. Out."

"L-T," Doc whispered after the transmission.

Brooks looked at the medic. He did not look good. He
looked worse than most of the others. "What's up, Doc?"
Brooks said trying to lighten his mood.

Doc shook his head slowly and said, "L-T, this a suicide

mission. Aint none of us gonna come back we cross that river again.''

"Doc," Brooks said soothingly yet with encouragement, "we've got Charlie Company two klicks west. They'll move in at dawn. Bravo's two and a half klicks east but they're tightening down right now. They'll NDP less than two klicks from our objective. Recon's on the side of 606 squeezing down. They'll be two klicks away. Those dudes in Delta are right above us, and thank God they're going to stay there. FO's got an arty prep lined up. We've got Tac Air and a pink team on call. This'll be a piece of cake. And I've got really good news. We're going to blow an LZ on the knoll and be extracted. We're scheduled for a week of firebase duty.''

The afternoon bore on. The sun had turned the swamp to steam. The steam wilted the boonierats. There was very little to do except lie and wait and hide. Because of the knoll observers Brooks had instructed Alpha to stay beneath cover and not move. The steamy stillness was as torturous as the cold stillness. Perhaps it was worse for in the cold wet they were stalking, trapping, ambushing. They had been the hunters. In the heat they waited and hid and knew that the NVA were now hunting. There was little to do except clean weapons and sleep and read the mail Major Hellman had thrown to Doc.

El Paso received his monthly letter from Father Raul. It contained inconsequential and insignificant news. His mother was well though worried as always. Cherry received a letter from his mother and father. His father said he wanted him to know that he was very proud of his son. There were assorted letters and small packages for twenty-eight others. There was nothing for Brooks.

El Paso confiscated the *Newsweek* that had come for Leon Silvers. It was the August 10th issue. He read the articles dealing with Vietnam and those about world politics. Red China, it was reported, was about to establish full diplomatic relations with Yugoslavia. The USSR had tested a Minuteman SS-11 ICBM which had decoy warheads and radar fooling metallic chaff. South Vietnam's President Thieu had finally agreed to devalue the piaster against the dollar. Ah, here's an interesting one, he said to himself.

HANOI TAKES NO CHANCES

Bombing raids against North Vietnam have been halted (except for a rare strike to protect scout planes) since November 1968, but Hanoi is not relaxing. It still maintains a net of 4000 Ack-Ack artillery and machine gun sites, almost 500 radar points and 40 batteries of Soviet missiles.

"Goddamn little rice-propelled bastards sure seem well equipped," El Paso mumbled. He jumped to the sports section. Vince Lombardi, coach of the Washington Redskins, formerly of the Green Bay Packers, had been hospitalized with cancer of the colon. Mexico's in the running in World Cup Soccer.

Jax slinked over cautiously and handed El Paso a stack of newspaper clippings he had received with a short note from his brother-in-law. "How far we from O'Reilly?" Jax asked.

"Fifteen klicks," El Paso answered. "Maybe, give or take two. Why?"

"Shee-it. Read this, Man," Jax said pulling one article from the stack. El Paso read the UPI article:

RED BUILD-UP IN NORTH OF VIETNAM

Saigon—Heavy fighting between North and South Vietnamese forces was reported yesterday in the jungled mountains of the far north near Ripcord, the abandoned United States artillery base.

More than 1000 enemy troops are believed to be massing for an attack on a South Vietnamese base.

U. S. and South Vietnamese fighter-bombers and helicopters attacked the North Vietnamese positions with bombs, rockets and napalm throughout the day. First accounts made no mention of casualties.

SIGHTING

A newsman reported from the South Vietnamese First Division Headquarters at Hue that four battalions of North Vietnamese troops were sighted Sunday along a ridge a mile west of Fire Base O'Reilly.

O'Reilly is a former U. S. 101st Airborne Division base reopened by the South Vietnamese First Division in March. It stands atop a 1500 foot ridge less than five miles north of Ripcord, the 101st Division artillery base abandoned under heavy enemy pressure July 23.

The article went on about enemy troop movements from Laos into the O'Reilly area and about South Vietnamese attempts to break up the troop concentrations.

"They doan even mention us," Jax moaned.

"We weren't even here when this was written," El Paso said. "It's datelined the eleventh. What else you got?"

"Here one on the Soledad trial," Jax handed him the article. El Paso began reading:

SOLEDAD TRIAL SITE IN DISPUTE

Presiding Superior Court Judge Carl A. Allen said yesterday he will do "everything he can" to have the Soledad Brothers murder trial transferred from San Francisco Superior Court to San Quentin Prison.

Trial of the three convicts—George L. Jackson, 28; Fleeta Drumgo, 25; and John Chutchette, 27, accused of last January's slaying of Soledad guard John V. Mills, 26 . . .

Jax interrupted El Paso with "Here one on the My Lai Trial. Read the last sentence there." Jax pointed it out.

"Man, that's old news. That shit was on the radio when we were on stand-down." El Paso went back to the Soledad article.

. . . Judge Allen's comments yesterday stemmed from last Friday's gun battle at the Marin County Civic Center in which Superior Court Judge Harold Haley was taken hostage in his courtroom by San Quentin convicts and shot to death.

Two of the convicts and a youthful confederate, Jonathan P. Jackson, 17, were also shot and killed in the melee. Young Jackson was a brother of George Jackson, one of the Soledad convicts . . .

"That ain't nothin," Jax interrupted El Paso again handing him a follow-up article from the next day.

THE MARIN GUNS—ANGELA DAVIS LINK
Purchase Records Traced
by Charles Raudebaugh

Investigators said yesterday that two of the guns used in the Marin county courtroom kidnapping tragedy last week were originally purchased by Angela Davis, 26-year-old former UCLA philosophy teacher.

Superior Court Judge Harold Haley of San Rafael and three other persons were killed in a gun battle which followed an attempt . . .

Jax interrupted again. "Whut we dowin ta end injustice?" Jax said to El Paso.

Doc came over and sat down with his two friends. He had heard Jax' question and he repeated it as he sat. Then he said, "We are injustice. We bein injust just bein here."

"You're soundin like Jax," El Paso told him.

"Maybe my eyes been opened," Doc said.

"You're feelin bad, Man," El Paso said, "cause a Minh."

"That's right, Mista. Over Minh. Over Soledad. Over the Panther trial. Over Nam. Over Nixon. Over law and order. I had it."

Egan had fallen into a deep sleep. He had wrapped his entire body in his poncho and snapped it tight from feet up over face. He had lain down beneath bamboo stalks, on his back, in his usual resting position, and he had fallen quickly to sleep. The afternoon's still heat was blown away by an early evening breeze before the dream mutated, before the pleasures of a fantasized future with Stephanie transformed to terror. It did not happen all at once. They had been in a strange land. They were marching away from nothingness toward a dark medieval castle of heavy stone, damp and moldy and old, toward the last bastion of ignorance and hate. Somehow they had become the leaders of a revolt against established, protocolled forms of deceit. They were on the verge of storming the Bastille with their hordes of bedraggled followers when Daniel lost sight of Stephanie. Then it was all nothingness, empty, barren. His bones quivered, his teeth chattered.

"The last bastion of hate?" he screamed, cried. "Nay," he moaned subdued. "It is not a bastion of hate. It is a bastion of wisdom and knowledge and love. Love and truth locked behind stone walls, hidden from a hateful world by massive enclave walls. What I lead is an army of hate set upon destroying it. Is that why you leave me? Are you inside? Were you a clandestine angel come to save my soul, and I, a recruiter for my devil? Why do I storm knowledge and love?"

The light flickered, flickered a single star in a black heaven. Then darkness and in the darkness the sapper. The star twinkled on the silver machete in his hand. It glittered on the blade as the dark form raised the huge knife higher, higher, cocked his arm and struck. Egan tried to move. He was immobilized, trapped in

the poncho. The machete hit his face, it hit him across the eyes.
Now he watched it from outside his body. The motion slowed.
The blade severed his nose, his eyes, impacting on his brain
slicing through severing the top half of his head cleanly.

Egan awoke startled, frozen. He dared not move. It was
dark in his poncho cocoon yet light seeped in at several cracks.
Slowly, very slowly he moved a hand to his head. He felt the
side, the bridge of his nose for the cut. Slowly he opened the
poncho. Cherry sat over him staring into his face.

Before they left Campobasso for the last time the boonierats
of Alpha ate dinner. Most ate slowly. Several men were out of
food but others shared the little they had left and no one went
without. At the CP after the tactical briefing the old-timers
silently prepared as elaborate a feast as their meager C-rations
would allow. Everyone contributed something, pork slices, pineapple bits, B-2 units. Egan added the *pièce de résistance,* a
two-pound DeBuque canned ham which he had received in a late
Christmas package and had humped for seven months. "There
aint been a good enough reason to eat it," he whispered to the
men about him. "But hell, with tomorrow probably being the
L-T's last day in the bush . . . well, that's better than good
enough."

Brooks organized the dinner. Thirteen boonierats had remained at the CP, the now six CP members, Lt. Thomaston,
Cherry, Jax and Egan from 1st Plt, Pop from 2d and Lt. Caldwell and Nahele from 3d. As Doc mixed a helmetful of mocha
he said to Brooks and Jax, "Minh would a liked this. You
remember that Cha Gio fondue stuff he made that night?"

"What stuff was that?" FO asked.

"This fondue stuff," Doc said. "Minh made it with rice
alcohol en vinegar en I think sugar. He had shrimp en beef sliced
almost so thin you could see through it. You dip it in the boilin
alcohol fo bout five second. That it. Sweet Mista. You aint never
tasted nothin like it."

Egan took charge of the meat. There was the two-pound
ham and three C-rat tins of meat that smelled like dog food.
Egan had poured a can of Cahalan's pineapple bits and a can of
Brown's peach slices over the top and he heated the whole thing
in a helmet on two C-rat can stoves using four heat tabs.
Cahalan, Brown and Cherry held ponchos over and about this so
the small flame could not be seen in the increasing darkness.

Egan stirred the contents slowly, trying not to dislodge the dirt stuck to the helmet. He was experiencing ominous premonitions like he had never felt before.

"Oh Man," Thomaston called to Caldwell and Nahele where they stood over Pop. Pop was concocting a chipped beef on bread dish from a can of Beef with Potatoes, two cans of meat slices and a can of Beans with Meat Balls in Tomato Sauce. The bread would be B-2 Unit crackers. "Oh Man, oh Man. Firebase duty. Tomorrow night we'll be kickin back lettin someone else do the humpin."

"Goina get us some beer, Sir?" Nahele asked.

"You bet," Thomaston answered. "On me. Hey Pop, what the hell you doing under there? That stuff smells like shit."

"Well, I aint pissin in it," Pop's voice squeaked out from under the ponchos.

When the food was ready they assembled in two facing rows with Brooks directing the helmets of food and drink from the center of one row. All the helmets passed clockwise. The boonierats scraped the food into empty C-rat cans with their plastic spoons or fingers.

"Man," Jax whispered. "This is good shit."

"My compliments to the chefs," Cahalan said.

"To the L-T," Egan said.

"To Minh," Doc whispered so only he could hear.

"Hey," Brown griped, "I didn't get any bread."

"Au! Brownie didn't get any bread," Cahalan chided him.

"Here," Brooks said breaking his last cracker in half, "take this."

"Oh shit," Brown said. "Thanks, L-T. I didn't mean for you . . ."

"That's okay," Brooks said. "I had plenty."

"Thanks L-T," Brown repeated.

They ate slowly for infantry soldiers used to ramming the food in and swallowing without chewing, yet they still finished in less than five minutes. They sat in silence. It was too dark to smoke. No one wanted to leave. They all felt close. Brooks glanced at them all. It was a great company, he thought. Quietly Brooks rose, went to his rucksack and returned with a single can of Budweiser beer. With his B-52 can opener he made two small holes in the top, took a drink and passed it. El Paso drank, then Doc, Jax, Thomaston, Egan and Cherry. Cherry passed the can,

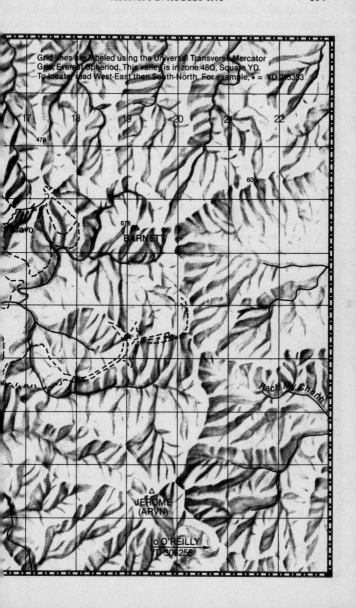

Grid lines are labeled using the Universal Transverse Mercator Grid, Everest Spheriod. This valley is in zone 48Q, Square YD. To locate, read West-East then South-North. For example, • = YD 215353

17 18 19 20 21 22

478

609

678
BARNETT

Bravo

Rach My Chanh

△
JEROME
(ARVN)

to O'REILLY
YD 306258

one half full, to Caldwell. "You gotta be kidding," the 3d Plt lieutenant said, grossed out by the half-dozen mouths on the can. He passed the can with two fingers to Nahele who took two sips. Pop, Brown, FO and Cahalan finished the can.

SIGNIFICANT ACTIVITIES

THE FOLLOWING RESULTS OF OPERATIONS IN THE O'REILLY/ BARNETT/JEROME AREA WERE REPORTED FOR THE 24-HOUR PERIOD ENDING 2359 24 AUGUST 70:

BEFORE DAWN ON THIS DATE ELEMENTS OF 3D PLT, CO A, 7/402 AMBUSHED AND ENGAGED A REINFORCED ENEMY SUPPLY TEAM, VICINITY YD 145324, KILLING SIX. ONE US SOLDIER RECEIVED MINOR SHRAPNEL WOUNDS.

AT 0720 A RECONNAISSANCE TEAM FROM CO A DISCOVERED AN UNGUARDED ENEMY AMPHIBIOUS CART. THE CART WAS AN EIGHT BY THREE FOOT BOAT WITH A SOLID AXLE ACROSS THE BOTTOM. TWO BICYCLE-TYPE TIRES SUPPORTED THE CART ON EACH SIDE. THE RECON TEAM REMOVED THE VEHICLE FROM ITS DOCKAGE AND PULLED IT TO AN EVACUATION POINT. THE CART CONTAINED SEVEN 122MM ROCKETS, FOUR ROCKET BOOSTERS, FOUR RADIOS AND DOCUMENTS. THE CART AND CONTENTS WERE EVACUATED.

AT 0915 AN ELEMENT OF CO A, 7/402 WAS MORTARED VICINITY YD 158317. COUNTER BATTERY FIRE SUPPORTED THE GROUND FORCE. ONE US SOLDIER WAS WOUNDED. A KCS WAS KILLED.

FIREBASE BARNETT RECEIVED 16 82MM MORTAR ROUND IMPACTIONS AT 1640 HOURS. TWO US SOLDIERS WERE KILLED AND THREE WOUNDED. AT 1730 HOURS AN ELEMENT OF CO D, 7/402 WAS AMBUSHED BY AN ESTIMATED REINFORCED SQUAD OF NVA. THE ELEMENT RETURNED ORGANIC WEAPONS FIRE KILLING ONE ENEMY. FIVE US SOLDIERS WERE WOUNDED AND EVACUATED.

ELEMENTS OF THE 1ST REGT (ARVN) ENGAGED AN UNKNOWN ENEMY FORCE IN THE AREA SOUTH OF FIREBASE O'REILLY KILLING 24 ENEMY. SIX ARVN SOLDIERS WERE KILLED AND EIGHT WOUNDED.

CHAPTER

30

25 AUGUST 1970

Alpha slithered away from Campobasso, slithered into the still night like one long segmented snake seeking prey. The boonierats had risen from their slumber, stretched the cold exhaustion from their weary backs, lingered until prodded, pulled by Brooks at point. They glided east, moving with no signs of movement, concealed beneath the renewed ground mist. The NVA too were on the move.

Where are they? Brooks demanded of his mind. Where are the little people? Have they been going there? Basing there? Hiding there? What will they do when we . . .

His thoughts shattered as fire erupted 1200 meters east. Audio concealment, he told himself. The noise from the east increased. Small arms fire, AKs, RPGs, maybe an SKS. Return fire, frags, claymores, M-16s and 60s. Alpha continued its slinking east then south toward the river.

Who's hitting Bravo? Brooks asked. Good, he thought. They'll be away from their base camp. Let Bravo take some. We'll go in and get their REMFs. Headquarters, huh? Who mans headquarter units? Clerks and jerks. Chairborne commandos. REMFs. Don't worry, Doc. This is not a suicide mission. Valley of death? Why? Why should it be? Why can't they make it easy on me? Why can't we agree on the plan? They know the score. Score? It is a language which translates war reality into clouds. I should write that down. Good fog. If we're lucky it won't clear before we cross the river. Stop it, Ruf. Just nice and steady, he said to himself. Easy, ease under the mist. Quiet. Lila, sweetie, when I get back, me and your Jody-boy are meeting one-on-one and my tactics are no longer limited to street games. I just may call in arty support.

Brooks had dived into his bag of tricks, had tried harder than ever to come up with a plan that would deceive the enemy and put Alpha in good attack position. FO's got every possible target listed "on-call," he thought. Instant fire. Instant support. No one hurt. Capture their headquarters, take prisoners.

Two hundred meters from the river the serpent's tail detached. Brooks led the CP, 3d and 2d Plts due south toward the river. Egan led 1st Plt southwest toward the riverbend on the east side of the knoll. The audio concealment continued. Mortar and artillery rounds exploded. Bravo's 2d Plt was on the hook calling for an urgent Dust-Off. Egan advanced with Marko, the M-60 gunner, at slack. "Need fire power," he had told Cherry. Cherry was fourth back. Egan slid through the valley brush, the bamboo, the elephant grass, as if he need not step, as if he could will his body three feet forward and have it materialize there without motion. The artillery for Bravo ceased. The thick valley air began to move, at first ever so gently, then a bit stronger until it became a breeze and bent the tops of the elephant grass and swayed the bamboo. Egan swayed with the bamboo, bent with the grass. Egan was born for the jungle valley, raised for a jungle valley war. He was the essence of the infantry. Marko looked at him from behind. All he could see was a boonie hat above a heavy rucksack and two legs below. He was impressed with the perfect balance of ruck and man. He would have been horrified had he known Egan's thoughts.

Egan's thoughts had deteriorated steadily since the high Stephanie's letter had brought. He had been uncharacteristically silent during the meal at the CP but he did not think anyone had noticed. They had all been quiet. Egan had covered it well. When Cherry had joked, "You know what I'd really like? I'd like a real roll of toilet paper. A nice soft roll of facial-quality tissue." And Brown had extended it by quipping, "Hemorrhoids gettin you?" Egan had whispered, "I think we just might be able to help you." He had risen, gone to his ruck and returned with a real roll. Everyone had been amazed.

After dinner they had slept, rested, waiting for 0200 hours, and Egan had asked himself again and again, "What the fuck have I produced? What the fuck makes him crazy like that?"

The thought of Cherry with his fingers in Minh's brain had made Egan retch. He had fought against the retching, fought against the feeling. Then he had gone over and spoken to Cherry: "Yer nuts, Mothafucker. Yer goin nuts. Get hold a yerself, Man. Think. Don't be an asshole." And Cherry had rolled back snickering and had grabbed his groin and laughed, "I got hold a myself. Hey Man, my bag is killin gooks." And Egan's thoughts had continued sinking. He had gone to Doc and had tried to talk to him but Doc wasn't talking. Then he had gone to Jax and Jax had sensed it before Egan had said it. They had exchanged a silent dap then Egan had said, "Jax . . . Jax." "It okay, Eg." "Man, do you . . . I don't think a dude's death bothers him after he's dead . . . not like just before he's scattered. If you can control your thoughts before . . . it won't bother you at all." "Cool it, Eg," Jax had said but Egan continued, whispered, "Everybody's got a life wish and a death wish. When the second's stronger than the first, Jax, then a dude eats it. Death aint random, Jax." "Shee-it EgMan, this aint even . . ." "I got it, Jax." "No fuckin way." "I got it," Egan had repeated. "I got it. Remember when Hutch got it before 714?" "Where yo guts, Man?" "It don't lie, Jax." "Aint yo got guts?" "It's cool now," Egan had said and he had relaxed. Jackson cried and barely listened as Egan talked. "I was just thinkin I'd like to go fishing. You know, go and just sit back, lie back maybe in the shade of a tree and let a clean breeze blow over my face. My shirt would be open and I could feel the breeze on my chest. I'd have a line in the water not ten feet in front of me and not a fish in the world would bother it. I wouldn't even bait the hook. I wouldn't even tie a hook to the line. Why should I want to go fishing, Jax? I never went fishing except as a little kid and then I never caught anything. I don't even think I like fishing. Funny, huh? Ya know, I was just thinking about fishing with Escalato. I can see that dude standin there that last night, standin there in the middle of the LZ directin in the Dust-Off while all that shit was flyin at him. He was really somethin, Man. It should a never happened. An ol Rafe, as much as I hate to admit it, that dude saved my ass twice. And Little Minh. And Garbageman and Silvers. I bet they all like to fish." Jax pulled his knees up and buried his face in them and he cried. Jax remembered Hutch getting the feeling. Others had too. Some died. Some survived. "Don't mean nothin, Jax," Egan whispered. He had cupped his hand over Jax' shoulder and had squeezed and shook it. "Really, Bro. Thanks. It's okay now. Don't say nothin, okay?"

During the night Egan had relaxed more and more and everything changed. He found he could think of himself as nonexistent, as dead. Egan had heard the radio call for them to move out yet he had not heard the words. He felt stronger as they left, stronger as they walked, very strong as he led 1st Plt toward the river. He was at peace. He was greatly aware of life, of the mist and the wind, of the wonderful lush green vegetation of the valley and the rich humus beneath his feet. He thought of himself in the third person. His fate is sealed, he thought. He can go forth without apprehension. He knows the future. It's okay. It's okay now that he knows it is coming. What terrible timing, though, just when Stephanie writes. Just when there could have been a future. Fuck it. Don't mean nothin. It's okay. Everyone dies sometime.

Before Alpha reached its river crossing sites Bravo was hit again. The medical evacuation had just begun when the NVA opened up with rifles and machine guns, and the helicopters had not been able to extract the wounded. The noise was ferocious. Helicopter gunships were attempting to strafe enemy locations but targets were not visible and the only known locations were those in very close and mixing with Bravo. From a kilometer away the small arms cracked and disguised any noise Alpha might have made. Alpha proceeded to its river crossing sites undetected. The wind had blown the covering mist off the river. Three huge explosions flashed, boomed to the west. Now Charlie Company was getting hit.

For nearly two days the NVA command had restricted the movement of its troops. Their thoughts had been simple. The Americans have been ambushing us because we have lost contact with several of their elements. We do not know the exact locations of all the Americans. The enemy has a temporary advantage. However the Americans resupply by helicopter and thus must give away their positions. We can pick them up at their LZs, adjust while we follow them and then hit them whenever possible. The NVA had adjusted. Charlie Company had two dead, two wounded. They too were calling for Dust-Off.

Beneath the aircluttering thwacks of the Dust-Off fleets Alpha prepared to cross the Khe Ta Laou. At the site beneath the knoll Cherry stripped. He sat in the rivermud, feet in the current, body concealed from the view of possible knoll observers with night scopes by the ragged foliage. The knoll loomed up like a tremendous monster before him. The summit seemed three hundred feet up, the sides appeared as vertical crevice-lined cliffs. At the top the tree looked like a horn on a monster's nose, a horn with a massive hood spreading over the top. Cherry sneered at the knoll. Eat it, fucker, he thought at the knoll. You'll get yours. Then he began a rhyme in his mind. He laughed as he chanted it silently.

> Here we go, up and down,
> over and out and over again.
> Here we go.
> I think that there shall never be,
> anyone crazy, as crazy as me.

Ha, Cherry laughed loudly within his head. The sound could not have been louder for him had it existed for him and all the men about him. He screamchanted in his mind:

> Men at war, once again,
> Peace's a bore,
> Let's have fun.
> Men at war, you and me,
> And I know,
> I'm crazy.

Glorious, he thought. That is a glorious rhyme. He screamed it twice as loud in his head until he felt certain every boonierat, every enemy, the tree, the knoll, God, they all must have heard it. Cherry stared into the dark jungle about him. No one was visible. He smiled. Poor Eg, he thought. Poor guy DEROSes in two weeks. He's goina miss all the fun. An Jax. Dude leaves in several months too. El Paso in a month. Even the L-T's leavin. Poor dudes. They oughta extend. I'm already becomin an old-timer. What a great bunch a guys. If I could only keep em together, we could do anything. It's sad. It's almost over. They're goina extract us and then these dudes'll split. I can keep em together, he whispered to himself. I can keep em together, he said, he shouted, he swore it before God. His inner voice building to a crescendo. I can keep em together in my head. They only exist in my head.

Then the voice crashed. Jesus Christ, he said aside to himself. Jesus Christ! If Jesus Christ was a man and all men are brothers, does not that mean Christ was my brother. He is the Son of God. Then it follows that I too am the Son of God and thus a God myself. I am immortal. I am immune to destruction. I am a man-God. If I get blown away I will resurrect myself. My friends, Leon, Minh, Whiteboy, I hold the power to destroy you, yet I love you too much. This is a love the others do not yet understand. My friends, we have become one being. Your cells are my cells, my cells are yours. I have this love in me for you, in me, through me, with me, in the power and the spirit of this man-god you are resurrected and you shall live. I am the Mangod and ye shall not raise false gods before Me.

The plan of attack at Khe Ta Laou had evolved with each skirmish, with each POW and document captured, and with each new report from aerial reconnaissance. Each information bit fit like a piece into a jigsaw puzzle, and with each piece placed the puzzle became easier. The Old Fox, brigade commander, had been certain Bravo's Comeback Ridge contained the NVA headquarters he so badly wanted. The GreenMan had disagreed and said the bunker complex would be at valley center. Each Intelligence Officer had his own idea. One by one the alternatives had either been proved wrong or simply, expediently, by-passed. Comeback Ridge had contained a hospital complex but no communications center or operation center were ever found. Areas of the north ridge went unexplored because of Delta Company's bungling. All attention turned to the valley center with the discovery of the amphibious cart. It was the last alternative. Perhaps, as the GreenMan later asserted, it should have been the first, with an entire infantry company having been inserted atop the knoll on 13 August.

Later the Old Fox would defend his initial planning by saying the 7th of the 402d had circled the valley on the first morning and no major enemy units broke out of the trap thus nothing was lost. The argument would be purely academic. The plan had evolved and by the 24th the final squeeze had begun. Bravo Company closed down from the east, Charlie Company from the west. At first light 25 August both companies were stalled in defensive positions with wounded. Delta Company descended the north ridge quickly under the direct leadership of the GreenMan. By first light Delta had closed off the enemy highway below the ridge and was advancing into Alpha's old AO. During the night Recon had descended the southern cliffs. First light found them disoriented and attempting to regroup among the mounds. NVA booby traps and snipers would hamper all four elements all morning. Alpha, which had not resupplied, had not been pinpointed by the enemy. They crossed the river undetected.

The sky is no longer black yet the brightest stars are visible. The earth is dark. In the hour before sunrise everything, everyone—the foliage, the earth, the mountains—takes on a blue-black tint, almost transparent. The wind is steady. The last remnant of fog has dissolved. It is the 13th day of the operation.

Egan leads 1st Plt. He is ecstatic. He is higher than he has ever been and he is at peace within. He has forgotten he is alive. He moves spirit-like, stealing along softly. His mission is to clear and secure the high feature, to cut an LZ on the knoll and to establish a base from which to support and reinforce 2d and 3d Plts if necessary. Behind him twenty-three boonierats advance cautiously. They are on a well-used trail, beneath canopy cover. Everything they see appears permanent. Everything is vacant.

No, Thomaston cries inside. No, we aint really doing this. I'm down to sixteen and a wake-up. Sweat rolls from his forehead into his eyes. Sixteen and a wake-up, he repeats. I'm a lieutenant. I'm not supposed to be in the bush with sixteen and a wake-up.

One mo step, Jax says to himself. One mo little step. His right hand twitches toward his pocket wanting to grab his hair pick. He resists. The ol right in front a the lef, he tells himself. Yo jest keep yo fuckin eyes all over the mothafuckin jungle. Jackson studies the trail briefly. His eyes dart up to the canopy. He keeps his head as still as possible moving only his eyes. A tree there, he says. Bush there. Grass there. If they opens up from the lef I jumps to that bush an do em a damn-damn. If they opens from the right I get in that depression. Jax, yo gotta git a job in comp'ny supply. What yo dowin fightin a white man's war? If they opens from the lef I can make that clump. If they opens from the right I goes back ta the depression.

1st Plt reaches a point approximately 100 meters in from the river at the knoll base. 3d Sqd breaks off and begins climbing. Cherry joins them, leads them. They form a three-man point with Cherry at center, Harley to the left and Hill to the right.

Centered behind them is Frye with the new XM-203, then in column, Andrews with the radio, Kirtly, Mullen and Lt. Thomaston at drag. They advance very slowly, letting the other squads continue across the base of the knoll. After 10 meters 2d Sqd breaks off and heads uphill into the knoll. 1st Sqd continues then turns. 1st and 2d form advancing arrows similar to 3d's. These three-man points have the machine gunners at center, riflemen to each side, grenade launcher just behind ready to lob rounds over the point. Now all three squads advance, begin the sweep up the knoll.

Brooks thinks, this is the last time. This is the last time I will lead an infantry company. Three and a wake-up. He leads 2d and 3d Plts in an arc away from the river, behind the knoll, behind 1st Plt. Their mission is to find, enter and destroy the NVA headquarters. Brooks thinks now without speech. He hears, feels, sees inside his thoughts, without words, the bunkers are west, northwest, at the base of the knoll. He leads the boonierats through brush and grass and into a nearly impenetrable bamboo forest. Brooks works slowly, quietly, patiently. He slithers with the patience of a hunter, the natural patience of a cat stalking prey, waiting for the moment to strike.

Behind Brooks no thoughts enter Pop Randalph's mind. He is part of the machine. He is a machine. He is an acute sensor with the responsibility of protecting the point, taking the shock when it comes.

At the middle of the column Doc Johnson's mind is full of thoughts, full of words. He is angry. They got no right, he thinks. No right. The oppressor got no rights the oppressed got to respect. Jax right. Cleaver right. They got no business sendin us down here ta be butchered. This aint a mission; this is suicide. Doc hears a twig snap. His heart freezes then beats one immense pulse which he feels throb down through his abdomen and up to his shoulders and on, building, surging, splashing up behind his eyes. He winces. He does not locate the origin of the sound.

Brooks breaks out of the bamboo thicket and leads them across a red ball. Bamboo frames an arch over the road concealing it from above. The platoons move into a mix of brush and bamboo and grass. 3d Plt begins spreading right, 2d left, the CP remains at middle. Nahele moves to the far right flank. He moves easily, cautiously. His M-60 machine gun seems to pull at his finger as if the weapon wants to be fired, wants to fire. He

fights the gun's desire. He pulls his squad, now his squad
without Ridgefield or Snell, right. Then he turns and advances
and begins the sweep northeast toward the river at the west base
of the knoll.

On the knoll 1st Plt reaches the mid-point of their ascent.
Every step has been quiet yet they feel a presence, are oppressed
with apprehension. They slow further. Cherry smells the air. He
smells them. Egan smells them. Cherry looks left right. He drops
to one knee and across the sweep they all drop into the brush
vegetation. 1st Plt's three prongs have closed from a thirty meter
width to a twenty. Cherry smells again. He looks up. The
massive tree is 250 meters ahead, 50 meters up. Its colossal
spreading limbs seem to stretch over him. He searches the
boughs and leafage. He becomes aware of warmth on the back of
his arms and neck. The sun is up, has crested the eastern ridge.
The noise of helicopters comes from the east and west. Medevacs,
he thinks. And the C & C. Suddenly pure white flashes cut
across his world. He whirls squeezing his 16, firing at the sight
before the sound registers, before he knows he is firing. Bursts
of AK-47 fire flashing from the right, then the sound erupts in
his ears. There is firing to the left, explosions, the crackcrackcrack
M-16s returning fire, his 16 barking.

"I'm hit," he hears Hill yell. Cherry and Harley leap, hit
the ground firing. They do not pause for Hill. Frye fires from
both barrels. He pays no attention to outgoing. Enemy rounds rip
up the dirt at his side. Cherry snaps a second magazine into his
16. He is charging, firing. Great whooshing noises tear the air at
his ears. RPGs. Rocket Propelled Grenades. Booming. The concussion rocks his eyes. His concentration does not break. He
continues firing. Andrews is screaming, "Bravo! Bravo!" Alpha's
code for medic.

To the left Egan is screaming, charging into the fire coming
down from above. He fires and charges quick, agile. He is
everywhere at once firing rounds like walls of lead. He whirls.
He kills. He does not linger on the sight of enemy death. He
swings firing right left. "For Minh," he screams. He does not
know he has yelled it. Marko and Jackson advance with him.
Sachel charges explode before them. The concussion dissipates.
Their ears ring. They do not know it. "Let um know they fuckin
with the Oh-Deuce," Egan screams. Marko shouts his battle cry.
No sound leaves his throat. They dive for concealment, reload.

Moneski from 2d Sqd dives in behind Egan. Beaford and Smith dive in behind Cherry and Harley. 2d Sqd has split up, five reinforce 3d Sqd, three 1st Sqd. The NVA do not capitalize on the split by driving up the center.

Cherry crashes forward, smashes forward, firing firing. He leaps a meter at a time and crashes down into the brush, the bamboo. Stalks stab him. Sticks rip his fatigues, his skin. Grass and vines trip him. He falls forward. Thorns rip his face. He does not know it, does not feel it.

"My toes! My foot! It's shot away." Hill is screaming. There is enemy fire coming from above and right. 1st Sqd is battling left. They are diverging. Cherry reloads. It is his fifth magazine. Hill crawls inward, toward the center, away from the firing. He slips under a bush for cover. His right leg drags. Blood is spurting from his ankle. "Medic," Andrews screams. "Medic!" Fuck codes. Doc McCarthy is with 1st Sqd. He and Numbnuts are pinned down. They do not fire. They do not move. Andrews lays his rifle down carefully. He strips the pants from Hill's left leg below the knee. Blood is everywhere. It shines brightly on Hill's white skin. It saturates Andrews' pants where it spurts. Andrews rips Hill's battle dressing from the wounded man's web belt. "My leg," Hill screams. "My foot. It's blown off." "Shut up," Andrews snarls. "Bite your tongue. You want a gook zeroin in here." Andrews slaps the dressing over the now flowing wound and wraps it over the holes. The ankle is shattered. Tendons are broken. The foot flops lifeless. "Aaaaahh," Hill cries, pain firing up his leg as Andrews clamps his hand on the wound. Direct pressure, Andrews thinks. Hill is thrashing, moaning, under the brush.

Fire from bunkers or fighting positions above slices through the brush, shattering it, smashing it. Marko sprays back into the noise, into the streaming lead, his machine gun ripping smashing ferociously. "Keep em down," Egan yells. He throws a frag at the bunker thirty feet away. He runs, dives, advances six feet, crawls. Marko keeps firing. Jax fires. Denhardt fires. "Move yer fuckin ass," Egan screams firing. The grenade explodes harmlessly below the bunker. Jax advances. Marko keeps firing, mixing fire with enemy fire. Jax throws a frag, his last. He fires. Egan rushes up left. Jax' grenade explodes. Trying to throw a one-pound grenade into a two foot wide slit from thirty feet while taking fire is impossible. Numbnuts with his XM-203 firing grenade rounds would not have been more effective, was he trying, but he had buried his head in a bush with the first volley. He is crying, weeping. "Let me go home. Let me go home." Doc McCarthy raises his eyes. He hears Andrews call. He can't move. He is trembling. An RPG round explodes above him. His stomach twists, he vomits. He tries to move away from his vomit. Machine gun fire cracks over his head. He drops flat, face-down in his own retchedness. He curses Numbnuts for infecting him with fear. "Medic!" he hears Andrews scream. I can, he says. I can. I got to. Doc McCarthy crawls. "Where ya goin?" Numbnuts cries. "No," his teeth chatter. "No, Doc." He hears, feels a sachel charge erupting up, up there, between Egan and Marko. He flattens, cries. He is sure he is pinned down forever. McCarthy's gone.

"Rover Two," Brooks' voice comes urgently over the radio. "Rover Two, Quiet Rover Four. Over . . . Rover Two, Quiet Rover Four. Over." Marko's firing steady. The barrel of his 60 is burning. Lairds and Denhardt firing bursts alternately. Reloading alternately. Most of 1st Sqd firing, Egan charging. At the bunker. Egan dives into the bunker with his 16 flashing. He sprays downward left right. It is not a bunker. He sees it immediately. Knows it immediately. It is a trench running horizontal, arcing about the knoll. There is no one in this segment. They can be anywhere. Move anywhere. Fighting is raging to the right.

"Rover Two, Quiet Rover Four," Brooks whispers frantic.

"Four, Two. Over," Hoover answers.

"Sit-rep? Over," Brooks asks urgently.

"We got em running. Over."

"How large an element? Over."

"Fifteen. Maybe eighteen. We can kill em. Over."

"What's your position from basket? Over."

"200 . . . maybe 150 mikes. They're running to the sidelines. Can we get ARA on them? Over."

"Affirmative. Will try. Cut to the basket. Direct your niner, cut to the basket. Set up number five. Over."

"Medic," Hoover hears Thomaston scream from the center. Thomaston is with Hill. Hill is still moaning. His dressing is slick with blood. Thomaston grabs him, unfastens his belt, makes a tourniquet about Hill's thigh groin-high. "Keep it tight," Thomaston directs Andrews. He grabs Andrews' radio. He hears Brooks and Hoover.

"Affirmative," Hoover says.

"Negative," Thomaston cuts in. "Right forward engaged. Double whiskey india Alphas. One priority. Over."

"Shoot for the hoop," Brooks comes on the net. "Set-up five. Over. Out."

1st Sqd sprints for the trench, leaps, jumps dives in. Denhardt leaps from the trench uphill, Lairds follows. They rush foot-by-foot, run crouched, meter-by-meter, toward the center. Egan stays in the trench, runs, fires semi-automatic, rounds splatting in the trenchwalls before him. Jax and Marko cover the left flank, one above one below the trench. There is no fire from above. There is an explosion in the trench. Egan's legs burn whitehot, his equilibrium lapses, he cascades forward still running. He has triggered a booby trap, a sachel charge, stone shrapnel burns in his legs. He drops his rifle. The sound of the explosion reaches his brain. He feels instant nausea. It is not a big explosion, he thinks. RPDs, AKs, RPG fire explode from the trench before him, beyond his sight, around the curve. He hears Harley scream, "Medic." Egan grabs his 16. Carefully now, he checks it. He ejects the magazine and inserts a fresh one. He chambers a fresh round then tries to crawl. His legs burn, his back feels hot, wet, sticky. Egan pulls his knees up under him, rocks back and stands. He charges down the trench.

Cherry charges the trench from below, his eyes blazing. He has enemy soldiers in his sights. He fires killing one. The other is fleeing. Cherry leaps. He is on top of the enemy. The soldier falls. He is small, lean, hard, but no match for Cherry. Cherry is on him gouging his eyes. *"Choui Hoi,"* the enemy yells cries into Cherry's madly punching fists. The man gashes at Cherry defensively. Cherry is infuriated. He digs his fingers into the enemy's face. The soldier bites Cherry's hand. Cherry bites his face, the nose crushes, Cherry bites, mad-dog, bites and rips the soldier's neck simultaneously thrusting his bayonet into the enemy stomach. Blood explodes in Cherry's mouth. He freezes. He feels Egan standing over him, staring at him.

Firing erupts sporadically all over the valley. The firebase is being mortared, the C & C takes fire. The NVA's coordinated plan is now being implemented. All four US perimeter companies are being attacked at once. It is costly to the NVA. They have at least thirty-six killed. American helicopters are strafing NVA concentrations. Red smoke is billowing from a dozen US marking grenades, marking US front lines or NVA positions.

American units do not advance. They are too close to each other
for artillery or tactical air support. The NVA are attempting to
have them fire at each other. From the C & C bird the GreenMan
sees their plan. He also suspects, as does Brooks on the ground,
that the NVA plan does not include Alpha Company, that Alpha
has indeed lost itself in the valley and the ruse of not resupplying
has worked. Only a skeleton crew of enemy soldiers is protecting
the headquarters complex.

They are sweeping northwest through the brushforest. The
sun is playing in the valley vegetation throwing dappled shadows
against vegetation and ground and men. The shadows seem to
dance in the stalks and leaves as the men sweep silently. They
are in three rough lines, the front line men seven meters apart,
too far, they think, yet that is how Brooks ordered it. The second
line is three to four meters back, splitting the distance between
the men in front, each second row man walking slack for two
front row men. Behind the third line are the reinforcers, the
reactors, and the co-ordinators. The sweep has advanced 300
meters. They have halted, listening to 1st Plt's fight, waiting to
be directed to help.

"Hey, L-T," FO whispercalls. "Hey," he gestures quickly
at a camouflaged mound, a swell not eight inches higher than the
valley floor around it. "Hey," he whispershouts, "we're on top
of a bunker complex."

Brooks looks. He stares. It is not FO's style to conjure up
nonexistent bunkers yet Brooks does not see a bunker. The
commander and the forward observer are fewer than two meters
apart. They are kneeling behind the front two lines. Brooks
stares. FO is covering the mound with his 16. He has risen and is
advancing on the mound. The immediate area is silent. 1st Plt's
battle for the knoll is quieting. Brooks stares, he sees nothing.
Then the form emerges from the camouflaging background. It is
like an optical illusion which, once seen, one cannot easily
reverse. Brooks scans the area. He sees what FO has seen. There
are bunkers everywhere, before them and behind. The camouflage seems to melt away, and there is a field of bunkers, a field
of low square mounds buried beneath growing layers of brush
and vine and some bamboo and some low trees. A few of the
bunkers are beneath what appears to be old Montagnard thatch
hootches that have collapsed and rotted.

It happens to Pop Randalph at the far left and to Nahele at

the far right. Some still see nothing even as others point out mounds to them. Never have any of them seen such perfect camouflage. There seem to be no openings. A spooky feeling sweeps across the invaders. Where are they? Brooks thinks. Where are the little people? Why haven't they hit us? He directs the unit to squeeze in at the flanks and bulge at the sides. "Have them form a perimeter," he tells El Paso. "We'll clear from inside out. Get Nahele up here. And McQueen. And Pop."

The boonierats react as if they were muscles in Brooks' body. They operate silently as if they communicate by telepathy and not by voice. Fear keeps them silent. Nahele is the first underground. He dives into a bunker opening that FO has found, one of only three discovered in all the square mounds Alpha has now investigated. With a .45 and a flashlight Nahele dives in as an underwater demolition expert on patrol might dive into a harbor across from his target. He comes out in only seconds. "It's empty," he whispers. "It's a vacant room. There's three tunnels leading out a it."

Brooks and Pop and McQueen follow Nahele back in. Brooks follows a tunnel south. The tunnel is large enough for him to walk hunched. It curves right then left and opens into a second room larger than the first. There is another tunnel leaving it. The sides are stacked with cases and crates. Holy fucken Christ! Brooks thinks. Pop is behind him. Then Nahele. McQueen has stayed in the empty room to guard against enemy coming from the other tunnels. Brooks comes from the second room with a case of mortar rounds. He pushes it up, out, above ground where FO grabs it and pulls it aside and helps Brooks from the hole. Brooks moves quickly now. He grabs Cahalan, grabs the handset of his radio and calls the GreenMan. In the second-long pause before the battalion commander answers, Brooks directs El Paso to tell Lt. De Barti that he, Brooks, wants Baiez' squad immediately. "Red Rover," Brooks addresses the GreenMan, "we've found it. We're in it." He continues explaining. "The tip of a iceberg," he says. He hears the GreenMan laughing joyously in his C & C bird circling three thousand feet over the valley. He hears the GreenMan laughing and saying, "This is it. Get it all out. I'll get up a back-up element for security. This is what I've been looking for." Brooks hears, feels the GreenMan's enthusiasm. It makes Brooks feel good.

And up it comes. Cases, cartons, crates. Cases of 82mm mortar rounds, each individually wrapped in corrugated cardboard.

Cartons of fuses. Boxes of paper-like explosive propellent discs that the NVA mortarmen used instead of the powder bags used by the US and ARVN forces. Baiez and Shaw are grabbing the supplies, stacking them, building piles. They are breathing hard, sweating. The day is becoming a scorcher.

Below ground it is cool. Pop is investigating a third set of rooms. I bet they're all connected, he thinks. I bet they're connected to Whiteboy's Mine up on the ridge. He and McQueen go into a fourth room. It is filled with radios and communication equipment. They take one radio and drag it through the tunnel network to the entry room. Brooks orders four more men below ground. The air is filled with discovery. Never have any of Alpha's boonierats seen such a cache, captured such quantities of equipment. They are smiling, laughing quietly, working eagerly. Brooks thinks, this is an NVA haven, a refuge for their battle weary soldiers. They could crawl into these bunkers and hide here for weeks. And it *is* their command and communication center. We have it. This is what it should be. Brooks is elated. This, he thinks, is the headquarters of the 7th NVA Front.

Jenkins on the right flank discovers another opening. He and Spangler slip in and find an entry room with tunnels leading northeast and south. They investigate moving south. More equipment. The C & C bird is now circling at fifteen hundred feet. Escort Cobras circle above the C & C. The stack of equipment grows. Chi-com claymore mines fill one entire room. Cases of 37mm anti-aircraft rounds fill another. There are RPG rounds and cans of RPD machine gun ammunition and three thousand sachel charges. The GreenMan can see the stacks growing from one thousand feet.

Suddenly fire erupts at the south perimeter. 2d Plt's CP and 2d and 3d Sqds are receiving fire, returning fire. All hell has broken loose. Molino is at the center. He cannot tell what is happening. He has hit the dirt with the first burst. He hears someone screaming, "Bravo! Bravo!" Then he sees Doc Johnson running across the top of a bunker. Doc is breaking his way through brush and small trees. He carries his medical bag in his left hand and he is firing his .45 pistol with his right. Doc disappears from Molino's vision. Molino cannot see the wounded because of the thick undergrowth. He sees Pop Randalph running. Pop has sprinted from Alpha's center. He is running in the direction Doc ran. He is screaming in his hoarse high voice, yelling at the top of his lungs. He has a grenade in his left hand

and grenades strapped to his web gear. He fires his 16 and yells.
Molino cannot understand the words. Pop disappears into the
foliage. The fighting is building. The noise is fogthick in the
steaming air. Molino hears shrapnel slashing into the vegetation
to his left. Someone is screaming. Molino looks leftright. He
cannot let them go it alone. He hunches his back, brings his legs
up under him, his hands are on the earth, his rifle is stuffed in
the muck. He is sprinting. He throws a grenade. He did not even
know he had prepared one, he did not know he knew the enemy
location. He is firing. He is with Doc and Pop and Calhoun. Doc
Hayes is wounded. Doc Johnson is applying battle dressings to
his chest. A horrible sucking gurgle is coming from Hayes'
chest. Blood froths from Hayes' mouth. It disgusts Molino. The
NVA disengage, disappear, dissolve. Pop wants to charge them,
pursue them. They have wounded his medic.

   "Negative that," Brooks is adamant. It has been his most
successful move ever. He does not want it ruined, he does not
want it to end. "Pop smoke in front of your position," he radios
2d Plt. Calhoun takes over from there. Red smoke is billowing
up from a smoke grenade before them. Calhoun is in radio
contact with the Cobras. "Dinks at two one zero degrees," he
radios and first one Cobra and then a second roll from the sky
diving across Alpha unleashing their mini-guns into and south of
the smoke, running cutting a swath on the 210° course. The
electric Gatling guns fire so quickly they sound like buzz saws.
The pilots report no kills. They do not see the enemy.

   Woods comes from the bunker opening. He is livid. He
wants to go back in. "There's a map room in there, L-T," he
says. "I just know there's goina be a full fledged TOC down
there." As he speaks firing erupts behind him where Lt. Caldwell and 3d Plt CP are manning the perimeter. Woods drops flat,
scrambles to his ruck and slips in. He grabs his rifle and crawls
toward the fight. Again the boonierats pop smoke and again the
Cobras dive in but Lt. Caldwell has retreated, has ordered his
men back and the NVA have followed. The enemy is on Caldwell's
side of the smoke. Kinderly is hit in the head by shrapnel from a
B-40 rocket. The skin is torn to pieces, the skull is splintered.
He is running, retreating. El Paso, Brown, L-T and FO run into
the fight. They overtake Woods. They sweep past Caldwell who
is still giving ground. They are firing madly. A shot grazes
Brooks biting a skin chunk off his left wrist. He fires. He sees
the man firing at him as he fires. The NVA skull bursts, explodes.

He is sweating, crawling, calling in air support. A Cobra pilot sees movement toward the bunkers from the east. He dives his ship firing rockets and mini-gun. Other gunships are diving to the west and the south, then rolling, circling above Alpha and diving again. The NVA are pulling back from hitting Bravo, Charlie and Recon. They are falling back to cover their headquarters complex. Brooks looks up and sees the C & C bird at twenty-five hundred feet. Rockets and Cobras and LOHs are everywhere. There is fire spewing from the sky over Alpha in every direction. The sky is darkening with smoke.

At the complex center Nahele is with the stacked munitions and equipment. He rigs two blocks of C-4 explosive to the radios and inserts a blasting cap. He works quickly, forcing his mind to concentrate, forcing his fingers to operate. Alpha is pulling back. Nahele sees Doc Johnson carrying Doc Hayes on his back. Nahele attaches his claymore wire to the blasting cap wire and quickly unrolls.

"Fuck that," Caldwell screams at him. "They can blow it with ARA. Dinks are poppin up all over." Caldwell is running, running for the knoll. Nahele checks his claymore firing device, looks once more at the bunker orifice. It is dark, black in the light of the day. The blackness explodes, Nahele's chest explodes with pain. He falls, is thrown backward. His body racks in spasms. He can hear the crunched bones. The pain ends quickly which surprises him. He can no longer feel it. He hears the impact of rounds slamming into his legs, abdomen, chest, but he does not feel it at all.

Brooks and FO, shouting orders that go unheard, try to organize the boonierats. Alpha retreats to the knoll behind a screen of ARA.

CHAPTER

31

There is pandemonium on the knoll but there is no firing. There is firing in the valley. NVA soldiers seem to be everywhere, firing from unseen everywheres. The four squeeze companies are again all being hit. It is as if Alpha has ripped the top off an anthill. 1st Plt is in a line at the knoll's south crest. 2d and 3d and the CP are coming in, collapsing.

Cherry is sitting beside Egan whom he has cared for since Egan passed out in the trench. Cherry had carried the platoon sergeant to the knoll's crest, had put him down and had helped set up the perimeter around him. Then he had stripped Egan's back and legs exposing a dozen holes seeping blood. He had cleaned them one by one as best he could until Doc McCarthy came and bandaged the wounds. Egan had moaned, had come to and passed out again. Then he had come to and his body had contorted, his back arching and twisting involuntarily from the pain. Egan had moaned horribly yet quietly, so inscribed is his mind with the need for silence. He tries to speak. His jaw draws back with each breath, the skin of his gaunt face stretches tighter. "Give him somethin," Egan hears Cherry saying to Doc McCarthy. "Yeah," Doc answers glumly. Egan moans. He can't remember how to talk, how to operate his jaw. He wants to speak but his lungs and mouth won't cooperate to produce the sounds. He tries again. He moans again. He thinks he is speaking. He thinks he is saying, Don't, Doc. Cherry, don't let Doc give me anything. No morphine. No pain killers. Godfuckendamn, he thinks the words are clear and is frustrated that McCarthy and Cherry do not seem to understand, that McCarthy is preparing to inject him. Goddamn, he thinks. If I'm going to have my shit scattered in the wind, I want to know it. "What's that, Man?" Cherry asks him. "You're goina be okay." Promise me Bro, Egan thinks he is saying. It aint goina help. Don't help. Like Hughes. Didn't help that fucker. He felt his fucken ribs go, en then you fuckers shot him up with dope. Then he died. Mothafucker didn't even know he died. I gotta know. I gotta know. McCarthy injects a syringe of morphine into Egan's thigh. Egan passes out again.

Cobra gunships are diving at the bunker complex, firing rockets. They are aiming for the huge pile of equipment and munitions stacked so neatly by Baiez and Shaw.

2d and 3d Plts have only just arrived at the knoll top. They are sweaty, filthy, blood-splattered and out of breath. McQueen drops Nahele's body in a clump of brush by Egan and collapses next to it. Doc Johnson lowers Doc Hayes next to him. Hayes is moaning, coughing blood and sputum. There are two more seriously wounded and half a dozen not so serious including Brooks. Around the entire perimeter exhausted frightened boonierats are regaining strength and courage and organization. Thomaston is directing the incoming platoons like a traffic cop. 1st Plt is set up across much of the south slope. It is the knoll's only real surface access. The knoll is a peninsula in the river surrounded on three sides by cliffs and water. From the valley floor and from the ridges the knoll had appeared small yet now the bulbous end with the titanic tree and the cliffs seems too large for one company to defend. The south side is a 100-meter wide ramp with tangled brush and small trees. The two paths that Egan, Cherry and McQueen had discovered on their recon have disappeared. Now 1st Plt squeezes down to cover sixty or seventy percent of the ramp. 2d Plt is directed to cover the east, 3d Plt the west. A few soldiers are scattered across the north overlooking the cliff and river. The defensive perimeter is an open end U-shape facing south. Everywhere the perimeter guards are checking their ammunition and weapons and clearing fields of fire. 1st Plt boonierats set up claymore mines across clearly visible approaches. The boonierats dig in. Marko and Jax erect a hasty position by rolling a thick log onto a tiny rise. They are staring down the peninsula. A thought hits them simultaneously.

They shed their rucksacks and scavenge through looking for more ammunition. They are almost out.

Brooks is shouting orders now. He has caught his breath from the racing retreat to the knoll. He takes over from Thomaston. Doc Johnson tries to inspect the L-T's wrist. Brooks looks at him then at his own wrist. There is a three-inch long gouge. He had forgotten about it. It is no longer bleeding though there are dried blood streaks across the back of his hand. "It's, ah . . ." Brooks tries moving his wrist. He winces. "It's a little stiff. Nothing." Doc snorts disgusted. He grabs Brooks' arm but Brooks jerks it back. "Later," he says. "See to the others. Get the wounded up to the tree. Make it a collection point."

"Mista, L-T . . ."

"Get the CP up there too," Brooks snaps. He breathes deeply. Suddenly he feels out of steam, run-down, not out of breath but out of fuel as if the adrenaline in his system has burnt up all the energy sources and there is nothing left to power his body. He does not shout now. He reverts to his characteristic soft voice. "Have the CP set up beyond the tree," he says. "Have De Barti furnish a squad to clear this place of booby traps, then have them get to work clearing the LZ. We sure as hell aren't walking out of here." Brooks walks up the knoll toward the tree. He stops, turns, looks at his perimeter and at the valley below. His presence and calm pervade Alpha's troops. They take strength from him. He turns again and looks at the tree. It is the first time he has been aware of it since he saw its shape from across the river six hours earlier. The sun is directly overhead yet he is comfortably shaded. Brooks looks up the straight smooth torso. It rises like a gigantic dark marble column from the knoll, branchless for, he estimates, 175 feet. Then the top mushrooms out huge branches, branches as large as trees, branches extending straight out then drooping. Looking at the tree makes Brooks feel peaceful. It is lovely, he thinks. And there aint no way in hell anybody's been climbing up that thing.

Suddenly Brooks, Alpha, the knoll and the valley are rocked by a concussion, a fantastic flash and explosion like none any boonierat has ever seen. Then comes a series of secondaries while the first explosion is continuing to erupt. The munitions at the bunker complex are exploding, a room below explodes. Shockwaves flip the diving Cobra that has initiated the explosions. The pilot is hanging on trying to regain control. There is a huge black cloud. More secondary explosions. Dirt and shrapnel gust up with explosive force then rain down. The flash burns from outside in, the edges turning immediately black, fire and flame roiling inside, breaking through. The huge cloud seems to detach itself from the ground.

Then it is over. It has not lasted a full minute. The cracking rifle fire in the valley seems to make no sound. A laugh cracks from Alpha's perimeter. Then another. "Gawd Damn!" Pop yells. Cherry whistles a blood-curdling shriek. They are laughing, cheering, clapping. "Gawd Damn!" Pop yells again.

"I ain't NEVER seen nothin like that," Calhoun squeals. He slaps Pop on the back.

"Gawd, that exploded quicker than a cat covers shit." Pop is dancing.

"God! That's like the time the ammo dump at brigade blew," Baiez laughs.

"Better." Shaw is hysterical. "Better en badder."

Brooks too is smiling. He is pleased. That's what we came to do, he thinks. He wants to let them enjoy it, enjoy the show. They've earned it, he thinks. They paid the price.

"Raggedy-ass mothafucka," Doc Johnson screams at him, drowning the applause. Brooks snaps his attention to Doc. Doc has come down from the tree. "Where my medevacs?"

"Where you going to land them?" Brooks snaps back.

"I got men need medevacs, Mista. Get me a fuckin bird."

"Show me what you've got," Brooks says firmly.

The perimeter positions settle down. A jittery tight-trigger tenseness settles on them. They are hot, thirsty, out of food and out of water. Ten men are hacking the brush from the knoll top and dumping it over the cliffs.

Brooks and Doc squat by the base of the tree. At the base gnarled roots splay across the knoll in a ten-meter radius humping and dipping and crossing themselves. Doc has the wounded lying in a protective cove, a canyon created by the root ridges and the tree trunk. Doc McCarthy and Doc Korman are administering to the wounded. The bodies of Doc Hayes and Nahele lay crumpled, not yet covered, at the cove edge. Brooks grits his teeth. Hayes didn't have a chance, he tells himself. He wouldn't have made it had he been shot that way right inside an operating room. Brooks gulps. No one looks at the dead.

Brooks inspects the wounded one at a time. Kinderly's entire upper head is wrapped, his eyes covered. There is blood on the bandages. Doc Johnson whispers to Brooks, "He gonna

lose both eyes, Mista, you doan get him out a here right now."
They move on to Bill Frye. He is conscious, not even dazed. He
is sitting scratching his chin, shaking his head. "You okay,
Cookie?" Doc says to him. Frye pulls his shirt open. His left
side is bandaged heavily. He looks up and nods. Then he says,
"I'm sorry, L-T. Really. I'm sorry."

"It's okay, Cookie," Brooks answers.

"I saw the fucker, L-T. I saw him shoot me. I shoulda got
him first. Crazy Cherry saved my butt." Frye shakes his head.

Brooks sees Egan. He did not know Egan had been hit. He
spins quickly to Doc.

"Fucked up, Mista," Doc says.

"He'll be all right," Doc McCarthy says. "I don't think
none of it went in too far." McCarthy is holding a bag of
plasmatine above Egan. Egan is conscious. His face is empty,
his eyes unfocused. He is lying on his side facing into the tree,
babbling deliriously.

"He all shot up with morphine," Doc Johnson says bending
over Egan, counting, timing his respiratory rate. "Dumb fucka,"
Doc Johnson raises his thick upper lip gesturing at McCarthy,
"shot em up twice. He lost lotsa blood an I think he gonna have
spine trouble."

"There aren't any holes near his spine," Doc McCarthy
says. "He hurts. That's all."

"Shud up, Mothafucka," Doc Johnson curses roughly. He
wants an immediate medical evacuation.

"What about Hill?" Brooks asks. Hill is moaning, lying on
his back with his right leg up on a high root hump. His head is
on a near-empty ruck. He is staring straight up, glassy-eyed.
There is a small break in the tree's leafage and the sun is shining
down, shining, illuminating all the smoke and dust particles in
the air, casting a beam all the way to the ground and to the base
of the tree.

"He's hurting but he's okay," McCarthy says.

"Mothafucka, I told you, shud up," Doc Johnson says.
There is anger and hate in his eyes. His body is tense like a cat
ready to spring. He has seen men with minor wounds die waiting
for medical evacuation. He does not like to see any of his
brothers wait.

Brooks puts his right hand on Doc's arm. "We'll get them
out as quickly as possible," he says. He stands. He walks to

where El Paso and Brown and FO have set up the CP. Cahalan is on guard overlooking the sparsely guarded north cliff.

Brooks talks to the GreenMan by radio. They converse in staccato radioese. They talk about extracting the wounded and all of Alpha. It will be dangerous to bring birds in on the south slope. "Blow the big tree," the GreenMan says. "I'll have a bird to you in one-five with a demo-kickout."

"Yes Sir," Brooks answers. He is pleased with the plan. It will save lives. No more wounded. No more dead. The wounded, he thinks, can wait. They are priority and routine. They are not urgent. Urgent means near death. Egan and Kinderly are stable—priority—evac ASAP but no heroics. Hill and Frye, priority. Hayes, Nahele, oh God, poor fuckers—routine.

El Paso is on the hook to the platoons with orders for the kickout. He is laughing to himself. He has just awarded a Silver Star to the GreenMan. In his mind he is watching Father Raul read the citation at an awards ceremony.

AWARD OF THE SILVER STAR

For heroism and gallantry in ground combat in the Republic of Vietnam, 13 to 25 August 1970. Lieutenant Colonel Dinky Dau GreenMan distinguished himself while serving as commanding officer of a bunch of dumbass troops during operations near Firebase Barnett. During the entire operation the GreenMan repeatedly supervised ground and air forces which got fucked up looking for a meaningless bunker complex. The GreenMan directed artillery and tactical air support against enemy hills, trees and grass. He listened on the radio repeatedly as his units were ambushed and attacked. After the enemy forces were routed, he, without regard for his personal safety, tabulated the reported dead. From the air he repeatedly urged boonierats on and he engineered attacks and counterattacks for them to carry out. During the operation the GreenMan also managed to take twelve hot showers in the rear, eat thirty hot meals and read twenty-seven Fantastic Four comic books. The GreenMan's personal bravery and devotion to duty are in keeping with the highest traditions of the military service and reflect great credit upon himself, his unit, and the United States Army.

Doc Johnson is sitting among the wounded in the root cavern below the giant tree. He has given them all clean water from two canteens he has saved just for the wounded. For three days he has been drinking riverwater or swampwater. Doc has also lit cigarettes for Frye and Hill and has held a smoke for Kinderly who is conscious though unable to see and afraid to move. "Hey, Eg," Doc says forcing a laugh. "I ever tell you bout the medics at Phu Bai?" Doc laughs a knee-slapping put-on laugh. "Heyhey. There ol Charles there in the dispensary. He say ta Dorf who standin near this microscope, Dig?, 'Dorf, you see anything on that slide?' Dorf look up an say, 'No. You see anything, Charles?' 'Naw,' say Charles. Then ol Charles pause an he say, 'Dorf, you look at the slide?' Dorf say, 'No, Charles. You look at it?' Ol Charles scratchin his head en he say, 'Naw. Ah, do that mean it's negative if we doan see nothin?' 'I guess so,' say Dorf. 'If we doan see nothin, it caint be positive.' 'Hum,' Charles go. 'I guess that right.' " Frye tries to control himself because it hurts his side to laugh but it feels so good to laugh with Doc. Doc winks at him. "Hey, Eg," Doc calls. "Dig it, Mista?"

Egan is staring into the tree. He has been in the same position for a year, he thinks. The morphine has dulled the pain in his legs and back and he is no longer angry with Doc McCarthy for having drugged him. He is not angry at anything or anyone. The morphine has hit him hard. It has warmed him, relaxed him, made him feel suspended. He is floating. The first injection had eased him but then the pain had built up higher than the drug effect and had spilt over tidalwaving impulses fought without success. His body shock reaction team was inadequate. He had been angry at that, at his body giving up on him. And then the second injection hit him and he was delirious, delirious with morphine and shock and pain and exhaustion and with the happy knowledge it was all over. The war is over, he had told himself. Just get me out and I'm gone forever from this bad mothafucker.

They had carried his body to the tree and had laid him down and given him blood. He had watched them do it though they did not know he was watching. He had heard Doc and Jax and the L-T and Doc McCarthy. How? he asks himself. I have been with Stephanie. He is with Stephanie now as Doc jokes behind him. "Wouldn't it be nice, Steph," he whispers to her, he is looking into her silver eyes, "wouldn't it be nice," he says, "if we could go back and relive some of those times. The beautiful times." Egan can see a village street with him and Stephanie skipping past a park. They stop. They kiss. She is singing, laughing. *"We'll sing in the sunshine, we'll laugh every day,*

*we'll sing in the sunshine, now that you've come back to stay.
Now your year is over . . ."* It stops. Stephanie is not here. He
is looking into a cavern created by the dark gnarled roots of a
large tree. He cannot see the top or the sides of the tree. He is
immobile, on his side, staring into the cavern. The place stinks,
he thinks. It smells of rancid meat. His eyes focus into the dark
chamber. It is clogged foul with spider webs. His chest ceases.
He tries to push himself back but he is immobile. The webs take
on a pattern. He can see a swelling of tree wood, the knoll,
surrounded by webs leading throughout the valley. A beam of
sunlight is glistening on moisture clinging to the silk threads.
Then he sees the creature. Again he tries to move, to react, yet
his body will not respond. Something is blocking his mental
orders and they are not reaching his muscles. The creature is
large and red, blood red. Egan thinks he can see through the skin
of the spider. It is almost translucent. No, he thinks. It is the
morphine. It is a hallucination. The creature moves. It is as large
as a hand. Its legs appear webbed. It is strangely delicate,
beautiful yet fearsome. The spider is devouring a mosquito.
Egan can see its jaws, its spinnerets, its claws. There are silken
wrapped insects suspended everywhere in the web network.
Egan closes his eyes. He thinks he is shaking his head. You
gotta be the biggest, baddest mothafucker in the valley, Egan
thinks he says aloud to the spider. Why the fuck doesn't Doc
come here, he thinks. He moans. He wants to run. Doc, he
wants to scream. He is immobile and mute.

"Hey, Eg," Cherry whispers. Cherry has left Marko and
Jax at the log on the perimeter. "Hey, Man," Cherry whispers,
"how ya doin?" He does not see Egan respond. "Hey Doc,"
Cherry calls, "can he hear me?"

"Course he can," Doc says.

"Doc, could you ask him if I can take his ammo? Anything
he's got left. We're pretty low on the berm."

"Jus take it," Doc snaps. "He ain't gonna use it."

Egan is not listening. He is watching the spider. It is
walking toward him. He moans.

Cherry looks at him. He puts a hand on Egan's arm. He can
feel the tension in the frozen muscles. Egan moans louder. "It's
okay, Man," Cherry says. "It's o . . . HOLY JESUS MOTHA-
FUCK! Holy Fuck. Okay, Man. Doc, get yer ass over here."
Cherry has seen the spider.

Doc springs over. Fear shows on his face. He is afraid he

has let Egan die. He grabs Egan's throat to check for carotid pulse. Before he can feel, Cherry shrieks, "WHhooeee!"

"Whut's it?" Doc is angry.

"Ugly fucker," Cherry growls. He spits at the spider. "Look at that ugly fucker."

The spider raises two side legs. They look mechanical snapping up and bending at the knee joints stiffly like marionette string puppets. The legs snap down to the web. Two front legs snap up. These legs vibrate tentatively, mechanically, above the web.

"Come on, let's get Eg back," Doc says. He does not want to look at the spider.

"Wait a minute," Cherry says. He is kneeling behind Egan's prone body, kneeling as if the body were a bunker parapet. He grabs a twig and tosses it toward the creature. It snags in the web. The spider jerks vibrating the entire network violently, defending his territory and snagging the intrusion. The spider eight-legs forward.

"Cut it out, Mista," Doc says hatefully. He gently slides one hand beneath Egan's head and the other beneath Egan's waist. Cherry does not move. Instead he searches the ground about Egan for a stick. He picks up a small branch perhaps eighteen inches long. He reaches over Egan and holds the end of the stick over the spider's head. Then like a drum beat he bops the spider. The spider dashes forward with incredible speed. Cherry jerks his hand back. The spider stops. Slowly it retreats on its mechanical looking legs.

"mmaghmm . . . kill," a faint moan-cry breaks from Egan's throat. His body is shivering. Doc eases him back a foot. Cherry does not move. Egan's legs touch Cherry's kneeling thighs and Egan winces. The pain is returning but worse is the spider.

"Get the fuck outa the goddamned way, cocksucka," Doc shouts releasing Egan and turning on Cherry. He shoves Cherry.

"Cool it," Cherry says calmly. "I'm goina kill that ugly fucker. I'm goina kill it for Eg, Man. For Eg. You know," Cherry laughs shrewdly, "Eg hates spiders."

"You a perverted mothafucka," Doc curses Cherry. "Get outa the goddamn way." He lifts Egan's legs ever so gently nudging Cherry with his own hips. Egan moans. Inside his head everything seems so clear. He can see everything, hear everything. He can speak, he can move. He knows he can yet he does not have the will. The will stops just before the muscles. It is all inside. He retches, upchucking bile burns his throat and lips. He can smell it, taste it, feel it. Get me out of here, he thinks he yells. Doc is cleaning his mouth. Get me away from that monster. His heart is beating rapidly.

"I'll give you a hand in just a second, Doc," Cherry says leaping right and immediately returning with a larger stick. This stick is twice as long, twice as thick as the first. Cherry now stands, crouches, between Egan and the spider. "Watch this," he says. Doc looks disgustedly. Egan watches. Cherry raises the stick twice as high as he had the first stick and he belts the spider twice as hard. The stick is rotten. It snaps against the tree, a section breaking, hitting the spider. The spider, wounded, retreats into the cavern.

"That bastard just don't wanta die," Cherry absolves himself. A chill runs up his back and neck and up behind his ears. He smirks, wipes his nose nervously. He picks up a larger, sturdier log and tests it on the ground. It is solid. "Come on you little fucker," he snarls. He swings hard inside the cavern, ripping years of webs, crashing hard solid against the inner tree. The spider eludes the blow and charges toward Cherry.

"Use this," Doc yells throwing Cherry a rifle with bayonet affixed. Cherry jumps back, jumps over Egan's legs, catches the rifle and spins, thrusts the blade into the spider's back. The spider squirms. It is inches from Egan's chest. Cherry slashes at it again and again. He leaps back over Egan and stomps the creature, grinding it into the mud. Cherry looks up, surprised, relieved. The sounds of machetes and ETs chopping at brush and vines are covering the hilltop. Egan is looking up at him, horrified. Doc is trembling.

"You guys going to sit here bullshitting or you going to help blow the LZ," El Paso calls coming down, joining them. "¿Que pasa, Doc? Come on, I'll help you move Egan to the other side. Stan, The Man, Kinderly, how are you doing, Man? Doc, if we're going to get a bird in here we got to take down the tree. Doc? You okay, Doc?"

The perimeter force has thinned. The valley has become quiet. Of Alpha's sixty-six able-bodied and semi-able-bodied men twenty are at work cutting, clearing, cleaning the landing zone. They are not carefully silent. They call to one another, joke, curse. Anyone in the valley who is interested can see exactly what Alpha is doing. There is no other way. Brush is slashed with single strokes or ripped up. Boonierats grunt with their straining. Small trees, up to six-inch diameters, are chopped down by machete. The cuttings are dumped off the cliffs or used for barriers on the south slope.

When Brooks had told De Barti that he and Pop were to blow the tree De Barti had emitted a high surprised "Blow that tree?!"

"That one."

"That tree?!" It was impossible to comprehend. It was not a tree, it was a monument.

"Blow it, Goddamnit."

"L-T!"

Then Doc and El Paso had moved Egan to the southern edge of the knoll top. Cherry had carried the wounded man's ruck and weapon and had rejoined the perimeter force. Now Doc brings Hill and Frye down while El Paso leads Kinderly. Others help to bring the rucks and Doc's gear. No one wants to bring Hayes' body so Doc returns. McQueen brings Nahele down. He has cared for him the entire time. He would not have it any other way. The knoll top looks strangely barren. Everything except stumps and leaf debris and the giant teak have been cleared. The ground is drying where the sun is angling beneath the teak's canopy.

Brooks comes down and talks to Doc and El Paso. He tells them the demo kickout is due in zero two. Then he tells Doc there will be two medevacs. "Get Hill and Frye on the first," he says. "They're going to take them to Eagle. Put Hayes and Nahele on that one too."

"What bout Egan and Kinderly?" Doc asks quietly.

"Second bird's theirs. It's going straight to Phu Bai. They'll take em to Da Nang from there."

"Hey, right on," El Paso says. Doc nods his head. He is pleased his most serious casualties are already scheduled to be evacuated to a major hospital complex. He does not care if it is true. He does not wish to ask. He wants to believe it. Instead he says, "L-T. That Cherry. He gone nuts. He crazy, L-T. You can see it in his eyes. L-T, Cherry becomin a animal."

Brooks looks at Doc and sighs, tired. "That potential exists in every man," Brooks says. He shakes his head. "The line between man and beast is very thin. He'll come out of it."

Brooks gets up, walks toward the exposed center of the south slope just behind the perimeter guards. The kickout point is well away from the tree to give the helicopter room to hover. Brown is there on the radio, talking to the approaching pilot. He tosses a smoke grenade a few feet from where he is standing.

Doc sits down among the wounded and dead and tells them what is happening. Then he says, "Dudes, it goan suit me jus fine ta stay in the boonies here fo the rest a my tour if I doan have ta treat one mo wounded. You dudes short now," he jokes with them. "Too short ta ee-ven write a letta."

The bird is on its way in. Thick violet smoke has covered the kickout point and obscured the L-T and the RTOs.

"I can't believe you dudes sometime," Doc continues his monologue. "You dudes was obsessed with gettin here. Why, Mista? Why?"

The GreenMan's C & C bird is circling at 4000 feet. Two Cobras are perhaps 1000 feet AGL. A LOH sprints across the knoll east to west at 75 feet. It loops gracefully, swings back, drops and hovers at 30 feet. The rotor wash swirls and diffuses the smoke casting the knoll in purple haze. The crewman on the hovering ship quickly shoves box after box of C-4 out the side. The boxes crash between Brown and Brooks. The crewman flips out two rolls of det cord and several small boxes of blasting caps. He works very quickly not looking at the ground troops. He taps the pilot. The LOH dives for the river, picks up speed and swooshes up.

Cherry has been circling back and forth behind 1st Plt's perimeter. He has checked every position, checked the ammunition situation and redistributed ammo from those that have to those who are out. Somehow he has missed Numbnuts.

"How's your ammo?" Cherry kneels beside him. He looks enviously at Numbnuts' new weapon. What firepower, he thinks.

"It's okay." Numbnuts looks up at him nervously. Cherry senses the nervousness. He does not know if Numbnuts is hiding something from him or if his reputation has made the thumperman nervous. Cherry knows he is being talked about. He has overheard soldiers saying, "That dude's crazy. He's a crazy fightin mothafucker." Cherry enjoys the spreading reputation and he is now enjoying Numbnuts' nervousness. Numbnuts does not look at him but stares ahead vigilant.

"How do ya like the over/under?" Cherry asks.

"It's fine," Numbnuts answers.

"You got some 79 rounds you can spare for Polanski? He shot most a his up comin up here."

"I ah . . . I ah . . . I got a few. How many does he need?"

"How many you got?"

"I got ah . . . maybe . . . fifteen. No twenty."

"Hey," Cherry says trying to sound very friendly, "can I see your weapon?"

Numbnuts turns. "What for?"

"Let me see it."

"Fuck you."

Cherry darts his hand out and snatches the XM-203. He lifts it quickly to his shoulder, aims it downhill. He lowers it slowly, juggling it, hefting it, then snapping it back to his shoulder. He rubs his hand over it. The weapon is dirty. He looks at the end of the barrel. The flash suppressor is clogged with mud. He opens the lower grenade breech and holds the weapon toward the sun. There are leaf pieces and moisture but no ash in the bore. Cherry ejects the rifle magazine and opens the bolt. A cartridge springs out. Cherry cleans the flash suppressor and holds the barrel to the sun. The rifling is rusting but otherwise clean.

"You motherfucker," Cherry says slowly, coldly. "You motherfucker."

"Hey," Numbnuts whines.

"This weapon's never been fired."

"I was pinned down," Numbnuts blurts.

"It's never been fired," Cherry screams at him.

"I was . . . I . . . what are you goina . . ."

Cherry punches him in the face. He hits him with a solid closed fist aiming for a point through Numbnuts' head. Numbnuts' head flicks over on his neck, bounces down to his shoulder and back up. Immediately the nose bleeds, the eyes blacken. "That's for Egan," Cherry says. He rips the ammo vest off of Numbnuts. The man is crying. Cherry scavenges his pack and takes the grenades and all but one M-16 magazine. "You bastard. You slimy motherfucker." He spits in Numbnuts' face. He grabs the XM-203, he thinks twice about it, it has not been battle-sight zeroed, he throws it onto the crumpled back facing him. Numbnuts is vanquished, defeated.

Egan is propped up, lying with his side across a ruck, staring blankly up the slope at the tree. He feels better now. He can feel the pain in his legs and ass and back. He is happy with

the pain. He knows he will not be paralyzed. He is still warm
from the morphine and he is not certain if he is hallucinating or
if indeed what is before him is real. He does not want to try
speaking. He is afraid he will not be able to speak and he is
afraid to try.

"Wow, Man," Jax says to him, sitting next to him, leaning
on the other side of the ruck. Jax is looking into Egan's eyes.
"Yo really strung out," he laughs. "Maybe Doc got some a that
good shit fo Jax too. Make him look jest like yo."

Brooks comes down and stands before them, looking uphill.
The demo team has the tree partially rigged and all the perimeter
guards and extraneous LZ cutters are moving to the south slope.

"L-T," Jax calls.

"Say hey, Little Brother," Brooks answers Jax.

"L-T," Jax says again, "we oughta put Egan in fo a Silver
Star."

"Yeah, L-T," Doc joins in. "They sayin he took this hill
by his self, the gung-ho fucka."

"Sounds fine to me," Brooks says. He is not paying attention to them. His concentration is on the tree.

Jax nudges Egan and says softly, "An fuck yo feelin. Crazy
fucka, yo gowin be okay in a whirl. They gowin ship yo white
ass back ta yo girl." Jax pauses. He kneels in front of Egan,
finds Egan's hand and taps his knuckles to Egan's three times.
"Yo be cool, Eg. Take care yoself. Yo one fine dude." Jax gets
up and moves back to his guard position.

Up the hill Lt. De Barti and Pop have packed two cases of
C-4 explosive to the far side of the big teak tree. Pop has
inserted two blasting caps and has wired them together and fixed
the loose ends to a claymore wire. Now he and the lieutenant
move downhill as far as the claymore wire will reach. They wait,
pause silently looking at the tree, then in unison yell, "Fire in
the hole. Fire-in-the-hole. Fireinthehooo . . ." There is a large
explosion. A ball of fire bursts across the knoll's north end and
rolls out over the river. Smoke billows skyward. Chunks of
wood fly in every direction. The big tree trembles, the knoll
quakes, the tree rocks then settles, still stretching straight and tall
toward the sky. A landline telephone set dangles unnoticed from
high branches.

"SHIT," Pop explodes. "That thang aint comin down."
He and De Barti cross the knoll top and inspect the wound in the
trunk. There is a jagged burned wedge deeper than half the tree's

diameter. "This valley's been one large pain in the ass, Sir," Pop bitches to De Barti. Baiez and Woods carry two more cases of explosive up to them and Pop crawls up into the wound and again sets to rigging the tree.

It is now Brooks' turn to sit with Egan. He sees that Egan's eyes are watering. Egan is moaning, rocking back and forth slightly. It has been 180 minutes since he was wounded. He has gone from pain to morphine delirium to immobility and now back toward pain. His body is in shock but it does not seem acute and Doc judges his blood pressure to be within an acceptable range. Brooks holds a towel over Egan with his right hand. His hand is sore from having helped cut the LZ. Egan can see blisters and broken skin on Brooks' hand and he thinks, L-T, you're number one. Number fucken one. He tries to speak. He tries to hear his voice. His head hurts and he cannot coordinate his mouth and jaw and breathing. A noise comes out but it is not speech. Egan tires and decides to rest. It will come, he thinks.

"Hey," Brooks says to Egan, "it's okay. You're welcome. That sun's becoming a bear but we'll have you out of here in no time now. All of us. They're terminating the mission. We're going back to Eagle." Brooks looks down at Egan and he feels sickened. Of all the men Egan was always most alive, most active. It sickens Brooks to see him lying immobile, wounded and stoned. "You know, Danny," Brooks says softly, "I've been thinking a lot today about that theory. It's part yours, you know. I was thinking if I could teach it, maybe . . . maybe if it spread . . . it could stop war forever. But maybe that's fucked. Maybe you got it right. What causes war? People cause war. People being people. It's that simple. Love causes war. Hate causes war. Hate of the love of war causes war. We war because we abhor war." Brooks moans shaking his head and looking at the ground. "Oh Danny, why have I led you all here? Leaders cause war. The shame of it. The crime of it. If you hate war; if you love war; if you try to stop war; you cause it. Even if you run from it you cause it because then you create a vacuum and the pressure about the vacuum rolls in and the turmoil is war. When there are no more people," Brooks says woefully, "then there will be no more war. War is part of being human. It's like love and hate and breathing and eating. And living and dying. Just like you said, Danny. 'It just is.' It is natural to strive for peace and not to achieve it. But Danny, it does mean something. The striving means something."

Pop is yelling again. There are two charges on the tree this time. Pop has stuffed two cases of explosives in the splintered gash, and on the south side, twenty feet up, he has stuck a twenty pound kicker charge. The charges are wired together. ". . . Fireinthehooo . . ." The concussion shoots across the knoll, fire and wood blowing madly. Everyone ducks. Everyone except Egan. He is staring into the explosion. He sees the tree lift from its stump and fly upright, north, then drop off the north cliff. "Fuck," he says.

The others look up. There is no tree, no shade. The sun burns down on the knolltop searing the ground. The bare land is suddenly torrid. "Hey, where's that fucker?" someone shouts.

"Hey, where's the tree?"

"Secure the perimeter," Brooks yells. "Get back to your positions. Brown, El Paso, get those medevacs in here."

The boonierats scurry to their positions. FO is the first to discover the tree. It has been blown off the north cliff and it is in the river, upright. The top of the tree is only slightly lower than the knolltop. "I'll be a horse's ass," FO mutters to himself. "That son of a bitch looks like it's been growing there forever."

The GreenMan had planned, detailed and coordinated the extraction with the Air Mission Commander of the 101st Aviation Group two nights earlier. He had anticipated almost every action. There invariably would be modifications, he knew, and he had planned for them. From high over the valley the fighting was going well, better than he had anticipated. He was happy though he knew it was not yet over. Below, his efforts were unseen and unappreciated by the boonierats of Alpha. He was the man responsible for them being there in the first place, they felt. He had volunteered them. They did not blame their predicament on Brooks, he was down there with them. It was the GreenMan they hated.

The GreenMan had arranged to have one set of Cobras for each of his companies. Now he directs the fleet from the C & C Huey at 4000 feet. He coordinates the incoming Dust-Off helicopters with the firepower teams and holds Alpha's extraction birds circling high beyond the north ridge, unseen by either Americans or NVA. He had explained to Brooks earlier the pick-up procedure and he had had the company commander repeat it back to him. "Get your wounded ready," the GreenMan now calls. "Let's keep bird exposure time to an absolute minimum." Artillery rounds begin exploding at the base of the knoll. The GreenMan co-ordinates this too. He has artillery salvos crunching into the valley floor at three locations, wary to keep the projectile flight paths and the incoming helicopters apart yet also eager to dissuade enemy gunners from firing at the medevacs. He assists Brooks in establishing unit-to-bird contact. Then he gets off the net.

"Mercy Eagle Six, Quiet Rover Four. Over." El Paso has assumed radio responsibility. Brooks is standing in the middle of the LZ with his rifle. He holds it with both hands, gingerly with the left, horizontal. One hand is at the front sight post, the other at the mid-point of the stock. He is facing the bird.

"Quiet Rover Four this is Eagle Six. Over." The aircraft commander sounds casual. He asks El Paso several questions which the RTO answers in haste. El Paso signals Doc Johnson to pop smoke and Doc pulls the pin on a smoke grenade. He tosses the canister toward the south end of the LZ. "I see banana smoke," the AC radios and the bird banks slightly left dropping quickly then levels and aims for the LZ. The bird approaches quickly. There are Cobras high to its left and right.

"Come on in," Doc is cheering. He is holding Hill at one side of the LZ. Andrews has Hill's ruck and weapon and is holding Hill's other arm, chattering, wishing him well. Across the LZ Kirtley is holding Frye, telling him to get a piece of ass for all of them. Baiez and Shaw are holding Doc Hayes' poncho-wrapped body. McQueen has Nahele in his arms.

"Next one's yours," Doc Korman says to Kinderly who cannot see what is happening but who has seen it before and understands. The sound of the helicopters hurts his head. Don White is sitting with Kinderly and Korman. He has Kinderly's gear ready to be thrown onto the second ship.

The Dust-Off comes in from the east, passes, shoots across the top of the knoll, seems to stand on its tail. Stopping, it rotates and drops left, turns around, hovers momentarily. Brooks lowers his rifle—the bird slides to a touchdown on the LZ before him. Debris is blowing everywhere. Men are running. Hill is helped aboard by the crew-chief, on the other side the medic pulls Frye in through the opened side. Gear is tossed in. Hayes' body bounces on the floor. McQueen is crying as he lays Nahele down. "Good-bye." Tears are streaming uncontrollably down his cheeks. Brooks jerks his rifle up. The bird lifts. It edges forward then dives off the east cliff picking up speed and swinging up left, up, up out of range of ground fire, out of the flight path of the second Dust-Off coming at the LZ full bore.

"Man, them dudes are fine," Jax yells to Doc. "One fine piece a flyin." Jax has Egan's ruck and weapon. Brooks and Doc are holding Egan. Egan is standing, shaky, pain in his legs, but feeling. Coming down over the north ridge are twelve Huey slicks. They are Alpha's lift birds. They are in line, two sets of six. They are coming in from the valley's west end. The second medevac bird crosses the LZ and begins turning. Doc and Brooks lead Egan toward the pick-up site. They are by the stump of the giant teak. The bird is coming at them, rotor wash lashing dust and debris into their faces. "I'm going to miss you," Brooks yells. "You're the best they come." "Stephanie," Egan murmurs. His eyes are tearing. Doc Korman and Don White lead Kinderly. White sees them first and pulls Kinderly down. There are NVA on the north rim of the knoll. "You're going to see that la . . . oh shit." Brooks is cut short by automatic weapons fire. They are firing at the medevac. Brooks and Doc pull Egan down behind the stump. All the boonierats have hit the earth. The helicopter shudders. Now there is return fire. Cherry is running up the LZ. There is steady firing into the helicopter. The bird shakes violently and drops onto the LZ. The tail rotor is dangerously close to the teak stump. There is firing coming from above, from across the river and up the south slope. An RPG round bursts into the bird's front Plexiglas windows. AK fire is spraying down on the bird from the rear. M-16s and 60s are returning fire, trying to suppress fire. The aircraft commander is hit bleeding slumped over the control stick, his shoulder harness holding him while rounds slam into his face and chest. The first Cobra rolls and dives raking the south slope with mini-gun fire. The medevac co-pilot is still fighting with the controls, trying to lift the ship. He pushes the stick forward increasing rotor angle. The bird does not respond. Oil lines are ruptured. The crew-chief and medic jump from the bird. The helicopter is on fire. Korman and White are pulling Kinderly back. Kinderly is frantic, blind, terrified. Brooks is lying over Egan and Doc shielding them with his body. The helicopter is being ravaged. All enemy guns are trained on it. Cherry picks off one then another and another enemy soldier coming up over the cliff. For him it is a shooting

gallery. The NVA are shooting only at the bird, trying to explode it, trying to jam the LZ so Alpha cannot be extracted.
Cherry and now Jax and Pop and half a dozen others are killing
NVA. AK rounds impact into the neck and shoulders of the
co-pilot. He is struggling. His body stiffens then drops limp.
Again an RPG smashes the bird. The bird explodes gushing
flaming aviation fuel. Huge chunks of helicopter slash through
the air like shrapnel. The NVA fire lulls.

"Bravo! Bravo!" Screams are coming from the south and
west sides of the perimeter.

"El Paso," Thomaston shouts, "have the lift birds come
in."

There is still firing from the south. Cherry and Denhardt
race down to help suppress it. Denhardt is hit. His leg blows up
splattering Cherry. Cherry thinks he too is hit.

The middle of the LZ is a ball of fire. In the flames Jax can
see the pilots burning. Then he sees Brooks and Doc. They are
lying lifeless on top of another body, on top of Egan. Doc's jaw
is sheared, bloody, raw. Brooks is moving. Egan's legs are
moving. NVA fire erupts again from the south. The enemy is
right in Alpha's lines. Boonierats low-crawl and fire on enemy
only feet away. Two Cobras dive. They swing in on tangents to
Alpha's perimeter so as not to undershoot and hit the boonierats.
They dive from west to east keeping the sun behind them. They
do not fire rockets. Their mini-guns are buzzing, nailing down
everything in forty foot wide swaths. A LOH is blasting away at
the north side of the knoll. El Paso has picked up the LOH
commander on his radio. The bird has caught a column of enemy
soldiers climbing in a cleft up the knoll cliffs. A Cobra pilot
reports seeing forty enemy on the valley floor streaming toward
the south slope. The GreenMan orders in the extraction birds.

The heat of the burning helicopter is incredibly intense. The
fire sucks air like napalm. Egan is trapped beneath Doc and
Brooks. He is conscious but stoned. He can see the flames but
the heat does not bother him. For a moment he smells Brooks'
flesh burning but then he can no longer smell. He is calm. He
has been waiting without anticipation. He does not see fire, he
sees energy. Energy, he thinks. Energy is reduced by the square
of the distance from its source. As his eyebrows and hair curl
and blacken in the heat like melting red plastic threads, he sees
an equation: $L_2 = L_1(d^2)$. It isn't energy, he thinks, it is Light.

No Sight. The power of sight decreases in direct relationship to the square of the distance from the source. Or is it, $S = D^2$? Oh, he smiles inwardly, it isn't distance, it is Daniel. It isn't sight, it is Stephanie. Egan sees his exposed skin peel, split, roll back from the splits and char. The surface of his eyes are boiling. The magnesium hulk medevac bird is changing from matter to energy in whitehot burning. "I don't feel we're saying good-bye," Egan says aloud. He does not hear his voice. "Stephanie, we'll see each other again. Haven't I always come back to you?" Egan hears a rhythmic hush rushing sound and a quick pumping. It is his own breathing and his heartbeat. He does not feel his skin. He thinks he sees. He sees Stephanie.

"Jax," Cherry screams. "Egan, Doc, the L-T."

The first extraction bird is coming in, landing, not touching down completely, below the kickout point. Thomaston is directing. 2d Plt is loading. Doorgunners are keeping steady fire pouring south. The bird departs, a second bird lands. Wounded are thrown on. Numbnuts jumps on the second bird. Jax and Cherry are sprinting up toward the burning ground near the medevac. Pop and El Paso race after them. Enemy fire is increasing with every lift bird touching down. Mohnsen is hit boarding. Thomaston directs 3d Plt to begin loading.

"3d Sqd out," Caldwell yells. He is backing toward the pick-up point. McQueen and 1st Sqd begin backing away from the ragged perimeter. They are firing suppressive fire trying to keep the enemy fire down.

"Get back to the perimeter," Caldwell kicks at McQueen's ass as both of them back up.

McQueen turns. "Eat it, Lieutenant," he snaps. "We're coming up now. You stay there."

"Sergeant, I gave you an order," Caldwell screams.

"No shit," McQueen growls. Another bird leaves, another sets down. McQueen snarls.

"Get down there, Goddamn it. That's an order."

"Like you gave to Ridgefield," McQueen explodes.

"I didn't . . ."

"Like Snell. Like Nahele."

"Sergeant . . ."

An ugly mask of hate contorts McQueen's face. "Like you always give." McQueen lowers his M-16, squeezes the trigger and puts three rounds into Lt. Larry Caldwell's heart.

"Pick up the wounded," McQueen yells to his platoon. He lifts Caldwell's body. 3d Plt is extracted.

"They aint dead," Jax is shouting, screaming. "We ken get um."

Lairds throws Denhardt onto the floor of the extraction bird. Marko, Hoover and McCarthy leap in. Cahalan jumps in. The bird lifts.

"Get on the fucken birds," Thomaston shouts at Jax and Cherry. Alpha no longer has a perimeter. Gunships are diving over the tops of the lift birds spraying mini-gun fire and now rockets. Thomaston reaches Pop. He grabs him, spins him hard. "Get on the bird." He seizes El Paso, shoves him. "There." Cherry and Jax are crawling forward toward Egan and Doc and the L-T. They are guarding their faces. Enemy fire is increasing. There are a hundred NVA soldiers coming up the south slope. A hundred dead NVA bodies give them cover to dive behind as the helicopters fire at them and they fire back. Cherry and Jax are hugging the ground inching into the heat. Jax' fatigue shirt bursts into flame. Mortar rounds are being walked across the knolltop by NVA mortar teams. Jax sheds his shirt, running, retreating from the flames.

"Get outa there," Thomaston shouts crouching, blocking the heat from his face.

"I'm Cherry," Cherry yells reaching, his face and hands burning. Cherry can see Egan's eyes. They are open. His arms seem to be reaching toward Cherry. Thomaston dashes in wildly, grabs Cherry's ankle and pulls. "No," Cherry screams. Thomaston stands, jumps clutching insanely, lifting Cherry and carrying him toward the last bird. They break for the helicopter. The doorgunners are burning the barrels off their machine guns. LOHs are buzzing. Pop and El Paso reach the bird, step on the skid and spin into the open side. Jax and Cherry jump in. Thomaston jumps, Pop catches him, pulls. The bird lifts up to his not yet falling body. The noise of the rotors slaps louder, the ship dips, the tail raises. Cherry's eyes are on the pile of US bodies. The helicopter is off.

Cool wind rushes through the open sides of the helicopter.

"Where in the fuck did the gooks come from?" Thomaston cries. "They were right on the knoll with us."

Jackson too is crying. His face is distorted, ugly. "We left em there," he screams. "We left em there. Egan woant dead."

El Paso vomits.

Pop is dazed.

Cherry is cold, breathing hard. He looks at Jax. He says at him, a smirk on his face, "Fuck it." He bursts out laughing. "Don't mean nothin."

SIGNIFICANT ACTIVITIES

THE FOLLOWING RESULTS FOR OPERATIONS IN THE O'REILLY/ BARNETT/JEROME AREA WERE REPORTED FOR THE 24-HOUR PERIOD ENDING 2359 25 AUGUST 70:

AN UNDETERMINED SIZED ENEMY FORCE ATTACKED 2D PLT, CO B, 7/402 AT THEIR NDP VICINITY YD 165325 AT 0217 HOURS. CO B RETURNED ORGANIC WEAPONS FIRE. THE ENEMY WITHDREW. CO B RECEIVED SEVEN MORTAR IMPACTIONS IN THEIR NDP AT 0235 HOURS RESULTING IN THREE US WIA. COUNTER-BATTERY ARTILLERY WAS EMPLOYED TO SILENCE THE MORTARS. AT 0305 HOURS, CO B WAS AGAIN ATTACKED IN THEIR NDP AND AGAIN REPULSED THE ATTACK WITH ORGANIC WEAPONS FIRE. THREE MORE US SOLDIERS WERE WOUNDED. THE WOUNDED WERE EVACUATED AT 0410 HOURS.

CO C, 7/402 WAS ATTACKED BY AN UNKNOWN SIZE ENEMY FORCE BEFORE DAWN VICINITY YD 133318. THE ENEMY INFILTRATED TWO POSITIONS OF CO C'S PERIMETER KILLING TWO US SOLDIERS AND WOUNDING TWO BEFORE THE ATTACK WAS REPULSED WITH ORGANIC WEAPONS FIRE.

AT 0712 HOURS 1ST PLT, CO A, 7/402, WHILE ADVANCING UPHILL ENGAGED AN UNKNOWN SIZE ENEMY FORCE DUG INTO A TRENCH, VICINITY YD 148318, KILLING FOUR NVA. THREE US WERE WOUNDED.

AT 0855 HOURS 2D AND 3D PLTS OF CO A DISCOVERED AN NVA HEADQUARTERS AND SUPPLY BUNKER COMPLEX CONSISTING OF APPROXIMATELY 28 UNDERGROUND ROOMS CONNECTED BY TUNNELS. THE ELEMENT ENTERED THE COMPLEX UNOPPOSED AND CARRIED OUT FOUR SOVIET-MADE GR-9 RADIOS, AND AN ESTIMATED SEVEN TONS OF AMMUNITION INCLUDING 18 CRATES OF 82MM MORTAR ROUNDS, 36 CRATES OF 61MM MORTAR ROUNDS, 24 CRATES OF RPG ROCKETS, 40 BOXES CHI-COM CLAYMORE MINES, 60 BOXES 37MM AA AMMUNITION, 55 CANS RPD MACHINE GUN AMMUNITION AND 3000 SACHEL CHARGES. AT 0935 AN UNKNOWN SIZE ENEMY FORCE EMERGED FROM THE TUNNELS AND ENGAGED CO A KILLING TWO US AND WOUNDING TWO. CO A WITHDREW ALLOWING AIR SUPPORT ACCESS TO THE ENEMY. 16 ENEMY WERE

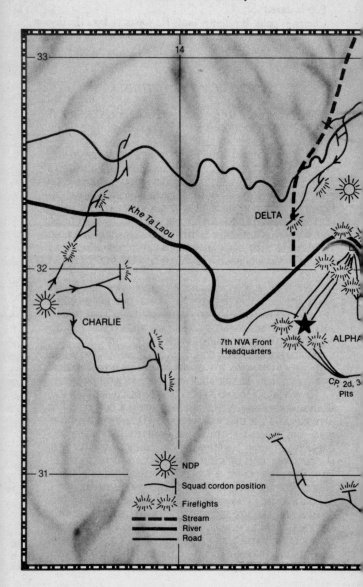

Khe Ta Laou

DELTA

7th NVA Front
Headquarters

CHARLIE

ALPHA

CP, 2d, 3
Plts

☀ NDP

⊣ Squad cordon position

Firefights

▬ ▬ Stream

▬▬ River

— Road

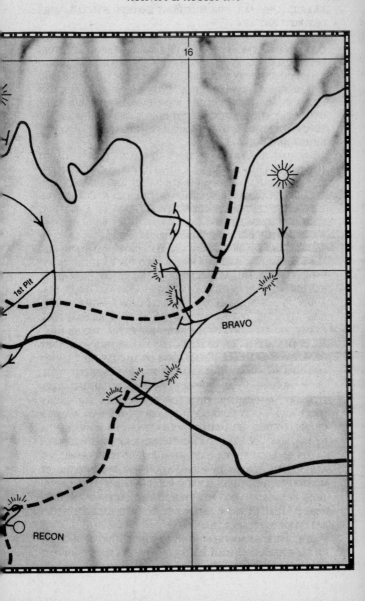

KILLED, 11 BY ARA. THE MUNITIONS EXPOSED BY CO A WERE DESTROYED BY ARA.

AT 1242 HOURS CO A WAS ATTACKED BY A LARGE WELL COORDINATED ENEMY FORCE WHILE THEY WERE EVACUATING PREVIOUSLY WOUNDED SOLDIERS. A MEDICAL EVACUATION HELICOPTER, HIT BY RPG FIRE, EXPLODED ON THE LZ KILLING THE PILOT AND CO-PILOT. CO A RETURNED ORGANIC WEAPONS FIRE AND ARA AND GUNSHIPS WERE EMPLOYED. WHILE STILL UNDER FIRE, CO A WAS EXTRACTED. ONE US SOLDIER WAS KILLED, SEVEN WOUNDED. KNOWN ENEMY CASUALTIES WERE 44 KIA, 30 BY ARA AND 14 BY SAF.

DURING THE PERIOD OF CO A'S CONTACT, COS B, C, D AND THE RECON PLT OF E ALL ENCOUNTERED SPORADIC ACTION. THE ENEMY INITIATED SEVEN SEPARATE DIRECT AND INDIRECT FIRE ATTACKS ON THESE UNITS AS THEY ATTEMPTED TO CORDON OFF THE VALLEY CENTER AREA BEING ATTACKED BY CO A. THE 7/402 COMPANIES ENGAGED THE ENEMY NINE TIMES WITH ORGANIC WEAPONS FIRE AND WERE SUPPORTED BY ARTILLERY, ARA AND TAC AIR. A SWEEP OF THE CONTACT AREA REVEALED 57 NVA KIA, 31 BY SUPPORTING FIRE. THE NVA SLIPPED THROUGH THE TIGHT-ENING CORDON AND ATTACKED CO B AND RECON FROM THEIR RESPECTIVE REARS RESULTING IN THREE US KIA AND TEN US WIA. AFTER CO A WAS EXTRACTED THE BATTALION'S OTHER COMPA-NIES ATTACKED OUTWARD FROM THE CORDON KILLING FOUR ENEMY. ALL ELEMENTS OF THE 7/402 WERE EXTRACTED BY 1600.

IN THE VICINITY OF YD 332239, TWO KILOMETERS SOUTHEAST OF FIREBASE O'REILLY, ELEMENTS OF THE 1ST REGT (ARVN) ENGAGED AN UNKNOWN SIZE ENEMY FORCE. THE ENEMY WITH-DREW UNDER HEAVY ARA SUPPORT BY THE 4TH BN (AERIAL ARTY), 77TH ARTY (AMBL). THE ARVN ELEMENT PURSUED THE ENEMY FORCE AND WAS IN CONTACT THROUGHOUT THE DAY. A SWEEP OF THE CONTACT AREA AT 1730 HOURS REVEALED 37 NVA KIA, 16 BY ARA. NINE ARVN SOLDIERS WERE KILLED AND SEVEN WOUNDED.

ON 25 AUGUST, THE 101ST AIRBORNE DIVISION (AMBL) RE-ALIGNED ITS FORCES IN PREPARATION FOR THE NORTHEAST MONSOONS. THE 7TH BN (AMBL), 402D INF TERMINATED OPERA-TIONS IN COORDINATION WITH THE 3D REGT (ARVN) IN THE FIRE-BASE BARNETT AREA, AND MOVED TO CAMP EAGLE TO BEGIN BATTALION REFRESHER TRAINING.

THE 1ST REGT (ARVN) CONTINUED CONDUCTING OPERATIONS IN THE FIREBASE O'REILLY AREA WHILE ELEMENTS OF THE

3D REGT (ARVN) CONTINUED OPERATIONS IN THE FIREBASE
BARNETT/JEROME AREA.

DURING THE PERIOD 13–25 AUGUST COMBINED OPERATIONS IN
THE O'REILLY/BARNETT/JEROME AREA RESULTED IN 614
ENEMY KILLED.

EPILOGUE

31 AUGUST 1970

With great dignity and military bearing Command Sergeant Major Zarnochuk mounted the stairs, marched to the center of the stage and halted. He executed a precise right-face and took two steps forward. In his hand he held a single sheet of paper. He glanced down at the paper, then called out, "Captain Matthew R. Kalemba."

"Here," a voice sounded from the bleachers.

The sergeant major paused. In a semicircle before him on the stage there were twenty-nine M-16 rifles with bayonets affixed. The muzzles were turned down, the bayonets stuck into the plywood. Atop each weapon was a helmet and in front of each, a pair of jungle boots. Someone had taken the time to spit-shine the boots.

"Captain Thomas M. Lopez," Zarnochuk called.

"Here," another voice answered.

Again there was the pause. The weapons and helmets and boots looked like a strange, morbid picket fence. The sergeant major was three steps behind the fence. Behind him was the colonel, the battalion XO and the chaplains. The brigade commander, the Old Fox, did not attend. He had already rotated to a duty station in the United States.

"Captain Peter L. O'Hare," Zarnochuk called.

There was no answer. He paused, looked forward, down. The remnant of the 7th Battalion, 402d Infantry sat in the sun, on the crude wooden benches before the stage. Cherry was in the fourth row back. Around him were Lt. Thomaston, El Paso, Jax,

Cahalan, Brown and FO. Squads, platoons, companies sat informally, partially mingled, yet generally the boonierats sat with the men they were closest to in the field. The sun was beating down harshly on the soldiers. The air was still. Zarnochuk surveyed the battalion.

"First Lieutenant Lawrence J. Caldwell."

Again there was no answer. The boonierats shuffled and fidgeted in the sun. They had been sitting there for an hour. The memorial ceremony had begun with Chaplain Gibson's invocation.

"In the name of the Father and the Son and the Holy Spirit," the chaplain had mumbled.

"Amen," the chaplain's assistant had responded from the first row of bleachers. Cherry had gritted his teeth.

"The grace of our Lord Jesus Christ and the love of God and the fellowship of the Holy Spirit be with you all."

"And also with you."

"Hey," Cherry whispered to El Paso.

"¿Que pasa?" El Paso nodded to him.

"You are, Bro," Cherry said. He smiled. "Hey, do you believe in reincarnation?"

The chaplain's voice rose as his tempo increased, ". . . Give our brothers peaceful rest in the Light of Your Resurrection, in the Glory of Your Holiness. May they see the Light of Your Divine presence, Lord Jesus, in the Kingdom where You live and where You will graciously allow them to abide . . ."

"Yes," El Paso whispered back to Cherry. "I think so. Everything in nature renews itself."

". . . Christ was the first to rise from the dead . . ."

"Shee-it," Cherry smiled, "you mean, they goina be recycled." He laughed. Jax laughed too yet he was angry with himself for laughing, for finding Cherry funny.

". . . He will raise up our mortal bodies to be like His in Glory on the last day . . ."

Cherry did not want to listen to the chaplain and was happy when the chaplain ended by mumbling the Latin, *"Benedictus qui veni in nomine Domini."* Blessed is he who comes in the name of the Lord. Cherry scratched his nose, rubbed his chin.

A new operation was to begin 1 September. He looked up toward the Oh-deuce pad to see what activity was in progress. The hilltop was buzzing with supply personnel and stacked deep in new equipment. The GreenMan's speech brought his attention back to the stage.

"I feel humbled to stand before so many brave and valorous men," the colonel began. He spoke with total sincerity, with real love and total belief in his words. "I want you men to understand what your valor has achieved," he said. "And for what your brave brothers have died. To each of these men represented here, we are awarding a Bronze Star. This may not seem like much. But these are symbols. It is a way the country has of saying, 'Thank you.' These men, you men, have made a significant contribution toward the accomplishment of our mission. These men we honor here today can rest in peace, assured that progress in Vietnamization, for which they gave their lives, is being made . . ."

Cahalan shook his head at the GreenMan's words. He found them sickening. He looked at Jax and Cherry. Jax did not seem to be listening. Cherry was listening intently now.

". . . I am fond of telling people that the job of the infantry in this country, this military region, this province, stacks up against the job of any infantry in any war that our country has ever fought. That includes the Winter Campaign in Germany in 1944 and the World War Two island hopping in the Pacific.

"I want you to know that you have been knocking against much of the NVA 7th Front composed of infantry, sapper and supply battalions. You ran head-on into a strong enemy in his own base area and you defeated him. You discovered what has probably been the biggest, most extensive, best camouflaged and, yes, most secure NVA complex discovered in I Corps during this entire war. You successfully exposed and neutralized the enemy, and you commenced his ultimate destruction. The headquarters you exposed has been completely destroyed by follow-up heavy bomber raids which produced numerous secondary explosions. Bomb damage assessment photographs indicate total destruction.

"Gentlemen, there are a lot of women and children in Hue and the surrounding lowland communities who are alive because of your sacrifices. The Vietnamese held national elections yesterday and because of your efforts there were no significant incidents in our coastal areas. There are also a lot of GIs in this division rear area who are thankful that you were out there . . ."

"They best be," Cherry said aloud.

". . . whether you like this unit or not," the GreenMan continued, "you owe it to yourselves to be proud of what you have accomplished. You men descended into a valley that no allied troops had ever set foot in. The enemy will never again be secure in the Khe Ta Laou. You men sitting here have faced possibly the toughest obstacle life can throw at you and you have conquered it.

"Thank you."

The GreenMan paused. Cherry sat ramrod straight in the seat below his commander. His chest swelled with pride. The GreenMan seemed to stare right at him. Then very solemnly the GreenMan said, "Sergeant Major Zarnochuk." The GreenMan's voice was now loud and clear and hard. "You are directed to read the roll call."

At that moment Zarnochuk had mounted to the stage. The roll call continued. No one answered.

"Second Lieutenant Roosevelt Wheltley.

"Platoon Sergeant Manuel T. Alvarez.

"Platoon Sergeant Washington C. Briggs.

"Staff Sergeant Johnny Cartney.

"Staff Sergeant Le Huu Minh.

"Staff Sergeant Rafer S. Ridgefield.

"Staff Sergeant Leon I. Silvers."

Jax could not help it. Tears were heavy in his eyes. He cried unashamed. El Paso cried too. On Cahalan's face the flow glistened in the sun.

"Sergeant Michael D. Bissett.

"Sergeant Anthony K. DiComo.

"Sergeant Joseph R. Escalato.

"Sergeant Woodrow M. Hayes.

"Sergeant Donald A. Nahele."

Behind Cherry, McQueen also cried. There were no tears in Cherry's eyes. He was pissed, indignant. "They are still here with us," Cherry whispered. The others are not listening to him. "They are here in these seats. Now," he said. "Now and forever. In me, by me, their spirits shall live forever."

"Specialist Jerome Clement.

"Specialist Charles T. Finton.

"Specialist Norman Rocca.

"Specialist Carlos Sanchez.

"Private First Class Daniel A. Dunn.

"Private First Class Juan Carmona.

"Private First Class Dewey C. Greer.

"Private First Class Wayne Z. Smith.

"Private First Class Justin Trumbull.

"Private Thomas Martinzelli.

"Private Thomas M. Southern.

"Private Stanley Wilson.

"Private Alberto S. Wong.

"From Eagle Dust-Off, Warrant Officer Robert Thatchman.

"Warrant Officer Brian E. Vaughn."

Zarnochuk paused for a long minute. The theater area was silent. Zarnochuk pivoted about-face and stepped to the back of the stage.

The GreenMan came forward again. He called out, "This is the last roll call for these men. From here forward, those men who have not answered roll call, Sergeant Major, I direct you to strike their names from the battalion roster."

The theater was silent.

"Hey, Jax, El Paso." Cherry nudged El Paso. "How come they didn't call out Egan? or Doc? or the L-T?"

No one answered. Cherry turned to Thomaston. The new company commander looked at him coldly and said, "Haven't you heard? They listed them as MIAs."

"Well fuck," Cherry smiled. He was happy they were not listed among the known dead. In me, he thought. He laughed. "Fuck it. Don't mean . . ."

Thomaston cut him off. "Don't say it, Soldier."

FINAL TABULATION

The following composite results were reported for the 101st Airborne Division (Airmobile) for Operation TEXAS STAR—1 April to 5 September 1970:

ENEMY LOSSES INFLICTED

Killed in Action (body count)	2053
POWs	38
Ralliers	14
Individual weapons captured	420
Crew served weapons captured	121
Rounds of ammunition captured	200,000
Rice captured (tons)	59

DIVISION CASUALTIES

KIA	349
Died of wounds	37
WIA	1978
MIA	7

G L O S S A R Y

AC: Also A/C. Aircraft Commander.
AGL: Above Ground Level.
AHB: Assault Helicopter Battalion.
Airmobile: Helicopter-borne. Those who jump from helicopters without parachutes.
Airborne: Parachutist. Those who jump from airplanes with parachutes.
AIT: Advanced Individual Training.
AK-47:   Also known as Kalashnikov AK-47. The most widely used assault rifle in the world. A Soviet produced semiautomatic or automatic 7.62mm assault rifle. Known as the Type 56 to Chinese forces. Characterized by an explosive popping sound.
ALPHA: The military phonetic for the letter A.
AO: Area of Operation. In rear areas this may connote a sleeping area or bunk. "MY AO . . ."
ARA: Aerial Rocket Artillery. A Cobra AG-1H helicopter with four XM-159C 19-rocket (2.75 inch rocket) pods.
Arty: Artillery.
ARVN: (Ar'–vin) Army of the Republic of Vietnam. Also a South Vietnamese soldier as in Marvin the ARVN.
AWOL: Absent without leave.
azimuth: A bearing from North.
B-40:   A communist bloc rocket-propelled grenade launcher. Also the rounds fired—B-40 rockets.
B-52:   A can opener (church key type). Also a heavy American bomber.
ballgame: An operation or a contact.
band-aid: A medic.

basketball ship: An illumination-dropping (flare) helicopter.

battle-sight zeroing: The process of adjusting a weapon's sights and windage to an individual soldier so the weapon, when fired, will hit the object of aim.

Battery: An artillery unit the equivalent of a company. Six 105mm or 155mm howitzers or two 8-inch or 175mm self-propelled howitzers.

BDA: Bomb Damage Assessment.

beaucoup: French for many. Boonierats usually pronounced this word boo-coo. Many thought it was Vietnamese.

berm: The perimeter line of a fortification—usually raised above surrounding area.

bird: A helicopter.

bird dog: A FAC or forward air controller, usually in a small, maneuverable single-engined prop airplane.

blue feature: Any water feature, so called because of the color used to designate water on topographic maps.

boo-coo: Beaucoup.

boonie hat: A soft hat worn by a boonierat in the boonies.

boonierat: An infantryman.

boonies: The field, the bush, the jungle. Any place the infantry operates that is not a firebase, basecamp or ville. From boondock.

bowl: A pipe used for smoking dope.

BRAVO: The military phonetic for the letter B. Also Company A's call for medic.

breaking squelch: Disrupting the natural static of a radio by depressing the transmit bar on another radio set on the same frequency.

Bro: Also Brother. A black soldier or soul brother. Also, at times, boonierats from the same unit.

BS: Bullshit. Also, BSing; Bullshitting, as in chewing the fat, telling tall tales, or telling lies.

C-4: A powerful plastic explosive.

C-123: A small cargo airplane, The Caribou.

C-130: A medium cargo airplane, The Hercules.

C-141: A large cargo airplane, The Starlifter.

CA: Combat Assault.

CAR-15: A carbine rifle.

CC: Company Commander.

C & C: Command and Control (helicopter).

CG: Commanding General.

CH-47: A Chinook.

CH-54: The largest of all American helicopters, strictly for cargo, The Flying Crane or Skycrane.

***CHARLIE*:** The military phonetic for the letter C. Also, the Viet Cong.

Charlie-Charlie: C & C.

Charlie Four: C-4.

cheap Charlie: A GI who is frugal with his money while in a bar.

cherry: A new troop.

Chi-Com: Also Chicom. Chinese communist. Used in conjunction with an object this denoted manufactured in Red China. Used alone Chi-com usually meant a Chinese manufactured hand grenade.

Chieu Hoi: Vietnamese for Open Arms. An amnesty program to encourage enemy soldiers to rally to the GVN.

Chinook: A large twin-rotor cargo helicopter, CH-47, often referred to as a Shit-hook because of the discomfort caused by the rotor wash to anyone in the vicinity of its landing. Wind velocity at the tip of the rotors reportedly is 130 mph.

Chuck: or Chas The enemy.

clacker: A small hand-held firing device for a claymore mine.

Claymores: Anti-personnel mines with one-pound charge of C-4 behind 600 small steel balls.

CO: Commanding Officer.

Cobra: An assault helicopter. AG-1H.

comics: Topographic maps.

commo: Communication.

CONEX: Corrugated metal packing crate of large dimension, often used as shelter atop firebases.

COSVN: Communist Office of South Vietnam. Thought to be located in the Parrot's Beak area of Cambodia, it was never found.

CP: Command Post.

CQ: Charge of Quarters.

C-rats: Combat rations. After two weeks they all taste the same.

Cs: C-rats.

DA: Department of the Army.

daily-daily: Anti-malaria pills taken daily.

dap: A soul handshake and greeting which may last up to ten minutes and is characterized by the use of both hands and often comprised of slaps and snaps of the fingers. Highly ritualized and unit specific.

dee-dee: Also dee-dee mau (Vietnamese, *didi*—to run). Get the hell out of here.

***DELTA*:** The military phonetic for the letter D.

DEROS: (Deé-rōs) Date Estimate Return from Overseas. The day a soldier is scheduled to go home or the act of going home.

dew: Marijuana.

dicks: A derogatory expression meaning or referring to the enemy.

dime: The number ten.

dime-nickel: A 105mm howitzer.

dinks: A derogatory expression meaning or referring to the enemy.

DMZ: Demilitarized Zone (a word game).

DRO: Dining Room Orderly.

drops: Reduction in length of tour caused by overall reduction and withdrawal of American forces from Vietnam.

DTs: Defensive Targets. Also known as Delta Tangos.

Dust-Off: Medical evacuation by helicopter.

DX: Direct exchange. Also, to discard or dispose of, to kill someone.

E-1: Private One. The lowest army pay grade.

E-2: Private Two. The E stands for enlisted. Pay grades run from E-1 to E-11.

Early-Outs: A drop, or a reduction in time in service. A soldier with 150 days or less remaining on his active duty commitment when he DEROSed from Vietnam also ETSed from the army under the Early Out Program.

ECHO: The military phonetic for the letter E.

Eleven Bravo: Also 11-B, the MOS of an infantryman.

EM: Enlisted Man.

ET or E-T: An Entrenching Tool, a small collapsible shovel, pick and mattock combined in one instrument.

ETS: Estimated Termination of Service. The scheduled date of getting out of the army.

F-4s: Phantom Jet fighter-bombers. Range—1000 miles. Speed—1400 mph. Payload—16,000 lbs. The workhorse of the tactical air support fleet. Often called a fast mover.

FAC: Forward Air Controller. See BIRD DOG.

fast mover: An F-4.

FB: Firebase.

FDC: Fire Direction Control. (Artillery)

firebase: An artillery firing position, usually atop a hill or ridge, which would be secured by infantry and supplied by helicopter. They could be established very rapidly and were often in existence for only a brief period of time although many were permanent all-weather bases.

FO: Forward Observer.

FOXTROT: The military phonetic for the letter F.

frag: A fragmentation hand grenade.

fragging: Using a FRAG to wound or kill a person, usually a LIFER.

freak: Frequency, radio. Also a junkie or pothead.

freq: Frequency.

fuck: Along with Fucked and Fuckin—the most commonly used word in a GI's vocabulary other than the article *a*.

fucked up: To be wounded or killed. Also, to get high on marijuana or other drugs. Also, to get drunk. Also, to be foolish or do something stupid.

funny papers: or comics. Topographic maps.

FWMAF: Free World Military Assistance Forces. The allies.

ghosting: Goldbricking or sandbagging.

GOLF: Military phonetic for the letter G.

gooks: An NVA soldier. Also, any Oriental human being.

grunt: A BOONIERAT.

gunship: Early in the war this meant any extra heavily armed helicopter used primarily to support infantry troops. Later, it referred to a Cobra AH-1H equipped with a particular configuration of rockets, 40mm cannons and mini-guns.

hardstand: A pierced steel plate (PSP) platform over sand.

HE: High Explosive. (Artillery)

heat tabs: An inflammable tablet used to heat C-RATS. Always in short supply.

H & I: Harassment and Interdiction. (Artillery)

HHC: Headquarters and Headquarters Company.

Higher-Higher: The honchos. The command or commanders.

hook: A radio; a radio handset.

hootch: A billet, sometimes a bunker, sometimes an office building.

horn: A radio handset.

HOTEL: The military phonetic for the letter H.

Hueys: UH-1 helicopters of various series. This Utility helicopter was the primary troop insertion/extraction aircraft for the 101st. Also used as Dust-Off birds and C & C birds. Called Slicks.

Hump: To patrol carrying a rucksack; to walk; to perform any arduous task.

I Corps: (The Roman numeral I here is pronounced 'eye'.) The northernmost military region of South Vietnam.

IG: Inspector General.

INDIA: The military phonetic for the letter I.

insert: To be deployed into a tactical area by helicopter.

Jody: The person who wins your lover while you are in the Nam. From the marching song, or cadence count, *"Ain't no use in goin' home/Jody's got your girl an' gone/sound off...."*

JULIET: The military phonetic for the letter J.

k: In lower case, pronounced kay; a kilometer.

KBA: Killed By Artillery.

KBH: Killed By Helicopter.

KCS: Kit Carson Scout, a Vietnamese working with an American infantry unit as an interpreter and scout under the Luc Long 66 Program.

KIA: Killed In Action.

KILO: The military phonetic for the letter K.

klick: A kilometer.

LAW: Light Anti-tank Weapon. A 66mm rocket in a collapsible, discardable firing tube. Effective against bunkers.

LEMA: The military phonetic for the letter L.

lifers: Career military personnel, derogatory.

little people: The enemy.

lit-up: Fired upon.

LMG: Light Machine Gun—the Soviet made RPD, a bi-pod mounted, belt fed weapon similar to the American M-60 machine gun. The RPD fires the same cartridge as the AK-47 and the SKS carbine.

Log Bird: Logistical (resupply) helicopter.

LOH: Light Observation Helicopter.

LP: Listening Post.

LRRP: Long Range Reconnaissance Patrol.

LSA: Lubricant, Small Arms.

LZ: Landing Zone.

M-16:   A gas-operated, air cooled automatic/semi-automatic assault weapon weighing 7.6 pounds with a 20-round magazine. Maximum range 2350m. Maximum effective range 460m. Automatic firing rate 650–700 rounds/minute, sustained automatic firing rate 100–200 rounds/minute.

M-60:   The standard American light machine gun. A gas-operated, air cooled, belt fed, automatic weapon. Often referred to by boonierats as THE GUN.

M-79:   An American single-shot 40mm grenade launcher. Called the thumper.

MA: Mechanical Ambush. A euphemism for an American-set booby trap.

mad minute: A weapons free-fire practice and test session.

MARS: Military Affiliate Radio Station. Used by soldiers to call home via Signal Corps and ham radio equipment.

MEDCAP: Medical Civilian Assistance Program.

Medevac: Medical evacuation by helicopter.

mermite: Large insulated food containers.

MIA: Missing In Action.

MIKE: The military phonetic for the letter M.

mike-mike: Millimeter.

Mini-Gun: An electric Gatling gun, 7.62mm. Capable of firing 6000 rounds/min.

Monday pills: Anti-malaria pills taken once a week on Mondays.

Monster, the: A PRC-77.

MOS: Military Occupational Speciality. Job title code.

MPC: Military Payment Certificates; GI play money.

Nam: Vietnam.

NCO: Non-Commissioned Officer.

NDP: Night Defensive Position.

net: Radio frequency setting, from network.

nickel: The number five.

no sweat: Easy. Can do.

NOVEMBER: The military phonetic for the letter N.

numba one: The best.

numba ten: The worst. Often said by bar girls to CHEAP CHARLIES.

numba ten thousand: An exaggeration of how bad things can be.

NVA: North Vietnamese Army. Also, a North Vietnamese soldier.

OD: Olive drab.

Oh-Deuce: Nickname of the 7th Battalion, 402d Infantry.

OP: Observation Post.

opcon: Operational Control.

opposition: The enemy.

OSCAR: The military phonetic for the letter O.

P-38:   A tiny collapsible can opener.

PAPA: The military phonetic for the letter P.

PIO: Public Information Office or Officer or a person who works for such office.

piss-tube: A vertical tube buried ⅔ in the ground for urinating into.

point: or pointman.   The first man of a patrol.

PRC-25: or Prick-25.   The standard infantry radio used in Vietnam. Carried by RTOs, the radio was heavy and considered an ass-kicker.

PRC-77:   A radio similar to the PRC-25 but with a kryptographic scrambling/descrambling unit attached. Sometimes called the Monster, it was a 'real ass-kicker.' Transmission frequencies on the PRC-77 were called the secure net.

PSP: Perforated Steel Plate.

PsyOps: Psychological Operations.

PZ: Pick-up Zone.

QUAD 50s: A four-barrelled assembly of .50 caliber machine guns.

QUEBEC: The military phonetic for the letter Q.

RBF: Recon By Fire.

redball: An enemy high speed trail or road.

red bird: A Cobra helicopter.

REMF: (rim-ph) Rear Echelon Mother Fucker.

RIF: Recon in force, a heavy reconnaissance patrol. Later, Reduction in force, an administrative mechanism for retiring career soldiers prior to the end of their 20 year term.

rock'n'roll: Firing a weapon on full automatic.

ROK: Republic of Korea.

ROMEO: The military phonetic for the letter R.

RPD: A light machine gun. See LMG.

RPG: Rocket Propelled Grenade. See B-40.

R&R: Rest and Relaxation.

RTO: Radio-Telephone Operator.

ruck, rucksack: Backpack issued to infantry in Vietnam.

rumor control: The most accurate source of information prior to the actual occurrence of an event.

RVN: Republic of Vietnam (South).

S & S: Supply & Service, designation of a support unit.

S-1: Personnel.

S-2: Intelligence.

S-3: Operations.

S-4: Supply.

S-5: Civil Affairs.

SAF: Small Arms Fire.

sappers: Enemy demolition/assault teams.

SEATO: Southeast Asia Treaty Organization.

secure net: See PRC-77.

SERTS: Screaming Eagle Replacement Training School.

set: A party.

Shake 'n' Bake: Sergeant who attended NCO school and earned rank after only a very short time in uniform.

shit-hook: A CH-47.

SIERRA: The military phonetic for the letter S.

sit-rep: Situation report.

SKS: A Simonov 7.62mm semi-automatic carbine.

sky: To leave. Also, sky up.

Skycrane: A CH-54.

slackman: The second man back on a patrol, directly behind the point.

Slicks: Hueys.

Snakes: Cobras.

soul brother: A black soldier.

stand-down: An infantry unit's return from the boonies to base camp for refitting and training. Later, a unit being withdrawn from Vietnam and redeployed to the US.

steel pot: A GI helmet.

Tac Air: Tactical air (Air Force) support. Fighter-bombers.

TANGO: The military phonetic for the letter T.

tee-tee: Very small or little.

Tet: Vietnamese Lunar New Year Holiday. As a result of NVA/VC offensives during 1968, the term took on a special military significance.

three-quarter: A three-quarter-ton truck.

TOC: Tactical Operations Center.

TO&E: Table of Organization and Equipment.

201 FILE: A US Army personnel file.

UH-1H: A Huey slick.

UNIFORM: The military phonetic for the letter U.

USAF: United States Air Force.

USARV: United States Army, Vietnam.

VC: Viet Cong.

VICTOR: The military phonetic for the letter V.

ville: A village.

WHISKEY: The military phonetic for the letter W.

wake-up: As in '13 and a wake-up.' The last day of a soldier's Vietnam tour.

weed: Marijuana.

white bird: A LOH.

WIA: Wounded In Action.

widow maker: An MA.

willie peter: Also WP. White phosphorus, usually an incendiary artillery round.

World: The USA or anyplace other than NAM.

X-RAY: The military phonetic for the letter X. Also, a reconnaissance patrol from an NDP.

XO: Executive Officer.

YANKEE: The military phonetic for the letter Y.

YD: The grid 100,000 meters × 100,000 meters square from the Universal Transmercator (UTM) Grid Zone 48Q. The UTM map of the world dispenses with latitude and longitude in favor of a system of metric coordinates (usually six digits) which enable the user of the map to specify a location to within 100 meters. Thus the center of the Khe Ta Laou river valley is located at YD 150320.

ZULU: The military phonetic for the letter Z.

11-B: See Eleven-Bravo.

16:   See M-16.

51s: A communist .51 caliber heavy machine gun.

60:   See M-60.

60s, 81s: US mortars (millimeters).

61s, 82s: Communist mortars.

79:   See M-79.

122:   122mm communist rocket capable of traveling, with booster, 22 kilometers.

HISTORICAL DATES

"We think ourselves into war. The antecedents are in our minds."
Rufus Brooks, 23 August 70.

2879 to 258 BC —The First Vietnamese Kingdom (Van Lang or Van Tang, The Country of Tattooed Men).
—The Bac-sonians, a wave of Australoids from the north settle in the Red River Valley area (Hanoi-Haiphong).
—First wave of Malays from Central Asia settle coastal area from Saigon to Hue.

500 BC —Han Chinese advance into Vietnam (Red River Valley) and force earlier settlers south setting off the first North/South conflict.

258 to 207 BC —The Second Vietnamese Kingdom (Au Lac). The King of Thuc conquers Van Lang.

207 BC —Au Lac overrun by Central Chinese peoples who establish the Kingdom of Nam Viet in the Red River Valley.

111 BC to AD 939—Chinese occupy northern portion of Vietnam, Nam Viet, a conglomerate of smaller states falls.
—Second wave of Malays.

87 BC —Han Wu Ti, Emperor of China, spreads Chinese territory south to Hue.

AD 39 —Trung sisters lead a two-year revolt against Chinese, reestablish Nam Viet.

45 —Nam Viet again overrun and annexed by China.

197 —Kingdom of Champa established by peoples from India and further west under Lam Ap settling coastal area from Da Nang south to Cam Ranh. A trading people.

220   —Han Dynasty of China falls.

542-4   —Ly Bon (Ly-Nan-De) leads successful rebellion against China. For the next 60 years there is constant pressure from the north and the 'Vietnamese' extend their settlements south along the coast.

602   —China again imposes foreign rule on Vietnam. During this period Chinese method of agriculture adopted. A poor land becomes rich, the people remain poor.

938   —Ngo-Quyen leads armies which decisively defeat Chinese at Bach Dang River. Independence lasts for most of next 900 years. Language reverts back to ancient 'Vietnamese' language.

1215   —Mongols invade the Red River Valley area without success. A few years later they invade again. This time led by Kublai Khan. They are partially successful and keep the pressure from the north on until 1287.

1284   —Tran Hung Dao writes *Essential Summary of Military Arts*. "The enemy must fight his battle far from his home base for a long time. We must further weaken him by drawing him into protracted campaigns. Once his initial dash is broken, it will be easier to destroy him."

1287   —Mongols withdraw from Vietnam.

                    —With the overthrow of the Chinese (in 939) and for almost 500 years, the peoples of the Red River Valley area direct their efforts to the colonialization of the South. The Chams are destroyed in a systematic genocide, city by city. The remaining terrorized Chams fled into the highland jungles and became the ancestors of the present Montagnard peoples.

1407   —Chinese under the Ming Emperors invade the Red River Valley area and gain control. They are eventually defeated by guerrilla warfare and attrition.

1418 to 1427   —Ming Chinese defeated by Viet King, Le Loi. Le Dynasty comes to power in northern Vietnam. Nguyen feudal lords come to power in southern Vietnam.

1459 to 1497   —Completion of destruction of kingdom of Champa by Le Thanh. This period is known as The Golden Age of Vietnam.

1535   —First Europeans, Portuguese, drop anchor at Da Nang. This marks the beginning of the era of colonialization by Europeans of Asia.

1540   —Vietnam politically divided into North and South (Le and Nguyen).

1590   —Vietnam reunified.

1613   —Vietnam again divides into two countries. The Nguyen rulers of the South construct two walls at Dong-Hoi. One wall is six miles long, the other twelve miles long. Both are 18 feet high. Dong-Hoi is less than ten miles north of the DMZ established by the Geneva Accords of 1954.

1615   —First Catholic missionaries, Italian and Portuguese Jesuits, land at Da Nang.

1636   —First Dutch arrival in Vietnam.

1672   —English open trading post.

1680   —French open first trading office.

1770 to 1776   —Revolt of the Tay-Son Village against the Nguyen Dynasty in the South. Trinh family defeats Le Dynasty in the North. Nguyen Anh, King of Cochin China (Southern South Vietnam area), holds on to his throne in South, very unstable, negotiates for French assistance and support.

1776   —Vietnam and the Thai Kingdom clash over Cambodia.

1790 to 1800   —New, unsuccessful, Chinese invasion of North.
                —Nguyen Anh and French force land in North (July 1789). Nominal reunification of country.

1799   —Nguyen Anh recaptures most of South and exterminates Tay-Son leaders.

1802   —Hue falls, the Tay-Son movement ends. Hanoi falls. Prince Nguyen Anh becomes Emperor Gia Long. Gia Long restores the name Vietnam to the entire country. Gia Long's rule is anti-European. Ends with his death in 1820.

1820 to 1841   —The Emperor Minh Mang: under his rule the last Europeans are driven from the emperor's service. He effectively isolates Vietnam from development (technological and military) during a period of rapid European advancement. Persecutes Catholic missionaries.

1827 to 1856   —A period of genocide. 130,000 Catholics put to death.

1839   —The Opium War. Opium had been brought into China by the British who found it very profitable. When the Chinese try to stop the opium trade the British attack and defeat China. This becomes a pattern for colonialization in Asia.

1841 to 1847   —The Emperor Thieu Tri loses part of Vietnam to the French.

1845   —USS *Constitution* puts into Da Nang. The Marines land to assist in halting the killing of a French bishop. Marines stay four days. America's first Vietnam involvement.

1847 to 1883   —The Emperor Tu Duc loses all of Vietnam to the French.

1850   —The French view Vietnam as a staging area and foothold into the rich markets of China held by the English.

1858   —French attack and capture Da Nang.

1861   —French capture Saigon.

1862   —Vietnam cedes Saigon and surrounding provinces to France.

1883   —French expansion continues until all of Vietnam is under French control.

1880 to 1920   —Major immigration of Europeans to America.

1887 —Vietnam, Cambodia and Laos grouped into the French Protectorate called the Indochinese Union.

1920 to 1936 —A series of ill-fated nationalistic uprisings.

1937 —From Mao Tse-tung: (compare with 1284)

The enemy advances, we retreat;

The enemy camps, we harass;

The enemy tires, we attack;

The enemy retreats, we pursue.

—Japanese capture Nanking (China), a war where only one side shows up—200,000 civilians murdered.

1939 to 1945 —Japan occupies military installations in Vietnam, allows Vichy France to administer colony.

1941 —Iraqis oust British.

—First Airborne Infantry operation in warfare, Germany invades Crete.

—Japanese land in Indochina. US cuts off oil to Japan.

—Viet Nam Doc Lap Dong Minh, THE LEAGUE FOR THE INDEPENDENCE OF VIETNAM, established by Ho Chi Minh.

1945 —Japanese intern French administrators.

—Viet Minh take control throughout Vietnam and inter Japanese occupation forces. Democratic Republic of Vietnam is established.

—British army enters Saigon, Chinese (Koumintang) army enters Hanoi, per Yalta agreement. The British will yield to the French, Chaing Kai-shek to Ho Chi Minh. Neither Ho nor the French will accept this result, and war begins in 1946.

1946 —US/USSR divide Korea at 38th parallel.

—19 December, Viet Minh launch attacks against French. The beginning of the First Indochina War.

1947 —The TRUMAN DOCTRINE pledges economic and military aid to any nation threatened by communism.

1948 —The Berlin Blockade and Airlift.

1949 —The creation of NATO.

—Mao Tse-tung rises to power in China.

1950 —A period of Civil Rights sit-ins and boycotts begins in the southern United States.

—The Korean War begins.

1952 —Korean truce talks get underway. US role is mostly defensive.

1953 —Jan-Apr, First Viet Minh invasion of Laos.

—28 July, French attack Regiment 95 of Viet Minh along Street Without Joy.

—22 October, French/Laotian Treaty of Association affirms Laos independence as a member of the French Union.

1954   —7 May, Fall of French Garrison at Dien Bien Phu marks French defeat in First Indochina War. Ten thousand French soldiers surrender to Viet Minh. France's attempt to send relief force fails. American (Eisenhower/Dulles) official response to request for relief is a telegram of encouragement. (American public revulsion to Korean War is said to have deterred Eisenhower from committing to intervention in Indochina.)

—21 July, Geneva Cease-Fire Conference splits Vietnam into communist North and non-communist South along historical line at 17th parallel.

—August, First Indochina War officially declared ended.

—24 August, Communist Party outlawed in the United States.

—US sends 200 military advisors to Ngo Dinh Diem, President of South Vietnam.

1955   —Warsaw Pact formed.

—The Eisenhower/Khrushchev Geneva Summit, the cold war begins.

1956   —Russian tanks crush Hungarian Insurrection.

—NAACP outlawed in Alabama.

—Last French troops leave Indochina.

—Scheduled elections on reunification of Vietnam not held.

1959   —The Second Indochina War begins.

—Laotian rebellion begins in earnest.

1961   —John F. Kennedy, "We will bear any burden . . ."

—Bay of Pigs.

—Berlin Wall.

—Cuban Missile Crisis.

1962   —MACV (Military Assistance Command, Vietnam) established.

—Neutralization of Laos under coalition government.

1963 to 1968   —Second Indochina War, troop build-up phase. Generally, the US public believes US is winning, dismay grows gradually. JFK to news media, "Get on the team."

1963   —John F. Kennedy assassinated.

1964   —Red China explodes nuclear bomb.

—Gulf of Tonkin Incident.

—5 August, first US pilot (shot-down) captured by North Vietnam. Navy Lt (jg) Everett Alvarez, Jr., becomes first POW. US Veterans Administration declares this date as beginning of American Vietnam Era.

1965   —First US ground troops land near Da Nang.

—US begins operation Rolling Thunder. Bombing of the North.

—Viet Cong attack US airbase at Pleiku, 70 US KIA.

—War in the Dominican Republic.

—May, first five-day bombing halt of the North.

—19 June, Air Vice Marshal Nguyen Cao Ky leads military junta, takes control of Saigon Government.

—27 June, first major ground action by US forces.

—30 June, LBJ announces doubling of US troop strength by addition of 44 battalions increasing strength from 65,000 to 130,000.

—29 July, 1st Brigade, 101st Airborne Division arrives in Vietnam.

—China states its support for Viet Cong as central strategy for world communist movement to encircle western world.

—First (clandestine) peace negotiations between Washington and Hanoi begin in Paris. Hanoi demands total control of all Vietnam. The negotiation issues never change.

—24 December, LBJ halts bombing of North, announces 'peace offensive.'

1966   —31 Jan, US air bombardment of North resumes after efforts to negotiate prove fruitless.

—10 March, Roman Catholic Premier Ky fires Buddhist General Nguyen Chan The, thus provoking Buddhists. The's troops revolt in Da Nang.

—Special Forces CIDG camps at A Loui, Ta Bat and A Shau (all in A Shau Valley) are closed because of VC/NVA pressure (overrun?). For the next two years the valley belongs to the communist forces who openly ship tons of supplies down Highway 548 which runs the length of the A Shau.

—7 May, Ky declares he will not leave office no matter what election results follow voting for constituent Assembly. Da Nang Buddhists demonstrate.

—15 May, Ky sends his troops to Da Nang to quell demonstration—meet resistance from 1st Division troops—near civil war in South. Hue becomes center of Buddhist resistance and anti-American demonstrations.

—29 May, Buddhist nun burns self to death at Hue pagoda.

—30 June, US combat strength in Vietnam increased to 285,000.

—Summer-Fall Viet Cong terrorism campaign attempts to disrupt and intimidate South Vietnam voters. Eighty percent of eligible voters cast ballots for 117-seat constitutional assembly.

—End of '66, general optimism prevails in US and South Vietnam.

1967   —July, Viet Cong surprise attack on US air base at Da Nang, 12 US KIA, 45 US WIA, 25 aircraft destroyed.

—General Nguyen Van Thieu and Premier Ky elected president and VP of South Vietnam.

—13 December, remainder of 101st Airborne Div arrives in Vietnam. At end of year US combat strength in Vietnam reaches 480,000.

1968   —20 Jan, Battle of Khe Sanh begins. Lasts 77 days.

—29-30 Jan, Tet offensive begins. This begins second phase of Second Indochina War which lasts to May 1972. US public shocked by NVA accomplishments. Chasm in US thought widens, great disillusionment will hit Nixon Administration.

—22 March, LBJ replaces Gen. William Westmoreland with Gen. Creighton Abrams as Commander, US Forces, Vietnam.

—31 March, LBJ halts all US bombing above 20th parallel. He announces he will not seek another term as president.

—Dr. Martin Luther King, Jr., assassinated.

—6 April, US troops break seige at Khe Sanh.

—May, 1st Cavalry Division and 101st Abn Div begin probing the A Shau Valley.

—June, Khe Sanh de-activated.

—Robert F. Kennedy assassinated.

—My Lai massacre.

—Spring-summer, Hanoi insists US stop all bombing of North before Hanoi will negotiate. LBJ halts all bombing of North Vietnam. Hanoi agrees to negotiate shape of conference table.

—October, US Marines begin pulling out of Vietnam.

—1 November, bombing of North terminated.

—Richard Nixon narrowly defeats Hubert Humphrey for US presidency.

1969   —101st Abn Div transformed to Airmobile.

—101st moves into A Shau and surrounding mountain areas for 167 days. Much of NVA ability to attack population corridor destroyed. I Corps becomes mostly pacified.

—Paris peace talks expand to include VC and Thieu government.

—July, first major US troop reduction and withdrawals. Peak strength hit 540,000.

—VC 10-point peace plan—unconditional US withdrawal of forces, material and financial support of S. Vietnam. US declines. US counter-proposal—US and Hanoi each withdraw all forces over next 12 months. Hanoi answers it has no troops in South.

—Thieu proposes VC participation in internationally supervised elections. VC decline.

—15 Oct, Massive war moratorium demonstrations in US.

—3 Nov, Nixon announces Vietnamization Plan.

—15 Nov, 250,000 anti-war demonstrators march on capital.

—My Lai story becomes public knowledge.

1970   —March, in Cambodia, Lon Nol deposes Prince Norodom Sihanouk in coup. He demands communists vacate his country. Communists do not leave. Lon Nol requests US assistance (at urging of US).

—30 April, Nixon announces incursion into Cambodian sanctuaries at Fish Hook and Parrot's Beak. Allied forces uncover hundreds of tons of food, weapons and ammunition—communist troops defer—shift west toward Pheom Phen.

—Massive US anti-war demonstrations.

—Four students killed at Kent State.

—Two students killed at Jackson State College.

—7/402 sweeps Hills 714 and 882 wiping out NVA build-up in central I Corps.

—30 June, All US troops out of Cambodia.

—7/402 battles at Khe Ta Laou.

1971   —4 Feb, NVA/VC close prison camps in S. Vietnam and move North due to ever increasing pressure from US/ARVN forces.

—Lam Son 719, ARVN incursion into Laos to cut Ho Chi Minh Trail.

—13 June, *New York Times* begins publishing *The Pentagon Papers*.

—End of '71, US troop strength in South Vietnam below 160,000.

1972   —30 March, Nixon orders new bombardment of N. Vietnam, plus mining of Haiphong Harbor. Renewed anti-war demonstrations in US.

—NVA invade northern South Vietnam. This marks beginning of Third Indochina War which is ground fought by Vietnamese.

—Spring, Le Duc Tho and Henry Kissinger secret peace talks. May; US proposes internationally supervised cease-fire, repatriation of all US POWs and withdrawal of US forces.

—1 May, NVA capture Quang Tri City, Quang Tri province and much of Thua Thien Province including all of A Shau and Khe Ta Laou and all firebases west of Hue. During remainder of year ARVN, led by 1st Inf Div (ARVN), recapture most of lost territory and expel NVA from I Corps.

—Oct, Hanoi agrees to US peace proposals. US bombing of North halts.

—Mid-Dec, peace talks break down.

—18-29 Dec, Around-the-clock surgically precise bombing campaign of Hanoi, Haiphong and other North Vietnam cities. This includes night B-52 raids.

1973   —27 Jan, Paris Peace Agreements signed.
             —12 Feb, 1st US POW in North Vietnam released.
             Remainder released over next month.
             —29 March, last US troops leave Vietnam.
1975   —NVA begin offensive which crushes South.
             —29-30 April, Saigon falls.
1975   —Anti-communist Popular Liberation Front established.

A NOTE ON THE MAPS

Although a novel, *The 13th Valley* is a real place where American soldiers fought and died in August of 1970; the author did participate in some parts of the operation upon which the story is based. During the writing of the book, copies of the U.S. Army topographic maps of the area were consulted and these became the basis of the battle maps printed along with each Significant Activities report. The author wishes to thank F.X. Flinn, the managing editor, who conceived of and directed the creation of the maps; Peter McQueen and Ivan Bacaba of Rand McNally & Company, who prepared the shaded relief art from information on the army maps; Gene Siegel, who prepared the daily activity art from tracings by the author and editor; and Barry Denenberg, Oscar Dystel, Barbara Cohen, Lou Aronica, Ethan Ellenberg, Barbara Alpert, Alan Rinzler, Lisa Nicoll and Sally Williams for their suggestions and encouragement.

ABOUT THE AUTHOR

JOHN M. DEL VECCHIO graduated from Lafayette College in 1969. He was drafted in September of that year and sent to Vietnam in June 1970 where he served as Combat Correspondent in the 101st Airborne Division (Airmobile). In 1971 he was awarded a Bronze Star for Heroism in Ground Combat. His novels include *The 13th Valley* and *For the Sake of All Living Things*, recently published in hardcover by Bantam Books. He lives in Connecticut, where he is at work on his third novel.

DON'T MISS
THESE CURRENT
Bantam Bestsellers